James Philip

———————

EIGHT MILES HIGH

———

Timeline 10/27/62 – BOOK FOURTEEN

The Timeline 10/27/62 Series

Main Series

Book 1: Operation Anadyr
Book 2: Love is Strange
Book 3: The Pillars of Hercules
Book 4: Red Dawn
Book 5: The Burning Time
Book 6: Tales of Brave Ulysses
Book 7: A Line in the Sand
Book 8: The Mountains of the Moon
Book 9: All Along the Watchtower
Book 10: Crow on the Cradle
Book 11: 1966 & All That
Book 12: Only in America
Book 13: Warsaw Concerto
Book 14: Eight Miles High

A Standalone Timeline 10/27/62 Novel

Football in the Ruins – The World Cup of 1966

A Standalone Timeline 10/27/62 Novella

The House on Haight Street

Coming in 2020

Book 15: Won't Get Fooled Again (2020)
Book 16: Armadas (2020)

For the latest news and author blogs about the
Timeline 10/27/62 Series check out
www.thetimelinesaga.com

In a wilderness of mirrors.
What will the spider do?
Suspend its operations,
will the weevil delay?

T.S. Eliot (Extract from *Gerontion*, 1920).

Diplomacy is the art of telling people to go to hell in such a way that they ask for directions.

Winston S. Churchill (A note of caution: although this aphorism is commonly attributed to the great man, others have legitimate claims to having first coined it!)

Chapter 1

Friday 27th January 1967
The White House, Washington DC

Forty-nine-year-old James Jesus Angleton, the prematurely aged, one-time student poet who had founded a literary magazine called *Furioso* while he was at Yale, publishing the work of Ezra Pound, had been Associate Deputy Director of Operations for Counter Intelligence (ADDOCI) at the CIA since 1954. Even after the cataclysm of the Cuban Missiles War, which he – a man whose paranoia about and hatred of all things *Soviet* and *Communistic* was legendary – had regarded as a price worth paying for holding back the evil tide of global Marxist-Leninism, he had nurtured a deep, very nearly visceral affection for the so-called 'special relationship' with the British. Granted, his personal love affair with 'the Old Country', dating from his time in England in the Second War and succoured by his long association with officers of the British Secret Intelligence Service (MI6), had become more than a little strained post-July 1964 when the two countries had very nearly gone to war but nevertheless, he remained among the least 'lapsed' of any former Anglophile who remained in the upper echelons of the US Intelligence community. However, that morning the implications of the briefing he had belatedly received, only late last night, about the outcome of the seemingly fractious Camp David Summit, were burrowing, canker-like, in his head.

Richard Helms, the Director of Central Intelligence, had been unusually terse. Worse, he had, in so many words although he had not spelled it out – because that was not the way he operated – that *Operation Maelstrom*, ramped up to such a degree that during and since the war in the Midwest it had become the Agency's primary global focus, had now 'served its purpose' and 'needed to be reined in.' Maddeningly, Angleton's vehement protests that there were still 'thousands of dissidents out there', and remark to the effect that *they* were 'laughing at us' had fallen on courteously deaf ears.

'It is not against the law in this country to express peaceful opposition to the executive,' Helms had observed, a little tartly, at one juncture.

Angleton had angrily railed against the pernicious influence of 'that commie stooge Harding-Grayson' and his 'poodle', Airey Neave but the Director of Central Intelligence had steadfastly refused to rise to the bait.

Other, that was, than to observe that the British Foreign Secretary, *Lord* Thomas Harding-Grayson, and the United Kingdom's Secretary of State for National Security, Sir Airey Neave, MP – their NATO ally's chief spymaster – 'obviously still enjoyed' the absolute 'confidence' of the 'Angry Widow'.

In other words; anything anybody else thought about those two, particular 'operators' was entirely academic. More than one American commentator had speculated that probably no other woman in British history, including Queen Elizabeth I of Spanish Armada defying fame, had ever enjoyed such unrivalled power in her kingdom as the Right Honourable Margaret Hilda Thatcher, MP, First Lord of the Treasury and Prime Minister of Great Britain and Northern Ireland.

Notwithstanding his irritation with Richard Helms, nothing that morning had remotely prepared James Angleton, for the unmitigated hostility implicit in the first question put to him by the White House Chief of Staff, forty-year-old Harry Robbins 'Bob'" Haldeman, within seconds of the younger man's West Wing office door, shutting firmly at his back.

Haldeman was crew cut, showing very little of the inevitable weariness he must have been experiencing after several gruelling days of apparently, fruitless bickering with the British in the Catoctin Mountains sixty miles north of DC. After hands had been cursorily shaken, Richard Nixon's pathologically loyal Chief of Staff had waved the CIA man to a chair in front of his desk, sat down and viewed Angleton thoughtfully for a moment.

"Director Hoover claims that somebody at Langley blabbed about Billy the Kid and the Angel of Death," Haldeman stated quietly. "And now the word is out that 'the resistance' plans to assassinate the President in San Francisco." He paused, sucked his teeth. "Did you or your people have anything to do with that, Mister Director?"

Angleton sighed, offended as much by the clumsiness of the interrogative as anything else it might imply, and took off his horn-rimmed spectacles. A rake-thin man with a prematurely lined and aged face that belied his forty-nine years, he unhurriedly re-positioned his glasses on the bridge of his nose and returned Haldeman's gaze with contemplative, customarily esoteric intensity.

He had no intention, interest or inclination of addressing Haldeman's crudely framed question

"You know *that* woman is," he posed, a flickering scowl threatening to settle in his eyes if not his face, "is, and always was, a Soviet plant. An agent provocateur..."

Haldeman grunted his impatience.

He sat forward, resting his elbows on the table.

There were times when he asked himself who was the real enemy within: the KGB, the CIA or the FBI?

"Lady Rachel French," he groaned. Why the fuck am I the one having to explain this to the Associate Deputy Director of Operations for Counter Intelligence? "Is the wife of a key man in the British establishment. If her 'status' was ever any kind of issue; it is not now. Do I make myself clear?"

Haldeman had seen the files proving that – depending on how one read them – the legendary spymaster had either been in league with, or, more likely, he was assured, been completely duped by, and stubbornly remained a close personal friend of the notorious British traitor Kim Philby, long after the man's own people had exposed him as the 'Third Man' in the Cambridge Spy Ring responsible for the deaths of countless – hundreds perhaps – British, American and many other of their allies' agents. But for Philby's unmasking had been interrupted by the October War, Angleton might have been fired when the truth came out.

Or possibly, not.

Trying to get a CIA-man to take responsibility for his actions, misdeeds and blunders was a classic Intelligence community oxymoron, insofar as it hardly ever happened. Heck, Allen Dulles had gone rogue a decade before the Bay of Pigs fiasco finally gave JFK licence to fire his arse! And even now, there was still a hard-core gang of malcontents at Langley more interested in taking its revenge on the Kennedys, than it was in combating foreign counter intelligence operations in the United States!

"Is that clear?" Haldeman asked again.

Angleton shrugged.

He did not particularly care what this, or that, political place man thought about...anything, really. Besides, he knew enough about Haldeman, and several of his closest associates at 1600 Pennsylvania Ave NW, to know that neither he, nor many of his cronies were likely to last much longer in their current posts than the next general election, whoever sat in the Oval Office when the electoral hullabaloo was over in November next year.

Bob Haldeman had to bite back on his ire.

"Premier Thatcher informed the President that her Administration," he went on, battling a growing sense of unreality, "was now aware that the surveillance, eavesdropping and other illegal operations mounted against the British Embassy in Philadelphia during Sir Peter Christopher's ambassadorship, and to a lesser extent against the embassy and its accredited officials since its removal to DC last year, were not wholly undertaken by the FBI. In fact, the Brits now – they refused to specify how they knew – know that *your* people were heavily involved at all times..."

James Angleton stirred in his chair.

Haldeman held up a hand.

"The only reason *they* have not, yet, lodged a formal complaint under the terms of the Vienna Convention on Diplomatic Relations of 1961, is because Premier Thatcher does not want to cause further 'substantial embarrassment' to the Administration. Just so there is no misunderstanding about this, Mister Director, British Secretary of National Security, Sir Airey Neave, passed a file to us - personally, to the President - graphically detailing 'examples' of the aforementioned malfeasances."

Angleton had already taken as read that Richard Helm's earlier terseness, was not unrelated to the interview he and the President must have had shortly after the conclusion of the Camp David Summit.

The ADDOCI would have been worried; except he did not think he had anything to be worried about. He had meticulously documented his interactions with the latter Eisenhower, the Kennedy, Johnson and now the Nixon White Houses. Like his predecessors, Haldeman and the others had been like kids who honestly believed Christmas had come early when they were briefed about Operation Maelstrom: the domestic counter-intelligence campaign – initially launched under the auspices of Operation CHAOS back in the fifties, re-invigorated after the Battle of Washington, and supercharged during the first rebellion in Wisconsin, which had subsequently sucked in all the resources now not required in Western Europe, the Mediterranean and the old Warsaw Pact countries including the Soviet Union, until now it dwarfed the FBI's ongoing domestic surveillance and counter-intelligence programs directed against the agents of the Kingdom of the End of Days, leftist and socialistic groups, the African American Civil Rights Movement and its fellow travellers in the NAACP, the ACLU and lately, un-American elements within the Democratic Party and its 'stooges' on Capitol Hill.

Angleton was frequently astonished by the moral venality, and the crass naivety of the political classes in general, and by the inability of the Nixon Administration in particular, to understand the mechanics of wielding power.

If all that had stood between the Administration and the disclosure of the true facts behind the cover-up of the involvement, of the Nixon for President Campaign, in the whole sorry Warwick Hotel episode, had been a few bungling FBI apparatchiks under the heavy-handed supervision of that idiot Hoover, Haldeman, his UCLA buddy John Ehrlichman, the crooked bond lawyer cum-Attorney General John Mitchell, and that kid Ron Ziegler's denials from the lectern as the White House Press Secretary, to name but a few, every second staffer at 1600 Pennsylvania Avenue NW would already be under indictment.

Richard Helms, the man who had walked into the Director of Intelligence's seat at Langley, practically on the nod, despite the potential for scandal surrounding the break-up of his marriage, had told Angleton that Richard Nixon was a man who understood that debts needed to be repaid, in full.

The order to ramp up Operation Maelstrom into overdrive at the beginning of the war in the Midwest had never been rescinded. So, the big question was: 'Why the fuck am I being given the third degree by a fucking eagle scout?'

Haldeman might have been reading his mind.

"Vice President Rockefeller had a call from Kay Graham," he explained, his frown deepening. He only relaxed his facial muscles with a deliberate effort of will.

The normally suave, positively debonair Vice President, a living, walking, talking scion of old-world grace and dignity, who placed a premium on politeness and decency in all his personal public dealings, had been so angry that he had toyed with intemperateness, outrage almost, in his briefing of the President and his closest men at the close of the Camp David farrago.

Kay Graham, the owner and publisher of *The Washington Post*, a family friend of the Rockefellers; and still, it seemed, of the Kennedy's and these days, if James Angleton's sources were to be believed – they usually were – of the developing Betancourt faction on the Democratic National Committee, had been bright, breezy, pleasantly chatty as befitted one member of the American aristocracy conversing with another.

Problematically, what she had had to say to him, had left Nelson Rockefeller reeling; but then, inevitably, any man who was Richard Nixon's VP was hardly likely to be in the loop when it came to the issues which most concerned the Administration. And in any event, Rockefeller and his people had never shown the slightest interest in getting to the bottom of, or in any way soiling their hands, with the Warwick Hotel Scandal.

After confessing that she, Kay Graham, felt that her call was 'highly unusual' and that in any other circumstances she might have agreed with Rockefeller, or any 'unimplicated' third party, that it might be, on National Security grounds, borderline 'inappropriate', she had got down to business. That sounded exactly like Kay; underneath she was all business, eyes on the ball, a frustrated newshound and as brave as a lion.

'*The Post* has obtained a tranche of documents concerning a massive, covert *domestic* – which must be illegal because it falls outside the CIA's Charter, doesn't it? Although, obviously, I'm no lawyer so I'm just passing on what Ben Bradlee said *The Post's* lawyers say – intelligence operation aimed at infiltrating universities, the legislatures of several US states, the widespread phone tapping of US citizens, routine mail intercepts, and the systematic, dare one say, automatic surveillance of the political opponents of the President?'

Nelson Rockefeller had been struck dumb.

This Haldeman knew because the call had been recorded and he had listened to it...several times because he had not believed what he was hearing the first three or four...

'Nelson, are you still there?'

'Yes... These documents?'

'They were generated by the CIA's Office of Security? Doesn't that come under the ADDOCI?'

That was probably when the Vice President had panicked, or possibly, realised that – horror of horrors – he might be president one day soon; a job nobody who knew him seriously thought he actually wanted for a single moment. Being Governor of New York had been bad enough...

Kay Graham had clearly been well-briefed.

ADDOCI...

Associate Deputy Director of Operations for Counter Intelligence: James Jesus Angleton, the most mysterious, secretive man at Langley.

'Surely, those papers must be classified?' Rockefeller had shot back, trying not to seem overly defensive.

Even by Rockefeller's own account, Kay Graham had been politely disappointed with this, obviously expecting much better of such a highly erudite, intelligent man of the arts and good causes, whom, even now that he was Vice President remained the nation's most generous patron of the arts and philanthropist.

Now Bob Haldeman was about to reiterate the ticking time-bomb question that the owner of *The Washington Post* had put to a stunned Nelson Rockefeller.

"Kay Graham asked, and it seems likely *The Post* is going to ask, along with an exposé of the documents in its possession," the White House Chief of Staff prefaced, "why exactly, the man who was in charge of the collapse of US spying operations in Western Europe between 1959 and 1962, and who has since been spying on millions of patriotic Americans, is still ADDOCI?"

James Angleton adjusted his glasses, viewing Haldeman very much with the curiosity of a cat watching a goldfish in a bowl; ruthlessly calculating the optimum moment to trail his claws through the water.

The insulting manner in which the interrogative had been delivered, presumably in full knowledge of the visceral pain it would almost surely re-awaken, did not provoke the reaction Haldeman was hoping for: in fact, Angleton's expression and the dull contempt in his eyes remained opaque as if he had not actually heard the question wrapped inelegantly around the ill-considered insult.

Just because the President and the Brits had 'made up' lately, was irrelevant. Angleton would never trust *them* again. Once bitten, thrice shy was the principle that applied. That he now accepted that the Soviets' success in shutting down CIA operations in Eastern Europe and Russia in the years before the October War, was the work of Kim Philby, the former acting MI6 Head of Station in Washington, *his* long-time friend, was a non sequitur. That the Brits had known – strongly suspected was too weak a description – that Philby was a Soviet agent for years and never admitted as much to their closest allies; well, that was a thing he was never going to forget, let alone forgive. Moreover, he had drawn a deeper lesson from his personal, and his nation's betrayal from the episode. People like Philby and the other 'Cambridge Spies' could not have acted alone and if that sort of thing could happen in England, it could as assuredly happen in North America. Thus, when a defector – KGB Major Anatoly Mikhaylovich Golitsyn - had posited, less than a year before the Cuban Missiles disaster, that there was a mole at Langley, he had begun the hunt. That Operation Maelstrom had subsumed the original mole hunt was simply an accident of history but the notion of leaving the imperative national task of the unravelling of the American resistance to those thick-eared idiots at the FBI had never been an option.

Not in James Jesus Angleton's book!

When later, it had been put to him that his 'mole hunt' had turned into a 'witch hunt', which threatened to cripple the Agency around the time of the Cuban Missiles debacle, and had almost certainly paralysed Langley in the months leading up to the Battle of Washington, he had retorted that if there was 'paralysis' then it was the work of 'bad actors', traitors in their midst. Nothing that had happened since, had in any way altered his perspective, or his guiding calculus; the country was full of dissidents and it was his job to stop them dragging the United States to perdition.

"What did you tell Kay Graham?" He asked, coldly.

Bob Haldeman brushed the question aside.

"I told her that John Mitchell would serve her, and *The Post*, a non-disclosure order and a subpoena for the return of all classified documents in their possession."

"And?"

"She laughed."

Chapter 2

First Captain Dmitry Kolokoltsev attempted and failed to focus his vision for what seemed like an indeterminately long period of time. He did not try to move; knowing intuitively that this would be both a painful and probably, a very, very bad idea. The atmosphere stank of disinfectant, acrid bleach, there was a constant whisper of voices, a sense of movement around him and in the middle distance the low rush of...engine room blowers. So, he was on a ship, presumably the Jean Bart and from the proximity of the blowers, somewhere above the main armoured deck level amidships...

"Welcome back to the world of the living, Dmitry," Aurélie Faure said gently, not stinting on her obvious relief.

The man felt the soft touch of her hand at his right shoulder and a moment later a cool cloth dabbed at his brow.

"You had us worried for a while after we pulled you out of the water," the woman explained, her cheerfulness of that particular weary beyond measure angel of mercy kind.

The Russian blinked at her.

Her face came into and out of focus, as nausea washed across him.

"Where am I..."

"We converted the crew space beneath the boat deck into a makeshift hospital," Aurélie Faure told him. "The sick bay was filled up almost as soon as the shooting stopped. We ran out of anaesthetics; thankfully, they operated on you while you were still unconscious."

"What is the damage?" He asked, unwisely seeking to form a rueful smile on his lips.

For the first time he recognised the grey exhaustion in the woman's face, and the uncertainty in eyes which had seen too many terrible things in the last few hours.

"You were shot twice." Aurélie put a finger to her right torso, and then to her abdomen. "Both rounds went straight through. There's a drain in your right lung, we don't think the belly wound hit anything important, they just sewed that up. You swallowed a lot of water when you went into the bay. And the water is very cold at this time of year... It may have been the cold that stopped you bleeding to death." Too much information, she decided. "Anyway, like I said, you surprised us all still being here this morning."

That said, she smiled and blinked away a tear.

"Fortunately, several crew members had small stashes of morphine. We threatened that we would leave anybody who didn't turn the stuff over to us behind, when we left, if they didn't do the right thing. We got a couple of ampoules into you before we ran out."

The woman sighed, viewed him fondly.

"What you did was unbelievably brave, Dmitry. We'd never have caught so many of the bastards in the open like that but for you..."

Kolokoltsev must have betrayed his utter bewilderment.

Aurélie was unsurprised that his memories were foggy.

"Somebody on one of the destroyers opened fire with an anti-aircraft cannon when you were almost at the top of the gangway," she said, trying to be helpful. "Things were a little crazy after that."

She grimaced wryly as she flexed her left shoulder.

The Russian noticed her right cheek was puffy as if she had walked into something...

Aurélie Faure sighed, and forced a wan smile.

"Oh, that," she said, raising a hand to her face. "When the shooting started Rene tackled me to the deck and lay on top of me until the others could drag us back behind the sandbags. Mon Amiral," she said with quiet pride, "got hit by shrapnel from a grenade, maybe from two grenades and a bullet, a spent one, thank God, knocked him out long enough for the surgeon," a frown, because the Jean Bart's 'surgeon' was a former second-year medical student press-ganged into his present post before Rene Leguay's time with the fleet, "to dig out the biggest pieces of metal from his back and his," she hesitated, oddly shy, "buttocks."

"Where is..." Kolokoltsev's strength was failing.

"*He* is on the bridge. The Fleet cannot stay here. We have to leave. There is a lot to be done."

That was the understatement of the age.

Seeing that the Russian had passed out, Aurélie patted his torso, softly called across the cots between her and the nearest nurse-orderly that she planned to return to the bridge, and quietly departed.

Rene would be relieved to hear that Dmitry had made it through the night and besides, she needed to be by his side. She discarded her bloody once-white smock and emerged onto the deck. The cold air hit her like an unexpected slap in the face. For a moment she tottered, reached out to steady herself against the nearest bulkhead.

The Front Internationale's Revolutionary Guards had had several big guns: 75-millimetre calibre rifles, she was told, probably mounted on light tanks, Char 13t-75 Modèle 51s most likely.

In the confusion the Jean Bart had been hit by at least ten, possibly twice as many rounds before her return fire, and that from the other ships in the bay had obliterated the threat.

Most of the hits had hardly scratched the side of the battleship or bounced off the impregnable main battery turrets but a small number of others, thankfully just a few, had crashed into the less well-armoured superstructure and bridge of the leviathan, killing and wounding over fifty of their people. One of the hits on the bridge had killed two of the flagship's officers, both had been standing on the compass platform rather than in the heavily-armoured conning tower; presumably to get the best possible view of what was going on around the ship.

Aurélie's uncle, an officer in the Reserve, who had been captured by the Germans near Verdun in May 1940, and spent the rest of the Second War in a series of grim prison camps, before returning to teaching history had once told her brother, Edward – she was the youngest of three children - that war was 'messy, random and unutterably brutal.' Eddy had been killed in Algeria just before Charles de Gaulle, after winning an election promising he would never betray France's dead, shamelessly reneged on his pledge. They said the British had revived the Gaullist so-called 'Free French' to fight the Front Internationale, the Gaullists always betrayed their friends in the end, for such was the nature of the beast...

My thoughts are a mess...

Aurélie allowed herself a moment to reconnect with the harsh realities of the present. Her memories would have to wait for another day.

I was alone in the World; my sister Jacqueline had been a stranger to me long before the war. My family is...gone. My old family, leastways. Now, I have only my new family. My brothers and sisters on the Jean Bart...

Aurélie looked about her, letting the cold air sting her awake.

Nobody had had time to wash the blood off the decks of the flagship yet, like so many things, that would have to wait for another day.

Dmitry Kolokoltsev would have been dead if the last thing Rene Leguay had done before he passed out had not been to stop their people shooting the men in the water.

'Prisoners! Get me prisoners! We have to know what's going on!'

Those tank guns on shore were still shooting at the time.

Nevertheless, their people had started hooking and hauling on board the bodies floating nearest to the gangway. Most of the men landed were already dead or too far gone, Dmitry would have been left for dead had she not found him bleeding on the deck.

It had seemed like an age before her shrieking had attracted attention...

Last night's battle – it could not have lasted more than ten minutes – was still an insane, unresolved melange of deafening explosions, blinding flashes, earthquake-like detonations, screaming, and the constant yammering of automatic gunfire.

One of the other ships had suddenly opened fire.

Tracers had sliced through the gloom.

There was shooting on the gangway.

Rene had tackled her as if he was on a rugby field, much as she had seen, many times, her brother crash into an opponent in her girlhood, cheering from the side-lines, hurling her to the deck and throwing himself on top of her.

The three 152-millimetre guns of the port turret of the ship's aft mounted secondary battery had roared, seemingly right above her head, although intellectually she had known the nearest gun was over thirty metres away.

In a moment the air above her head had been filled with more tracers, and the deafening racket of countless automatic heavy-calibre weapons. The red and blue and white tracers had raced towards the shore at impossible speeds; the whole bay was lit up by the continuous explosions.

And then the great guns of No 1 turret had spoken.

In that moment Aurélie had imagined the ship had blown up!

The deck had heaved beneath her by then prostrate body.

The sound of the four great 380-millimetres naval rifles discharging had been like standing right next to a clap of thunder, except fourfold.

The ship had recoiled, rolled perceptibly, steadied.

And for several seconds afterwards she had heard nothing but for the ringing in her ears.

The next thing she was aware of was being hauled, literally by the collar of her shirt, behind cover.

'Where is Rene? Mon Amiral...'

'We've got him! We've got him!'

Rough hands had instantly begun to roam her body. She had fought back, not realising that she was covered in blood and that the men and women who had rushed out onto the open deck to save her and Rene were, far from molesting her, simply trying to find out where all the blood was coming from!

Aurélie began to climb up through the ship.

By the time she limped, stiffly onto the bridge she was breathless, ready to collapse, lie down, curl up and sleep forever. Suddenly dizzy, breathless she tottered. Fortunately, strong hands grabbed her, picking her up and carefully putting her in a chair.

She felt foolish discovering that she was in the Captain's seat to the right of the binnacle. Making to get up, a hand on her shoulder restrained her.

"Somebody, bring Mademoiselle Faure a hot drink please. Something with brandy in it!"

Aurélie breathed a new, heartfelt sigh of relief to hear the strength in Rene Leguay's voice. Strength and a now unshakable authority.

"You look all in," the man sympathised.

"There is so much to do..." Belatedly, she remembered the first thing she had planned to tell her Amiral. "Dmitry is conscious. Sort of. He's in a bad way but," she shrugged, "but we haven't lost him yet."

"Good. That's good." Rene Leguay's hand still steadied Aurélie. "Okay. Now you've looked after everybody else you ought to try to get a little shut-eye. Have something to drink, then lie down in the sea cabin," he nodded towards his claustrophobic cubby hole built into the starboard side of the bridge.

"But there is so much to do," she protested.

"Things are under control," the man assured her.

This would have been a lot more convincing had Rene Leguay not looked like death half-warmed himself. Blood oozed and coagulated on the back of his jacket and trousers and she guessed he must have swallowed a handful of amphetamines to still be standing on his own two feet, more or less unaided.

The man met her concerned look with another half-smile.

"Serge Benois," he explained, "has got three of the four big guns in No 1 turret re-loaded. The secondary battery seems to be operational again. If anybody tries to come down the coast road, we'll blow them to bits. I've sent some of our people over to the Clemenceau and the other ships to see if they can make enough steam to get under way and in a couple of hours La Seine will come alongside. Sometime tonight she ought to be able to start putting some oil back into the bunkers of our ships."

Serge Benois was *Capitaine de corvette* – equivalent to a lieutenant-commander in the British Royal Navy – the battleship's Gunnery Officer, and now Rene's second-in-command. He was a man in his early fifties, grizzled, who had, like the ship's few surviving regular officers, given up, long before Rene had come aboard.

Until last night, the Jean Bart's big guns had not fired a shot since 1957.

Aurélie was almost falling asleep in the chair.

Rene Leguay's presence made everything somehow...all right.

Back on the bridge with *him* she felt safe again.

"Not all the ships will be able to leave," she murmured.

The man chuckled grimly.

"We aren't leaving anybody behind. If it comes to it the Jean Bart will tow the whole bloody fleet out to sea!"

It was said part in jest. No matter, it perfectly expressed Rene Leguay's intentions. The French Mediterranean Fleet was done with the Front Internationale.

"Where will we go?" Aurélie asked, faintly.

The man thought about it for a second, guffawed anew: "All I ask is a tall ship and a star to steer her by; and the wheel's kick and the wind's song," he whispered in halting English as if exchanging some private joke that only they understood.

"John Masefield," she muttered, impressed. She beckoned him to lean closer. "The next time you jump on my bones can we do it on a mattress, not the deck, Mon Amiral?"

The man vented a snort of startled laughter which made everybody else on the bridge turn around. He shook his head and waved for the others to carry on doing whatever they had been doing.

For a moment he nuzzled the top of her head.

"That's one promise I know I can keep, Mademoiselle Faure."

Chapter 3

Saturday 28th January 1967
British Aircraft Corporation, Filton, Bristol, England

Air Marshal Sir Daniel French stepped out onto the balcony surrounding the Flight Operations Tower at RAF Filton the moment the rain eased, itching to get the best possible view of the new American-built Kestrel IIAs as they flew in from the USS Bonhomme Richard (CV-31), steaming some thirty-five miles away in the Bristol Channel.

Around the RAF's Air Officer Commanding (Research, Development and Pre-Production), Boscombe Down, representatives from Pratt and Witney, Rolls-Royce's partners in the ongoing upgrading and proving of the Kestrel's remarkable power-plant, formerly the Bristol Siddeley Pegasus, and other senior engineers and executives from Grumman and Lockheed-Martin, the newly agglomerated British Aerospace Corporation's airframe and avionics collaborators, mingled collegiately with Filton's resident BAC contingent, men from Rolls-Royce's huge works at Derby, miscellaneous RAF and USAF officers, and in the absence of Ambassador Brenckmann – who was at home in the United States - his deputy, fifty-four-year-old John Nichol Irwin II.

Irwin was an Iowan who had been with MacArthur in the Second War, a lieutenant colonel by 1945, and an attorney by profession he had turned his hand to diplomacy in the years since. It was as yet unclear, whether Irwin would actually be Walter Brenckmann's successor, if and when he laid down his ambassadorial sword; nevertheless, Dan French was not the only man in England keen to get the measure of Irwin before that eventuality came to pass, or not.

The number two man at the US Embassy in Oxford was still something of an unknown quantity to him, a thing he hoped to remedy somewhat in the next day or two. In this quest he was, honestly, unsure if his wife's present sojourn in North America was going to be a help or a hindrance.

Rachel, for all her inestimable talents and charm, had an uncanny knack of unsettling some visitors to his official residence at Amesbury. Especially, those guests with a guilty conscience, a thing Tom Harding-Grayson had once suggested, rather too enigmatically for Dan French's taste; possibly, because he could not help but appreciate the underlying truth of the observation.

Dammit, he missed her...

The scream of approaching turbofans snapped him out of his momentary introspection, reminding him of the truly astonishing technical-industrial muscle of his country's refound US allies. Yes, *everything* to do with the subsonic Kestrel, and the supersonic Strike Eagle projects had been shared with the Americans but even so!

As if it was not enough that the latest joint planning committee meeting now scheduled initial squadron deployment of the TSR-2 HASBV - High Altitude Supersonic Bomber Variant – of the Strike Eagle *only* fourteen months hence; factories in California were already rolling Kestrel IIAs, the ground attack version of the remarkable VTOL, vertical take-off and landing, version of the fighter off the production lines at Pasadena at a rate of a couple a day. US Marine Corps pilots, a handful trained in the United Kingdom but most on state-of-the-art simulators developed by Lockheed's legendary 'Skunk Works', were queuing up to jump into the cockpits of the latest 'top ticket' weapon in the Anglo-US armoury.

Which, all things considered, was extraordinarily good news because the RAF simply did not have the wherewithal to magic fast jet pilots out of the ether, nor was it ever likely to have that capability again any time soon, certainly, not on the scale its American cousins seemed to take for granted.

The Kestrels had been ground and flight tested at Pasadena before being ferried to Galveston where after short 'proving flights' they had been flown on board the USS Bonhomme Richard, a much-modified Second War Essex class fleet carrier which had seen extensive service in the recent Korean conflict. Apparently, two aircraft and one pilot had been lost in training evolutions at sea in the Gulf of Mexico, prior to the carrier's ultra-secret transatlantic crossing. While President Nixon might not yet be minded to send GIs back to European soil; in the meantime, the US Navy, and as quietly as possible, the US Air Force was starting to move back into its old stomping grounds.

If the establishment of the Joint Nuclear (Deterrent) Strike Force based in Scottish waters was no secret; the basing of US Navy Polaris-armed SSBNs and hunter-killer SSNs, and the establishment of permanent support facilities at the Gare Loch on the Clyde, at Rosyth on the Forth, and the construction of sprawling Electric Boat Company and Westinghouse fabrication and production plants at Barrow in Furness, could hardly be hidden; the USAF's return to the British Isles was, for the moment, a more sensitive exercise.

The stationing of four EC-135 Looking Glass aircraft, two squadrons of F-4 Phantom IIs in Scotland, and KC-135 tankers at Fairford and Brize Norton had already largely relieved the RAF of the responsibility for guarding the northern approaches to its airspace, allowing the re-deployment of two of the three operational squadrons of English Electric Lightning interceptors to bases in the English Midlands, and lately facilitated the stationing of a quick response flight at RAF Manston in Kent.

Moreover, the re-opening of RAF Lakenheath, closed since the October War and unrepaired until six months ago – sitting as it did in a designated post-October 1962 'restricted zone' – for the mounting of U-2, Martin B-57 and occasionally, Blackbird SR-71 ELINT and photographic reconnaissance spy-in-the-sky missions deep into Central, Eastern and Western Russia, had thus far gone unremarked, unacknowledged by the British Government.

Yesterday, Dan French had given John Irwin a guided tour, replete with expert briefings from selected test pilots and boffins, of his Boscombe Down fiefdom.

Unsurprisingly, Irwin had been impressed.

Most visitors were, in fact.

And rightly so, because Boscombe Down, the place where British military aircraft had come to be tested, often to destruction, since the days of the Royal Flying Corps in 1917, these days hosted the re-formed RAF High Speed Flight, the Empire – now Commonwealth – Test Pilots' School, and the Aeroplane and Armament Experimental Establishment (A&AEE).

Boscombe Down was the visible tip of an ever-expanding technological iceberg, the beating heart of the re-shaped aerospace empire that oversaw, and increasingly controlled every single one of the previously disparate, company-owned, managed and financed independent planning, design, development and testing bureaus of the pre-1962 still grotesquely, and very expensively fragmented British military aviation industry. Everything from abstract university-based theoretical aerospace research to the test flying and operational proving of cutting edge, essentially experimental advanced airframes, engines and systems such as those embodied in the Kestrel and the TSR-2 *Strike Eagle* fell under Dan French's bailiwick.

Basically, he was God at Boscombe Down.

Perhaps, that was why John Irwin had been moved to confide in him that: 'All the Kestrels are flown by US Marine Corp and Air Force personnel who have volunteered for service in England in the new Eagle Wing that Prime Minister Thatcher and the President will announce ahead of the meeting of the United Nations in San Francisco.'

The story would be that the two allies considered the creation of an 'Eagle Wing', reminiscent of the Eagle Squadrons flown by Americans in the Battle of Britain before the United States entered the Second War, the best way to cement the new 'special relationship' and to 'prove' the latest marvels of 'western' technology.

Unfortunately, it would be several months - possibly not until the summer or autumn – that the three planned Eagle Wing squadrons would actually be operational, ruling it out of the plans afoot to take the initiative in France.

The last thing the Nixon Administration needed was having to explain US casualties in a European war...

Nonetheless, an unabashed celebration of US-Anglo rapprochement, a pill to soften the failure of the Camp David Summit of the last week, was going to make a big impression on Dan French's countrymen and women.

As to the Camp David Summit...

Nobody on either side had really expected *that* conference to go well; and right now, neither the British or the American side really needed the complication of the re-inauguration of the United Nations. So, given their outstanding policy rifts over China and South East Asia, and the bellicose rumblings of Warsaw Concerto, the shining beacon of Anglo-American aerospace 'co-operation' was too good a gift horse to ignore. Nevertheless, to know that under a secret protocol signed at Camp David, that the current arrangements were, at least for the foreseeable future – five years - to be set in concrete, was going to be a huge boost to the whole of the rapidly re-organising, rationalising British aerospace industry.

All in all, Dan French would have had to have been a man with a soul and a heart set in stone not to be warmed, damned nearly exhilarated, by the news. In fact, had Rachel been to hand to celebrate with him, his world would have been just about perfect.

The first section of four Kestrels whistled down the length of the single, great runway at Filton from west to east travelling at a speed in excess of well over four hundred knots.

The aircraft were still in their silvery, naked factory livery but for the large alphabetical identity letter and three-digit production numbers on their fuselages, and the Eagle motifs on their tails. Their under-wing munitions hard points were empty, likewise the mounts for their drop tanks – their giant Pegasus engines were mightily thirsty beasts – and when they climbed, unladen, they were like four glistening arrowheads against the broken overcast.

Idiotically, Dan French had started clapping before he knew it.

Immediately, everybody else was clapping, and slapping backs.

A few minutes later the first of the twenty-six Kestrel IIAs began to land; not as would normal aircraft but by approaching, one section from the east, another from the west, slowing, slowing until, nearly in the hover, each in turn dropped gently onto the tarmac, rolled a few yards and halted, prior to taxiing towards the entrance to the perimeter track leading to the hangar complex on the southern side of the airfield.

With her 'birds' having flown the coop, the USS Bonhomme Richard was scheduled to steam for Pembroke Dock, there to offload the four hundred and thirty ground personnel, five 'spare' aircraft and some three hundred tons of equipment, ahead of transferring, via rail, to RAF Cheltenham, where initially, the Eagle Wing was to be stationed.

Strictly speaking, the Bonhomme Richard's Kestrels could have flown straight on to Cheltenham but without their ground crews they were simply ornaments; at Filton the new aircraft would receive the tender loving care they deserved.

"My God," John Irwin muttered, watching two Kestrels slow to a hover, and descend vertically as it they were helicopters not high-performance interceptors capable of breaking the sound barrier in a shallow dive.

"It takes one's breath away the first time one sees *that* particular party trick!" Dan French chuckled.

The American looked to him, and then waved his arm around the sprawling Filton complex.

"With these birds you don't need any of this!"

"The designers say any old field will do," Dan French retorted cheerfully. "Practically speaking, a road or a concrete hardstand is preferable, so long as it is close enough to somewhere the kite can be moved under cover within a minute or so of landing. That's the whole point," he went on, "quite apart from the immense tactical advantage having aircraft that can take off and land vertically, and all that," he guffawed, warming to his thesis, "not only does a Kestrel not need a conventional airfield; the bally thing can put down in a clearing and be rolled into the trees in seconds. It can knock down an enemy fighter at a range of several miles with a Sidewinder or Top Hat air-to-air missile, make four or five hundred mile-an-hour strafing runs with Aden cannon pods on its under-wing hard points, or shoot rockets or drop bombs, and then, hey presto, it can literally disappear into the landscape within a mile or two of the front line, re-fuel, re-arm and be back in the fight in half-an-hour!"

Dan French left out the most implausible aspect of the Kestrel's existence; that, anecdotally, it had been conceived in a shed by the same design team – some of whom had worked for Hawker-Siddeley in the days when it was just 'Hawker Aircraft' in 1935 – who, under the stewardship of chief designer, Sidney Cam, had designed the immortal Hawker Hurricane.

Even over a quarter-of-a-century later the 'Hawker men' still proudly told anybody who would listen, that the Hurricane had shot down twice as many German aircraft in the Battle of Britain as that somewhat more famous, and certainly infinitely more glamorous 'pretty little aeroplane that Supermarine had produced'.

Prosaically, it was a little acknowledged 'fact', that notwithstanding the brutal rationalisation of the British aerospace industry – a process in which Dan French was, in effect, the Government's axe man in chief – mergers, cutbacks and drastic switches in direction were hardly unknown, or, in any way a new phenomenon to the industry. For example, back in 1935 Hawker Aircraft had, itself, been subsumed into a conglomerate formed by JD Siddeley - one of the first manufacturers of motor cars in England, and by the 1930s an engine and airframe maker - another car maker and engine builder, Armstrong Siddeley, and Armstrong Whitworth Aircraft. Around the same time the new Hawker-Siddeley combine had swallowed up both AV Roe and Company – better known as Avro – and the Gloster Aircraft Company and several other smaller, ancillary training and engineering concerns. Moreover, while many of its acquisitions had continued to operate under their own brand names, even before the October War the process of commercial and technological rationalisation had seen Hawker-Siddeley – itself a shortened version of the 1948 renaming of a much re-vamped post-Second World War *Hawker Siddeley Group* – calve itself into a number of more manageable 'divisions': an aircraft division called Hawker Siddeley Aviation; a guided missiles company operating as Hawker Siddeley Dynamics; and an engine design and production business called Armstrong Siddeley. As recently as 1959, when 'HS' had bought the struggling Folland company, it had merged its engine operation with Bristol Aero Engines to form Bristol Siddeley, the progenitor of the extraordinary Pegasus power plant which powered the fast-growing Kestrel family of experimental, and now increasingly, near-operational family of VTOL fighters and fighter-bombers. Most recently, De Havilland Aircraft and Blackburn Aircraft had also come into the fold in 1960.

Soon, Hawker Siddeley's still stubbornly disparate wings would be clipped further when, under Dan French's remit, it would formally go forward under the name of the British Aerospace Consortium (BAC), the management structure currently in charge of Filton. Wags on his staff at Boscombe Down had suggested the name *British Aircraft Group* but he had drawn the line at calling the new, slimmed down central component of the United Kingdom's Post-War aerospace industry 'BAG'!

For all that Dan French might be the merciless executioner of the old aircraft industry; cruel he was not!

The people at Filton had hoped to be the main movers and shakers of the 'new age of the air'. However, the Air Officer Commanding (Research, Development and Pre-Production) and his political masters, had other plans. In future, Filton was to be the nexus of Anglo-American co-operation, no longer the manufacturer of completed airframes. Engine research and production was to be concentrated at two locations, here in Bristol and at Derby, Rolls-Royce's base in the Midlands. The main airframe production and assembly plants would be at Kingston in Surrey and spread across existing facilities in Lancashire and Yorkshire. Radar and space development would be located in Edinburgh, co-located with the Royal Navy's Guided Weapons Research and Evaluation Establishment, in the Ferranti-Marconi Science Complex at Crew Toll, and at Ferranti's facility at Hollinwood in Lancashire, which would be developed as a discreet research wing of Manchester University commissioned to pursue 'blue sky', or speculative lines of 'pure scientific discovery', complementing research facilities hosted by Oxford and Cambridge Universities.

It went without saying that none of these schemes would be possible, practical or in any way 'wholly fundable' without American money and generous technology transfers. His civilian 'clients' might not get the message, even now. They would, eventually. Dan French had no illusion what the United Kingdom brought to the party: it was innovation, a large cadre of experienced aerospace engineers and designers the equal of any on the planet, ideas and a capacity to take unreasonable risks and now, thank the Heavens, in the Kestrel, it had a 'product' which had not so much caught, as transfixed the imagination of his country's refound transatlantic friends. If the United Kingdom wanted the 'partnership' to go on beyond the initial five-year term, it would need to bring a new Kestrel-type project to the table. Hopefully, when the TSR-2 Strike Eagle got into pre-production, it would be that first 'future project'; if not, it was *his* job to identify and develop the next 'big thing'.

"Of course," Dan French said mischievously, quirking an

apologetic grimace at John Irwin, cautiously confident that the diplomat would catch his mood, "the other thing you get with VTOL aircraft like the Kestrel is that all of a sudden one doesn't need half-a-dozen thousand-feet-long, multi-billion dollar floating airfields like the carriers your Navy, and mine too, given half-a-chance, wants to build in the next few years, to project air power anywhere in the world!"

The American looked to him thoughtfully.

"I wouldn't tell the Admirals that," he grinned conspiratorially.

Chapter 4

Sunday 29th January 1967
CIA Headquarters, Langley, Virginia

Lady Rachel French née Piotrowska had expected – when she got around to thinking about it, for no particular reason – to encounter Professor Caroline Constantis-Zabriski when she got back to Langley.

'Before she got on her flight to Nebraska, Caro stopped off at the White House to have a 'chat' with the Commander-in-Chief," Richard Helms, Director of Central Intelligence informed her, a faint, ironic smile playing across his handsome face. "She and the President really hit it off last year; I think *he's* missed her the last few months.'

It seemed that the remarkable former Assistant Dean of Psychiatric Medicine at the University of Chicago and ground-breaking FBI criminal profiler, was exercising her right to make regular marital visits to Offutt Air Force Base, where her husband, Nathan, was a navigator-communications officer serving with the 36th Strategic Reconnaissance Squadron, flying 'Looking Glass' ultra-top-secret Boeing EC-135 missions.

Given the Warsaw Concerto provocations of the last couple of months Operation Looking Glass had assumed – other than in the days after the Kingdom of the End of Days had nuked several American cities nearly thirteen months ago - a sudden, uncomfortable significance with its aircraft ever-watchful for Soviet hostile intent, and its crews reminded of the absolute need to maintain invulnerable airborne command and control of the global battlefield.

Rachel had shrugged.

"Some girls get all the luck."

The Director of Central Intelligence had already worked out that his guest was not in an overly sanguine frame of mind. He said nothing, braced himself.

"Why have you brought me back to DC?" Rachel asked.

Richard Helms opened his mouth to speak but a knock at his door cut him off. A buttoned up, bespectacled, middle-aged secretary entered the office to deliver a coffee tray.

Rachel counted the cups.

"Who else are we expecting?" She inquired suspiciously.

"Somebody who has been wanting to talk to you again for a long time, Lady Rachel."

Rachel was a little bit jet-lagged, irritated by having to wear her 'second' dress – she had only packed for a short stay and had not attempted, or rather, had not been permitted by her minders, to go shopping since she arrived in the United States – and she was feeling, although not looking, dowdy and a little tired.

The other thing, which she had not expected, was how much she was missing Dan. Not least the calming, pacific effect he seemed to have on her. Even after such a short separation, still only a few days, she was afraid she was inexorably morphing back into her former persona. The profession of violence became her; and she it. Disturbingly, having half-convinced herself that she was weary of hurting people, that weariness had faded, it was as if having rested, reflected, recovered from the nightmares of the Battle of Malta and only months later, the traumas of the Wister Park Siege, she was a little afraid that she was beginning to revert to type...

Perhaps, sensing this, The Director of Central Intelligence was looking uncharacteristically...*fidgety.*

With a shock Rachel suspected she might have inadvertently given Richard Helms a look which communicated a lot more than just feminine impatience.

"I asked the ADDOCI to sit in on this meeting," he said quickly.

Rachel, who like Helms had been standing, now poured herself into the nearest comfortable chair around the coffee table set to one side of the Director's airy, spacious room.

"That bastard put a price on my head the first time I was posted to Washington," she reminded her host, much like a cat raking its claws across glass.

"Yes, well. You killed *two* of his operatives..."

Rachel arched an eyebrow.

Okay, so this was about Operation Maelstrom; up until now she had wondered if, not how, Kurt Mikkelsen's re-appearance five years after 'doing a fade' and 'going black' – in trade terminology, disappearing – was linked to James Jesus Angleton's machinations.

Now she knew that Kurt's return home was anything but an inevitable, or a random consequence of his history.

This, she decided, was definitely not an interview the Director of Central Intelligence or his own, personal cloak and dagger Machiavelli, wanted a woman like Caroline Constantis-Zabriski sitting in on!

"So, what?" She mused, thinking out aloud. *"The Gray Ghost* is going to try to pretend that Billy the Kid's return is all some kind of a Soviet *counter-play?"*

Richard Helms passed her a coffee, unsweetened, no milk.

He stuck to the script he had prepared as soon as he had been notified Rachel had agreed to return to the United States. Only a fool, or worse, somebody with a death wish left anything to chance with a woman like...*her.*

"The United Nations thing has been on the cards ever since the end of the war in the Midwest. The Soviets always used to play the long game. Why wouldn't they be doing the same now? The Warsaw Concerto exercise makes very little military sense; other than to increase British pressure on the Administration to put GI boots on the ground in France, and inevitably, West Germany and Scandinavia, and to send a fleet back to the Mediterranean..."

Richard Helms's voice trailed off because the woman was suddenly studying him with the intensity of a Leopardess eying its next meal.

He was relieved when there was another knock at the door.

James Angleton walked straight in.

Rachel, who had had her back to the door – CIA Headquarters was the one place in the world, now the dungeons of the Lubyanka were an irradiated hole in the ground in the ruins of central Moscow – where not being able to see who came in and left through a given door was remotely pertinent to her prospects of survival. If the CIA did not want her to leave the complex that was that, there was nothing she could do about it. Thus, normal tradecraft was superfluous. Now, she rose slowly to her feet, smoothed down her frock and turned to confront the man who had once, and for all she knew, still had, or had again, put a price on her head.

From what she had gathered from one of Angleton's hit men – there was only so much useful intelligence one could glean from a man choking in his own arterial blood – the contract had not specified 'dead or alive'.

Angleton looked older than she had expected.

That might just have been a result of his brush with one or other of the war plagues, or a consequence of the wounds he had sustained during the Battle of Washington back in December 1963. Losing half a lung and nearly bleeding to death on a city sidewalk, were the sort of mishaps which ought to leave their marks on a man...

The Associate Deputy Director of Operations for Counter Intelligence halted in his tracks half-way into the room as Rachel rose to her feet.

He sniffed, scowled.

"We meet again," he observed dryly.

Rachel studied the thin man with the bearing and demeanour of an austere-faced college professor. Angleton was notorious for his inability to tolerate fools – a problematic flaw in a man whose role required him to interface with so many of DC's glitterati – not to mention his legendary arrogance and a propensity for secretiveness unusual even for a career spook. It was reputed that he kept his own set of files separate from CIA archives, for his eyes only and occasionally to be doled out to his shrinkingly small trusted inner circle of other confidantes. *The Gray Ghost* was just one of his Company and Capitol Hill handles; others were *Virginia Slim*, or *the Fisherman*, in the 1940s he had got addicted to fly-fishing in England. Other nicknames, few uttered other than out of spite were *Skinny Jim*, or the *Black Knight*. A man of well-known obsessive, compulsive habits, legendarily there was no lock Angleton could not pick. Hence, the sobriquet *the Locksmith*, reflecting a talent which had led to rumours that whenever he did one of his periodic morning, afternoon or evening 'flits', going absent without warning, that he was somewhere in Washington picking somebody's lock. However, his burglarious activities apart, Rachel had always thought that *the Scarecrow* fitted him as well as any, although the post-October 1962, MI6 files she had read at the new Embassy in Philadelphia, after the Wister Park atrocity seemed to favour *the Gray Ghost*...

Richard Helms had moved so that he could, at a pinch, step between the man and the woman; not that he imagined for a single second that if Rachel took it upon herself to conclusively right old wrongs there would be much, if anything he could do to stop her.

'Understand that the Angel of Death referenced in your files has not gone away,' Caroline Constantis had told him. 'For the moment, that persona, psyche, whatever you care to call it, is dormant within her. If you like, simply accept that presently the better angels of her nature are in control. No, I can't rule out that one day she might snap, become again the killer, the merciless hunter she was back on Malta or in the nightmare of Wister Park; but on balance, I think that is unlikely. If it happens it will be a progressive process, not an instantaneous flicking of a switch...'

Right now, this was a not wholly reassuring prognosis to the ears of the Director of Central Intelligence.

The tension in the room thickened.

And dissolved in a nanosecond.

Because Rachel quirked a smile.

"No," she corrected the tall, angular man wearing a suit which hung off his shoulders as if off a coat-hanger. "We have never 'met'. Although, we have been close, many times, Mister Director, without being formally introduced."

James Angleton thought about this.

"Yet, still, here we are..."

"The last time I was in America your people started calling me the *Angel of Death*," Rachel went on, her smile fading. "You ought to listen to what Caroline says to you. No psychopath likes to actually be called 'a psychopath'. That's a thing you should have worked out for yourselves, by the way."

It was as if the ambient temperature in the office had dropped twenty degrees and their breath ought, suddenly, to be frosting in their faces.

Now that Rachel had both men's whole and undivided attention, she turned to the probable reason for her recall to the East Coast.

"I assume that old faggot Hoover has finally fallen over Operation Maelstrom?" She asked rhetorically. "Or," she smiled tight-lipped, "he thinks he's entitled to hitch a ride on it as his personal getaway car when the Warwick Hotel Scandal eventually hauls him up before a grand jury?"

The two men looked one to the other, remaining silent.

Rachel felt an urge to vent a girlish giggle.

This was almost too delicious...

"Oh, I see?" She murmured. "It's even worse than that? Everybody thought that Operation Maelstrom was just about taking down the bad guys during the Civil War, a leftover from the failed coup of December 1963. Now *everybody* is going to find out that JFK flagged it in the days after the October War and like topsy, it has grown and grown ever since!"

Neither of the men in the room cared for her flippancy.

But... She was not the kind of woman any sane man took to task over a piffling little thing like that. A man's dignity and self-esteem were important; but not worth risking one's life to preserve, in a setting such as this.

"I'm sorry," Rachel apologised, perfunctorily. "This really isn't funny at all, is it?"

At last, something all three of them could agree upon.

It was then, materialising out of nowhere that Rachel suddenly recollected – for no apparent reason – an interview she had had with Ben Bradlee in Harrisburg back in the summer of 1964.

Bradlee, at the time was still the Philadelphia Bureau Chief of Newsweek. In those odd days after the US Government had shifted to Philadelphia in the aftermath of the Battle of Washington - ostensibly to allow the reconstruction of the badly damaged capital to proceed at breakneck speed under the direction of Secretary of Defense, Robert McNamara and the US Army Corps of Engineers – Bradlee had lived and worked in the big city five days a week, and tried to get back home for the weekends. Things hardly ever worked out that way; but like others within his privileged circle, most of whom had CIA or other, long-standing connections with the Kennedys – he came from an old 'Boston Brahmin' family, his wife was a Pichot, the sister of one of JFK's mistresses - he was not the only man who joked that 'the next time there is a nuclear war' that he was going to feel a lot happier about it knowing that Antoinette, 'Tony' and the kids were not living in a big city...

Those had been strange times; but then when had times not been 'strange' in the last few years?

Rachel remembered thinking that before the October War a man like Ben Bradlee, would have felt guilty about being a member of a class that could afford to *park* his family in the country, just in case there was another war. Back in June 1964, Rachel had been the de facto Head of Station of MI6 in North America, albeit in charge of a skeleton staff still barely a pale shadow of that decimated during the Battle of Washington, and barely recovering by the time it was practically wiped out, during the Wister Park siege. She had not been alone in wondering how 'the rebels' had contrived to target so many British Embassy staffers and their families during the fighting in December 1962, as it turned out, just a cruel prelude to the mayhem which was to transpire at Wister Park only seven months later.

However, that day she had met Ben Bradlee in Harrisburg, all that had lain in an unknowable future and she had been intent on reminding Bradlee – then being touted to be the next Managing Editor of *The Washington Post* – that his whiter than white liberal credentials, somewhat sullied because of his involvement in the CIA's propaganda-misinformation machine back in the day, were only a paper-thin shield in this brave new post-cataclysm world.

Rachel recollected every detail of that day, that meeting and of a brief, passing personal equanimity soon to be consumed by the madness...

As she and Bradlee had walked along the bank of the slow flowing Susquehanna River, at that time of year the river was beginning to fall again after the spring floods, exposing the muddy flanks of the scrub-topped islands in the stream, she was at pains to reassure him that she was no kind of skeleton in his cupboard. Quite the reverse. The last time she had been 'in town' – DC was actually more like a huge feudal village in those days before the war - she had been Hannah Ziegler, a German émigré courtesan, way out of his class. She had had burning red hair then, and a reputation for predatory conquests. Everybody had assumed that she was spying for somebody; but nobody had known for whom, and she had had so many powerful friends and patrons that nobody had been brave enough to ask too many questions.

Or rather, nobody except James Jesus Angleton, whom with his wife, a Midwestern lumber heiress, was another leading member of the tight-knit circle of Kennedy insiders, Democrat literati and CIA apparatchiks within which the Grahams, Philip and Kay, and the Bradlees had moved during the 1950s. Most of the people in that milieu had links to the CIA, or military service in common, or had simply been born into the wider, born to privilege Georgetown-based elite of the District of Columbia. They had all considered themselves to be movers and shakers, the conscience of their country, or at least, they had until the catastrophe of the Cuban Missiles War.

Except perhaps, James Angleton, who had always been convinced that the failed, bloody coup of December 1963, the first uprising in Wisconsin, and then the subsequent Civil War, had all been, in part, the work of the Soviets and 'traitors within' the DC bubble.

"No," Angleton grunted. "It is not funny at all."

Even at the height of the war in the Midwest there had been no little unease in some quarters about the reach and penetration, of the deep, surveillance state which had somehow, seemingly from out of thin air, been 'switched on' to hunt for 'End of Dayer' extremists and fifth columnists in our midst'. Most Americans liked to, or in any event, chose to believe that the 'police state' methods – like those their government had told them had been among the greatest evils of their Marxist-Leninist foes – were no more than a brief, transient wartime necessity. It was a thing that had had to be borne in order to defeat the fanatical, nihilistic evil doers of the Kingdom of the End of Days. The implicit promise had always been that, as soon as victory had been won, the 'extraordinary measures' employed during the period of hostilities would, as if by magic, evaporate.

Of course, that pre-supposed that the aforementioned 'extraordinary measures' were in any way exceptional, or in any sense, a strictly 'wartime expediency'.

This was, of course, a complete misnomer because neither clause had ever applied.

Thus, James Jesus Angleton had been, and remained, the high priest of the surveillance state he had begun building up as long ago as 1959, from around the time the true extent of his personal and professional betrayal by the British, 'Cambridge Spy', and close friend, Kim Philby had begun to warp, and eventually so twist his world view that his subsequent paranoia would have been instantly recognisable to any of the former denizens of the now, obliterated Lubyanka.

No man in the history of espionage had been personally responsible for the death of so many British, American and allied agents than Harold Adrian Russell 'Kim' Philby; yet, in some indefinable way, it would have been kinder by far if James Angleton had died with them when the dreadful truth of his betrayal became known.

It was not as if Angleton had been the only man taken in by the charming, debonair son of the famous Arabist, St John Philby, an advisor to the King of Saudi Arabia, Ibn Sa'ud. An old boy of Westminster School, a graduate of Trinity College, Cambridge; Philby had reported for *The Times* from the Nationalist side of the Spanish Civil War and enjoyed a stellar career in intelligence in the Second War. Later, Philby's stellar intelligence career had resulted in him being, for a short period, the de facto MI6 Head of Station in Washington in the early 1950s, and for Angleton those had been glory years, the happiest days of his life...

Angleton had come into contact with Philby, and fallen in love with the world of counter-espionage and the heavy-drinking, devil may care ways of MI6 while working for the X-2 – Counter-Intelligence - Branch of the Office of Strategic Services, in London in the winter of 1943-44. Philby, as no other man, had awakened Angleton's imagination to the possibilities of the secret world. Even when the first gossip surfaced about Philby, and then his alleged confederates, Burgess and MacLean, and of communist cells formed in the 1930s in their college days, Angleton had never believed his old friend was a traitor.

And then one day Dick White, then the Head of MI6, had had to make the fateful telephone call to Washington to break the awful news; and James Angleton's world had changed forever.

What had started as a mole hunt within the US security community – if the British could have been compromised so easily for so long; it seemed axiomatic that the CIA, the FBI and every organ of the Federal Government must also be similarly 'penetrated' – had gradually consumed more and more of the CIA's assets, ever-spreading its tendrils of inquiry and suspicion until, gripped by post-October 1962 paranoia, regularly fuelled by further national and international disasters and incontrovertibly confirmed by the evidence of the coups and rebellions, Operation Maelstrom had long ago, come to assume the proportions of a crusade consuming the resources of the greater part of the whole counter-intelligence community of the Central Intelligence Agency.

Ironically, by the mid-1960s, the CIA's operations had been subsumed, much in the same way the House Un-American Activities inquisition had relegated the FBI's crime-fighting role to that of an under-staffed public relations operation as progressively, its focus shifted towards a witch hunt for 'Commies' in the 1950s. Of course, when the McCarthy witch hunts ended, or more correctly, fizzled out in a welter of recriminations that left the reputation of the old FBI indelibly tarnished, J. Edgar Hoover, had simply shifted those 'anti-

Commie' resources to the 'fight against African-American subversion'. Essentially, in his eyes, the Civil rights Movement had become the exemplar of a new 'Un-American activities' threat.

The CIA, on the other hand, prided itself on never having lost sight of the ball.

The recent war had, inconveniently, cast an unwelcome spotlight on the scale and the range of its domestic activities; it had hoped that with the end of major hostilities in the Midwest, that the American people would complacently assume that it had gone back to spying on foreigners. Therefore, the notion that Operation Maelstrom was about to be placed front and centre of the national debate was nothing short of a...nightmare.

That was a given.

For Rachel, the real imponderable was why, exactly, she had been whisked back to DC – without a word of explanation other than that 'this had been cleared by the British Ambassador' – and why she had been driven straight from Andrews Field to the Headquarters of the CIA in Langley.

To meet James Jesus Angleton?

That hardly made any sense.

Unless, that was, he wanted her to kill somebody for him.

Chapter 5

Citizen Maxim Machenaud was sitting on the step below the platform where the great altar had once stood at the far end of the great medieval cathedral, when the Soviet delegation entered the building. Although a detachment of Republican Guards patrolled outside in the cold of the winter's day, the First Secretary and Chairman of the Front Internationale was almost - but not completely alone, today he was accompanied as he often was, lately, at a distance by the thin, severe-looking, lank-haired woman Machenaud called Comrade Agnès, who customarily recorded everything he said in shorthand in her note book – in the sepulchral stillness within, his breath frosting faintly in the clammy, frigid air as the Russians marched purposefully down the length of the knave, their booted steps ringing on the flagstones underfoot.

The Frenchman seemed not to hear them coming until, when they were still some ten or so metres away, he slowly rose to his feet. He had forsaken his normal civilian suit and donned the matt black uniform of the heavily armed storm troopers at the doors.

The expression of Sharof Rashidovich Rashidov, the Troika's Commissar Special Plenipotentiary to the Front Internationale in Clermont-Ferrand, was unreadable. The longer he was in the Auvergne, the better he understood the wisdom of his masters in the Sverdlovsk Kremlin, sending a man such as he, to such a godforsaken place as this. Nobody but a man who had come up the hard way, paid his dues sucking up betrayals large and small, fighting for everything he got, was going to stick it out among *these* people!

He glanced at the woman standing ready with her pencil and note book. He had not noticed her at the time, if she had been present, she must have been lost in the crowd that first day he arrived in the Auvergne. That was the day he had witnessed a middle-aged French woman hung with piano wire, and Jacques Duclos, the leader of the pre-Cuban Missiles War French Communist Party and Maxim Machenaud's last surviving rival, and a terrified teenage girl burned to death for the amusement of Comrade Citizen Machenaud.

Today, Comrade Agnès's face was a mask, her eyes seemingly dead. It was a look many Russians had had to cultivate in the Stalin years.

Rashidov focused his whole attention on Maxim Machenaud.

It was as if his whole life had been a preparation for this...test. His upbringing as the son of an impoverished peasant family in Jizzakh, in remotest Uzbekistan, born on the day before the Russian Revolution, his youth had hardened, tempered him to withstand suffering and cruelty. Despite being wounded so badly he was sent home from the front in the Great Patriotic War, invalided out of the Red Army, fifteen years later he had risen to First Secretary of the

Uzbek Communist Party, a thing no man without an excess of feral cunning and a streak of ruthlessness as wide as the Steppes themselves, could have possibly achieved and yet...the lithe, dapper, wholly evil man standing before him in the gloom of the ransacked *Cathédrale Notre-Dame-de-l'Assomption*, remained a dangerously closed book to him. A complete, lethally dangerous enigma, a mystery that beneath his stolid, poker-face mask, had the unique capacity to scare the shit out of Comrade Commissar Sharof Rashidovich Rashidov.

"Do you know what I did to the last Bishop of Clermont-Ferrand?" Maxim Machenaud asked urbanely. As always, he never bothered with civilities, for such were no more than 'false bourgeois reflexes', superfluous to the Revolution.

"No, Comrade," Rashidov intoned respectfully.

The Frenchman replied without waiting for the interpreter to do his work.

"I had Monsieur Pierre-Abel-Louis Chappot de la Chanonie crucified in the Place de Jaude," the First Secretary of the Front Internationale said, bloodlessly, as if it was nothing of any particular consequence. "Right next to that bloody statue."

"Oh..."

"The one of the noble savage Vercingetorix, the Chieftain of the Arveni Tribe who stupidly allowed himself to be captured by the Romans and paraded through the streets of the Eternal City. Do you know what Julius Caesar did to him afterwards?"

Rashidov shook his head.

"He was garrotted to death."

Sharof Rashidov listened to the translation. He had no idea where this was going; so, he waited, patiently. Some days, Machenaud communicated in his prissy Moskva Russian; today, he was pretending not to understand a single word said to him in Russian.

"J'ai pris les armes pour la liberté de tous."

I took up arms for the liberty of all.

The Russians had learned not to exchange looks, or to interact in any human fashion with each other, when Maxim Machenaud was in this sort of mood; apparently lost within his own twisted reality...

The Frenchman waved idly at their surrounds.

The great church's fixtures and fittings down to the last pew and icon had been stripped out, now the building served as a communal meeting place where the faithful stood corralled often for hours on end, while the First Secretary ranted and Kalashnikov-wielding Revolutionary Guards mercilessly watched for the minutest signs of inattention, or a failure of...*rapture.*

The Russians, having been briefed that the terror had been dialled down in the last year or so; had discovered that their arrival had in some, indefinable way, ramped it up again to a new apogee of random violence.

"Bishop Chappot pleaded to be closer to his God," Machenaud went on. "But we were in less of a hurry than he was. So, we nailed him to a cross. It took him four days to die. Amazing what the human body can withstand if you put your mind to it? Such is life, do you not agree?"

Rashidov shrugged.

"As I have explained previously," he reminded his ally, "the methods that you employ to further the cause of the Marxist-Leninist International is your affair, Comrade First Secretary."

Maxim Machenaud was hardly listening.

"We are standing in the fourth cathedral built on this spot, which was originally a knoll or small hill in the centre of the ancient town. Le Cathédrale Notre-Dame-de-l'Assomption took over a hundred years to build, substantially, that is. They were still building and rebuilding in the fifteenth century, and then again in the eighteenth, and for a period in the nineteenth. We make a mistake when we think that what we can achieve in the short span of a human lifetime can really change the course of history, do you not agree, Comrade Commissar?"

"The march of history is unstoppable," Rashidov retorted, doggedly, hardly crediting that he was having this conversation.

The smaller man shook his head.

"This place was inspired by Sainte-Chapelle in Paris; some say that it is Notre-Dame in black," Maxim Machenaud half-smiled, ghoulishly whimsical in that moment, "but my ancestors chose their building material wisely. The local volcanic stone is of the Trachyandesite variety of extruded igneous rock; it is the strength of that material which allowed the construction of such apparently slender, load-bearing pillars around us holding up the great vault of the ceiling."

Sharof Rashidov recollected that somebody had told him that the colour of the cathedral – black – was not a result of industrial pollution but of the rock from which it had been erected...

"Your man Kolokoltsev led my Revolutionary Guards into a trap at Villefranche," the First Secretary of the Front Internationale declared without warning.

Rashidov was caught off guard; and reacted angrily.

"What? What the fuck are you talking about?"

"*He* tricked my people into believing that he was going to help them seize the Villefranche Fleet. Instead, he led them into a trap."

Rashidov was sorely tempted to take the smaller man's scrawny neck in his muscular, calloused hands and to shake a little sense out of him.

He had seen Dmitry Kolokoltsev's preliminary report on the condition of what was left of the pre-war French Mediterranean Fleet, now holed-up on the Riviera. He had noted with interest but little surprise that the majority of the ships were in need of overhauls, time in dry dock and 'incidental' refits – whatever that meant, he was no Navy man and Kolokoltsev came highly recommended and seemed to know his business – and Rashidov had had no qualms passing a summary of the KGB man's report directly to his superiors back in Sverdlovsk. He guessed that Comrade Admiral Gorshkov would be interested, and assumed that the irascible Minister of Defence and First Deputy Secretary of the Communist Party of the Union of Soviet Socialist Republics would, in due course come back to him with the normal raft of queries, both technical and political. Frankly, he had thought no more of Kolokoltsev's guardedly optimistic report…until now.

"I have no idea what you are talking about, Comrade!" The Troika's Commissar Plenipotentiary complained, trying very hard not to lose his temper. "Why was I not informed that you planned to seize the ships at Villefranche? Surely, that would have been an operation best co-ordinated with the special forces troops attached to my delegation?"

Privately, he was thinking: "What the Hell was Kolokoltsev up to?"

Suddenly, there was animation in Maxim Machenaud's cold grey eyes.

"One hundred and fifty-seven men of my personal guard were flown down to Nice," he ground out between clenched teeth, trembling with rage, "where, assisted by the garrison at Nice, another two hundred and eighty men, they mounted a combined operation to secure the port of Villefranche, and under the leadership of *your* man, a force of over a hundred men was attempting to board the battleship Jean Bart, the flagship of the traitor Rene Leguay, when the whole fleet opened fire on the boats carrying my men, and upon the Revolutionary Guards and their vehicles parked along the dockside and the corniche!"

Neither Sharof Rashidov or any of his escorting KGB officers and Party officials, were any the wiser.

Their blank looks enraged the Frenchman.

"The bloody battleship opened fire with its big guns at point blank range!" Machenaud hissed accusatively. "My people had no chance. Then the survivors were ambushed by fighters in the hills as they tried to escape. Only about twenty men made it back to the fortified perimeter of eastern Nice and many of them were seriously wounded!"

Sharof Rashidov's mind was working overtime.

Admiral Gorshkov would be unbelievably pissed off; it had been a pipe dream but potentially, those ships at Villefranche might have tip the balance of power in the Mediterranean.

And as for Chairman Shelepin; he had sent Rashidov to the Auvergne to 'get a grip' and that was even less likely now, than it had been twenty minutes ago.

One of the reasons Rashidov had, to all intents, forgotten about the French Fleet, and decided against wasting effort fomenting more Soviet-friendly groups among the southern and coastal enclaves ringing the Bay of Lions and clinging, like sickly limpets to the rocky coast of the old Riviera, was that any idiot could see that apart from in and around Clermont-Ferrand, Maxim Machenaud was clearly not the only game in town. Increasingly, he was suspicious about claims the FI also had a tight grip on the larger, former industrial city of Lyon; all his intelligence suggested the place was a deserted ghost town.

In fact, contrary to the wishful thinking behind Warsaw Concerto, there was absolutely no evidence that the people in Toulon, or Marseilles, Perpignan or anywhere else in the south – with the possible exception of the fanatics in control in Bordeaux - wanted to pick a fight with the British, especially on their own initiative. As for the Villefranche fleet, even if the ships wanted to sally forth into the Western Mediterranean there was no bunker oil to keep their boilers firing, there was hardly any ammunition in their magazines; and besides, those fucking cretins on Corsica had already found out exactly what happened to anybody who was stupid enough to pick a fight with the English Royal Navy!

Fuck it!

One would have thought that after the Malta fiasco, even Gorshkov would have learned his lesson!

Warsaw fucking Concerto!

When Rashidov had explained his part in Warsaw Concerto, Maxim Machenaud must have wet himself. Hearing that the Sverdlovsk Kremlin planned – albeit at some unspecified future date - to send him enough arms and Spetsnaz to drive the Free French all the way back to the English Channel, must briefly, have been real music to his ears!

Of course, Machenaud did not want to wait; he wanted everything now!

Sharof Rashidov forced himself to calm down.

If that the little shit had ever been taken in by what the Troika had sold him, for a single moment, it said everything one needed to know about the severity of his psychosis.

Rashidov misunderstood the psychology of the olive branch his masters were dangling in front of their French comrades. All they had to do was hold on until the spring and then the Red Army and the Red Air Force would come to the rescue and together, the Front Internationale and the USSR would be triumphant...

That the object of the exercise was primarily to stop the FI imploding; to sustain it as a thorn in the side of the Free French and their English friends, ought to have been transparent from the outset.

Now, belatedly, it was clear that Citizen Machenaud had smelled a rat. The first consignment of weapons ought to have arrived by now. The Soviet submarines supposedly lurking in the Black Sea ought to have broken out into the Mediterranean, and lifted the British blockade by now. Russian gold ought to have persuaded the merchantmen trapped in Italian and Spanish harbours to begin to land heavy equipment, even crated Red Air Force jets, bombs and rockets of every description at Toulon by now.

None of that had happened.

None of that was ever going to happen.

Long live the Revolution!

Chapter 6

Sunday 29th January 1967
Nikolaev, Ukraine

Fifty-two-year-old Yuri Vladimirovich Andropov, the Deputy First Secretary of the *Komitet Gosudarstvennoy Bezopasnosti*, the USSR's second most senior secret policeman, always felt uncomfortable when he was required to leave behind the 'Sverdlovsk Lubyanka', and travel anywhere near the outlying regions of the New Soviet Union.

This was not entirely unnatural, given that he had very nearly been beaten to death in a Bucharest dungeon, been assigned the task of 'cleaning the stables' in Turkey – a euphemism for overseeing a genocidal campaign against Krasnaya Zarya and its associated clans which had left Istanbul in ruins and large areas of the Turkish littoral bone fields – and once, when he was at his lowest ebb, been sent to France to try to treat with that maniac Maxim Machenaud and that deluded, now dead fool George Duclos. He would bear the scars and the life-changing injuries inflicted upon him by Nicolae Ceauşescu's Securitate goons until the day he died, and carry the deeper, invisible, none the less indelible scars of his other 'missions' with him always.

Since his appointment as the number two man in the Sverdlovsk Lubyanka, Yuri Andropov had taken on many of the duties of his boss, Vladimir Yefimovich Semichastny, who was now firmly installed as the third, junior partner in the ruling Troika. Semichastny had acquired new responsibilities for the current Five-Year Plan and for maintaining internal party discipline; and Andropov had been invited to become the Troika's 'enforcer', a role he relished. Andropov, an ambitious but very patient man, had learned that although one day his time would come to climb the Politburo ladder, it was not now. Having earned the trust of his superiors for the foreseeable future he had dedicated himself to building his reputation for steadfastness and reliability, obedience and absolute loyalty to the Troika, and in particular, to the Supreme Soviet, Alexander Shelepin.

Nevertheless, when he received the peremptory summons to report to the peripatetic court of the Head of the Troika, Alexander Shelepin, at a half-wrecked city sixty kilometres north of the Black Sea, it crossed his mind that it might, conceivably, be his turn to be purged. Such a fatalistic attitude was characteristic in all echelons of the Party, the higher one progressed the nearer one was to the razor's edge. Although, thus far – if one excluded the ruthless purges which had followed hot on the heels of the July 1964 coup – Alexander Shelepin had shown an odd, positively counter-intuitive disinclination to conduct the regular 'sort out' or 'exemplary' winnowing out purges which had been the stock in trade of most of his predecessors.

"There's no need to look so worried, Comrade Yuri Vladimirovich," the Chairman of the Communist Party of the USSR said after the two men had swapped the obligatory public kisses, and separated themselves from their entourages, retreating into what had once been the State Shipyard Director's office in the ugly concrete block overlooking the derelict slips on the *Pivdennyi Buh.*

The forgotten shell of two warships, destroyers still lay rusting, forgotten in the near distance.

"It has been a while since you and I had a chance to talk in private," Shelepin declared, his manner strangely collegiate. "You do not need to waste time convincing me of your devotion to the USSR or the Party, or to me, personally. I know that you are a good man and that your work is of immense value to the Motherland. Vladimir Yefimovich has spoken to me about the desirability of formalising the separation of policy and operational functions within the Central Office of the *Komitet Gosudarstvennoy Bezopasnosti.* You and I, practically all of us in the Politburo, are of a similar generation. We grew up knowing only the Great Patriotic War and the iron rule of the Man of Steel. Comrade Stalin's methods worked well in those days but that was then and this is now, the World has changed and we must change with it or," he shrugged, "perish. Vladimir Yefimovich will speak with you on the matter of the reforms he and I have agreed to streamline the apparatus of state security. The KGB is too large, too labour-intensive and personnel will need to be redeployed to the Armed Forces and civilian policing roles. This will be painful but frankly, we can no longer support a *Komitet Gosudarstvennoy Bezopasnosti* which employs more agents than the Red Army has soldiers."

Yuri Andropov had been horrified when his boss had warned him what was coming. That had been over a month ago, and even now he was by no means reconciled to 'reforms' that almost certainly meant the wholesale dismantling of large parts of the state security apparatus. It was going to be a painful business.

"Vladimir Yefimovich assures me that you are the man to carry through the necessary reforms, Comrade Yuri Vladimirovich?"

"It won't be easy," Andropov nodded. "But I am the man for the job."

"Good. Good. We'll go ahead and promulgate the new organisational structure. Vladimir Yefimovich will remain Director, with responsibility for policy pending the appointment of a second Deputy Director for the Department. You will be confirmed as Deputy Director (Operations). Congratulations, I know we can rely on you."

The two men shook hands.

Andropov was waved to sit down in the hard chair before the room's one big desk. He noted that there was no dust on any surface, and that the building he had walked through seemed like a normal office, with men and women going about their normal daily business, whatever that was these days.

The mood in the room subtly altered.

"The Admiral," Alexander Shelepin prefaced, everybody on the Politburo referred to the irascible force of nature that was Sergey Georgyevich Gorshkov as 'the Admiral', the undisputed number two man in the Troika, "wants to start building the new Black Sea Fleet here, at Nikolaev. It actually makes a kind of sense now that we've got the nuclear submarine program in full production on the Amur, to centralise surface warship construction here."

The Politburo was worried that all their eggs were in that one precious, irreplaceable 'basket' in the Russian Far East, so close to China and those duplicitous bastards – pseudo Marxist-Leninists, dangerously revisionist – who controlled the People's Republic. However, Andropov knew for a fact that Shelepin did not take the recent setback in Sino-Soviet relations anywhere near as personally as many of his senior subordinates.

"We'd be starting from scratch again if we looked to the Arctic, or the Baltic ports," the Deputy Head of the KGB agreed cautiously.

Murmansk and Archangel no longer existed, Leningrad was a rubble field and any ships built, or salvaged in the Baltic would be trapped there.

"I had Mikhail overseeing a technical study of the possibilities for the Odessa-Nikolaev industrial complex," Shelepin continued. "It looks promising." He sighed, shook his head. "Always assuming *The Admiral* doesn't get us all blown up again in the meantime!"

Yuri Andropov blinked, wondering if he had misheard.

Mikhail was Mikhail Sergeyevich Gorbachev, Shelepin's thirty-five-year-old protégé, the child of a poor peasant family who had graduated from Moscow State University and made a name for himself working in the Komsomol at Stavropol before the Cuban Missiles War, an enthusiastic convert to Nikita Krushchev's anti-Stalinization reform program. The man had been dangerously close to the Brezhnev regime and yet, survived the July 1964 upheavals without a scratch, appearing almost immediately in Alexander Shelepin's personal retinue. Gorbachev had been the lead author of the Warsaw Concerto discussion document the Politburo had rubber-stamped in August last year; however, the implementation of the political and diplomatic objectives outlined in that provisional document had been the responsibilities of others.

Any mistakes which may have been made were, therefore, somebody else's fault, specifically, the over-reach of the Red Army on the ground in Western Europe, the Foreign Ministry's determination to muscle in, transforming a domestic propaganda initiative into an international cause celebre, and most egregiously, the Defence Ministry's ongoing unauthorised interference in the civil war in France, and less obviously, in Scandinavia. The big problem was that the Troika had lost control of the situation on the ground in Western Europe. It was not Soviet policy to risk the large-scale re-engagement of the US military on the European mainland. And it was *not* Alexander Shelepin's expressed intention, or wish, to throw fuel on potential flashpoints in Sweden, Norway, Denmark, the old Federal Republic of Germany, or the internecine squabbles of the various factions – rightist, leftist or criminal in Italy, Corsica, Sardinia or Sicily. The argument that by applying constant pressure to alleged 'Western pressure points' it must inevitably weaken and distract the Soviet Union's enemies was, to Shelepin's mind, specious. It was one thing to challenge western hegemony outside Europe, in Africa, or Latin America, or South East Asia but anything that looked like a resurgence of Soviet ambitions in Western Europe was clearly...unhelpful. It was probably already too late to forestall the eventual re-engagement of the United States in the affairs of Europe; a thing which might slam the door shut on any hopes of avoiding a new and disastrous Cold War that would leave the Motherland isolated and impoverished for generations.

That path had led to the catastrophe of the Cuban Missiles War. But never again!

Yuri Andropov had been in favour of the more aggressive stance inherent in the Warsaw Concerto policy. Right up until the moment he realised that 'the Admiral' had hijacked it and the Berlin 'demonstration' was supposed to be the end, not the beginning of the posturing. Like a good Party man; he had quickly re-adjusted. It was irrelevant if, personally, was in favour of a more aggressive – although not overly militarily provocative – stance against the West. It was his job was to run the security apparatus of the USSR, not to ponder upon or to tamper with the geopolitical chess board.

The First Secretary and Chairman of the Communist Party had stood, framed in the window, now he settled – a little fussily – behind the big desk and scrutinised the KGB man with thoughtful eyes.

No two men in the Soviet Union understood as well as Alexander Shelepin and Yuri Andropov that there would have been no coup of 1964, or possibly, no real opportunity to steady the ship of state, or to seriously begin to rebuild the USSR, but for Admiral of the Fleet and Defence Minister, First Deputy Secretary of the Communist Party, Sergey Georgyevich Gorshkov.

Gorshkov had been courageously, openly – everybody thought recklessly - opposed to the Brezhnev regime-inspired insanity of the Iran-Iraq adventure which had 'pissed away' the Motherland's last two tank armies and treasure so vast it was impossible to quantify in the rocky deserts of the Middle East. Nevertheless, ever the diehard patriot, it had been Gorshkov's brilliant counter-stroke which had very nearly destroyed British power in the Mediterranean, albeit at the cost of sacrificing most of what little remained of the Red Navy in the region; always acting as a good communist for the greater good. His daring attack on Malta had completely unbalanced the West and allowed the Iran-Iraq madness, Operation Nakazyvat - *Operation Chastise* – to commence with the Soviet Union's enemies in abject disarray. Moreover, it had been Gorshkov who had stepped in and by ordering the nuclear bombing of Basra, effectively halted the disastrous land war in Iraq, almost certainly preventing the complete rout of the surviving Red Army forces in that godforsaken, blighted country.

When presented with the news of the coming coup; back in July 1964 he had simply, stood aside, and let it happen, ordering Red Army, Air Force and Naval troops not to 'interfere in matters of politics.' In hindsight, that had been a masterful move; enabling

Shelepin to identify, right at the outset, who was and who was not to be trusted within the military-industrial complex. But for this, the purges would have had to go on, and on, and on, possibly without end. As it was, opponents in every arm of the armed forces had been liquidated within days. Undeniably, so much of that which had been achieved in the last two-and-a-half years would have been impossible, unthinkable without Gorshkov's support.

Problematically, there was a growing clique within the Politburo, and around Alexander Shelepin who suspected that *the Admiral* now had his own agenda. And that Admiral of the Fleet, Defence Minister and Deputy First Secretary of the Communist Party of the Union of Soviet Socialist Republics had got a little too big for his sea boots.

Alexander Shelepin's people had no scruples about reporting every disconnected piece of gossip, hearsay, or malicious rumour that came their way about Gorshkov's latest 'initiative' or 'brilliant idea', or whose arse he had just kicked, nose put out of joint or ribald comment he had voiced about the state of the Party in this or that fiefdom as he charged about the country.

Not that Alexander Shelepin believed that a little 'constructive tension' within the Troika and its subservient Politburo, was necessarily a bad thing. He was perfectly content to allow Gorshkov a certain leeway in offering succour to previously neglected, Soviet-aligned freedom and rebel movements around the globe intent on destabilising West-dominated or leaning governments in Africa, Asia, Latin America, and whole-heartedly supported his ongoing large-scale 'survey and salvage' operations in Central Europe. Because of Gorshkov they had a greatly improved feel for the situation on the ground in Poland, East Germany, Austria and even much of former West Germany. Forward camps and depots – in a small way – had been established and much useful technology and other hardware discovered and, in some cases, recovered. Moreover, Gorshkov's rag-tag, gunboat and three-old submarine Black Sea Fleet – its largest vessels a pair of two thousand-ton destroyers, recently, the eleven thousand ton Chapayev class cruiser Komsomolets had had to be laid up for want of spare parts at Odessa – had made the Aegean a quasi-Russian lake, and enabled the repair and reactivation of the war-damaged submarine base at Sevastopol, in preparation for the arrival of the first of the new Amur-built nuclear boats...

Which of course, was where ambition was trumped by hard reality; a thing Sergey Gorshkov was the last man in the new Soviet Union to accept, or in any way tolerate.

Nobody really believed any of those new nuclear-powered Pacific Fleet submarines could really evade the American blockade of the Sea of Okhotsk, let alone make the voyage submerged all the way to the Mediterranean to challenge the British. Even if they made it all the way; hardly anybody in the upper echelons of the Party really thought it was a very good idea to 'challenge' the British, and certainly not the Americans in an area where, clearly, they were bound to react very, very badly.

Except Sergey Gorshkov; whom Alexander Shelepin had realised, too late, had now employed Warsaw Concerto to subvert his own plans.

The first two leaky, accident prone vessels of the Amur-built and based Project 659 submarines – originally designed as hybrid attack-missile platforms capable of firing the P-5 *Pyatyorka* turbojet-powered cruise missile from deck-mounted tubes – had evaded the US blockade in mid-1964. One of those boats had *probably* torpedoed and sunk the American guided missile cruiser USS Providence in the Arabian Sea; nobody knew for sure because the boat which supposedly conducted the attack - the K45 - had not returned to base, and the K-59, assigned the impossible, path-finding role of attempting to steam underwater all the way to the safety of the Dardanelles and the Black Sea, was believed to have been attacked and sunk by the US in the North Atlantic, somewhere in the vicinity of the Azores. It was this operation which had been the final act of madness which had driven Shelepin to act against the old guard.

Characteristically, once 'the Admiral' had got used to the idea that Shelepin had no intention of reneging on their deal, he had continued to pour resources into his Far Eastern power base. Two further, improved Project 659 boats and a pair of Project 627 hunter-killers had joined his Pacific Fleet since July 1964, and three more vessels presently under construction in hardened pens on the slips of the Leninskiy Komsomol Shipyard, at Komsomolsk-na-Amur.

In October 1962, Amur had been targeted by at least one ICBM and at least four bomber strikes; two B-52s having been shot down within thirty kilometres of the yards. Fortuitously, the nearest big bomb had gone off twenty-three kilometres north of the yards, and the city around it had largely survived.

Initially, in the wake of the Cuban Missiles War new construction had been hamstrung by all manner of shortages, with reactor fabrication only re-commencing eighteen months after the catastrophe. However, none of that had deterred Sergey Gorshkov; who had been pressing for the reactivation of the Nikolaev and, or smaller, Odessa yards for the last six months. Gorshkov made no secret of his big plans for his new Black Sea Fleet!

Alexander Shelepin was of the view that the time for 'aggressive confrontation' at sea was not yet, nor would it be for many years to come. The enemy was far too strong at sea, in the air, and possibly, on land, also and the problem was that the irrepressible Admiral was full of plans!

It ought to have been entirely predictable that he would try to appropriate parts of Warsaw Concerto to promote and to progress his ambitions for the new USSR. That, after all, was to be expected of the never say die, never give a millimetre attitude that Gorshkov brought to the Troika.

Good enough is the enemy of better!

Nonetheless, Alexander Shelepin had decided that he must risk everything to put the Motherland on a better path.

He sighed.

"I have informed Comrade Sergey Georgyevich that his plan to induce the Front Internationale to hand over the French Mediterranean Fleet to the Red Navy is unacceptable," Shelepin confided to his chief secret policeman.

Yuri Andropov raised an involuntary eyebrow: his right eyebrow. Ever since Bucharest his left eyebrow had been permanently raised, much in the fashion that the rest of his physiognomy had been rearranged, and thirteen other bones below his neck had been cracked or broken by the Securitate.

Sergey Gorshkov had many plans, fingers in countless pies; the one-man dynamo who had single-handedly galvanised the Motherland's shattered and, after the Iran-Iraq disaster, dispirited Armed Forces was the one person who might, conceivably threatened the First Secretary's grip, or if he wanted, attempt to oust him. Confronting Gorshkov was a strategy fraught with dangers; unless, of course, Shelepin planned to eliminate him...

"No. The Admiral did not take the news very well." Alexander Shelepin scowled. "He was even less happy when I informed him that he was to order the Red Air Force to sink the French ships presently anchored at Villefranche. This, apparently, will take several days to organise; the only aircraft with the range to carry out the mission from bases east of the Urals are Tu-95s presently configured solely for strategic, nuclear roles. Sufficient of them to successfully achieve their objective, at least twenty, will need to be assembled at Chelyabinsk before the strike can go ahead. I have instructed Comrade Sergey Georgyevich that I don't care if we lose every aircraft, the French fleet must be destroyed by the end of the month."

Yuri Andropov absorbed this.

Against his better judgement he felt obliged to offer a warning comment: "Having had dealings with the FI and its leadership..."

"That psychopath Machenaud?"

"Yes, Comrade First Secretary," the Deputy Head of the KGB swallowed nervously, "Machenaud... I'm not sure I know how the Front Internationale I will react to the bombing of the fleet. My information is that the people in Clermont-Ferrand have been casting envious eyes at those ships for some time. Ever since a man called Leguay, one of their few competent Navy men, took command at Villefranche..."

"I don't care how the FI reacts, Comrade," Shelepin retorted, resignedly. "They need our support and it is about time somebody reminded them of their responsibilities. The air bridge to the Massif Central can be suspended or terminated at any time. Our policy is to 'appear' to contest our legitimate security and other territorial grievances in respect of the Warsaw Pact members all the way up to but not beyond, the line of the Rhine." For a moment his exasperation surfaced. "The Admiral was supposed to stop migration across that river line, not bloody encourage it!"

Without warning, Alexander Shelepin rose to his feet and stepped to the window. Behind him, Andropov respectfully got up and hesitantly, moved to join his leader.

"We have made certain undertakings to the FI," he reminded the other man. "If we abandon Machenaud now it won't look good around the World."

"No, it won't," Shelepin agreed. "But I am not going to go to war with the British, or the Americans, over a few mountains in France. Besides, our vital strategic interests *all* lie a lot closer to home."

"Yes, I agree." It deeply troubled Andropov that he still did not know how, exactly, his leader wanted to play things. Gorshkov was a powerful man. "Comrade Sergey Georgyevich has a lot of support within the Defence Ministry. The Red Army and Air Force think he is 'acceptable', but..."

"In the absence of a candidate they can both agree on," Shelepin growled, "they are quite happy with the status quo?"

"Yes, Comrade First Secretary."

It happened that having a Red Navy man as his deputy admirably suited Alexander Shelepin in all respects bar one, that the man in question was Sergey Gorshkov. However, regardless that Gorshkov's position in the Troika effectively prevented the Army and the Air Force obtaining a controlling influence over its affairs, and that Shelepin was, in some sense, still in the Admiral's debt, the time had come to put his over-reaching comrade firmly, and if necessary, brutally in his place.

Hopefully, without starting a civil war like the one the Americans had just gone through!

Pragmatically, if he demonstrated to the others around him, particularly the nascent trouble-makers in the Politburo, and all those generals desperately looking for a way to promote their causes, that he had Gorshkov under his thumb, or if it came to it, he was prepared to crush him, Shelepin's own position would be doubly secure for the foreseeable future.

"I wanted to talk to you, man to man," he explained to Andropov, "because we both know that while I have decided, at this time," he qualified coolly, "that I do not wish to appear to be harshly disciplining, or for that matter, actively demoting Comrade Sergey Georgyevich, I must be seen to be ruthlessly acting against those 'responsible' for recent real or perceived errors of judgement at the highest levels of the Party. In this connection I am of the opinion that we simply do not have enough good people, especially in the middle ranks of Party and Governmental administration, that we can afford, like in the old days, to indulge in indiscriminate purges."

Personally, Yuri Andropov was old-school about these things and he was a little shocked to hear such sentiments spilling from the Shelepin's lips.

"Oh..."

Shelepin was suddenly brisk, business-like.

"I have prepared two lists. You can do what you wish with the names on List Two, throw the families of the men and women on that list out of their homes, or send them to labour battalions. Whatever you want, I leave you to use your imagination. I know that you have a talent for these things."

Andropov waited.

"List two is a long list by today's 'liberal' standards," Alexander Shelepin explained, sensing the KGB man's suspicion of half measures. 'There's no need for executions. I want a handful of show trials. The Politburo will show clemency, commuting death sentences to life imprisonment or internal exile."

"No executions?"

"No. people who have survived the last four years don't fear death the way they did before the Cuban Missiles War."

Yuri Andropov had never really thought about it that way.

Notwithstanding that it was an extraordinary thing to say he conceded that his leader might have a point...

"List One," Shelepin went on brusquely, as if he was a tiny bit uncomfortable with what he was about to say. "Is a schedule of demotions and expulsions from the Party, included are several non-punitive redeployments. There will be no special measures enacted against any family member, friend, or associate of the people named on List One. Nobody on List One is deemed to be in any way an enemy of the people, or worthy of ongoing KGB surveillance. The names on List One will retain their current security clearances."

This seemed an entirely novel way of disciplining the scapegoats required to save Admiral Gorshkov's face. His expression must have inadvertently betrayed Andropov's misgivings.

"Is that clear, Comrade?" Shelepin demanded softly.

"Yes. Of course."

"Good."

The KGB man thought he was about to be dismissed.

However, Alexander Shelepin had not finished.

"If we are to survive," he said quietly. "If we are ever again to stand as equals to the Americans and their British lackeys we must change. We must strive for World Revolution; we must spread the Marxist-Leninist dialectic but that does not mean that we must go back to the bad old days of Stalin. Our people have been through so much, they deserve better. That," he concluded solemnly, "is why, while I am Chairman of the Party there will be no new *terror*."

Chapter 7

Monday 30th January 1967
Stanford, San Francisco, California

Sir Roy Jenkins, the United Kingdom's Permanent Representative Designate to the United Nations was finding life in California exceedingly convivial. He was not the 'Champagne Socialist' his accusers back home in the Labour Party had derisively labelled him but he did enjoy fine red wines, leisurely meals and the company of attractive, intelligent women and after surviving the various privations of life in the British Isles these last few years, he was very nearly, and unashamedly, in seventh heaven on the West Coast. That he also felt that for the first time since he had served - for over a year as Home Secretary - in Margaret Thatcher's Unity Administration, that he was actually 'making a difference' and again, very much a round peg in a round hole, rather than a square one in an irregular octagonal one trying to work, struggling pointlessly most of the time, within the Labour Party. An intelligent, academically inclined historian, superbly articulate in personal conversation if not in public due to a slight lisp, he was a man who prided himself on his command of detail and the reasonableness of his arguments. Basically, he might have been born for his present job.

Once US Secretary of State, Henry Cabot Lodge, had got used to the idea that he had more in common with his Democratic domestic detractors, than with the 'communistically inclined deadbeats' that hard-core Republicans associated with the British Labour Party, he and his English luncheon guest that afternoon in his rooms at Stanford, had got on famously. Both men were erudite, believed that there was nothing good men could not agree to disagree about, and that between them very few problems were going to be insuperable going forward. Which was exactly what the British Ambassador, Sir Nicholas 'Nicko' Henderson had told Roy Jenkins before he got on the plane for San Francisco.

It had not been decided whether Nicko would be accompanying his Prime Minister when she flew to the West Coast in a couple of days. She and the President's, separate arrivals in San Francisco had been delayed for at least another twenty-four hours; not a propitious sign. Everybody in DC had tacitly assumed that the Brits would row back from their undertaking to the Chinese Communists that, they would put a motion to the new General Council proposing Nationalist China – basically, the island of Taiwan, under the dictatorial rule of Chiang Kai-shek – should be removed as a permanent member of the Security Council, and that Communist China, the People's Republic, should be recognised and admitted as a full member to the United Nations. Whereupon, presumably, the British intended to propose that the People's Republic assumed the vacated Permanent seat on the Security Council.

Not one syllable of this proposition was acceptable to the Nixon

Administration, and there was some discussion to the effect that Nicko was going to be needed back in DC to do whatever he could to 'pour oil on troubled waters' while his Prime Minister and President Nixon 'duked it out' on the West Coast.

"Tell me what you honestly think about the China situation, Roy?" Henry Cabot Lodge invited, judging the Englishman had drunk just enough wine to be drawn out of the last vestiges of his immaculately constructed diplomatic shell.

"Honestly, Secretary of State?" People made the mistake of interpreting Roy Jenkins's earnestness for pomposity, for an absence of a sense of humour. It was neither, and as now, there was often a twinkle of mischief behind the lenses of his horn-rimmed spectacles.

"Yes, honestly."

"Very well." The Englishman put down his glass. "Well, if we are to be honest with each other then I think we must start by calling a thing, or things, by their real names and describing them as they are, not how we would wish them to be. Also, our reference point, our mutual starting point must be where we find ourselves now, not in that pre-October 1962 halcyon era one hears so many people who ought to know better, talking of as if in those days the land was criss-crossed with rivers of milk and honey and all was well beneath a sun that never set. If that World ever existed, it is gone forever and we are, as they say, where we are."

Henry Cabot Lodge thought about this, nodded for his guest to go on.

Roy Jenkins contemplated another sip of wine before he continued.

"Her Majesty's Government negotiated and has since ratified, a treaty in good faith with the People's Republic of China which, in my opinion, prevented a futile and ruinous conflict between Great Britain, and possibly several of our Commonwealth allies with the Communists over the future disposition of Hong Kong. In fact, the deal we agreed with the Chongqing regime is unambiguously advantageous to both sides and we firmly believe that the Chinese – the Communists, if you prefer – signed the pact in the same good faith as we did. Under that treaty we made certain commitments; commitments we *will* fulfil to the letter. We expect the People's Republic to do likewise with its side of the bargain. I must tell you, that thus far we have not one scintilla of evidence that they will do otherwise."

The Secretary of State allowed his nascent irritation with British intractability to show for a moment.

Roy Jenkins smiled ruefully.

"Now," he went on, "I wholly understand that the Administration holds the view that the People's Republic's aggression against Taiwan in January last year, not to mention its ongoing threatening pronouncements, in some way invalidates the Hong Kong Treaty. Forgive me, this seems to me something of an intellectual-diplomatic, and indeed, semantic nonsense. Sino-Russian aggression against a regime they view as an illegitimate, revisionist, insurgent threat, is neither mentioned, considered in any way, and self-evidently immaterial to the terms of the treaty agreed between Her Majesty's Government, its Commonwealth, the Portuguese and the People's Republic dealing with the disposition of Macau and Hong Kong. Similarly, constantly raising the issue of our non-involvement in the second Korean crisis is *not* helpful; anymore," Roy Jenkins grimaced apologetically, "than it would be if my principals were to constantly harp on about the untoward intervention of US Navy units in the Persian Gulf while Commonwealth servicemen were engaged in a life or death struggle against vastly superior Soviet forces. I think we had all hoped that we had moved on from *all that* in the thirty or so intervening months. Likewise, we negotiated the Hong Kong treaty with open eyes and we are not about to start re-interpreting its terms willy-nilly; any more than we would, for example, the US-UK Military Mutual Cooperation Treaty, or the re-instituted Five-Eyes intelligence-sharing agreement."

Henry Cabot Lodge stirred uncomfortably.

Roy Jenkins was in no mood to surrender the floor.

"As I am sure my Prime Minister communicated to President Nixon, please do not imagine that our interpretation of our treaty obligations to the people of Hong Kong, and the regime in Chongqing, is not shared by our Commonwealth allies. We are partners in the CMAFTA – the Commonwealth Mutual Assistance and Free Trade Agreement – not its guiding hand. Also, to paraphrase Mrs Thatcher's comments on the subject: 'the United Kingdom is not, and never will be, a short cut by which the will of the CMAFTA may be subverted or marginalised.' I would go so far as to say this is an article of faith to us."

The US Secretary of State was quiet for several seconds.

"But are we talking practical politics, Roy?" He queried presently. "Or statesmanship in the real world?"

"We no longer live in a global environment of masters and serfs, Secretary," Roy Jenkins observed gently, leavening his words with a wry smile.

"We're both going to look stupid next week?" The stalwart of GOP post-Second War politics complained.

"I think not. We will be as steadfast in our agreement over numerous other issues. Friends ought to be able to sustain their alliance despite their differences."

Cabot Lodge suppressed an inner groan.

It was common knowledge that White House insiders were demanding that President Nixon employ one or more of the sledgehammer bargaining chips at his disposal to persuade the Brits to 'get back on the team'. The argument was that if the White House threatened to cut off the United Kingdom's credit line, delayed, paused or temporarily halted deliveries of food or medicines, or if the Pentagon stalled the growing number of joint weapons-development projects, or the ongoing technology exchange programs, that the British would soon change their tune.

Cabot Lodge doubted it but then he fancied he understood their allies as well as anybody in the Administration, apart, that was from his President and Henry Kissinger, Richard Nixon's enigmatic National Security Advisor.

"The danger is that the Chinese will try to drive a wedge between us," Cabot Lodge observed.

"Which Chinese?" Roy Jenkins inquired urbanely. "The Communists or the Nationalists?"

The Secretary of State quirked a wan smile.

"The Communists won't be there," he retorted, knowing that was no answer. "Okay, what will you do if Generalissimo, Chiang himself turns up and personally takes his seat on the Security Council?"

"Is that likely?" Jenkins inquired dubiously. "My understanding was that the poor fellow is so paranoid about somebody mounting a coup in his absence, that he hardly ever leaves his compound in Taipei?"

Henry Cabot Lodge had not known his British counterpart was so well informed.

He repeated his question: "What will you do if Chiang walks into the conference room?"

Chiang Kai-shek was the only surviving member of the Second World War 'Big Five', the others, Winston Churchill, Franklin Delano Roosevelt, De Gaulle and Stalin were dead.

"We should not allow ourselves to be held hostage by the past," Roy Jenkins suggested. "In any event, Chiang and De Gaulle were junior figures in the wartime Big Five, in some ways, incidental to the ultimate victory, remembered mainly because sometimes, there are myths and legends which simply must be sustained, even in this brave new age. If the old man turns up *my* delegation will greet the man with the same courtesy and consideration that we will welcome Alain de Boissieu's man, Maurice Schumann, to the table when he takes the French seat on the Security Council."

Both men knew they were dancing on the head of a pin; there were no plans for the Security Council to convene at the forthcoming San Francisco rededication of the United Nations. Goodness, they had no idea if the Russians were even coming to the party!

Henry Cabot Lodge put down his knife and fork, sat back.

"And that's another thing, there is no such thing as a properly constituted French government, by what right do..."

"It was either the Free French or the Front Internationale at the table," the Englishman mischievously reminded his host.

Morally, it was a moot point which of the Chiang Kai-shek or the de Boissieu administrations, had less right to sit as representatives of their countries. Chiang ruled over a tiny minority of the Chinese population and an island – formerly Formosa – over a hundred miles away from the mainland; de Boissieu controlled less than a third of the territory of European France, and nominally perhaps half of the pre-war Fifth Republic's overseas colonies and departments.

"Putting that aside, there is a very simple way around the China situation," Jenkins offered, knowing that what he was going to say next was not going to go down very well.

"Oh, no, the make-up of the Security Council is non-negotiable," the US Secretary of State averred with a finality that boded ill for his digestion in the coming hours.

Roy Jenkins brushed this aside.

"The Security Council was a construct of the victors of the Second World War. If it was ever fit for purpose, it was, only briefly, in the particular circumstances of 1945. Forgive me for saying this," he recollected sadly, "we no longer live in *that* world. How on earth can we tolerate a situation going forward in which the permanent membership of the Security Council – and with it the five powers of unconditional veto – continue to rest with the globe's single major power, the United States, two badly damaged survivors of the October War, the United Kingdom and the Soviet Union, and two unrepresentative rump administrations, Chiang's and Alain de Boissieu's, when the two most populous nations on the planet, Communist China and India, the latter the largest democracy in history, are excluded from it, the Security Council's, deliberations and therefore can have no commitment to any of its decisions?"

"So, what? We abandon the whole thing?"

"No, but we might seriously consider a more rational settlement…"

"And that would be the British Commonwealth's preferred option?"

Roy Jenkins took a sip of wine, a very acceptable Californian red although not a patch on a good Burgundy.

When would there ever be another great vintage?

"Frankly, I would not care to speculate as to what the view of the Commonwealth is, or is not," he remarked, as if turning Cabot Lodge's question in his mind in the fashion of some abstruse geometric proof. "The broader 'Commonwealth' is an idea, not a fact. Within it, the signatories to the CMAFTA, several of whom, like Portugal and the Scandinavian countries, non-Commonwealth polities, have a generally similar approach to the broad sweep of international affairs. Please remember that Her Majesty's Government presumes no license to speak for, say, Australasia, any more than," he halted, dissonant thoughts momentarily cluttering his head, "the Argentine has to speak for any of the islands in the South Atlantic that it invaded in April 1964."

The US Secretary of State struggled to stop himself raising his hands to his head in despair. The Falkland Islands-South Georgia issue was the last thing the Administration wanted aired on the floor of the new United Nations!

"What I am saying," Roy Jenkins continued, "is that you and I are not the only people who will arrive on board the USS United States with agendas. In that we have more that we agree about than not, and many key interests in common, we will probably be the exception to the rule."

Roy Jenkins was very aware that Henry Cabot Lodge had flown to California not to oversee the final arrangements for the re-inauguration of the United Nations, rather to attempt to identify what, if any, room for manoeuvre remained in the British and therefore, the Commonwealth, stance on the Chinese question. More broadly, he was preoccupied with possibilities of re-establishing the US's pre-war global economic ties on a 'business as before' the October War basis, hoping to appease the loud and persistent Congressional demands ringing in his President's ears.

Problematically, several Commonwealth countries – especially those within the protective umbrella of a CMAFTA Treaty - had embarked on programs to re-nationalise factories, farms, mines and infrastructure hoovered up by American companies and banks in the fire sale confusion of the weeks and months after the cataclysm, in which global markets had crashed, international trade had stalled and traumatised governments had snatched at any credit lines they could find. In those dreadful days, as the denizens of the last great power still standing, Wall Street's robber barons had made hay and now, were feeling hard done by – and not a little sorry for themselves - on account of the brazen retaliatory measures 'unjustly' bearing down on US 'interests' throughout the New Commonwealth. Predictably, those self-same thieves – that was how Roy Jenkins and, unofficially, Her Majesty's Government privately regarded the men responsible – were now shamelessly applying pressure to the White House, Congress, and funding aggressive nationwide advertising campaigns to undo the 'socialistic conspiracies' which now sought to deny them the lucrative fruits of their opportunistic malfeasance in the winter of 1962-63, and the long springtime of greedy acquisitive opportunity which had lasted until the high summer of 1963.

'It is just business; and business is the business of America!'

A contract is a contract...

Of course, Standard Oil and all the other US 'drillers' unceremoniously edged, or just plain ejected, from Arabia and the Persian Gulf after the war of 1964, felt even more aggrieved, especially as it was no secret that cheap Arabian, and subsidised Texan oil was what was filling the United Kingdom's 'energy gap' while the wells and refineries of Abadan were recommissioned.

"I'm sorry, Henry," Jenkins shrugged, "there's no way to phrase this that won't come across as deeply offensive to you. Certain elements within the American business and banking community behaved disgracefully in the aftermath of the Cuban Missiles War. Now, the worm has turned and they are receiving their just deserts. It is profoundly unwise to conflate their mealy-mouthed protests with the broader foreign policy objectives of the United States." He paused, shrugging sympathetically. "I believe that the United States has made a terrible mistake not whole-heartedly embracing the re-establishment of the United Nations. At the present time, the World is looking to America for leadership in a way that, perhaps, it never will again."

One only had to look out across San Francisco Bay to where the USS United States was moored off the Alameda Naval Base to appreciate how little hope, or interest, the Nixon Administration had invested in the re-dedication of the United Nations.

The US Navy had not even bothered to give the great liner a fresh lick of civilian paint; the fastest transatlantic liner in history had been sent to the West Coast in her drab, battleship grey livery. And as to why the ship was anchored within two hundred yards of the nearest Polaris submarines of SUBRON15, great low-lying black missile-packed whales lurking ready to unleash untold global thermonuclear destruction, only a psychiatrist would know!

The huge grey slab of a ship in the Bay, the threatening presence of the nearby missile boats and in recent days, the public bickering of mid-level Administration staffers, the calculated, snide leaks to the DC press corps to the effect that everybody seemed to be 'leeching off America' might have been specifically designed to intimidate the visiting delegations and to sour the atmosphere.

Roy Jenkins put down his glass, regretfully.

"I seriously doubt that President Nixon will come away from the forthcoming events with anything to show for it," he decided.

Henry Cabot Lodge grimaced involuntarily.

And I thought Lord Thomas Carlyle Harding-Grayson, my counterpart in Oxford, was Machiavelli incarnate!

This guy is just as bad!

"Why the heck should we bother with the United Nations at all?" He inquired pointedly, albeit with impeccable courtesy and in the most level of correct, civil monotones.

"Because it is the last best game in town, Henry," Roy Jenkins told him, as urbanely. "NATO and the re-creation of a new 'special relationship' with the United States is what is in it for us; what's in it for you, the United States, is a rehabilitation settlement with the rest of the free World post-October 1962, and longer-term, the re-establishment of *legitimate* economic and strategic global partnerships which will ensure that *you*, and only *you*, remain the globe's solitary super-power for the rest of this century. That is not to say that you will not find this as onerous, and ultimately, as expensive and unsustainable a burden as we back in the British Isles, eventually found it to be in the decades before and after the Second War."

"China?" The US Secretary of State asked, archly.

"Sooner or later a US Administration is going to have to do business with the *real* China, not the fake one; you know that as well as I do. You also know as well as I do that an ongoing open-ended commitment to South Korea, or to the countries of South East Asia, had the potential to be a nightmare for the US taxpayers, not to mention a graveyard for the sons of those taxpayers. Again, I repeat, I am not telling you anything that you, or the President does not already know. Likewise, if I suggested to you that those same taxpayers' hard-earned dollars would be much better spent over the next fifty years rebuilding European civilization and markets for American manufacturers than fighting wars in Asia you cannot possibly, in the end, win: that such a new Marshal Plan would be the best investment your country had ever, or could ever make, I don't really think I would be telling you anything you had not already worked out for yourselves."

Henry Cabot Lodge was not about to split hairs about any of that. Notwithstanding, the Englishman's logic completely ignored domestic US political reality – the mood of Congress and on Main Street America was fundamentally intolerant, or at any rate, it was at present, of the bothersome sophistry inherent in what actually mattered 'long-term' to the country – he knew he was probably right. Those oil fields in the Middle East were not about to fall again like ripe, low-hanging fruit into the United States' lap, the pre-war booming overseas markets for US manufacturers were not about to magically re-open to Uncle Sam at the click of Richard Nixon's, or any other President's fingers.

America *first*, America *alone*, were slogans not strategies and sooner or later the country's continued massive re-armament, the root of the current seemingly runaway but in many ways false, economic boom, was going to have to slow down. There were already an awful lot of soldiers, airmen and sailors on the Federal pay check with not a great deal to do, and no real mission now that the war in the Midwest was won. True, a quarter-of-a-million US serviceman now garrisoned the Philippines, the Japanese archipelago and Taiwan, supported by a much enlarged Seventh Fleet operating out of Hawaii. But what was the role of the US military in the World as it was now when so much of the intellectual superstructure which still governed its existence belonged, frankly, to an ante-diluvian age that no longer existed?

Cabot Lodge had already had this conversation with Henry Kissinger, the US National Security Advisor. The trouble was that unlike the Harvard Academic, he had to factor in the complexities of the politics presently besetting the President.

Irrationally, trying to do the right thing in foreign affairs was invariably painted by one's enemies as 'weakness' and presently, with the re-emergence of the Warwick Hotel Scandal, and the rumours that Judge Warren Burger's stalled – because the Department of Justice had secretly ceased to bankroll it – 'Special Investigation' looking into evidence of cover-ups within the White House, Richard Nixon could not afford to show so much as a scintilla of weakness in San Francisco.

Right now, the American people and the suddenly very twitchy GOP majorities in both Houses of Representatives, needed to be reassured by the sight of a President banging the table and demanding that the United States got the respect it rightfully deserved on the global stage.

Henry Cabot Lodge reached again for his wine glass.

His problem was that he was the man who was supposed to lay the ground work for that 'table thumping'.

All in all, he reflected, it was hardly surprising that the President's pre-San Francisco summit with the British at Camp David had been, in his absence, a 'real car wreck!'

Chapter 8

Prime Minister Margaret Thatcher could never really make up her mind if she was talking to Lady Rachel French, the wife of one of the vital lynchpins of the new transatlantic concord; or Sir Dick White's most remarkable secret agent.

The problem was that this strange question, never far from her mind when she was in the other woman's company, was impossibly complicated by the fact she was one of the few people – anywhere – who actually was 'in the know' about Rachel's part in the savage fighting for Admiral Sir Julian Christopher's Headquarters in Mdina at the height of the Battle of Malta, and her now semi-mythic contribution to the eventual relieving of the siege of the Wister Park Embassy compound just three months later. Dick White, assisted by Airey Neave and more recently, by Sir Daniel French, in a confidential interview, had clarified...*everything*, about those two affairs, if nothing else.

Rachel's was a story that frankly, was so extraordinary that knowing 'everything' about a part of it, albeit a significant 'part', really resolved very little. She had been more than somewhat miffed that her 'security chiefs' had only told her a version of the truth *after* they realised that Dan French was determined to marry her, come what may. He had still been the Governor of Malta at the time, his name inked in for the extremely important, and sensitive post he now held at Boscombe Down; so, that had suddenly forced a lot of hands.

Subsequently, Sir Dick White, ailing fast by then had acquiesced to a face-to-face interview, something of a confessional.

Margaret Thatcher still suspected that but for the great spymaster's illness – he had seemed glad to confess his sins before it was too late – and Airey Neave's reluctant admission that basically, she 'had to know' or she would be in an impossible situation if later some kind of scandal blew up, she would still have been none the wiser.

But she was, wiser, that was.

It helped that the events of the spring and summer of 1964 seemed like very ancient history, so much water – and regrettably, blood and misery – having flowed, somewhat like a river, in full spate under the proverbial bridge in the intervening two-and-a-half years.

Overnight, the sad news of the death of Sir Richard Goldsmith 'Dick' White, under Airey Neave's watch at the Department of National Security, the Joint Director of both MI5, MI6 and the entire intelligence gathering machinery of the Government Communications Headquarters (GCHQ) since April 1964, had been received. Although, it was expected, Dick had been terminally ill and fading in recent weeks, the blow had left both Airey, and Tom Harding Grayson, possibly – along with First Secretary of State, effectively her deputy,

Lord Carington - her closest lieutenants and confidantes in government, understandably down in the mouth.

The Prime Minister had decided that she would break the sad news of the death of the nation's greatest post-war spymaster to his most illustrious agent.

Much to Margaret Thatcher's surprise, Dick White's death had brought tears to Rachel French's eyes and with a sniff of apology, she had asked for a few moments to compose herself before again presenting her customary, coolly watchful face to the world.

"Who will step into Dick's shoes, Prime Minister?"

"Sir Maurice Oldfield. He was appointed Deputy Joint Director a couple of months ago..."

A glimmer of smile touched the other woman's grey eyes.

Margaret Thatcher inclined her head in askance.

The two women were sitting a little apart from the others towards the rear of the aircraft, both having taken heed of their pilot's advice to arrange their seat straps across their laps.

Several rows away Major Sir Steuart Pringle, since the death of his predecessor in the IRA atrocity at Cheltenham in April 1964, the – sometimes suicidally – devoted head of Margaret Thatcher's personal security squad, tried not to eye the two women with too obvious concern. Preux chevalier to the core he had once been moved to admit to the Prime Minister that he did not, 'always feel comfortable' when she was in close proximity to Lady French, and nothing his principal had said to him to allay his fears had done a great deal to soothe his nagging worries.

Steuart Pringle was not privy to the real secrets of the lady, now enjoying a tete-a-tete with the woman whose life he, and every man jack of his AWPs – among themselves they were proud to retain the old nickname 'Angry Widow's Praetorians', a motivational handle coined by the man into whose steps Pringle had stepped – had sworn to guard with their lives. However, he knew enough, and had probably guessed enough of the rest of her story to know that the woman was nothing, if not a natural born killer. Although he had no idea how her marriage to a senior RAF officer – whom he knew to be a thoroughly good egg, a fine officer and a gentleman to boot – worked; if he was Sir Daniel, he would live in fear every waking second, minute and hour of the day. As for entertaining Lady French on a long continental flight in close contact with half-a-dozen of the key members of the British Government, well, that seemed to him to be just...bizarre, actually.

The Royal Marine's brooding thoughts were interrupted when the aircraft's intercom burst into noisy life.

'Rather than fly a lengthy diversion to the north into Canadian airspace, air traffic control has requested we fly about eight miles high for the first half of our trip today. The US Air Force is in the middle of a big exercise down below us, apparently. Anyway, it so happens that forty-two thousand or so feet, is quite close to Commonwealth One's safe ceiling, and the air being somewhat thin up at these rarefied altitudes, we are liable to *drop* or *soar* a few hundred feet without warning...'

As always, Group Captain Guy French's voice was marvellously laconic; as befitted the man who had dive-bombed the then biggest warship in the world in a Handley Page Victor V-Bomber and somehow, he claimed to have no idea or memory of how exactly, survived to tell the tale.

Rachel listened to the broadcast, a wry smile threatening to touch her eyes if not her pale lips. She half-suspected that there was an inner woman within the Angry Widow's complex psychological make-up, which was just a tiny, little bit tempted to swoon every time Rachel's unlikely stepson's cultured, insouciant tones came over the public address system.

Much to her surprise, all things considered she had always got on a lot better with Guy – who was only around ten years her junior - than was reasonable, although, not so well with his wife, a very self-possessed Japanese-American nurse he had met the day after the sinking of the USS Kitty Hawk on board the USS Berkeley. She was one of the team of US Navy doctors and nurses who had saved her future husband's life.

As the Prime Minister had been known to observe: 'It was a funny old world...'

"What is it?" Margaret Thatcher inquired when the intercom went quiet, and the two women continued their interrupted conversation.

"I imagine John Rennie would have expected to be given first 'dibs' at the job," Rachel suggested neutrally.

For the current head of MI6 (the Secret Intelligence Service, responsible for spying and counter intelligence abroad) to be passed, literally on the rails, by a man he must have thought he had seen off in the run-in to the winner's post, would not be an easy thing to swallow. Whereas, Martin Furnival Jones at MI5 (the Security Service, the watchers and the secret policemen at home in the British Isles) was a different case. The last Rachel had heard, Martin was still only 'Acting Director' of his service; presumably, happy just to be back in the fold after his exile in Scotland looking after the dwindling band of 'incurables': persons whom in other, less enlightened times might simply have been 'disappeared'; but these days were simply interned, far from the madding crowds, lest their secrets corrupt the minds or twist the attitudes of the general populous.

Both Wellington College and Baliol-educated Rennie, and Maurice Oldfield were old 'America hands', and therefore acceptable to the New Romans. Of the two, fifty-one-year-old Oldfield, a man from a less privileged background, who had studied under the historian A.J.P. Taylor at the University of Manchester, probably had the better connections in Washington and was by far the wilier of the pair. Rennie broadcast 'establishment'; Oldfield 'detachment' as befitted the man who was, or the two, the born case officer. Maurice Oldfield, who had been knighted, made CBE as long ago as 1959, must have been Dick White's nominee.

Rachel's pain to learn that the man who had been her 'controller' and at some level, her friend and a kind of strange father figure, right up until she was posted to America after the bloodbath on Malta in the spring of 1964, had passed, now.

Neither Maurice Oldfield, John Rennie at MI6 or Martin Furnival Jones were protégés, less still 'deep' confidantes of the departed spymaster. Among the 'old brigade' only Airey Neave and Tom Harding-Grayson might still have a sense of the work she had done for Dick White; or any real understanding of her history. True, they knew, or suspected that she was an assassin but it might well be that as a matter of operational 'necessity' or simply for reasons of plausible deniability, she had never officially existed. 'Officially' it was not beyond the bounds of possibility that Dick had never shared...*anything* about her with any of the three men – Maurice Oldfield, John Rennie, or Martin Furnival Jones -now at the fulcrum of the United Kingdom's national security apparatus.

Rachel's soul was unquiet.

It was odd, disconcerting to think that Dick would never be there, ever again, waiting to hear her report when eventually she needed to touch base, tell somebody...what she had done.

Much as she intuitively shied away from such thoughts, Dick White really had been the nearest thing she had had to a father since her own, dear, half-remembered Papa was dragged out of the house in Lodz to his death back in 1939. She had been eleven then, and not met the handsome, really quite dashing, young intelligence officer until she was nearly eighteen. And yet, he had often seemed fatherly, strangely protective of her; the one man in her life who had always been there for her. Apart, that was, from Dan French, only it had taken her a while to get used to the idea...

Rachel realised that the Prime Minister had said something to her. She blinked alert, fixed the other woman's face in her gaze.

"I'm sorry, I was...distracted..."

"That is quite understandable in the circumstances. I know you have hardly had a moment to catch your breath since you arrived over here."

Margaret Thatcher seemed a little older than she had even the last time they had met, when the Prime Minister and her husband – one of those very rare men who saw exactly through her; but then he was an ex-SAS man – had dined at Amesbury last autumn. Her hair, auburn not the 'blond' the papers used to claim for it, was tinged by a suggestion of grey at her temples and there were new worry lines at the corners of her steely blue eyes. The leader of Rachel's adopted country was just three years her senior, and even on the aircraft immaculately coiffured, outwardly magnificently assured. Rachel was aware that she was not wearing her own years as effortlessly as once she had; to the extent that of the two women she might have passed as the older. It was amazing how quickly the cracks began to appear when one lowered one's guard, allowed the world to see one, at least in part, unmasked.

Rachel had been the guest of the CIA until shortly before

Commonwealth One was scheduled to take off, and nobody in the Prime Minister's entourage had yet attempted to interrogate her on the subject. Which was peculiar, an anomaly; it suggested that either they already knew what Richard Helms and James Angleton had so desperately wanted to talk to her about and they were, as unlikely as it seemed, unworried about it, or that they had no idea what she had been doing at Langley the last couple of days. Clearly, neither clause was tenable, each as improbable as the other.

"Airey was unhappy sending you back to Washington," the Prime Minister announced without further preamble. "Frankly, everything he has told me about Operation Maelstrom is quite appalling!"

Rachel must, momentarily, have blinked in astonishment.

"But you authorised my recall, anyway," she said, recovering her composure in an instant.

"Yes. The Camp David Summit was a disaster. It was always going to be a disaster. I could hardly refuse what was, on the face of it, a reasonable request from," she hesitated, "an ally."

Rachel thought about it.

"Even though you knew that there was a possibility that once the Agency had me in its hands again, I might just disappear?"

The Prime Minister frowned.

"No, Airey and Tom thought that was extremely unlikely."

Rachel did not find that remotely reassuring.

That said, it was good to know where she stood.

She leaned a little closer to Margaret Thatcher, careful to move so slowly that she did not risk alarming Steuart Pringle – any more than he already was – or either of the two, apparently dozing but in reality, watchful Royal Marines waiting, like coiled springs, to hurl themselves into violent action at a moment's notice, five rows farther towards the tail of the VC-10.

"May I ask you a question, Prime Minister?"

"Of course."

"Do you have any idea at all about the things I did for Dick White," she quirked a wan smile, "and for the Service?"

"Yes," the other woman said softly, "and no. And, if it doesn't sound a contradiction in terms, not coming from a background remotely connected to the secret world, I perhaps, like to think I have a more human appreciation of," she shrugged, "things, than some of my male colleagues." Again, she hesitated, briefly considered saying one thing, then determining to say what she had meant to say all along. "The late Sir Julian Christopher, to whom you may or may not be aware, I was affianced at the time of his tragic death on Malta; was deeply troubled by some of the decisions he had been obliged to make in his short tenure as Commander-in-Chief in the Mediterranean. Your husband, passed Julian's confidential papers to me after his death. So, I know that several of those 'decisions' concerned you, and your work with the Red Dawn agent Arkady Rykov..."

Rachel did not react; her eyes were cold as winter on the Russian plain. She said nothing, knowing the other woman needed to say what she was about to say and had probably been waiting to say it, needing to say it, to somebody for a long time.

"Julian confided his regrets in a letter to me; a sealed letter only to be despatched to me in the event of his death. I chose to believe that had he lived he would have made a clean breast of...everything to me in due course. In the event, your now husband, Sir Daniel, passed that letter to me unopened. Later, when I visited Malta, he was so good as to fill in the gaps and to answer, as best he could, my questions. At the time of the Battle of Malta, I had no idea that he had been so completely taken into Julian's confidence, shortly after he arrived on Malta, although I could not but be aware of the real sense of the genuine friendship struck up by the two men during their relatively brief acquaintance..."

The Prime Minister realised that she had become a little over-sentimental.

"I never asked for, and Dick White never volunteered, an accounting of the service you have rendered your adopted country, Lady Rachel. *Until*, that was, you became affianced to Dan. Previously, honestly and truly, although I had no doubt both Airey and Tom had a good idea of the nature of the work upon which you had been engaged, I assumed Dick White would only have shared with them only what they absolutely needed to know. Which," she concluded, "in the times in which we live, is entirely the way it should be. And," she added, a little sternly, "before you ask, neither John Rennie, who has been standing in for Dick in recent weeks, nor Sir Maurice Oldfield, is aware of any file, or of any documentation of any description, in Dick's personal archive, relating to you or your work for him."

Rachel absorbed this.

She shrugged, weary now.

"But when Dick knew he was dying, *you* had to be told everything, anyway," she smiled, feeling very old.

Margaret Thatcher nodded.

Rachel made and held eye contact with the other woman and said, almost casually: "The Americans think that when they unmask me at the San Francisco conference that it will, in some way, alter your Government's policy on China."

The Prime Minister stared at her like she was an idiot.

Okay, so Mister Thatcher, her former SAS-man second husband whom Rachel had discovered, belatedly, was an old partner in crime with Airey Neave, and therefore, also of Tom Harding-Grayson's, had clearly not felt the need to mark his wife's card in respect of *every* dirty little secret of the pre-October 1962 Cold War.

This confirmed that not even Dick White had known everything about her 'grey times' working for Uncle Sam. Never mind, it was not the sort of thing she was going to hold against her adopted country.

Margaret Thatcher's sudden change of expression was such that Steuart Pringle instantly braced himself, and the two watching Royal Marines, seeing their commanding officer tense up, likewise began to move.

Margaret Thatcher waved distractedly at her guardians to relax.

"Which is why I need to get off this aircraft before we reach California," Rachel explained, as if that was not going to present any kind of insuperable problem.

Margaret Thatcher had been under the mistaken impression that she was in control of the interview, that she had initiated it; now she realised her error.

Biting back a complaint she listened, very hard.

Saying nothing.

Rachel was aware that time was short.

"Prime Minister," she murmured, "the CIA believes that a large number of documents relating to Operation Maelstrom – its large-scale counter-intelligence activities against ordinary American citizens – *and the activities of people like me, not just overseas but in North America*, will soon leak into the public domain. Specifically, the Department of Justice and the White House is trying to gag *The Washington Post* but Ben Bradlee, *The Post's* editor, and Kay Graham, its owner, are or rather were, part of James Jesus Angleton's circle. They don't scare easily, and after all the grief they've had the last year or so over the Warwick Hotel Scandal, I think they are beyond caring what the Administration tries to do to them." Rachel shrugged, almost but not quite apologetically: "So, to pre-empt *The Post's* scoop, it is likely that somebody in Langley, and possibly, at the FBI also, will leak *my story*, or at least, what little they know about my history, to one of *The Post's* competitors."

"Surely the Administration would not stoop so low?"

Rachel studied the Prime Minister, surprised that there was a note of genuine horror in her voice. Perhaps, in some respects, the Angry Widow was still the choirgirl people assumed her to have been in the early days of her premiership?

"If you were the Prime Minister of a Latin American government who had upset the White House, you might be dead now, Prime Minister. Please, do not make the mistake of thinking, for a moment, that you are dealing with 'decent' people. In England I was 'one of a kind'. In this country I was only ever one of many."

Rachel let this sink in.

"Look," she continued, "just as Dick White didn't tell you things that he knew you did not need to know, or if, had you known about them, you would have faced impossible dilemmas; so, it is with the US intelligence community. The only difference is that back home all you had to worry about was MI5 and MI6, over here, the CIA, the National Security Agency, the Secret Service and the FBI are just the tip of the iceberg. No one department of state controls more than one or two of the big players, CIA belong to the State Department, the FBI to Justice, other organs serve the Pentagon..."

"Angleton?" Margaret Thatcher interjected. The name was familiar but she could not recollect ever having met the man, although Airey Neave had mentioned him several times – in passing - in recent months. "James Angleton?"

"Since 1954 he has been ADDOCI, Associate Deputy Director of Operations for Counter Intelligence, at Langley. He was an Anglophile right up to the moment he got used to the idea that Kim Philby was a Soviet spy." Rachel thought about it: "Actually, he was one of the last people in the western intelligence community to accept that his old friend had been a traitor all the time. He tried to veto an operation to liquidate Philby shortly before the October War..."

"Liquidate him?"

"It was the last time I worked with Kurt Mikkelsen; the man *you* sent me to America to kill."

Now the Prime Minister was totally baffled and starting to get very worried. She would have protested that she had never sent anybody anywhere to kill anybody but that objection seemed somehow redundant in the present context. She was head of a government that did, or at least, had sent people abroad to kill its enemies in the past; it was just nobody had told her, or her predecessors about it at the time.

Rachel continued; her tone blandly matter-of-fact.

"He's the man the FBI believe – and our 'friends' at Langley – now believe, plans to assassinate the President during the re-dedication of the United Nations in San Francisco," she reminded Margaret Thatcher.

"You were *not* sent to America to kill anybody," the Prime Minister snapped with such hissing, outraged vehemence that half the people in the cabin of Commonwealth One turned their heads. "And how on earth does exposing you, assist in stopping this madman?" A gasp of air: "Or induce *My Government* to renege on a solemn treaty obligation to the People's Republic of China?"

Rachel was unmoved by the outburst.

"Forgive me, but I was sent to America to kill, or to be killed, by Kurt Mikkelsen, you just did not know it at the time you authorised Airey to approach me."

Margaret Thatcher was lost for words.

"And, for what it is worth," Rachel went on, her tone sympathetic, patient, "unless something changes in the next few days, the White House will allow the CIA to embarrass your government out of spite, regardless of whether it is convinced that it can alter your foreign policy in the Far East. And as for the CIA, well, James Angleton knows that when the truth about Operation Maelstrom gets out his career is over. So, he is doing what any normal, paranoid, megalomaniac, high-functioning sociopath in his position tends to do; he is conspiring to bring down as many other people around him, and presumably, in friendly foreign intelligence agencies, as he can before the axe falls."

"Surely, the President knows what is going on?"

Rachel was tempted to retort, acidly: "You've met the man, what do you think?"

Instead, she was a little, albeit only a little, more diplomatic.

Given that Richard Nixon had not invited his own Secretary of State, Henry Cabot Lodge II to participate in the main discussions at Camp David, preferring to send the elder statesman to the West Coast with the White House's advance guard, she had rather hoped that the Prime Minister had assumed, from the outset, that the Catoctin Mountain retreat was going to be no more than a Presidential photo opportunity, at which the Administration made strenuous attempts to publicly cover up the worst cracks in the vaunted new 'special relationship'.

Perhaps, the lady had worked it out for herself?

After all, *they* were having this conversation.

Rachel shrugged, deciding to ignore the Prime Minister's question.

"Dick is gone. I work for you, now."

"You no longer work for the security services..."

"People like me don't get to retire, Prime Minister. Ask Airey, ask Tom, Lord Harding-Grayson."

"I have no use for an assassin."

Rachel thought that was a naïve, and oddly ill-considered remark for any British Prime Minister to think, let alone say out aloud.

"Forgive me, we misunderstand each other," she said, resignedly. "I am already on a mission. I was from the moment I left England. You can order me to stand down. You can have me sent home in chains. What you cannot do, in any circumstances, is to allow our American 'friends' to take a picture of *you* in *my* company. Tomorrow, or by the day after, the media in this country is going to be so obsessed with the *Angel of Death* that briefly, possibly for several days, they will give James Angleton, the CIA and the President an easy ride on the revelations that the US Government has been systematically spying – driving a cart and horses through any number of constitutional rights and protections – on the American people."

As Rachel spoke her acquired, practiced Home Counties English accent had begun to re-acquire the Polish lisp and vowels of her youth.

"If I arrive in California with *you*, Angleton's creatures at Langley will drip feed everything they know about *me* into the press in the coming days. Destroying people is what they do best; a thing they have been doing at home and abroad ever since the CIA was created. Therefore, I cannot arrive in San Francisco with you. Which is why I needed to have this talk with you before it is too late. It is all a game, Prime Minister. I'm sure that Dick told you that; a brutal, nasty, immoral game and we must play it the way our enemies play it or...they will win and we will lose. If I am not on Commonwealth One when we land in California, the game will change again. *The Locksmith* will have to think of a new stratagem to buy himself time; or maybe, something else will happen. Either way, we will be playing our game, not their game. The decision is, of course, your's. But remember, the life that I thought I had in England is already gone now, possibly forever."

"I don't believe that. I cannot let that happen!"

"It has already happened," Rachel replied gently. "I am again what

I was. Major Pringle is right to watch me every moment; right now, I am dangerous to anybody around me. So, either you chain me to a seat, or you must let me run free."

Chapter 9

Contra Amiral Rene Leguay was on the point of collapse when he eventually reached the top of the Jean Bart's hastily repaired, somewhat scorched gangway that afternoon. It was one thing joking about not being able to sit down on account of his recent wounds, another entirely being on one's feet all the bloody time!

The Jean Bart's port side was painted – although in the main, hardly scratched – by the multiple impacts from the Revolutionary Guards' 75-millimetre anti-tank guns. Apart from a couple of rounds which had penetrated the thin, lightly protected strake above the tapering 227-millimetre armour which extended over three metres above the main belt – itself some 330-millimetres thick to the level of the first platform deck – and having failing to detonate, pinged around off armoured bulkheads before finally coming to a rest, the Front Internationale's supposedly elite Revolutionary Guards might as well have been shooting cowpats as high explosive rounds at the steely carapace of the leviathan.

If the idiots had stopped to think they might have realised that two or three rounds pumped into the unmissable hulk of the Clemenceau, anchored barely two hundred metres off shore, might easily have set the carrier on fire and left her a burning wreck. Likewise, the thin-skinned destroyers moored nose to stern in the northern part of the anchorage would have been susceptible to crippling damage even by the 20-millimetre anti-aircraft cannons mounted on a couple of the Revolutionary Guards' lorries. However, true to form the numskulls had just blasted away at the biggest, toughest ship in the bay instead of doing the logical thing; running away to fight another day.

Not that Rene Leguay was complaining.

For all its faults, his plan could not have worked any better; in drawing the fools' fire onto the Jean Bart – on which the majority of his people were safe behind virtually impenetrable cemented armour – he had minimised the fleet's casualties and ensured that perhaps, two-thirds or more of the FI's bully boys had been blown to pieces on the corniche or drowned in the cold waters around the flagship.

In total, there had been less than a dozen casualties – none fatal – on all of the other ships combined. Inevitably, Jean Bart had not been so fortunate, suffering seventeen dead and fifty-one wounded, including many with injuries which still threatened their lives.

Most of the battleship's casualties had been manning or sheltering in the lightly-skinned gun houses of the Jean Bart's 100-millimetre 55-calibre, or 57-millimetre 60-calibre anti-aircraft batteries. What little available ammunition on board had been transferred to two of the 100-millimetre and three of the port 57-millimetre mounts, all of which had shot themselves dry inside two to three minutes. So, notwithstanding that from a distance the Flagship seemed to bristle with 100- and 57-millimetre anti-aircraft cannons, it was now completely defenceless against air attack.

Warned that the gun houses of the smaller calibre weapons offered little protection from anything but infantry weapons, people caught topsides, or drawn to the upper decks through curiosity – or more likely, just wanting to see the hated Revolutionary Guards blown to smithereens by the ship's big guns – had had nowhere else to hide when the enemy's 75-millimetre anti-tank rounds, and heavy machine gun fire had started coming inboard.

Sadly, several people had been killed and injured on the bridge, watching the battle from the open wing of the compass platform.

Back in November 1942, when the Jean Bart had been moored at Vichy-controlled Casablanca, still fitting out, she had been struck by as many as seven 16-inch rounds fired by the USS Massachusetts – not to mention at least two bombs by US Navy dive bombers – and although 'sunk', in that she settled on the shallow, muddy bottom of the harbour alongside the dock, not one of the one-ton American shells had penetrated her main belt, or deck armour.

Knowing this, it was hardly to be wondered at that the relatively small-calibre artillery and anti-tank guns of the Revolutionary Guards – even shooting over open sights at very close range – had failed to strike a single telling blow.

From his low but unrestricted vantage point in the stern of the Clemenceau's captain's barge – practically all of the Jean Bart's boats had been destroyed in the battle - Rene Leguay had counted at least a dozen hits, none of which had so much as dented the castle of steel's outer shell. Unfortunately, the damage above the great armoured raft around which the rest of the ship had been built, was painfully obvious, even from a distance. The 75-millimetre shells and countless cannon and machine-gun rounds which had peppered the bridge, and raked the amidships superstructure, had made quite a mess and started several small fires. As the barge had approached the irregularly mottled flank of the leviathan, Leguay identified where stray projectiles of several calibres had bounced off the two giant, quadruple-barrel main battery turrets forward of the bridge, and aft of the superstructure, the port and central triple 152-millimetre secondary turrets.

He could see daylight through the big, ugly hole in the funnel. Men were still aloft trying to reconnect severed connections to the main mast radio and radar aerials. Incidentally, he was able to confirm with his own eyes the report that a direct hit had disabled the port boat crane; this at least was a thing he could afford to be sanguine about since most of his flagship's boats were splintered driftwood...

In his exhausted, pain-wracked condition the gangway steps were a sore trial to him.

Eventually, reaching the brow, soaked in sweat and trembling with exertion, he straightened to his best ability and saluted the officer of the deck, a weary, stern-faced matron wearing an Engineering

Committee armband at her left bicep over a greasy grey boiler suit. In common with his welcome on board all the other ships of the Villefranche Squadron, his orders to the effect that he did not wish to be ceremonially piped on and off deck, had been signally ignored.

Aurélie Faure had assured him this was a personal compliment to him from the crews of *his* fleet. The action of two nights ago was a defiant blow that every single man, woman and child of the squadron had been aching to strike. During his day-long tour of the fleet, on each ship the people evacuated from houses and streets destroyed by the Revolutionary Guards and in the subsequent battle, had surrounded Leguay and his ever-present companion. But for Aurélie's warning frowns and unashamedly possessive demeanour, they would have slapped his back and mobbed him so enthusiastically that his wounds might have split open, and given the severity of his wounds it was not beyond the bounds of possibility he that he could easily have bled to death on the deck of one of the warships; not a very dignified way for a hero to exit stage left!

"It is good to have you back on board, Mon Amiral," the matronly engineer – strictly speaking, only an artificer under training in the bowels of the monster – but today, like everybody else, called upon to do whatever needed to be done and thus, finding herself officer of the deck at the gangway.

The woman was clearly immensely proud to be the one with the honour of welcoming *her Amiral* back onto the flagship.

Indeed, it was a funny old world...

Yesterday, notwithstanding the chaotic aftermath of the previous night's desperate battle, the oiler La Seine had edged alongside the Jean Bart's undamaged starboard side and taken aboard two-thirds of the flagship's bunker oil, some twelve hundred tons, just enough tonnage to re-invigorate the rest of the fleet.

All the big ships in the anchorage bar the old cruiser, the Jeanne d'Arc, had managed to light off boilers, and to turn at least one of their screws. Now thin, grubby flutes of greyly translucent, shimmering smoke rose into the oddly still winter air above the other warships. The bay was again a scene of purposeful activity, with several patrol boats, ship's launches and fishing craft moving between the ships transferring personnel, shifting scarce stores and ammunition. Deeper into the bay La Seine, high on her load markings again having swiftly emptied all but the dregs from her bunkers was in the process of being lashed alongside the Jeanne d'Arc.

The Fleet had to escape Villefranche: the great natural anchorage had been its haven; at any moment it could become its prison and then its graveyard.

Privately, Rene Leguay was amazed that the FI had already granted him further two priceless days grace.

Even so, everything seemed to take so damned long...

That night the oiler would slowly drag the Jeanne d'Arc close to the Jean Bart so that a tow line could be carried across...

"You need to lie down, Mon Amiral," Aurélie commanded, her tone betraying that she knew, unlike most of their people that their admiral had been much more badly injured than they had known, or he was prepared to admit, in the battle. Only hours before his tour of the fleet a further, agonising surgery had been carried out to remove several further shards of detritus, shrapnel imbedded in his lower back. That seemed to have gone well but Rene Leguay had been as weak as a child in the following hours and was, even now, fortified by stupidly reckless doses of Benzedrine and Codeine, practically out on his feet.

Rene had been on the verge of collapse more than once that afternoon as he conducted one, agonising visit after another to his ships. Twice, at Aurélie's insistence, ignoring his feeble protests, they had had to take him out of sight, and hastily re-bandage his seeping wounds. Presently, he was ashen grey and fatigued beyond measure...

Standing, swaying on the deck of his flagship, Leguay realised belatedly that the only reason he was still on his feet, was that Aurélie had put her arm around his waist and he was leaning on her.

"Help me!" She called desperately; afraid he was going to pass out and, in a moment strong, gentle hands took the load.

Presently, Rene Leguay was laid, with strange tenderness on his lightly injured left side on the big bunk in the Admiral's day cabin beneath the quarterdeck.

"I have things to do," he protested, impotently, his words slurring.

"Sleep a couple of hours first," his anxiously watchful personal angel of mercy declared implacably. "I've sent for the surgeon to check your dressings. Keep still, man!"

In truth, by then Rene Leguay needed no encouragement to lie still, unmoving: it hurt a lot less than any of the other alternatives. Aurélie had moved behind him, her hands cautiously exploring his clumsily stitched gashes. Her tender touch seemed to make the aching go away...

"How is our Russian friend?" Leguay asked when the Jean Bart's exhausted surgeon arrived.

"Capitaine Kolokoltsev is very unwell. He's feverish. I'm sorry, there is not much I can do for him, sir. He needs anti-biotics and much more intensive care than we can give him." The other man apologised before, with a contemplative hesitation, he collected his courage. "You should be in the sick bay with him, Mon Amiral!"

Leguay protested feebly when the much younger man dug a small bottle of pills out of his pocket.

"These will help with the pain..."

"I thought we were out of morphine?"

"The Clemenceau sent over everything left in her medical locker." He must have looked to Aurélie Faure for support at this moment. "These will help you keep going..."

Leguay swallowed a couple of the pills, washed them down with brackish water from a cup Aurélie had to hold to his lips, and then he slept, painless in an opiate-induced oblivion.

Serge Benois, the battleship's greying Gunnery Officer, and by default, the Jean Bart's second-in-command, reported to the cabin about an hour-and-a-half later. He took off his cap, wiped his hands on his slacks.

"How is he?" He asked, nodding stoically to the unconscious fleet commander in the gloom of the big cabin lit by a single dull bulb near the hatch.

Aurélie vented a shuddering sigh, thankful that Serge Benois was one of the few people in the fleet with whom she could be honest.

"He badly needs to rest. I don't know how he got through today," the woman replied, not attempting to conceal her angst. "I really don't know...I thought he would collapse a hundred times..."

Tears trickled down her pale cheeks. She sniffed, a little ashamed of her weakness. The man patted her arm, nodding paternally.

"Look," he guffawed quietly, sighed. "I ended up on the Jean Bart because it was the only place in the Navy a drunk like me could go on drinking himself to death without doing any damage." At this point Serge Benois grimaced, chuckling lowly, self-effacingly. "Then I met *him*," he declared. "I thought he was just another FI shit from Toulon. A week later he threw me in the brig to sober up for a couple of days, then he had me brought to this cabin."

The flagship's second-in-command grinned.

"'I plan to save this fleet'," he said to me. "That was the day he threw a couple of those fucking pimps over the side," Benois smiled ruefully. "Remember that?"

Aurélie blinked at him. She had no idea where this was going...

"Yes," she agreed, "that was a good day."

The man shrugged: "Sorry, I know you had a hard time when you first came on board..."

Aurélie knew the man had not meant to remind her how she had inveigled her way on board the battleship. Or that, when Rene had first come to Villefranche, she had still been at the mercy of the Jean Bart's gangsters and pimps.

"That was the day things started getting better," she smiled, tight-lipped.

The lined, prematurely aged Gunnery Officer glanced again at the unconscious form of the one man at Villefranche under whom, all the disparate elements crewing the ships of the ghost fleet could, and thus far, had loyally coalesced.

He chortled gruffly.

"He said to me: 'Serge, the people in Toulon are shits and our Front Internationale comrades in the Auvergne are fucking lunatics. One way or another we have to save the fleet. Do you think you can stay sober long enough to help me?' And here we are. Still, more or less alive." He looked to the woman. "So, just so you know, you're not the only one on this ship, or in this fleet, who loves the Old Man."

Aurélie allowed Serge Benois to wrap her in a fatherly embrace; having sobbed on his shoulder for a few restorative seconds she swiftly recovered her composure.

"Let him sleep," the man murmured. He straightened, visibly focused on the business of the moment. "There are things le Amiral will need to know when he comes to," he prefaced. "Shipboard status: he'll have seen that the old girl looks a bit worse for wear topsides; but most of the damage is superficial. Basically, repairs are in hand and our people are doing their best; I've prioritised re-stringing the main mast aerials so we've got a working FM short-range ship-to-ship comms system again. Otherwise, things on board are as under control as they are ever going to be. Number One main battery turret: we've finally got all four big guns loaded again. Between you and me I've got no idea if the turret will traverse, or how fast, the next time we hit the switch." He grinned, piratically and rubbed the stubble on his chin. "On the bright side; while we're at anchor the big guns are pointed in more or less the right direction. What is it they say about being thankful for small mercies?"

Aurélie Faure had snatched up a notepad, her pencil scratched urgently.

"The surgeon told you about the Clemenceau suddenly discovering a locker full of drugs?" She checked.

The man nodded. "Better late than never."

"It is good that everybody is pulling together, Serge," Aurélie retorted mildly

"I suppose so." Having come to report the general status of the ship he got on with it. "We still have about six hundred and some tons of oil in the bunkers. That is enough to get us out into the Mediterranean and a couple of hundred miles from shore. Regrettably, nowhere near enough to get to Malta, or Gibraltar, and we don't want to go anywhere near the Spanish. I suppose Genoa is an option. Those bastards on Corsica would feed us all to the fishes..."

Aurélie stopped scribbling and gave him an impatient look, reminding him that he needed to deliver the rest of his report, if she was to properly inform the Fleet Commander when he awakened from his drug-induced slumber.

"Sorry. I'm still hopeful we can bring Number Three 152-millimetre turret back into service." He considered this, counting in his head. "We've got about fifteen reloads per barrel for the secondaries. The De Grasse and most of the destroyers have still got bullets in their magazines but like us, not very many of them. So, even after the other day's fight, we're not completely defenceless. Except against air attack, that is. In that regard, I've got people working to bring the air search radar on the fighting top back on line. That's no use to us in harbour but out at sea it might give us a few minutes warning of trouble." He changed the subject. "Rations. With several hundred more civilian mouths to feed that's going to be a problem in two or three days from now. There's resistance on some of the ships to sharing their rations, although Amiral Leguay's order for the flagship's stores to be opened to the rest of the fleet has temporarily taken the sting out of that for now. La Seine's skipper is hoping to start moving the Jeanne d'Arc sometime in the next hour or so. The Chief is getting ready to turn our screws just in case it looks like we're going to get rammed. On that subject, I'm fairly confident that we can manoeuvre if and when required. Not very fast, obviously, but we can probably move at about an hour's notice. Most of the other ships are hoping to be ready to move sometime in the next twenty-four hours."

Serge Benois sighed, continued soberly.

"Once we pass a line to the Jeanne d'Arc her deadweight is liable to make us drag our anchors. We may have no choice but to tow her out to sea if that happens."

"Why can't she anchor?" Aurélie asked brusquely, grimacing apologetically for her flash of impatience the next moment.

Serge Benois had not taken offence.

"She's going to have to cut her forward chains. Everything's seized up. Her capstan motor is a rusted heap of junk."

"Okay," the woman murmured, realising that she should have just listened in the first place.

Serge Benois ran a grimy hand through his thinning hair.

"Le Amiral is right about us having to get out of here in a hurry. The bastards have got two, maybe three submarines at Toulon, or wherever the Hell they've hidden them away the last few years. All they have to do is put them off the entrance to the bay and we're not going anywhere. Then they can starve us out, mortar or shell us twenty-four hours a day from the hills, or more likely *the other side* of the hills hereabouts, or try what they tried the other night, except plan it properly next time..."

"How long do we have?"

"Before those idiots get themselves organised? A day or two, perhaps. Longer, if we're lucky but we need to be gone before that happens."

In other circumstances Benois would be reporting to the ship's Executive Officer but he, of course, was dead. The man had put a pistol to his temple last autumn. His replacement had been killed in the battle with the Revolutionary Guards, cut in half by a 20-millimetres cannon shell as he stood on the bridge wing. In the absence of anybody else; Serge was reporting to *her* because...well, actually, she had no real idea why anybody was *reporting* to *her*, or for that matter even *taking her seriously!*

She was their Admiral's secretary, his steward, no more or less. Rene had not taken her as his mistress nor, had he given anybody the impression that she was his mistress.

And yet knowing that their Amiral was wounded the Jean Bart's people were looking to *her*...

The World had truly gone mad!

The flagship's unlikely new Executive Officer must have read her thoughts, some of them, anyway. He shook his head, touched her arm.

"Aurélie," he murmured reassuringly. "We all stopped being in the *Marine Nationale* after the war. We never had a leader until le Amiral came aboard the Jean Bart," he went on, lowly, as if he was afraid the fitfully sleeping man in the nearby bunk was hearing every word. "The

Worker's Committees put their own people onto the fleet. Nobody knows what happened to the original captains of the bigger ships, they were just purged most likely. The fucking Navy sat back and let it happen. But when *your* man," he went on, nodding at Rene Leguay's unconscious form in the nearby gloom, "came to us, things started to change. He was one of us, a real Navy man who cared about *us*. He didn't care about the state of the ships, or all the old rules we were breaking, or the ordinary citizens sheltering in the fleet. Right from the start he was our *Amiral*. He reminded us all how much we had missed the old *La Royale!*"

The Royal...

No real French Navy-man called his service the 'National Marine' when he was among his friends. To a son of the service it was always 'La Royale', a living, breathing tradition.

Aurélie Faure was staring at the man with eyes that must have been as large as dinner-plates by then.

"And you were his woman months ago, only we knew it, and you knew it before *he* did." Serge Benois declared with the authority of a fond, slightly disreputable uncle. "Whatever, whether I like it or not, I'm the *real* executive officer of this tub now. So, if it comes to it, I'll sail her, and I'll fight her as well as I can if our Amiral," another nod to the sleeping form in the nearby bunk, "needs me to. But I won't make the mistake of thinking this is *my* fleet the way it is *his*," he shook his head wryly, "or *yours*," he concluded, half-bowing his head: "la dame de mon Amiral."

My Admiral's lady...

Now Aurélie suspected she was blushing like a virgin backstage at the Folies Bergère!

She stared at the deck by her feet, nonplussed.

"So," the man sighed, "while the Amiral is sleeping; who else on board *his* flagship would I report to, Mademoiselle Faure?"

Much as she would have preferred to cry, Aurélie sniffed, straightened to her full height, her forehead just about coming to the man's unshaven chin.

"I thank you for your report, Commander Benois. I am sure that the Amiral will resume his duties as soon as he has rested. I will pass on you report when he awakes."

It was not until she was alone again with Rene Leguay that Aurélie became aware that she was shaking from head to toe. She folded her arms tight about her chest, squeezed her eyes shut and hoped, against hope she was not about to completely break down.

Rene had once remarked, in that self-effacing way of his that tended to take the sting out of even a stiff rebuke, that the difference between a real Navy man and a 'fair-weather' sailor was that a 'real' La Royale man always remembered that 'things can always get worse!'

There was just enough time for Serge Benois's booted footsteps in the passageway to fade to quietness.

Before the alarm bells started sounding throughout the ship.

Chapter 10

The old Fletcher class destroyer was quartering a six-mile square patch of sea, zigzagging just in case one or more of the Front Internationale submarines based at Toulon had managed to slip past HMS Onslaught, the diesel electric Oberon class submarine presently guarding the approaches to that eerily derelict port. Overhead the sky was overcast, and farther out to sea Campbeltown's air search and gun director radars picked out the two high-flying de Havilland Sea Vixen FAW2s of Task Force V1's combat air patrol. The CAP was operating twenty or so miles inshore of the invisible flagship and the cruisers of the gun line. Campbeltown's sisters, the Perth and the Berwick flanked their Leader at varying ranges of eight to ten miles respectively, to east and to west, with the other four Fletchers of the 21st Destroyer Squadron 'riding herd' on the Victorious.

Captain Dermot O'Reilly paced his darkened bridge, pausing now and then to remark about this or that, or to peer in apparently idle curiosity at the glowing green screens of the radar repeaters. The ship rode easily on the strangely placid wintery Mediterranean swells.

Campbeltown had been closed up to Action Stations – these days, really just a refined, nervier version of Air Defence Stations One – for the last hour as the destroyer's erratic zigzagging had gradually brought her closer to the rocky shores of the Cote d'Azur.

O'Reilly had been surprised by how little electronic 'life' there seemed to be on that still distant shore. No probing radar pulses reached out into the night, and apart from a few faraway echoes from small boats close inshore – fishing boats, perhaps – there was no coastal traffic, and there were no aircraft movements in the skies over France. Given that he had been sceptical of the reconnaissance reports about the lack of air activity, it was a little unnerving to discover how far France, less than five years ago, a modern, fast-growing industrial powerhouse, had descended back into the medieval darkness.

Yet now his radars left no doubt.

There was no distant glow of lights along the northern shore; and the invisible electromagnetic spectrum scanned by his radars was deserted.

The ship's C-I-C – Command Information Centre – reported occasional snatches of what could have been talk, or broadcasting; it was hard to pick anything out of the background mush, white noise which might have been jamming except, it was not.

Steaming north from Gibraltar, the distant Spanish coast had been radio 'quiet', not dead like this.

The minutes dragged past.

The destroyer's Captain fought back the urge to pester his Communications Officer.

They ought to have heard something by now, instead, his mind was turning through ever-darker possibilities.

He had proposed that the best way to avoid 'unnecessary unpleasantness' might simply be for him to take Campbeltown into the anchorage at Villefranche, and to attempt to establish navy-man to navy-man contact with whoever was in command...

'No, we're not doing that, Dermot,' Rear Admiral Henry Leach had decided. 'Not unless we know exactly what we're dealing with. The blighters might simply turn the Jean Bart's big guns on you!'

Nonetheless, neither man actually wanted to blast the French Fleet out of the water unless they absolutely had to; hence, tonight's attempt to communicate with the ships at Villefranche.

Thus far, to no good effect...

Suddenly: "The Comms Room have made contact with the Jean Bart, sir!" The bridge talker reported.

O'Reilly hesitated, realising that there was more.

"They say they are in communication with a lady calling herself *la dame de mon Amiral*, sir?"

Dermot O'Reilly had grown up a fluent French-speaker, his best friend as a teenager – the poor fellow had been killed at Dieppe in 1942 - had been of Quebecuar descent and although his command of his second language had grown a little rusty with disuse, he grinned at the talker's Anglicized accent.

'*My Admiral's Lady*," he guffawed out aloud, not remotely knowing what to make of it.

He had been handed a headset without having to request it.

He donned it.

"Patch me through. Headset only, please."

This, he decided, was going to be interesting!

He waited patiently to be told he was on an open circuit.

"This is in the *plain*, sir," he was reminded. It was a comfort to know that all the evidence of the last few hours was that there were precious few people listening; but not *that* much of a comfort. "Understood. Carry on."

The connection crackled and hissed, swooped and attenuated distractingly.

"This is Captain O'Reilly," he said. He thought about it: "C'est Capitaine O'Reilly!"

For several seconds there was silence.

"My name is Aurélie Faure, I am Secretary to Contra Amiral Rene Leguay, the Commanding Officer of the Jean Bart and the Villefranche Fleet."

The woman had spoken in French.

"Forgive me, my English is un-practiced," she added apologetically.

"That's all right, Madame. I speak French," Dermot O'Reilly replied sternly. He thought about trying to apply normal radio protocols. He decided using 'OVER', or 'CLEAR' or 'COPY' risked confusing matters possibly beyond all recovery. "Please explain why Amiral Leguay is not available?"

There was a hissing of static for some seconds.

"Amiral Leguay was wounded when the Front Internationale attempted to seize the fleet. That was two nights ago. He lives, he will be all right...I think, I hope. But at the moment he is incapacitated in his cabin and much of our radio," she paused, 'many of our intercom and public address system cables situated above the main armoured deck were shot through in the recent battle. I am speaking to you from the ship's radio room and it will take some minutes for my comrades to carry Mon Amiral to this place..."

Dermot O'Reilly was still digesting this when the woman asked him two obvious – in the circumstances – questions.

"Where are you, Captain O'Reilly?"

Axiomatically, he was not about to call out Campbeltown's longitude and latitude. This, the woman belatedly worked out for herself a moment later.

"Sorry, that is a stupid question..."

A burst of clicking and roaring drowned out everything for about ten seconds.

"Sorry, I heard none of that?" O'Reilly called.

The woman's question was stark: "Have you come to kill us all or to save us?"

Now *that* really was a good question!

"These are matters I must discuss with Amiral Leguay," O'Reilly said. "In the meantime, we need to find a 'cleaner' and a more secure frequency over which to communicate. I will keep this channel open. Please pass your headset to one of your radio people, my Communications Officer will advise him of alternative frequencies by which you may contact this ship if this channel is jammed, or unusable for any reason."

O'Reilly scowled as he handed back the headset.

"How far away is the Flagship?" He asked Lieutenant Keith Moss, Campbeltown's Navigator and by chance presently the officer of the watch.

"Victorious is over fifty miles to the south, sir. Beyond scrambled TBS range," he apologised, as if it was his fault.

O'Reilly glanced at the air search repeater.

"Request the CAP to fall back on Campbeltown. I want to piggyback their secure comms to the Flagship. As soon as the link is up, put it through to my sea cabin please."

Calling his sea-cabin a 'cabin' was to grotesquely malign the word 'cabin'. Cupboard or 'dog-kennel, would have been pejorative yet oddly apt names for the tiny space crammed into the starboard side of the bridge. However, it was home when the ship was under way and frankly, he would not have swapped it for a suite in a five-star hotel.

He switched on the overhead lamp, shut the hatch at his back and tried very hard, to think slowly, rationally. Contrary to their worst fears the ships at Villefranche might not be under the control of Krasnaya Zarya, the Front Internationale...

A buzzer rang.

He picked up the handset near the head of his narrow bunk.

"Captain speaking!"

"The flagship is on circuit two, sir."

O'Reilly flicked the toggle.

Rear Admiral Henry Leach sounded as if he had been half-expecting his call.

"What the Devil has gone wrong now, Dermot?" The other man inquired jovially.

O'Reilly recounted his short exchange with the woman claiming to be on board the Jean Bart.

"Fifty-fifty it is some kind of ruse, a trap, Dermot."

"I agree, sir. But..."

"Well. You had better have a chat with this chap Leguay," the Task Force Commander determined. "We shall take stock of the situation again. Carry on."

Chapter 11

Tuesday 31st January, 1967
Headquarters Free French 2nd Corps, Châlons-sur-Marne

Field Marshal Sir Michael Carver stepped down from the train, his booted feet sinking deep into the falling snow. As was his custom when he came to France or visited troops in the field, on training exercises or operations in Northern Ireland, he was attired in standard British Army battle dress absent any insignia of rank. He wore a tanker's black beret with the badge of the 7th Armoured Brigade; his one small concession to sentimentality in memory of his days in the desert in the bad old days of 1941-42.

The Supreme Commander of All Allied Forces in France – SCAAFF – was similarly decked out in battle dress, except unashamedly he was proudly wearing his General's tabs and medal ribbons on his left breast.

Alain de Boissieu crisply saluted the Chief of the Defence Staff and stuck out his right hand in welcome, as, in his turn, did the lean, moustachioed, smiling officer at his shoulder bearing the pip and crossed sword and baton tab of a major general.

For the cameras, Michael Carver, who had stuck rigidly to his self-denying ordinance that their ought to be only one field marshal in the British Army – otherwise the elevation the rank implied was meaningless, until the official retirement from the active list of his predecessor as CDS, Sir Richard Amyatt, now Lord Hull, gazetted a month ago, which was due to come into effect at midnight – exchanged fraternal kisses with his French host, followed by a manly handshake with de Boissieu's Chief Liaison Officer, Francis St John Waters, VC.

Yesterday afternoon, Carver had attended Woodstock Palace to receive his field marshal's baton from Her Majesty, the Queen, in a ceremony carefully choreographed before the assembled British and ever-growing international press corps in Oxford. He had found the whole thing an enormous strain, a genuine trial whereas the arduous overnight journey to France by train, ferry and train, again, as the Arctic blizzard now engulfing Northern Europe swept in from the east, had been a blessed relief and an invaluable opportunity to receive and digest the implications of the latest reports, while locked in conference with his Staff.

Carver had instructed his senior lieutenants that while they were in France, to conduct all discussions 'in French', and firmly reiterated his earlier mandate that there will be 'no suggestion of *us and them*' in allied deliberations.

Frank Waters, the Prime Minister's husband, was in a typically buoyant mood.

"Do you think the bloody weather is part of Warsaw Concerto, sir?" He put to the Chief of the Defence Staff.

This prompted hearty guffaws all around them.

Michael Carver noted that Alain de Boissieu had laid on a large honour guard; long lines of Legionnaires, Chasseurs to one side, and light tanks and armoured personnel carriers to the other, awaiting his inspection in the increasingly wintery scene.

The Chief of the Defence Staff reviewed the troops with keen alacrity, pausing a couple of times to complement a man on his turnout, once remarking that 'a White Christmas has come late again this year'.

Then the troops were dismissed back to their billets and the senior officers hurriedly sought the warmth and privacy of the Hôtel de Ville, formerly the mayoral offices of Châlons-sur-Marne, for the last year the Headquarters of the Eastern Command of the Free French Army, and now the home of the Staff of the Free French 2nd Corps, now briefly hosting SCAFF and his entourage.

Major General Guy Méry, a forty-seven-year-old veteran of the Second War Resistance, commanded in this sector of the front. A tall, distinguished-looking man he was noticeably stiffer in the presence of his English guests than his chief, Alain de Boissieu.

Frank Waters had warned Michael Carver not to be concerned if Méry 'seemed a little offish'. According to the ex-SAS man the 'Free French High Command is a bit like my wife's party, practically every senior officer, regardless of the abundant weight of evidence to the contrary, thinks he is top quality C-in-C material!'

The Chief of the Defence Staff had not planned to come over to France for the start of what everybody – bizarrely, given the climatic conditions – called the 'Spring Offensive'. But then he had been handed the latest meteorological reports.

A giant storm system from the east – all the way from Siberia, it seemed - was rolling across Western Europe and temperatures were predicted to fall as low, as improbable as it seemed, to perhaps minus fifteen or more degrees Celsius over parts of northern Germany, the Low Countries and much of France, in the next few days.

Roads would soon be impassable from the Channel coast to the Auvergne, the rebuilt railways of the Somme and Picardy were predicted to grind to a standstill within hours, and men in the open could easily freeze to death in hours...

Of course, the dreadful weather conditions would be the same for the enemy but, understandably, Michael Carver was wholly concerned only with the intractable problems the storm was likely to cause *allied* troops. Thus, knowing that if he travelled to the Marne Front, he was likely to be snowed in, at a minimum, for at least several days, possibly a week or more, he had deemed it essential that he take ownership, in person, of the decision whether to proceed, or to delay the planned offensive.

In fact, he had already decided that a seven-day postponement was inevitable. This was the third 'perfect storm' of the winter, in which apparently freak, once in a hundred or two or three hundred-year climactic conditions, conspired to produce 'super-hurricanes' in the North Atlantic, or in this case, to transport a Siberian blizzard to normally temperate Western Europe. Maddeningly, the generally clear, dry, frosty weather of the last fortnight had been marvellous campaigning weather.

Once the conference room had been cleared of junior officers and aides, Michael Carver wasted no time attempting to sugar-coat the bitter pill. In the room where the city council of Châlons-sur-Marne had sat, debated, haggled in the years of peace, the Chief of the Defence Staff looked around the table, his gaze settling on Alain de Boissieu's face.

"We must stand down until this storm blows through, gentlemen."

Guy Méry stirred unhappily.

"The snow might lay on the ground for days or weeks, and even when it thaws the ground will be heavy, and river obstacles swollen, in flood..."

Michael Carver listened patiently.

"I agree, conditions will not be ideal. They hardly ever are. However, for our irregular troops – the majority of our frontline forces – General Winter will be their death. I know full well that your professional units, like those of the BEF in the west, are fully capable of fighting in this weather. Unfortunately, two-thirds of our forces are not. Moreover, for so long as this storm lasts there will be no possibility of re-supply or reinforcement either from England via the Channel, or from the depots located around Calais and Boulogne. Tracked vehicles may be able to cope with the snow, wheeled fuel tankers and ammunition lorries cannot. Presently, we have a situation where our assault troops are billeted under shelter, protected from the worst of the storm." He let all this sink in, knowing that he was not telling any of the men present anything they had not already worked out for themselves. "Gentlemen, I am proposing to unilaterally order an initial seven-day postponement of northern element of Operation Mangle."

Much though this had been anticipated there was, nonetheless, a reluctant sigh of relief around the table.

"That said," Michael Carver continued, "the Royal Navy has been directed to delay its operations against the Front Internationale in the south by forty-eight hours; and then, when our offensive in the North gets under way, to hit the enemy with everything it's got, as planned." He smiled ironically. "It happens that this delay would probably have been inevitable. Apparently, the cruiser Belfast was unable to sail on schedule with the rest of Admiral Leech's squadron, and the assault ship, HMS Fearless, was held up by unspecified technical difficulties. Both ships should be on station in the next few days. Likewise, the two American nuclear submarines we asked for..."

Major General Guy Méry leaned forward, resting his arms on the table.

"Is the plan still to 'neutralise' the Villefranche Squadron, Sir Michael?"

The Englishman nodded solemnly.

It was Alain de Boissieu who broke the silence.

Carver was struck once again by the profound recent change in the man. His voice now rang with calm authority and clearly, he and the commander of the 2nd Corps had agreed to bury their professional and personal differences in recent weeks.

"As distasteful as it is to us all, Guy," he declared regretfully, "if that fleet was to break out into the Western Mediterranean it might threaten Malta, or Gibraltar. As for the possibility those ships might fall into the hands of the Russians, like all those Turkish ships did back in 1963 and 1964, well, frankly, that does not bear thinking about!"

"No," his compatriot agreed. "It is just that it brings back memories of July 1940 and the disaster at Mers el Kebir..."

Alain de Boissieu returned to the main issue.

"I agree with Sir Michael's appraisal of the tactical situation. Clearly, not the least of the problems with the weather is that it makes aerial reconnaissance and fire support for our ground troops impossible."

"Obviously," Michael Carver interjected, "you should continue raiding and other scouting, or intelligence gathering activities as you see fit during the period of postponement, Alain. It is not beyond the bounds of possibility that the coming storm will decimate our foes without us lifting a finger!"

Frank Waters chortled wickedly.

"That would be a damned shame. Nothing like seeing the whites of the other fellow's eyes when he knows you've got his number, what?"

"Yes," the Chief of the Defence Staff breathed, with markedly less blood-thirsty enthusiasm, "quite."

Chapter 12

Tuesday 31st January 1967
Battleship Jean Bart, Villefranche-sur-Mer

Rene Leguay had had to be carried through the ship. That afternoon, he had passed out the moment his head hit the pillow, of his bunk in the Admiral's cabin near the stern of the leviathan. He wanted nothing but to go back to sleep; even though he knew that Aurélie would not have allowed the others to rouse him unless it was a matter of life and death. Despite the pain he was still groggy.

As there was no coffee, an ersatz, vile chicory-flavoured brew was offered to him and obediently, he drank it down. Whether by accident or by design, it was so disgustingly bitter it partially snapped him out of his drugged stupor.

"Now I'm being poisoned," he groaned, determined not to show the pain he was in. Somebody had tried to arrange cushions on the hard chair in the radio room. It helped, just not very much. He met Aurélie Faure's concerned gaze. Her face was pinched with worry and this sobered him as nothing else could. "Please inform Captain O'Reilly I am ready to speak to him."

Very little that Aurélie had just said to him about her conversation with the British officer had sunk into, let alone stuck in his mind.

There was a delay as communications were re-established.

"He sounded like a Quebecois?" He checked with the woman.

She nodded.

With a sharp knife one could have cut the atmosphere in the compartment; everybody understood that the next few minutes would decide...*everything.*

"Put this on the speaker," Leguay directed, while they waited. "Everybody on the bridge needs to hear this, too."

He was passed a headset.

He held the microphone to his face.

And heard at last the voice of the man who was going to be, in all likelihood, his executioner sometime in the coming hours.

Yes, he was definitely a Canadian, Rene Leguay decided.

"This is Captain Dermot O'Reilly of Her Majesty's Ship Campbeltown," the other man declared in flat, unemotional French. "To whom do I have the honour to address, sir?"

That was a nice touch!

"You are speaking to Contra Amiral Rene Leguay, I command what was, until a few days ago, the Mediterranean Fleet of *la Marine de la Révolution.* My fleet successfully repulsed an attempt by forces of the Front Internationale to seize it two days ago. We are, therefore, now deemed enemies of the people, fugitives..."

"What is the status of the ships under your command, sir?" O'Reilly asked neutrally, his voice echoing around the bridge.

"Those of my ships which are capable of making steam are preparing to depart this place in search of sea room, Captain O'Reilly."

There was a pause.

"To what end, sir?"

Rene Leguay half-smiled.

"Thank you for your consideration, Captain O'Reilly," he said, grimly, sensing that the man at the other end of the connection had intuitively grasped the parlous situation of the Villefranche fleet. And, as one captain to another, had no intention of further denting his interlocutor's dignity. "My 'end' is simply to escape the tyranny of the Krasnaya Zarya maniacs who now rule my country. If you demand my surrender then you have it, sir. However, my personal preference would be to sail the fleet to a safe harbour where my people will be free to decide for themselves if they wish to join the fight against our mutual foes."

Leguay realised that this was quite a lot for O'Reilly to assimilate all at once, so, he waited patiently. In the event he only had to wait about five seconds.

When he spoke, Dermot O'Reilly's voice – despite the static and clicking of the connection – rang with command.

"I regret that I am operating under specific and non-negotiable rules of engagement, sir," he apologised. "I am obliged to require you to unconditionally surrender all your ships to British and Commonwealth naval forces. In this connection I am authorised to accept that surrender on behalf of my direct superior officer, Rear Admiral Leach. Is this acceptable to you, Amiral Leguay?"

The Frenchman swallowed hard.

He thought he was going to be physically sick for a moment.

Implicitly, if he cavilled then the British would destroy his fleet. His dignity, his sense of honour was not worth the blood of a single one of his people.

"Yes. That is acceptable to me in every respect," he said with a heavy heart.

"Thank you, sir," O'Reilly replied, clearly relieved. Suddenly, he was crisply business-like, there was no time to be wasted. "I must know if the Front Internationale or your people, have installed surface-to-air missiles to defend the city of Nice or the anchorage at Villefranche?"

"To my knowledge, no. I regret that I cannot be certain what air defence provisions have been made at Nice."

"Can you confirm that Nice is held by FI forces?"

"Yes. We anticipate that they will make another attempt to capture the fleet as soon as tomorrow…"

"Please list the vessels under your command, sir."

"My flagship is the Jean Bart. In company is the Clemenceau, the cruisers Jeanne d'Arc and De Grasse, and the destroyers La Bourdannais, La Galissoniene, Surcouf and Kersaint, and the frigates La Savoyard and Le Lorrain. The oiler La Seine and several smaller patrol boats and auxiliaries, including several fishing boats are also present in the bay. All are under my command and my protection."

"How many people do you have on your ships?"

"Perhaps, two thousand five hundred. That is, men, women and children. Few of my ships have much ammunition in their magazines for their main batteries, Jean Bart included. My magnificent flagship had not fired her big guns for nearly ten years until the other night."

To Rene Leguay's surprise, the other man chuckled.

"That must have been quite a thing!"

"It was, it was..."

O'Reilly sobered: "What happened to the submarines based at Toulon before the October War, Amiral Leguay?"

"Until recently, they were manned by skeleton crews. I would be surprised if at least one of them had not been fully re-activated by now..."

"So, one of them could be standing off Cap Ferrat as we speak?"

"Yes..."

"Very well," O'Reilly concluded. "Please continue to prepare your ships to get under way. Campbeltown will come alongside Jean Bart at first light. At that time, I will formally accept the surrender of your fleet. Thereafter, you and I will discuss what needs to be done, Amiral."

Rene Leguay acknowledged this without comment.

O'Reilly informed him that he was passing his handset to the Campbeltown's Communications Officer.

"We need to establish robust radio communications," he explained tersely. "Alternative secure channels, and so forth. Please keep this channel open. You and I will speak again in the morning."

O'Reilly hesitated.

"The Task Force's combat air patrol will extend its area of operations north to cover your ships. You should hear our aircraft overhead within the next few minutes."

On board the Jean Bart, Rene Leguay passed the headset back to a technician.

He tried to get to his feet unaided; a bad mistake.

Aurélie Faure and the two nearest men grabbed him as his knees buckled.

Chapter 13

Tuesday 31st January 1967
Washington Post, 1150 15th Street, Washington DC

Ben Bradlee was on the phone when Kay Graham quietly knocked at his door and slipped, as was her habit, almost shyly into her Managing Editor's office. Her friend's secretary had warned him that her boss was on the phone to 'somebody at Justice'. Which, obviously, did not sound like good news; but then the team of lawyers who had been camped out in the boardroom a floor above her head, for most of the last fortnight, was hardly a good omen either.

They had known they were about to stir up a hornet nest; but right now, it felt as if the White House was about to call in Strategic Air Command to level *The Washington Post Building*!

Yesterday morning, just before dawn the FBI and the Washington PD had turned up in force to 'seize' allegedly confidential documents that were 'illegally in the possession of the company'. *The Post's* duty attorney had pointed out two grammatical and three spelling mistakes in the two page-long warrant. Nevertheless, nobody had tried to stop the FBI agents and Washington PD detectives ransacking selected offices and newsroom desks, and when Kay had received a call asking if the boardroom safe should be 'cracked', she had meekly – as any good citizen would – given permission for it to be opened.

Of course, the searchers had found nothing remotely relevant to their warrant and by mid-day, given up. Although, not without attempting to 'steal' miscellaneous other papers and notebooks which had caught their attention. The resulting stand-off had only ended late last night, when the Special Agent in charge had been served with a subpoena demanding that he 'desist forthwith any searches or confiscations not authorised' by the original warrant.

Ben Bradlee's room was still a complete mess.

There were heaps of files on the floor, piles of typescript still lying unrecovered, the FBI had jemmied open all his desk draws and splintered wood still crunched underfoot. Only one of the three telephones in the office still worked. Similar damage – well, vandalism – had been inflicted elsewhere in the building although the main focus of the interlopers had been in the adjoining newsroom.

Kay Graham had no idea where, what *The Post's* staffers now called the 'Langley Papers', were. Day-to-day, certainly hour-to-hour, she suspected that not even Ben Bradlee knew where the three boxes of files were to be found.

Only an idiot – or in this case, a gang of idiots like the people surrounding J. Edgar Hoover – would think for a second that they would be dumb enough to keep the stash at 1150 15th Street!

But then, the evidence they had to hand was proof positive that the FBI was not alone in being run by megalomaniac, paranoid imbeciles with no regard whatsoever for the constitutional rights of their fellow citizens!

When the Langley Papers had first arrived on *The Post's* doorstep – actually they had been left in the corridor outside the apartment of a newly recruited rookie stringer, called Robert Woodward, who had previously been connected with *The New York Times* – Kay Graham had initially suspected that *The Post* was being 'hoaxed', either by the FBI or the CIA, possibly at the behest of the Administration, to discredit its ongoing investigation of the Warwick Hotel Scandal.

If anything, Kay had been even more suspicious than Bradlee; whom she had asked to check out 'this Woodward guy' before they risked putting their heads in what had every hallmark of being an 'Administration bear trap'.

Twenty-three-year-old Robert Ushur 'Bob' Woodward, had turned out to be an interesting young man. A native of Geneva, Illinois, he was the son of an attorney, and had studied History and English Literature at Yale under the auspices of the Naval Reserve Officers Training Corps, graduating in the summer of 1965. At Yale he had been initiated into the Phi Gamma Delta fraternity and been a member of the Society of Book and Snake, the college's fourth oldest secret clan. One of three children of his father's first marriage, he had grown up in a household swollen by the three children of his step-mother. Tragically, his father, the President of the DuPage County Bar Association, his stepmother, Alice and three of his siblings had disappeared in the days after the Soviet nuclear strikes on Chicago in October 1962, and of his two surviving sisters, Wendy had died of cholera and war plague in Madison, Wisconsin in 1963, and Anne, had perished in the atomic bombing of St Paul at the outset of the war in the Midwest.

Unsurprisingly, it seemed the young man had had some kind of breakdown, which had led the Navy to send him ashore from his first ship, the USS Northampton, and by the end of the war in the Midwest, he had been honourably discharged into the Reserve with the rank of Lieutenant, junior grade. His Yale contacts had got him introductions to *The Times* and *The Post*, and several West Coast papers when he visited friends in DC, where, it seemed, the young man had by design, or inertia, settled last autumn.

Ben Bradlee had told Kay from the start that: 'No, this is exactly the sort of thing that James Angleton would do if somebody was stupid enough to let him get away with it.'

Ben was convinced the CIA had wanted *The Times* to get the apparently too good to be true scoop. In any event, he had wasted no time instructing Carl Bernstein to 'take this guy Woodward up country and figure out what we've got.'

In the meantime, he and Kay had agonised over what to do with their possibly lethally poisonous chalice.

Kay had known James Angleton for many years. He and his wife, Cicely – née d'Autremont - were among her circle of long-standing DC friends. She had heard that the marriage was no bed of roses; a thing which struck a chord. James Angleton was one of those men who tended to bury themselves in old and new compulsions; he presumably poured the same intellectual curiosity and intensity into his work for the CIA, as he did into growing rare orchids or hooking trout in the rocky streams of New England. Kay knew each of the Angleton's children, again not well but by name and a little by temperament. Cicely and the kids had been out of town when their Georgetown town house was burned down during the Battle of Washington.

Even now, a part of her still wanted to believe that the relatively small number of documents she had had the opportunity to read, were the minutiae of some kind of cruel hoax, if only because it beggared credulity that the Associate Deputy Director of Operations for Counter Intelligence had employed – had been allowed to employ - virtually the entire apparatus of the CIA's Office of Security, to spy on the American people. There were, allegedly, over fifteen thousand 'live' investigations ongoing, and files on tens of thousands of other Americans, many of whom had been targeted primarily on grounds of their religious beliefs, or their affiliation with protest or civil rights groups. Many of the newest files dealt with individuals who had registered as Democrats since the defeat of LBJ in November 1964, with particular emphasis on new recruits or candidates with any connection to the Betancourt family.

Although only fragments of their files were included in the tranche of documents thus far in the possession of *The Post*, it was apparent that the patriarch of the clan, Claude Betancourt, and his daughter, Gretchen, were 'targets' of great interest to the CIA's Office of Security, and both were under constant surveillance, as was the US Ambassador to the United Kingdom, Captain Walter Brenckmann and his family, with the notable exception of the Ambassador's eldest son, a Lieutenant Commander in the Submarine Service.

Angleton's inquisitors seemed obsessed with the Brenckmann family; on account of their links to the Betancourts but also because the CIA was clearly highly motivated to 'gain insights' on the eventual findings and recommendations of the *Commission into the Causes and Conduct of the Cuban Missiles War* 'at the earliest possible time', which was currently being drafted by the Ambassador's second son, Daniel, a Clerk to the Chief Justice of the United States, Judge Earl Warren. The clear implication was that the White House was eager to steal a march on Congress; presumably with a view to, if it was possible, heaping even more opprobrium and humiliation on the Democrats ahead of next year's Presidential race.

Kay Graham had been moved to remark: 'You couldn't make this stuff up!'

It seemed that there were also files on hundreds of journalists, lawyers, and a whole department of the Office of Security had been created and tasked with infiltrating university campuses, and tracking the un-American activities of 'student leaders and disloyal teachers'. All of which was overshadowed by the machinations of the 'Political Warfare Division', a publicly acknowledged organ of the CIA, which had been responsible for rooting out End of Dayers – spies, sleeper agents, agent provocateurs, saboteurs, terrorists and fifth columnists – during the first rebellion in Wisconsin and the later Civil War. However, far from being wound down at the close of hostilities in the Midwest, the PWD had never ceased conducting its ever-expanding nationwide 'mole hunt'.   It seemed that everybody was under suspicion; and that denunciation was the CIA's new badge of patriotism because nobody was above suspicion.

According to the CIA the British Foreign Secretary was a KGB spy, as was Lester Pearson, the Canadian Premier...

It was ridiculous!

The *only* person in America who was not under suspicion was James Jesus Angleton...and in Kay Graham's candid opinion *he* was plainly delusional!

According to Ben Bradlee, Carl Bernstein's jaw had pretty nearly literally hit the floor when he read a report that the Warwick Hotel Team – whom the world now referred to as 'the plumbers' – sent to New York to 'bug and to conduct general surveillance' on Doctor Martin Luther King junior and his associates in 1964, had been a routine element in a continent-wide CIA-sponsored and financed operation, directed against the leadership of the Southern Christian Leadership Conference. As to the FBI's subsequent involvement, acting as a CIA sub-contractor in the actual bugging of the Warwick Hotel...it was all too insane!

The Managing Editor of *The Washington Post* hung up.

"That was Carl," Ben Bradlee explained. He picked up the handset again. "Hold my calls please."

Kay Graham's face creased with concern.

"He was calling from a box downtown," her friend lied with a broad grin. They both knew the FBI or the CIA, among others, would be listening in on each and every line coming in and out of the building. "They've found another memo from the White House requesting surveillance and phone tapping of the DC offices of Sallis, Betancourt and Brenckmann..."

Kay made to speak.

Ben Bradlee held up a hand.

"*And* Ambassador and Mrs Brenckmann's hotel room in Georgetown.   There's also a partial transcript of a conversation between Gretchen Betancourt and David Sullivan, Miranda Sullivan's elder brother and attorney in San Francisco. You can't even get a court order allowing you to listen in to client-attorney conversations! Anyway, the documentation pretty much proves that Angleton's plumbers are bugging the firm's California offices, too!"

The illegality of it all was breath-taking; straight out of the KGB play book!

Briefly, Kay Graham was afraid that she had lost the power of speech.

"That is just so...illegal," she spluttered. "Isn't it?"

"That depends."

"On what?"

"The White House has to know that you don't just wish a guy like James Angleton away. Bernstein reckons that all this shifted up a gear long before the war in the Midwest. Heck, for all we know it was LBJ or JFK who authorised the original surveillance of Doctor King and the other Civil Rights leaders back in 1963, or 1964. Those were crazy times, remember?"

"So, what? What are we saying? It might just be that Nixon carried on with Operation Maelstrom because he honestly believed this stuff was 'business as usual?'"

Ben Bradlee shrugged: "No, I'd guess it was more to do with realising that he could get away with it" he grinned, "and that green-flagged stepping up the level of malfeasance to a whole new level."

Kay Graham suddenly felt unbearably tired.

"They'll shut us down if we publish any of this, Ben."

"Maybe," he conceded. "Maybe, they'll just throw us in jail and throw away the key."

"It is not funny!"

Ben Bradlee's one surviving phone rang.

He scowled, picked it up anyway.

"Okay..."

Kay Graham noticed her friends posture alter, his eyes widen and brighten. She might have been watching a Pointer stiffen and focus when it detected the scent of a fox.

Bradlee signalled for her to come closer.

"I'm with Kay, Gretchen. I'd put the phone on speaker but the Feds smashed up my office yesterday and this handset doesn't do 'broadcast'. I guess the only reason the Feds left this phone connected was because they're bugging it." He paused, winked at his friend. "Gretchen says 'hi', Kay."

"I heard!" Kay Graham mouthed.

Just when you think the day cannot possibly get any weirder...

Guess what happens next!

Chapter 14

Wednesday 1st February 1967
HMS Campbeltown, Villefranche-sur-Mer

Dermot O'Reilly had conned Campbeltown into the bay as the first light of dawn cast long, gloomy shadows from Saint-Jean-Cap-Ferrat. The destroyer was closed up at Action Stations, every gun loaded, torpedo tubes swung outboard, primed, and every man on deck was weighed down by heavy flak jackets and modern 'tin hats.'

Two of HMS Victorious's Blackburn Buccaneer S2 strike aircraft had made passes over Villefranche-sur-Mer and loitered fifteen miles out to sea, just in case there was the least tincture of treachery; overnight Sea Vixens FAW2s had circled within easy earshot of the French fleet.

Nearing the battleship O'Reilly saw that her forward main battery turret was still trained to port, its four mighty rifles raised five or six degrees into their loading configuration. The monster had clearly taken a large number of broadside hits; however, nothing short of a torpedo hit or a very large calibre armour-piercing round could seriously hurt a ship like that. Not even HMS Kent's eight-inch guns were capable of penetrating her main belt other than at point blank range.

Presently, Jean Bart loomed over the old destroyer as Campbeltown slowly steamed down her port side.

"STOP BOTH!"

Dermot O'Reilly stepped to the starboard bridge wing.

"FULL RIGHT RUDDER!"

"HALF ASTERN STARBOARD!"

"HALF AHEAD PORT!"

The margins for error were tighter than he had expected but there was no appreciable breeze inside the anchorage, and notwithstanding her lean, greyhound lines built for speed, he had discovered that the Second War vintage Fletchers were unreasonably, pleasantly handy in enclosed waters.

All things considered...

The Campbeltown's bow began to swing.

He planned to moor along the port side of the Jean Bart with Campbeltown's bow level with the leviathan's stern chains, pointing directly out to sea.

Dermot O'Reilly heard the pipe for sea duty men to move into position to pick up their lines, and to stand ready with their ropes for coming alongside. On the deck of the battleship men, women and...children were gathering, staring fascinated at the dazzle-camouflaged hunter in their midst, bristling as she did with gun barrels, exuding a particularly raw menace for all that she was dwarfed by the dreadnought guarding the entrance to the bay.

Before first light O'Reilly had had the Campbeltown's battle ensign flown from the main mast halyards of his ship. To her Second War namesake's battle honours – North Atlantic 1941-2, and St Nazaire – had since been added 'Biscay 1967', and the proud list of actions and campaigns the ship had participated in under American colours in her former existence as the USS Schroeder (DD-501): including Tarawa Atoll, Kwajalein Island, Hollandia and Okinawa.

"STOP BOTH!"

"RUDDER AMIDSHIPS!"

A burst of revolutions on the port screw.

Ten degrees of rudder, this way and that.

And the destroyer was drifting, slowly, slowly towards the battleship.

The deck division were hanging old tyres and collision mats over the side of the ship; happily, in the event the Campbeltown kissed the immovable flank of the battleship so gently the meeting was barely perceptible on her bridge.

Ropes were thrown from both ships.

Presently, the Jean Bart put a gangway over the side where the difference in height between the battleship's quarterdeck and the destroyers fo'c'sle was only five or six feet. That differential would have been less had not the Campbeltown's bunkers still been seventy percent full and the dreadnought's ninety percent empty.

"You have the watch, Mister Moss," Campbeltown's commanding officer told the Navigator. "The ship will remain at Action Stations until further notice while I go aboard the French flagship. Inform the Executive Officer that he is in command."

Dermot O'Reilly had walked through how he planned to 'play' this morning's sortie into Villefranche-sur-Mer with Campbeltown's departmental heads. Once moored alongside the Jean Bart, he and a team of specialists would immediately board the battleship. The weapons, engineering and communication status of the big ship would be swiftly assessed while he and Amiral Leguay parleyed. At the first hint of 'back-sliding' by the French, Campbeltown would call down the loitering Buccaneers, put a brace of 21-inch torpedoes into the Jean Bart and the Clemenceau and 'engage targets of opportunity' as she attempted to remove herself from the anchorage.

'Don't wait. Leave me behind if you have to. Just so there is no misunderstanding, gentlemen," he had stressed, "that is a direct order.'

O'Reilly had inquired if his Executive officer needed it in writing. The other man, a reservist of about his own age, called back to the colours after leaving the Navy in the late 1950s, had shaken his head.

'No, sir.'

Lieutenant-Commander Brynmawr Williams arrived on the bridge as his captain was leaving. The two men nodded acknowledgement.

A bearded, bear-like man who had played rugby for the Navy against the Army at Twickenham two years running in the late 1940s, Williams had spent most of the last eighteen months of the Second War on board the fleet carrier HMS Formidable. Rather more lissom in those days, his most vivid recollections were of pushing wrecked aircraft over the side after the ship had been hit by a second Kamikaze. Formidable's armoured deck meant the bloody things caused a dreadful mess every time they crashed; but once the fires had been put out it was usually just a case of a little flight deck 'cleaning up'.

He had commanded a minesweeper around the time of the Suez debacle; after that it had looked as if he would spend the rest of his career steering a desk. And besides, his wife, Glenda – for reasons best known to herself – had seemed to want to see more of him, a decision she had lived to rue. They had agreed to divorce shortly before the cataclysm. He had been wondering how one got hold of a suitable tart to be 'seen with' so that the divorce papers could be filed when Glenda disappeared in the chaos...

Now he was the second-in-command of the ship that was about to take the surrender of what was left of the French Mediterranean Fleet.

Goodness...that was almost Nelsonian!

Hopefully, all would go well when the Captain met his opposite number; it would be such an infernal pity to have to put several torpedoes into the side of such a magnificent ship; even if the Jean Bart was, in reality, no more than an obsolete museum piece.

Which was pretty much the way Dermot O'Reilly felt about things as he strode purposefully up to the brow of the gangway, and to his surprise, given the raggle-taggle crowd at the battleship's rail, was piped aboard the Jean Bart.

His reception committee was, however, less than impressive and did little to qualm his nerves.

He was greeted by a creased and unshaven man in a commander's uniform standing beside a petite brunette in a grey boiler suit, flanked by four men in what might once have been the blues of French Navy Marines. However, he drew some small comfort from the business-like way the latter presented arms, and the shipshape fashion in which the bosun's pipe fell silent when he looked around and eventually spied a French tri-colour to salute, flying limply from the battleship's stern jackstay.

"I am *Capitaine de corvette* Benois," the man in the grubby officer's uniform announced in heavily accented English, his tone indicating that he was a little ashamed of his appearance. He looked to his companion. "This is Mademoiselle Faure, to whom you spoke...previously, Captain O'Reilly."

"Ah, yes," O'Reilly smiled. "La femme de Le Amiral."

Aurélie Faure blushed and lowered her eyes even though she realised, intuitively that the captain of the English destroyer had meant nothing by it.

The rest of the boarding party from the Campbeltown were spreading out on the deck at their captain's back. Six Royal Marines hefting FN L101 SLRs, and as many officers and senior rates from the destroyer's gunnery, engineering and communications divisions whom O'Reilly had briefed to conduct a whistle stop inspection of the seaworthiness, combat readiness and the condition of the ship's electronics suite, while, presumably, if all went according to plan, he was receiving the surrender of the French Fleet.

Involuntarily, he glanced skywards as two Buccaneer S2s roared low over the northern hills and skittered deafeningly across the anchorage from north to south at several hundred knots, the roaring shriek of their twin Rolls-Royce Spey turbofans reverberating across the bay long after they had climbed back up into the low clouds out to sea.

O'Reilly saluted Benois, nodded acknowledgement to the woman, who shyly offered her hand, which he shook, half-afraid to crush it.

"Amiral Leguay was badly wounded in the battle," she apologised. "Our sick bay was overwhelmed by the number of casualties two days ago..."

Dermot O'Reilly forced himself to pause for thought.

But not for long.

He turned.

He had warned the Campbeltown's Surgeon, a practical, four-square man who had been a year short of qualifying for general practice at the time of the October War, to be ready to receive casualties, or if the situation demanded, to assist the medical staff on board the battleship.

"My compliments to Surgeon Lieutenant Braithwaite. Please ask him to report to me on board the Jean Bart at his earliest convenience."

O'Reilly switched his attention back to the welcoming party.

All the time his experienced, tested Navy-man's eyes were absorbing information. Whatever the great ship's crew looked like – a crowd of waifs and pirates – somebody had ensured the decks were cleared of battle damage, and he could hear the fire room blowers whispering softly in the distance.

He re-fixed his attention on Benois and the woman.

Speaking in French he explained: "When Surgeon Lieutenant Braithwaite, the Campbeltown's doctor comes on board, please escort him directly to your sick bay. He will need to have an inventory of your medical supplies," he hesitated, "such as they are." He grimaced apologetically. "Regrettably, I must now demand the surrender of this ship and the Fleet."

"Amiral Leguay directed me to draw up a formal document," Aurélie Faure said nervily.

Serge Benois had tried to stand to attention.

"The Fleet is your's, Mon Capitaine," he said with gruff pride, attempting to put his shoulders back in a military pose he had not assumed in years.

"Very good," O'Reilly grunted, as uncomfortable in that moment as the Frenchman. "Please take me to see Amiral Leguay."

The commander of the Villefranche Squadron had to be gently restrained by Aurélie Faure and a another, older woman, who had been caring for him in her absence.

O'Reilly quickly signalled for his two Royal Marine bodyguards to leave the stateroom.

"Mon Amiral insisted upon touring the Fleet yesterday," Aurélie informed him, her face a picture of worry. "It almost killed him!"

"Stop fussing, woman," Rene Leguay complained half-heartedly, eventually struggling into a sitting position on his cot, and then levering himself to his feet.

Swaying, he met Dermot O'Reilly's gaze.

"Sir, if I still had my sword, I would offer it to you..."

"My surgeon will attend you shortly, sir," O'Reilly promised. "In the meantime, my people need to board and inspect your ships as soon as possible."

"I am fine," Leguay insisted. "Please, attend to my wounded first..."

"You are not 'fine'. Mon Amiral," Aurélie objected, frowning in exasperation.

Her concern was illustrated a moment later when Rene Leguay sagged back down onto his cot, beads of perspiration dripping from his brow and trembling from head to foot with the exertion of having got to his feet.

Breathlessly, he looked up at the tall Canadian to whom he had just surrendered the fates of all his ships and people.

"Will you scuttle my ships, Capitaine O'Reilly?"

O'Reilly pursed his lips, contemplated a white lie.

No, these people deserved the truth.

"I don't know. My orders are to prevent your fleet falling into the hands of the Front Internationale." He grinned ruefully: "Judging by the battering this ship took the other day; you and I feel exactly the same way about that!"

Chapter 15

Wednesday 1st February 1967
Santa Barbara, California

Joanne Brenckmann had never seen her husband *this* angry. True, she had only known her husband of thirty-two years – and some – for the best part of three-and-a-half decades and therefore, she could not discount the possibility he had been angrier at some time before that, or during his various spells in the Navy, and then there had been that time he had been in England in 1963 being completely ignored by an oafish ambassador and a complacent State Department; but all in all, she very much doubted if her patient, wise, profoundly decent, kind husband had ever been this angry about anything in his fifty-seven years and, give or take, around three-hundred and sixty days on God's Earth.

Joanne had come in half-way through the telephone conversation with Gretchen. She and Walter thought the world of both their daughters-in-laws; which was all the more remarkable because before the event neither she or Walter could have foreseen their younger sons would marry such, on the face of it, unlikely women. Their freewheeling, musician younger son, Sam, had married the most practical, sensible woman in Christendom and together they were already raising a brood of three very young children. Meanwhile, Dan, their bookish, undriven middle son had courted and wooed an American princess, the daughter of one of the richest men on the East Coast. Perhaps, it was simply proof positive that love conquers all? It was safer not to ask the reasons why; better by far to acknowledge that they had been doubly blessed with their daughters-in-law, and leave it at that. These things happened: Walter had got lucky with her, hadn't he? So, what was so odd about their sons hitting the jackpot too?

Sam's wife Judy was exactly the gentle and very, very forbearing lovely person he needed to balance the craziness of his life on the road: it came as absolutely no surprise to Joanne that there was not so much as a whisper of her youngest son philandering. Why ever would he? He knew damned well he was the luckiest man on the planet.

As for her middle boy, if anybody in Christendom had landed squarely on his feet after threatening to be the family's amiable under-achiever forever, it was Daniel. Dan had courted, with dogged, unflagging persistence despite more than one – more than moderately, and knowing Gretchen, probably quite cruel – rejection until Claude Betancourt's favourite little girl had finally seen the light. Gretchen, of course, was one of those people who were always going places, fast!

Fascinatingly, Gretchen was the one person in the family who could actually get Walter talking politics.

Joanne frowned as she heard her husband's spluttering attempt to get a word in edgewise; and worried briefly for his blood pressure. She worried even more when she walked into the study of the plush apartment they were renting down near the beach, and saw that Walter's normally measured, commanding – Captain on the bridge – composure was, only temporarily, she hoped, shredded. He was red-faced and for a moment she was a little afraid he was going to start chewing the Bakelite of the telephone receiver.

"Walter?" She mouthed. "What is it?"

This seemed to snap her husband out of the top circle of his rage, and calm his fevered brow a degree or so.

"Jo's just come into the room, Gretchen," he said gruffly. He shook his head and growled an exasperated: "Aaaargh!" Without another word he passed the handset to his wife and stalked out of the room.

Joanne blinked at the handset.

"Whatever did you say to Walter, dear?" She asked, mildly. It seemed like the logical thing to ask.

"The CIA was behind the Warwick Hotel Scandal and the Nixon For President people, Haldeman, Ehrlichman, Helms, Angleton and all the rest of the President's men were in on it from the start. The Administration, the CIA and the FBI have been running a huge criminal conspiracy to cover it up from way before Nixon's inauguration!"

Joanne thought that was dreadful; what right-thinking person would not? However, that did not even begin to explain why her husband – a man inured to the double-dealing of powerful men, he was, after all, a career attorney – should be on the verge of apoplexy.

"Oh, I see," she murmured noncommittally.

"That's not really the thing," Gretchen explained. She had first got to know, and trust, her mother-in-law many months before she had opened her eyes, smelled the coffee, and realised that Dan was the ready-polished diamond he was. Joanne had been there for her, supportive and understanding when she was feeling very alone, basically confronting the first real crisis of her life. It was likely there was nobody else in the world – Dan excepted, obviously – in whom she could confide her innermost thoughts.

Not that this was a thing she did very often...

"I did wonder. Walter seems unusually...*upset.*"

"This is the thing," Gretchen explained. "The CIA have been spying on the American people for years under the auspices of a program called Operation Maelstrom run by the Head of Counter Intelligence at Langley, a creep called James Jesus Angleton. He's involved in the Warwick Hotel Scandal up to his neck; but that's not the half of it. The scumbags at Langley have been spying on me, Dan, you and the Ambassador, Sam and Judy, all of us. I wouldn't be surprised if your apartment in Santa Barbara isn't bugged, or there aren't spooks working for Angleton listening to this telephone call. This is incredibly heinous stuff, Jo! Honestly, you couldn't make this up. I had to call the Ambassador to warn him that *The Washington Post* is splashing this on tomorrow's edition. Everybody else will pile in after that. The White House has tried to get the Department of

Justice, that fraud John Mitchell, to block it. Haldeman rang up Kay Graham and threatened to get her and Ben Bradlee thrown in jail!"

Joanne struggled to take this, any of it, in for some moments.

In her distraction she reflected on how sweet it was that Gretchen had always called her 'Jo' and Walter 'the Ambassador' and occasionally, 'sir'.

Shortly thereafter, she forced herself to face reality.

"You're saying that our own government has been spying on *my* family?"

"Yes. And tens of thousands of other patriotic families, too. As a matter of routine, standard operating procedure, lately under cover of hunting for End of Dayers and other terrorists but Operation Maelstrom actually grew out of an earlier surveillance project called Operation Chaos back in the late 1950s."

Joanne was starting to work through the ramifications.

"So, it is true that our own government deliberately set out to destroy the Reverend King's reputation and to make that poor girl, Miranda Sullivan's life Hell?"

"Yes," Gretchen replied tersely.

She hardly knew Sam or his wife Judy but all the other Brenckmanns, Walter senior and Dan's big brother, Walter junior, and Jo, of course, all caught on at lightning speed. Everybody else she talked to seemed to need her to draw a diagram for them, but not the Brenckmanns!

"Why in God's name would they want to spy on *our* families?" Joanne asked, still in shock.

If the Brenckmann's were in the spotlight then axiomatically, it was as nothing compared to the resources the government would inevitably, have devoted to the Betancourt clan.

Gretchen decided a little more exposition was required before she got to the nub of the matter. Facts were facts; context was everything. She had married a historian and he had gently put her right on this, and to her surprise, quite a lot of other things in the course of their as yet, blissfully happy marriage...

But first things first!

"We think it was LBJ who authorised the bugging operation against the leaders of the Civil Rights Movement," she told her mother-in-law, "so this isn't even just a GOP or a Democrat thing. Apart from the Warwick Hotel Scandal cover up, that is, that's all Nixon's own work!"

Pat was speechless.

Gretchen, realising as much gave her a few seconds to regain her equilibrium.

"Jo. When the Ambassador has calmed down, he and I need to talk some more. Everything will go crazy when *The Post* goes to print, probably tonight Eastern Standard. We have to decide what we're going to do..."

"Do?"

Joanne became aware of her husband's presence at her shoulder.

She looked to him, relieved to discover that his face was no longer flushed with angst and that he was his normal self again.

"Walter's come back into the room, I'll pass him the phone, dear."

This she did and hovered, arms folded tightly across her chest, unable to stop fidgeting nervously.

"I'm sorry about that, Gretchen," her husband apologised. "I needed a short time-out. This is bad." He sighed, took a long, weary breath. "I cannot continue to serve a President who spies on my family..."

"The other thing you cannot, must not do, is sit this out in dignified silence," Gretchen retorted, in the event with a brusqueness she had not intended. "The Administration will walk all over you if you let them. I know you have no plans to run for President next year but they don't know that; they'll still destroy you if they can. You have to get in the first punch..."

"I didn't have any plans to run for office," Walter Brenckmann told his daughter-in-law. "But that was then and this is now. I didn't know then that we were governed by a bunch of crooks."

Actually, that was not entirely true.

He had had his suspicions all along.

When he had heard his son, Dan's account of how the Republican majorities in both Houses of Representatives had effectively buried the provisional report of the *Commission into the Causes and Conduct of the Cuban Missiles War*, and applied pressure to its Chairman, Chief Justice Earl Warren, to 'come down harder on the Kennedy Administration' – threatening to haul him up before half-a-dozen different Congressional and Senatorial Committees in what sounded like quasi-McCarthy era type witch hunts, he had assumed this was just a return to politics as normal.

The whole Warwick Hotel affair had left a bad taste in the mouth. He had known something was not right about it from the start; and would have known it without *The Washington Post* ever having exposed even the smallest part of the scandal. The way that poor girl – Miranda Sullivan was hardly any older than his dead daughter, Tabatha, would have been now – had been treated, forced into hiding while heavily pregnant, hounded by the press and the FBI, threatened with Congressional interrogations of the kind thus far singularly lacking in the oversight of the current Administration, had been just plain disgusting.

Up until now he had believed it was his duty to keep his head down, to work for the good of the Union in England; taken loyalty to his Commander-in-Chief as read, inviolable. Whatever one thought of the man in the Oval office one respected and saluted the Presidency.

Yet all the time his Government had been spying on him and *his* family!

If he had learned anything in the Navy, especially when he was the man in command, it paid to think for as long as time permitted; and then to make hard decisions without regret or hesitation.

"Okay," he said grimly.

Joanne knew that tone; understood that her husband had just determined the right, and the *only* way to go forward.

She met his gaze.

They communed briefly, for a second or so and understood each other perfectly.

The decision was made.

"Okay," he repeated, suddenly the man in command. "Can I leave it to you to fix a flight that will get Jo and I back to DC in time for us to have a conference ahead of meeting the press, Gretchen?"

For once in her life this rocked Claude Betancourt's daughter back on her heels. She recovered fast.

"Are you saying what I think you are saying, Ambassador?"

Walter Brenckmann grinned ruefully.

"Yes," he confirmed. "And if we're going to do this thing, we're going to do it properly, no holds barred. Like we mean it. Are you on board, Gretchen?"

Both husband and wife could picture the smile spreading slowly across their daughter-in-law's face.

"Yes, sir," Gretchen said.

Chapter 16

Wednesday 1st February 1967
Andrews Field, Maryland

Although there had been a change of plan, Anatoly Fyodorovich Dobrynin had no idea if this was good, or very bad news. For him, or for his country; but then this was a situation he had got depressingly accustomed to over the last four years. In any event, he had bade farewell to his wife and daughter, and along with the man the Troika had sent to Washington to babysit him, sixty-five-year-old, and clearly ailing, Vasili Vasilyevich Kuznetsov, addressed the Embassy's hastily 'California Advanced Party', before they had all got on the State Department-supplied bus to take them and their luggage to the airport.

Either everything had changed in the last few days or he had really been as isolated, out of the loop, mistrusted by his masters back in Sverdlovsk as he had assumed all along. The only thing he knew for certain was that Chairman Shelepin and Minister of Defence, Admiral Gorshkov were both coming to America to attend the re-dedication of the United Nations in San Francisco, an event now planned for the weekend of the 10th to the 12th of February. Notwithstanding it was impossibly late in the day, he was supposed to fly to the West Coast and 'prepare the ground' for his leader's arrival in San Francisco on – or about, there was still a great deal of uncertainty about the travel arrangements – Wednesday 8th February, one very short week hence.

Both Dobrynin and Kuznetsov had been surprised, well, speechless initially, to discover that the two leading men of the Troika were coming to America. Much as they knew Alexander Shelepin had taken a vice-like grip on their still sorely wounded Motherland, the notion that the two key players in the post-July 1964 Party hierarchy felt secure enough to *both* be away from the Soviet Union for perhaps, as long as a week to ten days, took a lot of swallowing. However, now that the two men were getting used to the idea they were, like true Marxist-Leninists, obsessing over a whole range of likely conspiracy theories.

In the absence of the Troika's two leading men, the man in charge in Sverdlovsk would be forty-three-year-old Vladimir Yefimovich Semichastny, the Director of the KGB and the third, permanent member, of the ruling Troika.

Nobody doubted that Vladimir Yefimovich was anything other than Alexander Shelepin's – the Boss's – man. Heart, soul and body, his loyalty was as rock solid as it was possible for it to be in the USSR.

Semichastny was a Ukrainian whose studies at the Institute of Chemical Technology in Kemerovo had been cut short by the German invasion in 1941. Completing a degree in history at Kiev after his military service he had begun his ascent to high office in the late 1940s, before 'teaming up' with 'the Boss' in Moscow. The two men had become close friends, with Semichastny succeeding the older man as First Secretary of the All-Union Komsomol when Shelepin moved to the Lubyanka in 1958. Later, after a stint as Second Secretary of the Communist Party in Azerbaijan, Nikita Khrushchev, presumably at Shelepin's prompting, had recalled him to Moscow to 'chair' the KGB at the time the Boss had taken up his post as a First Deputy Prime Minister in 1961.

Semichastny, the man nominally responsible for co-ordinating intelligence at the height of the Cuban Missiles Crisis, had only survived the war because he had been ensconced in the deepest bunker in the Moscow Military District. In its aftermath, notwithstanding Alexander Shelepin's protection, he had not been fully rehabilitated by the Communist Party until he resumed his former duties in the hours after the coup which had decapitated the Brezhnev administration. As befitted a man who had first been promoted to oversee the security apparatus of the Soviet State at the improbably young age of only thirty-seven, nobody doubted that Vladimir Yefimovich was an astoundingly talented 'operator'; nonetheless, that the Boss had few, if any qualms trusting his 'friend' to 'mind the shop' in his and Gorshkov's absence abroad was nothing short of...extraordinary.

Anatoly Dobrynin stepped up to the half-a-dozen microphones bearing the badges and signs of the various US news broadcasters. He was uncomfortably aware that he was standing directly in front of a Boeing 707 in the livery of the United States Air Force. To be totally reliant on the charity of the Americans just to enable the party from the Soviet Embassy to attend an international conference, was a new humiliation. Unfortunately, the alternative, a three or four day road or rail trip, skirting around the Midwest, many areas of which were still closed off to civilians – while survey parties searched for atomic, biological and chemical weapons, and a myriad of suspected contaminated facilities left behind by those maniac End of Dayers – would have left virtually no time to lay any of the ground work necessary to ensure that, at the very least, the Chairman's visit to the West Coast was not a complete, organisational disaster.

A cable to the Secretary of State, Henry Cabot Lodge II – whatever his shortcomings a decent, courteous man who had always respected the dignity and the sensibilities of the invidious situation Dobrynin found himself in – had swiftly prompted a request for the US Air Force to make the necessary arrangements and twenty-four hours later everything had been in place.

A dozen cabins on board the USS United States had been set aside for the Soviet delegation and the Secret Service had appointed a liaison officer to be 'at Ambassador Dobrynin's disposal on arrival in San Francisco'.

Dobrynin had immediately asked for alternative accommodation to be provided 'on land'. Secure lodging at the Presidio had been offered, and his people would inspect those facilities when they got to California.

Apart from having to stand in front of a bloody US Air Force plane things had been relatively painless, until now...

The Soviet Ambassador brandished his notes.

Lately, his large-boned frame had filled out to become again the imposing, bear-like presence he had been in better times; although inwardly, he felt the chill as he had never done before October 1962.

Every survivor of war plague said as much...

The wind plucked at his papers as spots of rain began to fall.

Vasili Vasilyevich Kuznetsov stood shivering in the cold of the winter morning, longing to collapse into a seat on the jetliner and surrender to the blissful arms of a restorative slumber. He had been too exhausted, worn down by the exigencies of his original tortuous journey to Washington, the influenza which had touched him last week, and the inevitable march of time, to do more than run his eye over the momentous statement his much younger, heartier comrade was about to make to the American media.

When the two men had read the Troika's 'United Nations Directive' they had looked at each other for some moments before Dobrynin had voiced the thoughts they were both thinking: 'I can honestly say that I did not see this coming, Comrade!'

Now Dobrynin focused on the words already beginning to dissolve in the rain.

"Gentlemen, it is my honour to announce today that Chairman Shelepin and the Deputy First Secretary of the Communist Party of the Union of Soviet Socialist Republics will, in the next few days, be flying to San Francisco to take the Soviet Union's rightful place at the top table of international affairs."

Given the inherent leakiness of the State Department it would have been a minor miracle if most of the men and women gathered on the wet tarmac at Andrews Field, had not known that the diplomatic game was, well and truly, afoot several days ago.

In recent weeks the American media had been obsessed with rising 'gas prices', the ongoing revelations about the Warwick Hotel Scandal, not to mention the latest indictments posted by the US War Crimes Tribunal, detailing in still more egregious fine print, the depravities committed by the rebels before and during the Civil War. The forthcoming United Nations 'circus' had not been front page news, and the paucity of hard information seeping out of Camp David about the allegedly frosty US-British pre-San Francisco planning summit, had forced broadcasters and newspaper editors to look elsewhere for their headlines.

Anatoly Dobrynin suspected that yesterday would be the last 'quiet' news day for a while...

"Ever since the disaster of the Cuban Missiles War the United States and its allies have attempted to conduct themselves on the international stage as if my country no longer existed. Consequently, the risk of a new and even more terrible global conflagration has been ever-present in the last fifty-one months. Historically, after all great wars there has been a coming together of the parties, old enemies have come together to make pacts to ensure that the mistakes of our fathers are not repeated by we, the sons and daughters of war. President Kennedy, President Johnson and now, President Nixon, have refused to confront the great questions of war and peace which confront the World today."

Nobody had hurled a rock at him...yet.

That was probably a good sign.

"Chairman Shelepin will fly to San Francisco in search of a new global settlement. We have no wish, or desire to revisit the failures of Versailles in 1919 or of Potsdam in 1945; the one led to the Second War in which twenty million of my Motherland's sons and daughters perished, and the other to the Cold War and the cataclysm of the Cuban Missiles War, and all the miseries which have followed."

Dobrynin tried to speak slowly.

"It is my country's wish for there to be a peace between the great nations of the Earth. But not a peace between the victors and to the defeated; rather, a peace that respects the legitimate security and territorial imperatives of all the parties. A peace which outlaws great wars forever but which allows different economic and political systems to co-exist."

This was where it got...serious.

"The Soviet Union is prepared to respect the rightful sphere of influence of the United States. In return, it demands that the Soviet Union's rights in Europe be respected."

And even more serious...

"We must move away from the flawed settlement of the post-Great Patriotic War era and international forums must be re-configured to reflect the realities on the ground. Specifically, the Security Council of the United Nations must be re-modelled or scrapped. It is simply not tenable in this new era for France, a country that does not exist in any meaningful form at this time, or for the island of Formosa, to be allowed to continue to speak for the Chinese people, over ninety-five percent of whom live on the mainland of China in a completely different country under their own government."

Dobrynin had no intention of spending the next thirty minutes reading out a list of demands, many of which were at best fanciful, and few of which were actually anything other than provocations, a classic smoke and mirrors tactic. He would leave that for the negotiators at San Francisco.

"Ladies and gentlemen, there is a great prize to be won on board the USS United States in San Francisco Bay." This he asserted, his voice ringing with gruff gravitas. "If the United States and its allies will de-commission its nuclear arsenal, so will the Soviet Union. If the North Atlantic Treaty Organisation will turn its tanks into ploughshares and send its warships to the breaker's yards, so will the Soviet Union. If the West scraps its warplanes, so will the Soviet Union. If NATO disbands, so will the Warsaw Pact. As an earnest of its good faith, the Soviet Union is prepared to accept, as a starting point for all future peace talks the October 1962 demarcation lines. The Soviet Union will unilaterally undertake to withdraw its forces behind those boundaries if the United States will do likewise..."

Which was, as they all knew, hogwash.

US forces could not march back into South Korea, or reassert their pre-war influence in South East Asia, the geopolitical map of the Middle East had been redrawn by the Soviet invasion of Iraq and Iran, and the expulsion of US oil companies from the Arabian Peninsula. There were no 'boundaries' in Europe other than that of the Rhine, and the Alps guarding the passes into a fragmented and strife-torn Italian peninsular. The Balkans, Turkey and the Anatolian littoral seethed with civil war, partially under Soviet control. The old Warsaw Pact existed in name alone and nobody in Washington, or anywhere else in the West could put their hands on their heart and claim, one way or another, if Russia and China were friends, allies of any kind, or simply old enemies looking to take advantage of the other's weakness. Elsewhere, Krasnaya Zarya hold outs, the legacy of older Soviet inspired insurgencies and the exigencies of a world trade system which had still barely recovered from the disruptions of 1962, 1963 and 1964, had caused political, economic and vast humanitarian disasters, and hugely ravaged parts of the old colonial empires. Even unaligned, potentially mighty India – on account of its stalled wars with Pakistan and its ally, China over Kashmir and the Himalayan Ladakh - struggled just to feed its people.

"Or," Dobrynin called, much in the fashion of an enraged Grizzly Bear, "let us, let the World hear the peace proposals of the Government of the United States. Chairman Shelepin will come to San Francisco with no pre-conditions, with no red lines. The World is in crisis, let us together chart a way forward!"

Chapter 17

Wednesday 1st February 1967
Commonwealth One, Grand Forks Air Force Base, North Dakota

Within minutes of Margaret Thatcher completing her deeply disturbing interview with Rachel French, Guy, her disconcerting, frightening interlocutor's stepson – the pilot of Commonwealth One – had come over the intercom and with masterful understatement explained: 'There's nothing to worry about but several red lights have just blinked on up her in the cockpit...'

As if this was nothing anybody should concern themselves with, he had gone on to explain that he was requesting the US Air Force to escort the VC-10 to 'somewhere safe' where 'we can put down' and 'run a few *routine* checks'.

Margaret Thatcher knew she would remember the apologetic, almost hurt insouciance in her pilot's words; as if the fact that there was a problem with the aircraft was somehow Guy French's personal fault, a thing that clearly mortified him to his very core.

Commonwealth One had bled off height and speed, eventually flying on across the wasteland of post-war Wisconsin, across Minnesota to North Dakota, intercepted by a pair of F-4 Phantoms over the darkened, barren, ruined cityscape of Chicago some minutes after having declared an emergency.

Guy French had sent his co-pilot back into the main passenger cabin to personally explain the situation soon afterwards.

'The aircraft is flying happily,' he had explained cheerfully. 'It is just that some of the instruments are playing up and every now and then the starboard outer engine *surges* somewhat. So, we'll be switching that off in a few minutes. The kite can fly on two engines, or even one at a stretch, so going down to three is an absolute breeze. The Americans have offered us facilities at Minot and Grand Forks, or several nearer fields in the unlikely event we run into more trouble.'

Commonwealth One had made an unusually bumpy landing on the three-and-a-half-mile-long main runway at Grand Forks Air Force Base; a thing Guy French had subsequently fulsomely apologised for. It transpired that the reason the aircraft had rolled for so long after it touched down was that he had not wanted to risk touching the brakes on account of his instruments reporting an almost complete loss of hydraulic pressure in the undercarriage and braking systems. The bumpiness of the landing was attributable to his having had to turn off not one, but two of the VC-10's four Rolls-Royce Conway Mk 301 turbofans on the approach to Grand Forks. In fact, as soon as the jetliner had come to a halt, he had ordered – firmly but very respectfully - an emergency disembarkation.

'Dreadfully sorry about that,' he confessed, afterwards, downcast, 'I was afraid something might have broken when we bumped up and down like that on landing. I thought it was for the best that everybody vacated the kite pronto, just in case there was a fire...'

In the following hours Commonwealth One had been towed to the hangar complexes which normally serviced the B-52s of the 4133rd Strategic Bomb Wing, and the McDonnell F-101 Voodoo supersonic interceptors of the 478th Fighter Group, and it seemed, every aircraft engineer and mechanic in the US Air Force had fallen upon the stricken VC-10 in response to the Base Commander's gruffly unequivocal command to 'fix it fast'.

An hour after landing the President had been on the line to Grand Forks, personally inquiring after the safety and comfort of his British guests. An offer to send an aircraft to convey Margaret Thatcher and her entourage onward to the West Coast was forthcoming; and likewise, a suggestion that Air Force One, the modified long-range Boeing VC-137C flagship of the Presidential air fleet, might stopover at Grand Forks to collect the Prime Minister's party...

'No, no, I can't have you being put out in such a fashion,' the Prime Minister had objected.

In the end it was agreed that if Commonwealth One could not be safely repaired within the next twenty-four hours, the US Air Force would assume responsibility for safely delivering the British delegation to San Francisco. In the meantime, Grand Forks was pulling out all the stops to accommodate and to entertain its unexpected visitors.

The Base Commander, a large, phlegmatic man with a stern physiognomy and a growling laugh who had flown B-24 Liberators with the Eighth Air Force in England in 1943; seemingly both the grimmest and the happiest days of his life, treated the British Prime Minister as if she was the Queen.

Everybody had been put up in marvellously functional, comfortable, spic and span quarters in a wing of the Officers' Mess complex, royally attended by stewards and guarded by immaculately turned out military policemen (and women).

'How practical would it be for Rachel French to do a disappearing act before we leave this place?' Margaret Thatcher had put to Airey Neave and Steuart Pringle.

The two men had considered this for some moments.

'My chaps could smuggle her out on an expedition to the nearest town, Ma'am," the Royal Marine had remarked.

"I doubt of the locals would count our people out, and then in again, Margaret," Airey Neave had offered.

The nearest town – more a community straggling south of the nearby east-west state highway – was a place called Emerado. Grand Forks itself, was some fifteen or sixteen miles to the east, bisected by the north-south US Route 26.

'Perhaps, an expedition to Grand Forks?' Steuart Pringle prompted hopefully.

The Prime Minister had recognised that her personal guardian angel was immensely, albeit genteelly, keen to see the back of Lady Rachel French!

Nobody at Grand Forks AFB had batted an eyelid when several of the AWPs and a couple of the Prime Minister's junior staffers, undertook a jaunt into Grand Forks the next morning. Similarly, nobody seemed to notice that the returning party, all with diplomatic papers and thus immune from any of the normal base security checks, it seemed, was one short of their full complement.

Later, she had confessed to Tom Harding-Grayson that she felt she had betrayed Rachel.

'No, Margaret,' he had objected paternally. 'Things are what they are...'

'I should never have given permission for her to be approached in the first place!'

'Don't you think the Americans would have approached her, anyway?'

Her Foreign and Commonwealth Secretary had reminded her that as a result of the breakneck expansion of the Anglo-American aerospace partnership, Wiltshire was turning into an 'American camp these days'. He had speculated that as many as one in fifteen or twenty of the new arrivals from the United States either worked for, or were in some way secretly affiliated to the CIA.

'Trust me. Somebody, would have made the initial approach to Rachel, with or without our leave.'

This thought had done nothing whatsoever to alleviate Margaret Thatcher's nascent guilt, which lingered like a miasma low in her consciousness. Now, finally, everybody was strapped in as Commonwealth One taxied smoothly onto the main runway and halted at the threshold. Guy French was being overly cautious; today he ran up the engines against the brakes, throttled back.

There was a delay of several seconds.

"Captain to crew, prepare for take-off."

And then, to his passengers.

"Everything looks ticketyboo up here. We've been routed a long way west today, so the flight down to California will probably be in the order of about four to five hours. At some stage we should get a jolly good view of the Rockies; I'll come back on the intercom when we're a bit closer. Until then, I hope you enjoy the rest of our interrupted flight!"

In moments the jetliner was surging forward and in no time at all, leaping into the air like a rocket-powered salmon, climbing steeply away from Grand Forks after barely using a third of its great runway.

Not for the first time the Prime Minister found herself contemplating the wrecked landscapes over which they had flown, to reach the safety of Grand Forks.

Remembrance was their one inviolable defence against stumbling again down the road to ever more terrible future wars. When the spring came the wastelands would 'green' anew, like London, large tracts of which had already been reclaimed by the Thames; verdant scrubland, new growth feasting on the nutrient-rich ashes of the last metropolis.

That train of thinking brought to mind her most recent conversations with Miriam Prior-Bramall, the solitary Labour Party member of her Cabinet charged with oversight of the London Garden City Project (LGCP).

Miriam had always been sensitive to the contradictions of her position within Margaret Thatcher's Government. Her own Party had long since disowned her as a traitor, withdrawn 'the Parliamentary whip', effectively consigning her to internal exile and certain de-selection as a Labour candidate at the next election. She attended Cabinet, reported on her portfolio – London and other reconstruction projects and plans – but declined to vote and often excused herself when strictly Party-political topics were under discussion.

Once, or sometimes twice a month she lunched with the Prime Minister, alone the two women would – as unlikely as it seemed – enjoy each other's company, and almost although not quite manage to gossip, and review the progress of the LGCP. The last time Miriam's soldier husband, Major General Edwin Bramall was home from France, the Thatchers had entertained the couple at their rooms in Hertford College. Frank had got on like a house on fire with Edwin, while the women talked of the planned network of villages to be planted, or allowed to generically 'grow' within the sea of greening ruins of the former capital.

Several day's personal correspondence had caught up with the British delegation at Andrews Field, and a fresh slew of telegrams had passed through the communications centre at Grand Forks Air Force Base. By design only the highest priority communications had been allowed to interrupt the summit at Camp David, thus, if was as if the flood gates had suddenly been opened!

She and the President had had their senior advisors agree the text of an anodyne official communique which had shamelessly glossed over the most egregious of their differences, and enthusiastically highlighted those areas – which, whatever the naysayers claimed, were many and significant – where the parties stood 'shoulder to shoulder'.

All to no avail.

Already, much to the Prime Minister's chagrin, the DC press corps was damning the Camp David discussions as a 'car wreck'. That, in her humble opinion, was a travesty: just because the United Kingdom was unprepared to unquestioningly fall into line with everything the United States wanted was, she had decided, probably a sign of hope rather than a cause for despair going forward.

'The future is usually somebody else's problem, Margaret,' Tom Harding-Grayson had said, attempting to console her after one particularly ill-tempered exchange. He had warned her that China was the 'only thing' the Administration wanted to discuss and as always, in this, her Foreign Secretary had been reliably perspicacious.

Tom was such an old cynic sometimes!

He was convinced that the American's angst over China – which one was the real one, etcetera, which in itself was a stupid question, anyway – had more to do with ensuring that the new United Nations was a toothless talking shop, than anything resembling a coherent Far East policy.

'So far as the State department is concerned, the whole Hong-Kong-South Korea-Taiwan imbroglio was no more or less than proof positive that when it comes to global realpolitik, neither we, nor our Commonwealth friends can be trusted. Personally, I suspect the Administration is still far too traumatised by the Civil War, not to mention increasingly afraid of its own shadow over the Warwick Hotel fiasco, to think very far beyond November 1968 and the next Presidential race. It may be that our best strategy is to wait and see what happens next. Because of the CMAFTA and the blood and treasure *we* and our Commonwealth Allies spilled back in 1964, the White House understands – even if Congress does not – that the key to the US regaining its October 1962 pre-eminent global economic position, lies in Oxford.'

Margaret Thatcher had been much cheered to receive a bright, breezy cable from her knight errant husband, which had served to remind her exactly how much she missed his *bright, breezy* cheerfully insouciant presence; and a longer, as always eminently sensible and of late, sisterly, sympathetic missive from Lady Marija Christopher.

Marija was a marvel.

The Prime Minister was well aware that things had not been all tea and cakes down in Canberra lately but as was to be expected, the Governor-General and his wife had risen to the challenge as if to the manor born. Not that Marija's letter had troubled its intended recipient with any of that nonsense: no, Marija had focused on updates about the children – the Prime Minister's godchildren – new friends, Jack Griffin's forthcoming return to 'sea duty', and the ongoing social whirl of Government House in Yarralumla. Several photographs had been enclosed, a family group of the mother, father and the youngsters, with young Miles Julian in his baptismal shawl, and separate up-to-date portraits of each of Peter and Marija's bambinos...

Margaret Thatcher knew that among their other responsibilities, the Christopher's had taken on the role of chaperoning and generally acting in the capacity of locus parentis of their predecessor, Viscount De L'Isle's two youngest daughters. Nineteen-year-old Anne was at University, but Lucy, still only thirteen had, it seemed been taken under Marija's wing much in the fashion of the little sister she had always longed to have! Apparently, Lucy was positively thriving in her first experience of attending a normal day school, a thing suggested by the ever-egalitarian Christophers, and apparently, much-lauded by the Australian press.

Philip De L'Isle had mentioned to the Prime Minister that he had already received two 'very comprehensive reports' on 'the girls', which had done a great deal to reassure him that he had done the right thing 'abandoning them in the Antipodes!'

'Lucy sounds like she's having the time of her life...'

Under the tutelage of Lady Marija Christopher that did not surprise the Prime Minister one jot!

Nothing quite gave Margaret Thatcher more hope for the future than the constant, small reminders of the kindness of strangers.

To her way of thinking, the most malign underlying evil of the October War had been the way its aftermath had predated so mercilessly upon the old and the young, particularly upon babes in arms and toddlers. The war would leave a damaging demographic hole in the population for the generations alive today, it ought to be everybody's duty to do what they could to repair the...hurt.

Her Majesty the Queen had caught the national mood by producing another royal prince; in comparison, had she shirked her responsibilities by not providing Mark and Carol, her twins, a new sibling?

Of course, not every woman felt this way, and many like herself could legitimately claim a higher calling. If she was still an obscure, anonymous Member of Parliament everything would be so different. Or not. She might never have met Frank Waters, for example. She had never expected, for a single moment, that he would be so 'fatherly' towards the twins, or get on so well with both of them, especially Mark, who as special as he was to her, yet had not always been an easy child to like...

Margaret Thatcher became aware of a looming figure.

"You asked to be informed when the operation against the French Mediterranean Fleet got under way, Prime Minister," Ian Gow, her Chief of Staff murmured. "Our terms have been delivered to the French at Villefranche. We are awaiting further updates."

"Thank you, Ian."

There were times, many times, when Margaret Thatcher almost envied her predecessors from the ages before modern communications shrank the globe. Nowadays, the information flow was brutally continuous, literally blow-by-blow, relentless. Worse, the temptation to try to intervene, to double-guess the people on the spot could be dangerously seductive. Which was why she expected her most intimate confidantes to ensure she did not meddle once *she* had made up her mind. If she had learned anything in the last few years it was that one simply had to trust the man, or the woman, on the spot.

One intelligence report described the French ships at Villefranche as a 'ghost fleet' which was *unlikely* to be capable of conducting offensive operations; but others warned it constituted a clear and present threat to British Forces in the whole Mediterranean Theatre. Politically, there could be little doubt that 'neutralising' what remained of the pre-war French Navy, would send an unambiguous message to the regime in the Massif Central at the moment Allied Forces went onto the offensive in France.

Now that she had had a chance to think about it, the Camp David talks had been far more unpleasant than any of them had anticipated. It was doubtful any British Prime Minister and an American President had ever been so at odds over so many things. One way to look at it was that the air had been cleared; another was to accept that there was still a gulf, or as Tom Harding-Grayson remarked, 'a bloody great big ocean between us!' Had the memory of standing shoulder to shoulder last year, and the horrors of those terrible times when the two countries had almost gone to war with each other, not been so fresh in everybody's mind, those days at Camp David would have been truly bloody. As it was, very little had been resolved and deep rifts had been widened, not papered over.

Both sides had told each other a lot of things they really, really did not want to hear. Not even the introduction of Walter Brenckmann into the mix, effectively brought in to attempt to bridge new chasms threatening to open up between the allies, had achieved a great deal more than to ensure discussions were conducted in a civil fashion.

There had been times when Margaret Thatcher had felt horribly guilty. Nobody knew better than she how much President Nixon had done to accelerate and sustain the ongoing British recovery; honestly, without his and his country's selfless, remarkable generosity, things would still be unutterably grim back home and by now, the United Kingdom's ability to carry on holding the line in Borneo, the Persian Gulf, Arabia, in several struggling, recently 'independent' sub-Saharan countries and of course, in maintaining 'deterrent' garrisons in Denmark, Norway and Sweden, and going full speed ahead with a slew of major, very expensive economic mutual assistance and defence programs, would be in serious doubt.

In the air, large parts of the British aerospace industry were now locked into partnerships with US companies; the Kestrel vertical take-off and landing subsonic fighter program was a joint British Aircraft Corporation, McDonnell Douglas, Grumman venture, the supersonic version of the Kestrel, the P-1154 Raptor, was now a joint Lockheed 'Skunk Works' venture, and the TSR-2 Strike Eagle, sponsored in the US by McDonnell Douglas and Pratt and Whitney was undergoing proving and advanced evaluation in Texas and New Mexico.

At sea, the Polaris-armed Joint Nuclear Strike Force was about to commence deterrent patrols operating out of the Gare Loch on the Clyde, the Royal Navy's nuclear hunter-killer building program at Barrow-in Furness and at Rosyth was gathering momentum, and the continuing US Navy surface ship transfers begun in 1965, were finally filling the yawning capability gaps left by combat losses and the intolerable strain of constant operations for much of the last three years.

Basically, even while the US had been fighting the war in the Midwest transatlantic aid had been running first at tens, then hundreds of millions of dollars a month. Yes, there was the hackneyed argument – often pedalled by the left and by backwoodsmen in her own Party – by people who were always ready to point out that much of the American 'aid' was actually spent in the United States, employing American workers who would otherwise be unemployed; but that completely misrepresented the scale of the largesse of the American taxpayer.

Without once stating it publicly, the Nixon Administration had in effect, secretly committed itself to a modern-day equivalent of the post-Second War Marshal Plan. And despite the failures of the Camp David

Summit, nobody on the American side had whispered, let alone threatened, to even mention any possibility of turning off the aid tap.

Margaret Thatcher wondered, if she and the President's positions had been reversed, if she would have remained so staunch in her internationalist belief that whatever else happened – or realistically, whatever else went wrong – that the United Kingdom was, like Canada, an ally that the United States simply had, come what may, to sustain. It was almost as if, despite Richard Nixon's re-emerging domestic problems, now the war in the Midwest was already slipping into memory, America's best interests lay in rebuilding what could be rebuilt, of the former world order.

Tom Harding-Grayson quipped that Nixon had been Eisenhower's faithful lieutenant for so long that he saw no better global geopolitical model than that of the Cold War map of the 1950s: a web of alliances resting upon US wealth and military weight ringing and holding back the Red Menace...

Perhaps, Richard Nixon still viewed the World like that, perhaps not. Either way, Margaret Thatcher still felt awful about the way Anglo-American differences were going to be ruthlessly highlighted at the coming United Nations 'jamboree', when in fact, the White House and her own administration were in rock-solid agreement about so many more things!

Back home there were discontented voices on her own back benches; her own MPs complained that British soldiers, sailors and airmen were 'holding the line', and that the Americans were only paying *us* what 'we are due'.

How could people be so short-sighted?

"The darkness is a curse," Tom Harding-Grayson said softly, settling stiffly in the rearward-facing seat opposite his friend.

The Prime Minister blinked out of her reverie and flashed a brief frown at the Foreign and Commonwealth Secretary.

"This thing with the French Fleet must be done, Margaret," he said gently, sharing her misgivings.

"We don't even know if those ships are manned, or ready to fight, Tom!"

"We can't take the risk that they might one day steam out into the Eastern Mediterranean and cause God alone knows what havoc," the man sighed. "If that was going to happen then now, or in the next few days when the Front Internationale feels itself under threat from both the north and the south for the first time, is when those ships could do us the most harm."

"Yes, yes," Margaret Thatcher groaned. She dragged her eyes from the dark wasteland of the Midwest and affixed her friend in her sights.

Poor Tom, he was looking older these days. He had wanted to retire, fade into obscurity at the time of the March 1965 election; she had press-ganged him into carrying on. Now great tranches of the globe were allied, organised, at odds with each other because of his – and her – handiwork. Tom was like a master magician, full of surprises, always with another rabbit or dove to hand.

She sighed: "Like July 1940, Mers-el-Kebir and all that. I know that, I understand why we must be..."

"Cruel?" Her friend prompted.

"Ruthless," she objected mildly.

"It was ever thus," the Foreign Secretary sympathised. "Plus, ça change, plus c'est la même chose," he smiled thinly

The more it changes, the more it stays the same.

The Prime Minister shook her head.

"Warsaw Concerto," her friend reminded the Prime Minister. "It's all very well for Dobrynin to claim that it is just a propaganda film but we know there are Soviet troops in West Germany and Austria, and that they would be in Denmark too if the Danes were any less trigger happy. We know for a fact because of radio traffic analysis coming out of France, our listening stations in northern Italy and intercepts by Royal Navy submarines operating in the Bay of Lions and off the Cote D'Azur, that the Soviets are operating an air bridge to the Front Internationale..."

"I know," Margaret Thatcher agreed reluctantly. "I know..."

Her friend was not prepared to let the argument rest there: "Admiral Gorshkov has made no secret that he will use 'any tool that comes to hand'. Goodness, we have no way of knowing if one, or more, of those blasted submarines they've been building in the Far East, has managed to reach the Mediterranean!"

Privately, Tom Harding-Grayson was dubious that was even conceivable for one of the noisy, relatively primitive Project 627 or Project 659 nuclear powered submarines constructed at the Leninskiy Komsomol Shipyard, at Komsomolsk-na-Amur to get out into the North Pacific, evade the US Navy blockade and make passage, undetected all the way to the Mediterranean via the Indian Ocean and the Cape of Good Hope. The experts at the Pentagon thought it was just about impossible; and they laughed in one's face if one suggested a Soviet submarine might evade the US Navy blockade of the shallow Bering Strait, successfully circumnavigate the 'northern route' via the Arctic and the Norwegian Sea, break out into the Atlantic and somehow arrive off Gibraltar.

Perhaps they were right.

In any event, the Navy was confident that any enemy submarine attempting to 'break into' the Eastern Mediterranean through the Straits of Gibraltar, would be detected by a British or American submarine, or a sonar buoy, and thereafter, if it failed to surface and surrender, it would be depth-charged or torpedoed by a patrolling anti-submarine helicopter or frigate, or by 'one of our subs.'

Or that, at least, was what the Prime Minister had been told up until now, although not, in such categorical tones, by the one submariner whose opinion she valued over all others.

Vice Admiral Sir Simon Collingwood, VC, promoted and knighted in the New Year's Honours List, Flag Officer (Nuclear Submarines), who had earned immortal fame in command of HMS Dreadnought, the Royal Navy's prototype nuclear-powered hunter-killer submarine, on her first two war patrols, had not completely written off the possibility that one day, the Red Navy might successfully infiltrate one or more Project 627 or 659 boats 'into the mix' in the Mediterranean.

'Dreadnought went one hundred and one days submerged during her first patrol to the South Atlantic. She could have stayed down longer but the crew would have starved!"

Simon Collingwood had speculated that it might take a Soviet submarine between sixty and seventy days to make the 'southern passage' via the Western Pacific, the Indian Ocean, *well south* of the Cape, and *well out* into the South Atlantic before turning north for the run up to Gibraltar. He calculated as many as forty days for the alternative Arctic 'northern run'. However, he was less than sanguine about the prospects of transiting the Straits of Gibraltar without being discovered: 'We always have a sub, usually an 'O' or a 'P' class boat loitering in the vicinity most of the time. Those boats are devilishly quiet, we usually hear a US nuclear hunter-killer, coming miles away and we know Soviet nuclear subs are as noisy as express trains!'

The Prime Minister had asked her favourite admiral if he could have sneaked into the Mediterranean when he was in command of the Dreadnought?

'I might have got past the American boats. Always assuming that I had the nerve to dive deep enough, I *might* have been able to ride the eastbound current past the watchers.'

Margaret Thatcher had had no idea that there was an upper, westward current pouring out of the Mediterranean, and a lower, colder, eastward counterpart sweeping into it. The problem was that a submarine using, hiding deep in the latter might – there were an awful lot of 'mights' involved in this business – have to risk diving below its crush depth to utilise it...

'It would have been an 'iffy' affair in the Dreadnought,' Simon Collingwood had confided to her. Subsequent classes of British nuclear submarines had been designed to dive deeper but Dreadnought had never been certified below about five hundred feet and the bottom south of Gibraltar was over nine hundred deep in places.

'Or that was what I thought back in 1964,' Collingwood had chuckled ruefully. 'That second war patrol was so secret I was unable to draw charts for the Med before we sailed!'

"Tom," Lady Patricia Harding-Grayson scolded her husband. "What did I tell you about not pestering Margaret? Give the poor woman a chance to catch her breath!"

The Prime Minister snapped out of her wool-gathering introspection and smiled at her friend. Her Foreign Secretary took his cue and eased himself to his feet so that his wife could join her younger friend.

"This trip really isn't anything like the disaster that everybody said it was going to be," the older woman said brightly.

Margaret Thatcher smiled tight-lipped.

Her friend had been a successful novelist and a regular

contributor to left-leaning papers and periodicals before the October War; yet, in this mixed up, topsy-turvy age she had become the National Conservative Prime Minister's go-to speech writer, fashion guardian, confidante and in many ways, reassuring mother figure; the one person in Christendom that the nation's first female leader – since Elizabeth I, quite an act to follow – could say, literally, anything to. Although, not in such a public place as the cabin of Commonwealth One.

"That is as may be, Pat," she agreed. "But right now, that is not really terribly comforting!"

"That's because you've spent the last few days surrounded by all the President's men," the older woman commiserated. "My, my, what a complete shower! Lawyers, used car salesmen and flimflam men, all of them. Well, apart from Henry, obviously. And that nice Mr Laird. And Nelson..."

The Prime Minister suspected her friend had taken quite a shine to Henry Kissinger at Camp David. Of Richard Nixon's other associates, only Secretary of Defense Melvin Laird, and Vice President Rockefeller, whose wife Happy, Pat Harding-Grayson got on with like a house on fire, remotely stood up to her high standards.

Pat had positively flirted with Henry Kissinger, the charming Harvard academic – formerly a Rockefeller man - who had found himself the United States National Security Advisor in what was, as scandal began to fall upon the heels of earlier disasters, a less than stellar Administration.

The Prime Minister looked away, staring out across the darkness over which the VC-10 was cruising, six miles high at over five hundred miles an hour.

"I do hope Frank is taking care of himself in France, Pat."

"The poor man would have been bored stiff over here on this trip," her friend said. "As for the headlines in some of the papers, well, he would have been bound to punch somebody on the nose sooner or later."

Margaret Thatcher smiled. The American media had rediscovered the Angry Widow of yore, a handbag swinging witch, smiting her foes and detractors right, left and centre. These days the cartoons and the editorials stung, the pain was momentary, and the realisation that she was being taken with deadly seriousness by all and sundry, a little humbling. Whatever they said about her, she knew that most Americans respected her.

And that, was a thing beyond price...

Ian Gow materialised in the aisle, and leaned confidentially towards Margaret Thatcher.

"I thought you'd like to know the moment we heard from the Mediterranean. I am given to understand that the French Fleet at Villefranche has been surrendered to Admiral Leech's squadron, thankfully, without bloodshed," the Prime Minister's Chief of Staff said lowly.

Chapter 18

Thursday 2nd February 1967
HMS Campbeltown, Villefranche-sur-Mer

One of HMS Victorious's Westland Whirlwind helicopters had made two round trips to the anchorage to transfer four seriously injured men, two women and a child – an eight-year-old girl with multiple shrapnel wounds – to the assault ship HMS Fearless, cruising some forty miles off shore.

The Fearless had the best equipped and staffed surgical facilities on any ship in Task Force V1, and one of her roles in any major landing operation was to put ashore at the earliest opportunity, an emergency field hospital detachment. She also had a large helicopter landing deck.

Because of the clutter of mothballed 57-millimetre Modèle 1951 in twin ACAD Model 1948 anti-aircraft mounts on the quarterdeck, the casualties had had to be offloaded from the fo'c'sle; an evolution greatly assisted by the fact the battleship's Number One main battery turret was still traversed ninety degrees to port, thereby approximately doubling the amount of space the Whirlwind's pilot had to work with.

Lieutenant-Commander Brynmawr Williams had served on a battleship as a young man, as indeed, had his father, who had been a junior gunnery officer on the old Colossus at Jutland; a thing his mother always blamed for his deafness in later life. Now and then, as a boy, he had wondered what it would be like to command one of the leviathans.

Now – for a few hours at least - he knew.

It was surreal...

'These people want to join the fight with us,' Dermot O'Reilly had told him shortly after he returned from his first meeting with the French admiral. 'I intend to send as many people as we can spare over to the Jean Bart, and the Clemenceau, too, all being well. We're going to steam or tow as many of these ships out of here as possible. Ideally, sometime in the next forty-eight hours. But most of all I need you to go on board the battleship and act as my liaison with Admiral Leguay. And,' his commanding officer had added, 'take over if necessary. I should imagine things are a bit chaotic at the moment.'

Williams was too old a hand not to seek absolute clarity on one particular matter.

'Are these fellows our prisoners or our...'

'They are our allies," he had been informed, definitively, "unless or until somebody tells me differently; but in the meantime, we will proceed under *that* assumption.'

Once Dermot O'Reilly had sought and received the Task Force Commander's leave, the three detached Fletchers of the 21st Destroyer Squadron had set to with a will to care not just for the Jean Bart's sick and wounded, but to alleviate the near starvation rations the French had grown accustomed to regarding as a balanced diet. Over a hundred of the Campbeltown's men were presently aboard the battleship; the destroyer's galley and sick bay stores having been three-quarters emptied the previous afternoon and overnight, in a cross-decking exercise which had co-opted every spare man, woman and child on the French battleship.

HMS Perth and HMS Dundee had nosed into the anchorage around noon yesterday, the former tying up alongside the Clemenceau and the latter bow to stern with the La Bourbonnais, similarly freely transferring men and supplies to further cement Anglo-French relations and to hasten the readying of the Villefranche squadron for sea.

Unlike his Captain, Brynmawr Williams's command of French was non-existent; thus, he was heavily reliant on the services of his ever-present translator, Aurélie Faure, other than on those occasions, at roughly hourly intervals when she disappeared to check on her 'Amiral'. Rene Leguay was confined to his cabin – nothing to do with the perfidious English crawling all over his mighty vessel but upon doctor's and Mademoiselle Faure's diktat – receiving a stream of visitors and in between, being debriefed by two French-speaking members of Rear Admiral Henry Leach's staff who had cadged a lift to Villefranche on the Whirlwind mercy sorties. Each time Williams laid eyes on the intelligence men methodically sucking up every last bit of tactical, technical and political information about the Villefranche Squadron, the politics of the coastal region and the dangerous hinterland beyond, they were a little wide-eyed, and scribbling like men possessed.

At a little after three in the afternoon the sound of gunfire rumbled like distant thunder, coincidentally as Aurélie Faure returned to the bridge map room – where Williams and a somewhat spruced up Serge Benois – had just finished the latest of an ongoing series of mini-conferences. The two men had hit it off from the outset, they were both practical men with very little time for the staid, formulaic protocols that would normally have governed the working relationship of men from the two different Navies. Benois had touched his battered cap and smiled at Aurélie as he departed.

"Mon Amiral is having his dressings changed," she reported distractedly. "Now that he is feeling a little like his normal self, he didn't want me to be around," she admitted, not knowing whether to be relieved or a little miffed. All she knew for a fact was that her relationship with Rene Leguay would never, nor could it ever be, what it had been before the battle. "He is determined to come to the bridge when Lieutenant Braithwaite has finished with him."

"It only goes to show you can't keep a good man down, Mademoiselle Faure!"

Threading her way through the Anglo-French work parties and the stores and equipment heaped and piled in the passageways amidships, Aurélie had not noticed that the wind had freshened until she had taken a moment to compose herself on the upper platform deck, ahead of reporting to the map room buried deep in the armoured citadel of the bridge.

The normally millpond-still waters of the anchorage were flecked with spray, the chop running at perhaps half-a-metre, with small waves actually breaking in flurries of apologetic spume on the shores of Cap Ferrat. Moreover, she could see that several of the destroyers and frigates moored in the most protected part of the bay, were gently moving, working against their rusting anchor chains.

A couple of seamen on the nearby deck of the Campbeltown looked up and caught her eye, they waved and she mirrored their gesture, smiling before she could stop herself.

The British were supposed to be such a warlike people; yet everybody she had met in the last day or so, was as pleased 'as Punch', as was she, that everybody was friends again.

Rene said that the Campbeltown's radar was relatively ineffective within the anchorage, masked by the surrounding hills, nevertheless the curved aerial bowl atop the destroyer's forward superstructure turned constantly and above her stern deckhouses another smaller, greyly conical electronic eye moved from side to side, scanning relentlessly, tirelessly.

A couple of miles out to sea another British warship, a visibly more modern frigate with tall box-like masts fore and aft of her single funnel, both presumably topped with the most modern all-seeing electronic eyes, kept watch. Now and then this ship disappeared into the haze, or behind a rain squall.

"This is just the leading edge of the great storm that's afflicting England and the northern two-thirds of France," Brynmawr Williams explained cheerfully when she commented about the changing weather. "The worst of it will never reach this far south, the storm centre is drifting slowly across the northern foothills of the Massif Central at present having dumped several feet of snow up to a hundred or so kilometres south of the Loire Valley. By this time tomorrow we'll be on the wrong end of forty or fifty knot," he paused, converted the numbers to an approximation of the wind speeds in kilometres per hour, "that's gusting up to seventy or eight kilometres per hour, with a likely sea state of six or seven, that equates to waves from five to seven metres high by the time the storm has blown through."

To Aurélie, this seemed to be awful news.

How could the rusty, neglected ships at Villefranche survive in a storm like that?

"Can your Task Force fly its aeroplanes and helicopters in such weather?" She asked, thinking she already knew the answer.

"Probably," the man retorted affably, as if he really did not see what the problem was. "The storm is beginning to wear itself out. We might be lucky down here. It might not be anywhere near as bad as we fear."

Aurélie heard the distant thunder again.

"What is that?" Aurélie Faure asked anxiously.

"The Belfast is demonstrating off Nice," Williams reported. "She'll be out of sight of land, most likely. I think the general idea is to drop several salvoes of 6-inch shells onto the coast road and in and around the main port area, then withdraw further out to sea. If the Front Internationale has any plans to interrupt operations here in Villefranche Bay, we thought it might be a good idea to make them think again."

"Those people can still approach Villefranche through the mountains?" She pointed out, her voice a whisper.

She was still getting used, half-way through the second day after HMS Campbeltown had tied up alongside the Jean Bart, to the idea that the three lethally armed British destroyers in their midst were their saviours, not their executioners.

Aurélie felt as if she was walking through a dream; it was all she could do to resist the urge to pinch herself. It was going to be a long time before she got used again to being in contact with people who, regardless of their rank or the badge of specialisation on their fatigues, knew exactly how and what they were supposed to be doing, to whom they needed to report to, and who had, without fanfare, miracle of all miracles, had immediately set about reviving and repairing long dormant, apparently moribund equipment working again, if not like new then at least serviceably, throughout the ship. Apart from the helicopter which had lifted off the Jean Bart's most badly wounded casualties, two similar machines had since landed on the deck of the Clemenceau, offloading men from the British ships cruising somewhere below the southern horizon.

Brynmawr Williams flicked a glance to the heavens.

"If anybody in the hills makes trouble the Fleet Air Arm will settle their hash for them!" he promised grimly.

"This *Belfast*, is she a battleship like the Jean Bart?" Aurélie asked sheepishly.

This hugely amused the Royal Navy man.

"Good Lord, no," he chortled, "we sent the last of our dreadnoughts to the breakers yard a couple of years before the big war. The Belfast is a cruiser, an old ship built before the Second War. I suppose she's about the third of the size of this ship. Her main armament is the same calibre as this ship's secondaries but unlike the Jean Bart she's got the latest fire control and air search radars; so, she shoots her arrows right on the nail whatever the time of day or the state of the seas!"

The roar of the Rolls-Royce Avon turbojets of a pair of De Havilland Sea Vixen interceptors, and of the Rolls-Royce Spey turbofans of Blackburn Buccaneer strike bombers, loitering several miles high above the anchorage was always audible from the decks of the ships of the Villefranche Squadron.

The man and the woman had walked out onto the bridge wing to watch as the Campbeltown's crew recovered the last lines, water churning under her transom as she pulled, very slowly, clear of the behemoth, with the Aldis lamp on the port wing of the bridge blinking.

The plan was for the Campbeltown to go alongside the old cruiser

Jeanne d'Arc, pump a couple of hundred tons of bunker oil into the French ship, and to use her generators to power the equipment to test and restart the derelict's antique electrical systems.

Williams read the Morse code.

He shook his head, chuckled softly.

Moved to the rail and waved.

"*En attendant de nous revoir*," he explained, apologetically. "If I am not mistaken!"

"*Until we met again*," Aurélie grimaced.

"I bet the skipper had to spell that out to the yeoman at the lamp," Williams laughed.

Aurélie Faure opened her mouth reply.

Had she spoken her words would have been drowned out by the Campbeltown's fog horn, blasting deafeningly, repeatedly.

The woman started in alarm, and looked to the British naval officer whose easy bonhomie had suddenly been replaced with a grim, vaguely angry resolution.

"Oops, that's torn it!" Brynmawr Williams groaned, taking Aurélie's arm and striding to the port armoured hatch, dogged open.

Aurélie blinked into the spotting rain she had not noticed falling, glanced to the destroyer still less than fifty metres clear of the Jean Bart's massive flank, watching her men running to their battle stations. The ship's four 5-inch dual purpose guns began to elevate, their gun houses swinging around to bear towards the north east.

Brynmawr Williams bawled: "SOUND THE ALARM! COLLISION STATIONS! SHUT ALL WATERTIGHT DOORS! ALL NON-ESSENTIAL PERSONNEL ARE TO GET BELOW THE ARMOURED DECK! PREPARE FOR AIR ATTACK!"

Aurélie was rooted to the spot as the battleship's klaxons began to blare.

Air attack...

How could the man know that?

How could anybody know what was going on...

Campbeltown's main battery suddenly belched red-spotted fire.

The whip-like percussion of the broadside made her ears ring.

Aurélie could see that HMS Perth and HMS Dundee were casting off from their charges, their decks a riot of men clearing equipment and sprinting for the guns.

"They aren't going anywhere," Williams promised her, conversationally calm and collected. "Our ships need a little sea room to clear their 'A' arcs." A little too much naval jargon he decided: "So that we've got clear arcs of fire for all our big guns."

Campbeltown fired a second broadside, her guns pointing, it seemed to Aurélie, at an impossibly acute angle almost directly up into the looming clouds.

It was then that Aurélie heard the unearthly whistling.

She stared in startled, shocked, momentarily uncomprehending disbelief as the hillside above Pointe de la Rascasse, on the western side of the anchorage, began to sprout giant, dusty plumes of erupting earth. The sound of the huge explosions was delayed a split second and then they were reverberating around the anchorage. It was as if somebody was striking the surrounding hills with a godlike hammer. She felt herself being seized, unceremoniously manhandled away from the hatch but not before she saw the volcanic plumes of water, hundreds of feet high erupting across the neck of the bay.

It was all like a dream.

A nightmare.

She heard Brynmawr Williams speaking laconically over the TBS – Talk Between Ships – network that the first boarding party had set up even while Captain O'Reilly was formally receiving Rene Leguay's capitulation...

"Fourteen or fifteen heavies, yes..."

"The CAP has already taken down two, roger that..."

"Victorious is scrambling two more Sea Vixens..."

The whole ship shuddered, rang like a cracked bell, rocked and stabilised.

"A couple of near misses off the stern, yeah, we all felt them!"

Aurélie realised that Williams, who could not see what was going on from within the armoured citadel, was receiving a running commentary from the Campbeltown.

"Open the bloody hatch, I need to see what's going on!" He demanded, his frustration peaking. In a moment he was outside again on the port wing of the compass platform, with Aurélie trailing along; attempting very hard, to be anonymous in his wake.

She knew she had lost all sense of time by then.

Already she had no idea if the attack had been under way for seconds or for minutes.

All three British destroyers in the anchorage were blasting main battery salvoes into the northern skies every few seconds; their shooting radar-directed at invisible targets.

Campbeltown was idling in the waters at the neck of the bay, her Bofors heavy cannons rattling continuously. A stick of bombs marched ominously, unstoppably towards her and she disappeared behind monstrous walls of water and spray.

Aurélie could swear she saw rivers of foaming white water flooding off her upper works and over her sides as she slowly staggered back into the grey afternoon daylight.

Brynmawr Williams was bawling at men standing on the deck alongside the barbette of Number Two main battery turret apparently 'watching the fun' to go below.

"The CAP is engaging a formation of TU-95 Soviet bombers at Angels Two-Zero!" He reported, picking up his running commentary. "Our boys have splashed four of the beggars now!"

There was a new, terrifying whistling.

Nobody needed to be told what that signified.

Everybody dived for the deck.

Two sticks of one-thousand and two-thousand-kilogram semi-armour-piercing bombs, one of eight and the other of seven, dropped on a heading of approximately one hundred and ninety degrees – more or less down the length of the anchorage from north to south – began to plummet into the now churning, fouled grey waters of the bay.

One big bomb exploded on the corniche; others began to stride like the footsteps of an avenging colossus towards the helpless ships of the ghost fleet.

The bigger harbingers of doom, the two-thousand-kilogram death-bringers were already falling faster than the speed of sound, the smaller devices went silent as they fell to earth and water, wood, iron and flesh.

A bomb struck the destroyer La Galissoniene amidships, another somewhere on her fo'c'sle, both carved through the ship like two red-hot knives through butter, their fuses initiating at depths of fifteen and twenty-five metres beneath and slightly to starboard of their points of impact.

The first hit, immediately aft of the two thousand seven-hundred-ton T-53 class destroyer's bridge, had passed through the forward fire room uptakes, killed everybody in the boiler room through which it crashed and exited the vessel carrying away a seven-metre square section of keel plating.

The second hit penetrated the deck beside the forward twin 5-inch main battery turret, slicing down through the empty magazine, smashing frame six, compromising the stability of the bow section forward of it and tore out a ragged ten-spare-metre section of underwater hull plating.

The destroyer would probably have sunk even had neither of the two huge bombs actually exploded; but when they went off, less than milliseconds apart, La Galissoniene ceased to be a ship. Her back broken, her waterlogged bow floating apart from the wrecked carcass of the once proud greyhound of the seas, she died in less than a minute.

In the spray and fury of the drum roll of ear-splitting detonations nobody actually saw the bombs which bracketed and shattered the T-47 class destroyer Surcouf, like La Galissoniene, she was a sinking, smashed hulk by the time the smoke cleared.

A one-thousand-kilogram bomb exploded on impact with the roof of the old cruiser Jeanne d'Arc's Number Two double 6-inch main battery turret, instantly destroying the bridge and Number One turret and a large part of the fo'c'sle, killing everybody within fifty to sixty feet of the impact in every direction.

Several other very big bombs landed in the waters around the six-and-a-half thousand-ton cruiser and the oiler, La Seine, lashed alongside. One, possibly two or three of these exploded directly beneath, or penetrated the sides of the two ships. The massive underwater explosions probably stove in the tanker's starboard side, snapped the Jeanne d'Arc's keel and opened her up like a tin can from end to end.

Inside three minutes the cruiser had capsized, turning turtle before lingering on the surface for half-a-dozen dreadful minutes as survivors attempted to cling to her barnacle-encrusted bottom. Nearby, La Seine sank by the bow amidst a spreading morass of flotsam and evil-smelling bunker oil.

And then, as swiftly as it had begun, it was over.

Aurélie Faure and the others drifted out onto the bridge wing to stare, dazedly at the carnage, unaware that they were all drenched from head to toe and the decks all around them still ran, in places several inches deep in gushing water, from the towering near misses.

The foul, acrid tang of burning oil and wood, and the stench of cordite hung in the air as the cold wind began to blow with new, bitter ferocity across the scene of devastation.

Chapter 19

Thursday 2nd February 1967
Prince Street, Alexandria, Virginia

The body of sixty-nine-year-old Jay Lovestone, since shortly after the Cuban Missiles War, the Director of the American Institute for Free Labor Development (AIFLD), whose offices had relocated to Alexandria in the spring of 1964 after its old premises – having survived the Battle of Washington unscathed – happened to be in a block requisitioned by the US Army Corps of Engineers, was discovered by his secretary when she reported for her fourth morning, working as a temporary agency typist, for the AIFLD.

When the cops arrived on the scene she said her name was Adele Fleming – she also explained, chattily, that she had been born 'Mueller' but her father had changed the family name in 1942 when she was only four – and that she was covering for the absence of Mr Lovestone's normal secretary, a Miss Clara Schouten, a lady in her fifties, while she cared for her aged father, who had been taken ill in Connecticut the previous week...

No, she had no idea if Mr Lovestone had any enemies.

No, so far as she knew he never kept more than a few dollars, 'petty cash' in the office safe.

And no, she had not seen anybody acting suspiciously in the vicinity but then, she had only worked at the AIFLD office on Prince Street since Monday.

So, she had hardly known the dead man.

In fact, the Washington PD soon discovered that the AIFLD had had such a low profile that few of the workers employed in the building above and below its offices, or anywhere nearby in the neighbourhood, was aware of what it did, or even of who opened and shut up the premises every day of the working week. In fact, it soon became apparent that most of the AIFLD's former employees, laid off when the Corps of Engineers took over the organisation's former premises nearly three years before, had had no idea that Jay Lovestone – not a very well-liked man, it seemed – had even set up a new office.

The dead man had been shot twice in the back of the head, probably when he was on his knees. There was not much left of his face and there was a lot of blood on the floor, and splashed across one wall and two grey metal filing cabinets.

Later, a Washington PD homicide detective was to note, for the file, that Adele Fleming – the temporary typist – had been unaccountably calm and collected, unusually self-possessed when she rang the local precinct to report finding the body, and later when the first uniformed officers arrived in Prince Street. However, that note was only appended some days later, after the lady in question had disappeared without trace, and three women called Adele Fleming had been tracked down by investigators in the surrounding counties and the District of Colombia, none of whom had turned out to be the woman encountered at Prince Street that morning.

None of this came as any surprise to the handful of people who actually knew what went on at the anonymous office of the American Institute for Free Labor Development in Alexandria, nor to the man Jay Lovestone had worked for, since before the Cuban Missiles War.

"Do we have any idea whatsoever has happened to Clara Schouten?" James Jesus Angleton – still for the moment at least, although probably not for much longer, the Associate Deputy Director of Operations for Counter Intelligence of the CIA – as he sipped the tepid black coffee the slim, twentysomething brunette, who had ushered him into the ground floor parlour of the two-storey 1940s town house at Bellevue.

"No," the young woman retorted. She had held herself together until she got back to the house – one of two 'safe houses' nominated for the duration of her operational attachment to the Office of Security at Langley - but had poured herself several fingers of Bourbon since then. "All I know is what I was told when I was briefed to work for that slime-ball Lovestone!"

"Lovestone said nothing to you earlier in the week?"

James Angleton's companion had briefly planted herself in an adjacent arm chair, now she jumped to her feet, clunking her glass on a low table prior to folding her arms tightly across her bust and beginning to pace.

"The Police did not ask you for proof of your identity?" The man asked.

"No! I told you."

"Yes," Angleton agreed. "And there were no cartridge cases?"

"No. I told you. I looked before I called the cops."

At some level James Angleton was aware that the young woman was becoming more agitated, irritatingly tearful. However, if he had ever been overly concerned with the fears or the problems of subordinates, among whom his rudeness and arrogance was a given, that was a train long gone.

The woman was getting his nerves, now.

"I'm not an agent, Mr Angleton," she reminded him. "I'm just a junior case officer. Nobody told me I was likely to walk in just after a man had been murdered. For all I know I might have passed the killer on the stairs. If I hadn't been held up this morning, I might be dead too!"

The spymaster frowned at her.

"Yes. You were 'held up'. Why were you 'held up' this morning?"

The cold suspicion behind the curt interrogative startled the young woman. She stopped pacing, stared at the monster suddenly studying her as if she was an enemy.

"I got a call from a girlfriend just as I was leaving my house in Georgetown. She's expecting her first baby, it is due any day now, she was getting panicky." The Bourbon was beginning to work its spell. "Her husband is a klutz."

Angleton rose stiffly to his feet.

"You should stay here tonight. Make yourself scarce over the weekend. Report back to work at Langley on Monday. If anybody asks, stick to your cover story about 'running errands for my office'. Do not discuss this matter with anybody. Is that understood?"

Angleton left the house a few minutes later.

One of his people was dead; sooner or later the Washington PD, or some FBI-man was going to start joining up the dots, following the breadcrumbs back to Langley. Obviously, the Office of Security was firewalled but that would not stop the whispering, DC was gossip ground zero and once Operation Maelstrom became public property he was finished.

When the call came through about the killing, his first thought had been to check that the Angel of Death had disembarked from that British plane at San Francisco. He had refrained from making that inquiry; knowing Richard Helms would have warned him if she was still in DC.

Implausibly, that only really left Billy the Kid in the frame and so far as anybody could tell, he was still in California...

James Angleton had not noticed the rain sleeting in his face until he dropped behind the wheel of his car, a nondescript 1962 Chrysler, parked two blocks away from the safe house, and he was surprised to discover that he was dripping wet, and suddenly shivering.

He fired up the motor, cranked up the heater to maximum and waited as it blew frigid air for some minutes. He lived in a country which could drop an ICBM on a pinhead – well, within a few hundred yards of a pinhead half-way around the world – but could not build a car with a heater that actually worked!

Angleton thought about lighting a cigarette, discovered the pack in his jacket pocket was wet. He did not notice the matronly woman with two young children who walked past the car giving him a very, very odd look as he sat behind the wheel, with the engine rumbling, staring fixedly, blindly down the road.

Forget about Operation Maelstrom...

When his association with Jay Lovestone became national news, his career would end; inevitably, the AIFLD would be blown, and with it the CIA's covert money transfer and laundering operation in Latin America.

Everything was going to Hell...

It seemed that Angleton had no more understood Jay Lovestone than he had his old friend Kim Philby; the latter was a double agent, a traitor, Lovestone, was just a loser who had never wholly shaken off his past. Old Communists never die, they just plot their next coup...

Jay Lovestone had been born Jacob Liebstein, the son of Jewish parents in the Lithuanian province of the old Russian Empire sometime around the end of 1897. His father had come to America when he was six or seven, and he, his mother and three siblings had followed in 1907. Growing up in the Lower East Side and later the Bronx, he had got embroiled in socialist politics studying at the City College of New York. Back in those days there was no enduring stigma in this – in both the 1912 and 1920 general elections Socialist candidate Eugene V. Debs attracted nearly a million votes - nor in becoming a full member of the Communist Party, which the young Jacob Liebstein did in 1919, around the time he changed his name to Jay Lovestone.

Like so many American Communists Jay Lovestone had had, at practically every turn, demonstrated an uncanny knack of being on the wrong side of history. In a movement riven with factional feuds and arcane ideological schisms he had ended up on the Bukharin side of the 'Stalin question', albeit, only after burning his boats with a host of would-be allies after featuring prominently in the expulsion of so-called Trotskyite back-sliders in the movement. After visiting the Soviet Union in the 1930s he was expelled from the Party, mainly on account of his support for the theory of *American Exceptionalism*, a defeatist paradigm which held that capitalism was so well-entrenched in North America that, in effect, Marxism was never going to work 'over here'.

Lovestone had found a home, at first around the fringes, then as an organiser in the labour movement as long ago as the 1920s. In a career infrequently touched by success or meaningful, lasting achievements – possibly because he was forever serving the cause of International Communism at the same time he was supposedly representing workers – by the time the United States had entered the war against Germany (on the side of the Soviet Union), old loyalties had got warped and to a degree, Lovestone's communist past was rapidly becoming ancient, somewhat blurred history.

In 1944 he was the director of the International Affairs Department of the International Ladies' Garment Workers' Union (ILGWU), then still one of the biggest unions in the country. It had been while holding this post that he had been positioned on the American Federation of Labor's so-called Free Trade Union Committee. And it was out of this web of connections that the American Institute for Free Labor Development had emerged with a specific remit to promote and organise labour unions in Europe and Latin America which were deemed, *free* of all communistic involvement.

Jay Lovestone was one of those old communists who had been on a long, circuitous journey without ever really knowingly acknowledging that he had changed sides.

James Jesus Angleton could spot a conflicted man with deeply confused motivations a mile away; they were perfect fabric from which to weave his countless spider-webs of deceit.

The American Institute for Free Labor Development – fronted by a relatively prominent old-time, supposedly reformed American Bolshevik – had been James Jesus Angleton's pliant tool for over a decade; obediently working to sabotage Soviet influence within the international labour movement, and dripping leftist insider intelligence to the CIA. In the confusion of the immediate post-October 1962 era, Angleton had seized the opportunity to re-design the whole operations, turning the AIFLD into a full-blown cut-off through which misinformation and millions of dollars of aid had been fed to South American *allies*.

In the scale of things, the AIFLD managed by Jay Lovestone – a man who had needed increasingly onerous 'management' as time when by, and he got older and grumpier – was relatively small beer in comparison with the Office for Security's main responsibility, Operation Maelstrom. Such small beer, that even James Angleton could appreciate the irony in the AIFLD, not the vast spying machinery he had created to watch over the actions and the consciences of the American people, becoming the primary, initiating cause of his now inevitable downfall.

Gradually, he regained his senses, his mind slowed, calmed and as the Chrysler's heater suddenly began to pump out blisteringly hot air to warm his sparse, angular partially drenched frame, and the sleet began to turn to snow, accumulating on the windshield, obscuring the street ahead, he realised that only one question still possessed the power to torment.

Who had used the AIFLD cut-off to re-awaken the Agency's most dangerous assassin?

Or perhaps, pertinently, a better question might be: who had the most to gain by unleashing Billy the Kid on the rump of the Resistance – which, for the while, it had been deemed safer to leave in place and keep under surveillance than to attempt to roll up, on the grounds that it was better the Devil one knew than to risk driving it underground where it could do all manner of harm, and nightmarishly, morph into a 'real' threat again – and in the process, allow the maniac a gold-plated chance to settle every last blood debt?

Whoever it was, they had made a dreadful mistake.

Never a man overly concerned with collateral damage – who got hurt just because they were in the wrong place at the wrong time, through no fault of their own – it was an odd feeling for the Associate Deputy Director of Counter Intelligence to find himself suddenly, unexpectedly trapped helplessly in the firing line from a quarter he had least expected.

Somebody in the Office of Security must have betrayed him.

Nothing else made sense.

Forgive them...for they know not what they do...

Chapter 20

Walter Brenckmann only truly realised how 'old school' he was when he entered the packed second floor conference room of the Washington offices of the law firm he had worked for, on an off, most of his adult life and belatedly become a senior partner in two years ago. Not that he had done a lot of 'lawyering' since October 1962.

Gretchen had instructed her own father to 'stay invisible' in Connecticut – a good place to be invisible – until further notice; nothing was going to rain on *her* parade today. Moreover, she had advised her husband to 'keep his head down', a thing Dan was good at and besides, he was clerking for the Chief Justice for the next fortnight, with the Cuban Missiles Commission not scheduled to be in session again until early March, a thing contingent upon the level of Congressional harassment between now and then.

Gretchen had been busy, like a whirlwind, for much of the last twenty-four hours. Hiring a jet to bring her father and mother-in-law back to DC had been but the prelude to a never-ending round of telephone calls and hastily arranged meetings. She had had no idea how hard it was to get one's hair properly styled at four o'clock in the morning!

Dan had received the news that his father planned to run for President, and that she was going to managing his campaign in his stride. Not a lot fazed Dan and even though she had not consulted him in advance – given they had two very young children and most American husbands expected their wives to doing a lot more 'mothering' than she was going to have time for in the next couple of years – he had taken the news on the chin. And, as always, rolled with the punch. Because that was the sort of guy he was, had known exactly what he was letting himself in for, and loved her just the way she was.

Yes, marrying the Ambassador and Mrs Brenckmann's second son had definitely been one of her better life choices!

However, she would dwell on her good fortune another day; today, she was busy. She would feel guilty – well, a little, anyway – about handing off her kids to their nanny long before dawn that morning.

Actually, abandoning Louisa Tabatha – barely ten weeks old – was a bit of a wrench, even though she knew her daughter was probably in better 'mothering' hands than her own while she was rushing around Washington. Gretchen was also aware that 'getting back to normal' had been harder than after the birth of her son, Claude Walter, now eighteen months old. God, they were so lucky to have Sherry Marley, their African-American housekeeper, now full-time baby-minder and a lot of the time, their two little ones' 'mother.

Sherry was a wonder. Forty-seven-year's old with three grown kids of her own, divorced or separated – it was unclear which - many years since from her son and two daughter's father she had worked for the Betancourt family for many years before, in retrospect, she had attached herself to Gretchen. That was the best part of a decade ago now, seamlessly morphing from she and Dan's housekeeper in Philadelphia to the woman who now organised, well, everything domestic in their lives. Sherry was middlingly large, loud and Gretchen suspected she carried a flame for Dan: what sensible woman would not? In any event, without Sherry, whom she trusted, literally, with her babies' lives and whom, although she rarely articulated it, a friend, practically a family member, not an employee or retainer, Gretchen knew she would not have the life she loved.

In the twenty-four hours since her conversation with her father-in-law, she had succeeded in stirring the DC rumour mill to a fever pitch; unashamedly milking the pandemonium stoked by *The Washington Post's* revelations.

WELCOME TO THE SURVEILLANCE STATE!

Now that Kay Graham and Ben Bradlee had called the Administration's bluff, the second editions of most of the other papers had picked up the clarion call: put up or shut up, sue us, arrest us or confess!

The White House had gone silent; hurriedly circled the wagons while a couple of tame GOP stalwarts had brazened it out on the steps of the Capitol.

The CIA's 'information machine' was already in high gear, although mainly spinning its wheels because today, nobody was buying anything Langley wanted to sell.

A small, floodlit – for the TV companies – rectangle of floor space around a lectern with seven or eight microphones had been preserved for Gretchen's principals.

Magically, the buzz of conversation faded and the newsmen parted in a feeble imitation of the Red Sea draining aside, so as to allow Moses and his tribes to carry on to the Promised Land.

Gretchen was surprised, and despite herself, impressed, by the respect the DC press pack paid to Dan's parents.

My, my, Jo is smiling at these people like they are her favourite nephews and nieces and they...love it. And the Ambassador is radiating...decency and authority.

Please, please, nobody is to shout: "Captain on the bridge!" right now...

Gretchen wished she had had more time to rehearse her part in the forthcoming drama. Five run throughs would have to suffice!

She tapped one of the microphones.

There was a satisfying 'thump' over the room's freshly set up public address system which instantly got everybody's attention.

"Thank you all for coming to Pennsylvania Avenue at such short notice," she began, smiling with a genuinely mischievous twinkle in her eyes, "on such a busy news day!"

Even hardened news hacks chuckled.

"This morning we learned that our Government has been spying on us. Worse than that, that our Government has threatened, and presumably is still threatening to throw anybody who dares to make public its dirty washing, into prison. Whatever happened to the First Amendment, ladies and gentlemen?"

She let this sink in.

"But you have not come here to see me."

Gretchen noted that Walter Cronkite was giving her one of his 'patient uncle' looks, as if to say 'don't overplay this'.

Good advice!

This was not *her* day.

"So, without further ado, I am going to stand aside. Let me present Captain Walter Brenckmann!"

This caught both her father and mother-in-law a little by surprise, both were still soaking up the atmosphere, a febrile animal, when the spotlight, literally fell upon them.

Walter Brenckmann squeezed Joanne's hand as they stepped forward. He looked around. Right then he would much rather have been on the rolling, pitching deck of a destroyer in a storm than in the eye of the Washington media pack.

Joanne clung to his hand.

"We, um," her husband smiled, ruefully, "came stateside for a vacation and a chance to get to know our grandkids a little better. However, that was before I discovered that the CIA and the FBI were tapping my phone, and following me and members of my family as they went about their normal, lawful business."

He spoke with court room gravitas, precision. His voice would likely have carried into every corner of the room without amplification. Like an actor he had learned long ago to project his words; one could not persuade anybody about anything unless one was heard.

"We were told that enemies of the people had to be uncovered, spies and fifth columnists unearthed, terrorists hunted down before they could do 'the people' harm, and yet," he shook his head, sadly, "nobody seemed to see the coup d'état in this city in December 1963 coming, or the atrocity at Wister Park, or the first rebellion in Wisconsin, or the ten-one cowardly terrorist attacks in Philadelphia in October 1965, or the nuking of American cities and the Civil War in the Midwest. We were under surveillance by our Government all the time, and yet nobody in the CIA or the FBI, or any other organ of the police state, seemed to see any of the disasters which have befallen us coming until they were, tragically, already upon us. Nobody..."

He sighed, shook his head.

"My friends, I think we are all entitled to ask what went wrong? Sadly, one is bound to reflect that if the people we trust to keep us safe had been a little less preoccupied bugging hotel rooms in Manhattan and listening to the pillow talk of private citizens, they might just, have noticed that the Union was damned near broken."

Walter Brenckmann had anticipated a ragged salvo of questions by now. Nobody said a word, a problem because it gave him no clue as to whether or not he was striking the right note.

"I believe our country has a problem," he went on, more in sorrow than condemnation. "A country which spies on its own people; a country governed by men who have lost their moral compasses, a country in which the rule of law is routinely, systematically flouted by those we have elected to preserve and to guard that same rule of law, cannot be a happy country."

He was beginning to relax, breathe evenly.

"If what we read in *The Washington Post* is true, and I have no reason to doubt that, substantially, it is true; then we live in a country where those in power believe it is okay to spy on the Chief Justice, his clerk, his clerk's wife, on an Ambassador and his wife, or on anybody they want, in fact."

He started making eye contacts.

"I have worked, and fought, all my adult life to defend the constitution of the United States; I plan to go on fighting to defend the rights enshrined in that proud constitution. It is with a sinking heart that I tell you today that I cannot, in good faith, or in accordance with the oath I took as an officer in the US Navy back in 1940, continue to serve an Administration which is more interested in covering up its complicity in spying on its own people, than it is with serving *the people*." He stood ramrod straight, at attention. "It is with immense regret that I must inform you that immediately prior to attending this press conference, I telegraphed my resignation – with immediate effect - as United States Ambassador to the United Kingdom, a post I have been honoured and privileged to discharge, to the President. My formal letter of resignation should be delivered to the White House about now. In that letter, a copy of which has been lodged with the State Department, I lay out the legal and the personal reasons for my departure, and demand that the Department of Justice take the appropriate steps against several named persons."

"Who?" Barked two or three reporters in unison.

Walter Brenckmann pretended to be deaf; looked to his wife.

"Jo and I will miss all our friends in England. Although we served in Oxford in good times and bad, we were always treated with unfailing courtesy and respect. We both look forward to visiting the British Isles and renewing the countless friendships formed in our three years in post."

He suspected Gretchen would chastise him for drifting 'off message'.

"Director of the Federal Bureau of Investigation J. Edgar Hoover, Associate Deputy Director of Central Intelligence, James Jesus Angleton, and Richard Helms, Director of Central Intelligence," he said with a rising edge of indignation. "Each have presided over a corrupt regime, or been directly involved in heinous crimes against the people of the United States."

There were more shouted questions.

He ignored them.

"Ladies and gentlemen, it is never enough simply to 'cry foul' when one witnesses a crime. All it takes for evil to triumph is for good men, and women, to turn a blind eye, to walk on by on the other side of the street. Therefore, I do not propose to be simply a man with a grievance railing against the iniquity of an Administration in which I have lost faith."

Walter Brenckmann grimaced.

"Let us be frank, brutally frank, about this, ladies and gentlemen," he warned sternly. "President Nixon is barely half-way through his four-year term in office. He ought to be impeached but with the GOP in control of both Houses on the Hill, we all know that there is not a snow flake's chance in Hell of that happening this side of November next year. So, I hereby give notice that I plan to put my name forward to be Democrat candidate for the Presidency of the United States!"

Chapter 21

Thursday 2nd February 1967
Clermont-Ferrand, The Auvergne, France

The first Sharof Rashidovich Rashidov, the Troika's Commissar Special Plenipotentiary to the Front Internationale in Clermont-Ferrand, had known about the bombing raid on the ships anchored at Villefranche, had been when he received a panicky telephone call from the airfield to the west of the city.

It later transpired that the Troika had sent him a long, convoluted briefing paper about the raid, and how he was to present the destruction of the 'French Mediterranean Fleet' to his 'Front Internationale Comrades'. Unfortunately, the message had been broadcast in four separate parts and three of the 'parts', had been garbled, resulting in a long delay while the people in Sverdlovsk processed the requests for re-broadcasts. And then, inevitably, there had been a hold-up with the decoding protocols. This latter had occurred because it was not immediately recognised in the Soviet Mission's Communications Room that the re-broadcasts had – in contravention of normal practice - been re-coded in the 'transmission day code' rather than re-sent in their original coding. It made for a very unfunny comedy of errors; the upshot of which was that when Rashidov was peremptorily summoned to explain what was going on, all he knew for sure was that there must have been some kind of botched attempt to sink the Villefranche ships by the Red Air Force.

Then, as he prepared to leave the Soviet Residence situated in the Place de Jaude, more messages delayed his departure for his meeting with Maxim Machenaud.

It seemed that several Tupolev Tu-95 bombers had attempted to land at Clermont-Ferrand.

'The fucking French shot down one of them!'

The confusion would have been laughable had it not been so obvious that the Troika had decided to burn its boats with the Front Internationale; which left Rashidov in a more than somewhat awkward position.

The Commissar Plenipotentiary had still been digesting the – somewhat unlikely, barely plausible reports – when the man at the other end of the line, the Red Air Force Transport Division Duty Liaison Officer, at the airport blurted: 'The Revolutionary Guards have arrested the crews of the two aircraft on the ground. Another aircraft has just crashed. There's a bloody great big fire, I have no idea if any of the crew survived...'

'Why the fuck would the FI shoot down one of our aircraft?' The Commissar Plenipotentiary had demanded.

'They claim it didn't have its transponder switched on so the idiots manning the SS-75 batteries in the hills targeted it with a full salvo of missiles...'

Given that the last time Rashidov had spoken to Maxim

Machenaud, the First Secretary of the Front Internationale, he had spoken of the ships at Villefranche as 'my ships', Sharof Rashidov did not anticipate that there was going to be a great deal of fraternal back-slapping going on when he confronted the little shithead.

It transpired that 'Comrade Machenaud has already left for the airport' by the time the Soviet delegation arrived at the FI's headquarters at the old Michelin Factory.

Under the escort of grim-faced, Kalashnikov-toting Revolutionary Guards the Russians were 'escorted' out of the city and driven across the great, mostly empty expanse of the airfield. There was a large crowd gathered around the two big, silvery bombers parked on the northern side of the field. To the east a plume of black smoke still rose from the scatter of burning wreckage just short of the threshold of the main runway.

The convoy approached neither the parked bombers or the site of the crash; instead, it carried on across the runway and headed for the as yet still uncompleted bunker complex located to the south west, where the aerodrome butted up against Clermont-Ferrand's derelict pre-war industrial sprawl.

Rashidov thought it was stupid locating a command bunker anywhere near the airfield. The RAF had decapitated the Soviet leadership with a couple of big bombs back in 1964, wrecking a bunker complex far larger, far better-engineered and much deeper than the one Maxim Machenaud's people were building.

The convoy halted.

The Russians stepped onto the tarmac; grateful they had grabbed their heaviest coats when they left the Mission that morning. A fiercely gusting northerly wind was ripping at their faces, attempting to lance through their layers of warm clothes.

Rashidov glanced to the distant, burning wreck.

Any aircraft with significant damage would have struggled to land in weather like this. There would be unpredictable winds falling off the surrounding mountains, worse, to his untrained senses it seemed as if the wind was ripping directly across the runway...

"Those were *MY* fucking ships!" Maxim Machenaud screamed in Sharof Rashidov's face as he strode up to him.

The thin woman hovering in the background, three metres behind the 'great leader' was in her thirties, or perhaps, a little older, it was hard to tell these days.

Nobody seemed to know a lot about her.

However, since Rashidov's encounter with Maxim Machenaud at the *Cathédrale Notre-Dame-de-l'Assomption*, he had demanded to know more about her.

Rashidov's people had confirmed that her name was Agnès, or rather 'Comrade Agnès'. She was a member of the Central Committee of the Front Internationale, in charge of the Forst Secretary's Secretariat. She had no personal power base, no friends; she was usually with or close to hand at executions. There were also suggestions that she sat on the FI's 'Revolutionary Court'. This latter body had not been convened in recent months but up until a year ago, it had rubber-stamped, legitimised Maxim Machenaud's rule of terror.

There were rumours – gossip really - that she was Maxim Machenaud's 'squeeze'; Rashidov was sceptical; the little shit got his kicks hurting and killing people and besides, the woman was no kind of 'looker'.

Presently, the woman was looking at him with dull, dead eyes which betrayed not one scintilla of emotion, or...empathy.

Rashidov did not react to Maxim Machenaud's shriek of angst. Nor did he flinch as he felt flecks of the Frenchman's spittle on his cheek.

"MY SHIPS!"

"Comrade First Secretary..."

"MY SHIPS!"

Rashidov recognised that this 'interview' was not going to be a meeting of minds. Machenaud's retinue was bunching up behind him like a lynch mob and his troopers were fingering the triggers of their assault rifles.

Only Comrade Agnès was untouched by the madness.

She stood unmoving, inscrutable in her detachment.

"Where are the crews of the two bombers which landed?"

"They are in custody."

"I must debrief them."

"You can have their bodies after my people have finished with them!"

Rashidov knew he was losing his temper.

He eyed the crowd packing ever closer, threatening, vengeful.

"If you are not willing to allow me to speak to the crews of those two aircraft," he said slowly, carefully projecting every vowel in Moskva Russian which he knew only Machenaud and a handful of his disciples would understand, not waiting for the Frenchman's translator to catch up. "I will return to the Mission's quarters in the city and communicate your non-cooperation to Sverdlovsk. I expect any Red Air Force personnel in your hands to be surrendered to me," he glanced at his watch, "not later than four o'clock this day."

He turned on his heel.

"Where are you going?"

Rashidov turned back.

Enough was enough!

"There have been communications difficulties recently with the Motherland." He thought about complaining about the British 'jamming' of signals, another of the FI's lies to cover up its clumsy attempts to eavesdrop on the Soviet Mission. "Because of this I was not pre-warned about the Red Air Force's operation. I am confident that Sverdlovsk will communicate with me in due course, until then I can be of no assistance to you until my people have debriefed the Red Air Force men from those two bombers."

Rashidov shrugged, and fixed his gaze on the smoke in the distance.

He went on: "In this respect it seems to me that if Soviet aircraft are to be shot down – without warning - over the Massif Central, that I ought to warn my principals back in the Motherland to indefinitely suspend normal supply flights."

Maxim Machenaud stared at him.

His eyes burned, angry hot spots in his ashen, cold-pinched features.

Sharof Rashidov might not have received the signal about the raid on Villefranche, or the attached request to negotiate landing facilities at Clermont-Ferrand for any aircraft with technical issues, or in the (unlikely) circumstance of suffering battle damage; but he had received pre-warning from Troika member Vladimir Yefimovich Semichastny, that in future 'war and humanitarian' supplies for the 'FI Front' would no longer receive the 'priority previously assigned' to them.

This had been the first indication that his brutally candid assessment of the permanence and the resilience of the Machenaud regime, might conceivably, have been taken on board back home. He had pointed to the regime's over-reliance on a relatively small cadre of 'highly capable and motivated Revolutionary Guards', the majority of whom were stationed in and around Clermont-Ferrand, the obvious disconnect between 'legacy out of control Krasnaya Zarya' detachments in the countryside, prosecuting the war beyond the boundaries of the Massif Central. He had also identified the 'political and ideological separation' of the Central Committee of the FI in the Auvergne to the Workers Committees controlling much of the rest of the south, who – contrary to Maxim Machenaud's delusional assertions - regarded what was left of the former French Mediterranean Fleet holed-up in Villefranche-sur-Mer, as 'their' fleet."

That summary, despatched to Sverdlovsk before the news of the FI's attempt to seize 'the fleet' became known was, of course, already out of date.

Maxim Machenaud's attempt to steal away his southern allies' fleet might already have fatally undermined his last hope of uniting the south of France under the red banner.

Thus far, Rashidov's people had been unable to discover how badly the storms in the north were hitting the FI's forces below the Loire Valley, or even if the British were still probing threateningly along the north bank of the Gironde Estuary towards Krasnaya Zarya's last major bastion on the Atlantic coast, Bordeaux. Problematically, not only were the FI in general, and Maxim Machenaud in particular, almost wholly uncommunicative about 'their' military capabilities and ongoing operations outside the Auvergne; but what little intelligence Rashidov had seen since arriving in France, seemed to him, inherently suspect. Assurances that the Free French were on the defensive, trapped in their trenches along the Loire Valley in the west and in their 'enclaves' in Picardy, the Somme and the Ardennes, flew in the face of what little intelligence he had inherited. If the British were parked on the landward approaches of the Gironde Estuary, nothing about the FI-Krasnaya Zarya positions in the Loire Valley could possibly be remotely 'secure'. And as for the laughable claim that the Free French were on the defensive east of Paris; how on Earth did that square with hard and fast intelligence that the enemy had succeeded in halting infiltration into France across the Rhine?

That said, before the Siberian storm had swept across the continent, he had largely discounted any likelihood of a major Free French offensive before the spring at the very earliest. Moreover, the latest forecasts warned that even though the worst of the weather would linger over northern France and the southern British Isles, there was likely to be a freezing sting in the tail of the huge depression as it rolled south west toward the Atlantic. Heavy snow and Arctic conditions were likely even in the Auvergne in the next week...

Maxim Machenaud had stopped ranting.

So, Sharof Rashidov started to listen to what he was saying.

"Your people," the Frenchman said, accusatively, "say they sank several ships but that they were engaged by missile-equipped British fighters, and encountered heavy, very well-directed anti-aircraft fire as they commenced their bomb runs. They say Villefranche was obscured by clouds and that their bomb-aiming was probably degraded by an unexpectedly hostile 'electronic environment' as they made their attack."

One of Rashidov's aides coughed diplomatically.

"Modern warships routinely monitor and in combat will seek to disrupt a foe's electronic warfare suite," the man, attired in KGB green with a badge on his uniform left breast indicating he was a communications specialist, remarked respectfully.

"I understood that the Villefranche Squadron was virtually mothballed?" Rashidov queried brusquely.

"Just so, Comrade Commissar," the much younger KGB man agreed hurriedly. "It might indicate, therefore, that there were vessels from a foreign navy present in the anchorage at the time of the raid."

"The fucking English?" Maxim Machenaud spat.

"A British Squadron departed from Gibraltar several days ago, Comrade First Secretary," he was informed, cursorily in comparison with the caution the officer had addressed his own superior. "A carrier strike group commanded by HMS Victorious, which carries about twenty-five or thirty aircraft. Including," he added, "jet interceptors."

Machenaud scowled, looked to Rashidov.

"I am informed your people caught a glimpse of one of the fighters. It had an 'odd looking' tail plane..."

The KGB Intelligence man spoke up again.

"The Victorious carries Sea Vixen interceptors; they have a very distinctive twin boom tail plane..."

"How could they have approached so close to Villefranche without anybody knowing?" The Frenchman demanded angrily, his eyes blazing anew.

"Very easily," the KGB man observed. "It was assumed Victorious and her escorts were bound for Malta."

"What happened to those Red Navy submarines that were supposed to be guarding MY southern coasts?" Maxim Machenaud asked sourly, bitterly.

"That was last year, Comrade First Secretary," the KGB man explained guardedly. There had never been any Red Navy submarines within a thousand miles of the Bay of Lions or the Riviera. "They were redeployed when the British made no attempt to reinstate their blockade..."

"Order them to come back!"

Sharof Rashidov shook his head.

He knew that there were Red Navy conventional, diesel electric submarines, operating in the Black Sea, the Aegean and the Eastern Mediterranean. He also knew that there were never more than a couple, more usually only one, and sometimes, no vessels available for operations on a given day, and the Mediterranean was a big, big sea, even when local tactical conditions occasionally permitted free passage in and out of the Black Sea.

In any event, any Red Navy man who torpedoed a British or an American warship would be lucky if he was only shot when he got back home!

Notwithstanding that no Soviet diplomat or commissar ever went abroad with wholly unambiguous instructions; Sharof Rashidov knew full well that the last thing the Troika – leastways its chairman, Alexander Shelepin – wanted, was anybody starting an actual shooting war with the West.

It went without saying that Maxim Machenaud's perspective on such matters was radically, insanely divergent from that held within the Sverdlovsk Kremlin!

The leader of the Front International turned and pointed, right arm outstretched, at the two Tu-95s in the distance.

"I want those aircraft to attack the fucking English!"

Chapter 22

The crews of the Campbeltown, Perth and Dundee had done everything humanly possible to pull as many of the survivors of the four sunken French ships from the oil and wreckage-strewn waters of the anchorage. But the water had been cold, and many otherwise unhurt survivors had died from ingesting salt water and fuel. Less than an hour after the end of the attack there were only dead bodies to be pulled from the sea.

It was too early for a proper reckoning; but already Captain Dermot O'Reilly knew the body count was going to be in the hundreds. It was a mercy that nobody had been killed on his three ships, although all three destroyers had walking wounded and several more men more seriously injured by splinters or the blast of near misses. Campbeltown herself had been bracketed by big bombs from the stick which had damaged the Jean Bart as the action came to a sudden, shuddering end almost as quickly as it had begun.

A thousand-kilogram bomb had glanced off the side armour of the battleship's Number Two 380-millimetre quadruple main battery turret, lanced through the main deck and exploded between five and ten metres from the side of the leviathan as it hit the water causing only relatively minor blast damage.

Another thousand-kilo munition had hit the ship far forward, demolishing the Jean Bart's empty paint store and severing her starboard anchor chain before cleaving through an empty fuel bunker and screaming, without exploding into the depths of the bay. Presently the Flagship of what was left of the Villefranche Squadron was down two degrees by the head, having taken on several hundred tons of water between frames two and five.

The battleship had sustained four dead and another seventeen wounded, mercifully most of the latter having suffered only minor injuries.

Bizarrely, the one ship in the bay which had completely escaped damage or casualties was the Clemenceau. Throughout the attack the aircraft carrier had sat like a huge, seemingly unmissable target amidst the mayhem, a surreally serene witness to the tide of death and destruction threatening to overwhelm the rest of the fleet.

"We think there were at least twenty of the beggars," Rear Admiral Henry Leach told O'Reilly over the secure TBS connection in his sea cabin on board the Campbeltown, which was again back alongside the Jean Bart, offloading survivors from the sunken ships.

Apparently, the Fleet Air Arm contingent aboard the flagship were a little down in the mouth about their failure to shoot down *all* the Russian bombers.

Dermot O'Reilly had moved on past this; there was only so much two Sea Vixens could do against such a large formation of bombers.

"Our best guess is that twelve or thirteen of the bombers managed to unload somewhere in the vicinity of Villefranche. We think at least a couple of bomb loads probably fell long, maybe even into the eastern suburbs of Nice, sir," he offered, feeling unutterably weary.

"We think we shot down six of the Tu-95s," Henry Leach went on. "Unfortunately, they were on us almost before we knew it. Understandably, the CAP was loitering to your west where we all anticipated any threat might materialise from. But anyway, we between the CAP and your Fletchers we bagged at least six, and possibly another one. The enemy formation split into two sections after the raid, with three, possibly four aircraft heading off to the north west and the rest beetling off to the east. It may be that the bombers heading towards the Auvergne were 'winged' by your five-inchers. The consensus at this end is that the Red Air Force must have scraped-up every available Tu-95 to mount a show like this. Ergo, now they have shot their bolt we should not expect a repeat exercise in the near future. It also inclines me to the view that, after their botched attempt to seize the fleet the other day, our friends in the FI might not be in any position to further muck about with us at Villefranche either."

Dermot O'Reilly hoped he was right.

However, hope was a thing he had learned not to bank on in combat.

"I still think we need to get the French ships out of here as soon as possible, sir."

"I agree absolutely. While those ships remain at Villefranche we will be operating with our hands tied behind our backs!" There was a brief pause, presumably because one of the Task Force Commander's staffers needed to speak to him urgently. "Sorry about that, Dermot. Right, I want all those ships out of there tonight. Scuttle any vessel that cannot steam under its own power. Once you're at sea detach Dundee and Perth to escort the French to Malta. Any questions?"

Dermot O'Reilly chuckled to himself.

"No, sir. Get the French to sea and send them off to Malta."

"That's the ticket."

It was getting dark by the time O'Reilly went on board the Jean Bart to speak to Brynmawr Williams. Over a third of the Campbeltown's crew – among them many of his most experienced men - was still aboard the battleship and he needed as many of them back as possible before he re-joined Task Force V1.

His Executive Officer had anticipated as much and it was amicably, and speedily agreed which sixty-six of Campbeltown's people would remain.

"I need you back on Campbeltown, too, Bryn," O'Reilly informed his burly second-in-command. "Admiral Leguay and Commander Benois are perfectly capable chaps. I'll send over Keith Moss; they'll need a Navigator. He speaks tolerable French, I gather. Anyway, it will be useful experience for him."

The two officers had been conversing on the compass platform, their new French 'allies' careful to give them space, privacy and not to in any way intrude.

There was a polite cough.

Contra Amiral Rene Leguay, leaning for support on the diminutive form of Aurélie Faure, had stepped, unsteadily onto the bridge.

"So," the Frenchman asked, "what is the verdict? Are my ships to be sunk at their moorings?"

"No, sir," O'Reilly grimaced, shaking his head. "Any ship that can steam out of Villefranche under its own power before dawn tomorrow, will be escorted to Malta."

It was likely that the frigate La Savoyard, so badly damaged in the air raid that everybody was a little surprised she was still afloat; would be the only one of the surviving major units which would have to be abandoned at Villefranche.

Dermot O'Reilly went on: "At Malta, it is my understanding that any person prepared to swear allegiance to the Free French cause will be granted political asylum, and offered employment in the crusade to free your country from the curse of the regime in Clermont-Ferrand. As to your ships, well," the Canadian Captain (D) of the 21st Destroyer Squadron shrugged, "that will be a matter for naval surveyors and the Allied High Command. I repeat what I said to you the first time I came aboard the Jean Bart. You are *not* prisoners; you are free men and women. Today, we fought side by side. That, I think, is a good start." He glanced to Brynmawr Williams. "Bryn will be transferring back to Campbeltown," he smiled wanly, "I need him more than you do. I shall be sending my navigator, Lieutenant Moss across to you as senior Royal Navy officer. His status on board will be as a detached watch officer responsible for Campbeltown's personnel on board the Jean Bart. He will be under your command, sir. Once the squadron is out to sea, Campbeltown will probably re-join Task Force V1, leaving the Dundee and the Perth to escort you to the Grand Harbour."

Leguay was speechless.

Aurélie Faure smiled: "Mon Amiral did not believe you when promised not to take his fleet from him, Captain O'Reilly."

"We live in a world that is full of surprises, do we not?" The Canadian Royal Navy man observed wryly, drawing himself up to his full height and turning to Rene Leguay. "Sir," he said, formally, "'you have the deck."

After Dermot O'Reilly returned to the Campbeltown, he walked the ship. Today, was the first time most of his greenhorns had been in a real battle; and nothing prepared a man for that. The random brutality of it was what struck most men. Prepare as you might, death walked where it pleased across any seaborne, aerial or land battle, random quirks of fate determined who lived and who died. As for the reasons why, well, that was always a mystery.

Why had the Red Air Force sent – at huge peril - most, if not all, of its long-range heavy bomber force thousands of miles from the Russian heartland to destroy what survived of the French Mediterranean Fleet?

To keep it out of the hands of the Front Internationale?

That made no sense, the Soviets were obviously hand in glove with those maniacs.

To stop the West getting hold of those ships?

That was almost as nonsensical as any other explanation. *Those* ships had been rusting at Villefranche for years, nobody in Oxford or London had given them a second thought until the last few weeks. By spiriting the surviving ships to Malta, the allies – the British and the French – were as good as putting them out of the fight as if they had scuttled them at their moorings.

And yet the Russians had sent at least twenty bombers laden with ship-killing bombs to destroy *that* fleet. Was this some sort of reaction to the Front Internationale's failure to seize the fleet; or had the Russians intended to destroy the fleet sooner or later, if only to deny it to the allies?

But for the Victorious's Sea Vixens and the radar-directed barrage thrown up by his Fletchers, those Tu-95s would have had a field day...

Of course, the Russians had not expected to be confronted with fast jets, or murderously effective anti-aircraft fire filling the skies precisely where they planned to release their bomb loads. So, if neither the Royal Navy nor their new French friends had been expecting the attack; the Russians had certainly not anticipated running into fighters or three old-fashioned gunship destroyers spitting radar-directed fire in their faces. In other words, everybody was as blind as everybody else!

The wind was starting to whistle through the upper works of the old destroyer; even in the shelter of the anchorage he could feel the Campbeltown working under his feet. The trip to Malta was going to be a rough one for the people on the smaller ships. Nonetheless, at the moment he suspected most of Rene Leguay's people would steam into the jaws of Hades to get away from Villefranche and the hated Front Internationale. It was too early for the full shock of that afternoon's disaster to have sunk in, either for many of his people, or Rene Leguay's. While he and his French counterpart knew that this was what mortal combat was like, even in this brave new post-apocalypse world, many, the majority perhaps, of those who had not experienced the savagery of a sea battle, would need a little time to come to terms with their experiences. Even after the fire fight with the Front Internationale's Revolutionary Guards, the civilians on the battleships would have felt relatively secure, having witnessed how invulnerable the great ship was to the 'big guns' of their foes. Now, however, they knew the great ship could easily have been smashed like matchwood by the two-ton bombs falling like supersonic bolts from a grey sky, dropped by aircraft they never even saw.

Dermot O'Reilly was under no illusion how lucky his ships had been that afternoon. Even a relatively near miss by one of those bombs would have stove in the side of one of his thin-skinned Fletchers, a direct hit would have folded Campbeltown or one of her sisters in half and killed most of the men aboard.

It was around midnight that a hand touched Dermot O'Reilly's shoulder as he dozed in the captain's chair on the bridge.

"La Savoyard's splinter damage is too bad. Her engine room is still flooded, sir," Brynmawr Williams reported in the unearthly red lighting of the compartment.

The Villefranche Squadron and the three detached Fletchers of the 21st Destroyer Squadron were observing a total black out; the red lighting preserved the bridge watch's night vision.

La Savoyard was a thirteen hundred ton Le Normand class frigate capable of making twenty-eight knots, a relatively modern ship commissioned as recently as 1956.

Dermot O'Reilly sighed.

"Admiral Leguay has ordered her to be evacuated," Campbeltown's Executive Officer continued grimly. "She may sink before dawn. If she doesn't..."

"Notify the Jean Bart, that Campbeltown will sink La Savoyard with gunfire at dawn."

Using torpedoes within the enclosed anchorage was impractical, not least because the frigate was moored close in to the corniche at the northern end of the bay where the waters narrowed.

Campbeltown's 21-inch fish needed to run several hundred yards before their warheads activated, thus making it almost impossible for the destroyer to safely manoeuvre into a firing position without risking running aground, or fouling the wreckage of one or other of the sunken ships.

"Aye, aye, sir."

It gave neither man any pleasure to be contemplating delivering the coup de grace to any ship; but neither could they risk allowing the ship, her weaponry or any of her equipment falling into the hands of the Front Internationale, or their Soviet sponsors.

Most of the survivors from the sunken ships had been transferred to the Jean Bart, which, courtesy of Campbeltown's surgeon, assisted by sickbay attendants from both the Dundee and the Perth, and the ransacking of the contents of all three destroyers' medical lockers, was the best equipped of the French ships to deal with casualties. Ideally, helicopters from the Victorious or the Fearless would have airlifted off the most seriously injured casualties in the morning but because of the increasingly wild weather offshore, that was not going to happen now.

Jean Bart, her list stabilised by counter-flooding, and her head still down by a couple of degrees, would lead the Clemenceau, the cruiser De Grasse, the fleet destroyers La Bourdannais, and Kersaint, the frigate Le Lorrain and a motley collection of fishing boats out of the anchorage in the hours before dawn. If Le Lorrain's sister ship, La Savoyard was still afloat at daybreak, Campbeltown, which would remain behind in the anchorage until all the other vessels had safely departed, would sink her.

Even after Campbeltown had recovered every one of her people not essential to the operation of the battleship, there would still be over a hundred and seventy Royal Navy men – including sixty-six of

Campbeltown's complement on the Jean Bart, and a similar-sized contingent from the Dundee and Perth aboard the Clemenceau - aboard the French ships. Several of Rene Leguay's smaller ships were so bereft of competent, let alone qualified watchkeepers, and so short-handed that had the three destroyers not each have given up several experienced officers and petty officers it would simply not have been possible to operate La Bourdannais, or the Kersaint.

Mercifully, at the time of the bombing raid there had been no British personnel on either the Jeanne d'Arc or La Savoyard, and miraculously of the twenty or so men from the Perth aboard La Galissoniene and the Surcouf, had all survived with nothing worse than cuts and bruises and for two men blown overboard by near misses, a brush with hypothermia and exposure in the cold waters, survivable only because, fortuitously, they had been wearing life jackets when they went into the water.

Dermot O'Reilly blinked awake again.

He had been cat-napping, lost track of time.

Three bells in the middle watch: zero-one-thirty-hours.

A mug of cocoa was respectfully pressed into his hands.

"Thank you, Tompkins," he said gruffly to the young quartermaster's mate who had brought him the life-giving brew.

O'Reilly had once asked Peter Christopher how 'on earth do you remember everybody's name?' It transpired that his friend religiously locked himself away for a few minutes every day and mentally walked the ship, or the office, or the embassy or these days, presumably the Governor-General's Mansion at Yarralumla and the nearby Australian Parliament, picturing faces and naming the names. Apparently, Lady Marija did the same sort of exercise; and sometimes they tested each other.

Apparently, quite competitively!

HMS Campbeltown's commanding officer had still not got the faces and the names of each and every man of his three-hundred-and-four-man crew locked and loaded in his mind's eye. He was only about ninety percent of the way, the calculus complicated by the fact that thirty-one men had transferred off the destroyer at Gibraltar, mostly older hands or promising greenhorns going on board other of the 21st Destroyer Squadron's vessels, and forty-seven completely new men had joined the ship.

O'Reilly could only imagine what a nightmare it must be trying to remember names on a big ship like a cruiser or an aircraft carrier! Reconciling names to faces, ranks and duties on a ship the size of the Victorious must be akin to painting the Forth Bridge; no sooner had one finished one end and it was time to start daubing again at the other!

He tried very hard not to fret over everything that had to be done over the next few hours, if the ships in his charge were to be safely set upon their way to freedom.

The idea of sailing the French ships to Malta was, to his way of thinking, something of a stretch. Corsica and Sardinia, neither under the control of regimes friendly to Royal Navy surface ships trespassing anywhere near their waters, and Sicily – nobody knew what to expect from that Mafia-controlled island, or the Italian mainland if the fleet attempted to make a passage through the Straits of Messina – all lay between the French Riviera and the safety of the Grand Harbour, a transit of the best part of seven hundred and fifty miles. Granted, a voyage to Gibraltar, over nine hundred miles distant, would have been no picnic but at least they could be confident that the Spanish were not going to make any difficulties, not now that Generalissimo Franco was in the middle of gratefully falling back into bed with NATO.

Surely, it would have been better to attempt to park the French ships at La Spezia or Genoa; the people in charge of those ports – Fascisti, by all accounts – were badly in need of friends and there were big dry docks and shipyard workers crying out for gainful employment, capable of patching up the French warships…

Ours is not to reason why…

So, Malta it was; and it was his job to see the fleet – what was left of it – safely on its way.

O'Reilly sipped his cocoa.

'Chi,' they called it in the Royal Navy. His brew was laced with rum, a little something to help him get through the night. When he dined with his officers, he nursed a small glass of beer, and axiomatically, it went without saying that he drank the Queen's health with 'the real stuff', that apart, he was fastidiously teetotal these days.

At a pinch, the French ships had just enough oil in their bunkers to make Naples. Before the air raid he had been contemplating pumping a couple of hundred more tons of Campbeltown's fuel into the Jean Bart's tanks, little more than a drop in the ocean to a thirsty monster like the battleship. He had hoped similar 'top ups' from the Dundee and the Perth would have been just enough to get the French to Malta. All those plans had gone overboard when the first Russian bomb screamed down. Out at sea, even had the survivors of the Villefranche Squadron been equipped, or their crews trained to do it, oiling was going to be impossible given the predicted sea conditions.

O'Reilly tried not to obsess about all the things which could go wrong. If any of the French ships broke down, lost power, there would be no way a tow could be passed or secured, a stricken ship would be at the mercy of the seas, possibly even driven north onto a lee shore…

Another sip of his restorative cocoa.

Another sigh, oddly contented.

Whatever his worries these were the days any Royal Navy Captain worth his salt longed to live.

God in Heaven, how Peter would envy me if he could see me now!

Chapter 23

Thursday 2nd February 1967
The Oval Office, The White House

US National Security Advisor Henry Kissinger was in conference with Richard Nixon when Bob Haldeman had burst into the Oval Office, without knocking, and turned on the new colour TV in the corner near the door.

Bizarrely, nobody had mentioned *The Washington Post's* damning indictment of the Administration's competence, morals and grasp of legal proprieties that morning. Other, that was, than to despatch senior staffers to bad mouth Ben Bradlee and 'the traitors within' to the White House press corps, which, despite the furore, was oddly depleted, the building had been in a state of semi-denial.

That was not to say that the phones did not ring, maniacally.

"No comment..."

"That's horseshit..."

"No comment..."

"Which part of 'no comment' don't you get, buddy?"

"No, the President is working at his desk as normal..."

"No comment..."

"You need to see this!" Bob Haldeman informed the Commander-in-Chief, rattled, which was not like him. Other staffers had followed him into the Oval Office.

Richard Nixon's scowl of displeasure to be interrupted without a by your leave, morphed into something a lot closer to unmitigated horror as he realised what he was watching.

Walter Brenckmann and his wife were fielding – with courtesy and an uncanny 'down home' charm - a barrage of questions.

"He's just told the American people that we've been tapping their phones and bugging their houses," John Ehrlichmann explained breathlessly. He had spilled something, possibly coffee, on his jacket in his anxiety to get to the Oval Office. "And he's just announced he's running in 1968!"

"The general election is two years away!" Somebody objected derisively.

"It is in twenty-one fucking months," Bob Haldeman snapped irritably.

Joanne Brenckmann was talking.

"You really never know what life is going to bring next," she reflected. "A little over four years ago, we were planning to sell up our house in Cambridge – we were almost right next to the MIT campus - and go down to the Keys, and then," she shrugged and smiled that 'grandmother of the nation' smile that scared the living daylights out of the older campaigners in the Oval Office, "everything changed!"

"Oh shit!" More than one man muttered.

Joanne Brenckmann was not Jackie Kennedy, nor was she anywhere near as scary as Lady Bird Johnson. She certainly was not

Mamie Eisenhower, that most anonymous of presidential spouses in the last three decades.

No, she was more Eleanor Roosevelt reincarnated...

Except, happily married to her husband...

And as for the Ambassador: heck, nobody wanted to get into a man to man debate with the guy who had been Claude Betancourt's go-to fixer for all those years!

"No chance," another pundit offered, wandering into the Oval Office. "What about the beatnik son in LA. You know, the one who did jail time..."

"Even Hoover figured that was a fix up."

"Oh, right..."

"Shut up!" Richard Nixon barked angrily. "All of you, shut up!"

Coincidentally, that was when Pat Nixon entered the Oval Office, having been warned that something 'was going on'. Normally, the President's wife prided herself on being above the fray, that classic non sequitur, a 'non-political' political wife. She was no such thing, no woman married to a career politician who had been vice president for eight years in the 1950s could claim to be ignorant or untouched by the curse of political life.; all she could do was try to protect her daughters from the nastiness of the environment in which they lived.

She came to stand beside her husband's desk.

She too, frowned at the telecast.

Joanne Brenckmann had that natural common touch that simply could not be taught, or acquired. She just *connected*, instantly, her smile cutting through all the shit...

"*If* he runs," John Ehrlichmann speculated, "we hit him for his links to the Kennedys, we call him old man Betancourt's personal congressman, we dig up dirt on his kids..."

"Turn up the sound," the President snarled.

"I support my husband in everything he does," Joanne Brenckmann was saying. "No, of course we don't agree over everything. How do I feel about Walter running for President? How did I feel about bringing up three, and then a fourth young child during wartime when he was away in the Navy? Walter was doing his duty. He was defending us all. That is what he will be doing running for President."

A secretary scurried into the Oval Office and spoke to Haldeman. The Chief of Staff scowled, nodded curtly and the woman fled back into the adjacent secretary's room.

"Brenckmann and his wife are going to be on Walter Cronkite's show tonight," he reported to the room at large. "It gets worse. The word from her lawyer in San Francisco is that Miranda Sullivan will be holding a news conference this afternoon, local time. All the networks are going to carry it live tonight as soon as Cronkite winds up with the Brenckmanns."

Ronald Ziegler, the still absurdly youthful White House Press Secretary skidded into the Oval Office.

"There's hardly anybody in the press room," he complained,

"they've all gone down to Sallis, Betancourt and Brenckmann. What am I supposed to say to them all when they come back here?"

Nobody said anything.

"I've got to have something to work with," Ziegler pleaded. "There's a whole lot of blood in the water and all those guys down there at the Ambassador's conference are real sharks!"

"Former Ambassador," John Ehrlichmann said absent-mindedly. Like other members of the President's inner circle he was in shock.

"Did we sack the guy?" Ziegler queried, brightening a little.

"No. He quit."

"Oh, but can't we still say we fired him? For being such a klutz with the Brits, or something?"

"No," Henry Kissinger spoke for the first time in several minutes. The urbane Harvard academic was ashen-faced, clearly not himself. The US National Security Advisor seemed to be standing, physically and psychologically, apart from everybody else in the Oval Office. He threw a questioning glance at Richard Nixon. "You told me there was nothing to worry about?" He put to the President, disappointed.

"We did things during the war that," the Commander-in-Chief blustered uncomfortably, not meeting the other man's eye, "that we had to..."

Everybody in the Oval Office was looking at the National Security Advisor. Some resentfully as if to say: "What right do you have to pretend that you are any better than us?"

Kissinger was supposed to be the cleverest man in any room he walked into in DC; it was a bit late to try to claim that he had not known what was going on all along just because he himself had never, at any time, actually got his hands dirty.

"Operation Maelstrom started while Ike was in this office, Henry," John Ehrlichmann said. "JFK's people green-lighted it, LBJ was so pissed off with Doctor King and his people for keeping up the pressure in the South, that he signed an Executive Order authorising Hoover to start tapping phones..."

"But that was already going on, anyway?" This Kissinger retorted, his voice gravelly and pitched sotto voce in what, infuriatingly, sounded to those around him like incredulity.

"Yeah, but LBJ had just got past the Kitty Hawk thing, and the Kennedy people were still trying to shut him out of a lot of stuff at the time..."

Kissinger had latched onto the nuance that Johnson had not been in the Oval Office long enough to unravel the half of what had been, and was continuing to go on, out of sight and out of mind.

"So, LBJ never knew the scope and scale of Operation Maelstrom. What about JFK?"

"You'd have to go up to Hyannis Port and ask him, Henry?" Bob Haldeman suggested sarcastically, trying to listen to what Walter Brenckmann was saying on the TV.

"I might just do that, Bob," Kissinger replied levelly.

The White House Chief of Staff frowned, tried to tune out the background noise. They did not have time to swap recriminations or play the blame game; right now, they needed to work out how they were going to distance the President from the unprecedented shit storm that was about to hit the Oval Office.

"No, I have not spoken to President Nixon about this," Walter Brenckmann admitted. "Honestly, I do not see what good that would do. I believe that the Administration has been spying on its friends and its adversaries – I have no idea whether I and my family fall into the former or the latter category – it does not matter. What matters is that the whole nation has been misled about the Warwick Hotel Scandal, and so many other things that frankly, it beggars my imagination as it must do, millions of my fellow Americans. Our friends and allies must be looking on, watching this, wondering if they can believe their ears and eyes. Personally, I feel like I have been duped, and deceived. The current Administration has been using powers granted to it in war time to mount a Soviet-style deep state surveillance and counter intelligence operation *against* its own people. I do not care if spokesmen for the GOP – thus far, I gather, the White House has adopted the approach of hear no evil, see no evil, speak no evil, the approach of the three brass monkeys – are right, or wrong when they claim both Democrat and Republican Administrations are equally culpable. When my own government spies on me and mine, I don't care how much or little they are doing it; what I care about is that they are riding a coach and horses through the Constitution of the United States of America!"

Walter Brenckmann's denouncement was all the more damning for being enunciated in the quiet, sober voice of a man who patently felt he had been horribly let down.

Betrayed, in fact.

"Therefore, I cannot and I will not continue serve an Administration, or a President, whom I consider to be a crook."

Chapter 24

Friday 3rd February 1967
Odessa, Ukraine

The car ground over the previous week's partially cleared snowfall, now frozen solid by the bitter north easterly winds blowing straight off the Siberian tundra.

"It has been a while since you and I talked, Comrade Sergey Georgyevich," the Supreme Soviet, head of the Troika and Chairman and First Secretary of the Communist Party of the USSR, Alexander Nikolayevich Shelepin decided, staring out of the frosted window of the ancient Red Army car bumping and grinding along in the middle of the heavily armed convoy heading for the city's newly refurbished air base. "Perhaps, it may be that recent events, if nothing else, prove that this has been...counter-productive."

Admiral of the Fleet Sergey Georgyevich Gorshkov, Minister of Defence and First Deputy Secretary of the Communist Party, and since July 1964 the number two man in the Soviet hierarchy, grunted noncommittally, unconsciously running a nicotine-stained forefinger through his now grey moustache.

The two men sat alone in the back of the car, jolted painfully every time the wheels hit a bump or juddered on an ice ridge. The vehicle's heater blew lukewarm air fouled by the exhausts of the armoured personnel carrier leading the small procession of cars carrying the rest of the United Nations delegation out of the snowbound city.

The passenger section of the Supreme Soviet's rattling conveyance was partitioned off from the driver's cabin by a sound and bullet-proofed bulkhead.

Privately, Sergey Gorshkov was seething.

And not just on account of the first, inconclusive – albeit wildly optimistic – Red Air Force reports of the attack on the ships of the former French Mediterranean Fleet anchored at Villefranche-sur-Mer.

Forgetting for the moment the fact that Gorshkov and his Red Navy Staff had had plans for those ships, what ought to have been a straightforward – granted very long-range - bombing operation against targets unaware that they were under attack until it was too late, had, whatever the Air Force said, resulted in at best, only a partial success. More worrying, from the tone of the first reports passed to him, Gorshkov suspected that the raid had been far from the unopposed 'cake run' he had been assured it would be, and that several of the priceless, irreplaceable Tupolev Tu-95 strategic bombers – three-quarters of all the serviceable aircraft of their type, which had participated in the Villefranche operation – had been damaged, or disastrously, lost. That at least three aircraft, possibly four of the Tu-95s had diverted to Clermont-Ferrand, presumably because of battle damage, or mechanical failures, might yet turn out to be the sourest of sour icing on a very, very bitter cake.

And as for Warsaw Concerto...

The political and the military aspects of geopolitical policy were indivisible. Diplomacy was war by other means; conversely, war was diplomacy by other means.

Or was it?

If Gorshkov had not already known that his power and influence was on the wane when a third, permanent member of the Troika, one of Shelepin's protégés, had been anointed; the fact that the man whose name appeared on the initial draft plan for Warsaw Concerto, had not been summarily sacked, or he and his family deported to the Gulag, nor even consigned to house arrest or internal exile, but rather, he had been handed a cushy, high-profile job in the Russian Far East, would have hammered home the point.

Mikhail Gorbachev would have been the guest of the Lubyanka in the old days, beaten to a pulp and forced to confess his treachery in front of a show trial. Not treated with kid gloves; not treated in such a way that meant that one day he was going to return to Sverdlovsk like a fucking prodigal son!

Okay, he got it that the man had been removed, temporarily, from the Boss's inner circle. It would be a while before Mikhail Sergeyevich would again enjoy unfettered access to the head of the Troika. But Gorbachev had actually, if one was being pedantic about it, been promoted at least two ranks in the Party!

Shelepin had allegedly written the bloody man's wife, Raisa, a personal letter, exhorting her to do everything in her power to 'support Mikhail Sergeyevich' in his 'new and vital role' in Vladivostok!

Understandably, the old Admiral was reeling.

What did it all mean?

All the old certainties of the Soviet system seemed to be shifting under his feet like the deck of a destroyer in an Arctic storm. Nor was Mikhail Sergeyevich Gorbachev the only one who had failed to be punished for the misrepresentation of Warsaw Concerto – or rather, the way certain Party apparatchiks and middle-ranking Red Army officers had chosen to interpret its goals – and the fallout, mixed messages, and miss-steps which had subsequently caused so much confusion with both the Chinese and with the Americans.

Warsaw Concerto was supposed to be a fucking propaganda exercise to boost morale on the home front! Instead, some idiot, or cabal – probably in the fucking KGB, those bastards were still a rule unto themselves despite the Boss being one of them – had promulgated it across the fucking globe!

Gorshkov himself, had not really understood what was going on until the Boss had ordered the attack on the French Fleet at Villefranche, and in effect, cut off their French allies at the knees.

It was a mess.

Normally, this sort of shit heap would be covered up by a purge. But all that had happened was that a handful of Party apparatchiks and military officers, none very close to the Boss, had been sacked or transferred to Red Army units stationed in the frozen north. It was almost as if the Boss had used the whole thing as an excuse to get rid of a gang of time servers, to coppice out dead wood and the unproductive, redundant 'drag' that their families and hangers-on had represented within the Sverdlovsk-Chelyabinsk military-industrial complex. Obviously, the KGB had identified a handful of counter-revolutionary scapegoats, and things had not gone well for their families but otherwise, even the sanctions against the 'guilty' had amounted to little more than cursory metaphorical slaps on the wrists.

And as for Shelepin's, pretty near damned 'open letter', to Comrade Yuri Vladimirovich Andropov, the Troika's 'enforcer', telling him, basically, that there would be no more 'terror'...

What the fuck was all that about?

"When do I get to be purged, Comrade Chairman?" Gorshkov demanded gruffly.

Alexander Shelepin did not look at him; he continued to gaze, contemplatively out of the misted window.

"Purge you?" He echoed.

"Yes! Isn't that why we're both going to San Francisco? You don't trust me enough to leave me at home while you're away?"

Shelepin glanced to the other man.

Looked away again.

"In future, we must understand each other better, Sergey Georgyevich," Shelepin sighed. "If you and I, and the factions who look to us for guidance, cannot coexist, then what hope is there for the Motherland, or for the International Revolution?"

Gorshkov was a life-long believer in counter-attack being the best form of defence: "Why wasn't I forewarned of the change of policy over France?"

"Because you would have objected," Shelepin returned, bloodlessly. "As indeed you did when I ordered you to bomb the French Fleet at Villefranche. Which would have been communicated far and wide. As it is, if things have not gone as well as we hoped, we can both, justly and with clean hands, blame Comrade Konstantin Andreevich."

Chief Marshal of Aviation, the Head of the Red Air Force, Konstantin Andreevich Vershinin, had been a key conspirator in the overthrow, and swift liquidation of the Brezhnev regime back in July 1964. His reward had been to remain in command of the Red Air Force, subordinate in the Defence Ministry only to Gorshkov, and in that role he had served, grumpily, with bad-tempered ill-grace at times, but loyally, ever since.

Gorshkov changed the subject.

"Whatever happens, we must keep up, increase if possible, the support for the Front Internationale..."

Alexander Shelepin knew the other man was needling him, looking to revisit a decision which had already been made. He refused to rise to the bait.

"Propping up the FI even at the risk of forcing the Americans to send troops to Western Europe again?" He countered, reasonably.

"What makes you think they haven't already made that decision?"

Alexander Shelepin brushed this aside with a shrug.

"As you know, I have always accepted that there is merit in actions which continue to," he thought carefully, '*stress* the reactionary forces in power in the British Isles."

The two men lapsed into their thoughts for some seconds.

The car's engine rumbled and roared.

"Our last best chance of militarily confronting the West in Europe died when Brezhnev and his cronies pissed away what was left of the Red Army in Iran and Iraq," Alexander Shelepin said with a quiet, stinging bitterness. "Krasnaya Zarya ought to have been a dagger to the heart of our enemies overseas, not an enemy within."

Gorshkov opened his mouth to speak.

"No, no," Shelepin went on, shaking his head, "of course, I acknowledge that Red Dawn won great advances in the beginning. Nor do I discount that in France and to a lesser extent, elsewhere in the West, it remains a thorn in the side of our adversaries. But let us, you and I, not get carried away with the vodka talk of our staffers, and of those comrades who claim great deeds for their heroic Krasnaya Zarya brothers and sisters. We both know Red Dawn had little or no part in the American rebellion, or their so-called Civil War. We have no spies in America, and only a few in England. Krasnaya Zarya is a nightmare only to the Motherland; it kills Soviet soldiers and civilians every day of every week, because of Red Dawn we must fight a guerrilla war for control of our southern republics, the Anatolian littoral and the whole southern coast of the Black sea is a lawless wasteland denied to us. As many of us predicted in the days before the Cuban Missiles War, Krasnaya Zarya was always likely to become a repository of Islamic fundamentalism, and counter-revolutionary dissidents' ambitions in the Southern Republics. Now, as a result of the war in the Middle East so foolishly embarked upon by our predecessors, we face civil wars on our borders all the way from Afghanistan to the Adriatic. In time, our enemies in the West will, no doubt, do whatever they can to fuel those religious and separatist movements spawned by the nihilism and ethnic genocide promoted by Krasnaya Zarya. You know as well as I do that day-to-day, we cannot even keep the Dardanelles open, that it is only a matter of time before we must withdraw our remaining forces from the Anatolian Littoral and the Balkans, that we must re-trench, focus upon reconstruction."

Gorshkov, at fifty-six the older man by eight years, could never remember hearing such unmitigated exasperation in the Boss's voice. Or what, to his ears, sounded a little like...defeatism.

Wisely, he elected to say nothing.

"For all we know," Shelepin went on, visibly breathing hard, trying to keep the lid on his anger. "We have Krasnaya Zarya agents to thank for inflating Warsaw Concerto into a global challenge to the Yankees and their English poodles!"

The car slowed down to traverse a particularly pot-holed, crumbling stretch of road further ruined by that winter's frost and ice.

"If we cannot be honest with ourselves, you with I," Alexander

Shelepin put to his Defence Minister and de facto deputy, "who are we really deceiving, Comrade Sergey Georgyevich?

In a moment he answered his own question.

"Ourselves, I think. Certainly not our enemies. They must know that the surviving fragments of the USSR constitute less than forty percent of our pre-war mass, that three-fourths of our industry and agriculture was burned away by the firestorms. *We think*, we *choose* to believe that around thirty-five millions of our fellow citizens survive in those regions still under our control, possibly another few millions in the wastelands we no longer pretend to govern, existing in the margins within or beyond the bombed-out areas, or on the fringes of the former, now burned down forests. The reality of it is that many of the communities we call 'new republics' in Central Europe are in reality disparate Krasnaya Zarya colonies, loyal to Sverdlovsk only so long as we keep the railroads open and send them grain, and what little surplus of manufactured goods that we can afford from our re-located industries beyond the Urals and in the Far East. Thus far, we have lived in peace with the People's Republic of China but if that peace ever broke down, short of using nuclear weapons, we would surely lose Manchuria and the Amur industrial region; that would gut us, cripple us and probably condemn the Motherland to the status of an impoverished central Asian pauper for untold generations."

Gorshkov said nothing to this because he was struck dumb, literally lost for words. Never in his life had he heard a senior colleague, or anybody with any standing in the Party deliver such an excoriatingly bleak – and honest – critique of the Motherland's abject political, military and economic bankruptcy.

"We need to be worrying about feeding our people this winter," Shelepin ground on, his tone lowly malevolent. "Not wasting our time wringing our hands over how to promote the global march of Marxist-Leninism!"

The convoy drove onto the smooth concrete apron of the airfield. In the distance snow ploughs were churning up and down the main runway and attempting to keep the taxiways clear of drifting snow.

The car halted.

The door on Shelepin's side was opened.

"Shut the fucking door!"

The trooper standing in the snow was so terrified he inadvertently slammed it, coming within a millimetre of trapping the Chairman's left hand.

Shelepin took a series of long, deep breaths.

Then, turning to face Gorshkov, he spoke in a near whisper.

"We must look to the world as it is, not how we would wish it to be. The war may not have bombed us all the way back to the Stone Age, as some Americans no doubt still desire; but everything the Revolution achieved is in ruins. We must acknowledge that to become again a rival to the American Empire is the work of, perhaps, two generations."

His pale face was pinched with weariness.

"We have lost so much, Sergey Georgyevich. Frankly, there are few enough of us left to carry on the struggle. We must find a way out of the cycle of war. I don't know if that is even possible, or realistic," he groaned, "but we must at least try to make peace with our enemies."

Chapter 25

Friday 3rd February 1967
The Presidio, Sixth Army Headquarters, San Francisco

Fifty-three-year-old Lieutenant General Frederick C. Weyand, the acting Commander of the United States Sixth Army – he was also filling the post of Military Advisor to the Secretary of State, Henry Cabot Lodge II at the forthcoming United Nations re-dedication – was somewhat at a loss to know what to make of his British guests. All, that was, except the remarkable force of nature to whom the entire entourage deferred, and in some respects, seemed to worship.

Sitting next to the lady at dinner that evening he had very nearly become completely bewitched. And this, notwithstanding his carefully pre-scripted diplomatic conversation, and rehearsed short set-piece monologues and anecdotes, of the sort all men who reached high command in the service of the Union, failed to master at their peril. Somebody like Curtis LeMay, or that tearaway young tyro 'Storming' Norman Schwarzkopf, could probably get away with any number of faux pas; not so men of a less Herculean, nonetheless professionally accomplished warrior ilk of soldiers like Fred Weyand. In his experience, it paid for a man to know and the understand his limitations.

Fred Weyand was a product of the University of California, Berkeley ROTC – Reserve Officer Training Corps – program commissioned as an artilleryman in 1938. During the recent war in the Midwest, he had commanded all US and allied ground troops west of the Mississippi. It did not bother him that he had not emerged from the war with the kudos of young Schwarzkopf, or his old friend Creighton Abrams; he had been given the job of holding St Louis, wearing down and pinning a dozen Legions of the End of Days in the west, ahead of the massive armoured thrusts from the east, and the amphibious operations on Lake Michigan which had ended the war in damned nearly one hundred hours.

What those deskbound tacticians in DC thought about it was their problem. The war had been won fast, dirty and with negligible casualties on the US side, and that was all any *real* soldier ought to care about.

Margaret Thatcher had listened attentively, with – so far as he could tell – genuine fascination as he had rolled out his dutiful spiel about the long and illustrious history of the Presidio.

"There was nothing here until 1776," he had explained. "Although, I don't discount the possibility that in years to come archaeologists or historians of the Mesoamerican period, might dig up something or find an obscure reference in a dusty, crumbling old native text to prove me wrong!"

"1776," the lady had smiled. "Wasn't that around the time George Washington was having all that trouble with the Howe brothers at New York?"

Fred Weyand had been impressed by the reference to the Battle of Long Island, where, had George Washington not contrived, very much against the odds, to extricate the Continental Army across the East River to Manhattan, the Revolutionary War might have ended, right there and then.

In which case, he might he wearing a British, not an American uniform that evening...

"I don't think Juan Bautista was very concerned about that when he led a wagon train, from Tucson to the West Coast and first settled this piece of real estate," Weyand countered, smiling broadly.

The British Prime Minister, seemingly well-rested after her party's unscheduled stay over at Grand Forks Air Force Base in Nebraska, had drunk only still water, and daintily picked at the salad and then the main course, prime beef steak, put before her.

"The stories which have come down to us from the Spanish, pre-Mexican period, suggest that there were several earthquakes and a lot of bush fires in this part of California around the turn of the nineteenth century. We know more about the site after 1846. Around then American settlers had explored as far south as the northern side of the Bay but everything to the south was still Mexican, although, between us, I don't think the Mexicans ever cared that much for California, or as they called it Alta-California. Then a certain Lieutenant John Freemont crossed the Golden Gate by boat and captured the Spanish Fort, which was probably situated more or less where we are sitting. A year later gold was found in the mountains, and the rest, as they say, is history."

He had excised the normal 'tourist' gibberish from his dinner talk, sticking strictly to the curios and significant events in the Presidio's one-hundred-and-twenty or so – give or take a few months – relationship with the US Army.

"The first real fort was constructed in 1853, this eventually became – around 1912, if I recall correctly – officially, Fort Winfield Scott. Back at the start of the Civil War, the one in the 1860s, Colonel Albert Sydney Johnson defended the post against secessionists, yet later in the war he died at Shiloh fighting for the Confederate side."

"It is a funny old world, sometimes," his guest agreed, her blue eyes twinkling.

"The Modoc Campaign, the last of the Indian wars was conducted from the headquarters here at the Presidio. That would have been in the 1870s. In the late 1890s the Presidio became a training and embarkation point for troops fighting in the Spanish-American War."

The Prime Minister had been curious about the 1906 earthquake; most visitors to San Francisco were.

"The then commanding officer, a fellow called Funston, incidentally a decorated hero of the Spanish-American War took over the emergency response to the disaster. His soldiers fought fires and recovered poor souls trapped in the rubble of collapsed buildings. A large tented refugee camp was set up within the Presidio." Fred Weyand was actually enjoying himself. His officers were amusing the other British guests; he had the star of the show to himself.

"I read somewhere that your great First World War general, Pershing," Margaret Thatcher prompted him, "suffered a terrible personal loss at this place?"

"Yes, Ma'am. In 1915, while he was absent on an operation against the bandit Pancho Villa, his family was killed in a fire..."

"Oh, how awful!"

"Yes. General Pershing was at Fort Bliss, in Texas, at the time. His wife Helen, and his three daughters, Mary, Anne and Helen junior, all died, it was believed at the time from smoke inhalation. The girls were aged only three to eight years old. The only mercy was that the General's son, Francis Warren survived. Although the General was subsequently engaged at one time to Nita Patton, George Patton's niece, he only remarried very late in life, in 1936 shortly before his death to a lady he had met while in France in the latter stages of the Great War."

Thereafter, the Presidio had been a mirror of America's wars; a base, a staging point, a hospital, a headquarters, post-1945 a meeting place of friendly nations and during the denouement of the Second Korean War the object of student and popular demonstrations against the United States' participation in those foreign wars.

As the British party had been driven into the fortress that afternoon there had been demonstrators waving placards at the gates.

Lady Patricia Harding-Grayson had been button-holed by a Marine Corps colonel and his bubbly Hispanic wife; after the meal was over, she came and compared notes with her younger friend. The thing which had struck her most during the enjoyable, relaxing dinner as the guests of the US military, was that nobody had mentioned Operation Maelstrom; revelations of which seemed to be threatening to tear the American body politic apart, limb from limb back in Washington but which, seemingly, had been taken with a very large pinch of salt out here on the West Coast.

The other thing about the whole affair that had not been missed by the Foreign Secretary's wife, was that nothing in that morning's papers, nor in the cables thus far received from home in the short time they had been resident at the Presidio, had really come as any news to her husband or, his old partner in crime, Airey Neave. To say that both men were 'relaxed' about the scandal would have been the most arrant of understatements; it was as if nothing they were hearing, dreadful as it was, surprised or in any way worried them. In fact, she strongly suspected they had known all about Operation Maelstrom, possibly for many years!

Tom Harding-Grayson and Airey Neave had advised the Prime Minister that it was 'nothing to do with us'; that it was 'best not to intrude on our ally's personal grief', and that obviously, 'other than in the period of the post-war emergency in the United Kingdom, and in the exceptional case of fighting the ongoing Nationalist insurgency in Northern Ireland', *we do not do that sort of thing...*

"You and General Weyand seemed to be getting on like a house on fire?" Pat Harding-Grayson observed, mischievously.

Margaret Thatcher pulled a face.

"Oh, have I said something wrong?"

"No, no, it was just that the General told me all about how one of his predecessors, General Pershing, once went off on campaign and his wife and their three daughters were killed in a house fire."

"Oh, how gruesome..."

"Apparently, that was why they set up their own fire brigade on the base."

The two women agreed they might take a walk around the elongated part-circle of redbrick 'lodges', one of which had been given over to the British mission. During daytime, the lodges had a marvellous view of the Golden Gate Bridge. As it was, in the darkness, the two women had to make do with the bridge lights in the near distance, itself an impressive thing.

Even though they were inside a well-fortified military base surrounded by heavily-armed soldiers, marines and naval personnel, not to mention that the grounds were positively infested with Secret Service men, two of Steuart Pringle's battle-dress-fatigued AWPs hefting Stirling sub-machine guns, followed the two women as they walked.

"You're still feeling guilty about abandoning Rachel in the middle of nowhere, aren't you?" The Foreign Secretary's wife prompted quietly.

"Yes, and no. Frankly, I wonder if it was a mistake getting her involved in this thing in the first place, I suppose." The Prime Minister shook her head. "What will her poor husband think when he learns his wife was ejected from Commonwealth One in the middle of the night?"

"That wasn't exactly the way it was, Margaret," Pat Harding-Grayson objected, putting on her best Head Girl's tone. She had discovered when there were times that her younger friend needed a little tough love; and suspected that this was one such. "Rachel is hardly a defenceless little lamb lost in the woods..."

"Um..."

"What does Airey think about all this?"

Margaret Thatcher scowled momentarily.

Airey Sheffield Middleton Neave, MP, the Secretary of State for National Security thought it was all 'a jolly good wheeze', whereas, she did not!

"What on Earth is Rachel going to do? I mean, on her own..."

The older woman halted, and the two friends looked at each other.

"Margaret," Pat Harding-Grayson murmured, as if afraid they were being overheard. "Honestly and truly, had you considered that it might be in everybody's best interests, that it may well be for the best if you know absolutely nothing, or at least, as little as humanly possible, about whatever Rachel French gets up to over here?"

Chapter 26

As the grey pre-dawn began to turn the night to subtle shallower hues of darkling grey the Jean Bart cut her stern chains, the black water under her transom churned, and she began to move, drifting, crabbing towards Cap Ferrat for several anxious seconds before her screws began to drive water across her massive rudder.

Flooded down aft the great ship sat lower in the water than the day HMS Campbeltown had first come alongside her, if anything seeming like she was even more a giant castle of steel rising out of the sea. The old Fletcher class destroyer idled in the now lonely anchorage, flotsam occasionally bumping her camouflaged flanks, the waters fouled with oil still leaking from the bunkers of the sunken ships as the Jean Bart eased past the headlands guarding the entrance to Villefranche Bay, and took the first tall seas over her clipper bow.

Many men had gone to the port rail to watch the battleship get under way. Out to sea the other survivors of the Villefranche Squadron were limping to the south, shepherded by the Dundee and the Perth, with the modern Leander class frigate HMS Ajax still patrolling three miles off the mouth of the anchorage, her Type 965 air search radar probing deep inland.

Ajax was one of three Leanders rushed to Gibraltar from their Devonport home, to beef up Task Force V1, an acknowledgment that Henry Leach's operation brief seemed to expand daily. To his original mission, the relatively straightforward job of wreaking havoc along the Bay of Lions and the old French Riviera, and in so doing implement a close blockade of the same, had been added neutralising what was left of the French Mediterranean Fleet at Villefranche, mounting not punitive but 'seize and hold' raids on targets on and near the coast, deep ELINT and tactical strike missions, and now, the small chore of escorting Rene Leguay's leaking scows all the way to Malta.

Or rather, as Dermot O'Reilly had feared, that was a chore *he* had inherited. One plan had been for the County class destroyer HMS Hampshire, en route to Malta, to rendezvous with the Anglo-French fleet during the transit of the Tyrrhenian Sea, so that Campbeltown might 'pass the baton' to her, and make best speed back to the Bay of Lions to join Task Force V1, thereupon to retake command of the 21st Destroyer Squadron.

Instead, the Hampshire was now slated to join the Victorious; leaving the 'baton' firmly in Dermot O'Reilly's hands. Wickedly, he suggested to Brynmawr Williams he ought to have just recommended that the ships at Villefranche be scuttled...

No, that would never have done!

Not once he had met the remarkable people who had kept what was left of the once proud French Mediterranean Fleet in being all these years.

The frigate La Savoyard's listing silhouette began to clarify out of the murk as the dawn hurried into the bay. A near miss by a big bomb had twisted the thirteen-hundred-ton ship like she was a tin can in the hands of a greater God; both her shafts had been warped out of alignment so badly her engine room had been flooded within minutes. Her skeleton crew had wanted to try to pump out the water; O'Reilly's engineers had taken one look at the ship and known it was hopeless. Even had it been possible to tow the ship to a dry dock, any sane naval surveyor would have inevitably declared the vessel a constructive total loss. In fact, the only thing nobody understood was how a relatively small ship could have sustained such severe, terminal structural damage – her back must be bent or fractured for her stern to be pointed several degrees out of kilter – and still be afloat the next day. There was no accounting for it; one just had to accept that some ships fought harder than others to carry on living.

"Guns! Prepare to open fire on La Savoyard with the aft Bofors and the 20-millimetre auto-cannons. Warn Numbers Three and Four main battery gun houses to be ready to shoot Common HE if needed!"

The acknowledgments flowed back via the Bridge Talker from the Gunnery Officer at his post in the big rotating gun director station almost directly above Dermot O'Reilly's head.

"Permission to shoot in local control, bridge?"

"Affirmative. Aye to that!"

The Campbeltown was closed up at battle stations, her stern about two-hundred-and-fifty yards from the bow of La Savoyard. The frigate seemed visibly lower in the water at the stern now; perhaps, they would be able to let her succumb in her own time, without the indignity of first being pummelled by close range heavy automatic fire or high explosive shells.

The Jean Bart cleared the entrance to the bay, pitching into the worst of the weather at the minute and the hour that dawn was supposed to break over the Riviera. Beneath lowering clouds as the wind whistled across the two to three-foot swell in the bay despite the sheltering hills, darkness clung to the wilderness of the seascape off shore.

Suddenly, there was a clang of metal on metal somewhere within the Compass Platform behind Dermot O'Reilly, then another. This time something ricocheted within the steel confines of the compartment.

The ship juddered as the aft 5-inch guns fired and 40-and 20-millimetre cannons unleashed the first, short, aimed bursts at La Savoyard.

There was another 'clang' in between the rattle of gunfire from aft.

Dermot O'Reilly had stepped onto the starboard bridge wing to see La Savoyard trembling with impacts amidst a fine mist of spray from rounds exploding in, or skipping off the surface of the water.

There was a groan behind him, and the sound of a man dropping to the deck.

"SNIPERS!"

Dermot O'Reilly strode back onto the bridge as the splinter shutters were banging shut all around him.

Men were diving for the deck.

Dermot O'Reilly did not flinch.

He patted the Bridge Talkers shoulder.

"Stand up, son."

Another round hit a nearby bulkhead: starboard side.

"GUNS! FORWARD MAIN BATTERY MOUNTS AND ALL UNENGAGED ANTI-AIRCRAFT MOUNTS THAT WILL BEAR ENGAGE SNIPERS AND TARGETS OF OPPORTUNITY TO STARBOARD. COMMENCE FIRE IMMEDIATELY. ALL GUN CREWS TO FIRE AT WILL UNDER LOCAL CONTROL. EXECUTE!"

The aft main battery rifles barked again.

"ENGINE ROOM TELEGRAPHS! RING FULL AHEAD BOTH!"

He felt the screws bite in the cold waters of the bay, the destroyer began to shoulder into the light swell piling up at the entrance to the anchorage.

"PORT TEN!"

The hammering of anti-aircraft cannons shook the ship. Pound for pound no ships in the Royal Navy bristled, more or less from bow to stern, with as many guns as the transferred former US Navy Fletchers.

The ship was picking up speed, surging forward like a seagoing greyhound exploding out of the traps.

"LE SAVOYARD IS SINKING BY THE STERN!"

O'Reilly acknowledged this.

"ALL GUNS THAT WILL BEAR ENGAGE TARGETS OF OPPORTUNITY TO STARBOARD UNDER LOCAL CONTROL!"

The Campbeltown was pushing fourteen or fifteen knots as she crashed out of the anchorage into the roiling seas clear of the lee of the land.

O'Reilly ordered revolutions for fifteen knots and turned the ship's stem into the wind to allow his radar plot to update. Even though it was suddenly fully light, visibility was only two or three miles and apart from the Jean Bart and the destroyer Kersaint, the former muscling to the south west, the latter rolling horribly several hundred yards off the battleship's starboard quarter, no other ships were in sight from the bridge.

The Campbeltown's commanding officer refused to be distracted by the sick berth attendant and the other men kneeling on the deck around the downed man, an able seaman who had been on lookout duties on the bridge.

"The surgeon's mate reports three casualties on deck, sir," O'Reilly was informed as Campbeltown took the first big sea over her bow and the whole ship seemed, for a split second to halt before knifing ahead through the waves.

"Very good," he intoned. Then: "Helm. Come right to one-one-zero, if you please."

The guns had fallen silent as the ship had cleared the anchorage and the range to the snipers – any who had not been driven below ground by the ferocity of the destroyer's counter-fire – lengthened.

"Leading Rate Parkinson is dead, sir," apologised a bloody-handed sick berth attendant.

There were times when Dermot O'Reilly wished he was a cold-blooded, unfeeling martinet. He knew that the dead man had a wife and a two-year-old daughter back in Portsmouth. Sometimes, it was a mistake to know too much about the men one commanded.

"Damn," he grunted. "Dammit!"

His anger burned, he wanted to lash out.

He shut his eyes, fought to get a grip.

"Thank you," he murmured to the downcast man at his side. "You did what you could, Lewis," he said, placing a paternal hand on the much younger man's shoulder. "Carry on."

Twenty-six-year-old Sick Berth Steward 1st Class Wesley Lewis muttered "Aye, aye, sir" as his training kicked in. Other men were wounded and in the absence of Surgeon Lieutenant Braithwaite aboard the Jean Bart, he needed to concentrate on the living, not the dead for the next few minutes and hours, or however long it took, to do what he could for his injured shipmates.

He and Tom Parkinson had been in the same pre-commissioning draft which had come aboard the old destroyer soon after she arrived in England. Their wives knew each other better than they did; that was the way of it sometimes. Sandra, Tom's wife, was expecting their second child later that spring...

The Old Man would not necessarily know that; it was not on his papers yet. Unless, of course, his Divisional Officer, Mister Moss, or one of the Chiefs had mentioned it to the Master and Arms, and he had said something to him. Parkinson had joined up in 1958 aged seventeen, mostly been ashore until the war, been on the Agincourt when she was sunk in Sliema Creek, got himself a Blighty wound that day. He had almost been posted to the Tiger back in sixty-four; luckily for him, he had gone down with a bout of War Flu, missed that bullet, thank God! Now he was on Captain O'Reilly's ship – all the old-timers were proud to be on Campbeltown – serving with the man who had navigated the Talavera down the guns of those Russian battleships off Malta, and almost had the Cavendish shot out from under his feet in the Channel War, and then again by those Yankee terrorists in Philadelphia...

His crew loved it that the Old Man, with his beard and a face heavily lined standing watches on the bridge of whale ships in the Southern Ocean, an honest to god veteran of the Battle of the Atlantic – truly a character who might have stepped straight out of the pages of *The Cruel Sea* – seemed to them to be a throwback, such a piratical figure, albeit one they all knew, with a heart of gold.

Dermot O'Reilly had turned to the officer of the watch.

"You have the watch, Mister Rainsford," he said to the thirty-seven-year-old former merchant seaman and Cunard Third Officer, a reservist at the time of the October War, who had joined Campbeltown shortly after she had commissioned last autumn.

"I have the watch, aye, sir!"

O'Reilly allowed himself several seconds to study the radar repeaters. They were a juddering mess, the ship was rolling and pitching too badly apart from when she was taking the seas directly on her bow.

He stood over the plot table.

"Clemenceau, the De Grasse. La Bourdannais and Le Lorrain are approximately eleven miles south-south-east, sir," he was told crisply by the petty officer responsible for constantly updating and verifying the navigation plot. Dundee is in company with that group. Perth turned back to support the second group, the Jean Bart and the Kersaint, on receipt of Campbeltown's action alert, sir."

"Very good," O'Reilly murmured, studying the plot. He looked again to the radar repeaters. Nine fishing boats had accompanied the first group out of the anchorage; wind tossed, tiny radar targets they blinked in and out of existence. "I should imagine the fishermen in the fleet are the only ones used to this sort of weather," he grimaced.

Back on the bridge he called up his captains; first Commander Sam Todd of the Dundee, a thirty-four-year-old who had been serving on the Ark Royal back in October 1962, when she had been Julian Christopher's flagship in the Far East. He had stayed behind with the Anglo-Australian fleet fighting the communist insurgency in Borneo and Papua New Guinea, returning home only a year ago.

"It's a bit like herding cats, sir!" Sam Todd had reported, cheerfully. "None of these chaps seems to be able to steer a steady course."

Todd had married a widow a couple of years his senior shortly after being gazetted Commander; these days, it was almost a man's duty to get properly wedded before he went back to sea.

Dermot O'Reilly had resisted the temptation thus far but he was in a shrinkingly small minority within the brotherhood of naval officers. It happened that Sam Todd's new wife had not needed to marry to avail herself – or her ten-year-old son the protection of the so-called Military Compact – because as the widow of a serviceman she was already beneath that umbrella; but Sam was a good man and perhaps, his new wife, recognising as much, had dragged him to the altar before somebody else did.

The Perth's captain, Commander Nigel Woodford was, like O'Reilly a bachelor, although unlike his Captain (D), of the never-married, confirmed type. This was a thing that within the Squadron his fellow captains often teased him about.

'Dammit, what good woman would have me!' He would protest.

Woodford and O'Reilly were kindred spirits, real old sea dogs; the wilder the weather the happier they were.

"We suffered several casualties from sniper fire," O'Reilly reported.

"Bad show," the other man sympathised over the TBS. It was not a thing to dwell upon. "Now that were all at sea, so to speak, what's the form, sir?"

"You ride herd on the Jean Bart, Nigel," O'Reilly directed. He knew he did not have to micro-manage, or wrap either of his captains in spiders' webs of instructions. "Campbeltown will hang back for a couple of hours. I want the fleet to close up during the day but try to keep one thousand-yard gaps between ships."

"Understood!"

Dermot O'Reilly planned to reduce speed and quarter the seas astern of the fleet, conducting an anti-submarine 'trawl' before turning to the south.

Men were carrying Leading Seaman Parkinson's body off the bridge when O'Reilly handed the TBS handset back to the Bridge Talker.

"There were no other fatalities, sir," the officer of the watch reported. "Minor injuries were sustained by three men manning the amidships 20-millimetre mounts. Rifle rounds struck splinter guards and the resulting spalling caused a few superficial injuries. All three men are currently receiving attention in the aft casualty handling station, sir."

O'Reilly breathed a very obvious sigh of heartfelt relief.

"Secure the ship from Action Stations. Sound the bell for Air Defence Stations Two. Inform the galley to prepare to take hot drinks and sandwiches to the men who have to remain at their stations."

"Aye, aye, sir!"

Dermot O'Reilly listened to the bells, the warning 'pipe' and then the officer of the watch's voice booming over the Tannoy.

The bullet which killed Tom Parkinson must have passed within feet, more likely, inches of his head. If he had leaned forward at the wrong moment, he would be dead and the younger man, would still be alive...

Chapter 27

Sunday 5th February 1967
Georgetown Pike, Langley, Virginia

Kurt Mikkelsen had only realised how desperate the high priest of the Office of Security was, when he discovered the trap that James Jesus Angleton had baited and set for him at the Alexandria office of the American Institute for Free Labor Development.

His old boss must have had the snare ready and waiting, pre-primed in his pocket for a long time to have been able to suddenly pull the lever and set it up over the course of just a weekend. But then when you were a guy with the resources to spy on all of the people, all of the time, *resources* were probably the least of *the Locksmith's* problems, not the issue they were for an average Joe on Main Street.

Kurt assumed that the real Jay Lovestone must be shut up in some safe house in DC; crapping himself. Hopefully. The agent, or maybe just a stooge, the Agency had put in place at the Prince Street office of the AIFLD had been good; as fat as Lovestone, and physically, from a distance a good likeness. Kurt had got the distinct impression the man he had executed had not had the least idea he was in any kind of danger until he saw the gun. Briefly, he had thought about interrogating the imposter. Although, not for long; it was not as if the schmuck was going to tell him anything he did not already know and besides, killing him was going to send exactly the same message, or as near as damn it the same message, as ending the *real* Jay Lovestone would have done.

Kurt reckoned a man had to be a real shit to leave a woman like Clara Schouten literally, in the firing line. She had been a loyal, patriotic member of the Counter Intelligence 'family' at Langley right from the start. Heck, she had been with the Office of Strategic Services in DC and London before that.

The fucking *Locksmith* had not even warned her she was in a bad place.

'Jay's got business in Manhattan next week; why don't you go spend a little time with your folks in Uncasville?' Angleton had said to her, like it was no big deal.

Clara's Ma had died a few years back, just before the war, and her Pa, an old Navy man had heart trouble. He was in his seventies now, did not like the VA poking around his affairs, he preferred to get by on his pension and Clara paid for help around the house. She was the youngest of four kids, the only one who had cared enough to stay close to her parents the last twenty years.

Clara was a good person.

Kurt had felt bad putting her through...*this.*

That was new, or at least he thought it was before he started thinking about the other times he had, sort of, *felt* this way. Conflicted, as if nothing was quite as simple, straightforward as it used to be back in the day.

Rachel used to describe what it was like feeling bad – guilty, he guessed – about some of the things they did to folks. Obviously, their working assumption had always been that the people they killed, or hurt, had it coming to them. Although, thinking about it, most of the time they had had no idea what any of their victims, targets, whatever, had done wrong, if anything at all...

That was weird.

Lately, he had started worrying about stuff like that...

Rachel was right, it did not pay to 'over-think' shit!

Kurt remembered the unmarked turn off the pike, from the last time he had been in this part of the country. That had been years ago. It was still there, just a little overgrown, the tangle of bare wintery tree trunks and branches had thickened either side of it. The track disappeared into the trees despite the time of year. Thank God for evergreens, pine trees that ought not to be there!

He pulled off the pike and his old Dodge semi rumbled and rolled over the unmade surface of the track. From the map in the dash he figured the perimeter wall of the most secure compound in North America – well, after Fort Knox and NORAD under the Cheyenne Mountain – was about two hundred yards from where he planned to...*stop awhile.*

It was odd that he had not yet decided if he was going to kill Clara Schouten. There had probably been times during the last few days she had longed for him to kill her, end it. Again, back in the day he could never remember worrying about what a mark thought about anything.

If that was not weird, what was?

He parked up, got out a pack of cigarettes, Camels, lit up with the Zippo he kept in the driver's door side-panel – next to his Beretta M1951 – and smoked awhile, waiting to discover if anybody came along to see what he was doing.

In most countries there would be soldiers, regiments of them guarding a place like Langley; even here only a stone's throw from DC, there ought to be patrols in the woods, pressure pads underfoot, maybe even cameras. In Russia the woods would be a death trap, mined, the track he had just come down would be blocked off with sentry posts at the Georgetown Pike.

God save America!

The land of the free and the stupid...

That was the trouble with Angleton and the others; they honestly believed they were untouchable, that they could do whatever they liked, whenever they wanted and it would never, ever have any consequences.

He turned on the radio.

He hated country music, re-tuned, got a talk program. All everybody wanted to blab about was Operation fucking Maelstrom. If they had been paying attention they would not be so upset now!

Nobody came and knocked on his window.

After a second Camel he got out, tucked the Beretta into the back of his trouser belt, stretched, ground out the butt of his smoke under his heel and walked around to open the trunk.

It was cold and he wished he had a sweater, or maybe, a waistcoat under his sports jacket.

Never mind, this would not take long.

Clara Schouten's wide, terrified eyes greeted him when he opened up the trunk.

Kurt wrinkled his nose.

She had pissed and soiled herself.

Somehow, that made him feel bad...again.

Reaching down into his right boot he pulled out his switchblade, flicked the blade open, three-inches and some of razor-sharp steel.

Clara Schouten squeezed her grey-green eyes tightly shut and would have screamed but for the gag, which was a little bloody, in her mouth. She had tried to put up a fight when he put her in the car. Heck, the lady had a lot more courage than any of the arseholes she worked for...

"Fuck it, lady," Kurt complained, growling his mild exasperation as he leaned over her and slashed the ropes around her ankles. He was hardly going to slice and dice her in the trunk of the car!

He re-folded the blade, stuck it back down his boot.

'Don't make this harder than it has to be,' he had said to her when he snatched her seventy-two hours ago.

He had been angry by then because he had expected the Agency to send people to transfer her to a safe house. He could have made an example, sent a message, killing them. Instead, he had had no choice but to put Clara through the treatment.

She had tried to put up a fight when he picked her up, too. Tried to scratch, well, gouge out his eyes actually, so he had had to hit her a couple of times, then again, a lot harder than he had meant to in order to quiet her down.

Clara was a pretty lady, just past fifty, curvy; she had always been *above* the 'help' like him, with all the hoity-toity, airs and graces of the big men she had worked for down the years. People wondered how many of those bastards she had slept with; Kurt did not think she had screwed any of them. She had probably been a fifty-year-old virgin until he fucked her raw in that dirty shack off the Connecticut turnpike.

He had liked the idea of wearing out untouched pussy.

He had gagged her to stop her screaming.

She had just stared at him with contempt that first time.

So, he had turned her around and taken his own sweet time taking her again.

'Why... Why are you doing this to me?'

He had honestly believed she was better than that.

Had she not been paying attention at all for the last few years?

He knew she was more than just *the Locksmith's* secretary; so, all that shit about what her bosses did was nothing to do with her was just bullshit. According to her she typed the orders; she did not dictate them.   She was just a nine-to-five office girl; none of the heinous shit that came out of Langley was down to here...

Yeah, right, now that he had her full attention, he had planned to put her right on a few points.   Except, that had not happened.   She stuck to her story, looking at him as if she was something bad, she had stepped in on the sidewalk...

He had drilled a slew of holes in the bottom of the trunk so she would not suffocate on the journey back to DC, left her trussed up like a hog in the cabin out in the woods over towards Manassas.   There were always hunting cabins out in that country the owners never used in the winter.   Finding a suitable one had taken him only a day.

Before they left that morning, he had even let her clean herself up before he trussed her up again.

Shit, he was turning into a real gentleman...

The guy impersonating Jay Lovestone had had a Navy Colt in his top drawer, if he had had the courage to go for it, he would have died like a man, not crying, on his knees trying to tell Kurt secrets he either already knew or did not give a damn about.

Tap, tap...

And the guy was on the floor in a pool of blood.

He had waited a few minutes to see if Clara's replacement turned up; she had not.   That did not matter; he already had Clara, the real thing.   Whoever the dead guy's sidekick was, she would not be anybody important.   A nobody, expendable, with no secrets to burn.

After the hit, Kurt had stopped at a grocery store on the way back to Manassas; purchased bread, milk a couple of bottles of beer, breakfast cereal, tinned soup, and a bar of soap for Clara.

'If I let you clean yourself up you won't do anything dumb?   Right?'

Clara had got wise by then.

The cabin only had a couple of rooms, a bedroom with just a mattress on the boards, and a kitchen that only an old-time dirt farmer would have thought worthy of the name.   There was an outside John.   In the summer you would have to worry about rattlers every time you took a dump; at this time of year, it was just cold and everything was damp, the whole Goddamned country.   He had watched the woman strip off to her underwear, wash herself from a bowl of cold water.

There was an old pot-bellied stove in one corner, a little kindling and it was the work of only a few minutes to smash up the cabin owner's favourite rocking chair.

Clara had volunteered to heat up the soup.

Twice, that afternoon and night he took her out to the John, watched her do her business.   You never, ever let a prisoner out of your sight, or trusted them, or believed a word they said to you.

'Do you plan to use me again?'   She had asked as night fell.

'Yeah, do I have to tie you up again?'

'No,' she said but she had sobbed when he was done with her that first night at the cabin, like she had the previous night.   She went quiet on him after he took her again, and again; then he trussed her like before, except not so tight that the ropes pinched her any harder than they needed to.

She had got all tearful on him that morning even though he had been gentler with her last night. And then she had tried to run away...

He had caught her fast.

Slapped her about, open hand stuff, nothing likely to break anything or leave permanent scars; it was not as if he was any kind of hoodlum.

"Please, just get it over with,' Clara Schouten begged the moment he removed her gag. She stumbled as he lifted her to her feet and propped her against the side of the Dodge. 'Just kill me!'

Why am I just standing here?

Looking at her like I don't know how this has to end?

What was it that Rachel said?

'It shouldn't make any difference if they cry but lately, it does...'

Kurt stared at the woman he had kidnapped, beaten, humiliated, repeatedly violated as if she was a piece of meat and as the tears rolled down her cheeks, her left eye swollen, mottle blue and almost closed and her bottom lip fat and bloody, it was almost as if he had forgotten who and what he was...

What the fuck am I doing here...

He stared, and he stared.

He was paralysed by indecision and for the first time in his life, a numbing canker of...*crippling doubt.*

In a trance the switchblade was in his hand again.

Clara Schouten screamed and tried to shrink away.

It was impossible, she was hard up against the Dodge.

There was no room to move.

No place to run, or hide.

The blade flashed dully in the winter sun.

She shut her eyes and waited to die.

Chapter 28

First Captain Dmitry Kolokoltsev awakened to the feel of the new motion of the ship. Overnight – he was beginning to regain a sense of the passing of time, a thing Aurélie assured him was proof of his continuing recovery – the battleship seemed to be riding easier, working with rather than against the seas.

The former KGB man had only been dimly aware of the arrival of the British, of the sick bay and the dressing rooms being re-organised around him and several of the other seriously injured men and women being removed. He had been unconscious, drugged before, during and for many hours after the bombing of the fleet.

He had missed all the excitement...

Almost, because his dreams were vivid, lurid, haunting nightmares.

Around him was the infernal chaos, sounds of suffering, the moaning of the terribly wounded, the desperate response of crew members unable to cope with the casualties queued up on stretchers in the adjoining passageways. The absence of modern medicines had turned the sick bay compartment into a Hellish place. He remembered, or at least he thought he remembered – the last few days were a blur – things which he now suspected were just more bad dreams. Waking bad dreams as he slipped in and out of consciousness. He had no idea if had imagined the blood pooled on the deck, the discarded dressings, cut away clothing, the screams of those being operated on without anaesthetic other than, if they could keep it down, a few mouthfuls of the rotgut hooch distilled aboard...

Now, as he blinked at his surroundings, around him all was tranquility, antiseptic cleanliness and attendants, nurses for all he knew, instantly moved to the side of their cot-bound patients if they raised a hand or tried to speak.

Seeing that he was conscious a man stood over him, smiled comfortingly, took his pulse, felt his brow and made notes on a clipboard, returning the same to its unseen place somewhere at the foot of the cot.

"How do you feel this morning, Captain Kolokoltsev?" The man asked, talking slowly in English.

Learning English was a thing that every ambitious KGB officer knew to be essential to his future prospects but the one-time Red Navy Officer, having struggled for a couple of years to attain a basic proficiency in the language, had not actually spoken it for over five years.

"Not so bad," he muttered, focusing on the man, whom he determined must be one of the men the English had left on board the Jean Bart.

Aurélie had reported that the Royal Navy, their 'saviours', had originally transferred over a hundred of their personnel to the battleship; and that those remaining were mainly engineering, communications and medical orderlies under the command of a British surgeon. She had also informed him, without beating about the bush, that if the 'English had not emptied their medicine cabinets for our people', he and a lot of others would be dead by now.

Kolokoltsev had been astonished to discover that the British had sent helicopters to carry the Jean Bart's most seriously ill men and women, and a child also, to one of their ships which had 'proper operating theatres'. Apparently, there had been some question about his being airlifted but in the end Surgeon Lieutenant Braithwaite, who had already assumed the status of a minor saint aboard the flagship, had decided that his injuries were 'manageable' where he was, and that therefore, the considerable risks of moving him were unjustified.

The Russian licked his dry lips.

"We unhooked you from your saline drip a while back. You must be thirsty?"

The man held his head while he drank, sucking cool, cold water through a straw as if he was a man lost in the desert who had stumbled across an unmapped oasis.

"Steady, steady," he was counselled gently.

"Let me," another, feminine whisper interjected.

"He's better again this morning, Ma'am," the man murmured as he departed.

"Good," Aurélie Faure said simply. "That is good..."

"I still feel like a T-54 just rolled over me," Dmitry Kolokoltsev complained wryly as he enjoyed the woman re-positioning his pillows. "How is l'admiral?"

'L'amiral is having the time of his life!" Aurélie giggled. She was as tired as any of them, and actually, still a little seasick which she had not expected on such a big ship. But then she had not expected the Jean Bart to be tossed about like – an albeit – very large cork in the wilderness of white horses and roaring winds of the Ligurian Sea.

"I bet he is!" The Russian retorted, trying not to laugh because he knew it would hurt.

Aurélie grabbed the guard rail of the cot, waiting for the ship to roll back somewhere near to the horizontal. For much of the last twenty-four hours the surviving ships of the fugitive Villefranche Squadron had been sheltering in what Rene called 'the lee' of the northernmost island of the Tuscan Archipelago, Capraia, 'so that our people on the other ships, especially the smaller ones, can have a little respite'.

Finally, it seemed the storm was starting to 'blow itself out' and that 'it should be fairly smooth sailing from now on'.

Her stomach would believe that when it happened!

Although Rene made light of his injuries, Surgeon Lieutenant Braithwaite was unconvinced that he was anywhere near as fit as he claimed, as evinced by his regular treks up to the bridge of the leviathan to check up on his reluctant patient.

The rest of the time Rene sat in his command chair on the compass platform, the lord of all he surveyed, blissfully at peace with the world for the first time Aurélie could remember.

Serge Benois periodically reported to the bridge and stood a long watch, otherwise, Rene and the English officer, Lieutenant Moss carried the burden.

The two men, the haggard saviour of the Villefranche Fleet and the youthful Englishmen had already become firm friends, chatting away the long hours on the bridge.

Keith Moss had been stiff, wary when he first came aboard.

Now, like Rene, Aurélie could tell that he was having the time of his life.

"Rene says the fleet will need to take on fuel at Naples. Captain O'Reilly has detached HMS Dundee to make the necessary arrangements with the Italian authorities. I think the plan is for a tanker to come up from Malta to meet us in the Bay in two days' time, or maybe, three. The plan keeps changing because of the storm."

Dmitry Kolokoltsev knew he must be getting better because it was starting to worry him that he had only the vaguest idea what had happened in the last week.

"Forgive me, you must have told me all sorts of things but I have no idea how the British came to be here, on board..."

Aurélie pulled up a chair.

"You were very unwell. I talked to you just to talk to you," she smiled, her weariness evaporating, "as I did to the others, because I hoped it would help. Most of the time I did not know what I was saying,' she confessed, sheepishly.

She briefly recounted the fraught radio conversations with Captain O'Reilly, about HMS Campbeltown coming alongside, and Rene surrendering the fleet. Then the arrival of two more of the British destroyers, how Surgeon Lieutenant Braithwaite and his men had taken over the sick bay, and how in no time at all how supplies and specialists had transferred onto not just the Jean Bart but all the other big ships. She recounted the way the three British destroyers had blazed away at the bombers attacking the fleet, and desperately tried to rescue survivors of the sunken ships from the oily waters of the bay. Finally, she told him about the decision to sail for Malta, where everybody on board the French ships would be offered the chance to 'join the fight' or to 'return to civilian life.'

Suddenly things started making sense, with context and chronology approximately aligned, and Dmitry Kolokoltsev was, for the first time in a week or so, more or less, cognisant of the state of the world around him.

"What happens to mongrels such as me?" He inquired wanly.

Aurélie had already thought about that.

"You are an honorary Frenchman now; an officer of the Villefranche Squadron," she stated, and with a shrug, added: "You fought with us against the Front Internationale. The British know that. Rene thinks the British will want to 'debrief' you when we get to

Malta. However, we are not prisoners. That is a thing Captain O'Reilly made very, very clear." She reached for and held the man's right hand. "I have spoken to Lieutenant Moss, the senior Royal Navy officer on board the ship. He says that the 'normal drill' for any Soviet citizen who surrenders or who voluntarily hands themselves over to the British authorities, is that they are given the choice of 'joining the fight', and of living under the laws of 'the Commonwealth', whatever that means, or of returning home. He says quite a lot of former prisoners of war and refugees are already living freely in England, some may even have signed up to fight with the British forces. He admitted that he did not know a lot about it but he said that he thinks most of the Russians captured on Malta in 1964 – apart from the ones who murdered civilians – were eventually sent to the British Isles where so far as he knows, practically all of them were assimilated into civilian society and handed British passports."

The former KGB man frowned.

"Seriously?"

"Yes," she nodded. "I think the British are so tired of fighting that anybody who is an enemy of their enemies, is their friend. You are no friend of the FI, or those unspeakable Krasnaya Zarya bastards. Therefore," she concluded, "you are their friend."

This was all quite a lot to absorb.

Aurélie released his hand, patted his arm.

"Now, you must rest. You are safe, *mon amie.*"

Aurélie remained in the sick bay and the nearby, much modified casualty clearing station where the less seriously injured were being given their mid-day meals, helping as best she could, and just...being there.

She was, after all, la femme de l'amiral.

The Admiral's woman...

All pretence was gone now.

Oddly, there had been no moment when she had ceased to be the Admiral's faithful secretary and become, proudly, his woman. Nothing had been said.

Nothing had needed to be said.

As the Jean Bart had shouldered into the first big seas beyond the shelter of the Bay of Villefranche-sur-Mer, she had felt Rene's arm circling her shoulders, and leaned against him.

They were on the bridge, surrounded by their people and he had drawn her to him.

She had kissed his cheek.

And everything had changed.

Chapter 29

Monday 6th February 1967
Headquarters Free French 2nd Corps, Châlons-sur-Marne

"Ha!" Major General Francis St John Waters, VC, chortled happily as he digested the contents of the message flimsy a French staffer had just handed him.

It was about time they got some good news!

It seemed that the Senior Service had successfully spirited away what was left of the French Mediterranean Fleet, including a battleship and a modern aircraft carrier, from the clutches of those perfidious scoundrels in Clermont-Ferrand!

"My word," he sighed in satisfaction, '*the Lady* will be even more chuffed with her Admirals when she hears about this!" He observed to his companions in the Officers Mess at the Hotel de Ville.

The snow had finally relented twenty-four hours ago, and with the wind gusting at a mere twenty or thirty miles-an-hour, the blizzard was reluctantly loosening its grip on Picardy and the Marne Valley. A new spirit of optimism filled the air and provisional movement orders had been sent out to the leading assault battalions; orders to be confirmed around midnight if the current forecast for cold but clear weather for the next two to three days still held.

"My, my, another one of the Navy's Nelsonian cutting out operations, what!"

Truth be told, not all his French comrades were wholly of the same mind on the subject. The apparent Soviet bombing attack on the Villefranche Squadron – which might have cost as many as three or four hundred lives – and the subsequent 'escorting' of the undamaged French ships out to sea, presumably into internment somewhere in the Mediterranean, smacked to many Frenchmen of a re-run of the Mers El Kébir betrayal of 1940. True, the British had not fired on French ships in port but the whole affair still had a damnably unsettling ring about it.

Had the Villefranche Squadron not capitulated; would the Royal Navy have fired on it as it had on Admiral Marcel-Bruno Gensoul's ships in July 1940. Almost certainly, was the general consensus.

Fortunately, General Alain de Boissieu, the Supreme Commander of all Allied Forces in France (SCAFF), was less preoccupied with the what ifs of French mid-twentieth century naval history, than he was with the reality of the Soviet intervention at Villefranche, when Frank Waters strolled into the Supreme Commander's map room that morning.

Contrary to the ex-SAS man's jaundiced expectations, the fact that Field Marshal Sir Michael Carver had been trapped in Châlons-sur-Marne for nearly three days by the blizzard, had done a great deal to heal the lingering mistrust between the two men.

The Chief of the Defence Staff, notwithstanding he had proven himself to be the finest, most adroit and resourceful British battlefield tactician of his generation; was never going to be the most clubbable or personable man in Christendom. Superficially, he and Alain de Boisseu might have been made to rub each other up the wrong way. However, cloistered in the Hotel de Ville the two men had talked military history, strategy and tactics and unexpectedly, although they had differed over many things, clearly discovered, and developed an abiding respect for where the other man was coming from.

Frank Waters did not think it was anything to do with a meeting of minds, or any of that psychological mumbo jumbo. He had decided it was simpler than that.

It more to do with the fact that up until that point, Alain de Boisseu had never really believed that the great general who had Cannaed two Soviet Tank Armies, took him very seriously, let alone respected his own grasp of battlefield realities. In the Second War de Boisseu had led a cavalry charge against Nazi panzers; for a couple of days in the Western Desert in 1941 Michael Carver and a gang of relatively junior staff officers in XXX Corps had virtually been left to fight Afrika Corps on their own, because their own high command was all at sea. The one was an exemplar of reckless courage under fire, the other possibly the coolest, most calculating mind in the British Army. And yet they had buried the hatchet, agreed a modus vivendi, finally accepting that their fates were inexplicably locked together.

I never used to go in for any of this soul-searching guff...

It was *the Lady's* influence, of course.

He wrote his wife letters, chatty mainly inconsequential nonsense – she got quite enough remorselessly grim, serious, cerebral reading matter from her official cables and reports – which he hoped might cheer her up, brighten her days.

Her letters tended to be brief, a little formal, stultified, in fact. That was her nature, the very private public woman. Not that she could not be sharp, distanced in private; it was just that now and then she let him into her real, inner world and a scintilla of affection and intimacy from the woman he loved was worth a deluge of it from anybody else he had ever known.

That she was likely thinking a lot less about him than he was about her did not trouble the old soldier. His wife was the bally Prime Minister, after all, what!

That said, separation was beginning to play on his mind.

He missed her...

Moreover, all this sitting around waiting for the storm to abate had not helped; not one little bit!

Alan de Boissieu was contemplating the map, a coffee cup in hand.

"I wish I knew what to make of the Russians bombing the Villefranche fleet," Frank Waters confessed to his friend as he joined him at the big wall map of France.

"Yes," the other man agreed, a little absently. He blinked, emerged from his thoughts. "It is very curious. The timing, especially. They could not have known that the Royal Navy had already seized," he grimaced, rephrased this: "agreed the neutralisation of the ships at Villefranche. Thus, the attack must have been otherwise motivated...it is all very, curious." He sighed. "Sir Michael may be right when he suggests it smacks of a certain strategic dissonance on the part of our Russian foes."

Up until then the assumption had been that the Soviets – given that everybody viewed the Front Internationale as straightforward agents of the monstrous Krasnaya Zarya abomination – would fight tooth and nail to succour their 'ally' in France.

"If I may, an appropriate analogy may be the Mers El Kébir affair," de Boissieu remarked, a note of apology underlying his words, "that sad business succeeded in putting a part of the French Fleet out of reach of the Axis powers, but it did nothing whatsoever to weaken the grip of the Vichy regime in French North Africa, enabling those traitors and cowards to cling on to power for well over another two years. To bomb the fleet that way, it is almost like the Nazis attacking Mers El Kébir first. It makes no sense..."

Frank Waters was uncharacteristically contemplative for a moment.

"Maybe the Russians were afraid those ships would fall into our hands?"

"But that infers they did not trust their friends in the Auvergne to keep them safe?"

"True," the former SAS man agreed. "But either way, *we* have those ships and *they*, Maxim Machenaud's crowd in Clermont-Ferrand, or Admiral Gorshkov's merry men in Sverdlovsk, don't!

The two men could hear the armoured vehicles, jeeps and trucks in the main square starting up their engines, revving hard. The cold had been so intense that motors had had to be fired up every two or three hours to ensure that lubrication oils did not start to separate out or engine blocks freeze solid.

Snow ploughs had been deployed that morning for the first time in four days, to start to clear key roads behind the front, and work had also begun to re-open the rail lines from the channel ports. Engineer battalions stood ready to advance with the troops, repairing roads, rigging temporary bridges and re-constructing, if necessary, several railways to enable the Anglo-French logistical chain to keep up with the fighting troops. Having been stood down a week ago, everything was slowly gearing up anew, this time in a frigid, wintery world.

The winter storm had wrecked the original plan; presently, there was no prospect whatsoever of poorly-equipped militia units advancing side by side with the front-line assault battle groups, nor any realistic hope of Free French forces moving forward in an unbroken 'broad front'. In the snow and the anticipated thaw conditions a week hence, volunteer regiments would bog down, most likely suffer ten times as many casualties from the cold and the wet than from enemy action.

Pertinently, faced with an army of irregulars, fighters better attuned to guerrilla, asymmetric warfare, in those self-same – by any standards, diabolical campaigning conditions – the men of the British

Expeditionary Force on the right, and the mainly regular, well-trained and armed assault formations of the Free French Army supported by *all* the armour, artillery and the whole Army's supply train – which otherwise would have been dispersed along the whole front – might, conceivably, still sweep everything before them all the way to the foothills of the Massif Central in a matter of days.

The gamble – for that was what it was – was worth the candle.

And they were going to gamble the whole house on it!

Chapter 30

Monday 6th February 1967
USS United States, San Francisco Bay

Sir Roy Jenkins, the United Kingdom's Permanent Representative to the United Nations (Designate), had been caught unawares by the Prime Minister's delayed arrival on the West Coast, having arranged – as a connoisseur of fine wines - for a visit to the Napa Valley to get better acquainted with Californian viniculture. Unknown to the Prime Minister he had also received a note from his putative boss, the Foreign Secretary suggesting that since there would be little opportunity for confidential discussions on the first evening at the Presidio that he join the party that morning on the USS United States.

The full United Nations Assembly was not due to be called to order until Friday afternoon; the coming days were reserved for 'arrival' and 'familiarisation' sessions, and to allow the delegations staying on board the former Atlantic Blue Ribbon holder to settle in and to conduct pre-conference 'get-to-know' and 'exploratory' off the record encounters and meetings.

Margaret Thatcher viewed the long, black shapes of the two Polaris submarines moored outboard of the twenty-thousand-ton depot ship USS Hunley (AS-31) off Almeida as the British convoy and its escorts drew up at the quayside. Now anchored only some sixty yards offshore the USS United States filled the visible horizon, blanking out the city of San Francisco on the opposite side of the bay. The drive across the city and the Bay Bridge to Oakland and thence, down to the naval base had taken – notwithstanding police outriders hurrying the cavalcade through the traffic - the best part of fifty-five minutes, seemingly a further disincentive for the British delegation to base itself at the Presidio.

Where to 'call home' had been a subject of discussion that morning at breakfast, the Prime Minister having indicated that she had found her lodgings 'most satisfactory' and 'enjoyed the view' from her apartment window of the Golden Gate Bridge. The length of the journey to the Almeida Naval Base had complicated the debate but those close to her knew she was not easily going to be swayed. Nevertheless, there was an odd disenchantment within the group at the idea of being 'cooped' up on a boat for as long as a week with a bunch of potentially quarrelsome strangers. Moreover, that morning Roy Jenkins had put a call through to Tom Harding-Grayson confirming that the US 'top team' planned to base itself in a mansion 'in the hills', rather than 'slumming it' with the 'hoi polloi' on 'the big boat'.

Jenkins saw absolutely no profit in the Prime Minister making herself a sitting target for 'all comers' aboard the converted liner, especially given the absence of the President and his Secretary of State, speculating that: "Perhaps the US Navy or the Marine Corps could be prevailed upon to provide a fast boat or possibly, a helicopter, to speed daily transit to and from the conference venue?"

This had swiftly hardened into a specific request by the time one of the Navy launches loitering in a line to carry dignitaries, had ferried the party out to the USS United States.

The request somewhat perturbed the State Department's Head of Protocol.

"We shall remain at the Presidio," the British Prime Minister declared when the man had politely begun to make difficulties.

The Administration's attitude, disdain if one was being brutally honest about it, for the whole 'Rededication Process' at the acrimonious Camp David Summit had sparked unhappy memories of the abortive Manhattan Peace Process initiated in JFK's time, quietly allowed to run into the sand by LBJ and subsequently, abandoned by the Nixon Administration after the old United Nations Building had been badly damaged in the New Year's Eve nuking of the Empire State Building.

At one level the Prime Minister – and everybody in her party, also – understood the Americans' natural preference for bilateralism rather than internationalism; after all, the US was the top dog in the World militarily, industrially, economically. Foreign compacts such as the Commonwealth Mutual Assistance and Free Trade Agreement, the Hong Kong Treaty with the Communist Chinese, the developing internal Commonwealth trade 'understandings' excluding or limiting the freedom of operation of US companies, not to mention the web of British and Commonwealth highly secret 'relations' with powers across the Middle East, had already, in its view, unfairly shut the US out of many of its post-1945 markets, and artificially inflated the prices of many of the raw materials desperately needed by its now booming economy. Moreover, it had come as no surprise that the Americans had been selectively deaf to the British – reflecting the perspective of the new Commonwealth – position that if the US negotiating posture was that it should be free to attempt to 'pick off' or 'cherry pick' weaker nations at will, expecting the rest of the world to sit back and do nothing, that was no way to justly conduct international relations, and certainly no good reason to frustrate the re-inauguration of a global forum for the settlement of disputes between nations. Which actually, somewhat ironically from the US Administration's bilaterialist perspective, in a world ungoverned by general tariff and security arrangements, ought to be a common sense way forward.

Tellingly, at Camp David the US side had clearly regarded its idea to build on the presently ruined, inactive framework of the 1948 General Agreement on Tariffs and Trade (GATT), a 'world-wide organisation to regulate trade', as deserving of a much higher priority than setting up a new 'talking shop of the nations.' As it happened, the British were in no way hostile to the concept of creating a bigger, better, more inclusive GATT, especially if its long-term objective was the progressive elimination of all disincentives to international trade. That is, if it sought to get rid of tariffs and taxes and to open up all markets to British exports. When it came to discussing trade, nobody was selfless, and nobody's motives were snow white.

Richard Nixon had taken offence when Margaret Thatcher had likened the US model of international relations to a 'cartel designed to disadvantage smaller countries.'

In fact, there had been broad areas of agreement, genuine concord on a large number of issues: defence, technological transfers in a raft of spheres, and educational exchanges practically all of which were in the British favour. Undertakings to continue the ongoing diplomatic rapprochement between the US and the Commonwealth, and heads of agreement had been signed permitting Gulf Oil, Standard Oil of California (SoCal), Standard Oil Company of New Jersey, Mobil, and Texaco to buy back into the Arabian oil fields and the re-building of the Abadan Oil Refinery complex by buying stakes – short of a controlling holding - in British Petroleum and Anglo-Dutch Shell. On paper, despite the discordant headlines, in the round, the two allies had agreed on vastly more than they disagreed about; problematically, where they disagreed, they seemed literally, oceans apart.

Unfortunately, because the Nixon Administration had not got, nor was likely, to get everything it wanted from its British allies, or from the forthcoming United Nations gathering, it was sulking. Which was extraordinary, given even a cursory glance at the credit side of the international ledger.

For example, it was taken as read that the two country's policy towards the Soviet Union was in lock-step, and likewise, that their mutual commitment to NATO and a raft of other security-related concordats, rock solid. North America and the United Kingdom already formed what was, in effect, a free trade zone in which it was assumed the three economies would automatically become more integrated, regardless of the Canadian and British commitments under the CMAFTA umbrella. Practically speaking, exporting and importing via Canada and the United Kingdom, or setting up overseas offices in either country was a free pass for American manufacturers and financiers into the whole New Commonwealth Free Trade Area, in itself a much better deal for North American manufacturers and agricultural producers than before under the old GATT arrangements.

An unbiased, disinterested observer would have concluded that the British and the American governments had pretty much 'stitched up things' between them, and possibly, been minded to discount the few remaining dissonances in the allies' relationship as of minor, relatively insignificant bearing on their vital local and strategic geopolitical interests.

Inevitably, this ignored the reality; neither the UK nor the US were unbiased, or disinterested parties in the 'handful' of disputatious areas separating them.

The United Kingdom was maddened by the Administration's attitude to the Irish situation. From Oxford the US was both too involved, and in key respects, far too disengaged about the ongoing *Troubles*. American politicians were far too keen to rabble rouse and condone the activities of Irish Republican insurgents and terrorists, playing to their domestic East Coast Irish lobbies, and the American body politic had at no time acted decisively to stop the flow of cash and arms to the Irish Republic which was fuelling the war in the North. In the last couple of years, the imbroglio had become a nightmare not just for the British Government but for that of the Republic of Ireland also.

If it was not for the low-level war in Ulster, demanding the deployment of over twenty-three thousand military personnel and costing a hundred or so lives – in 1966 there had been two-hundred-and-ninety-four British servicemen and Northern Ireland police officers and nine-hundred-and-fifteen civilians, killed, excluding the sixty-one fatalities believed to be IRA men or active sympathisers - most months; in a shattered Europe, the twenty-six undamaged counties of the South, Eire, would by now have been a magnet for old and new industries, a heaven-sent gateway to the New World. Instead, the republic of Ireland was a country under siege from its own people, unable or unwilling to confront its enemies within and therefore, a pariah state to its nearest, over-powerful neighbour. Eire's economy was not so much in a state of collapse, as of slow disintegration yet it was the United Kingdom, not its avowed ex-patriot allies in the United States, which sent food ships, not cash and guns for the Irish Republican Army, a Mafia-like criminal organisation first and freedom fighting movement second, which seemed Hell-bent on destabilising both the government in Dublin, as well as that of the six counties of Ulster.

'Help us resolve the security problem in Northern Ireland," Margaret Thatcher had put to the President, "and there would no longer be any UK objection to the inclusion of the island of Ireland in both the CMAFTA *and* our existing free trade zone with you in North America."

Unfortunately, much though popular support for the Irish cause ran high in many cities of New England, the appetite of American entrepreneurs and tycoons for investing in what many still referred to, ignorantly and in the Prime Minister's opinion, unforgivably, as a 'potato economy' remained negligible.

If the Irish problem was seemingly intractable, the American disdain and real anger, was reserved for the Hong Kong Treaty and its implications for the constitution of the re-convened General Assembly of the United Nations, and the make-up of the future Permanent Security Council. This above all else, was the bugbear at the heart of the Administration's mistrust and lack of enthusiasm for the whole 'UN Project'.

Under the Hong Kong Treaty protocols, providing the Chinese stuck to their side of the agreement, the United Kingdom was obliged to vote – not lobby or in any way proselytise, just *vote* – in favour of the removal of Nationalist China, Chiang Kai Shek's rump regime on Taiwan (to the People's Republic the fraudulent 'Formosan running dogs'), and the elevation of Communist Mainland China to the Security Council. This had been no more than a potential embarrassment in the absence of the Russians but hawks in the Nixon Administration had always assumed that the Soviet Union would reclaim its place at the UN table, and now they had been proven right. Sooner or later, the Soviets were bound to question France's right to sit at that top table, and it was not beyond the bounds of possibility that the General Assembly would agree. In that event the United Kingdom and the United States could, conceivably, find themselves in a minority at the top table of the organisation that they had championed back in 1944.

Which was unthinkable...

Thereafter, the conversation about the third area of contention – the South Atlantic Question - between the two allies had been brief, ill-tempered and on the US side, offensively dismissive.

Margaret Thatcher had sought an undertaking from the Administration that it would support the UK's call for an international tribunal to determine the fate of the Falkland Islands (previously claimed by both the United Kingdom and the Argentine), South Georgia and the South Sandwich islands (both still internationally recognised British Overseas Territories), and the destruction of the British camp on its allotted slice of Antarctica, by force majeure by the Argentine in April 1964.

Further, the United Kingdom sought, on behalf of the one thousand, three hundred and ninety-seven surviving Falkland Islanders dispossessed and deported from their homes on the archipelago restitution and compensation, and justice for the three-hundred-and-eighty-seven islanders who had been killed, or disappeared during the invasion, during the process of forced deportation, or who had simply disappeared in transit and never reached either the United States or the United Kingdom.

There was also the small matter of the brutal liquidation of the small Royal Marine detachment based at Port Stanley at the time of the invasion, many of whom were suspected to have been executed by their captors after laying down their arms and surrendering.

The Prime Minister also raised the numerous documented cases of rape and torture reported by mainly women, but also by several men, by Argentine troops on the Falkland Islands, and – in the main – by Argentine military policemen and militiamen while they were detained in Argentina.

Henry Kissinger had been the least derisory of the President's inner circle. He had explained that the promotion of good relations with Argentina and other Latin American nations was an Administration foreign policy imperative; given, he apologised, that so many other parts of the globe were wholly or partially shut off to US commercial interests due to Commonwealth 'protectionist' policies.

It had made for an uncomfortable last day at Camp David and soured what ought to have been one of those summits, where otherwise good friends agreed to disagree, and parted on relatively sunny terms. Instead, reading the press the next day the British delegation had discovered it was totally to blame for the quote:

'FAILURE OF THE CAMP DAVID TALKS!'

In any event, nobody was in a particularly accommodating mood that morning on the deck of the USS United States.

"No," Margaret Thatcher decided, looking the US State Department Head of Protocol in the eye. "We shall be staying at the Presidio for the duration of the United Nations!"

It was at that moment that a shell-shocked Henry Cabot Lodge had made a delayed appearance.

"Henry, old chap," Tom Harding-Grayson said, a little concerned, "you look like you've just seen a ghost. Are you quite well?"

Standing on the promenade deck of the great liner the British party gathered, almost protectively, around the clearly very shaken US Secretary of State.

"Forgive me, I apologise for not being on deck to greet you," the grand old man of American foreign policy said, still visibly distracted. "I was called to the phone by the President."

Chapter 31

Tuesday 7th February 1967
North 12th Street, Bismarck, North Dakota

May Ellen Constantis's second life – everything before she and her daughter, Sally Jane, who was still not yet eighteen, had been thrown into that obscene baby farm at Madison three years ago – had begun the day she met her second husband. Of course, she had not known that he was going to be her second husband at the time. And neither had he; but they had been making up for it ever since.

She laughed and hugged the trim, grey-haired woman in the blue Air Force uniform on the doorstep, and quickly ushered her in from the cold of the late afternoon.

"So, you stayed over at Offutt with Nathan?" She queried rhetorically, leading the older woman into the neat, warm house. Outside, the snow lay a couple of feet thick on the sidewalks, piled up every morning before the local kids walked or jumped on the tired old Yellow School buses for the day's lessons.

"Yes, I'd meant to stay a little longer but the 'ops rotation' schedules got changed and he pulled a couple of missions a week early," Caroline Constantis-Zabriski explained. "I could have hung around and caught up with a little reading; but I'd only have distracted him."

Not only did her husband's job entail flying eighteen to twenty-four hour Looking Glass missions but in between regular spells of R and R, there was a punishing regimen of seemingly endless training and intensive preparation. Nathan's life had got even busier lately with his promotion to Group Navigation Officer, a thing which gave Caro a warm glow of pride.

Nathan had looked well, content, happy in his duties. Her time at Offutt had been a constant round of introductions, including dining with her husband's Group Commander and his Texan wife. And several rounds of newly-wed type sex; which she blushed involuntarily just to think about.

"My dear," she laughed, looking approvingly at her younger friend, "you're bigger than ever!"

May Ellen patted her belly.

She was about five-and-a-half months pregnant and the last week or so, starting to think – although not yet done anything about it – slowing down a little.

"Like I said in my letters, your favourite nephew didn't waste any time knocking me up!"

Again, the women laughed.

"Sally Jane had a special study session today, otherwise she would be home by now. Sam promised to swing by the school on his way back." May Ellen checked the clock on the parlour wall. "That won't be for another hour. So, there's plenty of time for us to gossip."

Caroline's favourite nephew, her older brother, Seth's son, Sam, had never been much for school books; he had wanted to be a football quarterback until his knee got crocked when he was fourteen. Apart from making it through ROTC – the Reserve Officer Training Corps – he had flunked college, settled at nothing and then, the October War had come along. Caro was still not entirely sure she knew the whole story about how her nephew had ended up in the US Rangers, operating as a spy behind enemy lines in the Kingdom of the End of Days.

Sam would have talked about it with May Ellen; Caro guessed they had the sort of relationship in which they talked, literally, about everything.

These days, Caro liked to think that she was the best wife she could be for Nathan, notwithstanding she was still damned nearly twice his age; but she *knew* that May Ellen was the best thing that had ever happened to Sam. Forget the age difference, not so pronounced as the one between her and Nathan, nonetheless, a dozen years was a lot, May Ellen and her nephew just 'got' each other.

"We all went up to the State House to have a family lunch with the Senator and Mrs Burdick a couple of weeks back," May Ellen reported with no little pride. Sam had looked so fine in his new uniform.

Caro's nephew had been temporarily promoted twice during the wars in the Midwest; and the Army Department had recently confirmed his substantive promotion to major, backdating his seniority and – a real bonanza – his pay checks all the way back to September 1964. May Ellen worked part-time at the local VA office as a case worker; not a well-paying job, so Caro reckoned the unexpected windfall was a godsend, given that the couple were busy sorting away every spare dime and dollar to build up a proper college fund for Sally Jane.

Not that it was likely May Ellen's daughter would elect to leave Bismarck any time soon, or perhaps, ever. After what the kid had been through even the thought of being separated from her mother, who had shared every minute of her nightmare, and the protection of Sam, their surviving knight in shining armour was probably still too...terrifying.

Caro and May Ellen corresponded regularly, now and then about business – including the various dates being mooted for the first sitting of the Minneapolis War Crimes Tribunal – but mainly about family, personal stuff.

Both women agreed that Minneapolis, which had survived the obliteration of its eastern twin, St Paul and of all the mostly intact cities of the Midwest, closer than any other to the nexus of evil that was the Kingdom of the End of Days was, like Nuremburg in 1945, the only place which had a right to try and to dispose of the cases against the several hundred members of Edwin Mertz's dark cult who had thus far, fallen into Union hands. Caro had promised to be with May Ellen, and if she chose to testify, Sally Jane every single minute they were in Minneapolis. Initially, the Administration had hoped to commence the WCT Proceedings later that year; now a date in early

1968 was much more likely.

"I've been warned that I may need to start setting up my department of the Judge Advocate's Division in Minneapolis perhaps as soon as April," she told her friend.

"You'll be a lot closer to Nathan," May Ellen sang happily.

Caro grimaced, deliberately somewhat theatrically.

"What?"

"You've probably read about the allegations about the CIA and the Administration in DC?" She prompted.

"Most people in North Dakota think everybody in the government is crooked all the time," May Ellen retorted, as if to say: "What's new?"

"Well. At the moment I am working a day or two a week as a consultant for the Office of the Director of Central Intelligence, and my name is still on the President's 'call at any time' list, acting in the capacity of a special advisor."

Caro bit her tongue; knowing she had very nearly strayed into confidential areas.

"Honestly and truly, if any of the things *The Washington Post* published are even half-true, I can't go on working for the CIA or the White House."

"Oh." The two women had wandered into the kitchen at the back of the house and now, carried coffee cups back into the parlour. "Where does that leave you, Caro?"

"Well, as a result of the war last year I was recalled to the active list; so, officially, I'm still an Air Force Colonel on detachment to the Office of Personnel Management at the White House, pending posting to the Judge Advocate's Department in Minneapolis. So, I'll be okay," she smiled wanly.

May Ellen and Sally Jane had met Senator Quentin Northrup Burdick when he and his wife had visited them at Grand Forks, shortly after their escape from the then Kingdom of Wisconsin. It was the Senator and his wife, Jocelyn, who had offered mother and daughter sanctuary under their own roof, and subsequently got May Ellen the job – clerking at first but 'clerking' had soon turned into case work and visiting families, which May Ellen enjoyed – at the VA office on East Capital Avenue.

In the beginning Sally Jane had tagged along some days. Lately, her daughter had started to make new friends. As was to be expected, for May Ellen – for them both - some days would be better than others. May Ellen was under no illusion she or her daughter would ever really 'get over' what they had been through at the hands of the Kingdom of the End of Days. It did not help to know that they had been among the luckiest of the lucky ones; survivors of the 'genocide of the peoples of the Midwest'.

At first the house on North 12th Street had seemed too big for them, three bedrooms and a family-sized parlour and kitchen – old-style but with an east-facing window which meant it was always sunny, apart from three seasons of the year because they were in North Dakota, after all – and a basement originally still full of somebody else's stuff but it had been home. It had been theirs, and behind its doors they did not have to pretend to be okay for other people all the time.

And then Sam Constantis had got back, still beaten up but in one piece from the war, and everything had turned out all right in the end!

The front door opened and a moment later, Caro felt her feet lifting off the floor as she was enveloped in her favourite nephew's hearty embrace.

"Don't forget me!" May Ellen chided her husband.

He put Caro down and rather more carefully, hugged his pregnant wife, with the couple exchanging wet kisses.

Sally Jane was not, understandably, a very tactile young woman. She allowed her mother to peck her cheek, and stuck out her hand to greet the eminent lady who had befriended them, in what now seemed like another age, back at Grand Forks Air Force Base.

Caro had been working for the President, and soon afterwards, got to be famous; not a thing that appealed to the slim, shy, old before her time teenager.

"Hi, Aunt Caro," she murmured, instantly glancing to her feet.

"You look more like your mother every time I see you, my dear."

"Inheritance, what can you do?" The girl said, quirking an ironic smile. She turned thoughtful: "All the stuff in the papers, is it true?"

Caroline pursed her lips.

"I don't know, but," she shrugged, "But I wouldn't put any of it past some of the people around the President."

Chapter 32

It transpired that it had taken the White House the best part of twenty-four hours to track down, or rather to catch up with, Caroline Constantis-Zabriski; with a harassed Air Force Captain arriving at the house on North 12th Street as she was helping her hosts clear away the dinner things. So, instead of enjoying a coffee and if her nephew had anything to do with it a couple of fingers of Kentucky Bourbon, she had found herself in the back of an Air Force Lincoln driving fast to the recently opened Municipal Airport just south of the city.

The Air Force had already called at the hotel she had booked into that afternoon before taking a cab to visit her nephew and his family. Never mind, she sighed, at least they will have folded everything nicely before they repacked my case!

She had pulled rank, insisting on time to say goodbye properly to Sam, May Ellen and Sally Jane. Caro was deeply touched when the girl hugged her.

So, as the car sped away into the night she sat alone in the back seat, quietly moist-eyed, knowing the next time she saw the women and her pesky nephew, might probably be in Minneapolis sometime during the lead up to the convening of the War Crimes Tribunal.

Her journey was going to give her plenty of time to carry on reflecting upon the White House milieu into which she had so suddenly been inducted into a little over a year ago.

What did I know?

What should I have known?

In many ways it was a self-defeating internal debate; she had been one of many outsiders parachuted into the White House machine to help to manage an unprecedented monumental national disaster. Yes, she had asked herself why Richard Nixon or any of the clever men around him had not seen that cataclysm coming but at the time, that had been academic. In all truth, she had been too busy trying to get inside, and stay inside, Edwin Mertz's twisted psyche to bother with ephemeral side issues; winning the war as fast as possible had been the only mantra and even now, she did not think that could have possibly been done any better or faster.

Even now, although the Commander-in-Chief might be a complete shit surrounded by crooks and charlatans; when he wanted something to happen, it happened!

This she knew for a fact because there was a US Army Bell UH-1 Iroquois helicopter waiting for her at the airport – which presently, was actually just one low building, a couple of hangars and a wide, open snowy field – with its rotors already slowly turning. A gas tanker was being driven away, having just topped off the Huey's tanks.

'Where on earth are you taking me?' She had demanded, working on the well-established principle that in the military if you did not ask, you never got to know anything!

'Minot AFB, Ma'am,' she was told with immaculate respect by a man in flight gear who saluted as crisply as any Marine in history.

She threw a sloppy salute, no more than a sad approximation of something she had seen other people do, in return.

Minot was up near the Canadian border, a hundred or so miles north, that was not even in the right direction for DC!

'Minot?'

'Yes, Ma'am. The Air Force have a Learjet 23 waiting on the runway to take you directly to Andrews Field. You should be in DC about zero-one-hundred-hours local.'

Perhaps, on another occasion – that is, not in the middle of the night and being the solitary passenger on a bumpy flight half-way across North America when she was already dog-tired – she might have enjoyed the flight, or the experience, leastways. As it was, by the time she fell into the car waiting at the foot of the three or four steps down from the plush cabin, she was seriously testy.

"Oh, God," she groaned, recognising the handsome man in the seat beside her as she dropped into the waiting limousine.

Even in the middle of the night a matter of days after his brilliant career began to irretrievably crumble to dust around him, Richard McGarrah Helms, presently although possibly not for much longer, the Director of Central Intelligence, was urbane and composed.

"I won't ask you how your flight was, Caro," he apologised. "Things have been a little hectic around here," he went on, "as I am sure you will have heard, even out in the boondocks of the Great Plains."

Caroline very nearly retorted that she had not got around to seeing the 'Great Plains' because they were currently buried underneath several feet of snow; and besides, when she was not being entertained by friends or working, she had been on her back being pleasured by her husband!

Strangely, much to her exasperation that remembrance took the edge off her angst; because she really, really wanted to be unspeakably rude to Helms!

Another time, perhaps...

"Is it all true?" She asked. It seemed like the logical question.

"It all depends on how one looks at it," the man retorted mildly.

"Have you and that snake Angleton been spying on the American people, Richard?"

"Yes, but not just for the Hell of it, Caro."

The car, a Lincoln, moved forward with purring power.

"And the Warwick Hotel business?"

"That would be a 'no comment' one."

"Claiming the 5th Amendment?"

The man shrugged.

"You really mustn't believe everything you read in the newspapers, Caro."

Remembering that it was pointless asking a man like Richard

Helms questions when one had no idea what he was actually hiding, Caro changed the subject.

"Why do you need me back in DC, Richard?"

"Billy the Kid has been in town for several days. He killed an agent in Alexandria a few days ago. He abducted, brutalised, raped another of my people before dumping her in woods within site of the Langley complex..."

"He killed her within sight of..."

"No," the man interrupted her. "He didn't kill her. He put her through Hell and then he released her. She wandered around, dazed and confused until she almost got knocked down walking along the Georgetown Pike. Nobody knew who she was, she was delirious for a couple of days. We've got her in a secure wing at Walter Reed. Physically, apart from a few cuts and bruises, she's okay..."

"No, she's not!" Caroline snapped.

Why did so many men have shit for brains?

"You said she'd been abducted and raped?"

"Yes..."

"How would you feel if that had happened to you?"

"Not so good, obviously..."

Sensing that something else was going on, Caro waited to see what Helms was going to offer her. After an uncomfortable silence as the car cruised through virtually empty streets, the Director of Central Intelligence, realised that unless he told her more, the President's favourite shrink was not going to play ball.

"We had reason to believe that 'Billy' would return to DC, doing what any operative would do, following the money trail. Sometimes, it is impossible to completely conceal, or eradicate the daisy chain of contacts which link an agent in the field to... *Control*. In this case, we created a false trail which, as it happened, our man followed back to its source, where, of course, from his perspective, the trail goes dead..."

"You laid a trap for him, he sprung it and now you're back to square one?"

"Possibly."

"And in the meantime, the CIA has a rogue assassin on the loose in the nation's capital?"

At the Walter Reed National Military Medical Center, Caro was guided through endless corridors, into a lift and eventually into a waiting room on the third floor. She had no idea which part of the sprawling complex she was in; not that she cared.

Richard Helms passed her on to a woman in her thirties. Caro was pleased to see that she looked as weary as she felt.

"Did Director Helms tell you about the sting in Alexandria, Professor?"

"Yes," Caro returned, irritated. She glared at the Director of Central Intelligence. "But right now, I'm not sure how much credence to place on anything you people tell me. Not now that I know I've been working for a bunch of two-bit crooks!"

The other woman looked blankly at Richard Helms.

"Professor Constantis was enjoying a little R and R in Nebraska and North Dakota," the man explained pleasantly. "We had to haul her all the way back to DC in a hurry, Jeanne," he went on. "None of us have got a lot of sleep lately."

Caro snorted her derision.

"The dead man," the other woman, called Jeanne, said cautiously, "was standing in for an agent called Jay Lovestone, who is currently in hiding. "There was a woman standing in for the lady who normally worked at the office. That agent was not present at the time of the killing, and therefore, was unharmed. Although, naturally, she was somewhat alarmed by the whole thing. The lady who normally worked with the intended victim, Clara Schouten, is here at Walter Reed."

"Clara Schouten?"

"Age fifty-two, unmarried. She transferred from the OSS to the Agency 1947, first as a typist and then GS9, currently she is graded as GS12, which means she has access to her department's most sensitive material..."

"Her department?" Once one had served at Langley or in the White House one got used to the fact extracting information from a CIA or an FBI staffer was like pulling teeth!

"The Office for Security, Professor."

"Okay, so she was in hiding..."

"No, she wasn't in hiding, she was on compassionate leave in Connecticut. Her father is in hospital at present..."

Caroline knew that the reason the CIA did stupid things was not because it employed inherently stupid people; to the contrary, some of the best minds she had ever encountered had been working in 'intelligence'. No, the problem was that the CIA worked in silos, nobody ever talked to anybody else, and everybody tended to be focused on their own sphere of interest, their own personal responsibilities, project, or pet obsession. Whoever was running the 'Alexandria sting' had been uninterested in the consequences, foreseen and unforeseeable of *his* operation to anybody else in the Company. Tunnel vision never helped the planning process; invariably it ruled out a rational assessment of the operational risks.

And Billy the Kid, the man whose real name was supposedly Kurt Mikkelsen, would have known this and would be, at this very minute, exploiting it.

Caroline looked back to Richard Helms.

"I still don't understand what I'm doing here?"

"Clara Schouten is alive. We don't know why. Mikkelsen clearly took her to the Georgetown Pike to kill her, specifically, to dump her body right next to Langley. But he let her go."

Caroline looked around for a chair.

She was exhausted.

The woman called Jeanne pursed her lips in thought.

"You've seen Billy the Kid's file?" She inquired, clearly under the impression Caro was a lot better informed than she actually was.

"No," Caro said, shaking her head. She looked to Richard Helms. "All I've seen is what the Director allowed me to read prior to interviewing Rachel Piotrowska-French, I have no idea if I have *seen* Kurt Mikkelsen's file…"

That was when Caro cottoned on.

"Oh, my God, it's not just that this poor Clara woman is still alive, which you don't give a shit about," she spat with contempt, hurling an accusative look at Helms, "you've lost track of Rachel as well, haven't you?"

Chapter 33

Thursday 9th February 1967
Grand Harbour, Malta

Despite all the assurances to the contrary, having half-anticipated being greeted by a detachment of Royal Marines and most likely, being taken into custody Contra Amiral Rene Leguay had been very nearly struck dumb when the Governor of Malta, Field Marshal Lord Hull and the Commander-in-Chief of the Mediterranean Fleet, Vice Admiral Sir Samuel Gresham had come on board the Jean Bart in all their ceremonial finery, smiling broadly.

The stormy, grey seas of the previous week had turned to tranquil aquamarine blue as the fleet had finally straggled into Naples Bay, where the seventeen-thousand-ton Royal Fleet Auxiliary tanker Orangeleaf, and her guard ship, the Battle class destroyer HMS Dunkirk, were waiting.

There had been a festive mood onboard the French ships the last couple of days as – having bade farewell to the Orangeleaf and the Dunkirk, both Gibraltar-bound - their three escorting Fletchers had shepherded them south, past the Aeolian Islands with Stromboli smoking on the western horizon and , eventually through the Straits of Messina, with Vesuvius, brooding threateningly in the fading light to the south west, down past Gozo at the northern extremity of the Maltese Archipelago, before the triumphal early-morning entrance to the Grand Harbour.

The Clemenceau had passed through the breakwaters first, and been guided to a deep water anchorage in Kalkara Creek beneath the cliffs topped by the Doric columns of the Royal Naval Hospital at Bighi, the smaller ships had preceded the De Grasse and finally the Jean Bart while Dermot O'Reilly's destroyers quartered the seas off the entrance to the finest natural harbour in the Central Mediterranean, suspicious, protective of their charges until at last they rested at their moorings beneath the ramparts and curtain walls of the mighty citadel of Valletta.

Rene Leguay, walking stiffly, as hurriedly as he was able to welcome his distinguished visitors aboard the flagship, acutely conscious that the Jean Bart, still showing her recent battle damage, her paintwork knocked about by the heavy seas, and with her crew – no matter that he was proud of every man, woman and child on his ship – an outrageously motley assembly as they peered at the approaching barge from every available vantage point on the battleship's starboard rails.

A contingent of men from the Campbeltown had got the main gangway over the side amidships. Keith Moss, the quietly spoken, extremely able navigator and watchkeeper Captain O'Reilly had loaned him – in what seemed like another lifetime back in Villefranche-sur-Mer – had rung down 'finished with main engines', and was patiently coaching a pair of cack-handed makeshift French seamen in the small matter of which flags to run up the mast to honour their guests.

Nothing had so deeply impressed Rene Leguay as the unfussy confident professionalism of the Royal Navy men aboard his ship.

"I hope somebody told Serge Benois to get his arse in gear?" He demanded with forced gruffness, as he stepped, painfully, off the bottom rung of the angled steps leading down to the quarterdeck of the leviathan.

"Serge is on his way," Aurélie Faure hissed. After all they had been through, it was ridiculous that *her* Admiral was panicking – very clearly, he was panicking - over the visit of a few British dignitaries!

Both she and Rene Leguay relaxed a little when they spied Dmitry Kolokoltsev sitting – well-wrapped in blankets with a sick bay attendant close at hand - near the gangway. Somebody had found the Russian a battered French Navy cap.

Leguay sighed with immense relief when he heard a bosun's pipe sounding. That would be their English friends who had organised that!

A dozen Royal Navy men came smartly to attention as the pipe trilled.

"I'm coming, I'm coming," Serge Benois, Leguay's second-in-command muttered breathlessly as he joined the reception party, still tucking in his grubby shirt. "So much for us all being arrested, Mon Amiral," he observed chuckling ruefully.

"We may still be arrested, my friend," Rene Leguay warned him. "The day is still young."

"Either that," Aurélie observed, suddenly less than sanguine, spying the photographers in the boat nearing the gangway, and the horde of other people in the two launches just casting off from the quayside, "or we are soon to be movie stars!"

"Voila," Dmitry Kolokoltsev whispered, contemplating rising to his feet, and instantly thinking better of it, "I think we are all about to become *Free* Frenchmen, and women," he grimaced at Aurélie.

"I have always been a free Frenchwoman," she murmured.

"But now you don't have to pretend any more, mon amour," Rene Leguay declared very nearly under his breath, doing his best to adopt a vaguely military bearing as he anticipated the appearance of the heads of the highest-ranking member of the British boarding party to appear above the level of the deck.

A handful of seconds later and he was swapping salutes and shaking hands.

Lord Hull, the Governor General spoke excellent, albeit schoolboy, French.

Soon, the quarterdeck teemed with photographers and became a minefield of trailing TV and radio cables. Things got a little confused for a while. Everybody wanted to shake the Governor's and the British Admiral's hands.

"Might I suggest we continue below, Admiral Leguay?" Sir Samuel Gresham called.

A large table had been manhandled into Rene Leguay's stateroom because he had been convinced that there was going to be some kind of formal surrender ceremony. Soon, Leguay, Aurélie, Serge Benois, Keith Moss – the latter looking sheepish and a little awed to be in the company of the C-in-C Mediterranean Fleet – to him God's direct representative on planet earth – Lord Hull's aide-de-camp and Sam Gresham's flag lieutenant, were alone in the sudden quietness.

"We ought to sort out the ground rules, I suppose?" Lord Hull suggested affably. "But perhaps, if we all sit down, things will be a little more relaxed, what?"

"We have English tea, a peace offering from Captain O'Reilly, My Lord," Aurélie Faure said, her courage evaporating.

"That would be marvellous, dear lady," the Governor of Malta smiled.

Aurélie waved at the door and heard movement in the passageway. One of HMS Campbeltown's Royal Marines and a young woman brought in trays.

"We only have powdered milk," Aurélie apologised, shame-faced, remembering how the English took their tea.

Samuel Gresham, the C-in-C Mediterranean Fleet, chuckled with such low-pitched enthusiasm, that it was a surprise to the others that nothing seemed to vibrate in sympathy.

"This, I think, sir," he prefaced for the Governor's benefit, "is the young lady who convinced Dermot O'Reilly and Henry Leach not to just sink these fine ships we have just welcomed into port today!"

Lord Hull beamed paternally at the diminutive figure still standing, a little embarrassed by all the eyes focused on her, between Rene Leguay and Serge Benois.

"I was indisposed at the time," Leguay said, by way of explanation.

Everybody sat, contemplating their 'tea' with mutual suspicion.

Still, it was the thought that counted.

"Let us not beat about the bush, Admiral Leguay," Lord Hull announced, taking charge of the meeting. "My Government has decided that it will treat you – everybody on your ships – as Free French allies, and that your ships will remain under French command, albeit for the moment reliant on the resources of the Mediterranean Fleet and the Admiralty Dockyards of Malta for their re-supply and mechanical repair and upkeep. I know that many women and children, and numerous male civilians sought sanctuary on your ships. All persons who wish to come ashore may do so without let or hindrance, there to continue their lives as they wish with the proviso that they undertake not to aide our enemies, namely the Front Internationale or any factions loyal to them, or to promote the interests of the Soviet Union in the Mediterranean theatre of operations. Is that acceptable to you Contra Amiral Leguay?"

Aurélie nodded unconsciously.

Rene Leguay grinned, glanced to her.

"That is settled, then," he sighed. He stood up and stiffly, extended his right hand towards Lord Hull.

The two men shook on the contract.

"Good. Sir Samuel's people will want to crawl all over your ships, and I imagine it will be a while before we sort out which ship needs whatever, and before we can free up dockyard time and resources to attend to all your squadron's needs. In the meantime, any of your people who wish to go ashore may so do, with immediate effect although I suggest not everybody lands at once!"

Courtesy of the Royal Navy crate upon crate of Maltese-brewed beer was sent on board the Jean Bart and the Clemenceau that evening, just to seal the deal.

After dark, Aurélie found her Admiral alone on the bridge wing gazing at the lights on the ramparts of Valletta. Earlier, she had seen Dmitry Kolokoltsev safely onto one of the lighters taking the battleship's sick and wounded across the water to the landing dock below the cliffs, where, one by one, stretchers were loaded into the lift carrying them to the hospital on the cliff top overlooking the harbour.

"I think Dmitry was upset to miss the party," she confided to the man as she joined him.

She took his hand and he turned.

Practically a head taller he looked down into her face.

Rene Leguay was momentarily lost for words.

He stood on the deck of a great ship, which he commanded, safe in a harbour among friends; and feeling like he was eighteen all over again. It was as if the last four years had been a bad dream, leavened only by the accident of crossing paths with the woman whose brown eyes seemed to heal all his woes.

"I must make one thing absolutely clear, Mademoiselle Faure," he said with every last ounce of mock severity he could gather, trying not to grin like an idiot.

"And what would that be, Mon Cher?" She asked, the lights around the Grand Harbour twinkling in her eyes.

"I have no intention of sleeping with you until we are man and wife," he said. He had never been one to sweet talk the ladies, he was no gallant preux chevalier. So, since being true to his own conscience had worked quite well recently, it seemed sensible to carry on in the same vein.

"Oh," she smiled. On tip toes, she kissed his chin and when he lowered his face, his mouth. She patted his chest above his heart. "Your wounds are still not healed. I would not like to be the death of you, mon cher."

"It is agreed?"

"Yes," she said, tears welling in her brown eyes as she buried her face in his chest. "But please...let us not wait too long."

Chapter 34

Thursday 9th February 1967
Philip Burton Federal Building, San Francisco

When Associate Director of the FBI Clyde Tolson had flown back to Washington three weeks ago, supposedly to 'brief' his boss, J. Edgar Hoover, he had handed the Billy the Kid investigation over to forty-year-old James B. Adams, the recently appointed Assistant Special Agent in charge of San Francisco.

In mid-January, Adams had been under the impression that Tolson would probably be back, possibly within a week or so. However, not only had the number two man at the Bureau not returned, a couple of long-distance telephone terse conversations apart, Adams had been left almost completely to his own devices. *Almost completely* because in the FBI there was always somebody looking over your shoulder and attempting to beg, borrow or just plain steal, a part of a big case because, not to put too fine a point on it, that was how a man – there were not a lot of women in J. Edgar Hoover's FBI other than in the typing pool – got ahead, got noticed, and made a name for himself.

James Adams was, by now, so familiar with former Special Agent Dwight David Christie's personnel 'jacket', he had developed a sneaking, never to be spoken, grim admiration for the way the man sitting in front of him had 'played the game' during his, in retrospect, more than middlingly brilliant career in the Bureau. Christie had made sure he was close to the people who mattered, that he got his share – and more - of the kudos when things went well, and he had an uncanny knack of not having, or adroitly removing, his fingerprints on anything that did not.

Go well, that was.

Christie had earned a reputation for good, solid investigative work, for sticking to the book and making damned sure nobody wrote it up when he went 'off-piste' and did his own thing. People who worked with him regarded him as a natural detective, a loner who had mastered the art of team work, and, more importantly demonstrated positively savant gifts when it came to navigating the Bureau's Byzantine red tape. Out on the West Coast, far enough away from the stultifying stasis of J. Edgar Hoover's aging dead hand in DC, practically every man who had ever worked with, or for, Dwight Christie had said he was a 'regular guy', a 'great boss' and a 'real friend', who 'always squared away the paperwork!' In the FBI there could be few greater accolades than this last compliment.

Right up to the moment he hired a Mafia hit man to murder his closest buddies in the San Francisco Office, the guy had been a model G-man...

"I don't get it, Christie," Adams admitted, swivelling in his chair to face the other man. The two of them were of an age, by rights ought to have had a lot in common and they were – in terms of their FBI careers – patently, both very good at their jobs. "The last thing you did before you went bad – openly bad, that is – was to make sure that the young woman you were holding at the safe house on Telegraph Avenue, was safe at her place in Oakland?"

Dwight Christie did not know where this was going; however, it was good not to be locked up in an eight by five windowless cell in the basement of the Bureau's Oakland Office.

That said, the last week or so they had turned the light off at night which told him that Clyde Tolson had not yet returned from DC. Agents tended to remember they were human beings when the big bosses were not around. They had given him the daily papers to read; heck, that was entertaining lately! It did not surprise him that the President was a crook, that after all, had been his underlying assumption about them all - from FDR through Truman, Ike, JFK and LBJ's - there was nothing different or out of the ordinary about Nixon, he had been a two-timing SOB back in his days as Eisenhower's sidekick, the guy was hardly going to change his spots when he got the top job!

"Darlene Lefebre," he recollected. "Nice kid, a bit mixed up. What happened to her?"

"She married a school teacher and these days they live on an old boat moored up off Sausalito with their kids, latest I heard she'd just had a third baby. Her married name is Sullivan."

Dwight Christie arched an eyebrow in honest curiosity.

"Yeah," the other man nodded. "She married Miranda Sullivan's brother, Gregory."

"Good for her!"

James Adams had been tempted to 'park' Christie. The man had been at Quantico two years before Clyde Tolson sprang him. If, as he suspected, that even the guys at Quantico had failed to clean him out in all that time, maybe, just maybe, the guy really was a genuine closed book.

The trouble was that every now and then, talking to him, Adams got the oddest feeling...

So, now he was trying something new.

Normally, Dwight Christie was cuffed when he was out of his cell. Not today. He had been issued with a new suit, and allowed to wash and shave with warm water for the last week. Not to soften him up; men like him were impervious to tricks of that sort. Simply, as an act of, well, human kindness, man to man because Adams was in a position to do his prisoner good turns, if for no other reason than it made him feel better about himself.

"You'd never have been caught down in Texas if you hadn't risked taking that girl to a hospital?" He went on, trawling cautiously through his man's back story.

"She'd been through Hell. She'd have died, it wasn't any kind of choice," Christie explained dully.

"And you did your best to defend the women at Wister Park, too?" That was the thing about Christie, he was not evil.

Bad, perhaps but certainly not evil.

He had done good, brave things even when he was on the run. There was no reason to doubt that he actually felt bad about beating up on a fellow agent that time he had escaped from the Bureau in Philadelphia back in sixty-four. The contradictions refused to add up, the real man hiding behind his eyes was always elusive.

"Yeah, well, I didn't make a very good job of it," Dwight Christie confessed.

James B. Adams sat back in his chair. Behind him the ninth-floor window opened onto the hazy vista of San Francisco Bay and in the middle distance the great grey liner, the USS United States.

"I don't get it," he admitted.

"About what?"

"You. You work for the Reds but you still keep trying to do the right thing," the FBI man shrugged, "even though it gets you caught, or bust up?"

"Put it down to a character flaw."

Adams thought about this.

"I was a Democrat member of the Texas House of Representatives back in the day," he informed the prisoner. "I trained to be an attorney at Baylor University Law School. I played football at Baylor. All that was before I joined the Bureau in July 1951, of course."

Dwight Christie still had no idea where this was going. However, he was curious and it was not as if he had anywhere else that he needed to be.

"Were you in the Second War?"

The other man nodded.

"Yeah. Not as a GI, although I did the basic training. That was pretty rough!" Adams eyed Christie thoughtfully. "I speak Japanese. Used to, anyway. I was a translator. Mostly behind a desk, but sometimes face-to-face." He picked up the phone on his desk. "Hi, we could do with coffee in here. Yeah... That would be good, thank you."

He returned his attention to Dwight Christie, jerking a thumb over his shoulder to the liner moored off Alameda.

The silhouette of the huge grey ship with her two massive, distinctive round smoke stacks suggested power and forward motion even when she was riding on her chains in harbour. The giant funnels were only partly for show, down in her bowels the liner had four Westinghouse double-reaction turbines powered by eight Babcock and Wilcox boilers, generating upwards of two-hundred-and-forty thousand shaft horsepower. The excess smoke and heat from a machinery set like that had to go somewhere!

"They say the Russians are coming to the party. Maybe the new guys in charge with thump the table like Khrushchev did a few years back? What goes around, comes around, right?"

Dwight Christie knew all that was way beyond Adams's pay grade, therefore it had to be smoke and mirrors, look at this hand while I smack you in the chops with the other one. Except, something told him that his interrogator was not that dumb. He tested the theory.

"The last time I was in the loop," he grunted, staring past Adams's shoulder across the bay at the USS United States, "and still getting to read the personnel circulars headquarters sent out, you were in Washington State, Seattle, right?"

"I was out of town when the bombs hit. After that I was posted to Minneapolis."

"What about your family?"

James Adam's face darkened.

"They weren't so lucky."

"That's bad. Sorry, none of my business..."

"I've since re-married. We have a son, James junior. He was born in Fresno shortly after I was transferred down here."

"Minneapolis must have been tough?"

Adams half-smiled.

"Carrie-Ann and me, we reckoned we had a duty to see things through. We were out of town on New Year's Eve when the bomb went off in St Paul, staying with an old football buddy of mine from Baylor. Crazy really, he has this summer place – had, anyways, it got burned down by raiders, or deserters, same thing, in the war – outside of St Cloud. I guess we were eighty, ninety miles away from the bomb in St Paul. Jeez, it lit up the night for a split second like somebody just turned on the noonday summer sun at midnight. Our place in Minneapolis was undamaged, weird that, all the houses nearby had busted windows..."

"You family still in Fresno?"

"No, we're renting this place at Berkeley nowadays," Adams replied. "Carrie-Ann's hoping to get a teaching job at the college. Night school, something like that. She's an English major, and speaks Dutch and German like a native." He paused, grinned. "What else do you want to ask me?"

Christie blinked, momentarily his confusion must have touched his eyes.

"People have been asking you questions for the last two years," Adams said. "That must have got old a while back now?"

The former Special Agent said nothing.

"You and me," Adams went on, amiably, "are the same – okay not in all things or in all ways – but we're both always trying to figure out what really goes on beneath the surface. Why things happen the way they do. Tell me I'm wrong?"

Dwight Christie shrugged.

"The killings out West have stopped, haven't they?" he asked.

Adams nodded.

"What do you think that means?" Christie pressed.

"I don't know."

"But the number with the rifle bothers you, doesn't it?"

Adams hesitated: "Yes," he conceded.

Kurt Mikkelsen had not spent several days in San Antonio – probably out in the desert, or one of the valleys up country - experimenting with, and intimately familiarising himself with the

Remington Arms Model 700, US Army designation M24 .30-06 hunting – slash – sniper rifle just for the Hell of it. And yet, leaving that gun in the house where he had raped, tortured and eventually murdered the daughter, and heiress of one of the richest men in Texas, had made no sense at all unless he already had another identical weapon waiting for him somewhere else...

"Me, too," Christie concurred sympathetically. "He might well have killed several people since he left San Antonio, of course? I assume the Bureau is checking all unattributed killings in the state?"

Adams nodded.

"Arizona, New Mexico, Nevada, and California. We're also monitoring missing persons reports. We've drawn a blank, so far. It takes a long time for all the reports to get back to HQ, and then they need to be sent out to Field Offices." He grimaced, shook his head. "The same way they always used to be back in the good old days..."

"The Pony Express," Dwight Christie sneered; although not at Adams and the other man knew as much.

The bureaucracy of the FBI still operated at pre-Second War speeds, eschewing any of the new – baffling to the Director – modes of electronic communication. Telegrams still flew hither and thither; mostly everything proceeded at the pace of the Mail unless somebody had the gumption to pick up a phone and risk the ire of his boss by incurring the cost of a long-distance telephone call. To be fair, things were changing – probably because the Hoover-Tolson axis was losing its grip – although not fast enough.

"You got CIA liaison on this one?" Dwight Christie asked, out of curiosity.

"Yeah, sort of. No way to tell if it's worth anything."

"That figures. But they still let you talk to Rachel Piotrowska?"

A rhetorical question...

James Adams hesitated, decided he needed to gamble because he had to know if he had a card in the game or if, as he feared, he was already holding a busted flush.

"Yeah, the *Angel of Death...*"

"What did you say?" Dwight Christie almost lurched to his feet, as if stung by a hornet.

"The Angel of Death," James Adams remarked. "That's what the CIA's Office of Security calls the lady. Why? Is it important?"

Adams wondered how much of the other man's sudden agitation was real; some of it, for sure.

"What happened to her? Where is she now?" Christie demanded.

"I don't know. Nobody knows. She was called to DC but afterwards they think she got off the plane bringing the British delegation from DC to the United Nations summit on the USS United States at Grand Forks. It had technical problems had had to divert to Nebraska ..."

"Did they actually find anything wrong with the aircraft?"

Adams frowned. "I don't know."

"It doesn't matter," Dwight Christie comforted him. "It doesn't matter."

The FBI man tried not to reveal his excitement.

Somehow, some way, he had punched Christie's button; that magical sweet, or soft spot – depending upon how you saw these things – more by accident than design. The man could retreat into his shell any moment if he made a bad move.

Adams said nothing, that was safest.

"I don't think Kurt Mikkelsen's gone rogue, I think somebody brought him in from the cold to 'tidy house'," Dwight Christie declared, a little breathlessly. "They just didn't reckon on the Operation Maelstrom story breaking, especially at the same time as the United Nations thing was happening. By now, Mikkelsen will have figured out that his mission is busted. He's not worried about us, the Agency or the Bureau, his mission is busted and he thinks he has been betrayed. You, or me, if we were in his place would do a fade, do a disappearing act. Not him. Not Billy the Kid; he's in hunter-killer mode."

"Is he working with the Piotrowska woman?" James Adams asked, if only because it seemed like the obvious question to ask.

"No, no, think about it, Mister Adams. Think about it!"

"I am," the other man rasped. Then, he realised he had been asking all the wrong questions. It hit him between the eyes and briefly, he was a little dazed.

The enemy within...

And before he could open his mouth Christie was walking him through his own thoughts and fears.

"He butchered that woman in Texas to metaphorically gut the Resistance, well, what's left of it in the South. There will be other targets in California, most likely but to Kurt Mikkelsen *the enemy within* isn't out in the boondocks, its back in DC, at Langley and wherever that old faggot Hoover hangs out these days."

The trouble was that every time James Adams thought he understood he discovered that he did not. He shut his eyes, tried to order the sum of his thoughts.

"Okay," he sighed. "Okay," trying to walk, not run through the field of ideas jostling like ripe stalks of wheat in the field as he marched forward, "Mikkelsen had to have had an accomplice on the West Coast. Maybe, even in the Bay Area, or down Los Angeles way; whatever, nobody knew where the United Nations event was going to be held until the last few weeks and we have to assume this thing was planned months ago. Would there be another 'partner' waiting for him in DC?"

"I doubt it," Dwight Christie shrugged. "The whole thing with the gun is bizarre...unless the gun was never *his* idea..."

Adams hesitated, hating what he was thinking.

"Where does the Angel of Death fit in?"

Dwight Christie chuckled unfunnily.

"You need to be looking at files you're not authorised to see, my friend."

The idea horrified James Adams: "Why would I do that?"

"You played college football at Baylor. So, you know you don't want to get blind-sided by a three-hundred-pound line-backer."

"Very funny!"

Instead of switching off in response to Adam's flash of irritation, Christie seemed re-energised.

"Look, think about it. The Company has its Angel of Death; why wouldn't the Bureau have another, one it identified before the October War but allowed to remain active at Los Alamos and in the experimental reactor program at Hanford, just in case it needed to pull a Soviet A-bomb spy out of the hat, to take the heat off J. Edgar and his boys if anybody discovered they were part of the problem, not the solution..."

"Yeah, well," Adams complained sourly, thinking the interview was effectively, over, "you can cut the Commie spiel..."

Dwight Christie was viewing him with a mixture of sympathy and...triumph. As if he had just won a private bet, or was in the middle of an absorbing game of Chess, declared: 'CHECK' out of the blue.

"Her name was," he said, smiling smugly, "and probably still is, unless she's gone to the electric chair yet; Karen Mathilde Czerniawska, the daughter of a Hungarian physicist who worked on the Manhattan Project with Oppenheimer."

James Adams stared at the former FBI man like he was threatening him with a meat cleaver.

For his part, Christie was smiling now like a cat that had just swallowed a mouse.

"Files. I read files. I remember everything. Sometimes, I make connections that you *real* special agents don't, and never will because you don't think 'crooked' enough."

Adams could live with that, he let the other man go on, uninterrupted.

Christie fell silent when a woman brought in a tray bearing two cups of coffee and a bowl of sugar cubes. She scurried out and the former Special Agent dropped two of the cubes into his cup, as if there was nothing at all odd about his surroundings, or his situation.

"You see," he continued, perhaps suspecting that James Adams's silence had a lot to do with his not wanting to risk breaking what he, presumably, thought was some kind of 'spell'. "Some jerk back in DC mistakenly added her name to a file list sent out to State Field Offices. That doesn't mean a mess of beans, obviously. Not of itself, but once you know a file designator and identify who owns, or originated it," Christie explained casually, "getting hold of it, or persuading somebody to have sight of it, and gossip about it at a bar is a lot easier than you'd imagine. Like I said, I'm lucky, I don't forget stuff. Show me a file and something in my head goes 'click' and it's all there, stored away for future reference. Photographic memory, although only ever in black and white, nobody's ever figured that out."

James Adams was reeling.

Karen Mathilde Czerniawska was among the twelve lead

defendants at the forthcoming War Crimes Tribunal in Minneapolis, charged with crimes against humanity and genocide. Herself horribly scarred in the Sammamish strike which had wiped out Adams's own family, it was suspected that she had personally armed the Las Vegas, Manhattan and the Philadelphia nukes on New Year's Eve 1965, and actively facilitated the arming of all the other bombs, the ghastly harbingers of the War in the Midwest.

And now Dwight Christie, who had been in a maximum-security jail under round-the-clock surveillance since the autumn of 1964, was telling James Adams things he could not possibly know...

"She's J. Edgar's trophy war criminal. She belongs to him. Even though it was Army Intelligence who tracked her down, she's the FBI's shield against the accusation it was asleep on at the wheel on 31st December 1965. And," Dwight Christie grinned, spreading his arms wide, "we both know that even though the FBI is up to its neck in its own version of Operation Maelstrom – which is why there are never anywhere near enough agents actually investigating crime – it never talked to the Company about people like Czerniawska. I don't know it for a fact but the reason, I'd speculate, that the War Crimes trials haven't started yet, even though the Administration will have lit a fire under the Department of Justice's arse – if only to distract attention from its own problems – is that getting the CIA and the FBI's files 'together' to build coherent prosecution cases against people like the Czerniawska woman, is like trying to get blood out of a stone. Rachel Piotrowska was in DC for several months in 1961; she made two contacts – maybe three but that third report was ambiguous – with Czerniawska. A 'brush contact', probably to pass some kind of message or to receive intelligence from her, and they met at a house in Georgetown one afternoon..."

"Why didn't you tell the people at Quantico about this?"

"What makes you think I didn't, Mister Adams?"

The two men stared at each other.

"You think the Piotrowska woman is a Red agent?" Adams asked softly.

Christie shrugged.

"Maybe. That or Krasnaya Zarya."

"Red Dawn?" Adams did not want to go there. "Why would the British turn her loose if she was Red Dawn?"

"I didn't say they'd turned her loose, Mister Adams."

The Special Agent held up a hand in apology.

"No," he conceded. "But she wasn't on that aircraft when it landed here on the West Coast?" He had another thought. "Why wouldn't the Bureau have moved against her if they thought she was a spy back in sixty-one?"

"It did," Christie said. "She killed two cops who were part of the snatch team. When she turned up again in 1964 the Brits requested, and the State Department gave her full diplomatic accreditation. The Bureau objected but somebody at the top, probably Tolson or J. Edgar himself, refused to share what was in the files with State."

James Adams rose to his feet, unable to keep still.

He turned his back to Christie, gazed out of the window.

"What are you telling me, Dwight?" He asked, his tone, his body language speaking to the shock half-paralysing his brain.

"People at Langley, and close to Hoover, had to have known there was an Angel of Death on their payroll long before 'Lady Rachel' showed up again. It was almost worth having the Battle of Washington just to lose Czerniawska, Karen Mathilde's file, don't you think? Otherwise, if something went wrong later, how the fuck do you think that old faggot Hoover was going to explain to the American people that the woman he employed to spy on all the good folk at Hanford, was a crazy woman who worked for Red Dawn all along?"

James Adams stared at the other man as if he was raving, a lunatic writhing inside his strait-jacket, frothing at the mouth and smashing his head against the wall in his raging against the world.

There had once been a time when he would have discounted what he had just been told as intelligence community mythology, outright misdirection. Literally, the rantings of a madman. The trouble was that in the last few years all the things he had honestly believed that not even a madman could possibly make up, had happened. No matter how implausible it seemed, the disgraced former Special Agent might actually be telling the truth, or leastways, a part of it.

And that was so far beyond frightening he thought the other man's madness was in danger of engulfing his mortal soul.

Chapter 35

Sir Roy Jenkins, the United Kingdom's Permanent Representative to the United Nations (Designate) had – somewhat reluctantly, because he was not really a morning person – allowed his twenty-nine-year-old Appointments Secretary, the man who was effectively his day-to-day chief of staff, to schedule a breakfast meeting with his new United States counterpart, George Bush.

This had meant rising at dawn for the irksome car ride through San Francisco, across the Bay Bridge and a thankfully short boat trip, across grey, ominously choppy waters to the conference venue, the USS United States. Given that his lord and master, Tom Harding-Grayson had kept him up half the night; he was not in the best of humours as the US Navy barge came alongside the great liner that dull morning.

"I apologise if I was a bit testy earlier," he confessed to his immensely competent, and even after only a few weeks acquaintance, utterly irreplaceable Appointments Secretary.

"I hardly noticed, Sir Roy," the younger man smiled.

Robin Butler was one of Sir Henry Tomlinson's – the Cabinet Secretary and Head of the Home Civil Service's - protégés. Until last summer he had been the most youthful Permanent Secretary in the land, working with the marvellously ebullient and debonair Minister of Sport, the former England cricket captain Edward 'Ted' Dexter. The two men had become the firmest of friends and it had seemed natural, when Dexter announced he planned – with the full support of the Prime Minister - to take a sabbatical from government, and tour with the England XI in South Africa that winter, that Butler should move on to better, greater things.

Everybody agreed that Butler had done an exemplary job guiding his 'first minister' through his relatively stormy tenure at 'Sport'. Ministers in their first post, regardless of their familiarity or otherwise with their departmental portfolio were, generally speaking, accidents waiting to happen; thus, it paid to keep a very attentive and protective eye on them until they had shown that they were up to the job.

The other thing everybody agreed was that, even if Ted Dexter had not set houses afire, and hardly been sure-footed, especially in his first year in the job, the successful organisation of the 1966 Soccer World Cup in England had been a triumph of political will, and behind the scenes one of exceptional organisational prowess. Naturally, Dexter had taken most of the public kudos but the Home Civil Service knew exactly who had been the power behind the throne; and recognised a coming man when it saw him!

Robin Butler, who had joined the Treasury in 1961, was that most 'civil' of civil servants – the unflappable, effortlessly competent, chivalric product of Harrow School, where it went without saying he had been Head Boy, and a graduate of University College, Oxford where he had achieved a double first and in his spare time twice won a Rugby Blue – had leapt at the chance to work with, and for Dexter.

Roy Jenkins did not need to be told – although he had in fact, been 'told' several times – how lucky he was to have been sent a rising star like Butler, and flying in the face of his fears, the two men had, after a hesitant beginning, struck it off in recent weeks. It helped no end that Robin Butler had a knack of getting on famously with practically everybody, even, improbably with the hard cases at the State Department who tended to treat Henry Cabot Lodge as if he was a man constantly pursued by assassins, whom nobody could approach or converse with other than after a positively Ruritanian rigmarole.

"What do we think is going on, Robin?" Jenkins asked his young colleague.

"I strongly suspect that there is simmering discord in the American camp, Sir Roy."

To say that Secretary Lodge had been 'off his game' throughout the interminable bilateral and multilateral meetings on board the liner in the last few days, would be an understatement of monumental proportions. The poor fellow had looked like somebody was walking, and now and then, jumping up and down on his own grave most of the time, and as for the rest of the 'Nixon gang' – as the West Coast newspapers were calling the inner circle of the Administration – they had been noticeable only for their absence. Apparently, the President and his advisors – Henry Cabot Lodge apart – were securely locked away in their Californian White House up in the Claremont Hills.

The US Secretary of State was waiting to greet his British visitors, flanked by a tall, lean familiar-looking man whom neither Englishman could have put a name to only forty-eight hours ago.

Forty-two-year-old George Herbert Walker Bush, Massachusetts-born but a man who nowadays combined New England poise with easy, sincere, Texan charm, smiled as hands were shaken.

Henry Cabot Lodge made no attempt to elaborate on why the younger man was standing next to him on the deck of the USS United States, jointly welcoming the representative of his country's most important foreign ally, was at his side.

Neither Jenkins or Butler thought this was amiss; important matters were not to be discussed on the promenade deck of an ocean liner!

George Bush fell into step with Robin Butler as the group followed a US Navy officer deep into the heart of the great ship, wondering how 'the Brits' were going to respond to the Secretary of State's news and his own, suddenly, literally out of the blue, injection into the mix.

However, it was not as if his life to date had not hardened him in preparation for the trials to come. He came from a banking family imbued with Republican politics; his father had sat in the Senate, representing Connecticut since 1952, bar a two-year period after unsuccessfully attempting to reverse his decision to stand down in 1962 in the immediate aftermath of the Cuban Missiles War, a thing put right in 1964.

Although not himself such a high-profile personality in GOP circles as his Senator father, Bush was a well-known – if only infrequently spotted – DC figure, not least because he was an honest to God American hero.

Back in 1942 he had volunteered for flight training with the US Navy as soon as he graduated, aged eighteen, from the Phillips Academy at Andover, Massachusetts. Commissioned an ensign in June 1943, at the time one of the youngest fliers in the Navy, and assigned to Torpedo Squadron 51 (VT-51) piloting Grumman TBM Avengers, and flying off the USS San Jacinto he had fought in the Battle of the Philippine Sea. Not long after that, attacking shore targets in the Bonin Islands he had been shot down, bailed out and spent several hours bobbing up and down in a small inflatable life raft – while US fighters circled overhead – wondering when the sharks, or the Japanese would get him, before being taken on board the submarine USS Finback.

He later discovered that scuttlebutt had it that the other men shot down on the raid, who had fallen into enemy hands had been executed, and their livers eaten by the Japanese. Understandably, when after a month, the Finback was able to return him to the surface navy, Bush was a man touched if not by revelation, then changed indelibly, with a conviction that God had saved him for some special, as yet unarticulated purpose.

After re-joining the San Jacinto, he had completed no less than fifty-eight combat missions, earned a Distinguished Flying Cross, a clutch of Air Medals and a little piece of the Presidential Citation awarded to his ship. Bush had married in 1945, gone to Yale where he had graduated in two-and-a-half years, been elected president of the Delta Kappa fraternity, captained the University baseball team and met Babe Ruth.

He had gone into the oil industry after Yale, becoming a millionaire by the end of the 1950s, which was about when, everybody assumed, he had got into bed with the CIA...

Of course, that was not the way he saw it.

George Bush had damned nearly got himself killed a dozen times as a young man in the Pacific; since then he had made his fortune, secured a sound foundation for his family – he and his wife, Barbara, had a brood of six children – and now he was returning to public service. He had been lucky in life and it was high time to pay his dues.

Having never resigned from the Navy Reserve, he had applied for active service within days of the October War, serving on the Operations Staff of the Seventh Fleet at San Diego and later in Honolulu in 1964 and 1965. Thereafter he had split his time between his business interests, GOP campaigning ahead of last year's mid-terms, and 'running errands' for the State Department, mostly in Latin America where he had formed a number of potentially significant relationships with political and military leaders.

The four men were suddenly shut up, alone, in a relatively Spartan compartment without portholes somewhere two or three decks down in the bowels of the monster.

"This is," Roy Jenkins began to remark, adjusting his horn-rimmed spectacles, 'cosy...'

"I apologise," Henry Cabot Lodge said quickly. "This is highly irregular, I know." He grimaced distastefully. "I must inform you that Doctor Kissinger and several members of the State Department mission in California, have resigned their posts overnight."

Neither Roy Jenkins or Robin Butler thought it appropriate to offer a comment on this, remaining determinedly silent. It was intolerably bad form to intrude upon another man's grief.

"Gordon Gray will be assuming the role of acting US National Security Advisor. Captain Bush," he nodded to his younger companion, "will henceforth, act as our Ambassador to the United Nations. Obviously, in the circumstances, you will understand that when I say 'acting' this merely reflects the urgency with which these, and several other appointments have been made to ensure the continuity of the good governance of the Union."

Roy Jenkins took off his glasses and extended his hand to Bush.

"Let me extend to you the heartiest congratulations of Her Majesty's Government, Mr Bush..."

"George," the other man said, smiling as hands were shaken. "Just call me George."

Chapter 36

James Jesus Angleton had looked as if he had not slept for several days. He was visibly dishevelled and Caroline smelled stale alcohol on his breath.

Frankly, she did not have a lot of sympathy for him: in her humble opinion he was every bit as bad, if not much a worse monster, than the man who had submitted Clara Schouten to such a prolonged, sadistically bestial calculated ordeal.

At least Kurt Mikkelsen had looked his victim in the eye, not hidden for years behind the fig leaf of so-called national security, and duty. Both men were bad men, Angleton was, in her opinion just as sick as Billy the Kid. What kind of self-obsessed coward neglected to tell a long-time, loyal servant of his department that she was in clear and present danger and, apparently, so as not to make her suspicious or overly anxious, not bothered to put any arrangements in place to keep her safe?

Several years ago, Caro had refused to participate in CIA-sponsored mind-control experiments, involving the use of psychotropic and other 'truth' and 'mind-altering' drugs, electing to concentrate on her profiling work with the FBI. In truth, working for the Bureau she had had to hold her moral nose to carry on at times. Right now, she was beginning to feel as spiritually violated as poor Clara Schouten had been physically and emotionally tormented by Kurt Mikkelsen, the CIA's creation and creature.

Caro was spitting mad: that she had once admired Richard Nixon's steadfastness and resolution, and applauded him for his courage in taking upon himself the responsibility for the war in the Midwest, and thereafter in her country's darkest hour tried to serve him selflessly, with her whole heart regardless of the cost to her professionally, and potentially in huge peril for her life, now made her want to puke.

How could she have been so fucking gullible?

She had been duped, taken for a fool.

Now, she would forever be associated in the public mind with a bunch of creeps and criminals. To think that she had once been seduced by the glamour and the kudos of working for the President, entranced like a stupid schoolgirl by her induction into the Commander-in-Chief's inner circle!

How could she have been so fucking stupid?

Learning that Operation Maelstrom, in the guise of a humbler abomination called Operation Chaos had its origins in 1959; when Nixon was the man Eisenhower was sending around the globe – because Ike was a whole lot happier on the golf course than in the Oval Office by then – bad-mouthing all those foul Marxist-Leninist 'dictatorships' who spied and unjustly subjugated their own people.

What a fucking hypocrite?

Well, she was through with the Administration.

And after today, she was through with the CIA, too!

She had no idea why James Angleton had wanted her to talk to Clara Schouten; the woman was in a mess, which was understandable but she was coherent, lucid. Yes, she would benefit from counselling, and she would need her friends to rally around. Presently, the horror of it all had not really sunk in; understandably, she was just relieved, happy to be alive.

What she did not need was an academic physician who would probably never see her again, attempting to deconstruct a psychosis which might never manifest itself if she was only given half-a-chance to get on with things, without constant reminders of the worst three days of her life. The saddest thing was that Caro strongly suspected the most destructive aspect of the whole awful business would, in time be, the certain knowledge that the man she had worked for, pretty much worshipped and held in awe with a mixture of platonic infatuation and unlikely girlish innocence, had so coldly, callously betrayed her.

James Angleton had reacted very badly when Caro told him exactly what she thought of him.

The spineless little shit!

'You violated that poor woman every bit as inhumanly as Kurt Mikkelsen; he's a fucking psychopath! What's your excuse?'

It was not perhaps, the sort of language one would find in a medical text book; however, apt and appropriate it had been in the circumstances.

Caro had lost her temper and said a lot of other things to the alleged 'great spymaster'. People like the Associate Deputy Director of Central Intelligence – it was no real comfort to know that he would not be that much longer – were contemptible.

When Nixon and all his men got back from California, Caro knew, she just knew, they were going to scapegoat Angleton, and pretend Operation Maelstrom was just a wartime expedient that was temporarily extended to complete the compilation of evidence for the forthcoming War Crimes Tribunal proceedings in Minneapolis. The White House would blame 'bad actors', Communists, journalists, political activists, the leaders of the Civil Rights Movement; in short, all the people they had been spying on and gratuitously denying their constitutional rights!

She refused the offer of a car to take her back to the first-floor CIA apartment in Georgetown that she had been allocated. She planned to pack her clothes and book into a hotel. Working for these people was no better than accepting blood money, thirty pieces of silver...

It took several minutes to flag a cab outside the gates of the complex; and she was still seething as she stomped up the steps to her soon to be vacated front door and turned the key in the lock.

She barged the door open, shouldered inside and slammed it hard, at her back.

"AAAARGH!"

This cry from the heart, was vented in spontaneous surprise and alarm from her lungs, as she squeezed her eyes shut and leaned back against the door.

She had been wanting to scream out aloud for the last two hours!

"Aaaargh...."

She opened her eyes, mostly to look around for something to kick.

"Aaargh..."

Suddenly Caro's eyes widened in alarm.

The other woman was sighting in an armchair, watching her with faintly amused, limpid eyes.

Caro froze, staring at the Navy Colt resting in the younger woman's lap.

"Oh dear," Rachel smiled wanly, "dear, dear me. I get the distinct impression that you've had a bad day, Professor."

Caro went on staring.

"How..."

"I'm good with locks," her unexpected guest apologised. As she spoke, she casually put the Colt into her handbag, an expensive-looking creation of the kind Caro had seen in the windows of the most exclusive shops in the rebuilt capital city. "Sorry about the gun. I didn't know it was you who would be the first person to come through the door."

Caro began to...unfreeze.

Rachel Piotrowska was dressed in a designer fawn two piece, still wearing a stylish – a-la Jackie Kennedy – and sensible, pair of new patent leather ankle boots.

The footwear was no doubt a trousseau compromise on account of the icy conditions outdoors; a girl in her business never knew when she was going to have to sprint for one's life...

Rachel rose to her feet and beckoned for Caro to follow her into the bathroom. Obediently, the older woman trooped after her. Therein, the younger woman closed the door and turned on the bath faucet and the shower.

"That's better," Rachel decided, putting down the toilet lid and sitting down, folding her right leg over her left knee and placing her handbag on the floor. "Now we can have a nice, private, long-overdue chat, Professor Constantis."

Chapter 37

International diplomacy is about accentuating the positive; or when there is nothing optimistic to be said about what divides the parties, agreeing to talk about something else.

There was only one common thread running through all the pre-conference discussions: namely, the USS United States was appallingly unsuited to host the gathering of the nations. There were ninety-two national delegations ranging in size from two or three persons to the twenty or thirty plus of each of the Chinese parties, the twenty or so of the British and Soviet contingents and the dozen plus of many of the other participants. With the crew of the ship doubled in size by translators, clerks, Secret Service and other national security detachments, and with the need to supply facilities for upwards of one hundred and fifty US and international journalists, not to mention seven or eight TV broadcast crews and their equipment, the whole ship was a crowded, ill-tempered circus.

It took up to three hours for all the delegates who had not made the mistake of basing themselves aboard the liner, to get to Alameda, then aboard, having to form long lines to have their credentials checked and for escorts to be summoned to take them to those areas of the vessel they were actually permitted to enter. Given that the USS United States was moored well within a couple of hundred yards of several Polaris submarines, the US Navy was understandably paranoid about security and heavily armed Marines guarded every corridor and communal hatchway. Throughout the ship there were huge signs in English, Russian, Mandarin, French and Spanish proclaiming 'NO ENTRY UNDER ANY CIRCUMSTANCES' and warning that 'INTRUDERS MAY BE SHOT ON SIGHT'.

It did not make for a conducive environment to conduct sensitive diplomatic conversations. Nor, with so many missions – about a quarter - led by national Heads of State or Premiers, was there a great deal of scope for good old-fashioned behind the scenes arm-twisting by professional diplomats. Or leastways, not without risking multiple international incidents.

Of the old, pre-October 1962 Security Council members, only the Soviet mission had elected to partially base itself on the USS United States. Claiming that the Soviet Union's last-minute notification that it planned to attend the San Francisco Conference limited the options, the US State Department had come up with a list of inherently unsatisfactory possible locations, including military bases and buildings on the campuses of Berkeley and Stanford. Quite apart from the fact such locales made it far too easy for junior members of the Soviet mission to defect, virtually at will at a time of their choosing, the KGB judged each 'insecure'.

Thus, Chairman and First Secretary of the Communist Party,

Alexander Shelepin had killed off further discussion with a curt: "The secretariat will stay on that bloody ship!"

Only the senior members of the Soviet delegation would be accommodated in the comfort of one of the lodges at the Presidio; and even then, the Russians were horrified to discover that they were being put up within a long stone's throw of the British!

Alexander Shelepin took it for granted that the Americans would bug their quarters, and spy on them every minute of every day that he and his people were in California. There was nothing they could do about that and anyway, the KGB would have done exactly the same thing to the Americans had the tables been reversed. That was, in a funny way, something of a return to business as normal. The only thing that mattered was that the Soviet Union was visibly, demonstrably a major player at the forthcoming event. It was his country's best chance since the war to make a real diplomatic impact on global affairs.

Shelepin and his deputy, First Deputy Secretary and Minister of Defence, Admiral of the Fleet Sergey Gorshkov had made their way to the uppermost public deck of the liner to watch the constant traffic of launches to and from the Alameda quayside.

Both men had eyed the long, low, black forms of the Polaris boats moored in the middle distance, and the continual helicopter take-offs and landings at the Naval Air Station less than a kilometre away. All around them San Francisco Bay thronged with activity and the cities ringing it were vibrant, breathing, ever-expanding, great engines of self-evident wealth and prosperity.

"We cannot fight *this*, Comrade Sergey Georgyevich," Alexander Shelepin observed, very quietly, without anger, knowing that there was more treasure and industrial capacity in the San Francisco Bay Area and the other cities of the American South West than there was in what remained of the whole former Soviet empire. There were small towns in Ohio and Pennsylvania which produced more steel than the entire Soviet Union; and aircraft factories within twenty miles of where the two men stood which produced more, and vastly technically superior war planes than the whole aircraft industry of the Motherland. Now, just looking at the great city across the bay, with the tall red girders of the Golden Gate Bridge just visible through the haze beyond it, the Soviet Leader hoped, above hope, that the men and women he had brought with him to America would see, like he had seen and already understood, that thoughts, talk of fighting the Yankee behemoth – stupid ideological pipe dreams even before the Cuban Missiles War – was futile. How could Nikita Khrushchev have believed, for a single moment, that he could directly confront such an all-powerful...colossus?

The Soviet party's Tupolev Tu-114 had eventually landed at Beale Air Force Base some thirty-six hours ago after technical difficulties had forced an emergency landing at Calgary, and US Air Traffic Control had subsequently diverted the aircraft to Offutt in Nebraska, presumably to show the Russians the lines of B-52s standing ready and waiting to carry on bombing the Motherland back into the Stone Age.

Making Shelepin's aircraft land at Beale, forty miles north of the state capital of Sacramento, and over a hundred from San Francisco, had probably been another calculated insult.

That said, Anatoly Dobrynin, who had greeted the party at Beale had explained that the Americans had probably offered it as a landing site because of its very long runway. This might, actually, have been true given that Shelepin's plane's 'hydraulics issues' had only been patched up at Calgary and the endless runways at Offutt and Beale Air Force Bases had meant its pilots had not needed to rely on their brakes to bring the giant aircraft to a safe halt.

Shelepin had only met the Soviet Ambassador to America a couple of times; that had been in passing, back before the Cuban Missiles War, not to talk. Gorshkov and the others thought he ought to recall Dobrynin; he had an open mind. He would decide for himself if the jovial Russian bear of a man who had greeted him at the foot of the steps on Californian soil had gone native, or not.

It was not lost on Shelepin, that Dobrynin had left his wife and daughter in Washington.

Presumably, just in case he was suddenly manhandled onto the Chairman's aircraft, out of reach of his alleged Yankee friends. The Tu-114 was diplomatic territory, as were, allegedly, the staterooms assigned to the mission on board the USS United States.

At Beale Air Force Base, Dobrynin had explained that the US State Department and the American Secret Service, had organised a convoy of armoured cars to transport Shelepin and the rest of the mission to San Francisco. Again, they had driven through sprawling urban landscapes broken by great factories along roads heavy, in places, with traffic and mighty, silvery lorries thundering in their countless profusion.

'If California was a country,' Dobrynin had commented, "it would be the fourth largest economy in the world." He had reeled out the numbers to back up this assertion.

Listening to the statistics, Alexander Shelepin, unable to deny the evidence of his own eyes, accepted that the 'sunshine state' was vastly more productive, and many times wealthier than the whole of what was left of the Russian Motherland.

The US Navy had moored a battleship and a huge aircraft carrier in the channel north of the Bay Bridge opposite the Berkeley shore, just to hammer home the point about who was the bully on the block.

"They are so powerful," Shelepin sighed, "yet still, they fear us. That is all we have on our side. We must work with that; we must find some way to co-exist with the monster we share this planet with."

Sergey Gorshkov scoffed ruefully.

"What makes you think they even want to co-exist with us?"

"Dobrynin says Nixon has his back to the wall," Shelepin retorted. "That may be good, or very bad for us."

Both men found it cruelly ironic that their adversary, supposedly the land of the free, was wringing its hands having finally awakened to the fact that its government had been spying on it – somewhat in the fashion of a pre-war Warsaw Pact state – for years. To the Soviets, the naivety of their American hosts was breath-taking.

Gorshkov was eyeing the long, elegant lines of the seven thousand-ton Leahy class guided missile destroyer – he made out the number '16' on her bow - moored a couple of kilometres south of the USS United States, her fore and aft twin-Terrier rails loaded and elevated forty-five degrees. He could not imagine what terrible threats the Americans imagined might materialise out of thin air in the middle of this great military camp!

Nevertheless, he admired the modern warship from afar with covetous eyes, wondering yet again: "How can these people not know how powerful they are?"

Anatoly Dobrynin had speculated that if the new General Assembly voted for the membership of the Security Council to be discussed the replacement of the Formosans with the People's Republic of China – he thought this was by no means a given, in fact on the balance of probabilities it was unlikely – and if either or both of the Soviet Union, or the British stood by their treaty obligations to the Chongqing regime, then that abominable Thatcher woman was likely to counter-propose that India and possibly, Australia should join the United Nations' top table, at least temporarily in lieu of France.

Alexander Shelepin thought that was all a bit tautological even for a professional diplomat; however, he was warming to Dobrynin. The man only rarely talked like a diplomat; in private he had about him the jovial ruthlessness of a gangster who only cared about realpolitik. He got the impression that Dobrynin was impatient, angry with the attitudes and policies coming out of Sverdlovsk.

'Disengagement has been a mistake,' he had said, bluntly.

Shelepin had uses for men who were not afraid of him.

Providing they knew their place…

Dobrynin had cut through the sophistry; explaining why he recommended Shelepin do 'whatever it takes to make sure there is no serious discussion of the Security Council.' There were 'elements within the Nixon regime' in favour of attempting to vote the USSR off that august forum.

It was not known what the British response to this would be.

That bloody woman was nothing if not…unpredictable!

Notwithstanding, Gorshkov was tickled pink about the rumours of discord within the enemy camp. Translators had gleefully read out whole screeds of the last couple of days editions of the San Francisco papers. Nobody knew for sure but it seemed that several of the President's men had decided, like rats, to jump off the sinking ship. Presumably, so they had more time to hire and brief their attorneys before policemen began to knock down their doors!

It was all hilarious!

If the gossip was to be believed, and since their arrival in California the air had been positively buzzing with the wildest of stories, a psychologically inebriating experience for many in the Soviet party, nobody was going to know who actually spoke for the United States until the 'last man standing' opened his mouth at that afternoon's opening plenary session of the General Assembly.

He mentioned this to Shelepin as the two men began to pace the open deck. The sun had broken through the overcast and from their vantage point they could now clearly make out the tops of the soaring red steel towers of the distant Golden Gate Bridge beyond the glinting windows of the San Francisco cityscape.

"Perhaps,' Gorshkov suggested sarcastically, "we will be confronted by Mickey Mouse!"

Chapter 38

Friday 10th February 1967
Sequoyah Country Club, Oakland, California

When it was feared that busloads of students and 'beatnik' protesters planned to descend on the Claremont Hills, the Secret Service had demanded that the President's party re-locate to the leafy foothills east of Oakland. At least here the narrow roads and the championship golf course south and east of the main clubhouse could be inundated with California State Troopers and Marines, and in extremis, the fairways and greens, provided multiple helicopter landing zones.

Margaret Thatcher was welcomed by Vice President Rockefeller as she stepped down from the cabin of Marine Two as the rotors of the Sikorsky SH-3 Sea King came to a standstill. She was closely followed by her Foreign and Commonwealth Secretary, Tom Harding-Grayson, blinking in the bright light as the sun poked dazzlingly through the otherwise leaden overcast for a moment. Ian Gow, the Prime Minister's ex-officio Chief of Staff followed, offering the older man a supporting hand as he threatened to stumble.

The invitation to fly to the unscheduled meeting with the President had come after the United Kingdom's advance guard had already departed the Presidio for the onerous journey by car to Alameda.

Commander Alan Hannay was the last man out of Marine Two. Dressed in his best uniform, he and his wife, Rosa, had brought their two youngsters to the Presidio to pay their respects to the Prime Minister – a pre-arranged five-minute engagement, just for form's sake – before they left San Francisco.

Unwittingly, the couple had walked into an, albeit bloodless, diplomatic minefield. Staffers had been running in all directions and US Marines were marking out a landing field on the lawn in front of the British party's 'lodge'.

"Why, Commander Hannay!" The Prime Minister had smiled maternally. And then beamed delightedly at Rosa who was cradling little Sophie Elisabetta in her arms, while eighteen-month-old Julian Alan, was trying to clamber out of his father's arms onto his shoulder, clearly determined to knock off his cap. "Marija would never have forgiven me if I hadn't found time to see your bambinos while we were here in San Francisco!"

Alan Hannay smiled proudly.

The Hannays did not know the Prime Minister as well as their friends Peter and Marija, and had never presumed to be on familiar terms with *the lady*, even though they had both gained the impression that in some way she regarded them as being a part of the same extended family to which the present Governor General of Australia and his wife belonged.

Margaret Thatcher had almost immediately been brought back to reality by the crisis of the moment.

"Admiral Pollock has gone on ahead to the USS United States,

Prime Minister," Ian Gow, balding and dressed in city pin stripes rather than his normal immaculate Hussars rig, reminded his principal. "Protocol probably demands we turn up with a military escort." He had looked meaningfully at Alan. "Commander Hannay perfectly fits the bill. And the Americans already know him."

Thus, Alan had kissed Rosa and his bambinos and marched purposefully out to clamber on board Marine Two when, a few minutes later it landed fifty yards away.

He had turned and waved to Rosa; phlegmatically hoping he would be returned to the Presidio in time for them to set off, bright and early tomorrow morning for their new home in Pasadena, where he was due to commence a training course he confidently expected to kick-start anew, his career as a 'proper' naval officer.

Alan had met Nelson Rockefeller a dozen times in Philadelphia and in Washington, now the philanthropist billionaire, seemingly a little under the weather, brightened momentarily as he received the younger man's salute.

"I'm standing in for Admiral Pollock, sir," Alan explained. "He had left for the UN *event* prior to the Prime Minister's change of plan."

Then Alan was trailing after the real players, barely having an opportunity to take in his surroundings.

Sequoyah Country Club?

Didn't Miranda Sullivan's parents own the place?

Yes, of course they did...

Protocol satisfied Alan shrank seamlessly into the background while his principals were wheeled in to meet the Commander-in-Chief. Soon, he and a US Navy four-ringer twice his age were chatting affably about their respective spells in the Mediterranean, and less professionally fulfilling, in DC...

Margaret Thatcher was a little shocked to find Richard Nixon haggard, round-shouldered, old-looking. He was staring sightlessly out of the windows of the club house, gazing into the distance down the length of the eighteenth hole.

She did not recognise the man beside him.

"Why, hello, Gordon," Tom Harding-Grayson chirped, approaching the stranger like he was a long-lost friend. "What on earth have you been doing with yourself lately?"

The President seemed to rouse himself.

"This is Gordon Gray," he said, introducing the middle-aged man who was torn between grinning at the Prime Minister's Foreign Secretary, and solemnly greeting the leader of his country's – despite their many differences – closest global ally. "Kissinger decided that he could no longer give his all to his role in the Administration," the President said morosely, "and that now would be a good time to return to academic life. Gordon has stepped into his shoes as my National Security Advisor."

Margaret Thatcher detected more than a little ongoing existential dissonance.

With a Herculean effort she contained her curiosity.

"Several others have not made the trip to California," the President went on, sombrely. "As you know, George Bush, Senator Bush's boy, has stepped in as our Ambassador to the United Nations. Oh, and Ron Ziegler has stepped down as White House Press Secretary..."

The British Prime Minister was momentarily stunned.

Just before the October War, she had been a shocked bystander – a relatively lowly parliamentary undersecretary at the Ministry of Pensions and National Insurance at the time of Harald Macmillan's famous 'night of the long knives', when Supermac had ruthlessly culled a third of his Cabinet one day in July 1962. But that had been a long overdue exercise in cutting out dead wood; right now, she was suddenly suspecting she was sensing the reverberations of some kind of dreadful schism inside the US Administration.

If British newspapers had published the sort of scurrilous gossip, and leftist-inspired anti-government propaganda the White House had been subjected to in the last few days, she would have damned them to do their worst and carried on as normal. One simply could not be blown from one beam to another by passing storms in the night, or entertain, for a second all this nonsensical conspiracy theory gone mad stuff about a Gestapo state run by the CIA!

While it was entirely credible that individual officers in that organisation, and in the FBI may have been over-enthusiastic in the performance of their duty – goodness, they had had their troubles with MI5 and MI6 in Britain since the Second War - and one had to recognise that there were always bad eggs in any walk of life, she really had not taken all the hyperbole in the American newspapers that seriously. As for the TV coverage of the alleged scandal, well, she had better things to do than dwell on that sort of thing!

Moreover, nobody around her had got very excited about it. Admittedly, Tom Harding-Grayson was not one to go overboard about any sort of scandal, and Roy Jenkins had wanted to 'wait and see' what developed.

Pat Harding-Grayson had observed: 'This is exactly the sort of thing that dreadful man Hoover has got away with ever since the Second War. The American people put up with all that McCarthy malarkey in the 1950s without saying boo to a goose. They've just had a civil war, for goodness sake. Of course, their government is going to be paranoid about getting caught out like that another time!'

There was a tacit agreement within the party that there was at least an even chance that the whole thing would probably turn out to be a storm in a tea cup...

Except, right now, that was not the message she was getting.

Fifty-six-year-old Gordon Gray was no stranger to government service, having served under Democrat Harry S. Truman and Republican Dwight Eisenhower. However, his recall two days ago had come as something of a surprise to him.

Born to a wealthy Baltimore family – his father, uncle and his brother had all been, in turn Presidents and Chairmen of the R.J. Reynolds Tobacco Company – he had obtained his law degree at Yale in 1933. He rose to the rank of captain in the US Army during the Second War, served as Secretary of the Army between 1949 and 1950, and later as Director of the Psychological Strategy Board responsible for coordinating 'psychological operations'. A former President of the University of North Carolina, Eisenhower had appointed him to the Atomic Energy Commission, and then to lead the Office of Defence Mobilisation before making him his US National Security Advisor in 1959.

His were a safe pair of hands.

And now, a little over six years later her was back in his old job and he could tell that Tom Harding-Grayson, a lot less spry for all that he was infinitely more dangerous these days, had to be viewing his return as the unmistakable signature of the Administration's possible disintegration.

Gordon Gray broke the ice.

"The President has raised concerns with me about the direction of travel of Anglo-American policy regarding the Security Council...*situation?*"

Richard Nixon seemed to stir out of his lethargy.

"Yes," he decided grimly.

Chapter 39

Professor Caroline Constantis-Zabriski had wasted no time packing her bags, getting a cab and booking into a hotel she had stayed at a couple of times last year. It was early evening by the time she went down to the bar and ordered a Bloody Mary.

I am getting paranoid in my dotage!

Nobody was following her.

However, Rachel had suggested she hang around the bar for twenty minutes; just to see if there was anybody killing time she recognised.

'I know a lot of people in DC!'

'Not the sort of people I'm worried about.'

She had a second drink, which did nothing to quieten her mind.

Rachel Piotrowska had wanted to know about Clara Schouten and the killing at the office in Alexandria. It never occurred to Caro to lie, or to dissemble. Everything she was learning about Kurt Mikkelsen, and now the small, piecemeal insights Rachel had inadvertently betrayed were beginning to build profiles. None of which was ever going to make for good bedtime reading. Strangely, although she had never met Billy the Kid; she felt she understood his underlying psychosis better, many times better than she did that of the Angel of Death.

Rachel's psyche was multi-layered; it was almost as if there were different personalities, different Rachels, vying for control, each seeking self-expression. It was no mystery to Caro that the woman could sustain – for long periods, possibly indefinitely – a happy, stable marriage. In fact, she suspected that given the right relationship, assuming no adverse, or a bare minimum of negative external stimuli, she might actually be perfectly capable of living a normal life. As to whether that was what she wanted, or sought, that was a different question. The Rachel that she was dealing with was not that pacific, reconciled woman with a brutally dry sense of humour; to the contrary; the one she had met and conversed with, for over an hour in the increasingly humid, foggy bathroom of her CIA apartment in Georgetown, was a coolly driven psychopath.

'You need to not be in DC,' Rachel had told her.

It had not been a suggestion, or any kind of advice; it was a statement along the lines of 'get out while you can!'

It was a thing that Caro planned to do first thing in the morning.

Rachel had asked her why Kurt Mikkelsen had not killed Clara Schouten. They both agreed that he had taken her to the woods off the Georgetown Pike to dump her lifeless, probably mutilated body close to the boundary of the CIA's Langley complex.

'Kurt was looking at me as if I wasn't there,' Clara had told Caro. 'That was the really weird thing, he didn't always look at me that way.

Even when he was…violating me. I got the feeling the times he took me from behind…he was sort of, ashamed. When he hit me it was cold, very deliberate, so as to not, I don't know, to damage me? I know that sounds strange. Except that one time he seemed to get angry. I shouldn't have tried to get away. He really hurt me, that time. Later, I could tell he wasn't proud of that. Apart from the first time he…violated me, he didn't try to hurt me. He was rough the next day but not, I don't know…sadistically?'

Confusion…

Caro had always known which buttons to press, and not to press, obviously, with Edwin Mertz; and figured out other criminal psychopaths in essentially similar ways. But none of that seemed applicable with Kurt Mikkelsen, and as for Rachel, well, she too, was a relatively closed book to her. She seemed to have the ability to shut Caro out at will, and none of the normal triggers worked.

Caro could see that there was a deep psycho-sexual component to Mikkelsen's behaviour, and conceivably, something causal, or at least, contributory buried deep in his war experiences. But he had been past childhood by then; not a brutalised teenage girl cut adrift in a nightmare like Rachel…

"You should have told me you were booking out of the Company house, Ma'am."

Caro almost jumped out of her skin.

She had been so buried in her thoughts that the world around her had gone silent, with all extraneous stimuli tuned out.

"Erin?" She blurted over-loudly.

Captain Erin Lambert, of the elite US Air Force Military Police 'blue caps', was out of uniform, slim and elegant in her off the peg dress beneath her open Camel-hair coat, wearing sensible shoes beneath legs concealed by thick blue tights against the winter cold.

The younger woman smiled.

They hugged.

Belatedly, Caro realised she had missed something really important.

"Did you follow me here from the apartment?"

The military policewoman shook her head.

"No. I got a report you'd moved out, and the number of the cab. I called up the company, they put a radio page to the driver and he rang in where he'd dropped you."

"Why you?" Caro asked pointedly.

"Because you'd have told anybody else who turned up tonight to go to Hell, Colonel," Erin Lambert shrugged. "I'm on assignment to the Internal Security Division at the Pentagon. I get to liaise a lot with CIA, FBI, and other offices you won't ever get to hear about. As of a couple of hours ago, I'm on your case. And," she pursed her lips philosophically, "my boss outranks you; so, even if you tell me to go to Hell, it ain't going to happen."

Caro was thinking straight for the first time in twenty-four hours.

Her friend was hefting a stylish black handbag just big enough –

like Rachel's - to accommodate a purse, the normal womanly compacts and cotton wool buds, *and* an automatic pistol.

"ISD at the Pentagon?" Caro checked.

Erin Lambert nodded.

"Have you ever been involved in any of the," the older woman caught herself, "*bad stuff* that's been in the papers the last couple of days?"

"No, Ma'am. That's not what my office does. We look for real spies and chase down real security issues at Department of Defence bases. Everybody in the military signs up to being under the microscope; that's how we all stay safe at night." She half-smiled. "Well, mostly. And no, we don't co-operate with any of that Operation Maelstrom...shit."

"What about now?"

The younger woman had settled on a bar stool next to Caro.

She signalled the barman.

"Any chance of a coffee in this joint?"

"Sure thing, lady."

Erin Lambert returned her full attention to her friend. The two women had grown very close last year when she was her bodyguard.

"While you wear the uniform, the Air Force owns you, Ma'am..."

"Cut that out, Erin!"

"I'm on duty, Caro."

The older woman raised a hand to order a third Bloody Mary.

"Sorry, she doesn't need that," Erin told the barman.

"Erin!"

"I've been ordered to not let you out of my sight until I've delivered you to your allocated married quarters at Offutt Air Force Base."

Caro stared at her in bewilderment.

"I have your orders in my handbag. They were cut this afternoon. You are hereby attached – until further notice - to Strategic Air Command's Operational Research Group as Officer Commanding the Office of Psychological Factors."

"You just made that up!"

"Sorry. But yes, somebody else may have just made it up, not me. If I have to, I'll cuff you, Caro. We fly out of Andrews Field at fourteen hundred hours local tomorrow."

Chapter 40

Friday 10th February 1967
4936 Thirtieth Place NW, Forest Hills Washington DC

There was only the one man who could disturb J. Edgar Hoover's evening, especially at a few minutes before midnight after the Director had already retired to bed. Over the last quarter-of-a-century there had been, in theory, one or two others for whom he would have deigned to rise – President Eisenhower, or FDR, perhaps although not Truman, and certainly not that young upstart JFK – but now there was only one man permitted to call him at any time of day, and it was not the President, Richard Milhous Nixon, it was Clyde Anderson Tolson.

"I'm sorry about this," Hoover's deputy apologised, getting to his feet as his best friend, mentor and long-time boss, entered with a face-wide scowl on his jowls and the tails of his dragon-motif silk dressing gown flapping in his wake. "If this could have waited for the morning..."

"That's okay, Clyde," the Director of the Federal Bureau of Investigation growled. Anybody else he would have bawled out for five to ten minutes before he listened to a word they had to say; but that was not the kind of relationship he had had with Clyde Tolson for the last couple of decades. They had covered each other's backs like brothers, blood brothers, everything they had achieved they had achieved together and although Hoover had always been the guy absolutely in charge, his partner's recent illness had illustrated that – as he had feared – without him he was vulnerable, incomplete and his control over the great sprawling empire of the Bureau was in some way, critically undermined. "That's okay, I know it has to be important. Whatever it is?"

"Adams called me from San Francisco. He tried to get straight through to you..."

Hoover's scowl had morphed into a frown, now he scowled anew.

"Did he?" He murmured menacingly.

"But that's not the thing, Chief."

"Okay," what is?"

"A few days ago, at his request I sent him several digests, and selected interview transcripts prepared by the people who had been processing that scumbag Christie at Quantico..."

Hoover, who had slumped into an easy chair began to rise to his feet, spontaneously enraged by the mere mention of that...bastard's name.

Clyde Tolson, who had settled in a chair opposite his friend in the house's old-fashioned, rather crowded and floridly furnished parlour began to rise also, except he had raised a hand to warn Hoover to try not to get too upset, over this, preliminary piece of information, at least.

Nobody other than Hoover spent as much time at 4936 Thirtieth

Place NW, as Clyde Tolson. His friend had moved into the house back in 1940, following the death of his mother. Therein lay another ghost in the Director's past which Tolson, had adroitly managed and largely, successfully conspired to conceal down the years.

Lately, the greying, still handsome Associate Director of the FBI, found himself thinking overlong about things buried deep in the past; as if wondering how many of their – his and Edgar's - secrets would one day come to haunt them. Hopefully, it would not be until they were both dead and gone.

John Edgar Hoover was supposedly one of three siblings, the son of parents of German-Swiss ancestry, born on New Year's Day 1895. Although listed on the 1900 Census, as living at the family's former address at 413 C Street SE, Hoover's birth – of which there was to this day no official original or contemporaneous record...*anywhere* – had not been registered until a certificate was filed, in the wake of his mother's death in 1938.

It had *always* astonished Clyde Tolson that this 'anomaly', which would have been of enormous interest in any Bureau investigation, where identity was invariably crucial to ongoing inquiries, had never really been the subject of close public scrutiny. Hoover and his mother had always been very close. Although Tolson had not met the father until several years after his death, he had got the impression that Edgar and the old man had been, in some way, mutually estranged. In any event, after his passing in 1921, Edgar, then aged twenty-six, had moved back in with his mother in the house where he had been born and continued living there, even after he became the famous gang-busting Director of the FBI.

In 1939, Hoover, by then a big man in DC, had had the house at *4936 Thirtieth Place NW*, specially designed and built for him at a cost of $12,000 only after his mother's death. It had been his hideaway ever since, where he lived in mostly blissful anonymity – or as anonymously as any man who was driven to and from his place of work in a gleaming limo – usually one similar to that in use by the changeable incumbent of the White House – every day. Out here in Forest Hills, Tolson knew that Hoover could relax, that to his neighbours and their children, he was anything but the ogre so many DC insiders assumed him to be. Heck, the Chief gave old folks rides to the local bus stops, and sometimes he stopped to talk to kids on the street...

For a moment, Clyde Tolson paused to organise his thoughts; that had got a lot harder lately even though he knew he had recovered as much as he was ever going to, from the stroke which had laid him low last year.

He stared at the stuffed animals, trophy heads on the wall; oddly juxtaposed with Hoover's favourite – by DC standard's avant-garde and esoteric – actually rather tame erotic paintings.

If only his enemies understood that Edgar was a complicated guy...

"Adams is a good man," Hoover mused aloud.

"Yeah, he's had a lot of face to face time with Christie in San

Francisco," Tolson returned, his mind slowly focusing on how he was going to tell his friend the bad news. "It may be that Rachel Piotrowska levelled with Adams before she came back to DC..."

Hoover raised a suspicious eyebrow.

"Have we found her yet?"

Tolson shook his head, waited patiently to defuse an explosion that never happened.

"No," he told his friend. "We reckon she probably got on a Greyhound at Grand Forks bound for Fargo. She could have got a flight from there..."

"How would she have paid for that?"

"I don't know, Chief."

"She could be anywhere!"

Tolson nodded. "Agent Adams is sending me the notes he put together after he talked to her. I think she got him thinking, questioning some of the assumptions we've been making about Christie."

Hoover had stopped frowning. "Such as, Clyde?"

"Adams used to be an attorney. He says we'd get our fingers burned if we tried to indict Christie for nine-tenths of the crimes he *claims* to have committed..."

"We ran polygraphs on the guy at Quantico?" The Director of the FBI objected. His voice was never quite so rat-a-tat when he was alone with Tolson. His persistent, childhood stutter virtually disappeared when he was in his friend's company. "The bastard passed them all."

"But there were anomalous results on several of the tests."

"There always are," Hoover shrugged.

"Adams said he thinks the psychological profiling for Christie is," Tolson continued, hesitating momentarily, "incomplete."

Hoover, the older man by some five years sighed, suddenly grey and worn despite his artificially boot-blacked head of only belatedly thinning hair.

"What the fuck does that mean, Clyde?"

"Agent Adams thinks that Christie may have been," he halted, distaste quirking his pale lips, "systematically falsifying Bureau records throughout his career," he shook his head, "and doing pretty much the same damned thing before that, when he was in the Army in the Second War as part of the Department of Defense's Central Office of Procurement Control."

Now J. Edgar Hoover raised a severely trimmed eyebrow.

Tolson continued: "Adams wants to bring in specialists, people from Stanford to forensically examine specimen historic files and records compiled during Christie's time as Assistant, and then Special Agent on the West Coast between April 1957 and December 1963..."

"How long will that take?"

"Months, maybe," Tolson admitted apologetically.

The two men stared at each other.

There was a rogue CIA operative on the loose in DC; a man clearly on some kind of wrecking ball mission. Operation Maelstrom was out in the open and it was only a matter of time before Special Council – in reality the previous Congress's 'Prosecutor' – Judge Earl Burger, sought to re-convene the grand Jury at which both Hoover and Tolson had systematically perjured themselves last year, and the whole, ghastly Warwick Hotel disaster came back to haunt the Bureau.

And now they were facing the possibility that Dwight Christie may have been doctoring the Bureau's most secret files, perhaps for many years...

It raised the nightmare possibility that whole tranches of records might just be flimflam, and if that became known outside the Bureau hundreds, or more likely, thousands of convictions would suddenly become suspect.

The old man realised he was hyper-ventilating, feeling dizzy. He forced himself to take several long, slow breaths.

They had to get a handle on this; and fast!

Not for the first time the irony of the situation pressed upon both Hoover and Tolson. Whereas, in the past they could always rely on Eisenhower, or even JFK in some things, and LBJ to protect them and their people from meaningful public and judicial scrutiny, he had no faith whatsoever that Nixon or the Chief Executive's incompetent California frat buddies filling most of the key posts in the White House, would lift so much as a finger to deflect the heat this time around. And, if that was not bad enough, the Piotrowska woman had disappeared, and nobody had figured out where that fucking Remington 700, M24 .30-06 sniper rifle fitted into the picture.

Hoover tried to take stock.

That the President and all his men were out of town, still half-paralysed by the Operation maelstrom shit storm raging in and around Capitol Hill was just another cruel accident of fate. Even the wiser DC-insiders were still too shocked to have noticed the storm generated by the initial *Washington Post* revelations had probably peaked. Or that, already, the attention was sliding off message to zero-in on the resignations and the sackings at the White House. Within hours of US National Security Advisor Henry Kissinger's resignation, 'sources close to the Administration' had retaliated, disseminating details of the eminent academic's womanising and 'wild partying', and put about a rumour that 'the Doctor' had been about to be sacked, anyway. Nobody cared about the US Ambassador to the United Nations (Designate) stepping down; and everybody had known Ron Ziegler was expendable, likely to be the first sacrificial offering to Earl Burger's investigation.

No, the thing that was still rumbling, like a low-intensity earthquake that just went on for ever and ever, it was the Good Captain, Ambassador Walter Brenckmann, jumping ship just at the moment the storm generated by *The Washington Post's* muck-raking was breaking around 1600 Pennsylvania Avenue!

That was not going to go away any time soon and if anybody was stupid enough to try to retaliate against the Brenckmann family, they were inviting a full-scale war with the Betancourt clan. Nobody in DC needed that right now!

In fact, nothing worried the veteran Director of the FBI as much as the thought that one of the President's men might get caught having a pop at...the Good Captain.

Hopefully, when the President got back from California things would have settled down again; and perhaps, he might try having a confidential word with the Commander-in-Chief about the best way to play...things.

If there had been anybody close to the President with his head in gear, who was capable of stepping back from the car wreck and looking at what else was coming down the road, somebody ought to have reminded Nixon that a GOP-dominated Hill, was not about to impeach the man who was the Party's last best shield against picking up the tab for Ike's carelessness – vis-a-vis Operation Maelstrom's parent project, Operation Chaos - back in the late 1950s. The political reality was that nobody was going to give a shit that JFK and LBJ had played along with Operation Maelstrom; the guy who had set the hares running in 1959 was Eisenhower, and full disclosure had happened on Richard Nixon's watch. Right now, the GOP on the Hill was in damage limitation mode; it was high time the Administration caught up!

Maybe, Hoover would tell the President the lay of the land.

Somebody ought to tell him he was playing this thing all wrong.

Paper-thin lies that Operation Maelstrom had had its roots in the Eisenhower-JFK years and had only been revived as a wartime 'exigency' to cope with the wars in the Midwest, were being pumped out by every Nixon staffer, spokesperson and every mealy-mouthed apologist left in the Capital. And as for the House of Representatives, presently nearly wholly-owned by the GOP, the silence had been positively, and very sensibly, deafening!

No, even if the President did not know it yet, he could ride this one out. His poll ratings were going to take a ten-point hit but that still left him odds-on to walk back into the White House in November 1968. Richard Nixon might think he had a headache but the Bureau and the Central Intelligence Agencies 'problems' were likely, very soon to become the real focus of the inevitable witch hunt. Especially, when somebody in the Administration got his finger out of his arse, and realised that the only logical thing to do was to blame it all on the guys who had been in charge of US intelligence and internal security in the Eisenhower-Kennedy years.

Hoover had it all worked out.

Richard Nixon was not going to turn on his best boy, Richard Helms. Helms had only got to be Director of Central Intelligence last autumn. No, the CIA's fall guys would be his predecessor, John McCone – people said he was a sick man on the way out – and the man JFK had sacked after the Bay of Pigs fiasco, Allen Dulles, the true architect of what later became Operation Maelstrom, and the man who had entrusted its execution to his faithful lieutenant, James Jesus Angleton.

Problematically, Hoover had no real feel for whether Nixon had the balls, knowing or suspecting he, and he assumed, Angleton both had to have 'the dirt' on him, would go for the 'nuclear option' and try to throw him and the Bureau under the bus. Or worse, simply allow Earl Burger and the army of investigators yet to be appointed – and there would be a lot more of them than before – to condemn his reputation and the whole FBI to a lingering death by a thousand cuts. He was trapped. There was no guarantee that if he resigned, which was unthinkable, the President would give him a free pass.

He suspected that while he still controlled the Bureau, he still had a weakened, brittle bulwark against evil; but the moment he put that shield down, or his grip on it faltered, the wolves would surely tear out his throat.

So, the big question was, does the President have the guts to sack me?

The problem with that shithead Christie and the CIA's mislaid assassins were, in the scale of things, if not manageable then peripheral to the tsunami of grief coming down the road towards him, Tolson and the shared love of their lives, the Federal Bureau of Investigation.

"That woman," Hoover said, his voice distracted. "Constantis, Zabriski, something like that..."

"What are you thinking, Chief?"

"How about it we send her out to San Francisco to do her profiling thing with Christie?"

"She's CIA..."

"Didn't she walk away from one of their programs – one of the ones the college boys at Langley didn't want to admit existed, even in those days - back in the fifties before she got to head up the psycho profiling task force?"

Clyde Tolson nodded, deciding not to correct his friend, whose memory, like his own, was not all it had once been. Professor Constantis, as she then was, might have thought she was working for the Bureau on *that* mind-bending program at the time. She was a clever lady; she would have figured out who she was actually working for; that was why she had invested so much energy working with the Bureau after she had had her little professional tantrum...

It seemed like ancient history now but before the Cuban Missiles War Professor Caroline Constantis had been on the Bureau's payroll as Associate Deputy Director of the Criminal Profiling Office of the FBI in Illinois, a part-time consultancy role which she combined with her teaching and research work with the Medical School of the University of Chicago. She had signed on the dotted line, taken the oath; if it came to it, the Bureau still owned a little bit of her.

"Yes. I recollect that she cited ethical concerns, Chief."

Hoover grunted an unkind snort of laughter.

Tolson, not knowing where this was going injected a cautionary note into the exchange.

"The work she did getting inside Edwin Mertz's head for the President would not have been possible but for the Bureau ensuring that she had had unrestricted access to the mad SOB for all those years…"

"True, very true. She's in DC, now, right?"

Clyde Tolson nodded.

"Do we know where?" His friend asked him.

"Yeah. The Secret Service usually has eyes on her when she's in DC; they're kind of stretched at the moment. We took up the detail, as a favour to the White House."

Hoover's eyes narrowed.

"Do you think she'd run her eye over former Special Agent Christie for us?"

"I don't know, Chief. What's your thinking on this one?"

No other man in America could have asked that questions and actually expected a frank answer. Especially, as it was the second time that he had asked it.

"I," Hoover replied, thoughtfully, "need to stay focused on the Administration, Clyde. Like we agreed, you and I can't be everywhere, fighting every fire with this Operation Maelstrom shit coming at us from all directions. But Christie's testimony has got our people in Texas and California running every which way. If it turns out he's been yanking our chain, we need to know about it before those parasites on Capitol Hill do. The Company's in the firing line at the moment; we don't want that to change."

Clyde Tolson fought of a sinking feeling.

"There is one problem," he confessed. "She's also got Air Force security on her case, Chief."

"Okay, okay," Hoover was on his feet. "We'll have to do something about that. We both need to be in the office. We've got some calls to make!"

Chapter 41

Whoever had decided that the one-time First-Class Dining Compartment of the former luxury transatlantic liner ought to be employed as the General Assembly Room, deserved to be keel-hauled.

In that, if not a lot else, Lord Thomas Carlyle Harding-Grayson, Foreign and Commonwealth Secretary of the United Kingdom of Great Britain and Northern Ireland, and the majority of the delegates and dignitaries crammed into the already stickily humid space, was relatively confident that there would be universal agreement.

Apparently, a small electrical fire somewhere in the bowels of the great ship had 'killed' the air conditioning plant serving the amidships compartments of the vessel.

As the day progressed, most of those present began to think that keel-hauling was far too good a fate for whoever was responsible for configuring the totally inadequate, and in every way, unsuitable General Assembly Room much in the fashion of a large, and particularly unconvivial speakeasy!

What might have been dining tables had been turned towards the forward end of the compartment, where officials sat on a slightly raised stage. Microphones with cables snaking to all parts were laboriously transferred from one table to another when each nation got its say, and Marine Corps troopers stood at every hatchway, serving as guards and assistant tellers whenever there was a vote.

On the first afternoon it had been agreed - although, by no means unanimously – that each member of the pre-Cuban Missiles War Security Council would address the General Assembly. No speech was to take more than twenty minutes; a stricture already breached by the representative of the Republic of China (the People's Republic had not been invited to the conference), the United States (with its newly designated Ambassador, George Bush, clearly reading from the script his predecessor had prepared), and by Maurice Schumann, who had been flown to California by the RAF only as an afterthought, when it was determined by the Free French political caucus in Oxford, that it was inappropriate for the Anglo-French position to be 'jointly presented'.

The purpose of the opening 'declarations' had been to re-affirm the purpose of the United Nations and to outline the main issues facing the re-dedicated organisation. Instead, thus far, there had been three wildly divergent, logic-defying proclamations denying that World War Three had happened and that they needed to deal with the World not as it was now but as it had been on Saturday 27th October 1962.

Tom Harding-Grayson, unlike the three previous speakers – each addressing the gathering from their seats among their delegations, practically unseen, had risen to his feet and surveyed his surroundings. Having in younger days, rather envied fellows who could casually wander a stage, with a microphone in hand in a club, strutting their stuff, crooning to their heart's content, he had – just to see what happened – lifted the microphone the technicians had planted on the United Kingdom's table, tapped it and raised it to his lips.

"I do hope everybody can hear and see me?"

This drew a subdued response.

"Jolly good. In that case I shall begin. I shall not exceed my allotted time; frankly, I take the view that in a forum such as this we owe each other all due courtesy and civility. In short, if we act towards each other without respect, what example does that broadcast around the globe?"

Members seated at the nearby US table shook their heads.

"It is the position of the United Kingdom that in its functions and established practices that the United Nations should resume unchanged. However," he went on, ignoring the mutterings from certain quarters, "that it should not be located on the territory of its most powerful and dominant member. Like other nations the United Kingdom wishes to bring certain matters to the attention of the General Assembly; and hereby gives notice that it is not content to go forward supporting the former constitution of the Security Council. The World has moved on since 1945 and the five permanent members of the pre-October 1962 council – the victors of the Second War – do not reflect the geopolitical realities on the ground. The United Kingdom's ally, France, is presently a country divided and clearly, no country so divided can speak with one voice. Therefore, it is my Government's recommendation that until such time as the war in France is over, France should not speak or vote in the forum of the Security Council."

Maurice Schumann stared fixedly to his front while other members of his delegation fulminated. He remained in his chair; that was the deal, the only realistic way his country could hope – in the long-term - to remain at the top table of international affairs. Schumann was older than most of his staffers, of a generation who, in the 1940s, had trusted to the British and the Americans to liberate his country and in the end, after four interminably, long years of humiliation and anguish, they had been true to their word. So, like his counterpart and the de facto leader of the Free French, General Alain de Boissieu, he had had no alternative but to accept this new, hopefully temporary, fait accompli. Their British allies, to whom they owed so much in blood and treasure, had had to have something to bring to the table. Given that there was no realistic prospect of the Security Council sitting at this gathering, Schumann and de Boissieu had agreed the 'negotiating tactic', and hoped above hope, that they were not going to be sold down the river.

There were no heads of state, no Prime Ministers at this first session; sensibly, they would only take their turn later when the dirtiest of the double-dealing was over and the United Nations was either reborn, or splintered anew.

"Consistent with its approach to the position of our French allies, with whom we are presently waging a war against the evil forces of Krasnaya Zarya in southern France and along the Rhine; my government applies the same judgement of Paris," Tom Harding-Grayson smiled wanly, "to the ongoing Chinese dilemma."

There was renewed head shaking around George Bush; who simply nodded, as if totally immersed in his thoughts and unprepared to offer hostages to fortune.

"Who speaks for China? Or who speaks for the greater part of the Chinese polity?" The British Foreign Secretary let the question hang in the air for a moment. "Who indeed? If there is to be only one China on the Security Council, surely, it is reasonable for the voice that speaks for ninety-five percent of all Chinese, to be the one that rightfully speaks for the Chinese nation? And that, is the view of my government."

Clearly, a lot of people who ought to have known better, had honestly not seen this coming.

Tom Harding-Grayson shamelessly added another element to the shock in the room.

"One is also bound to ask: what is the value of a Security Council which excludes the most populous democracies on the planet?"

No, very few people had seen that coming!

"After the People's Republic of China, India is the most populous nation on the globe. What of her inalienable rights to be heard?"

"Seriously?" Somebody on the US table asked, angrily.

"Unlike Ambassador Bush and the gentleman from Taipei," Tom Harding-Grayson continued, for all his talk of 'respect', referring to the representative of Chiang Kai Shek's Nationalist Chinese 'republic' with barely veiled contempt, "we view the Union of Soviet Socialist Republic's membership of the Permanent Five of the Security Council as a non sequitur. Let us not forget that the Grand Alliance of the Second War years might have been victorious but for the Soviet Union; either that or we'd still be fighting that war today, which surely would have been a catastrophe even worse than that of the war of 1962!"

He shifted the microphone, a large, lumpy stainless-steel implement from his right to his left hand as his arm threatened a spasm of cramp.

"Sincerely, I welcome the delegation of the Soviet Union to this international forum. It is my most profound hope that it has come to America to cement the global peace. If this is so, then I promise that the United Kingdom will treat with them with the utmost good faith. Further to this, my Prime Minister has asked me to extend an unconditional invitation to Chairman Shelepin to meet with her here in San Francisco, or in England, or if he prefers, at a place and at a time of his choosing, in the Soviet Union. We were co-belligerents in a war which resulted in the death and misery of millions of our own people a little over four years ago, it is our duty to ensure that nothing like that ever happens again."

The British Foreign Secretary was still a little irritated that his

French opposite number, Maurice Schumann, had elected to issue a formal complaint about the Red Air Force attack on the Villefranche Squadron, and the Sverdlovsk Kremlin's 'succouring' of the terrorists 'infesting my country'. Much as he understood the Frenchman's angst; it was unhelpful to express it publicly in this arena.

Of course, George Bush had parroted a familiar line; spoken of grand peace treaties, the assignation of blame and demanded the retrenchment of alleged Soviet infiltration globally in general, and particularly in Latin America with the blithe arrogance of a man who had read; but obviously not inwardly digested the now comprehensive CIA and US Air Force damage assessment reports of what had become of Soviet military and industrial capacity.

"Ladies and gentlemen," Tom Hardin-Grayson went on. "I will not pretend that the United Kingdom does not have its own, pressing issues to bring to this Assembly. The European security situation remains the biggest single obstacle to reconstruction in my country. Likewise, instability throughout the Mediterranean and the Middle East poses national and international threats to ourselves, and many of those nations represented in this room."

He sighed.

"And there remains, the question of the illegal seizure of British crown territories in the South Atlantic and Antarctica by force majeure, by the Argentine in April 1964, the deaths of British servicemen in Argentine hands and the deaths and mistreatment of civilians in the following months. I must, sadly, give this Assembly, notice, and the Argentine due warning, that my government will pursue justice and restitution in this matter without let or hindrance in the months and years to come."

Chapter 42

Saturday 11th February 1967
Soviet Residence, Place de Jaude, Clermont-Ferrand

Sharof Rashidovich Rashidov, the Troika's Commissar Special Plenipotentiary to the Front Internationale, had only just returned to the city from Maxim Machenaud's command bunker at the airport when the sirens began to sound.

He demanded to know if there had been further reports from Northern France while he had been away; there had been nothing of substance since the flurry of mostly garbled, panicky messages of the morning.

The enemy had attacked around Angers and Troyes, and 'in great strength' with 'tanks and rolling artillery barrages' in the Champagne towards St Dizier, and 'broken out of the Ardennes' supposedly 'sweeping towards the Rhine!'

There had also been less panicky reports from units in West Germany detailing a series of air attacks on depots, vehicle parks and communications targets, with the enemy apparently homing in on transmissions from radio wagons and even individual backpack radio sets.

It was alleged that Napalm had been employed in several of these strikes but then it was not as if the Red Army was going to squeal about that in public, given that it had no right to be anywhere near the Rhine...

Rashidov knew – well, he was convinced – that the Front Internationale had a much better idea what was going on to the north and the east, and probably, even an approximate tactical 'feel' for the real weight, and lines of advance of the enemy. Albeit, Rashidov's own advisors were scoffing at the foolishness of the 'Frenchies and their English lackeys' going on the offensive while the tail end of the recent blizzards were still blowing through 'the battlefield', and battering at the foothills of the Massif Central.

Foolish or not, from the chaos surrounding Maxim Machenaud that afternoon; the 'Frenchies' down here in the Auvergne were seriously rattled. Not so much caught on the hop, unawares, as completely taken by surprise and suddenly, badly in need of real leadership.

The Commissar Plenipotentiary did not think that Citizen Machenaud and his motley crew of bully boys and lickspittles had the remotest idea what 'leadership' actually meant.

Sharof Rashidov's quiet suggestion to the 'leader' of the Front Internationale that perhaps, he might consider going on the radio to broadcast an upbeat rallying cry to his people, had been brusquely rejected. Instead, the idiot had begun to rant about issues which had suddenly become at best peripheral, and at worst, irrelevant. Somebody was about to set fire to his castle; it was far too fucking late to obsess about the colour of the paint on the battlements!

And now the sirens were sounding across the city.

It was starting to get dark; dusk swiftly turned to cold night at this time of year.

"Comrade Commissar, we should go to the basement!"

Rashidov scowled in exasperation.

Sometimes, it was like being surrounded by old women!

There had been an air raid warning drill; a desultory affair in which hardly anybody hurried anywhere and was over inside twenty minutes, shortly after Rashidov and his people had flown into Clermont-Ferrand. But none since; despite – what had been thought to be low-level skirmishing, rather than serious - fighting in the north and the British advances down the Biscay coast. There had been no actual air raids inland, or anywhere within the Massif Central, or the south. Despite the air raids on Bordeaux, the Front Internationale's last surviving bastion in the west; the clowns in Clermont-Ferrand were convinced the English would never bomb the city, or any of its southern, Mediterranean enclaves!

Sharof Rashidov and his military experts thought that was not so much wishful thinking, as the self-evident manifestation of a worsening delusional psychosis. The only reason the British had not bombed targets in 'the south' was probably because, thus far, they had not got around to it. Clearly, any escalation of the war in the north was likely to signal a sea change in the enemy's operational thinking, and therefore, it was inevitable that Clermont-Ferrand, Lyon and the big cities on or near the coast, Toulon, Marseilles, Nice, Perpignan and other targets, like rail yards, docks, road bridges and suchlike would soon come in for the same sort of medicine the RAF had meted out to the Chelyabinsk bunkers and key infrastructure objectives in Iraq a couple of years ago.

Needless to say, Maxim Machenaud was totally unreceptive to this line of argument!

The First Secretary of the Front Internationale was concerned only with 'the threat' of further attacks by the *Red* Air Force!

It was...*unbelievable.*

The man was insane!

The two surviving interned Tupolev Tu-95s, both of which had suffered splinter damage from near misses over the Riviera: in one case a punctured fuel tank, and in the other suffered damage to the control surfaces and control cables of its starboard wing, had, in accordance with mission orders eschewed any attempt to immediately make the return journey to the Soviet Union and put down at Clermont-Ferrand to assess and if possible, to make repairs. This was the safest course before attempting the long flight back to their bases in the Chelyabinsk Military District. Both bombers had been moved to the western side of the aerodrome where around them, massive blast berms were still in the process of construction. Their crews, fourteen men and two women, notwithstanding Rashidov's angry protests, were still being held incommunicado in a disused block at the FI's headquarters in the old Michelin plant.

Having spent most of the afternoon kicking his heels waiting for Maxim Machenaud to make an appearance the two men had had a blazing row. The Frenchman had ranted about Soviet betrayals; Rashidov had demanded, yet again, the release of his imprisoned personnel, and information about the fate of several other Red Air Force crewmen suspected to have bailed out of the crippled bomber which had crashed attempting an emergency landing at Clermont-Ferrand.

Eventually, he been allowed to see – but not speak to or approach closer than a few metres - the sixteen prisoners, or more correctly, hostages. The crews of the two bombers looked hungry and dirty, and were being held in a cold room with a bucket for a communal toilet but had otherwise, not *yet* been harmed.

Maxim Machenaud had thrown a an even more violent tantrum when Rashidov had angrily renewed his complaints and warned him that 'our alliance hangs by a thread'.

The general tenor of the debate had proceeded to go faster and faster downhill after that, if such a thing was even possible.

Machenaud had threatened to start executing the Red Air Force prisoners, one every day that a supply plane failed to land at Clermont-Ferrand; Rashidov had told him that if that happened, *he* would be held personally responsible!

Sharof Rashidov had turned on his heel. He had no intention of wasting further time arguing with a sick man in a dank, stinking cellar, when the priority of the moment was to compose a communication with Sverdlovsk confirming what his masters already knew: that any ongoing investment in the alliance with the FI was futile.

The time had come to engineer Maxim Machenaud's downfall or to leave the FI to its fate. His opinion was that overthrowing Machenaud would be a less than straightforward project, and bloody to boot because the hardcore leadership of the Revolutionary Guards – scum of the earth but well-armed and used to all the privileges of belonging to a well-fed, feared elite – would probably put up a fight. There were hundreds of Soviet military 'advisors', many of them Spetsnaz trained and equipped; unfortunately, they were spread all over the south of France, and assembling in and around Clermont-Ferrand ahead of a coup to unseat Machenaud, would be almost impossible to conceal, and thus, the element of surprise could not be assumed.

An assassination might work, it all depended on how the Revolutionary Guard's dispersed command structure responded. The formation had no identifiable chief, each troop or company had its own leader, command hierarchy and broadly speaking, loathed and distrusted all the other troops and companies. For all Rashidov knew, if anything happened to Maxim Machenaud, they might simply liquidate his delegation, or simply hold *him* hostage. Then everybody would be back to square one again; and he would be in a cell at the old Michelin Works.

So, he planned to do what all good apparatchiks did in a situation like the one he found himself in. He was going to pass the decision upstairs and await instructions from the 'big men' in Sverdlovsk.

As to his recommendation to the Troika, that was easy: there comes a time when you simply have to admit to yourself that you cannot argue with a rabid dog. Maxim Machenaud had to go; or the mission in France ought to be abandoned.

In retrospect, now he was back in the relative safety of the mission's headquarters, the only thing which surprised the Commissar Plenipotentiary was that after his stand-up shouting match with Maxim Machenaud, he had not, personally, been taken hostage by the little shit.

Perhaps, he reflected sourly, somewhere in some unscrambled corner of the maniac's head he retained the memory of Leonid Brezhnev's decision to obliterate Bucharest when the Rumanians had – for reasons nobody had ever satisfactorily explained to him but which probably had a lot to do with the local Party leadership having suffered some kind of communal psychotic episode – arrested two visiting members of the then Troika, and tortured that arsehole Yuri Andropov to within an inch of his death.

The sirens were wailing all across Clermont-Ferrand, their unsynchronised banshee cries rolling in discordant waves from one horizon to the other, confined within the ring of mountains surrounding the ancient city.

But now there was another sound.

A fast approaching whistling scream...

Sharof Rashidov barged past the men around him and stepped out onto the cobbles of the Place de Jaude, just at the moment the first two jets thundered overhead so low that tiles showered down around him, and across the square, were ripped off and lifted into the air by the back draft of the ultra-low-flying bombers' thundering turbofans.

Rashidov heard the tiles crashing down, hardly noticed a man standing next to him grunting, and collapsing onto the ground. The deafening roar of another pair of big, dazzle camouflaged aircraft, their under-wing hard-points laden with evil black bombs and what looked like the sort of missile pods carried by the latest MiG-17 and 21 ground-attack variants he had seen demonstrated at the ranges in the Chelyabinsk Military District last year, rocketed over the roof tops at breakneck, impossible speed less than three or four hundred metres away.

He felt the first big explosion through his feet as the earth flinched and the supersonic pressure waves rattled windows before he heard it, a massive, rumbling detonation, the prelude to a drum roll of smaller, repetitive thudding, thumping impacts.

Some part of Sharof Rashidov's mind registered that what he was hearing was a long – a very long line - of bombs striking the earth, or more likely, the tarmac of the airport, three or four kilometres away.

Another pair of fast jets raced across the Place de Jaude.

Rashidov guessed the attackers were using the square and the nearby cathedral as way markers, possibly flying as close as possible to the great twin spires – the most visible position markers in the whole city – to draw them precisely to their targets.

But the bombs he was hearing falling were not from those aircraft...

A second drum-roll of detonations was walking across the volcanic soil of the Auvergne, a little farther away to the east.

"They're shooting off SS-75s," a man said, tugging at Rashidov's sleeve.

Trailing boiling pillars of grey smoke, multiple missiles were ascending into the darkening heavens in search of prey eight miles high. One, two...three four; with at least two widely separated launchers firing salvoes converging on an unseen target...

All the while the sirens were still sounding, a little forlornly, redundantly now.

Faraway, heavy anti-aircraft cannons began to saw at heavens.

There was a new whistling sound.

And a deathly, ear-splitting shriek.

And then an eerie silence, as the falling bomb sliced through the sound barrier and fell, dragging the impossible cacophony of its fall behind it, knifing down silently to all those unknowingly beneath its terminal dive.

The next thing Sharof Rashidov knew he was being picked up off the ground. He gazed in shocked bewilderment at the randomly strewn bloody body parts in the near distance, the great swath of destruction across the other side of the Place de Jaude, before an impenetrable bank of roiling grey smoke choked with pulverised masonry dust roiled over the carnage and he lost consciousness...

Chapter 43

Saturday 11th February 1967
USS United States, San Francisco Bay

Fifty-nine-year-old Lin Chieh, the Permanent Representative to the United Nations of the Republic of China, was the last man to arrive in the stateroom for the late morning meeting his government had been unwilling for him to participate in until less than an hour ago.

George Bush, the United States' Ambassador – why on earth the Americans could not call him 'Permanent Representative', his actual United Nations title, nobody knew – had finally prevailed upon him that 'it would look bad' and 'disappoint the President' if he was a 'no show' at the meeting mooted by the British, and consented to by Bush because it would have been discourteous to have refused.

It went without saying that Lin Chieh was attending under protest. And that he also thought it was a completely pointless exercise.

Whatever game the British were playing it would take a two-thirds majority of the member nations of the United Nations to remove the Republic of China from the 'big five' Permanent Members of the Security Council, or to vote the Communist People's Republic into the UN itself, let alone promote it to, or replace the ROC on the Security Council. Nobody seriously believed that was on the cards, and besides, Lin Chieh would not have the slightest compunction about vetoing any application by the Communists to join the 'UN family'.

In fact, he would not have turned up at all had George Bush not personally reassured him that the People's Republic could stay out in the cold forever, so far as the Nixon Administration was concerned. So, despite his near permanent frown, Lin Chieh was actually, a significantly happier man now than when he had boarded the US Air Force plane which had transported him to San Francisco, via Hawaii, three weeks ago. With the fortuitous departure of Henry Kissinger, what little pressure there had been to include the Communist usurpers in Chongqing in the mainstream of the international community had effectively, evaporated.

The 'United States stands by its commitments to the Republic of China, our Second World War ally,' Bush had unequivocally declared.

Lin Chieh was in no mood to sweeten the pill; he had come to the meeting to 'humour' the British.

Sir Roy Jenkins, his host, was perfectly well aware of this: 'Rome was not built in a day, Margaret,' he had reminded his Prime Minister.

'No,' she had retorted waspishly, 'but we have treaty obligations to the Mainland Chinese and I do not intend to be remembered as one of those British Prime Ministers who reneged on their word. Nor,' she had added, 'do I intend to bow to pressure from the White House on this.'

From What Roy Jenkins had divined, the meeting with President Nixon at the Sequoyah Country Club in Oakland, had been another, albeit smaller scale 'car wreck' on the model of the near disastrous non-meeting of minds at Camp David at the end of last month. The American side had been preoccupied with their own domestic woes and it had been a testy affair all around; hardly a good omen for the two sides co-operation at the United Nations get together.

Today's meeting was a deliberately semi-informal, relaxed occasion with just the Permanent Representatives and a couple of translators in the room, mainly for the benefit of Vasili Vasilyevich Kuznetsov.

The aging, patently unwell Russian had hardly said a word to anybody outside his own Soviet circle since he had been in America, leaving all the talking and the haggling over quarters, security and the domestic arrangements, to Anatoly Dobrynin, whom personally, Kuznetsov knew would be much better employed in the UN role than to go on being wasted as Ambassador in Washington. Not that the Troika listened to an old Foreign Ministry apparatchik like him!

Unfortunately, he got the impression that more than one Politburo member, and perhaps even Alexander Shelepin, did not entirely trust Dobrynin. Old ways, old attitudes died hard. Dobrynin had not stepped foot in the Motherland for five years now; for over a year he had been under house arrest in the United States. Had he been turned? In the good old days, he would simply have been called home and liquidated.

Roy Jenkins had been ambivalent about holding this meeting but Tom Harding-Grayson had insisted. If the Chinese or the Russians boycott it, we can at least say 'we tried', that we 'sought to mediate'; and if they,' specifically, Lin Chieh, 'turn up, you can have your first and probably, last, frank face-to-face exchange of views with representatives of every member of the current Security Council. Trust me, there will not be many opportunities to have a good, old-fashioned row in private going forward!'

The Foreign Secretary had reminded him that if he managed to get the Chinese and the Russians in the same room at the same time, it would be a thing that Cordell Hull, and Lord Halifax, respectively the US Secretary of State and British Ambassador to Washington had failed to do at Dumbarton Oaks in 1944, when the first conference had been held to discuss what should replace the failed League of Nations after the Second War.

Lin Chieh, an Oxford-educated lawyer, had been an advisor to the Chinese delegation at the conferences which had established the League of Nations after the First World War. Later, he had served as First Secretary at the Chinese Embassy in London before the Second War, and as ambassador to the Philippines and Canada, and represented his country at the Dumbarton Oaks Conference in Washington, and at the subsequent San Francisco conclave in 1945 which set up the United Nations.

However, back in 1944, the original United Nations talks had had to be conducted in two separate phases: the first with all the other parties and the Soviets; and the second with the Chinese!

At the time of the October War, like Vasili Vasilyevich Kuznetsov, Lin Chieh had been his country's Permanent Representative in New

York.

"Gentlemen," Roy Jenkins prefaced, waving his guests to seats around the table in the middle of the stateroom as fresh coffee was served by two of Steuart Pringle's immaculately attired Royal Marines. On board the USS United States only US Navy personnel and Secret Service men were permitted to carry firearms, so the Marines probably felt stark naked. Notwithstanding, unaccustomed as they were to stewarding duties, because the two men were Royal Marines, they performed their duties with aplomb. "Thank you all for coming to this tete-a-tete."

He waited briefly while Vasili Kuznetsov's translator caught up.

"It is the British Government's position that the United Nations failed in its primary task in October 1962. Frankly, we are lucky to have a second chance to get things right. I am aware that Lord Harding-Grayson put everybody's nose out of joint yesterday. Deliberately so, gentlemen. If the United Nations is to be a grand talking shop, all well and good. Jaw, jaw is a lot better than war, war. However, if it is to be more than that, the United Nations cannot continue to be an adjunct to world affairs, it must be able to act on, and to genuinely influence the course of events on the world stage."

George Bush stirred.

"That's very high and mighty," he said, "but Congress won't ratify anything I sign up to here on the basis of high-minded moral principles. Heck, twenty years ago Congress would have thrown out the whole Bretton Woods settlement if they hadn't been told, and believed that the US was running the show!"

The United Nations Monetary and Financial Conference, attended by over seven hundred representatives from forty-four nations under the umbrella of the Grand Alliance fighting the Germans and the Japanese, held at the Mount Washington Hotel at Bretton Woods, New Hampshire in July 1944, had established the future regulation of the post-war global financial system. Both the International Bank for Reconstruction and Development, and the International Monetary Fund had emerged out of the Bretton Woods talks, as had systems to manage the convertibility of national currencies, and general commitments to global 'open trade' and to the removal of artificial barriers to free trade. The Bretton Woods settlement remained the basis of international monetary regulation, despite the years of the Cold War, World War III over the Cuban missiles, and the volatile and often bloody chaos of international relations since October 1962.

No diplomat could do much better than to dream of one day designing a treaty which, despite everything thrown at it, had shown such fundamental resilience. In fact, the underlying driving force behind the gathering of the nations on board the USS United States, had a lot more to do with shoring up the Bretton Woods 'system' than it had to do with celebrating 'World peace'.

Restoring order to the international currency markets, attempting to reinvigorate the GATT – General Agreement on Tariffs and Trade – process, and moving to a situation in which the US and the Royal

Navies could stand down, at least in part, from their onerous trade route protection roles; all stood much higher on the British, Commonwealth and American agendas than arcane questions about who, exactly, should sit on the Security Council of a body that had not actually, sat in session for over four years when the World was reeling from a nuclear war.

"I agree that Bretton Woods must be our 'bottom line', George," Roy Jenkins agreed. "However, one cannot help but suspect that had those protocols agreed in New Hampshire been respected more in the spirit than the strict letter, many of the tensions which tore us asunder in 1962, might not have been quite so," he grimaced, "dangerous. Bretton Woods," he extemporised, with scholarly regret, "disadvantaged the poorer, and the less open economies of the post-1945 players..."

George Bush grinned.

"Heck, we're not going to have one of those 'our system is better than yours' fights, are we, Roy?"

Jenkins shrugged.

"No, of course not, George. All I am saying is that mistakes were made back in the 1940s, mistakes we have it in our power to avoid repeating. Whether by design, or from choice, the Soviet Union was excluded from the economic and commercial benefits of the peace of 1945; and inevitably, that deepened the resulting Cold War and was instrumental in what later transpired. In any event, we are where we are," he concluded, unconsciously pushing his glasses back up onto the bridge of his nose.

Aware that he had fallen into the trap of speaking only to one of the other four representatives, Roy Jenkins decided to carry on striking while this, particular iron, remained hot.

"Forgive me, George," Roy Jenkins continued, "I have been in politics most of my adult life. I recognise that it is very easy to be cynical about things. Nonetheless, while I fully understand that President Nixon feels as if he has enough on his plate already, closing off foreign policy options which might be the saving grace of his Presidency in the months and years to come, would be a mistake at this time."

George Bush was intrigued.

"Okay, I'm listening, Roy."

The two men had met last night over drinks in the US suite on board the liner, while the rest of the British Party had returned to the Presidio, where, to everybody's surprise it had been discovered that the senior members of the Soviet delegation had also found sanctuary. As it happened, in a 'lodge' only a couple of hundred yards from that which it occupied.

Apparently, Steuart Pringle's Royal Marines and their KGB counterparts had circled each other warily until the Prime Minister had called off her AWPs, and to a degree, somebody on the other side had told his own security people to do likewise, much to the relief of the US Army and Secret Servicemen terrified of being caught in the middle of a huge diplomatic incident.

Jenkins had already decided that George Bush was a man with whom he could do business; and hoped, fervently, that the other man had come to the same conclusion.

"Several days ago, a force of Red Air Force heavy bombers attacked Villefranche-sur-Mer on the French Riviera," he reported to his fellow representatives.

A flicker of irritation crossed Lin Chieh's face.

Maurice Schumann – who, of course, like the Americans, was fully 'in the know already' about the incident and the subsequent 'rescue' of the surviving ships of the pre-war French Mediterranean Fleet - inadvertently smiled like a Cheshire cat for a moment; then he sobered.

Vasili Kuznetsov's face was unmoving, his eyes inscrutable; unsurprised that nobody had thought fit to keep him abreast of purely 'military matters', regardless of how they might impact, or blow up, ongoing diplomatic initiatives.

George Bush sat back, clasping his hands over his belly.

Apart from the Frenchman none of the others knew where this was going and privately, admired the way Roy Jenkins let them wonder a few seconds longer.

"The objective of the Red Air Force Raid was, presumably, to destroy the surviving ships of the former French Mediterranean Fleet anchored in Villefranche Bay. Several ships were indeed sunk during this attack." Roy Jenkins met Vasili Kuznetsov's granite gaze and held it. "At the time of the attack, three Royal Navy warships were present in the anchorage, and Fleet Air Arm Sea Vixen Interceptors armed with Top Hat air-to-air missiles and thirty-millimetre Aden cannons, were, flying combat air patrols above the Riviera."

Vasili Kuznetsov felt physically sick.

This he tried to hide.

Had British vessels or war planes been damaged or destroyed?

What would that mad woman Thatcher do?

Several nightmare scenarios began to flash before his widening eyes.

Roy Jenkins decided not to keep his guest in suspense overlong. That sort of thing was strictly for the movies. So, with a melodramatic flourish he looked to his wristwatch, an ancient thing with a cracked face.

"About now," he declared, his tone regretful, "strike forces from two Royal Navy fleet carriers, HMS Eagle operating in the Bay of Biscay, and HMS Victorious in the Bay of Lions, and Vulcan V-bombers and Canberra medium bombers - between thirty and forty aircraft, all told – are conducting operations over the Massif Central, attacking targets in and around the city of Clermont-Ferrand, the capital of the so-called Front Internationale."

Jenkins leaned forward, fixing Vasily Kuznetsov with a genuinely sympathetic scrutiny.

"The attack will have lasted about three minutes. In that time higher flying aircraft will have dropped a large number of bombs on the air base at Clermont-Ferrand and precision low-level strikes will have been conducted on a number of military targets within the city. Simultaneously, ground attack and strafing operations will have been conducted against far-flung targets all across the Auvergne. I am also advised that other 'special' operations are presently in progress in the south of France in support of the Free French general offensive in the north."

Roy Jenkins did not have leave to tell, nor did he see any profit in telling, his colleagues on the ad hoc Security Council of the United Nations, that the Prime Minister had, after much soul-searching, green-flagged the Chief of the Defence Staff's request to authorise bombing missions to attempt to decapitate the leadership of the Front Internationale.

"At this time," Roy Jenkins concluded, "After several days of patrolling and skirmishing operations, Allied forces in France are on the move en masse in a general offensive against enemy forces in the south and to secure the Rhine against interlopers from the east."

Vasili Kuznetsov feigned disinterest.

"Why are you speaking of this?" His interpreter stuttered.

"Because several of the aircraft that attacked *Anglo-French* naval forces at Villefranche, flew on to Clermont-Ferrand, to where they were, presumably, given succour by the Front Internationale, a Soviet Krasnaya Zarya proxy."

The Soviet minister shrugged.

However, beneath his mask of indifference he was privately appalled.

Stoically, he said: "I know nothing of this."

Chapter 44

Saturday 12th February 1967
HMS Victorious, 43 nautical miles SSE of Montpellier

The first of the returning De Havilland Sea Vixen FAW2s thumped down onto the carrier's deck far overhead, as Rear Admiral Henry Conyer Leach surveyed the situation board in the dimly-lit Command-Information-Centre (CIC) of his flagship.

The Victorious had launched her aircraft – five Blackburn Buccaneers S2s of 801 Naval Air Squadron and eight De Havilland Sea Vixen FAW2s of 893 Naval Air Squadron - approximately two-hundred-and-twenty nautical miles to the south of Clermont-Ferrand, within fifty miles of the coast near Montpellier.

Simultaneously, out in the Bay of Biscay, HMS Eagle had launched – eleven Buccaneers of No 800 NAS and ten Sea Vixens of 899 NAS – from a position some thirty-five miles off the mouth of the Gironde Estuary, the best part of two-hundred-and-fifty miles, more or less due west of the target. Both carriers had put three Fairey Gannet AEW3 unarmed turboprop aircraft of 849 Squadron, from Flights B and C respectively, in the air nearly an hour in advance of the strike to reconnoitre the routes to the target, and to be in position at the critical moment of initial contact over the Auvergne, to attempt to electronically suppress enemy radar, communications and anti-aircraft and surface-to-air missile guidance systems immediately before, during and afterwards, in the withdrawal phase.

Throughout the operation information uplinks from the Gannets had kept both the Eagle's and Victorious's CICs updated in real-time as to the progress of the mission, including, during its latter stages, painting the ground tracks of the three Avro Vulcans of No 617 Squadron based at Scampton in Lincolnshire, the seven English Electric Canberra B5s of 100 Squadron flying from Wittering in Cambridgeshire, and the three unarmed electronic warfare countermeasures Canberra B6s of 360 Squadron, from Watton in Norfolk.

The Eagle's and the Victorious's Buccaneers had been carrying four one-thousand-pound iron bombs on their external hard points; the Sea Vixens a pair of Top Hat air-to-air missiles and two pods loaded with sixteen 68-millimetre unguided ground attack rockets. Fuel consumption had not been mission-critical for the Buccaneers – which were capable of striking targets up to a thousand miles distant – but all the Sea Vixens were operating with under-wing fuel tanks, which impacted their straight line speed and manoeuvrability by perhaps five percent; but importantly, meant that they could, if necessary loiter over the Auvergne for up to half-an-hour after the end of the attack.

The RAF Vulcans were carrying 'maximum mixed HE' loads of thirty-five five-hundred, one-thousand, and two-thousand-pound free-fall high-explosive iron bombs. Each Canberra carried a single modified four-thousand-pound bunker-busting bomb in its bomb bay, and four five-hundred-pound anti-personnel munitions on under-wing hard points.

The attack plan, although simple in concept was anything but *simple* in execution; not least because it had been developed by three separate staffs – at Strike Command back in England, and by the Operations Staffs of the Eagle and the Victorious – and then had had to be 'aligned' by the Joint Services Operations Group, chaired by the Minister of State, Sir Fitzroy Maclean, MP - at RAF Brize Norton, before being promulgated back to the men charged with carrying it out.

Essentially, the RAF was 'up high' and the Navy was 'down on the deck', with hopefully, the twain never meeting in the target area. The carrier-based Gannets would monitor the 'low' side of business; 360 Squadron's Canberra B6s, one of which was nominated as 'master of ceremonies' would control the 'high' end of the 'party'.

Timing in war, as in life, is everything.

If the Fleet Air Arm's Buccaneers screamed in low over the rooftops of Clermont-Ferrand thirty seconds early, they would attract the attention of every single gun in the city; if they turned up just thirty seconds late, they could easily end up flying through five-tenths falling bombs.

The Vulcans' job was to crater runways and to generally obliterate Clermont-Ferrand airport. The Victorious's Buccaneers were tasked to mop up anything the V-bombers 'missed'. Meanwhile, 100 Squadron's Canberras were going after 'command, control, and infrastructure' targets in and around the city. Among 100 Squadron's targets were command bunkers, a power station, two bridges, a communications tower and several large buildings inside the city thought to be Front Internationale headquarters, barracks, depots or vehicle parks. The big two-ton blockbuster munitions would do their worst; the anti-personnel munitions would prevent assistance reaching the hardest hit targets for hours, possibly days.

War was not nice; and nobody in England or aboard the two aircraft carriers was minded to think otherwise.

Nobody needed to tell the C-in-C of Task Force V1, Henry Leach, exactly how nasty and unpleasant war was; his whole adult life had been turned upside down that day in December 1941 when he had desperately searched the dockside at Sembawang Naval Base at Singapore, as the destroyers Electra, Express and the Vampire landed the bedraggled survivors of the battleship Prince of Wales and the battlecruiser Repulse, sunk by Japanese aircraft the previous day. As each destroyer docked and offloaded its cargo of shocked and injured men, he had searched in vain to be reunited with his father, John Leach, the captain of the Prince of Wales: to no avail, for he had gone down with his ship, one of the three-hundred-and-twenty-seven men who had perished on the battleship in what was, for the Royal Navy, probably the most humiliating defeat of the 1939-45 war at sea.

All things being equal, Henry Leach accepted, it was as well not to allow human frailty, or even decency to enter into military planning. One's duty was to one's own side, one's own men, and to be extremely careful in whom one trusted, and intensely suspicious of any blandishments to rely upon luck or good fortune to make good any deficiencies in one's preparation or professional competence of others.

Given that no air-to-air interdiction – that is, fighter intercepts – were expected either en route to, or over the target, the two carriers' Sea Vixens had been assigned a particular role all of their own. Previous ELINT - electronic surveillance - flights over the Auvergne had identified the signatures of short-range guidance radars consistent with those of the deadly Soviet surface-to-air missile systems encountered over Iraq, and elsewhere since the October War. It was the Sea Vixens' job to hunt down the suspected SS-75 batteries sited in the extinct volcanic mountains surrounding Clermont-Ferrand. Once a battery flushed its birds there was no way to hide its location; and that was where the rocket pods under the fighters' wings came in.

Henry Leach was in a bullish frame of mind.

To his mind the Clermont-Ferrand show was just the ticket.

Planning for it had commenced several days before Task Force V1 had departed Gibraltar and the need to keep his 'strike assets' rested and ready, and to avoid operations likely to deplete his squadron's 'punch' in the interim, had very nearly forced him to order the premature destruction or scuttling of the French Fleet at Villefranche. In retrospect, that would have been a damned shame but thankfully, Dermot O'Reilly, with his customary good sense and a large slice of luck, had managed to extricate the surviving French ships and mother goose them all the way south to Malta with a bare minimum of casualties. Well, leastways, on the Royal Navy's account, the unfortunate French had lost well over three hundred dead and missing, presumed drowned, according to O'Reilly's latest count, in that blasted Russian bombing raid.

Leach comforted himself with the knowledge that but for Dermot O'Reilly's Fletchers throwing up a distracting barrage the Soviets might have done for the whole French fleet!

It paid to be grateful for small mercies.

He guessed the public relations people in Malta were having a field day with the new French recruits to the cause! No doubt, when the news broke about today's operation the papers back home would shout headlines proclaiming the double body blows inflicted on those Krasnaya Zarya bastards in the Auvergne...

It seemed that a 100 Squadron Canberra and one of the Eagle's Sea Vixens were missing over enemy territory. The fate of the crews was as yet, unknown.

There was another thud overhead.

That was another aircraft down safely.

Even with the under-wing fuel tanks his Sea Vixens would be getting thirsty soon. The weather had been marginal earlier in the day, and it was no better now. The first time he had served on board a carrier he had spent endless hours watching air operations in all weathers, marvelling at the skills of the men who hurtled off the bow, hurled like a crossbow bolt, and landing back aboard, seemingly throwing their screaming steeds at the stern traps...

Thump!

The roar of jets, throttles pressed up against the stops, faded instantly telling all those below that the aircraft had caught a wire. Already, the fighter's wings would be folding inward, and deck crews waving it towards a parking space or the forward elevator; the next aircraft would be approaching, the traps – steel hawsers raised off the wet deck, tensioned hydraulically – would be scraping back into position across the wet steel. There was nowhere at sea, or possibly, on land, more intense than the deck of an aircraft carrier at sea at night recovering its birds.

Thump!

In the background the 'Air Circuit' was open so that the men in the CIC could remain, viscerally, in contact with the real world of carrier flight operations in their cocooned, de-humanised cave buried deep in the bowels of the ship.

"WAVE OFF! WAVE OFF!"

For several of the pilots in the returning planes this would be their first experience of real, shooting operations. It was to be expected that even men with tens, possibly scores or more of carrier landings in their log books, having recently undergone the trial of battle – life or death – faced with a night landing back on Victorious as the ship battered into a relenting, none the less fierce 'blow', were on high-energy personal journeys of pure, unremitting self-discovery.

Henry Leach glanced up at the radar repeaters on the nearby bulkhead. The Kent and the Belfast were giving the Flagship a wide berth, respectively one and two miles to starboard and port. Farther out the four destroyers and two frigates of the 21st Destroyer Squadron formed the outer ring of the Task Force, with the assault ship, HMS Fearless just inside the protective screen some seven miles to port.

More than once Leach had considered peremptorily ordering Dermot O'Reilly and the Campbeltown to re-join the fleet at best speed; stopped himself each time. However, once the French ships had been extracted from Villefranche, politically, they had assumed near iconic stature amongst the Free French and getting them to safety had suddenly become Task Force V1's absolute top priority.

Henry Leach chuckled under his breath.

Dermot O'Reilly's three Fletchers would have topped off their bunkers by dawn; after that he might be back in contact with the Task Force within as little as twenty-four hours. For Dermot's speedy greyhounds, a fast seven to eight hundred mile run in a day was nothing.

Thump!

The instant a pilot felt his wheels touch he thrust the throttles into the red.

High-performance jets did not so much land, as crash onto the deck of a carrier and were brought to a sudden, juddering halt within fifty yards by the traps, throwing crewmen forward into their straps like rag dolls.

Arrested, the pilot swiftly throttled back to idle.

The aircraft moved off the traps.

Already the Landing Deck Officer (LDO) and his crew would be studying the next aircraft lining up for approach. The pilot would already have his eyes on the landing board: red was too high, green okay, yellow too low. Multiple reds or yellows meant a fly around; yet everybody knew that men who only watched the lights, or fixated, counting the dots were the sort of men who flew into the stern or regularly overshoot the traps.

Attitude, speed, rate of descent, am I on the right flight path...or not.

The LDO would be watching the lights like a hawk, the wave off man with his big white paddles constantly acted as if he was in the cockpit, indicating if the incoming aircraft's wings were level. Just before landing he would fold those paddles across his chest to authorise the pilot to put down; if something was wrong, he would be the one that did the waving off.

Him, the Flight Crew in the Operations Centre in the island bridge superstructure and anybody else who had arms to wave!

If in doubt: wave off!

Every deck landing was analysed, assessed, picked over by the LDO and his team. It sounded arcane, to be judged by one's peers every time one survived a landing but when you were dumping a fifteen-ton fast jet – 'empty' a Sea Vixen was thirteen tons and a Buccaneer fourteen, so both would be around fifteen or sixteen tons for most landings, especially if a fellow still had ordnance on board - on a tiny, moving metal airfield in the middle of a big, cold sea that did not give a damn if you lived or died, it paid to remember that your first bad mistake was liable to be your last one too.

Thump!

Henry Leach thought that landing sounded different, heavier.

That had to be one of *his* Buccaneers landing.

Chapter 45

Sunday 12th February 1967
United Kingdom Embassy, Washington DC

Sir Nicholas 'Nicko' Henderson had been looking forward to tucking into a relaxed family luncheon on his arrival back at 3100 Massachusetts Ave NW, from church that morning. However, he and his wife Mary and teenage daughter Alexandra had been intercepted as they entered the residence, rudely spoiling any notion of a quiet family meal.

It seemed that a certain Lady Rachel French had, apparently 'turned up unannounced', if not to say, 'out of the blue' and asked to speak to the Ambassador.

The Duty Officer, a relatively junior member of Chancery Section newly arrived from England, had not really known what to do with the lady. Nor had he asked her for proof of her identity, asked the Security Department to do more than simply accompany her to the waiting room in the public area of the main building, nor had they had her searched, as was the normal drill for any person not expected at the compound.

"She claims to be the wife of Air Marshal Sir Daniel French..."

A claim made problematic to the young officer since the lady had a discernible 'Eastern European accent' and was dressed 'somewhat in the fashion of a...model.'

Henderson had apologised to his wife.

"I shall be late joining you for lunch," he bemoaned ruefully.

Mary Henderson accepted this without demur; life was never dull at the Embassy in Washington!

The Ambassador gave orders for 'Lady French' and any belongings she had brought with her to be searched in the normal way; and, assuming nothing untoward resulted, thereafter for her to be escorted to his office.

He would have asked the chargé d'affaires to join him but his deputy was staying with old friends in Connecticut that weekend; the poor fellow was still recovering from his latest brush with ill-health since his arrival in America last year.

Sir Nicholas was still a little miffed not to have been 'in on the ground floor' at the re-inauguration of the United Nations in San Francisco. That said, from what he was hearing the whole affair was something of a dog's breakfast. Foreign Office colleagues accompanying the Prime Minister on the West Coast, were appalled by their hosts' attitude and the cack-handed organisation on board the USS United States with diplomats and delegates being treated as 'virtual prisoners.'

In any event, no matter how he felt about missing out on the West Coast jamboree – Mary and Alexandra would have loved to visit San Francisco – as things had turned out, it was probably for the best that he had stayed behind in DC to 'mind the shop.'

In fact, the more he thought about the aftermath of the Camp David summit, and the mixed messages which were still seeping out of the woodwork, vis-à-vis the still, moderately rude health of the US-UK reconciliation, contrasted with the astonishing revelations emerging about Operation Maelstrom, he was ever more convinced that he was almost certainly, in the right place at the right time. His deputy was a fine fellow with immense experience of government and pre-October 1962 diplomacy but he had yet to establish good relations with key operators on the Hill, and he really had not come to terms with the changed realities of the modern age, bless him...

For example, he would definitely have got so hot under the collar about *The Washington Post's* allegations concerning the CIA's surveillance operation, and the activities of the 'dirty tricks department' of the Office of Security at Langley, directed in the main at the persons of Henderson's predecessors in Philadelphia and DC, Sir Peter and Lady Marija Christopher and their staff, that he would have almost certainly sparked a new diplomatic rift with the Nixon Administration. Yes, on balance, it had been for the best that he and Mary had still been in Washington to face down, and generally play down the outrage Her Majesty's Government was entitled to express, and to blithely assure all and sundry that the 'special relationship' was alive, kicking and all in all, in remarkably fine fettle.

Nicko had been careful not to rise to the bait; to answer every barbed question from the press pack encamped outside the Embassy gates that: one, nobody in England took the allegations very seriously, and; two, that even if there was 'some minor substance' in the 'rumours', it was nothing that 'good friends' could not 'get over.'

Privately, he was mightily disappointed with more than one 'old friend' at the State Department and elsewhere in the DC machine. There had been times in recent days when he had been too angry to talk to anybody at State, and only yesterday he had registered a formal, albeit confidential, letter of protest to the Deputy Head of Protocol demanding a full explanation of his hosts' blatant flouting of the Vienna Convention on Diplomatic Immunity. In fact, the more he learned about Operation Maelstrom and the CIA's, and the FBI's, failed attempts to spy on Peter and Marija, and their closest friends and colleagues, digging for dirt, anything to discredit, or possibly, to blackmail them with, the more disgusted the British Ambassador became. So, underneath his easy-going, Devil may care public persona that he continued to present to the American media, he was silently fuming. Moreover, he very much doubted he was going to forgive, let alone forget, any of the transgressions against him, his family, his friends or his country, suffered at the hands of his country's...*allies*.

Only one thing about the whole sorry affair really mystified him. By all accounts, the Prime Minister had remained, relatively speaking, beatifically 'calm' about the whole dismal farrago. It probably helped that he had Tom Harding-Grayson and Airey Neave at her side, and between them those two old rogues were no angels, both rascals on a par with Allen Dulles and J. Edgar Hoover any day of the week; albeit Nicko suspected rather shrewder practitioners of the dark arts, and, heaven forfend, nowhere near as brazen as their American counterparts.

Henderson had long ago, determined not to inquire too deeply into the world of the late Sir Dick White, the United Kingdom's spymaster supreme. It was salutary to remind oneself that the CIA and the FBI did not have the monopoly, any more than the KGB, on duplicity and the foulest of foul double-dealing...

"Nicko," Rachel smiled impatiently, "it is positively freezing in that dreadful waiting room your people put me in!"

Henderson waved for his guest's escorting security man – a middle-aged, balding former Special Branch officer – to leave the room before coming around his desk to greet his unwanted visitor.

"You'll forgive me if I am almost afraid to ask what I can do for you, Lady French," the British Ambassador admitted, shaking Rachel's hand and planting a cursory peck on the cheek she offered. "Or are you presently operating under one of your more arcane aliases?"

Rachel shook her head.

"No," she replied.

"Hopefully, Mary will be organising a pot of tea for us. The normal staff don't work on Sundays. We shut down most of the Embassy over the weekend these days, we can't afford to pay the American clerical and ancillary staff, you see. Hopefully, the pound will clamber up to parity with the dollar one day before I retire!"

Rachel smiled.

If Nicko Henderson had been a typical Foreign Office apparatchik she would not have risked coming within a country mile of the Embassy. However, if he had been just another diplomatic time server, hide-bound and unimaginative, his life dictated by red tape and the latest FCO dogmas, Tom Harding-Grayson would never have sent him to the USA, or so forcefully have insisted that he was the best man to buttress, and subsequently replace the Christopher regime. The Machiavellian Foreign Secretary had never been a big fan of Sir Peter Christopher's regime, the man he called 'the accidental ambassador'; in hindsight a rare misstep by the old fox, because Peter and Marija had been exactly the sort of people, possibly the only people in Christendom who could have plotted, or stumbled – it hardly mattered which – through the catastrophic denouement of Anglo-American diplomatic relations in the wake of the Wister Park atrocity. And thereafter, somehow save them all from the consequences of the unmitigated disaster of the Kennedy Administration's bizarre – she assumed, drug-induced – policy in the Middle East back in 1964.

Back in July 1964 maniacs had stormed the Embassy and murdered Lord Franks, his wife and practically the whole British diplomatic community in America while, to all appearances, the Philadelphia PD and the US Army, who were supposed to be protecting the Wister Park Compound, had looked on, reluctant to fire live ammunition into a rioting crowd. And then the news of the battles in the Persian Gulf had exploded across America; British and Commonwealth ships had been attacked by the US Navy, in retaliation the RAF had sunk the USS Kitty Hawk, by a few feet and tons, at the time the biggest warship in the world and savagely mauled the great ship's escorting task force. Thousands of American Navy-men were dead; the two old allies were seemingly on the verge of nuking each other's cities...and then Peter and Marija had bearded LBJ, then only hours into his brief, crisis-riven Presidency on the steps of the Philadelphia White House, and on nationwide, networked TV, implored Johnson to 'give peace a chance.'

Most Americans had instantly fallen in love with Peter and Marija, particularly the little sparkling-eyed Maltese princess...

All Nicko had tried to do since his friends had departed was to carry on the good work, despite having been sent a deputy, the former Conservative politician Sir Arthur Soames; a grandee appointed to the Washington mission as a concession to his ill-health, possibly with a view to his gentle rehabilitation ahead of re-joining the political mainstream in a ministerial post in Margaret Thatcher's government at some stage. Unfortunately, Soames, although a gentleman to the core, clearly thought he ought to be the Ambassador and often, seemed to regard Henderson as a usurper, and for reasons best known to himself, felt that a 'much harder line' needed to be taken with 'the Americans'.

It did not help that Soames represented that contrary – flying in the face of all the evidence – faction within the FCO that honestly believed, God alone knew why – that the 'Christopher Regime' had been a disaster.

Sometimes, it occurred to Nicko Henderson that all the wrong people had got blown up on that night back in late October 1962!

The Ambassador settled in a deep chair opposite Rachel and viewed her with thoughtful wariness. Peter, Marija, Alan and Rosa Hannay had befriended Rachel. That went back to their time together on Malta, of course. Although, he did not know the lady very well, mostly by hearsay truth be told, he struggled with the notion that his friends could ever have been so friendly, or at ease, unafraid of the woman sitting in his office. There were fools who claimed this was because they had had no idea who, or what she was; wrongly in his estimation, because Peter and Marija had known exactly what Rachel was and what she was capable of, long before the Wister Park bloodbath. Peter Christopher had turned up at the hospital when the US Marine Corps was guarding Rachel like 'Christ come to cleanse the Temple,' according to more than one account...

"I heard that your number two, Sir Arthur, was out of town," the woman said. "I don't think he'd approve of me paying a house call."

"No, possibly not."

"He's old school, Nicko. There are still a lot of people like him around, even now. You'd think the last four years had never happened." She sobered. "Is it true you went with Anthony Eden to visit Hitler's bunker in 1945?"

Henderson guffawed.

He had known enough spooks, brushed shoulders with countless of their kind down the years; he was not surprised that the woman probably knew a lot more about him than he ever would about her. That was the nature of the game.

Okay, Rachel wanted to shadow box for a while before she got down to business.

It cost him nothing to oblige her.

"Yes. When I came back from Cairo in 1944, Sir Anthony was kind enough to take me on as an assistant private secretary. When the war in Europe was over, Sir Anthony took me on a trip to Berlin. The whole city was in ruins, much as it is again now, I suppose. The Fuhrer Bunker was a dreadful mess, there were still clothes on the floor, the place had been ransacked by the Red Army. I think the ruins of the Chancellery left a deeper lasting impression on me; there were piles of Iron Crosses on the floor," he paused, met Rachel's stare unflinchingly, "but then you know what Berlin was like just after the war. For all I know you might have been one of the scarecrows I saw scavenging in the rubble when I was with Eden."

"After the end of the war?" Rachel considered a moment. "I never needed to scavenge. The Yanks paid well for a skinny girl who didn't cry."

Henderson sighed, opened his mouth to speak, shut it again when there was a knock at the door.

Mary Henderson and the Ambassador's daughter, grimacing shyly brought in a tea tray.

Rachel rose to her feet and hugged the other woman.

"My, you've grown up," she smiled to Alexandra who must have shot up several inches since she had seen her last.

Rachel understood how hard it was for them not to stare at her. It had been so much easier to believe that she was a normal person when Marija and Rosa had been around; people had had plenty of time to fill them in on precisely what manner of evil, they had inadvertently tolerated in their midst in...the old days.

"I don't bite," she promised. "Whatever they've told you since I left."

Soon she was alone again with Nicko Henderson.

"You are right to be afraid to inquire what I might ask of you, Nicko," Rachel remarked, watching the man pour tea into a bone china cup.

He passed her the cup and saucer before dribbling milk from a small silver jug into his own, and splashing tea into it. He raised the cup to his lips, viewed Rachel over the rim.

"I was being facetious earlier, dear lady."

"No," she disagreed, pursing her lips. "I think you're sitting in the hottest diplomatic seat in the world because Tom Harding-Grayson, bless his twisted little heart, thinks that you're the cleverest man he knows. Either that, or you know some of those nasty little secrets from the good old days that he tries so hard to hide. And if you know any of those kinds of secrets, then well, you're probably one of the shrewdest men left standing these days. So, no, I don't think you were being facetious, dear man."

"Oh, that's a shame," Henderson sighed, "in that case, you'd better put your cards on the table. Or do I need to drink poison first?"

Rachel smiled sweetly.

"Hemlock," she suggested.

"On second thoughts, I'll wait and hear what you have to say. If it's all the same to you."

Rachel hesitated, which was ridiculous. She knew what she had to say, how she was going to say it and why she could no longer freelance.

She needed Henderson's help.

Yet she hesitated.

The reason the Prime Minister had *not* wanted the Ambassador in the mix in San Francisco was because James Angleton's people were searching for ways to undermine and discredit him, just as assiduously as they had tried and singularly failed, to damage his predecessor. Except, unlike in the 'Christopher case', in Henderson's case – a man with a twenty-year history in the Diplomatic Service – the CIA had a career ready-made to be falsely embellished, with hearsay and manufactured evidence inserted at strategic points, a narrative ready and waiting to be spun to take the heat off the Administration if the United Nations talks went as badly as people in the State Department anticipated.

Henderson had been President of the Oxford Union in his time at Hertford College; openly socialist in his youth, the member of a Fabian circle that included contemporaries like Sir Roy Jenkins, he had been a personal friend of the pre-war leader of the Labour Party, Hugh Gaitskell and still was with Anthony Crosland, a minister in Margaret Thatcher's original Unity Administration of the United Kingdom. Having survived childhood tuberculosis, he had been rejected by the armed forces in the Second War, serving as Assistant Private Secretary to both Sir Anthony Eden, and his successor as Foreign Secretary, Ernest Bevan. In a varied and successful career, he had worked in Athens, Vienna and Santiago, Chile, as well as serving a stint in Washington before the October War, at the time of which he had been Head of the Foreign Office's Northern Department.

There was nothing remotely suspicious or untoward in Henderson's diplomatic service; but that would not have stopped the CIA's Office of Security warping innocent facts, or chance contacts into question marks, or more likely, falsifying and inventing 'evidence' to use against him...*at need*.

"You haven't asked me why I'm not in California with the Prime Minister's party?" She asked.

"Somebody tampered with the cockpit controls of Commonwealth One," Henderson retorted quietly. "That was what I was told, anyway. In any event, it gave you an opportunity to do a flit."

"Somebody?" Rachel murmured.

The Ambassador shrugged, put down his cup and saucer and swept the rebellious, a little overlong lock of hair off his brow,

"Possibly, a maintenance issue," he reconsidered. "One tends to be overly suspicious about these things nowadays, especially when they are so conveniently timed. Who else knows you have returned to DC?"

"Only the people who followed me after I met Professor Caroline Constantis-Zabriski in Georgetown. CIA, FBI, I have no idea which. It could have been the Mob, or the Teamsters, for all I know. This country is a lot more messed up than it thinks it is, Nicko. And no, I don't think I was followed here. They won't know I'm here, or was here, until tomorrow. As you say, you can't afford to employ Americans at the weekend."

"Okay, but I'm still none the wiser, dear lady."

"Sorry. Just so that you know, this isn't one of Dick White's little legacy wheezes. I saw him six months ago, before the cancer had hollowed him out. Just to say goodbye."

"You're working for Airey now?"

"Yes and no. This is more a personal sort of thing. I think I may have stumbled over something. Something big. A conspiracy, I suppose. Everything's got a little mixed up because of *The Post's* big scoop about Operation Maelstrom. I could have done without that, it has..."

"Muddied the waters?"

Rachel nodded.

"I think the CIA had, probably still have, people imbedded in what's left of the so-called resistance. Whatever... They brought back a man I know from the old days – Kurt Mikkelsen - to," she quirked a grimace, "*disrupt* the bad guys, which he's done. Very successfully, actually. Except, not in the way it planned. That woman he murdered down in San Antonio, Marilyn de Witt, the heiress, I reckon she was working for the Company, embedded in the resistance, what was left of it. When her father died – he's dying of cancer now – she'd have been perfectly placed to starve the Southern Resistance of funding, then people like Angleton would have rolled it up and flaunted the CIA's success in the FBI's face. I have no idea if Kurt knew what he was doing; or even if Angleton and his reptiles told him whose side that poor woman was on. Anyway, far from rolling up the resistance down in the South, I suspect the whole network – what's left of it – will have gone underground now. But that's somebody else's problem..."

Nicko Henderson blanched at this.

A possibly innocent, patriotic citizen working for the Central Intelligence Agency had been murdered, literally hung out to dry, left to her fate, by her own Government and Rachel was shrugging it off as if it was some kind of tiresome, incidental detail!

The woman was viewing him thoughtfully.

"Don't be so shocked, Nico," she soothed. "Nixon's the sort of man who appoints an operator like Richard Helms to run Langley. The White House was fine about Angleton feeding it dirt about its political opponents back around the time of the California Primary in the summer of 1964. It was before your time in America but if somebody hadn't leaked all those nasty rumours about that crooked bond issue when Nelson Rockefeller was Governor of New York... Remember, the one John Mitchell wrote the false prospectus for? Maybe Nixon wouldn't have polled well enough to even remain in contention? Who do you think told his campaign that the Reverend King was involved with a white woman? Angleton, Helms, all the others, Hoover too, I should imagine, were all pining for the good old days under Ike again by then. So, it's not as if we are dealing with people who give a damn if an asset, here or there, has to be burned for the greater good of the Company, or the Bureau, or," Rachel shrugged, "the Presidency. Marilyn de Witt was just collateral damage to these people. It'll be budget setting time again soon: why would they roll up the Southern Resistance when its continued existence justifies year-on-year increases on CIA and FBI funding estimates? Set against that greater *good*, what's the rape, torture and murder of a woman half-a-continent away?"

Henderson took a deep breath.

"Do you know any of this for a fact, Rachel?"

"Now that Dick White is gone, nobody knows the real 'facts' about the things I have done for," Rachel quirked a wry smile, "my adopted country."

The British Ambassador vented a sigh.

"The trouble is," Rachel went on, "that Kurt's gone rogue. I think he's figured out he's being used. It is not beyond the bounds of possibility, that he's gone after the people he's decided are the real 'enemies within'."

Nicko Henderson was parsing what he had been told.

He was still waiting to hear what any of this had to do with him.

Or his country.

"How did you get back to DC from Nebraska?" He asked, genuinely curious.

"Airey handed me the roll of greenbacks he keeps for emergencies. He's an old softie at heart. I don't think wanted me 'bushwhacking' innocent passers-by to survive."

"Why wasn't I warned you were coming here?"

"The Embassy? That wasn't part of the plan. Kurt Mikkelsen isn't the only one who has gone rogue, Nicko. But now I've spoken to Professor Constantis – you don't need to know why that may turn out to have been very important, by the way – I've come to the conclusion that hiding is going to be counter-productive."

"Why?"

"Because I intend to help you to do the Administration, the CIA, the FBI and whoever else is involved in this filthy business a huge favour. One day, people in this town will remember that, even if they'll never say it in public. Not ever."

Henderson was getting impatient.

"Don't look so disapproving, Nicko," Rachel comforted him. "In a wilderness of mirrors; what will the spider do? Suspend its operations, or will the weevil delay?"

This simply added to the Ambassador's bewilderment.

Now the bloody woman was quoting T.S. Eliot at him!

"The problem is that I haven't a snowflake's chance in Hell of tracking down the man, Kurt Mikkelsen, I am hunting. Not before he's killed again and again, leastways."

This, Henderson concluded was not a conversation the woman would have conducted with Peter Christopher!

But then Nicko had never pretended he was that gallant, understandably honourably naïve knight errant hero; he was, despite all appearances to the contrary, a seasoned and very hard-nosed diplomat, who had had more than a passing acquaintance with the secret world in the last two decades.

"So, what's the plan?"

"The man I plan to kill," Rachel said unemotionally, "or be killed by, is known to the CIA as Billy the Kid. He is the most dangerous man I have ever met. We were once, briefly, partners. Shortly, he will know that I am in this city. And then I will become the hunted, not the hunter."

"I repeat, what's the plan, Rachel?"

"Simple, I make it very easy for *him* to find me."

"That's no plan at all!"

Rachel gave Henderson a disappointed look.

Men, why did one always have to draw them a diagram!

Chapter 46

Sunday 12th February 1967
Headquarters, 4th Royal Tanks Battle Group, Blaye

All things considered, twenty-five-year-old Royal Marines Lieutenant Jeremy John Durham 'Paddy' Ashdown, had had a very busy time of it since the world went stark staring, raving mad that night in late October 1962. He had been in Singapore at the time, where he had learned to speak Malay, he would claim in the mess because one day he was told – possibly apocryphally – that there was a single word in that language for 'let's take off our clothes and tell dirty stories!' Subsequently, he had discovered he had an unsuspected natural flair for learning languages. In Borneo he had mastered Dayak, in the Mediterranean he flirted with Maltese, a baffling Semitic tongue descended from Siculo-Arabic and corrupted over the centuries by Sicilian and English, and since he had been in France, taken to colloquial French with the alacrity that a 'real' Royal Marine takes to canoeing!

His corps' special forces had been members of the Special Boat Section when he joined it, these days it was a fully-fledged *Squadron*. This however, was probably the least significant of the countless changes he had witnessed in his still relatively short military career; but then they lived in strange and more than somewhat troubled times, and he was at heart, a very sensible, very professional soldier.

The eldest of seven children – five of whom had initially survived the Cuban Missiles War but only three, himself included remained alive today – he had been born in New Delhi, the son of an officer in the Indian Army, 14th Punjab Regiment, and a mother who had been a nurse in the Queen Alexandria's Royal Army Nursing Corps. Brought up on a pig farm in County Down in Ulster after the Second War, he had been sent to Bedford School in England aged eleven, where his Northern Ireland accent had given rise to his nickname, a thing he had always embraced with pride, of 'Paddy'. From earliest boyhood, always destined for a military career he had joined the Royal Marines in 1959.

Another thing he was proud of was – because anybody who got to know him recognised he had a stubborn, contrary streak a mile wide when it came to matters of principle, what was right and what was wrong, and so forth - that his father had *almost* got himself court martialled on the honourable grounds that he refused to leave men behind on the retreat to Dunkirk in May 1940. Moreover, he was unrepentedly unapologetic about having never been a heart and soul team player at school. In his book, no man was no use to man nor beast if he was not true to himself.

This mantra had long since, become his solace in a world gone mad.

In Malaya he had seen the bodies of men and women murdered because they adhered to the 'wrong' religion; in an Indonesian creek he had canoed around the wrecks of a Dutch aircraft carrier and its escorts, and on the nearest shores, discovered the mass graves of the hundreds of murdered men who had survived the mining and missile attack on those gutted steel carcasses, half-sunk in the shallow inshore waters where the fleet had taken shelter in the immediate aftermath of the war to end all wars.

Axiomatically, as soon as he got home to England, he had trained to be a swimmer-canoeist to qualify for his corps' elite Special Boat Squadron. He had been doing his level best – off and on, with short spells back in the United Kingdom on R and R, or training in the Highlands or on Dartmoor - to thoroughly confound Her Majesty's enemies in France, for most of the last eighteen months.

He had heard about the former Red Army general attached to Brigadier Edwin Bramall's staff; but not met him until that day, having been out and about in the country – on one or other of the banks of the flooded Gironde Estuary in the last fortnight – reconnoitring in preparation for Operation Blondie.

Presently, he was not wholly comfortable delivering his report in front of Major General Sergey Fyodorovich Akhromeyev, the forty-three-year-old former Spetsnaz officer, and commander of the now defunct White Brigade, by far the most resilient and 'awkward' of the 'independent' groups that he and his men, had had the misfortune to encounter last summer and autumn.

Ashdown had spent a month in hospital back in England after one such chance 'meeting' with Akhromeyev's fighters. One of his men had not been so fortunate. Now he was being expected to treat the Russian as a friend and ally!

Edwin Bramall had introduced the two men.

"Lieutenant Ashdown lost a man in a skirmish with your people last August, Sergey," the commander of 4th Royal Tanks informed the stoic Russian, who looked fit and lean in his British Army battledress fatigues. "Paddy himself was wounded in that affair."

"I lost good people, men and women, every time we 'skirmished' with your Special Forces, Edwin," Akhromeyev retorted unapologetically. "This is a stupid bloody war and the faster *we* win it the better!"

Paddy Ashdown tried not to make a habit of interrupting a conversation between two general officers, so he held his tongue, reserving judgement. He noted that Akhromeyev's English was a little laboured, which raised questions about how well he understood what was being said to him.

He realised the Russian was looking directly at him.

"Operation Blondie? I wish to come along," he frowned at Ashdown, searching for the right words, "to observe."

"I can't have my chaps worrying about an *observer*, sir," Ashdown retorted. "Especially, not a General!"

Not so long ago, Sergey Akhromeyev would have reacted violently to this challenge. However, apart from the fact his new English friends would have regarded this as intolerably 'bad form', and just not the 'done thing', he accepted that intemperance on his part would do nothing to help his case.

He grimaced, fixed the young Royal Marine officer in his level, unblinking gaze.

"You think the war in France will go on for another six months, or a year. Maybe longer, no?"

Both the other men nodded.

"You are wrong. From what I have learned, and what I have seen here in the last few days, I do not believe my Commando back in Hereford," again the Russian struggled to trawl up appropriate words, "will not be needed here. I wish to strike a blow against those FI bastards before it is all over..."

"Operation Blondie is a raid, sir," Paddy Ashdown protested. "A raid and no more. We go in, we knock out specific targets, we get out again, get back to base to report, debrief and update the global intelligence picture..."

Sergey Akhromeyev groaned in mild frustration: "If it was not for the flooding the war would already be over in the west."

Edwin Bramall coughed.

The three men were standing at a map table studying a relief of the Gironde Estuary, which showed the dispositions of 4th Tanks and the suspected enemy 'strong points' on the south bank above Bordeaux. Very little was known about the defences of the city itself. However, Akhromeyev, having had several days to assess the situation on the ground, viewed the absence of stay-behind insurgents, and the relatively small number of booby traps left behind in the villages and along the roads of the districts around Blaye, as indicative of a disorganised enemy who had left in a hurry and who did not plan on coming back any time soon.

Therefore, now was the time to hit the enemy as hard as possible with whatever forces could be scraped together; the enemy was not just playing dead; he might already be as good as expired!

"Besides," Sergey Akhromeyev grunted, "I don't want to have to go home and explain why I didn't kill any of the bastards while I was in France!"

Paddy Ashdown had to concede that he saw where the former Red Army man was coming from, even if he did not wholly agree with him.

"We have some indications that the Bordeaux garrison has been reinforced since the autumn, General," he objected. "We also suspect that supplies from outside France were probably getting into Bordeaux and the Medoc from the outside world until at least last summer. Personally, I don't hold with rumours that the city is the Front Internationale's 'Stalingrad of the West', I think that's probably just Krasnaya Zarya propaganda; but I do think there may be tens of thousands of people still in the city and possibly a larger garrison than that of say, Clermont-Ferrand or Lyon, of as many as several thousand combat effectives..."

Edwin Bramall called a halt to the debate before it got overly heated.

"Paddy, you and General Akhromeyev find a quiet corner and draw me up a plan to find out what we're up against in Bordeaux. By all means blow things up and snipe at the leadership cadre, if the beggars are identifiable. Just remember that what I really want to know is if Sergey's 'feel' for what's going on to the south and across the other side of the Estuary, is a better appreciation of the tactical situation than the one we're working with at the moment." He drew breath. "Whatever form Operation Blondie takes *you* will remain in command. General Akhromeyev, if he accompanies you will be present in a supernumerary capacity only. Any questions?"

Chapter 47

Sunday 12th February 1967
USSR Lodge, The Presidio, San Francisco

Vasili Vasilyevich Kuznetsov had got to his feet and walked out of the interminable now two-day old plenary session of the Grand Assembly. This was not on account of having to listen to the repeated contentions of most of the representatives of the smaller and all of the unaligned nations, not to mention those under the thumb of the People's Republic of China, that both the Soviet Union and the United States were equally to blame for the October War, and should henceforth make full restitution to 'the whole of humanity' for their heinous transgressions. No, he got to his feet and led his small delegation off the USS United States because he had been instructed to so do, at an appropriate juncture in the middle of a speech by a 'country of no consequence'.

It happened that the Prime Minister of Botswana, Sir Seretse Khama had been speaking, eloquently and with none of the bile of previous delegates, at the time Kuznetsov had risen, stiffly to his feet. Khama had been appealing for a more just world in which intellectual and natural resources were shared fairly and the latest medical and scientific discoveries were used for the benefit of all Mankind.

Vasili Kuznetsov would have been sympathetic had such a world order been remotely feasible, which it was not because everything he had learned, during his over-long life, had taught him that the human condition mitigated against it.

It was crystal clear that the United Nations was not going to be in any sense, 'united', other than on paper, here in San Francisco. The indifference of the Americans, the intransigent attitude of the British and the general atmosphere of recrimination and resentment presented towering, unassailable hurdles. Cynically, the reconstitution of the United Nations in an incarnation similar to that prior to October 1962 suited none of the big players. The international chess board had changed out of all recognition since 1945, and the Cuban Missiles War had kicked over an already discredited, failed geopolitical system. The only country that had not come to terms with this new reality was the United States.

It had taken over an hour to get back to the 'lodge' allocated to Chairman Shelepin's mission at the sprawling military base; and Kuznetsov was still in the middle of reporting the events of the depressingly predictable day aboard the great liner moored in San Francisco Bay, when Sergey Gorshkov burst into the room.

Vasili Kuznetsov rose, respectfully but due to his increasingly arthritic knees very stiffly, almost in slow motion.

Alexander Shelepin did not so much as arch an eyebrow.

"Comrade Sergey Georgyevich," he observed, with a cool detachment that in any other man an observer might have characterised as 'laconic', "you seem...*agitated?*"

The greying Minister of Defence and second man in the Troika never quite seemed comfortable in civilian clothes; it was as if his uniform became him and he it, even though he had never gone in for the routine overkill of a chest weighed down with medals he could not possibly have earned or won.

Gorshkov was the man who had sacrificed what was left of the Red Navy's Black Sea Fleet and its Turkish prizes in a suicidally desperate attempt to seize Malta, and successfully drawn the eyes of the World's off the opening moves of Operation Nakazyvat, the doomed, disastrous invasion of Iran and Iraq. He was also the man who had ordered the thermonuclear obliteration of Basra to halt the British advance into Iraq, and thereby book-ended the Motherland's disastrous attempt to seize the oil of the Middle East. More pertinently, he was also the man who had coldly decided to stand aside while Shelepin's coup swept away the old guard.

It took a lot to get Sergey Gorshkov excited.

The newcomer pulled himself together.

"The British Minister is downstairs!"

Alexander Shelepin frowned.

"Lord Harding-Grayson! He says he is here to pay his respects to Comrade Alexander Nikolayevich!"

"Is he alone?"

"No, he came with his wife!"

"To pay his respects?"

"That is what he said," Gorshkov confirmed. "In very prissy Moskva!"

"Where is he now?"

"In the reception room on the ground floor guarded by two of my boys..."

Alexander Shelepin's mind was suddenly roiling with doubts, suspicions and possibilities.

Thomas Carlyle Harding-Grayson...

The man who had shut the Soviet Union out of Egypt and much of the Arab world for a generation; and had somehow contrived to turn the People's Republic of China off the one true path of Marxist-Leninism, while simultaneously somehow engineering the rebirth of the North Atlantic Treaty Organisation; and, this was the really remarkable thing, convinced the Nixon Administration that it was its idea all along, *was waiting downstairs to 'pay his respects' to his sworn enemies!*

The First Secretary and Chairman of the Communist Party of the Union of Soviet Socialist Republics was half way to the door, with a still disconcerted Gorshkov stepping out of his way before his conscious brain had instructed his body to move.

Lord Harding-Grayson and Lady Patricia were standing by the window, admiring the lights illuminating the nearest, southern tower of the Golden Gate Bridge begin to take full effect in the gathering dusk.

The British minister's wife, a slim, elegant, elderly woman with platinum grey hair and intelligent, perspicacious blue-grey eyes fixed Alexander Shelepin as he halted a bare arm's length away from the couple.

"Kak pozhivayete, tovarishch Pervyy sekretar," she smiled, extending her pale, white right hand to the Russian leader.

How do you do, Comrade First Secretary?

There was nothing 'prissy' about the woman's command of his mother tongue; it had a melodic Latvian lilt.

"Moy muzh tak mnogo rasskazal vam o vas, kak priyatno nakonets vstretit' vas vo ploti!" The lady went on, smiling serenely.

My husband has told me so much about you, it is marvellous to finally meet you in the flesh!

"I am flattered, dear lady," Shelepin replied in halting English. No Head of the KGB could function properly without at least a conversational grasp of that infernal language. It was, after all, the language of the Motherland's two most implacable post-Second War foes.

The woman beamed with pleasure.

"Forgive me, I was afraid my Russian would make me an object of no little fun," she confessed, reverting to her own tongue with evident relief. "I do my best to be a good Foreign Office wife but I have never had my husband's extraordinary gift for languages."

Alexander Shelepin belatedly remembered he was supposed to be sizing up Lady Patricia's husband; not allowing the mendacious old rascal – a man who would have been totally at home in any medieval Medici court – to study him at his leisure.

He nodded to his adversary.

Switching back to Russian: "You will understand that my people did not know what to do with you when you turned up at our door, Lord Harding-Grayson?"

The other man grinned ruefully.

"Given that our two missions are such near neighbours it would have been positively rude of us not to make a house call, Comrade Chairman."

Vasili Kuznetsov had trailed breathlessly behind his leader and was only now gathering his second wind; a lucky accident because Alexander Shelepin was looking at him expectantly.

"This is a little irregular, Comrade Chairman," he gasped.

And then the most bizarre thing happened.

The British Foreign Secretary's wife stepped forward, past Alexander Shelepin and took a firm hold of Kutnetsov's elbow and inquired, with convincingly genuine, maternal concern: "Tovarishch posol, vy v poryadke?

Comrade Ambassador, are you quite well?

"This is all quite a shock," the veteran diplomat murmured, allowing himself to be guided to the nearest chair. His face ashen with exhaustion, beads of perspiration peeling off his brow.

"Fear not," Tom Harding-Grayson promised. "This is but a short visit. Just long enough to ensure that *our* friends and *your* adversaries start to question *our* loyalties and *your* motives. Diplomacy, was ever thus."

Alexander Shelepin understood the Englishman.

"This conference has been, and will be, the disaster we all confidently expected it to be," the British Foreign Secretary remarked. "But then, I doubt if any of us, will be ready to sit down around a peace table in good faith for many years to come. However, that does not mean it is not in our mutual best interests to cobble together an armistice of some sort. Then, at least, we can leave the future to our successors, the next generation."

"You speak in riddles, Comrade Minister," Shelepin retorted with only mild irritation.

"Tomorrow," Tom Harding-Grayson said, abandoning artifice, "my Prime Minister, the President of the United States and," he quirked a crooked smile, "you, Comrade Chairman, will address the General Assembly. I humbly urge you to take into account the turmoil in *this* country, and to reflect upon the mistakes *we* have *all* made in Western Europe and France since the Cuban Missiles War. I also urge you to take advantage of this passing moment of American vulnerability, to draw back from the brink in Europe and to give President Nixon a sign, preferably an unambiguous sign, that you are prepared to contemplate at least, a...*dialogue.*"

The Soviet leader's eyes narrowed.

The Englishman shrugged.

"I would not be here if I had not already concluded that your presence in the United States was not, in itself, a solemn earnest of your willingness to make concessions to achieve a lasting peace, Comrade Chairman. I simply tell you that in my opinion – for what it is worth – now is the time to be seen by the World to be making the first move."

Shelepin absorbed this.

"And what of your own leader? What will she propose tomorrow?"

"Hope, tinged with fire and brimstone, Comrade Chairman." Tom Harding-Grayson hesitated; this was the time to turn and leave. He hesitated. "If you choose to see it in such terms, the conquest of France and the securing of that country's eastern borders for all time, may be the limit of the United Kingdom's territorial ambitions in Europe. Beyond that, stasis is acceptable to my government, given peace."

Now, he began to turn to leave, with his wife patting Vasili Kuznetsov's arm and rising to follow.

"Central Europe may never again be an armed camp as it was before the Cuban Missiles War," her husband sighed, his eyes sad, "if it ever becomes what it was before that war again, then I foresee only unimaginable grief. If I may, I will leave you with this thought: the man, or the woman, who proposes a thousand kilometres neutral buffer zone between the West and the Soviet Union in Europe may well go down in history as the saviour of us all."

Chapter 48

Sunday 12th February 1967
Place de Jaude, Clermont-Ferrand, France

Sharof Rashidovich Rashidov had been knocked unconscious for several minutes; otherwise, he had been one of the lucky ones when the big bomb had hit and comprehensively demolished the disused Opera House on Boulevard Desaix, its now shattered, burning frontage looking out on the famous statue of Vercingetorix. Several other smaller missiles had struck, set ablaze, and briefly, swept the surrounding streets clean of life.

Several hours after the attack the city was still reeling, in chaos. Here and there big fires burned; nobody was fighting them or it seemed, making any attempt to prevent them spreading. Bodies lay where they had fallen in the surrounding streets, and out across the square, the injured one by one falling silent in the cold and the ashes, falling like wet snow onto the frigid ground.

And there were no Revolutionary Guards on the streets...

Smoke and the sick stench of scorched flesh hung in the flickering darkness like a curse, as the Troika's Commissar Special Plenipotentiary to the Front Internationale in Clermont-Ferrand read the last decrypted reports to have been received before the raid.

The Free French were advancing in the north, slicing through the pathetic remnants of the Front Internationale's forces everywhere. There were even reports from Krasnaya Zarya-held city of Bordeaux – Maxim Machenaud's so-called 'Stalingrad on the Garonne – that it too had been bombed and that there were 'raiders fighting outside the city'.

In the near distance the small generator powering a few of the surviving lights within the blast-wracked, windowless, otherwise intact, Soviet Residence, rumbled and chugged feebly. The Mission's communications equipment was undamaged, unfortunately, all bar one of the operatives who knew how to operate it, code and de-code traffic, were dead or maimed. Outside, only the flames lit Clermont-Ferrand and fragmentary reports apart, Rashidov had no knowledge; other than that, the attack had probably had a catastrophic impact on the whole city, likely wrecking the airport and key industrial sites, striking key depots and communication links and killed hundreds, perhaps, thousands of people...

The aviation fuel tanks at the airfield were still burning, the glow in the east dully lit up the skyline.

There was a commotion in the square.

"What happened to that bloody woman?" Rashidov demanded, irritated that he had forgot all about the member of the Front Internationale Central Committee who had surrendered herself to his bodyguards earlier...hours ago, probably *yesterday* evening.

"She's still downstairs, Comrade Commissar!"

"Bring her here."

Presently, a familiar, scarecrow woman in the fatigues of the Revolutionary Guard, was thrust into Rashidov's presence.

"Comrade Machenaud lives," the woman blurted. "Or at least he did when he sent me here."

Rashidov had not risen to his feet from behind his candle-lit desk. The breeze infiltrating the room fanned and sucked at the candles, making for an eerie, ethereal atmosphere. Faraway, there was an explosion from the general direction of one of the FI's munitions dumps in the northern part of the city.

"That is good to know," Rashidov grunted. "What else did you come here to report to me, Comrade Agnès?"

At least Machenaud had sent him a Russian-speaker.

That might have been an accident; it all depended on how many of the lackeys in his inner circle were still alive.

"The British targeted the Michelin Works, the aerodrome and..."

The woman seemed to choke on the words.

"The First Secretary's bunker?" Rashidov inquired sourly. Only fucking idiots built a bunker complex in plain sight with nothing else for hundreds of metres around it. The FI might as well have painted a giant cross on it!

"Yes..."

"What about *my* people at the Michelin Works?" The man demanded.

"Regrettably, the Red Air Force personnel accommodated at the facility were killed in the bombing."

Sharof Rashidov was on his feet, his fists balled.

"And?" He ground out between clenched teeth.

"That is all I am able to tell you, Comrade."

"Seriously?" The man asked, knowing he ought not to be surprised by anything in this madhouse!

"Yes, Comrade."

"Not good enough," Rashidov snarled. "Guards!" He yelled.

Kalashnikov-wielding green-uniformed KGB troops rushed into the room.

"Take this little piece of shit away. I want to know everything she knows about everything, and I want to know it fast. I don't care how you get her to talk. Fuck her to death with a bayonet for all I care!"

"No!" The woman squealed as strong arms began to haul her away. "I will tell you whatever I know. That is the only reason I came here! Nobody ordered me to come here..."

"Bring her back!" Rashidov bawled, waiting until the KGB-men had dragged her half-way down to the cellars.

"What is your name?" The Commissar Plenipotentiary asked, re-taking his seat. This he asked although though he knew exactly who the woman was: she was the witch who had constantly been at Citizen Machenaud's side in Rashidov's time in Clermont-Ferrand. The woman who, according to who one talked to was either the madman's 'secretary' or his 'mistress', or both. However, when one commenced an interrogation one began from the beginning, followed the standard protocol, took nothing for granted and treated the subject, at the outset, with cold contempt, as if they no longer existed as a living, breathing human being.

"Comrade Agnès..."

"Do you have a proper name, Comrade?"

This utterly bewildered the woman, it was so long since she had used her real surname, let alone her baptised name, that they sounded strange inside her head.

As if they belonged to somebody else.

If the Front Internationale had ever discovered her true identity, they would have liquidated her in a heartbeat, and yet now, she was on the verge of confessing without hesitation...as if it was the end of the world and she was running out of time to atone for her sins.

She fought to control her terror.

"Just Agnès..."

Having threatened to have the woman beaten and raped to death, Rashidov, neither a trained interrogator nor a man who owed his position to abject thuggery, retained the presence of mind to understand that information obtained without violence, or violation, would be inherently much more reliable than that squeezed out of the woman by torture.

"Tell me what do you do for Comrade Machenaud? Apart from write down everything the mad fucker says?"

"I am a translator and clerk in his secretariat..."

She knew this was not going to be enough.

"I am his whore, too..."

Rashidov sucked his teeth.

"Have you seen Citizen Machenaud since the bombing raid?"

"Yes..."

"Where is he?"

The woman hesitated, glanced anxiously at the KGB men around her.

"I don't know. He plans to leave the city. I believe he may be in the chateaux once infested by the traitor Duclos..."

"Tell me what else you know?"

"The English have destroyed the airport and all the aircraft. They also attacked the rocket batteries in the hills. They knew where every headquarters building was located. When they bombed the power station, they dropped anti-personnel devices, many of them with delayed action fuses..."

The woman shivered uncontrollably. Her thin FI fatigues were no defence against the frigid bite of the winter evening. She was very hungry and had no need to feign her fear. In the near distance a long burst of automatic gunfire rent the night.

The woman's eyes were hunted, haunted.

And Sharof Rashidov realised he had missed something very important.

She might not be lying.

"The bastard didn't send you here, did he?"

Comrade Agnès shook her head.

"No, Comrade Commissar."

Rashidov waited patiently.

"It is all over," the woman went on. "The First Secretary and his personal guards have fled the city. They will go to Bordeaux; the people there are not like they are here in the Auvergne. All our best fighters are in that place. In Bordeaux they will fight to the death."

A man entered the room.

"Comrade Commissar," he reported tersely. "The Cathedral is on fire. Everywhere the fires from the bombing were previously burning themselves out, there are new fires!"

There was more machine-gun fire, seemingly less than a block away this time.

Rashidov pushed back his chair, turned to his aides.

"Make sure everybody has a gun; anybody who blinks at us in the wrong way; just shoot them."

The Commissar Plenipotentiary had heard bad things about what happened to Soviet citizens caught on the streets of Budapest back in 1956, and in a lot of other places since where law and order had broken down. If Maxim Machenaud and his crowd really had fled, the mob was likely to look for others upon whom to take their revenge.

"We can't stay here!" He decided, fixing his stare on Comrade Agnès's face. "How well do you know the city?"

"I lived here before the war, Comrade..."

"*We* need to get out of Clermont-Ferrand." He paused to listen to the shooting, this time hundreds of metres away. "Will you help us?"

The woman nodded jerkily.

"What about our wounded, Comrade Commissar?" One of the KGB men asked quietly.

"If they can walk, they come with us."

Comrade Agnès swallowed hard, feeling sick.

Everybody in the room knew that they could not leave the seriously wounded behind at the mercy of the mob. Within minutes the survivors of the Soviet Mission were hurrying across the Place de Jaude past the shrapnel-gouged statue of Vercingetorix, with the muffled reports of the headshots which had put the injured men and women in the cellar out of their misery, ringing dully in their ears.

Chapter 49

Colonel Caroline Constantis-Zabriski had awakened with a fierce hangover that morning to be informed that there had been a 'change of plan' by an unusually sheepish, Captain Erin Lambert.

'I'm sorry, Caro,' the younger woman had apologised. 'If there was a good way to say this, I would. The Air Force wants you to go to San Francisco to assist the FBI.'

'Seriously?'

Just so that there could be no misunderstanding, the orders – delivered to the Commonwealth Hotel overnight – were signed by the Chief of Staff of the US Air Force, General John P. McConnell and there were two more of Erin's people, unmistakably military, in their civilian suits outside in the corridor when Caro eventually surfaced to go down for breakfast.

'A sealed file will be waiting for you on the aircraft,' Erin had explained. 'I don't know its subject; furthermore, you are not authorised to share anything in it with me and I am expressly forbidden to question you about its contents. I will be accompanying you to California, and remaining with you as your bodyguard but operationally I will be handing you off into the care of FBI Special Agent James B. Adams...'

Inevitably, Caroline had tried to find out what was going on.

Her friend had shrugged.

'I don't know, Caro.'

It got worse.

Arriving at Andrews Field they had discovered that although their flight would be stopping over – to drop off personnel, correspondence and to top off its tanks – at Offutt Air Force Base, while the aircraft was on the ground, Caro was not permitted to attempt to make contact with her husband.

The first leg of the flight, from Washington to Nebraska would be on the same Air Force DC-8 Caro had been scheduled to board all along, the second 'hop' to the West Coast would be on an Air Force Lockheed Jetstar. She would not get an opportunity to read the report Erin had had to sign for, in a metal attaché case, until they were in the air after take-off from Offutt.

The two women had settled in their allotted seats, Caro next to the window and Erin between her and the isle. The younger woman had debriefed her charge *twice* about her visit to CIA Headquarters at Langley, Clara Schouten and everything she had learned about the rogue assassin Kurt Mikkelsen, and then dragged every last nuance out of her friend's encounter with Lady Rachel French, who seemed to her, even scarier than 'Billy the Kid'.

"You can't get your head around *that* woman ending up married to a senior British RAF officer, can you?" Caroline prompted as the DC-8 climbed away from Washington.

And not just *any* senior officer, either.

Air Marshall Sir Daniel French had been the Governor of Malta, and for a spell, C-in-C of all Commonwealth Forces in the Mediterranean, now he was the top dog in the US-UK Joint Aerospace Development Group and responsible for – give or take - all British aircraft, guided missile and airborne radar and communications research, development and operational trialling; the sort of job any US Air Force man would kill for if such a single post was ever created stateside.

Lady Rachel French had not only interrogated Caroline Constantis, undeniably, the two women had had a real conversation building on the tenuous relationship established when Caro had first interviewed the other woman at Langley.

"Yes and no," Erin's friend groaned. "There are two sorts of people in the world; those who are terrified of her, and those who aren't. If you fall into the latter, very small group, and you are a man then I should imagine that she is..."

"Fascinating? Seductive?"

"If you like," Caro conceded, staring out of the window as the clouds enveloped the climbing jetliner.

Around them were mostly service personnel returning to the Midwest, some with family members, and there were several unattached women, civilians, clearly travelling to join loved ones stationed on one or other of the great Strategic Air Command (SAC) bases, constructed miles from anywhere, out on the fastnesses of the Great Plains.

"Actually, *beguiling* is probably a better word," the older woman went on, distractedly. "It is very rare to meet somebody who understands who they are. Who they really are, that is; self-knowledge can be a dreadful thing, I suppose?"

"That doesn't sound very professorial?" Erin teased gently.

Caro turned away from the window and smiled at her friend.

"No, but then these days, I like to think I stopped being that fuddy-duddy old blue-stocking academic the last time somebody blew up the world!"

The women laughed softly.

"How's your headache now?" Erin asked.

"I shouldn't have drunk so much."

Erin let this pass without comment.

"*You* shouldn't have encouraged me!" Caro added.

"Not guilty. You were steaming by the time I caught up with you!"

The older woman grimaced.

The last time she had got drunk was when she was in an agony of indecision over Nathan; her feelings for him had got out of control, she was his physician and he was half her age...

That particular late mid-life *crisis* had turned out okay in the end. A spasm of rough, angry sex had broken the flood gates of angst for them both and afterwards, they had been...well, at peace with each other.

She had no expectation that this present 'situation' was in any respect, as amenable to such a happy denouement. In fact, she could do with getting drunk again right now.

Very drunk...

At Offutt Caro managed to put a call through to the married quarters she got to share with Nathan a lot less frequently of late than she would have preferred. The number diverted.

"Major Zabriski is currently unavailable, Ma'am."

In other words, he was on duty, training, in a briefing or in the air...eight miles high.

An hour later, the only passengers on board the Jetstar as it thundered down the endless runway built for SAC's B-52s, were Caro and Erin Lambert.

At cruising altitude, the younger woman unlocked her attaché case, handed Caro the inch-thick sealed Manila folder bearing the legend TOP SECRET and moved to the rearmost of the eight seats. The aircraft had originally been designed with six but the Air Force had installed smaller, functional seats instead of the original plush, deep leather ones.

Caro, who had slept most of the way to Offutt, still felt tired and hung over.

I should definitely have stopped after the third Bloody Mary...

She broke into the envelope.

There was a letter on the front page of the file.

She read it cursorily.

Basically, it promised that if she divulged anything herein to an 'unauthorised party' she was going to Sing-Sing for ninety-nine years.

Yeah, yeah, yeah...

She began to speed read.

Dwight David Christie, aged forty-three...

Until December 1963 FBI Special Agent, South California...

The man had confessed to complicity in the pre-meditated murder of two fellow FBI agents and a...professional hit man...

And to working for the Soviets from 1947 onwards...

And that was just the preamble to the file!

Caro had looked up, tried to catch Erin Lambert's eye but the younger woman was trying to nap, sensibly assuming that the next two or three hours would be the last time she got an opportunity to catch up on missed sleep for a while.

By then Caro had forgotten all about her hangover.

And a question was forming in her mind.

Dwight David Christie...

Who the Hell are you?

Chapter 50

Monday 13th February 1967
Manassas, Virginia

The rifle had arrived yesterday around noon.

The couriers, a young couple from San Jose had been nervous; they seemed nice enough kids, just starting out and when they got home and collected it, five thousand bucks in addition to the five hundred Kurt Mikkelsen's step-father had given them 'for the trip', was going to make a lot of difference to their lives.

'Don't let me hear you hurt them people, son,' the old man had said, finishing their brief conversation. Kurt had gone down to the town, put the call through on a pay phone in the square in front of what passed for City Hall out here in the boondocks.

'That ain't my plan, Pa,' he had replied woodenly.

'I mean it, son. I need you to promise me.'

It had taken three-and-a-half days for the boy and the girl, neither of them was much past eighteen, to drive their old Chevy across North America. They had taken it in turns driving, probably fallen asleep at the wheel more than once. The car was dusty, and they were frightened and elated all at once when he saw them drive past, brake, back-up and eventually turn onto the track south of Bull Run. He had followed them, flashed them and they had halted.

"Stay in the car. Don't follow me. Don't go anywhere until I get back," Kurt had told the kids, wearing his bad-arse face.

Then he had taken the long, heavy case holding the disassembled Remington into the woods. Checked the kids had not followed him, before unhurriedly opening it with the key he had brought with him from California, and looked over its contents, satisfying himself that nobody had opened the case since it was closed up in San Francisco.

He had gone back to the track.

'Where are you kids going from here?'

'Maybe check out DC before we head home, sir?' The boy, a tanned, wide-eyed surfer type, had replied uncertainly.

Mikkelsen had shaken his head.

The girl was brunette, curvy with Latino blood; she was the one who would try to make whatever the two of them had together, work.

'No. That doesn't cut it for me,' Kurt had told them. "You were never here. The last few days you've been up in the mountains screwing your brains out. You never saw me, or that box you brought me. You tell anybody about this and it'll fuck your lives. You dig?"

The youngsters had nodded.

'Where do you want us to go, Mister?" The girl had asked, sensible kid.

'Back where you came from,' he had said. 'Nice and easy, just so nobody ever knows you went out of state.'

He had gone to his semi, come back with the envelope containing one thousand dollars in used notes. Also, inside the envelope was a key and a note.

'The money is a bonus for getting here inside four days. The key in the envelope is for a deposit box at Wells Fargo Bank on Market Street back in San Francisco. In one month from today, my associates will place another five thousand dollars in used notes in that box." That was a lie, the money was already there; but it was important to put a little separation between the coast to coast drive and the pay-off. That was basic field craft. "Blab a word about any of this to anybody in the next month and that money will go up in smoke.'

Kurt had viewed the kids with cold, emotionless unblinking eyes until each had looked away.

'But you won't worry about that because you'll both be dead.'

He had told them to count the money in the envelope in front of him. The kids had not known whether to be yipping for joy or pissing their pants.

'You can rely on us, sir," the boy had blurted.

'Today never happened, understand?'

They understood.

Kurt Mikkelsen had trailed the old Chevy for twenty miles west before, in the darkness he had pulled off the highway, waited twenty minutes in the event the kids were stupid enough to double back, and then driven the hour or up country to the hunting lodge in the forest where he had 'entertained' Clara Schouten.

Normally, he would have found another place by now, kept moving after he had released her. However, he doubted the woman would have been able to tell the searchers anything liable to enable them to quickly, if at all, pinpoint the cabin in the woods; DC was surrounded by 'woods' and once picturesque, now industrialising country towns like Manassas and Bull Run. Of course, Clara Schouten would not have been able to tell her paymasters anything, if he had cut her throat the way he had planned, right up until the moment...he did not.

He told himself that killing the woman had not actually been operationally necessary; and that leaving her wandering around the woods with her hands trussed was enough. He had wanted to send the Office of Security and that bastard Angleton a message; killing that jerk in Alexandria, and fucking *the Locksmith's* secretary had sent plenty of messages!

Right now, Angleton would be obsessing over what Clara Schouten had blabbed to him to save her life. He would be terrified that the woman had spilled the beans on one or other, perhaps all, of his current operations in DC; perhaps, that was the plan all along, to uncover his most dangerous secrets and drip-feed the poison into the media, day by day. Actually, Clara had wanted to tell him everything.

'Why don't you want to know?' She had asked, despairing.

'Would it make any difference?" He had retorted.

Like he cared a fuck about what one bit of the US Government did to another, or all the sick games people like *the Scarecrow* played with all the other sick bastards in DC!

He spent most of that afternoon cleaning and checking the balance of the Remington M24 .30-06 rifle, and the old German telescopic sight his Pa – heck, Hans was the only man he had ever known for a father – had adapted for the gun. The old guy was the best gunsmith he had ever known, a true artist.

Neither of them had been entirely happy with the idea of modifying the Remington to permit the use of a heavy-duty screw-on silencer.

'First shot may not do it, Pa,' he had apologised. 'Got to reckon on needing to get off two, three, four shots off and that ain't going to happen if the mark and the whole goddamned Secret Service hears the first shot.'

Obviously, if he missed with the first round the target and everybody else, would probably hear the 'crack' of the bullet rushing past, or might even feel the perturbation of the air. Some people said bullets 'sang' as they went by; he had never been sold on the 'singing' deal. He just listened to the 'crack' and moments later, the 'bang' or more likely, the 'dull thud' that might tell him the direction from which a shot had originated. The different sounds were to do with velocity; often a round was flying faster than the speed of sound. The 'crack' sound of a near miss was simply an aero-dynamic by product of the air being shouldered out of the way along the initial, supersonic trajectory of the bullet, the 'bang' or 'thud' of the gun firing, travelling only at the speed of sound, then caught up...

Therefore, using a silencer meant the target had no idea as to which direction the bullet had come from. And no idea where to safely go to ground...

Kurt had identified a meadow where the ground sloped gently for nearly four hundred yards protected by trees on three sides, a place where he could zero-in the Zeiss-Jena sights.

Twilight fell as he was walking back to the cabin.

It was fully dark when he went out to his semi, turned on the radio to catch the news on Public Service Broadcasting.

...Lady Rachel French, the socialite wife of a senior Royal Air Force Officer Dan French gave an interview to reporters at the British Embassy a couple of hours ago. She said rumours about her parachuting out of Prime Minister Thatcher's private aircraft over the Midwest were nonsense. She had been at the Embassy all the time, quote 'nursing a head cold'. She said she planned the stay in DC a few more days 'settling a little unfinished business.' Now for the rest of the news on the hour...

Chapter 51

Monday 13th February 1967
Headquarters, 4th Royal Tanks Battle Group, Blaye

Sergey Akhromeyev had discovered that the great storm which had shut down the majority of offensive military operations, and suspended normal life over most of Northern France for better than a week, flooding not just the Gironde Estuary, but every other watercourse in Brittany, the Poitou and the ancient lands of Aquitaine south of the Garonne and Dordogne river systems and their confluence at the Gironde, had already led to several postponements in launching the original Operation Blondie.

He and Lieutenant Paddy Ashdown had retreated to a corner of the Mess in the old, rather knocked-about Town Hall of Blaye, sat down and pored over maps of the Gironde Estuary, the Medoc and the pre-war port city of Bordeaux. Vexingly, all the maps were quite old and took little account of the post-1945 urban sprawl and the modern industrial sites which had sprung up along both banks of the Garonne.

Operation Blondie had started life around the turn of the year as a modern-day variation on a famous Second War raid – Operation Frankton - on the port of Bordeaux led by Paddy Ashdown's personal hero, the remarkable Major Herbert George "Blondie" Hasler, Royal Marines.

Sergey Akhromeyev had never heard of the man, or the relatively minor 'nuisance' action against blockade-running merchant ships in November 1942. Apparently, the operation had been the subject of a very popular British movie, *The Cockleshell Heroes*, in 1955 and in Britain was proudly regarded as a classic small-scale commando raid by every Royal Marine.

'Blondie' Haslar had come up with the idea for the Second War raid, planned and led it – the name 'Cockleshell Heroes' came from the employment of six two-man 'Cockle' Mark 2 kayaks in the operation - navigating from the mouth of the Gironde Estuary over sixty miles up-river to Bordeaux. Thereupon, the limpet mines placed on the hulls of a number of ships had damaged, or sunk several of the perfidious 'blockade runners' at their moorings in the river. Operation Frankton had not exactly gone off without a hitch! This had only served to paint up the bravery of the men involved in the popular imagination. One of the six canoes having been damaged, launching from the casing of a submarine several miles off the coast, only two of the ten canoeist-commandos involved in the 1942 operation, had survived, of the others six commandoes had been executed by the Nazis, and another pair had died of exposure. Haslar himself, had only survived by walking all the way to the Spanish border, over a hundred miles south through enemy territory. He had been awarded the Distinguished Service Order to add to the Order of the British Empire and the French Croix de Guerre he had earned at Narvik in 1940.

Akhromeyev thought Haslar sounded like an interesting man. Apparently, after he left the Royal Marines in the late 1940s, he had become a well-known single-handed sailor, and the inventor of a self-steering system for yachts which he perfected so well that by the time he participated in the first Observer Single-handed Transatlantic Race from Plymouth to New York in 1960, it had been adopted by the majority of his competitors. It seemed that Haslar had not cared for *The Cockleshell Heroes,* loathing the title of the film, the narrative of which, completely ignored the fact that a simultaneous, botched operation by the Special Operations Executive – mounted in ignorance of the Royal Marines' raid – had very nearly resulted in his men and their brave SOE counterparts, very nearly 'falling over' each other.

Operation Blondie was to be focused upon the presumed headquarters of the Front Internationale within the city's massive concrete Second World War BETASOM U-boat pens.

It was a little-known adjunct to the Battle of the Atlantic that at one time over twenty Italian submarines – badly needed by Mussolini to fight the British in the Mediterranean – were, to curry favour with Hitler, based at Bordeaux, the most southern of the Kriegsmarine's bases in the Bay of Biscay. The great, complex – the acronym 'BETASOM' derived from the Italian *Bordeaux Sommergibile* (Bordeaux Submarine) - which had become operational in January 1943, hosting the 12th U-boat Flotilla, still dominated the inner basin of the port of Bordeaux, its anchorage secure behind still functioning locks isolating its waters from the tidal ebb and flow of the Garonne and the seasonal inundations of the flood plains of the Gironde Estuary.

Like similar structures at Brest, Lorient, La Rochelle and other places along the French Atlantic coast, the BETASOM complex had been left abandoned after 1945. However, if nothing else, the old U-boat pens were magnificent bomb shelters, impervious to all but the largest conventional bombs and virtually indestructible other than by a very adjacent, very large nuclear bomb. At the end of the Second World War 617 Squadron – the Dambusters – had attacked and damaged, but not destroyed, U-boat pens at Bremen and other places with six-ton 'Tallboy' bombs and a handful of ten-ton 'Grand Slams'. Post-war inspections of the U-boat pens which had been 'hit' by these big bombs invariably discovered that hits by single, or even by two or three 'big bombs' rarely caused more than local structural damage. Basically, structures like the BETASOM complex were the toughest over-ground targets imaginable. Therefore, it was hardly surprising that the Front Internationale, Krasnaya Zarya and other criminal gangs had gravitated towards the old Nazi monuments, colonised them and stocked them with weapons, food and fuel, much in the fashion of medieval warlords preparing to withstand a siege.

In the circumstances, it was logical to assume that the people 'in charge' in Bordeaux would have done likewise.

Paddy Ashdown's original plan had been to collect intelligence on a forty-eight hour-long infiltration of the city on the way to the BETASOM complex, and once there blow up the lock gates protecting

the outer basin, hoping to flood the dock complex and hopefully –
because of the unnaturally high level of the Garonne - the whole area
around the old U-boat pens. Or, failing that, just to blow up 'targets of
opportunity' in the vicinity.

Sergey Akhromeyev had hated everything about the younger man's
scheme, except that was, the use of helicopters to transfer Ashdown's
hand-picked 'team' of eight desperadoes across the swollen Gironde to
its 'start point' at Blanquefort, or more specifically, a wooded area a
couple of kilometres to the west of the village, which was situated
approximately ten kilometres north-north-west of the FI's suspected
headquarters.

The former Red Army man was not exactly overly enthused with
the idea of a jumping off point in the middle of nowhere in a probably
waterlogged, sodden landscape either. Especially, not when there was
a another, much better alternative staring them all in the face.

'Why don't we just land on top of the U-boat pens?' He had
inquired.

Paddy Ashdown thought about the proposition.

'We'd all get killed before we got anywhere near the target,' he
observed, although not in a tone of voice which indicated he ruled it
out simply on that basis.

Akhromeyev had objected, albeit mildly to his objection.

'Not if somebody can keep the bastards' heads down while it's
happening.'

The younger man pursed his lips, thinking aloud.

'The Fleet Air Arm mounted several hit-and-run raids in the
outskirts of the city before the storm front came over us,' he mused
out aloud. 'Presumably the Eagle will have remained close inshore
now the worst of the weather has passed over.'

Neither man had any idea if the big carrier had steamed out into
the Atlantic, searching for sea room as the storms blew through, or a
sheltering port, or if she was back on station fifty miles off the mouth
of the Gironde.

The germ of an audacious plan up to the standard set by Blondie
Haslar back in 1942 had, by then, begun to form in their minds but
first, they needed to establish whether or not 'keeping the bastards'
heads down' was going to be a practical proposition.

The two men had gone to see the 4th Tanks' GSO3 – staff officer
responsible for operations – whose office was in a requisitioned cottage
nestling beneath the shelter of the old city walls. It seemed that HMS
Eagle was back 'on post', somewhere out in the Bay of Biscay.

Sergey Akhromeyev explained why they had wanted to know.

'Um... That sounds like a jolly good way to get yourselves killed,
chaps,' they were told candidly.

Undeterred, Paddy Ashdown and his unlikely comrade in arms
continued their deliberations over hot drinks as they studied the maps
strewn on the table before them. A few minutes later they heard the
thunder of low-flying fast jets rocketing over the Gironde, possibly
following the course of the river.

Somewhat vexed, they had marched back to the GSO3, who was grinning like a Cheshire cat.

'The Fleet Air Arm and the RAF are mounting another big show. Right now, as you've just heard. The High Command has decided it is time we gave those comedians in Clermont-Ferrand a wake-up call!'

Both Ashdown and Akhromeyev were by now muttering about shades of Operation Frankton in 1942, the left-hand not knowing what the right-hand was doing, ever more united in their common purpose.

'How soon can you be ready to go?' The Russian had demanded.

'Any time for tonight onwards,' Ashdown replied without hesitation. 'We've been ready to go for over a fortnight.'

That had been two days ago.

Chapter 52

Monday 13th February 1967
USS United States, San Francisco Bay

A dozen or so delegations had either already departed, or not bothered to attend for the final session of the General Assembly. Many leaders had stormed out in protest when it was proposed that while the conference would continue for another week, or perhaps longer, the Assembly itself, would not gather again until its ceremonial dispersal on Friday.

Alexander Shelepin planned to return home – or rather, if possible, to commence his tortuous return to Sverdlovsk sometime tomorrow. He had come to California for one reason; to deliver the speech he clasped in his right hand as he got to his feet and walked, slowly to the stage.

Sometime yesterday the Americans had restored the ship's air conditioning plant to working order and for the first time, the air in the old First-Class Dining Compartment was coolly fresh, and not humidly oppressive to the First Secretary and Chairman of the Communist Party of the USSR. A less cerebral, more impulsive man might have taken this as a good omen but the Head of the Troika was not a sentimental man.

As he approached the lectern with its barrage of microphones, he raised his right hand and tapped his left breast with two fingers; a signal which prompted members of the Soviet delegation to rise to their feet and to begin to distribute the small stack of envelopes on their mission's desk to the other representatives in the room.

Each envelope was addressed to a named delegate or ambassador, and in that recipient's own language bore a request: PLEASE DO NOT OPEN UNTIL AFTER CHAIRMAN SHELEPIN HAS BEGUN TO SPEAK.

Among other factors, the whole United Nations enterprise had been hamstrung by the inadequacy of the translation arrangements, and a plethora of technical problems. Phones and microphones had, routinely, not worked, the relatively small cadre of US Navy and State Department translators had been unable to cope with the demand for their services, and for many delegations without an English speaker, many of the speeches and significant parts of the debates in the chaotic General Assembly had been incomprehensible. In this climate of rumbling dissatisfaction, rumour, so-called Chinese whispers, aggrieved national sensibilities and entirely natural exasperation on the part of a large number of the protagonists, had produced a febrile, volatile cocktail of mistrust and resentment, aimed particularly at the apparently disinterested organising country, the United States.

The suggestion, widely disseminated in the General Assembly, that President Nixon intended to make his one speech of the event at City Hall in San Francisco that evening before flying back to Washington, DC, threatened to be the straw that broke the camel's back. Many delegations were already bringing forward their plans to depart the city. It was likely that the only thing which had stopped the majority walking out and an unseemly premature exodus, was the panoply of obstacles placed in their path.

Aircraft seats and berths on ships had been arranged for the beginning of next week, and the State Department seemed pathologically incapable of bringing forward any of its hastily botched plans.

All this the Soviet leader knew as he stepped forward.

"Dobryy den', damy i gospoda, tovarishchi i druz'ya. Menya ogorchayet, chto eta smelaya popytka," the Soviet Leader began in Russian, his voice mechanical and seemingly lacking in inflexion.

Good afternoon ladies and gentlemen, comrades and friends. It saddens me that this brave attempt to restore a fundamental building block of the new post-Cuban Missiles War global settlement, is destined to end in failure.

Margaret Thatcher's expression was frozen.

"It will be all right," Tom Harding-Grayson murmured complacently. Counter intuitively, it was a non sequitur that the British Foreign Secretary was the only man in the room who was actually looking forward to Alexander Shelepin's offering.

An aide had torn open the Soviet envelope.

To get around the problems of translation the Russians had given everybody a text in their own language – or in the case of recently 'liberated' or 'independent' former colonies, in the language of their former imperialist masters - of what their leader intended to say in the next few minutes. This was at once immensely pragmatic, and a pre-meditated slap in the face to the US 'facilitators' of the conference.

"We live in a deeply troubled world in which a display of restored national pride in a ruined city in Germany can raise fears of a new war," Alexander Shelepin went on.

His delivery was flat, remorselessly bloodless as befitted a career apparatchik and former KGB technocrat. But then it was his words, not his emotions which he wanted, needed to communicate to his global audience.

Nearby, the US Ambassador to the United Nations, George Bush was scanning the pages of typescript with studious insouciance. It was unlikely that any man in America was angrier, or more humiliated by his country's inability to competently host the 'USS United States' event, than the new man, who had already struck his British allies as an operator of real substance, with whom they could look forward to doing business.

"We live in a world where the legacy of the Cuban Missiles War still curses us all; and in which old enemies are still, at war with each other. That is the reality we confront. Perhaps, our enemies wish this to be so forever, if only to stop my country beginning to rebuild from the ashes. But are we to return to the days of the Berlin Wall or the Bay of Pigs? None of us has lily-white hands; none of us is without blame for the global catastrophe of October 1962."

Margaret Thatcher noticed that her Foreign Secretary was no

longer slouched in his chair; he was leaning forward, listening like his life depended on hearing every word in the original Russian as clearly as possible.

She consulted the English transcript again.

The bloody man is casting himself as an international statesman...

The Soviet Union's one-time chief torturer was re-inventing himself as a man of peace!

"My country has a right to survive. My people have a right to be safe in their beds at night, and for their children to be fed, and to be proud of their Motherland. Please, please, do not expect me to come to a global forum and play the role of a colonial supplicant, a defeated enemy, the serf to mighty Uncle Sam."

The Prime Minister arched an eyebrow reading ahead...

"President Nixon, where are you today? Where are you? Where are you, *my friend*," he continued, "will you not look me in the eye. Will you not look me in the eye and give peace a chance?"

Margaret Thatcher was asking herself who had written this speech for the Soviet leader. And tantalisingly, how long had it been laying on the ground, waiting to be picked up while the battlefield was salted, in order that Alexander Shelepin could stand up here, today, and deliver it to the whole world?

Weeks, months?

Possibly, many months, or even a year?

She was remembering a conversation she had had with her Foreign Secretary before leaving England. She had wondered if her friend was just flying a kite, testing her out in some way.

'Leaving Dobrynin in place in Washington, only drip-feeding arms to the Front Internationale in France, the abandonment of territory in Iraq and Iran, the failure to pursue the treaty with the People's Republic of China,' Tom Harding-Grayson had speculated, 'might conceivably, amount to a deliberate attempt to reduce international tensions, Shelepin's way of signalling that he is no Stalin, or Khrushchev or Brezhnev, or even a known hawk like Sergey Gorshkov.'

At the time, Margaret Thatcher had suspected this was unlikely, implausible interpretation of the facts. However, her friend had alluded to this theory again last night.

'How does the attack on Villefranche fit in with that, Tom?' She had objected.

'Perhaps, the objective was to cripple the Front Internationale's fleet? Perhaps, the Troika was sending us a message? True, if one of our ships had been sunk that might not have been helpful; but the Soviets had no way of knowing our ships and our aircraft would be in the vicinity at the time of the raid...'

The Prime Minister had allowed her thoughts to drift.

Faraway, in France the British Expeditionary Force, the assault brigades of the Free French Army and the Royal Navy, operating in the Bay of Biscay and the Mediterranean would be in action against the Front Internationale, wreaking havoc, sowing fear, death and destruction. The assault would be all out, and continue for as long as the ships and sea and the troops on land could sustain the attack.

Realistically, that gave the allied forces a few days, perhaps, a week or so – a fortnight if they were very lucky - to kick the legs out from beneath the enemy. Privately, her generals and admirals had warned her that although 'huge damage might be inflicted on Krasnaya Zarya, it might be over-optimistic to hope that the regime would simply collapse.' Sir Michael Carver had counselled her that: 'Isolating the Front Internationale in the Massif Central' and making its southern coastal enclaves unviable,' would be a major step forward.

Whatever happened in the next few days; hopefully, it would shame the Nixon Administration into action.

Grand strategy operates at both the military, and the political level and the Prime Minister knew her Foreign Secretary was right to advise her, time and again, that ultimately, it was the political calculus that mattered above all else.

Alexander Shelepin was no public speaker; he droned on with all the charisma of a man reading a telephone directory.

"If President Nixon was in this room, I would say to him," he went on doggedly as all around the compartment delegates urgently turned to the next sheet of their transcripts. "Come to the Soviet Union. Fly over the wastelands. See us for what we are. Visit Sverdlovsk. Sit with us around the negotiating table and let us talk of peace, not ideological conflict or war. Let us start anew. Let us each bring blank sheets of paper to the table. Let us together begin to dismantle our great arsenals of weapons of mass destruction which have caused both our great nations such pain. Let us each, two great nations, develop in our separate ways in peace. Let us respect each other's inalienable right to exist. Where we differ, let us differ in the future in a spirit of peaceful co-existence where formerly, we clashed and walked, like sleepwalkers, down the road to perdition a little over four years ago!"

It was hard to do a head count from where she was sitting; Margaret Thatcher guessed at least two-thirds of the people in the room got to their feet and began to applaud as the Soviet leader completed his speech.

"Don't you dare get up and clap, Tom," she whispered to her Foreign Secretary.

"It would be polite to at least clap," her friend murmured.

"No!"

She glanced across to the United States' table and to her consternation discovered that George Bush was looking directly at her. He shrugged imperceptibly, otherwise he remained studiously poker-faced. Around him his colleagues were clearly angry, embarrassed also. From where she sat the Prime Minister could not see the expression on the faces of the Nationalist Chinese, or of her French allies.

This, she decided, was probably for the best.

Chapter 53

Monday 13th February 1967
Clermont-Ferrand, France

The woman Maxim Machenaud had only ever known as Comrade Agnès did not know when the idea had lodged, weevil-like in her head. So many of the things she had done, the decisions she had taken, or perhaps realistically, had had taken for her or imposed upon her since the war, had just happened without her conscious intellectual engagement, or any act of deliberate will. In retrospect, she realised she had been operating at a primal, flight or fight level for so long that she had begun to lose her sense of self, of any real recognition of who or what she had once been. Her mind had largely switched off, existentially she had survived on her wits without reference to a moral compass, done terrible things, become callous, and behaved like a feral, cornered animal.

Obedience and survival were synonymous in the insane world of the Front Internationale's upper circles; to be in that depraved hierarchy was a testimony to one's capacity to shed one's humanity like it was a redundant skin. To be close to the monster at the heart of the regime for any length of time was to sink ever deeper into a black pit of unremitting...evil.

Yet *she* had survived.

Not because she was pretty, or young like those whores who had betrayed the Revolution in Vichy; or even because she had convinced the madmen – and women – around her in the Auvergne that she was particularly intelligent, for had her 'comrades' even suspected as much, she would have probably been dead, hung or burned, shot or bayoneted to death on the execution grounds at the now cratered, wrecked, carnage-strewn airfield to the west of the city, one, two or even three years ago. No, she had survived because above all she had proven herself to be competent, efficient and unswervingly loyal, gifts few of Citizen Maxim Machenaud's most maniacal disciples ever displayed for long.

From what she had experienced in Clermont-Ferrand, psychosis and stupidity were common bedfellows, the hallmark of the Krasnaya Zarya plague that had fallen, like a random, corrupting epidemic across the South.

Everything was suddenly falling apart, the hated Revolutionary Guard, its leadership humiliated and bloodily purged after the fiasco at Villefranche, was disorganised and panicking, its aura of invincible untouchability as ruined as key parts of the city, which itself was under assault from all sides by a population driven to desperation.

It was as if the sudden shock of the English bombing had bust a dam of long-suppressed rage; the people had turned on their overlords...

The events of the last twenty-four or thirty-six hours; she had lost all sense of time; reality was a fluid thing and she no longer trusted her short-term memory. Sometimes the mind was subjected to too much stress, there were too many conflicting horrors and nightmares got confused with the waking, here and now when exhaustion began to erode one's sanity.

'What the fuck are you doing?' One of the Russians had demanded as she began to strip off her filthy, bloodied Revolutionary Guard uniform.

'I need ordinary clothes if I am going to be your guide out of the city!' She had snarled. 'Hurry, if we don't move soon it will be too late!'

She had told the Russians lies.

Lies were simpler than the truth.

Nobody had Headquarters had sent her to tell the people at the Soviet Residence what was going on, or to warn them. After the Michelin Works had been wrecked by the bombs, she had known the Front Internationale had become the hunted, not the hunter, predators turned prey. She had run from the mobs, kept on running until she nearly collapsed and discovered she was close to the Soviet Residence. All she had known was that the mobs were roaming the streets turning on anybody suspected of being a member of the old regime. One moment she had been a member of the loathed Central Committee, the next hunted, a dead woman walking as she had stumbled into the rubble-strewn Place de Jaude.

She had had no 'good' options; so, she had snatched despairingly at the first 'least bad' chance of survival, knowing that the Russians had Spetsnaz and KGB troopers stationed at the Residence to protect the Commissar Plenipotentiary and his people. Conceivably, the Russians might protect her if she could convince them that she was useful to them.

The Russians had to have known, or suspected, that Maxim Machenaud had always had a plan to flee to Bordeaux; people like him spent a large part of their lives obsessing over plots and conspiracies, they never felt safe without knowing they had a bolt hole ready and waiting if everything went wrong. That was why the Front Internationale forces in the Massif Central had been bled white to build up the 'citadel on the Garonne', the last redoubt where, if it came to it, the enemies of the Revolution would be made to pay in blood for every millimetre of every street. The whole city was supposedly a giant booby trap; the FI had long ago, virtually abandoned the South, and thinned-out its forces in the Auvergne and belatedly attempted to turn Lyon, the regimes 'Eastern Bastion' into a garrison town fast sucking the life out of the surrounding countryside, a fragile bulwark against the refugees from the East but not much more.

It had been clear to Agnès, if not to the other idiots on the Central Committee, that Maxim Machenaud had seen the future coming for him last autumn as the FI's dwindling number of volunteer fanatics, and the original Red Dawn companies withered away from hunger, disease, and the constant slow attrition of the war on the Loire Front, and slowly, inexorably drowned in the tide of humanity pressing against its eastern, Rhine flank. Last November and December, the ease with which the British had rolled up the last of the Krasnaya Zarya enclaves along the Biscay Coast and camped, threateningly on the northern bank of the Gironde Estuary, had sent a jolt of panic through the high command in Clermont-Ferrand.

The reign of terror that Maxim Machenaud had turned back on to celebrate the arrival of the latest Soviet Mission, had failed to stem the bleeding, desertions had continued; even members of the Central Committee had been captured attempting to flee the city.

The woman who had called herself Comrade Agnès when, eventually she had returned to the Auvergne eleven months after the war, had sensed the brittleness of the FI's hold over the city, interpreted Maxim Machenaud's suddenly rampant paranoia, the ramping up again of the terror, as the symptom of that ever-increasing vulnerability. It was as if Maxim had seen his power leaking away, drip, drip, drip and had no answer but to turn inwards upon his own supporters.

The savage revenge he had meted out on the Revolutionary Guard leadership cadre for its failure to seize those useless, rust-bucket ships at Villefranche, had been an incredibly stupid, and possibly, fatal self-imposed wound. When the Red Air Force had, literally, out of the blue, bombed those recalcitrant ships of the old Mediterranean Fleet, everybody could see that the emperor had no clothes, and that he had lost control of...*everything.*

Maxim Machenaud had jealously hoarded the levers of power to himself, liquidated anybody who challenged him, or worse, threatened to one day rise to threaten his position. When things went wrong there was nobody left to blame but the great dictator; a thing Comrade Agnès suspected Maxim had never, ever thought about. Until, of course, it was far, far too late and nemesis was upon him.

There was an odd, cruel irony in that.

It was just a pity it had taken a river of blood and untold grief to reach this day...

It was as if the bombing had flicked a switch, fractured and splintered what little remained of the regime's inner steel, and now, it was tearing itself apart, it was every man and woman for themselves now. The last she had heard before she slipped, quietly out of the chaos of the wrecked, burning Michelin Works, had been that terrified technicians were asking to whom they should report the panicky messages coming in from Toulon and Marseilles about men of the Naval shore brigade and workers on the street, burning the Red Flag, and attacking the Front Internationale's offices.

Sharof Rashidovich Rashidov, the bullet-headed, blood-spattered Commissar calling the shots at the Residence had bawled for clothes to be found for Agnès.

Without self-consciousness – considerations of ephemeral niceties like feminine modesty had gone the same way as decency and reason in the last few years – she stripped naked to the waist and tugged on the shirt the Russians around her had probably removed from a corpse. In a moment she had disappeared into an over-sized fur-lined greatcoat.

And then she had led the band of Kalashnikov-armed toughs and pistol-toting Communist Party hacks out into the night.

All the while Rashidov had hurled questions at her.

Stepping out into the gunfire-shattered darkness she had, at last, begun to think clearly, weigh again her options. Running into and hiding in the Soviet Residence had bought her time, and kept her from being recognised on the streets and torn to pieces by the mob.

Now, she had lost her uniform, become again anonymous.

What twinge of guilt she had experienced knowing she was going to betray her temporary saviours at the first opportunity; had passed when the bastards had started shooting their injured comrades.

Not even the English would do a thing like that!

These people deserved whatever they got!

The Soviets had supported first one, then another even worse faction in the civil war in the South. But for the curse of Red Dawn the farms and industrial cities of the Aquitaine, the Poitou, the Limousine, the Auvergne, the Rhone, the Midi Pyrenees, the Languedoc in the south, with Provence and the Cote d'Azur, ought to have been the salvation of La Belle France. Instead, the maniacs had condemned the decimated populations of the provinces unbombed in the catastrophe of October 1962, to a never-ending nightmare of internecine predation, its peoples conscripted into berserker robber bands to fight in the north and the east, leaving its fields untilled, its factories lying silent with starvation and disease stalking the land in a year in, year out cycle of death and misery.

There were no children on the streets of Maxim Machenaud's new Jerusalem, that Marxist-Leninist paradise on earth he talked about creating out of the ashes of the old, corrupt France.

Nobody had dared to tell the fool that the southern enclaves no longer paid more than passing lip service to the 'madman on the hill' in the Auvergne, or that the leadership in Lyon, and probably in Bordeaux too, considered themselves independent of Clermont-Ferrand, their ideologies having long ago, diverged from the one truth path. Comrade Agnès had never understood why the Soviets dealt solely with the Machenaud rump of the Front Internationale, or had, for reasons beyond her ken, remained convinced that there was still any such thing as the 'Front Internationale' as a coherent, organised regional movement. There had never really been a Front Internationale 'state' in Southern France, it had only ever been a gang of old Communist Party discontents, the rabble who had never found a home in the sclerotic semi-Stalinist 'Internationale' presided over by Jacques Duclos and his cronies in the old days.

But for Russian meddling the whole disgusting apparatus of the Front Internationale might have imploded two years ago; even under Duclos and his grasping lieutenants, life for the people of southern France could not possibly have been any worse than it had been under Maxim Machenaud.

Duclos was no iconoclast; he was an old-school leftist who probably yearned for things to be, more or less, the way they had been before the war...

Comrade Agnès tried to excise all the 'what ifs' from her consciousness as she led the Russians through streets turning into killing grounds, as the people of Clermont-Ferrand vented four years of pent up rage and vengeance upon their tormentors.

"Keep together!" She yelled, her voice cracking with raw fear.

"Close up!" Bawled somebody behind her. "Don't get separated from the main group!"

Chapter 54

Monday 13th February 1967
City Hall, San Francisco

Major Sir Steuart Pringle, the commander of the Prime Minister's personal protection squad, had been appalled when he was briefed about the security measures in place around and at City Hall and now, as he shepherded his charges through the crowds, he was a very worried man.

The problem was nothing to do with the unstinting wealth of resources their hosts had devoted to the 'security plan' – there seemed to be hundreds of armed San Francisco Police Department, Marines and State Troopers carrying shotguns, automatic weapons and any number and variety of handguns, nightsticks and tear gas canisters – but with the overwhelming impression of utter chaos. Nobody seemed to be in charge, or rather, nobody anybody who could be immediately identified. Moreover, while there were concentric cordons at eight hundred, four hundred and one hundred yards from the empty ground in front of the post-1906 earthquake building, civilians milled everywhere, even inside the police lines closest to City Hall where cars were continually pulling up, disgorging their human cargoes and parking up in the loom of the dazzling floodlights illuminating every arrival for the benefit of the TV cameras.

Steuart Pringle yelled at his men: "STAY IN TOUCHING DISTANCE OF OUR TREASURE!"

This meant that he expected his men to literally surround and protect, with their bodies, the Prime Minister. Normally, in the event of a problem, *the lady* forbade him to open fire in a crowd. This was something of a vexation to Steuart Pringle and his men, to whom only one thing mattered: the safety of their 'treasure'.

'I do not want innocent people killed or hurt because somebody sneezed at the wrong time, Sir Steuart!'

Tonight, in direct disobedience to his Prime Minister's diktat, Steuart Pringle's men had their Stirling submachine guns set on full-automatic with orders not to wait for his command to 'return fire' if there was 'an incident'.

Nobody was going to lay a finger on a single hair of the Right Honourable Margaret Hilda Thatcher, MP, on *his* watch!

The press of bodies, the constant flash of camera bulbs, the rattle of shutters firing and the general hubbub of the surrounding throng was horribly, dangerously disorientating. The whole ghastly accident waiting to happen, smacked of improvisation and a profound lack of attention to detail which immensely offended Steuart Pringle's Royal Marine soul.

The US Government had not wanted to host the United Nations re-union, a GOP Administration had squabbled with the State of California and the City of San Francisco, both controlled by Democrats, and at the last minute thrown resources at the problem as if planning and preparation were dirty words.   Worse still, the Americans had refused to divulge their 'full security plan' for this evening's Presidential address, citing 'confidentiality concerns' to anybody who had the temerity to inquire: "What the Devil is going on?".

Steuart Pringle had strongly advised the Prime Minister to remain at the Presidio.

'This is far too dangerous, Ma'am.'

The Prime Minister had long ago, stopped reminding her Royal Marine guardian angel that only the Queen was 'Ma'am', and that she was either 'Prime Minister' or 'Mrs Thatcher'; but eventually given up the unequal fight last year.

'Sir Steuart, I am not going to watch the most important speech of the year on television!'

Now, Margaret Thatcher's AWPs were trying to pilot her safely through a chaotic melee just to reach the small, cleared space in the crowd where the TV broadcasters had set up shop.

Steuart Pringle had one arm protectively about *the lady's* shoulders and the other firmly gripping the butt of his Browning .45 automatic pistol.

Like his men's weapons, his pistol was locked and loaded, 'safety off'.

This was one of those tricky situations where normally, he would have relied on 'the Colonel', Frank Waters, to take care of the really close protection 'duty'.   It went without saying that he would not have dreamed of laying hands on *the lady* had it not been in his professional opinion, such a decidedly dicey scenario that he was unprepared to be separated from her for a split second.

Frank would not have hesitated biffing anybody who got too close to his 'treasure'; and with a sinking heart, Steuart Pringle recognised that was exactly what the developing security foul-up might very well soon demand.

Behind their commanding officer other Marines were physically walking their charges, the Foreign Secretary and his wife, the Prime Minister's Chief of Staff, Ian Gow, and Sir Roy Jenkins, the United Kingdom's Permanent Representative at the – more or less – reformed, somewhat dysfunctional United Nations while others of Steuart Pringle's men tried to create a narrow, crushed cordon sanitaire around the group.

A shadow emerged from the dazzled and stepped directly in front of Steuart Pringle and Margaret Thatcher. The shape lurched towards the Prime Minister.

Steuart Pringle's pistol whipped the man across the face and kicked him, hard, as he went down, simultaneously, very nearly lifting his 'treasure' off her feet as they stepped over the writhing body on the ground. Behind him he heard his men reacting to his lead, elbowing and kicking out to clear a path through the suddenly very threatening pressing mass of bodies.

"HALT!" Steuart Pringle shouted in his most formidable parade ground voice. "RAISE WEAPONS!"

As if for emphasis several Marines re-cocked their Stirlings.

"ON MY COMMAND! ONE ROUND IN THE AIR!"

"Sir Steuart!" Margaret Thatcher protested, breathlessly, having been momentarily winded by the press of bodies.

"FIRE!"

The volley rang out in the night.

Nearby there was brief panic; farther away, that panic turned into a stampede. As the sea of surrounding bodies retreated, many falling, or barged to the ground by people suddenly fleeing the scene, Steuart Pringle regarded the stampede as 'somebody else's problem!'

The space around the British party miraculously widened as San Francisco PD men and women and the crowd shrank back from the *crazy English.*

Margaret Thatcher did not even think about pausing for the TV cameras as she and her colleagues were rushed, at the double, up the naked steps of City Hall and bundled inside the building. Later, she and Pat Harding-Grayson swore that there had been moments when their feet had not touched the ground!

Steuart Pringle took one look around, and up at the balconies surrounding the entrance hall and said: "This place is a nightmare, Ma'am. I *will not* allow you to go anywhere unescorted."

More than once the Prime Minister's husband had whispered in her ear: 'Pringle's a good man; if he tells you to do something, promise me that you will do it!'

There was nobody there to greet either the British or the other delegations hurrying into the building because, hearing gunfire outside, the Secret Service had already hustled President Nixon down into the basement.

Roy Jenkins surveyed the scene thoughtfully. He adjusted his glasses, sniffed a little irritably.

"We were given to believe that there was going to be some kind of reception before the President addressed us. A glass of red wine would be most acceptable, right now."

Chapter 55

Tuesday 14th February 1967
Saint-Dizier, Haute-Marne, France

Major General Francis St John Waters, VC, picked up the field telephone while still attempting to stamp the cloying snow off his feet and lower legs. His boots felt like they were filled with ice water and he was undoubtedly, as dirty and rank as a skunk, after spending most of the last forty-eight hours with Two Corps' advancing spearheads.

Notwithstanding it was past two o'clock in the morning and he was as sober as a Lord, the former SAS man was in impregnably good humour. He missed *the lady*, obviously; otherwise he was having the time of his life!

"I gather you've been charging about the battlefield like a proverbial blue-arsed fly, Frank?" Field Marshal Sir Michael Carver inquired laconically.

The Chief of the Defence Staff had hoped to speak directly to Alain de Boissieu but the Supreme Commander of all Allied Forces in France was not due back at HQ for another thirty minutes or so, having been visiting several forward units.

The line clicked and hissed, angrily.

However, given that the CDS was speaking from Oxford, over land lines passing around London, through Dover under the Channel to Calais, and thence over two hundred miles farther south to the forward headquarters of the 19th Chasseurs on the outskirts of the ruined town of Saint-Dizier, some forty miles south of that unit's initial jumping off point at Chalons-sur-Marne, the quality of the connection was tolerable.

The Free French were advancing against an enemy who was melting into the snowy wilderness, surrendering in pathetic, starving, freezing penny packets and only here and there, putting up any meaningful resistance, all things considered everything was going ticketyboo.

Well, apart from the roadside bombs which periodically took out a vehicle and some or all of its occupants, and the booby traps the enemy liked to leave behind. In fact, the enemy's gift for improvisation was proving somewhat more than an inconvenience. In a couple of towns, the enemy had pulled out leaving scores of carefully prepared very nasty surprises; everything from a half-ton culvert bomb, to fragmentation grenades set-off by tripwires concealed in the ruins.

At Vitry-le-François, north east of Saint Dizier, a town astride the road from Chalons-sur-Marne, and thus an obvious line of march for the advancing Free French forces, it was suspected that a small suicide squad had remained behind when most of the starving garrison decamped. There were accounts of insurgents barricading themselves into buildings and blowing everything up, themselves and as many of their enemies as possible.

The SAS man and the Chief of the Defence Staff had come across this sort of thing, or similar abominations, albeit on a smaller scale in Cypress, Malaysia and other places, including Ulster, in the years before the October War.   Thus far, it was possible that the Front International irregulars had only mined and 'set-up' a small number of towns and villages situated on major roads.   Hopefully, the gathering pace of the advance would make it impossible for the bastards to booby-trap the battlefield farther to the south.   However, depressingly, commanders now had to assume that whenever they came upon a settlement, they must fear the worst; and inevitably, this was going to result in delays.   Which, in turn, gave the defenders time to set more booby-traps...

War was, when all was said and done, a filthy business...

This Frank Waters proceeded to convey to the architect of the defeat of two whole Soviet tank armies in the Middle East, even though he was telling him pretty much what he had expected to hear.   Michael Carver was the man who had, imagined and pushed for this very offensive because he had been the one man in England who had understood how enfeebled their enemies in France had become; and that they were ripe for rout.   It only went to prove that it was far too easy to accentuate the negative when generally, the big picture was middlingly rosy.

From where Frank Waters stood, half-way between Paris and Strasbourg, with Free French forces advancing at will on either side of the 19th Chasseurs, there seemed to be nothing to stop the Allied armies in France from rolling the enemy all the way back to the Massif Central in the centre and Lyon on the left, with the British Expeditionary Force, still somewhat hamstrung by the need to garrison the territory it had occupied and to secure its lines of communication back to Brittany, and understandably, in a state of near exhaustion after conquering much of the Poitou and rolling up the enemy's coastal holdouts all the way south to the Gironde Estuary, gathered its breath.

The situation on the Atlantic right of the line, was further complicated because winter storms had thus far stymied all attempts to fully resupply and to significantly reinforce Edwin Bramall's operations-depleted 4th Royal Tanks Battle Group, presently parked on the north bank of the Garonne north of Bordeaux.

The great storm, the third of the winter had left the Poitou and Aquitaine flooded, the marshes of the Dordogne impassable and the lower Garonne and the Gironde Estuary in spate with towns and hamlets on both northern and southern banks isolated islands in the midst of what seemed, locally to be archetypally Biblical inundations.

Notwithstanding, Edwin Bramall had been game to do what could be done; however, all thoughts of a full-blooded crossing of the swollen waters to mount large-scale operations against Bordeaux, only ever a pipe dream, had now been abandoned for the time being.

Fortunately, ever since Alain de Boissieu had returned from England to announce the decision to go onto the offensive, a new mood of optimism had swept through the Free French high command. As for the rejuvenated Supreme Commander, Alain de Boissieu was suddenly sanguine about his forces 'taking the strain' while his British friends, 'rested' in the west. For once, practical politics and tactical reality were aligned and everybody was happy. Well, as happy as they were ever going to be. With the 'stand-to' in place along the Gironde Estuary line, Frank Waters chatted to the CDS about the 'juicy little scheme' the SAS's rivals, the Special Boat Squadron, had cooked up; just to keep the pot boiling.

The C-in-C 4th tanks had been guarded in his reporting of this latter operation: other to say that he planned unleash some of his 'ruffians' on a raiding and reconnaissance in strength 'south of the river' Security was so tight that nobody could tell Frank Waters if *Operation Blondie* had even kicked off yet!

Boys will be boys!

The one thing he could say for sure about it was that Edwin Bramall would certainly have squashed it if he had thought it was any kind of fool's errand. So, presumably, they would hear all about it *when* and not a moment before, they all needed to know!

There were many elements of the last couple of days operations that remained opaque to the men at the sharp end. Knowing this, Michael Carver attempted to throw much-needed illumination on the salient operations.

"The first indications are that the big Fleet Air Arm-RAF raid on Clermont-Ferrand went very well. It seems we caught the blighters with their trousers down and got away with very light casualties. Down in the Mediterranean, Henry Leach will be sending his gun line inshore again tonight to encourage the diehards along the south coast to carry on considering their positions."

"Everybody at this end is chuffed to bits that the Navy managed to get the big ships at Villefranche safely to Malta, sir."

That had been a very big secret from everybody – apart from the French down on the old Riviera and they seemed to have stopped talking, even for the sake of form, with the idiots in the Auvergne after those goons from Clermont-Ferrand had arrived in Nice and attempted to steal away 'their' ships - until those Villefranche ships had been safely moored in the Grand Harbour.

"Good, good," Michael Carver guffawed in an untypically jovial fashion. "The C-in-C Mediterranean Fleet tells me that practically every able-bodied man on those ships has already sworn an oath of loyalty to the Free French Government."

Frank Waters was loath to speak of less tractable, sordid matters. However, since he was married to the Prime Minister, he felt he ought at least to show willing. He ought at least to show an interest in his wife's work, and all that.

"Is there any news from California?"

"No," the Chief of the Defence Staff said tersely. He changed the subject. "What's your feel for this, Frank?" He asked bluntly, focused entirely on the situation on the ground in France. "Do you think we have those Red Dawn beggars on the run?"

Michael Carver was asking *him* because, for whatever reason, very few men in the British Army had had a finger in so many of the nasty little colonial wars, marking the post-Second War retreat from Empire, as Frank Waters.

"I've been thinking about that, sir," the ex-SAS man admitted. "I don't doubt that there may yet be a hard core of fanatics out there; real Red Dawn zealots and presumably, no end of good, honest, misguided Communists and suchlike... I don't think there was ever any such thing as a Front Internationale Army, just a bunch of these Revolutionary Guard chappies who either fight to the death or push women and children out in front of their lines and bravely run away in the other direction. Insurgency, guerrilla warfare is a damned funny thing; it is hard to know what one is dealing with at the best of times. For what it's worth, I suspect that the farther one travels from the centre of command, down in the Auvergne, it may be that true believers are few and far between and that explains why we've carved through them like a knife through butter in the last forty-eight hours."

Carver said nothing, patiently waiting for the other man to continue, knowing he had spent a lot of time in the last few days interrogating prisoners of war and deserters.

"From the fellows that I've talked to," Frank Waters offered, "between you and I, a real shower, I can tell you; they all seem to have known their number was up months ago. Some of the cheeky sods even had the gall to ask me why we hadn't attacked last autumn! Anyway, the rub is, I don't get any impression that the FI is built or mentally acclimatised to a long, hard slog. This isn't going to be like trying to chuck the Nazis out of Normandy or the Rhineland in the last show. That said, for all I know the chaps down south have got better guns, or the latest Russian kit, and they'll fight better but seriously, I rather doubt it. It may be that the Navy turning up off the coast and a few more raids like the one on Clermont-Ferrand, will do the trick..."

"Interesting," the Chief of the Defence Force mused. "I'll leave you to get on, Frank. Please give my most cordial regards to Alain."

Chapter 56

Monday 13th February 1967
City Hall, San Francisco

The Secret Service and the San Francisco PD would have made more of a song and dance about the Prime Minister's bodyguards firing live rounds in the air, and causing a stampede in which several people had been injured, had it not been for history.

In December 1963 the Secret Service had allowed a deeply troubled woman employed as a White House secretary to assassinate Edward Heath in the Oval Office, when the British premier was standing next to President Kennedy.

It later transpired that the woman responsible, Edna Zabriski, had had a long struggle with mental illness, and had finally been pushed over the edge by her husband's disappearance in the Sammanish strike on metropolitan Seattle during the night of the October War. Thereafter, she had been preyed upon and come under the spell of a mysterious 'preacher', who had later turned out to be the same evil, Svengali type leader – Galen Cheney, the notoriously psychopathic would be messiah to the religious zealots who had stormed the British Embassy and for twenty-four hours, carried out a reign of terror, rape and murder at the Wister Park compound. Galen Cheney had supposedly been killed by the Marine Corps when they finally lifted the siege. What was *not* public knowledge was that Cheney had actually died of his wounds, wounds inflicted by Rachel Piotrowska, some hours *after* the Marines stormed the Embassy.

However, this latter was not relevant to the reluctance of the authorities to make an issue of the AWPs firing a volley over the head of the press corps and the members of the public who had been allowed, inadvertently, inside the security cordons. No, the memory of the grotesque failure of the Secret Service to protect a foreign leader in the Oval Office – because of which, Edward Heath had been shot to death by the aforementioned 'crazy woman', Edna Zabriski – meant that it was going to be a very long time before any American was going to even think about laying down the law to the officer in command of a British Prime Minister's security detail.

It spoke not just to the chaos outside in the streets around City Hall but also to that within the Administration, that Richard Nixon should be making what his staff promised would be a major foreign policy announcement, early in the evening on the West Coast at a time when most viewers had already gone to bed on the East Coast and back in Washington DC. Normally, major speeches were timed to hit the network TV and radio channels when the whole country was awake.

Sensibly, the Soviet delegation had declined its invitation to the evening's main event; presumably, Alexander Shelepin and his comrades were settled around a television set in the comfort and security of their lodge at the Presidio.

Lady Patricia Harding-Grayson had reminded her younger friend what 'a lucky so and so' her Soviet counterpart was!

Soft drinks and liquor were served at the over-crowded, noisy reception in the rotunda, a hurried, sweaty affair with dignitaries mingling uncomfortably around the base or on the lower steps of the giant staircase. Everything was running behind schedule and it was necessary to get everybody seated in the main chamber ahead of the President's grand entrance. So, the Prime Minister and her party assumed their seats in the front row of the North Light Court.

And waited...

Inevitably, looking round at her surroundings, Margaret Thatcher found herself wondering if one or other of the great lecture halls at Stanford or Berkeley, or a theatre in the city might not have served better for the purpose of the President's first, belated appearance in San Francisco since his arrival last week.

"Ladies and gentlemen, the President of the United States!"

Richard Nixon made a courageous attempt to make an entrance, smiling and waving as if for a moment he had forgotten where he was and this was an election rally, not a solemn international gathering.

A broad lectern stood centre-stage, with two relatively slim steel microphones standing proud, rather like twin Cobras ready to strike, spitting venom in his eyes...

The President gripped the lectern, and steadied himself.

Rumours that the Commander-in-Chief had been unwell had been circulated, no doubt in the forlorn hope of defusing the widespread anger that he had failed to attend any of the sessions on board the USS United States. Indeed, to many of those closest to the stage, Richard Nixon did not look like a man in the rudest of health; he seemed hangdog, a little jowly and his make-up people ought to have done something about the bags under his eyes. He was like a man still suffering the tail end of a bout of influenza, or a bad hangover, or who had not slept properly for several days, or perhaps, an unfortunate soul afflicted by all three contingencies.

"I will start with an apology," the most powerful man in the world declared, his voice belying his physical appearance, ringing with practiced sincerity and gravitas. "You may have heard that I travelled to California against the advice of my doctors. Influenza these days is not to be taken lightly I was warned, and so it has proved. I am pleased to say that I am much recovered and Pat," he grimaced, referring to his wife whom he had wisely left back in Washington with his daughters, "reluctantly, I might say, gave me permission to rise from my sick bed when I spoke to her by telephone this afternoon."

This actually raised a murmur of amusement, albeit of the world-weary jaundiced variety in the high-ceilinged North Light Room of City Hall. Nobody in the room could realistically claim to be completely unaware of the President's 'little local difficulties', some probably even had a degree of sympathy for him; he was after all, the man who had just won the war in the Midwest, defeating a truly malevolent enemy and older, wiser heads among the national movers and shakers in his audience would have recognised that whatever Richard Nixon's domestic opponents said about him, his problems were by no means all or even substantially, of his own making. More pertinently, Richard Milhous Nixon was *not* actually the American President who had set the hounds of thermonuclear Hell upon the northern hemisphere at the end of October 1962. Nor was the resignation, or some said behind their hands, overdue removal of Henry Kissinger, from the President's circle of advisors viewed by all of those listening that evening, in any way unwelcome. In fact, to the majority of those present, the unalloyed gently patrician 1950's attitudes and experience of veteran Gordon Gray was infinitely preferable to the less ideological, stony pragmatism of the departed cerebral Harvard academic.

Moreover, given that only a minority – twenty-two of the ninety-two delegations which had eventually arrived in San Francisco – had been led by a national leader, or even an equivalent head of state figure. So, President Nixon's semi-detached approach to the gathering had not exactly been exceptional, and in contrast to three-quarters of his fellow heads of state, he at least was in San Francisco.

The President began to tick off the normal diplomatic niceties which always prolonged any major diplomatic gathering, employing a standard formulaic hyperbole praising the motives and the diligence of the participants, speaking to a generosity of spirit – of which there had been virtually none on display aboard the USS United States – and everybody's general good intentions, evidence of which was in even shorter supply. Seasoned politicians and rapporteurs, kept straight faces and tuned out the weasel words, waiting patiently for something of substance more in hope than expectation.

"To my mind this has been a good start," the President declared. "A positive first initiative to repair the fabric of international relations in the aftermath of the most catastrophic war in the history of Mankind."

Oddly, the prevailing mood of the British party in San Francisco was that although the event might not have been a 'good' start, neither had it been a complete disaster.

Viewed in the round, the Soviets had attended; and not walked out half-way through. The United Kingdom's observations about the make-up of the Security Council had caused much offence; but again, nobody had stormed out, packed their bags and immediately flown or sailed home.

The appointment of George Bush, whom members of the delegation had got to know a little better, as Ambassador to the rededicated United Nations augured well for the future. The man was clearly engaged in the process started on board the USS United States, and no kind of unthinking mouthpiece for the Administration, right or wrong. True, it was a pity Henry Kissinger had felt unable to carry on; but again, his successor was a tried and tested man with real standing in Washington, so not all was lost. And there had been no little quiet, 'soft' diplomacy going on in the background.

For example, Margaret Thatcher had lunched with the new Indian Prime Minister, Indira Gandhi, and it had been arranged, although not announced nor would it be for some days, that she would 'call in on' her fellow premier in Delhi on her way back to England from her next port of call, Australia. Further to this, the presence of so many senior figures from the New Commonwealth had been a boon, with Tom Harding-Grayson assiduously 'doing the rounds.' Commonwealth business would also be front and centre when she entertained both the Australian and the New Zealand delegations, both led by their respective Prime Ministers, on the long flight back to Australasia on board Commonwealth One, via a refuelling stop at Honolulu in the coming week...

Margaret Thatcher guiltily realised she had been wool-gathering, lulled into a sense of false security by the President's overlong introductory spiel. She hated to think it, and certainly would not admit it but frankly, on the evidence of the last few days, Soviet Leader Alexander Shelepin presently had a better speech-writer than the President of the United States.

Of course, in Pat Harding-Grayson, by profession a very successful pre-October War novelist, it went without saying that *her* own personal wordsmith was the queen of expression!

Even though at heart, Pat was every bit as incorrigible an old socialist as her rascally husband!

"We learn things by meeting and listening to others, our friends and our opponents, those who agree with us and those who do not, and perhaps, can never agree with us. We also learn by experience," Richard Nixon continued, quirking an unconvincing self-deprecatory smile. "Most of all we learn that one should not believe everything one reads in the papers, hears on the radio or sees on the TV. International relations are a lot more complicated than the Editor of *The Washington Post* will ever admit, as he should well know as a former CIA man!"

Margaret Thatcher did not know if this was supposed to be a witty aside, or a stiletto-like stab at his leading critic. Either way, it seemed wholly inappropriate in a setting such as this to be airing one's own dirty linen. She could not imagine Tom Harding-Grayson or Airey Neave allowing a line like that to survive in a draft of one of her speeches; or indeed, that Pat would for a moment, contemplate including such a reckless hostage to fortune in one of her carefully crafted scripts.

The President had obvious anticipated that his barb – rather clumsy character assassination of a known political rival - would go down a lot better than it actually did, and momentarily, in his chagrin, he lost his flow. He shuffled the papers on the lectern, possibly abandoning the next paragraph of the speech he had intended to deliver.

"Trust is the hardest thing to earn and the most dangerous thing to risk losing," he declaimed with grating pomposity, picking up the pace. "After previous great conflicts the nations came together to discuss the post-war settlement. Sometimes, this worked out better than others. For example, at Vienna the powers which had defeated Napoleon brought peace to Western Europe for two generations and established, possibly for the first time in history, protocols and rules by which we still conduct diplomacy. At Versailles after the First War of the twentieth century, a less successful settlement emerged. At Yalta and then Potsdam, the victorious Allies arrived at another pragmatic, nonetheless imperfect agreement, having already agreed that the United Nations should replace the old, failed, League of Nations. However, even though none of these post-war solutions were ultimately successful in outlawing wars between the great powers, each at least guaranteed a breathing space. One view of history might be that Mankind wasted those 'breathing spaces' and another might be that we are an inherently self-destructive species."

Margaret Thatcher blinked, glancing to her Foreign Secretary who contented himself with a raised eyebrow, obviously content to ignore the President's half-baked attempt at existential soul-searching.

"I choose not to believe this," the President decided, his tone increasingly stentorian. "I do not believe that we are destined to repeat, time and again, the mistakes of our fathers. We must believe that we have the power – in our own hands – to decide our destiny. War and peace are conscious choices that nations must take; not accidents of fate or even, as historians claim, commonly the consequence of miscalculations, or accidents of circumstance."

He paused, perspiring now under the glare of the TV lights.

"Words alone are not enough. Truly, actions speak louder than any words. The pen might be mighty but deeds are mightier. We have come together here in San Francisco to re-dedicate the United Nations. Let us never allow this august body to become again a witness to catastrophe, powerless to halt the march of events. In 1964 and 1965 many of the nations represented here today met and attempted to address the great issues of our time at the Manhattan Peace Process, so brutally cut short by the war-mongering of the fanatics of the End of Days cult. I know that many still harbour recriminations about the failure of that process. Attaching blame is wasting time that we may not have. We must commence anew a meaningful global peace process."

"This will be good!" Tom Harding-Grayson muttered sarcastically, clearly with little real expectation.

"I remain convinced that the United Nations is the best, last, only global forum capable of hosting comprehensive peace talks between the parties and the victims of the Cuban Missiles War."

Given the United States' apparent indifference to the United Nations in the last few days this came as something of a shock to many in City Hall that night.

However, what came next positively electrified the President's listeners.

"Chairman Shelepin has generously issued an invitation to me to visit him in Russia," Richard Nixon bored on relentlessly, "an invitation that I will be pleased to accept in the coming months. In this connection I am able to inform the Assembly that earlier this evening Secretary of State Cabot Lodge met with, and agreed with his counterpart, Ambassador Kuznetsov, that Chairman Shelepin will be my guests at the White House later this week. It is the hope of both our governments that these meetings, in Washington and later, in Russia, will lead to a general relaxation of tensions between our two great countries and ultimately, to a long-term peaceful rapprochement which will guard against us ever again, stumbling into the nightmare of a new global nuclear war."

Everybody was clapping.

People began to get to their feet.

Margaret Thatcher stood up and turned to her Foreign Secretary.

"Is this good or bad news, Tom?" she whispered out of the corner of her mouth, trying to keep on smiling.

"Frankly," her friend sighed, "I haven't a clue, Margaret."

Chapter 57

Tuesday 14th February 1967
HMS Campbeltown, Bay of Lions, Western Mediterranean

Dermot O'Reilly had led his three Fletchers, the Dundee and the Perth pursuing the Campbeltown north through the Straits of Messina, up the Tyrrhenian coast of Italy past Sardinia and Corsica, and across the southern quarter of the Ligurian Sea to re-join Task Force V1, at breakneck speed. Clearing the Grand Harbour breakwaters at dawn the previous day, and rushing north at near flank speed for several hours before the heavier seas had forced him to reduce speed to twenty-five knots, it had been a real rollercoaster ride. Any destroyer man lived for those days when his captain ordered the engine room to 'open up all the taps' and his ship careened through the waves with a giant bone in her teeth, her stern dug deep into the insanely foaming waters under her transom. To be in company with two other sister ships likewise charging headlong was to be in destroyer-man heaven...

"Signal to Flagship," Dermot O'Reilly said, chuckling contentedly as he turned to the Officer of the Watch, Lieutenant Keith Moss, a young man whom he knew to still be walking on water after his experience aboard the Jean Bart, "Campbeltown, Dundee and Perth have re-joined the fleet."

"Campbeltown, Dundee and Perth have re-joined the fleet, aye, sir," the younger man acknowledged with a broad smile.

Both O'Reilly and Keith Moss had been on the bridge from the moment the ship had cleared the Grand Harbour, neither yet touched by the weariness which would, inevitably catch up with them later when the exhilaration of the 'run north' slowly leeched out of their systems.

In a moment the yeoman manning the port Aldis lamp was clattering the signal to HMS Victorious, still over a mile-and-a-half distant as the Campeltown and her two sisters heeled into racing turns to take up position off the carrier's starboard quarter.

The destroyer's Engineer stomped onto the compass platform shortly afterwards to report on bunker levels. Notwithstanding the Fletchers' boilers were monstrously thirsty when 'all the taps were open', Campbeltown would have no need to seek an oiler for several days. The class had been built to rove the massive expanses of the Pacific, designed to operate for days on end at full, or damned nearly full, speed ahead. Moreover, despite their war service twenty years ago, O'Reilly's Fletchers were relatively 'young' ships, or, as he had once explained it to a politician, twenty-year-old sports cars that were flogged to death for a couple of years and have been resting, fully restored ever since. So, Campbeltown suffered little from 'old-boiler-syndrome', had few clogged or furred pipes, nothing rusted or seized in her fire rooms and her turbines, meant to work hard for a decade or two, were still lightly used, efficient, working as per specification or as near as damn it. Yes, at high speed she drank prodigious quantities of heavy bunker oil; but her machinery remained in 'good enough nick', in the Engineer's words, to get 'real value for money out of every drop of the black stuff!'

"How are things down there, Chief?" O'Reilly inquired as he signed off the bunker level report and handed the clipboard back to the Engineering Officer.

"We'll need to let Boiler Number Two go cold the next time we're in port, sir. Nothing to worry about." The other man grinned. "Just don't ask me to make smoke before then or the whole fire room compartment will be like a chimney sweeps' reunion when my boys crawl around inside the works!"

Making smoke involved deliberately injecting water, tinkering with the air blowers and not making optimum adjustments to the amount or the pressure under which oil was pumped into the boilers. In fact, a smoky ship was either a ship with boiler troubles, or an incompetent operator at the injector controls down in the bowels of the vessel.

"I'll bear that in mind if we come under attack, Chief," O'Reilly promised. "In the meantime, make sure your chaps know what a nailed-on good job they're doing down there!"

The Engineering Officer departed, smiling broadly.

Now that the enemy knew the task force was operating off its coast radio silence had been abandoned. Strictly speaking, O'Reilly's Aldis lamp signal was superfluous, both Campbeltown and the flagship having been exchanging signals for several days and the approach of the three returning destroyers having been monitored by one or other of the Victorious's Fairey Gannet AEW3 airborne early warning aircraft for the last three or four hours.

Nevertheless, there was something right and proper about the traditional 're-joining the fleet' signals.

Victorious was replying in kind.

"GOOD TO HAVE YOU BACK DERMOT!"

Not entirely as per the rule book but everybody on the destroyer's bridge was grinning from ear to ear.

A few minutes later the Dundee and the Perth relieved the Leander class general purpose frigate Ajax and their sister ship, the Berwick, and the Campbeltown stood towards the north, with the Ajax and the Berwick, working up to twenty-one knots to rendezvous with the Kent Bombardment Group, led by the heavy cruiser Kent, the former USS Des Moines (CA-134), currently in company with only a single escort, the newly arrived Leith, of O'Reilly's 21st Destroyer Squadron. Approximately thirty miles to the east, the old cruiser Belfast was in company with two more of Dermot O'Reilly's Fletchers, the Dunbar and the Stirling.

Task Force V1 was now split into three dispersed groups: the Kent and Belfast bombardment squadrons loitering within about twenty-five miles of the coast, the former in the Bay of Lions, the latter off the old French Riviera cruising south of Nice, Villefranche and Monaco; and the Victorious with the Assault ship Fearless, several destroyers and frigates, a Royal Fleet Auxiliary oiler and two general supply ships, generally about fifty miles out to sea. The big County class destroyer Hampshire – she was the size of a Second War light cruiser – was never far from the flagship, effectively acting as the Victorious's guard ship or 'goalkeeper', ready if the worst came to the worst to physically impose herself between real and present danger and the carrier.

At most times there was a Fairey Gannet AEW3, and a pair of De Havilland Sea Vixen FAW2s in the air. Notwithstanding the Victorious presently had only five of her seven 'Vixens' available for operations, 899 Naval Air Squadron had embarked eleven pilots and twelve navigator EWO – Electronic Warfare Officers – to ensure continual turn and turn again operations.

Last night, both the Kent and the Belfast had steamed within five or six miles of the coast and bombarded targets in and around Toulon and Marseilles, Montpellier and suspected 'regime objectives' up to fifteen miles inland all along the Bay of Lions.

While Campbeltown had been away, Westland Whirlwind helicopters flying off the Fearless had flown half-a-dozen missions to insert two and three-man Royal Marine SBS – Special Boat Squadron – teams, in some cases many miles inland to reconnoitre the ground, identify targets for naval bombardment and air attack, and to gather general intelligence.

Within a couple of hours, Dermot O'Reilly was chatting amiably with the man commanding the Kent Bombardment Group, forty-two-year-old Captain John Treacher, over the scrambled TBS network as the Campbeltown ranged up alongside the huge former US Navy heavy cruiser HMS Kent.

The two captains had first met in April 1964 when O'Reilly had been on that dreadful post-Battle of Malta public speaking tour. He had discovered that he and John Treacher were both 'foreigners', and 'half Canucks', Treacher having been born in Chile to an Anglo-Argentine father and a Canadian mother. They had hit it off from the outset and kept in touch, sporadically, ever since. Strictly speaking Treacher – in this situation his commanding officer – was actually Dermot O'Reilly's junior by a few months, seniority-wise, his commission having been awarded a few months after Dermot's RNVR, 'wavy-Navy' sub-lieutenant's ring back in the Second War years.

The two men joked over this.

Laughed together, oblivious to the fact their respective bridge crews were greedily overhearing every word.

Treacher had been on the old battleship HMS Nelson as she bombarded the defences of the landing beaches off Sicily in 1943, and served on the destroyer Keppel on the Murmansk Run. After 1945 he had trained as a naval aviator, flying Seafire Mk 47s off the aircraft carrier Triumph with 800 Naval Air Squadron. In the first Korean War he had flown raids over the North, later, he had been Executive Officer of HMS Protector, the Navy's Antarctic guard ship, and commanded the crew transferring the light carrier Hercules to the Indian Navy, served in Washington DC, and at the time of the October War been Naval Assistant to the Controller of the Navy.

Sadly, his wife, son and daughter had not survived the war.

"You, lucky blighter! Giving your ship her head all the way north from Malta!" John Treacher exclaimed. "I hope somebody took some photographs? I suppose you want to come alongside and top off your bloody bunkers now?"

Dermot O'Reilly chortled.

"No, we're good for a few days, John."

Soon they got down to business.

John Treacher had been anticipating his reinforcements and thinking about how best to use them the next time he took the Kent inshore.

"Guns tells me we your Fletchers ought to be able to slave your main batteries to Kent's secondary fire director control. Can your ships cope with that? I'm not convinced? What do you think, Dermot?"

O'Reilly thought about it.

"Perhaps, we ought to test his theory," he returned. "I'll get my CIC working on it. How about if I fall in astern at say, two thousand yards," he was working out the approximate gunnery trigonometry in his head, "that ought to give us sufficient separation for Kent's fire control radar to work out the relative deflections."

The business end of the big cruiser's radars – its aerials - were at least three times higher off the water and therefore, farther seeing, and less prone to degradation due to sea conditions than those just above Dermot O'Reilly's head on board the Campbeltown. Therefore, if the destroyer's main battery fire control could be successfully slaved to the Kent's, her gunnery ought to be more accurate, especially at longer ranges shooting over her own visible horizon, or targets at night.

The two men chatted a while longer then handed the problem over to their respective gunnery officers, who quickly asked for their EWOs to be brought into the discussion.

Treacher signed off with the confirmation that: "We're still awaiting tasking orders for this evening."

O'Reilly had just got sat down on his cot in his claustrophobic sea cabin when the collision bell started ringing.

Stepping back onto the bridge he was informed: "Perth reports a possible submarine contact bearing one-seven-five true, range eight thousand yards, sir!"

O'Reilly did not hesitate.

"Helmsman, full right wheel."

He nodded to the Officer of the Watch.

"Make revolutions for twenty-seven knots!" Dermot O'Reilly set his jaw, and added: "The ship will come to actions stations, if you please!"

Chapter 58

Tuesday 14th February 1967
Château Frédignac, Blaye

Sergey Akhromeyev had been introduced to Paddy Ashdown's band of eight hardened cutthroats – proud brigands all - only that afternoon. The Royal Marines had formed a presentation line, their cap badges aligned on their green berets as they stood to, at ease, before the stranger.

'This is Major General Akhromeyev, formerly of the Red Army, now the Officer Commanding the Vindrey Commando, currently forming in Herefordshire. Henceforth, he had requested that we all address him as 'Sergey' until the conclusion of Operation Blondie,' Ashdown had declared. 'He is not a Royal Marine, not everybody is that fortunate. Get used to it. However, Sergey is an experienced soldier accustomed to the ways of special operations, who has a lot of experience fighting Krasnaya Zarya. He will be coming with us to Bordeaux tonight.'

The Russian had thought it was all a little bizarre.

Ashdown was at once familiar with and yet wholly in command of his men.

'I have explained to Sergey how the Royal Marines won their badge and what is expected of him as an honorary member of our tribe.'

Akhromeyev had blanched at the lecture.

'The Lion and Crown at the top of the badge denotes that the Corps is a Royal Regiment. We were granted that honour in 1802. Included on the badge is a single battle honour, Gibraltar, which *we*, with a little help from the Dutch, captured from the Spanish in 1704. There is a globe device at the heart of the insignia, awarded to *us* by His Majesty King George IV in 1827 in recognition of the Corps' world-wide exploits. About it is a laurel wreath motif, granted to the Corps in 1761 after the Battle of Belle Island. The fouled anchor was added to the original badge in 1747, acknowledging the Corps' intimate relationship with the Royal Navy. Finally, you can make out *our* motto in Latin: *Per Mare, Per Terram*. Which translates as *By Sea, By Land*!'

The Russian had listened respectfully.

'That,' the younger officer had informed him, 'is what *we* are. My father was very nearly court martialled for refusing to leave men behind. Like father, like son. Whatever happens on the coming operation, we leave nobody behind, General Akhromeyev.'

The Russian had learned a lot in the few short hours he had been in the company of Ashdown's band of brothers. There had been twenty-three of them when they came to France. Three of the 'originals' were presently filling staff or liaison roles at the 4th Tank's headquarters, one was on board HMS Eagle, assigned to the carrier's Special Operations Staff, five men had been killed, another was missing presumed drowned on active duty, and another four invalided home, three with combat wounds, the other man having broken both his legs on a training exercise.

Akhromeyev had asked why the men lost had not been replaced. Ashdown had smiled wanly.

'There aren't that many of us left. Here, or in England, or elsewhere. The SAS lot,' most Royal Marines regarded their Army, Special Air Service counterparts as scruffy, lower forms of life, 'are, for once, in the same boat as we are. The priority is Operation Watch on the Rhine. That's where all the replacements go.'

The Russian had been impressed, as he was constantly being impressed, by the way in which it was accepted British practice to ensure that even junior officers like Ashdown, had a basic, sound understanding of the bigger strategic-tactical situation. *Need to know* tended to be restricted to current or ongoing operations that men really 'did not need to know' about to perform their roles locally. Everybody seemed to have a real sense of where they, personally, fitted in and exactly why they had been asked to do what they were doing. If he wanted to be, the lowliest private soldier could be a grand strategist, in his own head, at least. It made for an ease of inter-unit and service co-operation and a level of inter-arms integration that was unthinkable in the Red Army, and clearly, this way of war intrinsically strengthened unit cohesion and promoted high morale.

Paddy Ashdown's little army had a formidable stash of weaponry.

Several of his men hefted AK-47s.

'The locals didn't know what to do with them so we relieved them of the problem,' one broken-nosed man explained gruffly, handing a 'spare' to Akhromeyev. 'That's a good one. Made in Bulgaria before the war, not one of those cheap knock-offs from the factories in the Ukraine!'

The Marines knew a lot about the Avtomat Kalashnikova gas-operated, 7.62-millimetre assault rifle designed by Mikhail Kalashnikov back in the late 1940s. Only the 'traditionalists' still used the British Army issue Sterling sub-machinegun.

'Give me an AK any day,' one man chuckled.

Paddy Ashdown had listened to the exchange.

'Some of the chaps swear by them,' he confided, 'most reliable piece of kit I've ever used,' he added, grudgingly.

But then Sergey Akhromeyev already knew all about the capabilities of the AK-47. Rain, snow, hail, mud, sand, dust, grime, it could cope with them all. Drop it, sit on it, shake it all about and it would still keep putting rounds down the barrel. It was a real 'working gun'; moreover, with a standard magazine of thirty 7.62-millimetre rounds, a muzzle velocity of 700 metres a second – faster than a supersonic jet - and a rate of fire of around 600 rounds per minute, what more could a trained killer possibly ask for?

Operation Blondie had turned into one of those insane adventures it hardly bore thinking about, well before the approaching thrumming of the rotors of the first of the two Westland Wessex's tasked to transport the strike force to Bordeaux, began to rattle the windows of the old chateau that Paddy Ashdown's battle-hardened veterans called home.

There was still over ninety minutes to go before four De Havilland Sea Vixen FAW2s and four Blackburn Buccaneer S2s flying off HMS Eagle, forty miles out to sea strafed and bombed targets in and around the inland port of Bordeaux, and hopefully, dropped flares and ground markers to guide the Royal Marines' helicopters 'right onto the money'.

"Normally," Paddy Ashdown explained to his new Russian comrade, 'we'd set off on this thing in our boats carrying up to sixty or seventy pounds – say thirty plus kilos – of equipment, because we'd be planning to live off the land for an extended period. Tonight, we'll just go in with our personal weapons, demolition charges and ropes to allow us to abseil off the roof of the U-boat pens. That'll be a pleasant change, getting stuck in straight away without any of the normal creeping around trying to stay unseen in the landscape.'

Getting 'stuck in' was clearly a thing Ashdown was looking forward to! However, while this was commendable in any soldier, Akhromeyev was thoughtful about the runaway enthusiasm with which his new British friends embraced what he viewed as a semi-suicidal enterprise. This made it all the odder that although, on balance he would rather live than die, he had no personal reservations about taking part in this 'reckless' mission. He had thrown in his lot with his former enemies, knew in his heart that he could never return home, and understood also that if he was to have a life worth living in 'the West', and to be a respected leader of those other former Red Army, Air Force and Navy men who had made similar choices, he needed to do something, ideally spectacular, to cement his standing.

It was as simple and as cynical as that; either he grasped this transient opportunity or he, and his people, would become irrelevant adjuncts, and in time an embarrassment to their hosts in England.

If he had to get killed to secure a place in the West for *his* people, well, that was a price worth paying. He just hoped that if and when he got back to Hereford to explain himself to Vera, that she would not shoot him for being such an idiot.

Sergey Akhromeyev had decided he was going to marry Madame Vera Bertrand. He should have done it before he left England; they had been as good as man and wife for over two years, partners, each other's closest, best friend and most trusted confidante. Yes, he ought to have tied the knot a long time ago. She would be incredibly pissed off with him if he got himself killed...

Turning his mind back to the radically stripped down and re-focused objectives of Operation Blondie, the trouble with 'the plan', audacious as it was, was that it could all go horribly wrong in the blink of an eye. Not just because the best photographs they had of the old U-boat pens were twenty years old; or because the only intelligence to hand in any way strongly suggesting that they were being used as the Front Internationale's headquarters in the city, came from one, seriously wounded prisoner. They had no way of knowing if this information was simply another piece of Krasnaya Zarya misinformation, a ruse to persuade the British to bomb the wrong buildings, or real gold dust. On the other hand, the Front

Internationale leadership seemed to have a penchant for hiding underground, or under concrete and leaving all the fighting and the dying to its conscripted and terrorised foot soldiers, many of whom were only fighting under its banner because they believed their families were being held hostage.

Sergey Akhromeyev had been fighting the twin curse of Krasnaya Zarya and the Front Internationale for a lot longer than his new British friends; and understood the nature of the beast intimately. That was why he was less worried than Paddy Ashdown's superiors about where precisely, the leadership of the FI was likely to be found in Bordeaux. To him, it seemed axiomatic that even if the BETASOM U-boat pens were not the actual city HQ; it would be an important FI target. If it happened that the top dogs were hiding in the complex, all the better; either way attacking it, and killing as many of the bastards hiding in it, would be a good start!

In any event, it seemed that the British were content to risk the lives of nine Royal Marines and a renegade Red Army cast-off to establish, one way or another, to establish the truth about the BETASOM base from which those Regia Marina submarines had operated from between 1941 to 1943.

True, the RAF or the Fleet Air Arm might wreck the place with bunker-busting bombs and kill everybody inside. But then nobody would be the wiser as to whether the place had been a bomb shelter, a stores depot or a headquarters. And in any event, a bombing raid from a high enough altitude to optimise the chance of a big bomb bursting through the several metre-thick reinforced concrete roofs of the old U-boat pens would be an inherently perilous undertaking. There were known to be SS-75 high-altitude surface-to-air missile batteries defending Clermont-Ferrand and the possibility that there might be more, hidden inside the urban sprawl of Bordeaux, waiting to target high-flying bombers making precision attacks, clearly lessened the British appetite for risking scarce fast jet assets on what was, after all, a purely speculative operation.

Akhromeyev liked the pared back economy and simplicity of the operational plan: under cover of the attack by the Eagle's Sea Vixens and Buccaneers, the two Wessex's, each carrying a five-man assault team, would rattle in at rooftop height from the north, using Blanquefort not as a drop point but as a way marker, and land on the roof of the BETASOM complex.

Since there was absolutely no profit decamping from the three to five-metre thick reinforced concrete roof onto the landward side of the complex, the assumption being that the occupants would by then, understandably have locked themselves in behind half-a-metre thick steel blast doors, the strike teams were going to have to gain entrance to the facility via the 'wet side' of the establishment, abseiling – hopefully – onto the docksides of one or other of the eleven 'pens', all of which were believed to be flooded.

Sergey Akhromeyev had blanched somewhat when he discovered that what his new comrades described as 'abseiling' – supposedly controlled descents on a line coiled about one's waist – was in their parlance, actually the most reckless form of rappelling; basically, donning leather gloves and sliding, or more likely falling, down a rope, a thing he had not done for years. Now, while this might be all in a day's work for Paddy Ashdown's – much younger - men, all of whom were in peak physical condition, it was not going to be a lot of fun for a forty-three-year-old veteran of the great Patriotic War!

Ashdown casually, and Akhromeyev suspected, a little sarcastically, had generously offered to 'lower' him off the roof.

"Niet," the Russian had growled. "If I fall in the water, I fall in the water!"

"Oh, don't do that, old man," the Royal Marine had counselled earnestly. "You'll almost certainly drown."

Akhromeyev had agreed to do his best not to do that!

Ashdown had concisely summed up 'the drill' as the thrumming beat of helicopter rotors approached the landing field outside the Château Frédignac.

"We get inside, we kill everybody, we grab any interesting paperwork, and take a few holiday snaps," a man in each of the two sub-teams, one in each helicopter carried a small Leica camera, "and we bug out of there. No prisoners. Then we head for the pickup point on the bank of the river."

The helicopters were supposed to approach at 'zero feet' following the line of the River and lift off the survivors from a rendezvous located about a kilometre north of the BETASOM complex in the Bacalan neighbourhood of the city.

Sergey Akhromeyev had remarked that it was all a little...haphazard.

'Yes,' Paddy Ashdown admitted, privately as the two men had briefed Edwin Bramall. However, not caring to be out-done by the Royal Marines the RAF were 'game for it' and the commanding officer of the 4th Tanks had been itching to 'keep up the pressure' on his enemies.

Sergey Akhromeyev got the impression that his allies had got very, very used to making the best of a bad deal in the last four years. And now, at a few minutes before midnight he was clambering into the cabin of a Westland Wessex beneath slowly churning rotors as the rain began to fall.

At times such as this a man could do no more than take a firm grip of his gun and get on with it.

Chapter 59

Wednesday 15th February 1967
Clermont-Ferrand, France

Comrade Agnès had led the Russians away from the flaring fires consuming the roof of the Cathédrale Notre-Dame-de-l'Assomption, initially guiding them west along Rue Blatin. She really only had the one thought: to get out of the city, better to freeze or starve to death in the woods than to be lynched from a lamp post or... *worse.*

She had never been a very recognisable member of the Central Committee, active only in the under belly of the madhouse based in the heart of the old, mostly idle and abandoned Michelin Works less than a kilometre northeast of the now burning black-lava-stone cathedral. Despite her rank and two-year-long membership of the ruling council of the FI, most people outside the hierarchy assumed she was a drone-like secretary, a menial clerk dragging around after Maxim Machenaud like all the other beaten dogs. It had assisted in her quest for anonymity that she was pretty, affecting girlish attractiveness had never bothered her when she was younger, and the ravages of the new age had made all that frippery academic. She was a classic 'Plain Jane' in the parlance of the American academics she had rubbed shoulders with in the old days; blond, lithe not willowy, a little flat-chested, androgynous, she had always been a tom boy in her girlhood, happier in the rough and tumble games of childhood with her brother, and later, had never seen the point in embracing the coquettish ways of her much younger little sister.

She and Aurélie had never been that close as youngsters. Her sister was eight years her junior, a big gap between sisters and by the time they had both grown up, made their own lives, it had been too late to make up for lost time.

Edward, her brother, the younger by a mere fifteen months, had, like her, been separated from their mother in the Second War, sent to live in the country, brought up, by kindly strangers, old friends of their father. They had been strangers to their mother, who had married less than a year after the death of *their* father – swept off her feet by the 'bravest of all aviators', Aurélie's father within a year of his death. She remembered her step-father well, maddeningly, even better than she did her own father.

François de Seligny, the dashing, raconteur and adventurer son of a famous family, and in his spare time, the commanding officer of one of the elite fighter squadrons of the *Armée de l'Air*, whose Dewoitine D.520 fighter had crashed and burned in a field near Verdun less than forty-eight hours after the German's invaded France in May 1940. Her mother had always loved *that* man in the way she had never loved Eddy, or her, or their father...

Perhaps, she had blamed Aurélie for that.

Perhaps, not.

It had all seemed so pointless after Eddy was killed in Algeria; and then soon afterwards, the sky had fallen in and the whole world had gone to shit...

Nevertheless, she gone to Lyon to search for her sister a year or so after the war; but nobody had heard of her, or knew what had happened to her or her husband, Pierre, who had always had such grand plans, and talked about taking his wife to live with his family in Paris...

She had assumed that Aurélie and Pierre had gone back to Paris just in time for the bomb...

She had never seen what Aurélie saw in Pierre, the man was a handsome, charming waster, a spoiled rich boy brought up always expecting something to turn up.

Comrade Agnès kept walking, trudging along the track in the woods as the moisture dripped frigidly off the bare, overhanging branches.

The Russians had followed her like children...

Granted, cursing and complaining, spiteful bad-tempered, resentful brats desperately pretending that they were not scared shitless. Whatever they said, she just kept walking faster, trotting or jogging, stopping without warning if she sensed danger. The idiots must have honestly believed she was leading them to safety; using her intimate knowledge of the city of her birth – although they would not have known that – to spirit *them* to safety.

But then that was the way those children in Hamlin had probably felt about the Pied Piper.

Aurélie had always been the one for fairy stories.

And why not?

She was the pretty one, elfin with twinkling brown eyes to charm the pants of any man. Not, to be fair to her, that she had ever been that sort of girl, just different in every way to Agnès as sisters often can be except in their case, so different as to seem hardly related at all.

Aurélie had disappeared; these days that meant she was dead, too.

Two of the KGB troopers had fired at her as Agnès had suddenly sprinted into a narrow alleyway. One bullet had ricocheted off the brickwork and peppered her with masonry chips, filled her hair with dust and chips that had grazed her skull, and stung abominably for a few minutes. She had carried on running, following the bewildering warren of narrow streets through the old pre-Second War town, where so many of the Michelin workers and their large families had lived in polite poverty. Nowadays, hardly anybody inhabited the derelict district, which was impassable to wheeled vehicles because so many of the streets were still choked with the uncleared rubble from the fighting between the old Communist rulers, and the first Krasnaya Zarya zealots back in the winter of 1963-64.

That old fart Jacques Duclos had had her thrown into a makeshift cell in one of the basements somewhere around here. He had known who she was; and saw in her a collaborator who could one day help him obliterate his enemies. Her crime had been to swear never to help him or his 'filthy Stalinists'. Her reward had been a savage beating and being sentenced to starve to death, forgotten in a hole in the ground as the fighting raged above her head.

She had left her principles, her pride and the high moral fabric of her life behind her in that stinking, slowly flooding cellar; had she done otherwise, she would have been dead these last two-and-a-half years.

Maxim Machenaud's people had almost killed her out of hand.

Somehow, she had found the strength to scream: 'Duclos condemned me to death!'

That was enough for the surviving fanatics; after that she was for evermore, one of them.

My enemy's enemy is my friend...

There had been a lot of shooting behind her as she fled through the deserted quarter, prolonged bursts of automatic fire, several explosions; and grenades going off. In the darkness she had eventually blundered out of the city onto what must have been overgrown open ground to the west. Snow had begun to fall for a while, or so she thought. Actually, it was ash blowing on the wind from the fires spreading unfettered across large swathes of the city at her back.

That everything had gone to Hell, that all organisation and authority had collapsed around her like a building suddenly crumbling to the ground in a powerful earthquake ought to have come as a surprise to her. However, that all it had taken was a single, admittedly, devastating air raid and rumours of defeats elsewhere, scores, hundreds of kilometres away, was not, the more she thought about it strange at all. What had really triggered the disintegration of the Front Internationale's hold over the city and by now, several hours later, probably its grip on the South was the story, possibly a rumour, that Citizen Machenaud had himself, fled. Or was it that he was making preparations to transfer the FI's headquarters to Bordeaux, his vaunted Stalingrad on the Garonne in faraway Aquitaine?

Agnès had been the monster's secretary, his amanuensis, the plain, unremarkable, obedient, sexless servant to whom he dictated his thoughts. Those 'thoughts', recorded in a score of notebooks, were still most likely, locked in a safe in the basement of the anonymous concrete two-storey office inside the Michelin Works. Filled with 'thoughts' to torment any sane psyche, best treated like some terrible mis-reading of one of Grimm's fairy tales, real and yet unreal, unless you actually had to witness the abominations described upon each page. She had been spared most of that; yet seen enough with her own eyes to be traumatised forever.

And now, very soon, she would be dead.

Exposure, hunger, or a marauding gang from the city would surely transport her, if not to a better place, then one without so much pain and unbearable existential angst.

Legend had it that these woods were full of bandits, men and women who would cut one's throat at the drop of a hat.

As if I would be that lucky!

Maxim Machenaud had boasted that he had conquered France from the Pyrenees to the Loire Valley; a lie. His followers had laid claim to most of the big cities and towns, the peoples of the Biscay coastal enclaves had pledged allegiance to him and accepted his 'ambassadors'; the country had never actually been under the control of the Front Internationale. Bordeaux had been the first major city seized by Krasnaya Zarya in mid-1963, long before Clermont-Ferrand and Lyon had nominally switched their allegiance to Machenaud's faction of the communistic gangs vying for power in the Auvergne. In the beginning the Workers and Navy Committees that controlled the big ports had sought to create their own local 'Soviets'; only ever nominally becoming a part of the state controlled from the Auvergne for no better reason than to end the continual bloody border 'turf' wars with the FI.

Agnès had always assumed that Machenaud – a man with a brutally feral intelligence behind his mask of psychopathy - understood the limits of his power and how easily he might alienate the people in control in Toulon and Marseilles. The people of the Massif Central depended on the fish and grain sent north from the Mediterranean coastal margins to survive; that was the deal, smuggle, grow grain and fruit, and fish for the food that keeps the Revolution alive in France or face again a never-ending war. Attempting to seize those ships down at Villefranche had been a monumental blunder, a pyrrhic turning point; those ships had belonged to the commune of Toulon and by trespassing on the territory of the clans, the Franco-Italian criminal conferences which controlled much of the old Riviera coast, the Front Internationale had succeeded in doing the impossible, uniting the hole of the South against it.

That the ships in Villefranche were now either resting on the bottom of the anchorage or had been spirited away, god only knew where, by the English, had been like holding up a huge sign saying: 'THE FRONT INTERNATIONALE IS POWERLESS IN THE SOUTH!"

Now, with Clermont-Ferrand burning from end to end and with English warplanes bombing as they pleased; nobody but a fool or a madman, could think that the Front Internationale was in control even here in its alleged capital!

Agnès had carried on walking.

All the energy, the last failing warmth of life, was draining from her with every, exhausted step.

The ground beneath her feet was rising slowly.

She felt as if she was treading on quicksand; hardly moving forward and everything was happening excruciatingly slowly. Her head was sticky, wet, and it was a long time before she realised it was not just the cold, sleeting snow. Blood had dripped down the left side of her face.

She had no idea how long she had been stumbling through the trees, climbing ever higher.

She thought she remembered falling, passing out.

It had been daylight then, or was I hallucinating...

Regaining consciousness, heaving herself to her feet; being violently sick but she might have imagined, dreamed that because she was so, desperately tired.

She blinked up at the sky through the bare, wintery leaves of the forest. It was fully light, the sky leadenly overcast seemingly so low that she could almost reach up and touch the clouds.

Breathless, she turned and looked back.

There were too many trees: she could see nothing of the outskirts of the city which she guessed to be seven or eight kilometres distant.

She knew she could go on no further.

I have been walking around in circles...

For how long?

One day, or two...

She slumped down onto the ground, her back against the bowl of a tree. She would have wallowed in her misery had it not been for her conscience. Five years ago, she had had a brilliant career, her membership of the Académie des *Sciences* was assured, one day she might even have become a latter-day Marie Curie, a hero of the Republique for altogether different reasons. She might have been, or rather, possibly become a woman that all young French girls might aspire to be. Not an actress, a society harlot, or the wife of a great man, no, but a leading woman of the Republique in her own, inimitable right.

All those dreams were dead...

Now she was a bag of bones freezing to death in a forest in the Auvergne, alone, hunted and ashamed to be alive. She was so cold she had stopped shivering, stopped feeling the pain wracking her emaciated frame.

As she fell into the arms of sleep, Agnès heard footsteps, and lowered voices approaching along the path she had climbed a few minutes earlier.

However, she thought no more of it because she was suddenly irresistibly weary.

Far, far beyond caring.

Chapter 60

For the third morning running Rachel had ordered a cab to pick her up outside the Embassy at 3100 Massachusetts Ave NW, asked the driver to drop her off 'somewhere at the Foggy Bottom end of Constitution Avenue', and walked, depending on where the cabby had actually dropped her off, down either 23rd Street or across the park to the Lincoln Memorial.

Where she waited, and waited...for something to happen.

Nothing had happened on Monday, or yesterday.

The weather had been wet, windy and today it was bitterly cold but then, it was Washington in winter.

Nicko Henderson's words had been echoing in her head since the weekend.

'This isn't Malta and you are certainly not trapped in the middle of a siege like you were at Wister Park,' he had observed when she refused to discuss why she had returned to Washington, and what, exactly, she had planned.

In fact, the British Ambassador had got royally miffed with her after that.

'I haven't a clue what you and Dick White got up to in the old days,' he readily confessed. 'That was then, this is now and frankly, I don't need people like you muddying the waters here in DC!'

He had also told her that if he had known she was going to detach herself from the 'United Nations Party' and come back to haunt him, *and* that the Prime Minister had let it happen, presumably to 'keep Airey happy', he might very well have tendered his resignation.

'I might still!' He had added, heatedly.

Rachel suspected Nicko was behind the cable she had received on Monday from her husband.

She had arranged to speak to him via a scrambled transatlantic link yesterday afternoon.

Dan was flying out to America tomorrow, initially spending at least a week in DC 'finessing and generally charming fellows on Capitol Hill' ahead of visiting aerospace facilities in Philadelphia, Houston and New Mexico, on the way to California where he was scheduled to stay at least ten days. It was a work, work, work trip but he 'craved' her company.

The thinly veiled concern in her husband's voice was with her every waking minute. Sentimentally, she wondered if something so ephemeral and unquantifiable as her feelings, her attachment to Dan could have wrought some kind of change in her. Nonetheless, she comforted herself with the recognition that she had *needed* to get off Commonwealth One. Had she disembarked in San Francisco she was convinced that *the Locksmith* would have unleashed the hounds upon her, and everybody would have been horribly embarrassed by the resulting media feeding frenzy. The only thing which really surprised her was that Angleton and his cronies at the Office of Security had not yet 'outed her' since she resurfaced in DC.

That was not to say the nastier end of the Washington rumour-mill – the one that operated at the level of the publishers and editors of the big-circulation papers, the network TV chiefs, the old Kennedy mafia, infiltrated by those insufferable Boston Brahmins, and the real deal-makers on the Hill – was not already agog with the gossip about CIA and British assassins on the loose, and the near celebrity status of the mysterious wife of the famous RAF Air Marshal...

It would have been unbearable had not Rachel's world closed in around her; and had she not recognised that she had to get out of her bloodily gilded cage, if she was ever to start to breath freely again.

Oddly, well, bizarrely, she had only really begun to understand what was going on when she had casually scared the living daylights out of Caroline Constantis.

That was unforgivable...

The woman she had imagined that she still was, would not have cared, or even thought about a little thing like that but then she knew now, incontrovertibly, that woman had died at Wister Park...

Rachel had just not known it until now.

Maybe, one day in an ideal world, she would lie down on the eminent professor's couch and let her trawl through the ashes of her psychosis...

Now there was a weird thought!

That morning she sat on a bench overlooking the length of the Lincoln Memorial Reflecting Pool with the Memorial itself to her left as the cold, moist wind blew off the Potomac, ruffling her hair, and pinching her pale cheeks.

She was so deep in her thoughts, oblivious to her immediate surroundings that the man walked right up to her without Rachel being aware of his presence.

He stood over her, suspecting that she was in some kind of trance.

He sighed loudly, breaking the spell.

"He's not going to risk a meeting at a place like this," James Jesus Angleton remarked irritably as he slumped down on the bench as far as was physically possible, about two feet and a few inches, away from Rachel.

The man had tried to make absolutely sure – seemingly to no avail – that she had seen him coming from a long way away; there were some people you never, ever surprised.

"He's probably watching us," she retorted, tartly, unable to wholly overcome a listless, lifeless weariness. "Somebody in the Bureau, or the Company, maybe even in your own office, will have told him where I came yesterday and on Monday."

"Maybe, maybe," the man grunted, not knowing what to make of the woman's lassitude.

Rachel glanced at the Associate Deputy Director of Operations for Counter Intelligence. The *Locksmith* was looking old, like he was not sleeping too well these days. He had always been one of those angular men who wore suits as if he was a human coat-hanger.

"The funny thing is that there probably are moles in the CIA," she said, as if she was no more than floating a stray idea. "Just not mole's working for the Russians. That's the trouble with you 'patriots'," she went on, unable to stop herself sneering, "you can't tell your brand of patriotism from the real thing."

James Angleton said nothing.

He was too busy not getting angry.

Rachel decided it was oddly piquant that the great American spymaster was terrified she was about to kill him. She was not armed; she had dumped the forty-five she had had when she picked the lock to Caroline Constantis's apartment before she surrendered herself to the Embassy on Sunday. She did not have a blade, or knuckle-dusters, anything at all to attack Angleton, or anybody else who wished her ill except her handbag. Okay, so if it came to it, she knew how to, and was very proficient, hurting or killing with her bare hands, elbows, knees, feet, et al but somehow, she knew, she just knew, she could not do that. It took a particular mental attitude, adjustment, whatever, to deliberately, in cold-blood hurt or kill another human being and she simply did not have that animus in her soul. Not today. Perhaps, she never would, ever again. Of course, the Associated Deputy Director of Counter Intelligence at Langley, did not know that. Or, from his demeanour, suspect it.

"I was the one who told Dick that Philby was a double agent," she said, idly. "He didn't believe me either. Not at first. I should have just put a bullet in his neck anyway. It would have saved us all a lot of trouble later. Don't you think?"

If she had been unsure how ripping the scab off an old, unsightly, unhealed wound still hurt, the CIA man wasted no time confirming as much.

"You hardly knew Kim," the man objected, bloodlessly as if the fight had drained out of him.

"Neither did you, it seems."

"He deceived us all. Each and every one of his friends."

Angleton leaned forward, half-stretching and planted his gloved hands on his knees, staring into the bleak, wintery distance of the cityscape beyond the park.

"Aren't you afraid Mikkelsen will bring you down with him?"

"No," Rachel shrugged. "I quit this game back in Malta. I just didn't know it at the time."

"People like you..."

Angleton's voice trailed off; he shook his head.

"Heck, maybe people like you do quit. What do I know?"

"I came back because I wanted to see him one last time," Rachel confessed. "Don't ask me why, I just wanted to see him one more time. To look him in the eye and say, I don't know, I was sorry."

James Angleton shook his head.

"What's this? Honour among assassins?"

"Something like that. Back in the day, I warned him I'd been sent to kill him. It would have been better if I'd killed him, or he'd ended me." She changed the subject. "I met Dwight Christie again in San Francisco. Was he ever one of your guys?"

"No. Why?"

"Nothing..."

"It's something, or you wouldn't have asked?"

Rachel sighed.

"They say that after the White House and the Smithsonian, this is the place every visitor to DC should visit," she said, musing aloud. "Well, what's left of the Smithsonian. They say all the things looted from it during the uprising of December 1963 are flooding the antiquities black markets of the world. Perhaps, the Battle of Washington wasn't about overthrowing the government; it was just a great big heist after all? What do you think?"

"Most coups are criminal conspiracies: land grabs or worse."

"You should know, you've supervised a few in your time."

"What the fuck is going on, Rachel?"

She ignored the question, gazing instead at the marble white Doric-style temple at the western end of the National Mall housing the nineteen-foot-high statue of the sixteenth President of the Union.

Rachel had discovered as a child that nothing was ever quite what it seemed to be. For example, here in the land of the free, at the very heart of the Empire of Liberty, Congress had so cherished the remembrance of the victor of the Civil War of the nineteenth century that it had rejected the first six attempts to fund a monument to the great emancipator of the Southern slave nation; even the reflecting Pool had been an afterthought, not seriously contemplated until after Chief Justice William H. Taft had dedicated the 'temple' in May 1922 in a ceremony in which he then, 'presented' it to President Warren G. Harding.

Lincoln's only surviving son, Robert Todd Lincoln, then seventy-eight years old, had been a witness, possibly standing not a million miles from where she and *the Locksmith* reminisced about...old times.

Rachel wondered where the President's son, who had died only two years before she was born, had actually stood that day; had she unknowingly walked in his footsteps the last three days?

"I don't know what's going on," she confessed.

The architect who had designed the Lincoln memorial and the Reflecting Pool, Henry Bacon had campaigned for over two decades to erect a proper memorial to the man who had saved the Union; fighting apathy, parsimony and at times, callow indifference in a country that then, as now, prided itself on being the bastion of democracy. Like Lincoln's son, he too only just lived to see his vision come to fruition.

I never used to get distracted like this...

"Do you know that the man who designed the Lincoln memorial also designed the Confederate Memorial in Wilmington?" She posed, rhetorically.

Angleton, never a man overly sensitive to such social cues, got to his feet and standing over the woman, and vented a little of his pent-up exasperation.

"What's that got to do with anything?"

Rachel looked up at him, a twinge of pity twitching at her lips.

And then, as she knew it would; *it happened.*

The first bullet must have exploded as it passed through the spymaster's chest cavity. It fragmented, exiting in a blossom of gore, spattering Rachel.

James Jesus Angleton stood there for a moment, dying, a look of stupefaction in his eyes, his arms, already disarticulated from his ruptured nervous system twitching.

He swayed.

The second round took off most of his head as he fell.

As the spymaster's lifeless corpse collapsed onto Rachel she screamed.

And screamed.

And went on screaming for nearly a minute after the first uniformed Washington PD officer arrived, pushing through the small crowd of shocked, mute witnesses.

Chapter 61

Operation Blondie threatened to unravel shortly after the two helicopters lifted off. As they skimmed across the dark waters of the Gironde, racing along the left bank of the flooded river, up ahead the sky sparkled with tracers and the flash of explosions.

The Eagle's Sea Vixens and Buccaneers were doing their stuff; the problem was that the two Westland Wessex's were late!

This meant that by the time the two helicopters clattered across the flooded Garonne and turned over Blanquefort, settling upon their approach to the target, the bombing raid was over and the defenders, angry and ready, were standing to their guns.

"Go or no-go?" The pilot of the lead aircraft asked tersely over the open intercom circuit.

Paddy Ashdown did not think about this overlong.

"GO! CONFIRM GO!"

The flares over the port area had gone out by then; and the remnants of the white phosphorus markers strewn across the roof of the bunker and dozens of surrounding buildings spat and fizzled like guttering blue-white candles as the Wessex's suddenly flared, lost forward momentum and plummeted towards hard landings.

"Oh, fuck!" The pilot muttered. Then he shouted: "The fucking roof's not flat!"

"Hover, we'll jump out!" Paddy Ashdown retorted, as if leaping out of an aircraft in the middle of the night onto a concrete roof that was 'not flat' was but a minor inconvenience.

In the event the wheels bumped something solid and Sergey Akhromeyev found himself propelled out of the door by the man behind him, landing in a heap on the man who had preceded him into the darkness.

Paddy Ashdown yanked him to his feet.

"ALL IN ONE PIECE?" He bellowed in the Russian's face.

"Da," Akhromeyev grunted, dazed, disorientated, unconvinced. He was struggling for breath and his ribs hurt.

"Oh, shit!" The man he had fallen on muttered, rising to his feet.

They all turned...

The second Wessex was on fire, tracer ripping into it as it struggled to reach the BETASOM Bunker.

It fell – as if in dreadful slow motion - into the eastern end of the unyielding monolith of the BETASOM complex.

Tracer fell into it, it lurched sidelong.

In a moment it disintegrated into a maelstrom of flailing rotors, rending metal and a terrible, dazzling bloom of exploding aviation fuel.

The first Wessex was attempting to lift off.

The blast wave tipped it sideways for moment, the aircraft staggered, banked away, dipped below the roof line and then miraculously, flew on, perilously low over the cold, unfeeling neutral waters of the inner basin with small arms fire kicking up geysers in her wake.

The five men on the roof knew the Wessex was not going to make it.

Yet they still watched until the instant the helicopter nosed into the water and her main rotors ploughed the blackness into frenzied spume in the chaos of the crash. The machine settled, for a moment, upright. Not that there was any hope for her three-man crew as a single searchlight wobbled across the basin, captured the downed aircraft and automatic gunfire began to fall into the mist of spray around her.

Paddy Ashdown was the first to react.

"Get weaving, chaps. Nobody knows we're here yet!"

Sergey Akhromeyev was sorely tempted to remind the younger man that the whole of Bordeaux knew they were 'here' by now, and that once the defenders got bored shooting up the wreck of the rapidly sinking Wessex out in the basin, they would – with their blood well and truly up – surely come looking for the survivors from the two helicopters.

Acrid smoke drifted, biting his throat and stinging his eyes.

He stole a glance at the port around him: there were fires burning a hundred metres away, otherwise the city was blacked out, wholly dark.

Two of the other five men on the roof had secured lines.

One man had already thrown himself over the edge.

Another swiftly followed.

"You next!" Akhromeyev was commanded. A rope had been tied around his waist as he stared at the distant fires. The next thing he knew he was jerked to a gut-wrenching, agonising stop and he was swinging, winded, struggling to catch his breath, with his feet two or three feet above the water, his torso a sea of fire. He felt as if every bone in his body had just been jarred out of its socket.

He remembered the hand in the small of his back.

They had thrown him over the side of the bunker...

A body slid down a second rope right beside him.

They really did that!

The other man swung into him, hard.

They threw me over the edge...

Something rasped painfully against his ribs and he was being pulled sideways. Iron-strong hands grasped him and without consciously contributing to the process in any way, he was standing, swaying unsteadily on solid ground. Another man thumped down behind him.

"Everybody okay?" Paddy Ashdown asked cheerfully.

In acknowledgement there was a metallic chorus of gun breeches being snapped back.

Belatedly, Sergey Akhromeyev, operating on muscle memory, locked and loaded his Kalashnikov.

"Jolly good!" Ashdown declared in a hoarse whisper. "Follow me, chaps!"

While he and Paddy Ashdown had been drawing up their plans, the Russian had offered the thought to the young Royal Marine officer, that if the old U-boat pens were really being used as a headquarters, then it was likely that all the heavily armed troops in the vicinity would be posted *outside*, guarding it. Thus, if they – he and the nine Royal Marines - could get *inside* the complex *quickly*, the raiding party would have a short 'honeymoon' period in which they might conceivably encounter very little, or if they were very lucky, no serious resistance, before the men guarding the complex realised what was going on.

The dream scenario was that *all* the external blast doors would have been automatically closed when the air raid started, totally isolating the less heavily armed 'insiders' from the 'tough guys' outside.

'We will know if we are attacking the right place if it has its own generators, because inside it will be reasonably well-lit.'

There were dim lights, night lights, at the inner end of the pen. The four surviving SBS men and their Russian 'guest' were drawn to them like moths to the fire.

Of course, had the defenders taken the elementary step of shutting and barring the doors to the old U-boat docks; that would have been it, game over.

However, finding the heavy steel door wide open, possibly rusted in position since the Second War, the Marines around Sergey Akhromeyev whooped with delight almost but not quite under their breaths.

Nonchalantly lobbing a grenade ahead of him, pausing momentarily to wait for the sharp, ear-splitting detonation in the confined space, Paddy Ashdown plunged into the smoke, his men following without hesitation with the eagerness of hunting dogs desperate to get to the front of the pack.

Kill everybody; take no prisoners...

Sergey Akhromeyev almost immediately stepped over the bullet-riddled, dead and still twitching bodies of dying Revolutionary Guards in their grey-black fatigues.

Shadows moved in the gloom in a side passage.

His Kalashnikov bucked in his hands.

Ahead of him the Royal Marines quickly, efficiently, mercilessly cleared room after room, each seemingly identical, white-washed, now damp-infested concrete-walled cubes. Some had desks, other were clearly store rooms, one or two had bunks or palliasses on the floor, most now were sprayed with the blood of Revolutionary Guards. There were dead women, too. There was no way of knowing if they were Front Internationale stooges, 'comrades', whores or merely innocents caught up in the madness.

Suddenly, the strike team emerged into a long, low compartment, probably long ago a workshop with lathes, hoists; there were narrow rail tracks criss-crossing the floor, strong points in the roof and several doors leading off it, presumably into offices and store rooms.

The thump of a generator reverberated around the complex.

The lights were turned down low, somewhere air was being circulated by a pump. Already the atmosphere was tainted with cordite and the unmistakeable iron tang of blood.

In one of these rooms they discovered several men in the green of the FI leadership cadre cowering in a corner behind a shield of four shivering, half-naked terrified women.

Paddy Ashdown signalled Akhromeyev to stay with him.

"This seems to be the central area of the bunker," he observed, coolly, addressing the other three Marines. "Everybody will have gone to ground now. Root around a bit, if the bastards try to retake this area fall back, otherwise, anybody who doesn't look like a combatant gets a chance to surrender. Search everybody. If in doubt, shoot first and ask questions later. Any questions?"

He turned back to the women and the scum of the earth hiding behind their skirts.

Calmly, he pointed the barrel of his Sterling at the group with his right hand as he retrieved a grenade from his webbing with his left, and pulled the pin with his teeth.

"If any of you miserable beggars," he barked in French, "are armed, lay down your weapons now. If you shoot me, I will drop this grenade and you'll all be blown to bits!"

Weapons clunked to the concrete floor.

"Ladies, go outside please!" Then, without looking at him he said to the Russian. "Frisk the women for weapons. Don't be shy about it."

Akhromeyev stepped aside to permit the four women to file out of the room. Outside, he herded them against the nearest wall, waved for them to face it.

"Hands on the wall, spread your legs! Stand still!" He barked in French, the language which had become very nearly native to him in the last few years.

He searched each woman, careless of their modesty. One woman snivelled, flinched, the others were as still as statues.

The Russian stepped back two paces and lowered his Kalashnikov.

"I am sorry," he said gruffly, stepping back. "I have lost too many friends to madmen and women they ought to have searched to take risks. You may turn around now. Over there, go over there. Don't move from there," he directed, pointing at an abandoned pile of metalwork nearby. "Keep out of the way. We will not harm you." He hesitated. "You are safe now. Nobody will molest you. We are British Commandos."

The women, a pair in their twenties or thirties, he guessed, and two, possibly barely pubescent teenage girls, were all dressed like tarts for the entertainment of the 'great men of the Revolution'.

The women were dirty, the kids had been crying, and any fool could tell that none of them had had a square meal for a long time.

One of the other SBS men stuck his head around the door of the room where Ashdown was mulling whether to shoot one of his prisoners; so as to encourage the others to talk.

There's a comms centre down the corridor, we reckon most of the bastards went down to the level below when the shooting started. They've locked themselves in. There's nobody else around, Boss," he reported to Paddy Ashdown. "The whole place is locked down tighter than a duck's arse. I reckon they'll need demolition charges to break through the blast doors on the landward side."

Ashdown gave orders for the external exits, of which there were three, to be patrolled by one man, and the door to the lower-level bunker to watched by another. Sergey Akhromeyev and the remaining Marine were, meanwhile, to start searching the complex for maps, documents, and...food and water.

Both men reported back within less than ten minutes.

They had located other offices and a small, surprisingly well-stocked food store. There was running water in the taps, they assumed, piped from a rainfall tank somewhere in the roof structure.

"Right," the man running Operation Blondie declared, "there's been a change of plan. Unfortunately, our rides back home won't be waiting for us. So, we might as well try to contact base and make ourselves comfortable. And when it happens, stand by to repel borders."

He looked around the faces of the other men.

Made eye contacts.

Nodded.

"In the meantime, Sergey and I will have a nice, cosy little chat with our green-coated friends."

Chapter 62

Wednesday 15th February 1967
HMS Campbeltown, Toulon

HMS Stirling had very nearly run down the submarine which had suddenly surfaced less than a mile off its port quarter. The destroyer had fired two salvoes from its forward 5-inch rifles before it was seen that the vessel's - which turned out to be the Roland Morillot - crew were desperately waving white sheets from her conning tower, and precariously from her wave-swept casing. Later, it was discovered that the submarine's commanding officer had been attempting – without success - to radio his surrender for some thirty minutes before, as a despairing gesture, he decided to surface before the surrounding warships, all actively 'pinging' the depths, got around to raining depth charges on his head.

The Stirling's captain had put the wheel over at the last minute and missed, literally by a coat of paint, the stern of the wallowing submersible.

It seemed that the French Navy had wrested back control of Toulon from the handful of Revolutionary Guards, and Front Internationale zealots who had not fled during, or shortly after the previous night's bombardment of the port, public buildings, the main railway station and two road junctions north of the city. Apparently, several 'big shells' had landed inside the barracks complex of the hated Front Internationale storm troopers, with one, apparently penetrating a packed bomb shelter killing everybody inside it.

The Task Force Commander had come over the TBS and suggested to Dermot O'Reilly, that 'as you did such a good job at Villefranche, I think that you're just the man to receive the surrender of Toulon!'

The Campbeltown's Captain had politely thanked Rear Admiral Henry Leach for his 'kind consideration'. The two men had chortled briefly, and then after a short conversation with John Treacher on the Kent, two other ships had been detailed off to 'escort' the Campbeltown into Toulon, while the Kent would linger, threateningly on the horizon due south of the port.

Just in case...

Although sunset was supposedly over an hour distant the light was fading fast as Campbeltown, followed by the Leander class frigate Galatea, and the Stirling began to round the long, thin breakwater guarding the approaches to what had been, prior to the October War, the largest naval base in the Western Mediterranean.

People were on the sea wall at Point de la Vieille less than a hundred yards to port, and flags were waving. A signal lamp flashed erratically from the emplacements of Fort Balaguier, a little over half-a-mile to the north west.

The main batteries of the Campbeltown and her two consorts were trained fore and aft, albeit their crews were closed up at action stations, and all watertight doors were firmly dogged shut throughout all three ships. The two Fletchers' air search and gunnery radars turned from side to side, the Galatea's Type 965 bedstead revolved slowly, and the merest plume of grey haze rose from the stacks of the three warships. With their paintwork battered and rust streaked, the three British ships must have looked battle-hardened, threatening, ready for anything; the Fletchers bristling with guns, the Galatea with her clean lines, tall radar mast and helicopter hangar, a contrast in modernity.

"Mister Keith," O'Reilly grinned. "You have the Deck."

"I have the Deck, aye, sir!" The younger man acknowledged, stepping over to the binnacle to re-check the angle to the line of buoys marking the deep-water channel.

Dermot O'Reilly stepped out onto the port wing of the bridge.

He gently tapped the shoulder of the youthful yeoman manning the Aldis lamp as the destroyer began to turn to the north, to enter the main harbour.

The Campbeltown's captain swung the lamp towards Fort Balaguier, briefly glimpsing the silhouette of Fort Napoleon on the rising ground inland.

He clattered out a message.

"VIVE LA FRANCE!"

He noted the yeoman he had displaced watching, learning.

The signaller on shore replied.

"I think that fellow said 'WELCOME' or 'LIBERATION'," he remarked to the man next to him, grinning wolfishly.

O'Reilly re-sent VIVE LA FRANCE!

"Think you can send that?" He asked the yeoman, who nodded. "Good man," Dermot O'Reilly chuckled. "Every time somebody signals, return 'VIVE LA FRANCE'."

"Vive la France, aye, sir."

O'Reilly went back inside, waited until the rudder was amidships and reclaimed the Deck.

"Mister Keith," he declared cheerfully, apparently without a care in the world. "Find me a dock to come alongside. I'm buggered if I'm going to get my feet wet tonight!"

Campbeltown was scarcely making headway as she drifted north, almost parallel to the breakwater passing Fort de l'Éguillette to the west where a rusting merchantman lay half-capsized against a derelict quayside.

Dermot O'Reilly knew that the French had attempted to scuttle their fleet at Toulon when the Germans occupied Vichy France in 1942. The big ships had been salvaged but he had no idea whether there were more recent wrecks lurking beneath the cold grey surface of the waters around him.

"Switch on our running lights, Mister Moss," he said, stepping forward to raise his binoculars to his eyes and to peer into the gathering gloom. "Signal Galatea and Stirling to do likewise, if you please." There were still a couple of fires burning in the city, further degrading visibility as the winter's day drew in. "Close up all searchlight crews."

It had crossed Dermot O'Reilly's mind that not everybody in Toulon was going to be ecstatic about the Royal Navy steaming in to 'liberate' the port.

The harbour might easily be mined...

No, nothing I can do about that...

Although guns from the shore batteries defending Toulon back in the 1940s had been scavenged by the Nazis, and many of those that survived the liberation in 1944, subsequently removed or neglected long before the October War, he was painfully cognisant that a handful of relatively small anti-tank guns on the surrounding hills and promontories, might take a horrible toll upon his thin-skinned flotilla at point blank range...

Photographic reconnaissance sorties by the RAF, and earlier that afternoon, by one of the Victorious's Gannets reported that apart from the helicopter carrier La Resolue, sunk at her moorings, a couple of old destroyers being used as accommodation ships, and a flotilla of minesweepers, the great port was practically empty.

O'Reilly thought he saw the shortened silhouettes of other small warships, a couple of Le Normand class frigates and nearby them, a tanker and several merchantmen.

"Two surfaced submarines bearing three-three-zero one thousand yards!"

Several sets of glasses turned in unison.

Both low, indistinct, black forms were flying white flags.

One of the submarines appeared to have a bulbous rounded 'nose' at its bow; that was probably the Arethuse class boat that Rene Leguay had mentioned.

All around the widening bay as Campbeltown cautiously nosed north at little more than steerage speed, walking pace on land, was darkness.

Not for the first time in recent years the commanding officer of Her Majesty's Ship Campbeltown asked himself; exactly who had bombed who back into the Stone Age that night back in late October 1962?

Chapter 63

Thursday 16th February 1967
Philip Burton Federal Building, San Francisco

The old man had been picked up by the San Francisco PD on Tuesday night down near Fisherman's Wharf. They had assumed he was a hobo, vagrant, he was drunk, incoherent and had pushed an officer into the bay; this latter probably being the thing which had attracted the attention of the local plain clothes inspector.

When the man sobered up the next morning, he claimed to be Tobias A. Little of Irvington, Portland, Oregon revisiting the Bay Area, where he had served in the Navy in the Second War. He said he was ill and that he must have taken the 'wrong pills' the previous day. He seemed contrite, embarrassed, and a little ashamed of himself.

As indeed, would any self-respecting veteran who had disgraced himself re-visiting the scene of his military service in time of war nearly a quarter-of-a-century later.

'Even back when I was in the Navy, I never had no trouble with the Shore Patrol!' The old man insisted, sheepishly.

He said he was dying of lung cancer.

'Probably because of all the hot stuff that's in the air these days!'

By then the guys at the local station were starting to feel guilty about putting the old guy through the wringer, just because he had pushed one of them into the bay. No real harm had been done an nobody liked screwing around with a veteran who had fallen on hard times.

However, because he had been held two nights – the first sobering up without being interviewed - and nobody had actually ruled out the possibility of preferring charges against him for assaulting a police officer, he was still in custody the morning after his second night in after his arrest. There had been a delay finding a doctor to give the old man the once over; the boys at the station were worried about him and they did not want to be wrongly accused, at some time in the future, of not doing their best for the old guy.

By that time Tobias A. Little's file had already been sitting on a detective's desk for several hours and, because that detective knew that a uniformed buddy had been half-drowned, that detective had made several phone calls which otherwise, he might not have made.

According to the Veterans Administration, the Tobias Albert Little on the old guy's VA card, the only identification he had had on his person at the time of his arrest, had died in Little Rock, Arkansas in July 1957.

So, more – and progressively more urgent - calls had been made, including one to the VA office in the Mission District, which the Tobias A. Little, whose papers falsely claimed that he had been invalided out of the US Navy on 3rd January 1945, had registered as his forwarding address while he was in California.

It was quickly established that, notwithstanding he had initially claimed to have no fixed abode, a VA case officer had actually visited 'Little' at a flat in a tenement in the Fillmore District, ostensibly to ensure that the old man received all the benefits due to him.

Around mid-day two beat cops had checked out the address.

The building's manager, always glad to help the police because he did not want any trouble with the local precinct – he ran a 'clean house' – had let the uniforms into the one room, third-floor apartment.

Less than an hour later, the box containing what they had found at the old man's 'place', including what was probably his 'real' VA Identity Card, was sitting on the duty Inspector's desk at the station and shortly after that, the FBI had been called in.

'Son of a gun,' Special Agent James B. Adams had whistled down the line. Collecting his faculties, and still not entirely convinced that he believed his own luck, he had declared: 'My people will be over to pick him up, we'll take it from here!'

Now, the old man was sitting in front of him.

Hans Mikkelsen was unrecognisable as the man pictured in his stepson's FBI file. He seemed smaller, half-broken, and old before his time. Some of that would be the cancer but Adams suspected he had let himself go first, and then the illness had taken over. The man had given in, possibly years before the Cuban Missiles War, and allowed the habits of a lifetime to wither, his standards slip. Okay, he had been in holding cells the last couple of nights, but that did not account for, or excuse, the week's stubble on his face, the lankness of his hair, thinning, tangled and down to his greasy collar at the back. The plaid lumberjack shirt stank of sweat and although his denims may have been a lot cleaner a couple of days ago, there was dirt under his untrimmed nails and his physical frailty, briefly surmounted by whatever alcohol and pills, likely amphetamines, he had taken the other day, was obvious.

James Adams pulled up a chair opposite the old Marine.

The room, which had a large mirror on one side was windowless, warm, although in the background the air conditioning whirred. The table between the two men was bolted to the floor, as was the prisoner's hard, backless bench.

The old man, he was sixty-three in a week or so, had been leaning forward with his cuffed hands on the table, as if in prayer except the FBI man did not think he was a man who had ever put much stock in the existence of a merciful God.

Adams reached over and unlocked the cuffs, retrieved them and folded them into the right pocket of his dark sports jacket.

Hans Mikkelsen rubbed his wrists.

"Well," Adams prefaced, "one way or another, I reckon you and I have a lot to talk about, Gunnery Sergeant Mikkelsen."

The old man raised a grey eyebrow.

"You reckon?"

"Hey," Adams grinned ruefully, *"you're* the old Marine masquerading as a former cook on the USS Franklin who died ten years ago, not me, friend!"

"If you say so."

Adams did not react to being blanked; that was to be expected. Once a Marine, always a Marine. Forget the wreck of a man sitting across the table, there was a real hard-arse in their somewhere.

"I was in the Army in the forty-five war," Adams confided, allowing a self-deprecating note to seep into his voice. "Not that anything I did was a patch on your combat service. How many Purple Hearts did they give you? Two for Guadalcanal, another one for Saipan? Is it right you went ashore with the 2nd Marines at Tarawa? On Betio Island?"

"That's all just history. It doesn't mean a thing."

Adams shrugged.

"If you say so, you're the one who got so badly wounded at Iwo Jima the Corps discharged you when you got back stateside." He finally opened the folder he had brought with him into the interview room. "But they gave you a Silver Star for that, didn't they?"

"A medal doesn't mean squat when all your buddies are dead."

"No, I suppose not. Was that why you decided to be Kurt's wingman?"

That was a stretch, the sort of leap in the dark the Bureau's old-timers tended to give young tyros a slap over the knuckles for. However, Adams got the sense that time was running out and doing things by the book had not worked out so well on this case. Leastways, not yet.

"Kurt was what, about eighteen months old when you married his Ma?"

The old man shrugged.

He had never stopped viewing Adams with unblinking, inscrutable, oddly cold eyes. Eyes that were rheumy, more grey than green and...mocking.

That happened sometimes; some people were just plain bad. Out there on Main Street most folk had no idea what sort of evil the FBI was protecting them from. Right now, James Adams was getting a very bad feeling about the old man sitting opposite him.

"Kurt told the Army his Pa was drowned in a shipwreck on the Great Lakes in the winter of 1926? In a big storm?" Adams asked, as if he was just checking an inconsequential note on the file in front of him.

"Yeah."

"What ship?"

"The *Nisbet Grammer*."

"Yeah," the FBI man sighed. "She was the only big ship that went down that year. But that was in May 1926, on Lake Ontario, she was in collision with another ship."

Hans Mikkelsen shrugged.

"There were no casualties," James Adams went on. "The *Nisbet Grammer's* crew was rescued before the ship went down. So," James Adams prompted, "so, what really happened to Kurt's Pa, Hans?"

The old man was silent, brooding.

"You were a Chicago boy like him, right?"

Still nothing.

"Okay, you joined the Marine Corps in August 1927, right?"

"I'd just married Martha, the boy's Ma. It was a good job..."

"That was after the pair of you, and Kurt, got to Portland, Oregon," Adams interjected, reasonably, as if he was trying to help, "travelling from Chicago to the West Coast wasn't that easy in those days?"

Another contemptuous shrug of the shoulders.

"Okay, okay, I'll cut to the chase, Hans," Adams declared. "I can't prove it but I think you killed *Martha's* husband, Kurt senior. For all I know, the two of you, you and Martha, were in on it together, either way, when her husband was gone you married her, adopted young Kurt, who is probably your natural son, anyway, and moved to Portland – probably before anybody started making the sort of dumb comments people make, like: The kid looks just like you? Ain't that a thing? - where you joined the Marines. Once you got posted overseas, after a while you got to take Martha and your son away from the old country, hundreds, thousands of miles away from all the awkward questions that, by then, had followed you all the way to Oregon?"

Adams had heard the news of the shooting in the National Mall on the TV late last night; then, angrily, because he had realised Clyde Tolson and the Director had been playing him for a patsy, made the first of several calls to DC which had gone on into the early hours of the morning, eventually managing to get to speak with the high and mighty Associate Director, Clyde Tolson in person! Tolson had been angry too, threatening also; actually, James Adams did not give a damn! The CIA's Head of Counter Intelligence had been assassinated near the Lincoln Memorial standing right next to the Angel of Death and he had had to hear the news on the TV! What in God's name were those old farts in Washington doing?

Adams was fully aware he had not done his career prospects in the Bureau any favours last night; old men did not like being informed – no matter how diplomatically – that they needed to get their act together.

Like I care...

In contrast, dealing with Professor Caroline Constantis-Zabriski earlier that morning had been like a breath of fresh air. She had been as shocked as him and, frankly, equally astonished to hear the news.

However, unlike Adam's superiors in DC she had not needed him to join up the dots for her. To the contrary, she had begun, unprompted, providing him with sharply observed, very precise, targeted insights and new lines of interrogation within minutes of their introduction.

It seemed the lady went nowhere these days without her constant shadow, a trim, prim very protective Air Force Blue Cap who still contrived to look very military in her blue housewifely two-piece jacket – tailored to conceal the forty-five she toted in a shoulder holster - and pleated skirt.

Presently, Captain Erin Lambert was with Caroline Constantis in the adjoining room watching the interview. The two women were obviously very close, if not mother-daughter then sisterly, genuine friends.

'Erin was with me last year," the older woman had smiled, glancing fondly to her bodyguard, making absolutely sure that Adams did not jump to any conclusions that her companion was 'just her Air Force minder'. More, in fact, that she was her confidante and in her own right, a highly competent investigator. "One way and another we went through a lot together."

James Adams was a man who had got used to being, and if truth be known, a little complacent about being the smartest guy in the room; however, he intuitively accepted that when he was in Caroline Constantis's company, he was...not.

Hans Mikkelsen was studying the FBI man with half-lidded, dead eyes.

"It's started, right?" He asked, his voice rasping lowly.

Adams nodded.

The old man pursed his lips, sniffed, folded his arms across his hollow chest and fell silent.

The FBI man waited.

And waited.

Several minutes passed in silence.

Then there was a knock at the door, which opened.

Hans Mikkelsen's eyes flickered with interest as Erin Lambert entered, positioned a hard-backed chair next to James Adams, and stepped aside as an attractive, older, grey-haired woman came into the room and without a word, settled opposite him.

The old man viewed the younger woman thoughtfully as she moved to stand by the door, her back against it; her stare never wavered from his face.

"This is Professor Constantis," Adams announced, introducing the woman who had sat down beside him. "You may remember her from her TV appearances during the war in the Midwest last year."

"Never had much time for TV."

"Me neither, Mister Mikkelsen," Caro admitted. "The camera does not do one any favours as one gets older," she went on, "although my husband adamantly, and gallantly refutes this. But he's biased, of course."

"I'm done here," the old man retorted wearily.

"Is that so?" Caro sat back. "Semper Fidelis," she whispered. "*Always faithful*, whatever became of that, Gunnery Sergeant Mikkelsen?"

The old man snorted, shook his head.

"I spent the last couple of years of the forty-five-war trying to put back together the Army Air Force's lost boys," Caro explained. "The most destructive thing for most of *my boys* was the guilt they felt for having survived when all their buddies were gone, not the traumas that they themselves had lived through. After the war I went back to 'normal' life again; for many years I worked for the FBI developing psychological profiling protocols based on actual case histories and interviews, with most famously, among others, Edwin Mertz." She smiled thinly. "And people like you."

The old man was resolutely mute.

"Then, after the October War I got a call from Curtis LeMay. *Old Iron Pants* had found out that I'd worked with some of his boys back in 1944 and 1945. So, he asked me to do the same sort of work, very secretly, with some of the boys, mostly grown men this time around, who came back from that night over the Soviet Union with...issues. Funnily enough, that was how I met my second husband. The current one. His Ma tried to murder the President, JFK; then Nathan, my husband, got sold a hospital pass by the Pentagon but he didn't turn into a sad, sick fuck-up like you, or Kurt. He stayed loyal to his oath; he still serves."

Caro did not flinch from the pitiless darkness in the old man's eyes. He had warned James Adams not to expect much from this interview; or from her attempt to prick something other than undiluted hate out of Hans Mikkelsen's twisted psyche.

"Like father like son," she mused. "Wasn't that the way it was. Right now, the Navy Judge Advocate's Department, is conducting an urgent document search for cases involving unsolved killings or unexplained disappearances at your duty stations in the 1930s up to the outbreak of war in 1941. And," she added, "the FBI is doing the same sort of exercise for all the places you've lived since 1945. Unfortunately, this search will take several weeks, possibly longer to complete. You may not even live to be charged with the half of the crimes you have committed, Hans. However, I think that what we'll discover is that you, and Kurt, began your *careers* a long time ago. Tell me I'm wrong?"

Caroline nodded to the FBI man.

"A senior Central Intelligence Agency officer was assassinated in Washington yesterday," he informed Hans Mikkelsen.

"Angleton, right?" The old man checked, hoarsely.

James Adams nodded acknowledgement.

"Figures..."

"Who else is Kurt going for?" Adams demanded, suddenly a little breathless.

Hans Mikkelsen looked to him deadpan for a moment and then, very slowly, he began, hurtfully, to laugh.

Chapter 64

Thursday 16th February 1967
Manassas, Virginia

Kurt had held *her* face in the cross hairs of the Remington's telescopic sights for perhaps, as long as fifteen or twenty seconds before the first bodies began to flit across, and soon, completely obscure his line of fire.

James Jesus Angleton ought, by rights, to have crumpled to the ground like a broken rag doll after that first round tore out his chest. Yet the man had remained standing, swaying stubbornly like a tree cut through at its base, ready to topple for an interminable, impossible time.

Kurt had identified the mass of scaffolding on the roof of the old Federal Reserve Building on Constitution Avenue as a possible firing position on Tuesday afternoon; guessing that if Rachel had repeated the previous day's movements she would return at least once more, on Wednesday to the Lincoln Memorial.

'Same as Monday,' the man at the other end of the line had reported when he rang the DC number from the call box in the nearby town. 'Like she's waiting for somebody. Same bench. Stayed there half-an-hour, like before...'

Kurt had hung up.

The same voice, a guy with a Bronx hard-arse twang had answered both days. Years ago, it would sometimes be a woman with a sing-song voice. Clara Schouten had confessed that she remembered *that duty* one week when *he* was down in Caracas, Venezuela. Usually, he had got to speak to a guy, somebody hard-bitten like the man on the desk this week.

The Company did not care about the cops Rachel had taken down back in sixty-one; that was just inter-agency bickering. No, those idiots at Langley just wanted her dead, gone because she knew too much. If he did not do it; somebody else would. The weirdest thing was that he had been okay with that right up to the point...he was not.

So, he had ended *the Locksmith*...instead.

He had not known Angleton planned to meet Rachel; or even why he would take a risk like that. That was why he had waited; just to see if she was going to put a bullet in the evil bastard's brain. However, when it had become clear that she was out of the game, he had not hesitated.

Waiting just long enough to see *the Locksmith's* skull disintegrate in a spray of blood and bone; unaccountably, he had hesitated, stared through the sights...

All the buildings along Constitution Avenue had been burned out or fought over, wrecked, ruined, or looted during the fighting in December 1963; and several, like the Federal Reserve Building, on which restoration had only begun in the fall, were chaotic construction sites which, for one reason or another, had been left fallow, briefly forgotten when the Corps of Engineers – who were still in charge of the great reconstruction project to rebuild the capital – had moved resources to pacify one or other vested interest on the Hill, or simply, run out of men. Whatever, the old Federal Reserve Building had been deserted and last night he had parked up over a mile away, carried the disassembled Remington in a shapeless canvas bag like a workman wearily trudging home, broken into the site, set-up and grabbed several hours sleep knowing that the dawn would surely awaken him.

He had not *known* for a certainty that *she* would repeat the routine she had followed, with minor alterations, on Monday and Tuesday, nor did he have any way of knowing if the FBI, or the CIA, or any other Federal agency would again follow her to the Memorial, on Wednesday morning. However, when an operator like Rachel telegraphed her movements it was always for a reason; so, it was odds-on she would return to the bench overlooking the Reflecting Pool at least once more.

And that the other watchers would suspect as much.

Thus, if *they* were going to contact her; it was likely – if not probable – that they would do it that morning.

Ifs, buts, maybes, imponderables without number were the currency of an assassin's life. Like a big cat hunting prey on the African plains, many hunts failed. The mark never showed up, or something unforeseen happened. Fog, haze, a change of schedule, bodyguards on duty who actually knew what they were doing. No plan was rock solid, sometimes there was a kill-no kill split second.

Yesterday morning he had tracked *her* in his sights for perhaps, fifteen minutes. Another five and he would make the shot, break down the gun and bag it – that would take twenty-two to twenty-six seconds, he practiced with his eyes shut over a dozen times every day – and walk out onto Constitution Avenue like a curious pedestrian trying to find out what all the fuss was about. By then there would be blues and twos charging down to the Lincoln Memorial from every direction, ambulances and people milling around. Everything for the first fifteen to thirty minutes would be confusion. Nobody would even notice an unshaven, nondescript guy in greasy overalls trudging up 21st Street to catch the bus to Arlington.

He still did not know why he had not killed *her*.

He had planned to kill her and anybody who made contact with her, or just *her*, if nobody else turned up.

He had had other plans for Angleton and his family...

She had come to DC to kill him; there was no other explanation for her return. Knowing that *she* would never find him unless *he* wanted to be found *she* had made it easy for him, and incidentally, inevitably, for anybody else who wanted to catch up with *her*.

The trouble was, the more he thought about it the less he understood what had happened at the Lincoln Memorial.

The second round had been aimed dead centre of Angleton's torso but that was when he had begun to crumple to the ground. Between squeezing the trigger and impact the man had slumped between a foot and eighteen inches, and the bullet had smashed into the back of his head.

Rachel had already been sprayed with blood, flesh, spits of lung tissue; now she was showered with fragments of cranial bone and brain matter as the dead man's lifeless cadaver fell across her and bled out.

Through the Remington's sights she had looked like *she* was the one who was bleeding out, like she had been dragged along an abattoir floor.

And she was screaming...

He had cursed, recognising he had wasted several seconds. He broke down the rifle, hitched his bag over his shoulder and with an urgency he knew might attract unwanted attention, made his escape. He had decided to leave his semi where it was parked; hotwire a faster ride in Arlington.

The morning after, he now knew that had been a mistake.

The old black Dodge he had stolen from a lot near the great cemetery would have been reported missing by now.

In retrospect, he ought to have declined the shot; taken Angleton another day. The plan had always been to look into the bastard's eyes as he twisted the knife in his guts...

But only when he had buried his wife and kids.

Never use the same rifle for two hits.

That was two missteps in a day...

He had parked the Dodge behind the hunting lodge just to make sure it was invisible from the road, a track leading past the cabin.

Until he fired that second round, he had been the one in control. He still was, or that was what he told himself. So, why do I feel hunted?

The car's radio was crackly, the tuning knob loose.

"...the Chief of Police," the announcer declaimed as the volume rose and fell, "told the press that the woman apprehended at the scene of the shooting at the Lincoln Memorial is still in custody. He refused to confirm that she is Lady Rachel French, the wife of senior British Air Force Officer Sir Daniel French. The British Ambassador and his wife arrived at the Cleveland Park Police Station shortly after ten o'clock this morning. Sir Nicholas Henderson spoke briefly to reporters to voice his condolences for the family of James Angleton, the former Associate Deputy Director of Operations for Counter Intelligence at the CIA, at this sad time..."

Kurt switched off the radio and clambered out of the Dodge.

His feet squelched coldly in the sodden leaf matter and mud as he stamped back to the cabin, his rage boiling, threatening to consume him.

He was so distracted, roiling inside that he did not hear the car draw up in the road until it crunched gears. He glimpsed the white and blue paint job as the vehicle, a Highway Patrol Ford, reversed, halted, and moved forward again, turning up the soggy mud path to the cabin.

That was when habit, ingrained responses took over.

Suddenly, Kurt was glacially calm.

He was focused on only what he could do.

Everything else, all the myriad of things that were beyond his control were irrelevant.

Chapter 65

Thursday 16th February 1967
BETASOM Bunker, Inner Basin, Port de Bordeaux

At around the time they established radio contact with the Headquarters of the 4th Tanks at Blaye, the SBS men had discovered that there were, in fact, two 'doors' to the bunker in the roof. On inspection, one of them had probably been jammed shut 'since the war' – presumably the Second War – leading to ladders and other hatches which zigzagged, to prevent a bomb or shell following the route of the stairway, down into the heart of the bunker, emerging within a few yards of where the leadership of the Bordeaux 'Collective of the Front Internationale' had been captured.

The *gentlemen* in question considered themselves as belonging to a completely different organisation to that in the Massif Central or down on the south coast.

They were 'more pragmatic' socialists only 'loosely aligned' with their comrades in Clermont-Ferrand and with no direct contact with their 'Soviet brothers and sisters' back in the USSR. It was all hogwash, of course, judging by the number of Kalashnikovs and the other items of Red Army kit lying about inside the BETASOM complex.

Apparently, all the real Krasnaya Zarya fanatics were out 'in the countryside', doing whatever 'they did'. By their own lights the chaps running things in Bordeaux, were just a bunch of well-intentioned patriotic Frenchmen doing their best for their people.

Most remarkable of all, these were claims made with absolutely straight faces.

Paddy Ashdown, angrily unimpressed, had had explained to his prisoners that either they told all their 'people' in the city to lay down their arms or he would leave them alone in a room with a sack of live grenades.

White phosphorus grenades!

Specifically, he demanded that the Revolutionary Guards were to throw their weapons into a heap outside the bunker, an exercise the SBS men could observe from the relative safety of the roof. Thereafter, the disarmed fighters were to corral themselves in plain view at the dock gates to the inner basin of the port. The first trickle of men had begun to surrender within an hour of their leaders beginning to broadcast the call to capitulate.

From the roof of the bunker white flags, sheets were flying and soon, similar blankets, rags were showing from other buildings in the near and middle distance.

Pessimistically, Ashdown's prisoners had been worried about a popular uprising, or wide-scale reprisals.

'That's not my problem,' he had retorted.

Sergey Akhromeyev felt the same way as his new English comrades – no, brothers – in arms about men who used defenceless women and children as human shields.

It was a tactic he had come up against time and again in the White Brigade's running battles with the FI. And when the women they had liberated in the bunker had accused the 'commissars' now in the strike team's custody of 'pleasuring themselves' with the two youngest girls among their number, he had asked Ashdown to leave him alone in a room with the two 'perverts' at whom the finger had been pointed.

He had been astonished by the younger man's unequivocal, unbending response.

'No, we are better than these people,' the Royal Marine had said decisively. Besides, they needed one of the men, the alleged leader of the FI in the city, to carry on broadcasting to 'his people'.

Akhromeyev had wanted to press the point.

Paddy Ashdown had shaken his head.

"Sorry, Sergey. We're Royal Marines, we fight Her Majesty's enemies. We aren't judge and jury. Those beggars surrendered to us and therefore, we are responsible for their welfare. I know that sounds stupid, but," he shrugged, "like I said: we are better than these people."

The people of Bordeaux did not feel the same way about things.

The reprisals had started around mid-day.

Fires began to burn in the streets, thankfully only a few, a little later.

"The rioting doesn't appear to be too widespread, sir," Paddy Ashdown reported to Edwin Bramall when, eventually, the very surprised and relieved commanding officer of the 4th Tanks eventually came on the line.

Bramall's initial cheerfulness quickly sobered.

When neither of the Westland Wessex helicopters had returned last night, he had feared the worst. The confirmation of the circumstances of the loss of the aircraft and their crews, and of five of the SBS men, was a sickening punch in the solar plexus; one only made bearable by the extraordinary good news from the BETASOM Bunker.

"The people in charge in the city don't seem to have had any control over, or feel for the situation on the ground outside it," Ashdown went on. "It may be that a lot of the people out there were simply keeping their heads down, waiting for us to arrive; probably, they wish a plague on both our and the FI's head."

"Hopefully," Bramall suggested, "they won't take too many pot shots at us when we occupy Bordeaux. I'm going to fill up that old ferry moored at Blaye and get a few more of our ruffians across the river to give you a hand. There must be a few helicopters hanging around, too... Do you have any idea what's going on in La Bastide, on the other bank from where you are now?"

"None at all, sir," Ashdown apologised.

Bramall signed off by assuring the younger officer that he was going to send him every available man to 'secure the city'.

Afterwards, Paddy Ashdown climbed up to the roof to join Sergey Akhromeyev.

"What do we do with the people in the lower bunker?" The Russian asked as the two men surveyed the smoky cityscape beneath the low, threatening grey overcast.

According to the captive 'leadership cadre' there were as many as twenty men and women sheltering behind the barricaded blast doors of the lowest level of the BETASOM complex. There were just empty store rooms, unused for many years, down there.

There were spits of rain in the air and a bitter westerly wind plucked at their faces.

"They can stew where they are for the moment," Ashdown shrugged. "There aren't enough of us to guard any more prisoners and still man the communications room."

A couple of the women they had rescued had volunteered to cook up a porridge-type gruel for the Royal Marines' breakfast and kept pressing chicory-sour mugs of 'coffee' on their liberators and protectors.

The Royal Marine sighed.

"How are your ribs, Sergey?"

"I'll live," the Russian grimaced. It hurt to breathe but that was okay; he was still breathing so Vera would not be that angry when he got home...

Home.

Home was England now.

Paddy Ashdown chuckled ruefully

"Pity it was so dark last night. I'd have loved to have seen the expression on your face when we pushed you over the edge of the roof last night!"

Chapter 66

Thursday 16th February 1967
Philip Burton Federal Building, San Francisco

This time it was Special Agent James B. Adams who was in the observation room, and Caroline Constantis and her ever-present guardian, Erin Lambert who sat opposite the prisoner.

Dwight Christie was in an affable, chatty mood and clearly enjoyed being in the company of two, very intelligent, not to say, attractive women. He was particularly attentive to the younger of his interrogators which was odd, because Adams had assumed, he was smarter than that. Especially, since he had to be aware that it was the older of the two women who was the one who was trying to get inside his head.

But then Christie had been locked away with little or no feminine contact for the last two-and-a-half years, and even though the man was at best a scumbag traitor, he was only human. Adams guessed that Caroline Constantis had primed her younger friend to make eyes at the stocky, prematurely going to seed, former FBI man.

"I had a very interesting little chat with Rachel before I came out west," Caro prefaced, smiling.

"Rachel?"

"The Angel of Death, yes."

From his vantage point in the next room James Adams had to stop himself venting a chortle. *She* was good. I must work with Professor Constantis again. A man could learn a heck of a lot just sitting next to her, listening awhile. Less than five minutes in and she was already hitting all the buttons Dwight Christie *did not* want her to press!

"And," Caro went on, matter of factly, "the FBI has kindly given me access to your personal file." She met Christie's gaze, smiling wanly. "The whole file, not the expurgated, abridged version. My, my... I must say, it reads like a novel, Mister Christie." She sighed, her expression turning gently disappointed. "But not, unfortunately, in a good way."

James Adams had suggested to Caro that there was 'an unusually *significant* proportion of uncorroborated material' in the files which had been under Dwight Christie's control, in the two California offices at which he had been based for much of the latter 1950s all the way through to December 1963.

'Hearsay?' She had queried, just to be clear what they were talking about, and to confirm her own suspicions.

'No, more like the illicit padding of existing cases and possibly, the deliberate fabrication of other files the majority of which never reached a conclusion *but* which, when they read them, would have given his superiors the impression, he was a heck of a lot more active than he really was...'

Adams had not wanted to be specific.

However, Caro got the impression that Christie had exaggerated his role in successful cases, gratuitously erased his presence from others, and 'invented' and extensively documented, including with fictitious witness statements, non-existent investigations.

Investigations which were no more or less than figments of his fertile imagination.

What was the mantra that applied?

If one repeats a lie enough times one forgets what is false, and what is real?

Inevitably, this raised a plethora of questions about the value of the testimony he had supplied to the Bureau's interrogators at Quantico, and cast into varying degrees of doubt much of what until then had previously been taken as gospel about the man's FBI career.

"Dwight?" Caro inquired, leaning towards the former Special Agent, as if they were speaking confidentially. "If that is really your name?"

The man blinked, opened his mouth to speak and thought better of it.

"We know there is, or at least, *was* a real Dwight David Christie, date of birth 3rd June 1923," Caro explained. "He had two brothers who were killed in the Second War, one in the Pacific War, and another in Europe. Meanwhile, he, 'Dwight', served, with anonymous distinction in the US Army Office of Defence Procurement in the North West, mainly in Washington State and at the Pentagon, in DC, until he was discharged in early 1946. What we do not know," she qualified, "is if it was actually *that* Dwight David Christie who later went on to college and subsequently joined the FBI."

The man blinked at Caro, whose smiled faded.

"So, I have to ask. Are you Dwight David Christie?"

"Who else would I be?"

"We don't know. That's the problem. As you would understand, from your time with the FBI, identification is key to the whole investigative process. I don't know if you are who you claim to be. From what I can gather, Agent Adams has opened an investigation to establish exactly that," she smiled, tight-lipped, "one way or the other."

Caro knew little about the minutiae of the cases the man who called himself Dwight Christie had investigated, solved or failed to resolve in his decade-and-a-half with the FBI, she had focused on the story he had told, and largely sold to the FBI when he graduated to the Bureau 'Ten Most Wanted' list in early 1964 when it was suspected he was complicit in the pre-meditated, cold-blooded murder of at least two of his closest colleagues.

"Of course, if you are not the real Dwight David Christie, then the question arises as to what happened to the real one; and your culpability in his disappearance?"

"Seriously?" The man groaned, throwing up his arms a little too melodramatically in a parody of exasperation.

The only thing Caro could not understand was how and why Christie's 'history' had been tacitly accepted, more or less, in toto, until now.

Surely, somebody must have been paying attention in the FBI's Office of Personnel Management between 1946 and 1963?

She and James Adams had discussed how 'Christie' – if it turned out he was a fraud - could have flown under everybody's radar for so long.

'Two possible reasons, I think," James Adams had offered. 'Firstly, the Bureau has had other things on its mind the last few years and the top brass, Hoover and the people around him in Washington now view Christie as a huge embarrassment that frankly, they wish would just go away. Secondly, a great deal of what we know – or think we know – about the alleged Communist infiltration of the Bureau, and the Reds' links with what is generically referred to as the American Resistance, a catch-all name for home-grown insurgent or terroristic groups, turns out to be based on information supplied by Christie, or by persons who have worked with him down the years. If I'm right about this guy, it's going to turn out that either he wrote those reports and notes, signing them with somebody else's name; or he 'sold' a crock of shit, if you'll forgive my language, to other, honest agents and they submitted cockamamie reports in good faith.'

Caro had not been convinced.

'But surely, after over two years of intensive expert interrogation all these things would have been thoroughly explored and where possible, corroborated?' She had objected.

'Yes,' Adams had agreed, 'you would think that, wouldn't you!'

Caro did not need to be told that even the best interrogators could be persuaded to believe exactly what they wanted to hear, if their subject was skilled enough, and understood the way the questioners' minds worked.

Neither of them had mentioned the Elephant in the room, the fact that the CIA and the pre-ponderance of FBI resources had been dedicated to Operation Maelstrom for the last few years. Conveniently, everything Dwight Christie had told the people at Quantico, confirmed the worst suspicions of the paranoid conspiracy theorists in DC. Therefore, they were hardly going to risk deconstructing his 'confirmatory evidence'.

Caro sat back.

"Erin, this is going to take longer than I anticipated. Do you think you could persuade the FBI to bring us some coffee, please? Preferably, drinkable coffee?"

The man on the other side of the table was frowning.

"What's going on here?" He asked.

Erin Lambert hesitated.

"It's all right," Caro assured her. "Mister Christie knows that there are armed FBI men on the other side of that mirror and that if he lifts so much as a finger against me, or you, things will not go well for him."

Dwight Christie's frown turned to one of deep offence at the suggestion he might raise his hand to a woman.

"The FBI has shared its most recent profile of you with me," Caro explained patiently. "I am here to test it and if necessary, re-write it. Actually, I could probably do that now. However, were I to do that without properly documenting the reasons why, I'd never be able to quote my report in future academic papers. So, whether you like it or not I am going to do this by the book. When I've finished, the FBI can have you back. Obviously, if you elect to co-operate with me that might later form the basis of a plea for clemency, or whatever is applicable, if at all, in your case..."

"The DOJ cut me a plea bargain back in..."

"I'm no attorney, Mister Christie," Caro reminded him waspishly. "But a plea deal based on falsehoods isn't worth the paper it is written on."

The man thought about this.

He shrugged.

"You said you talked to Rachel?"

"Yes," Caro confirmed. "She told me that she knew the moment she laid eyes on you that you were a complete fraud, Mister Christie."

In fact, Rachel's exact description of the man sitting in front of Caro now was: 'He's some kind of Walter Mitty character...except, on Benzedrine!'

Chapter 67

Just before he left the Embassy for the drive to Cleveland Park, Sir Nicholas Henderson had received one of the odder phone calls of his long, and of late, illustrious career in Her Majesty's Diplomatic Service.

'You don't know me, Mister Ambassador,' the man at the other end of the line had explained, his Yankee drawl laconic, world-weary and somehow, immensely reassuring to Nicko Henderson, because he was already having a very bad day and given that it was still only nine o'clock in the morning, there was plenty of scope for it to get even worse.

Sixty-one-year old William Henry 'Bill' Sallis II was a large well-fed distinguished man with very old-fashioned, almost Southern, courtly manners. Moreover, it transpired that he was the 'Sallis' in *Sallis, Betancourt and Brenckmann, Attorneys at Law*. More pertinent to the moment; he had been Claude Otto von Betancourt's trusted right-hand man for well over three decades and therefore, knew where all this, and every other Administration's since Calvin Coolidge's back in the 1930's had 'buried all their bodies'.

And, in this time of travail, he was volunteering his services to 'the Crown' as an act of 'friendship across the oceans'. To wit, his own services and those of the mighty law firm he had led for the last twenty years. The law firm which was in effect, the executive arm of the sprawling Betancourt family empire.

Bill Sallis explained that 'it would not be appropriate for Gretchen, who has had, I believe, past dealings with Lady Rachel, and in whose debt she feels herself to be, morally at least, to become publicly involved in the present, unfortunate, circumstances; so, to cut a long story short, she sought my advice in the matter and I agreed to substitute my own, humble person for that of my goddaughter...'

The British Ambassador had had no idea what 'Bill' Sallis was talking about until he discovered him waiting for him at Cleveland Park, with a gang of muscular Betancourt family retainers pre-positioned to hold back the surging throng of reporters, photographers and the agitated front men of about a dozen TV news stations.

Mercifully, Nicko Henderson's Greek-born wife, Mary, in a former career a war correspondent and photographer for Time-Life, was able to fill in a few of the yawning gaps in his knowledge and general awareness about who was who in the Betancourt clan. Obviously, he had met Gretchen, the favourite daughter of the great magnet and nowadays, Democrat man of affairs, and her husband, Daniel Brenckmann, Clerk to the US Chief Justice and the middle son of the sadly, now ex-American Ambassador to the Court of Woodstock. However, Nicko had not realised that Bill Sallis was 'Uncle Bill' to all the Betancourt siblings, or that his socialite cousin, Eleanor Louisa Winthrop – the daughter of a wealthy Boston Brahmin family -

Gretchen's mother and the second of old man Betancourt's four wives, was presently the wife of President Nixon's Secretary of Commerce.

'Bill Sallis is one of the best-connected men in this city, darling,' his wife had chided him, adding a pithy comment to the effect that if he did not spend so much time reading Thucydides – a reference recollecting their early courtship in Athens when she would often encounter him dressed in a crumpled suit, a silk scarf about his neck despite the ferocious heat of the Greek summer, invariably with a *History of the Peloponnesian War*, or some other ancient classical tome under his arm – he would have a lot more time to listen to gossip.

Bill Sallis had already requisitioned the local Police Chief's office by the time the British Ambassador arrived on the scene.

"I talked Gretchen out of being seen around the station," he stated with gruffly fond good humour. "She needs to remember she's supposed to be Walter Brenckmann's campaign manager these days," he shook his head, "even if Walter doesn't intend to get out there on the stomp until the fall."

Nicko Henderson had watched with fascination, and no little horror, as the Operation Maelstrom storm had continued to play out. It was as if somebody had thrown a huge rock into the DC pool of politics and giant waves were still crashing, hither and thither, in all directions. Every day there was a new, seismic shock, it seemed.

Right now, the Russians were in town and had it not been for the assassination of James Jesus Angleton, the feared and variously loathed 'national spy', the unchallenged big story today, would be of the meeting of First Secretary and Chairman of the Communist Party of the Union of Soviet Socialist Republics and the President, in the Oval Office of the White House later that afternoon. That had been set up as a veritable media feeding frenzy; sadly, it was all rather put in the shade by the shooting at the Lincoln Memorial.

After fighting his way into the Cleveland Park Police Station, the British Ambassador was left reflecting, that it was a pity that the American press and broadcasters had not shown as much interest in the United Nations gathering in San Francisco!

Still, he reflected, one should always be grateful for small mercies: if Gretchen Betancourt had made an appearance this morning there would probably have been a riot!

After much coming and going Nicko Henderson's people had established that Rachel French had originally been conveyed to the George Washington University Hospital on 23rd Street. Although seemingly catatonic, it was established that, after she had been cleaned up a little that she was not physically injured, she had been transferred – in cuffs, no less – to Cleveland Park sometime during the night.

"The cops think she was involved in the killing," Bill Sallis announced, his tone suggesting that all cops were idiots. "They think she was the bait in the trap, enticing the victim to the Lincoln Memorial. I've been trying to explain to them the difference between probable cause – which they don't have, nor will they ever have in this case – and the stuff Perry Mason gets away with on TV!"

Mary Henderson, who had doggedly clung to her husband's arm as they were buffeted into the police station, at last felt safe to detach herself from her husband's arm, and appraised the broad – she had to admit, immensely solid, comforting – presence of the famous attorney.

Bill Sallis, that was, not the fictional Los Angeles small screen defender...

At that moment a stooped, grey-haired man smoking a cigarette knocked at the open door and walked into the office, with a rolling, stiff-kneed gait that spoke of a life of regular, hard knocks.

"I'm detective McCready. Tom McCready," he introduced himself. His tie was at half-mast and he clearly was not impressed, or in any way over-awed by the people who had commandeered his Captain's room.

Bill Sallis introduced Henderson and his wife.

McCready ran a hand through his thinning hair. He was in his fifties, and nothing he did happened in a hurry.

"Okay," he said eventually. "What we've got is your woman sitting on the same bench opposite the Lincoln Memorial three days running. Same time of day, near as dammit. Just sitting there, waiting. She says she didn't know the dead guy was going to turn up but she won't say who she was expecting. It doesn't look good for her, does it?"

Bill Sallis glanced at Henderson, who shrugged, wordlessly.

"Now I'm being told the lady worked for the Company?" The detective went on, taking a long, lung-filling drag on his cigarette, and exhaling with a sigh. "The FBI say this is their case. Two of their people are in with her now..."

Nicko Henderson and his wife blinked.

Bill Sallis was on his feet, brushing past Detective McCready, who watched the big man shoulder out of the door with a rueful grin playing on his lips.

"Okay," he groaned, shaking his head wearily. "I know your woman is involved in this thing up to her neck," he said, without a scintilla of angst, "but you don't need to be Chief of Police to figure out this isn't going anywhere. Trouble is, in this city everybody thinks they're smarter than everybody else. If it was me, I'd just have driven the lady up to the gates of your Embassy and washed my hands of it. Now, the way things are, there will be records in notebooks, custody documents, court papers and sooner or later everybody in DC will know what they 'think' they know about what happened yesterday."

He stubbed out his cigarette.

"And... They'll all be wrong. Because this is DC and that's just the way it is."

"My, my," Nicko Henderson half-smiled. "You are quite the philosopher detective, Mister McCready."

"No," the other man took no offence at this; to the contrary, he recognised the oblique compliment the remark implied. "I've got fifteen months to retirement. I plan to go fishing a lot. I need this shit like I need a hole in the head."

He shrugged again.

"You folks need to come with me; the Captain will be signing your woman over into your custody in about five minutes." He chuckled. "He doesn't want to lose his pension, either."

Chapter 68

Thursday 16th February 1967
BETASOM U-boat pens, Port de Bordeaux, France

Two of HMS Eagle's Sea Vixens had begun to fly noisy circles over the city that afternoon while, distantly, two of the carrier's Fairey Gannet AEW3s had flown lazy patterns across the suburbs, the surrounding villages and ventured over the southern valleys of the Dordogne and Garonne rivers. The arrival of the Sea Vixens, rocketing low over the roof tops at around six hundred knots, threatening to barrel through the sound barrier in long, low, shallow full-power dives, had driven the majority of the rioters, who in any case, had already had their fun, off the street or underground.

Some fifteen hours after they had tumbled out of their Westland Wessex onto the top of the BETASOM U-boat pen complex, the great still mostly intact river port city of Bordeaux was in the hands of four Royal Marines and a former Red Army defector. By rights, the situation ought to have been getting somewhat fraught by now.

Fortunately, those Krasnaya Zarya or Front Internationale fighters who had yet to give up their weapons, had no way of knowing that Paddy Ashdown's bandits were alone, out on an improbably thin, precarious limb, or the true paucity of Allied forces in the region.

The 4th Tanks might only be twenty miles away at Blaye but Edwin Bramall was fully aware that he might as well have been on the dark side of the Moon!

The flooded Gironde was between him and the city, an old ferry which had been moored in an inundated creek for four years, a few rowing boats and kayaks apart he was well and truly 'stuffed' when it came to riverine transportation. Worse, the two helicopters lost last night comprised half his available 'air force', and the two remaining aircraft were unserviceable, both in parts in barns.

He was so hard-pressed he had had to go down on his knees and beg the Senior Service for help.

To be fair, the Navy had been very good, quite charming about his dilemma and had promised to do what they could to help.

It was still galling to have had to go to cap in hand...

Out in the Bay of Biscay the County class destroyer HMS Devonshire, had stripped out the cabin of her single Westland Wessex helicopter and flown it to Blaye. Now it, and one of the Eagle's smaller Whirlwind's, similarly stripped down, were approaching the river port preparing to discharge their combined cargo of twenty Royal Marines – minus their normal kit, hefting personal weapons only - onto the quayside between the inner and outer tidal basins of the port of Bordeaux.

The plan was for the helicopters to shuttle backwards and forwards transferring every available man Bramall could scrape up as quickly as possible. To add impetus to the enterprise, he was travelling in the Wessex on the first flight.

A second pair of HMS Eagle's Sea Vixens rocketed over the port ahead of the approach of the Wessex and the Whirlwind, as if warning anybody stupid enough to take a pot shot at the approaching aircraft exactly what the consequences of such foolishness might be.

Edwin Bramall had informed Paddy Ashdown that he, Sergey Akhromeyev and his surviving Marines would depart Bordeaux on the second return shuttle to Blaye. They were to hand over to the reinforcements without delay. Bramall would brook no debate on the subject.

'You've just captured the last major city still in enemy hands in Western France, Paddy! I'm damned if I'm going to let you hog all the bloody glory!"

More to the point, the country badly needed a few more living heroes, instead of all the dead ones, it seemed to have been piling up lately.

"The Front Internationale seems to be disintegrating everywhere," Ashdown confided to Akhromeyev. "Like a house of cards; a couple of good, hard knocks and the whole thing is falling down. You were right all along. It doesn't look like they'll be anything for your Commandos up in Herefordshire to do, after all."

Sergey Akhromeyev thought about the proposition.

He shook his head.

"I wouldn't be so sure about that."

"No?"

Again, the Russian shook his head as the two men watched the first helicopter, the Devonshire's Wessex flare out and touch down, rolling a short distance and coming to a halt. Men immediately spewed from it, sprinting at a crouch to defensive positions at the neck of the dock before moving, suspiciously forward.

"You must understand that France was never a big thing for the people back home. It was always a test of how much the West cared; of how much blood it was willing to shed to defend its sphere of influence. Germany or Italy will be the next battleground, probably Italy because the people in Sverdlovsk aren't idiots. Krasnaya Zarya, the Front Internationale, these are just agents of proxy, names behind which the Party can hide. If the Americans give Chairman Shelepin what he wants in Central Europe he will turn his gaze elsewhere; that is the way this game is played. That business attacking the ships at Villefranche, that was an aberration. Mixed messages inside the Troika; don't count on that happening again. For all I know that was just politics, Soviet style. It weakens Gorshkov, even though I doubt Shelepin wants to get rid of him. Not yet. For the moment the military weakness of the Motherland can be blamed on the old Admiral, even though none of it is his fault. As I say, that's just Soviet politics. Sometimes, I think that only you British really understand us..."

Paddy Ashdown had been listening with mounting curiosity.

"In what way? I'm not sure I'm with you, General?"

Sergey Akhromeyev grinned, shook his head.

"Oh, I think you understand me. You just don't know it yet."

The first helicopter was lifting off, banking to turn away.

More soldiers, dark, distant forms were moving away from the second aircraft.

Sergey Akhromeyev smiled.

"The thing that the English and the Russians have in common is a sense of the gallant lost cause, and, a ruthlessness that singles us out from all other nations. The Americans wrote your little country off after Suez; now they will keep you close because after what happened back in the Persian Gulf, and since, they fear what, left to your own..."

At last Akhromeyev's vocabulary failed him.

"Devices?" The younger man offered.

"Yes, I think so. Left to your own devices," another smile, "they fear what you may do next!"

Chapter 69

Thursday 16th February 1967
RAAF Amberley, Queensland, Australia

The news from Washington had burst upon the Anglo-Australasian Party an hour before Commonwealth One, her tanks topped-off, was scheduled to take-off on the ten-hour long-haul south. What had been, until then, a most convivial flight from San Francisco to the Hawaiian fuelling stopover with the British, Australian and New Zealand Prime Ministers in conclave, and their staffs socialising, the wheels well-oiled by Steuart Pringle's Royal Marines smoothly adopting their secondary roles as stewards, was instantly over-shadowed by the looming scandal thousands of miles to the east.

Airey Neave had been shoe-horned onto a scheduled Pan Am flight back to Los Angeles, from whence he would fly straight on to Washington. Problematically, everybody knew that by the time he got to his destination it would be too late.

'We'll just have to let Nicko smooth things over as best he can, Margaret,' her friend had assured the Prime Minister as they said goodbye.

Tom Harding-Grayson had been uncharacteristically quiet on the flight south and had it not been for his wife, Pat, assuming the duties of hostess the trip would have been even more thoroughly miserable than it had been. For the British contingent, leastways.

The Australasian passengers mostly took the Prime Minister's word for it that it was 'all a storm in a tea cup', and tried to enjoy the journey, or even better, attempted to catch up on all the sleep they had missed in the last few days.

Group Captain Guy French had come over the intercom eight hours into the flight: 'I do apologise but we've encountered rather strong headwinds and detoured quite a long way around a nasty storm, which means it would be rather more touch and go, fuel-wise, to carry on all the way down to Canberra. I have advised the Royal Australian Air Force that we will need to land at Amberley, before a final 'hop' down to our final destination.'

As laconic as ever, it was apparent to all his listeners that he felt that he had, in some undefined way, let them all down.

At Ian Gow's suggestion, earlier in the flight Margaret Thatcher had gone up to the cockpit, posed for photographs sitting in the captain's left-hand seat while the Officer Commanding No 10 (Transport) Squadron flew the Super VC-10 from the co-pilot's right-hand chair, casually explaining the controls to the Prime Minister. At one point he had invited her to 'take the wheel'.

The small gang of journalists from British and Australasian papers had been most appreciative, as Ian Gow had hoped, in fact positively eating out of the Prime Minister's hand on account of the unexpected photo-opportunity, and the two or three page spreads their editors would lap up as soon as they got a chance to post their copy. A BBC radio man had waxed lyrical at one stage, his soundman chuntering to himself as he tried to exclude as much as possible the background noise of the jet in flight out of the recording.

For about half-an-hour the cockpit diversion had partially distracted Margaret Thatcher from the unprecedented, unmitigated diplomatic disaster unfolding in Washington DC.

Normally, she would have found the hastily organised welcoming ceremony at Amberley Air Force Base a little tiresome, that day it was a blessed escape.

The base commander and honour guard stood to attention as the Prime Minister of Australia, Sir Robert Menzies, who had seemed terribly tired and worn in California, briefly re-invigorated, led the British Prime Minister and his Kiwi counterpart, the Right Honourable Keith Holyoake down to the tarmac. Afterwards, while Commonwealth One was being re-fuelled for the short 'hop' down to Canberra, where, in comparison, a truly regal reception had long been planned, the premiers and their senior colleagues, including the leader of Her Majesty's Loyal Australian Opposition, Arthur Calwell, who had probably enjoyed the American trips a great deal more than his long-time opponent, Menzies, looking fresh and sounding optimistic, enjoyed drinks and a light meal in the Officers Mess.

'It will be very nice to see Peter and Marija again,' Pat Harding-Grayson had reminded her younger friend as Commonwealth One lined-up for take-off.

The Prime Minister brightened a degree; she had a new godson – Miles Julian – born shortly after the Christophers arrived in Australia last year whom she had never seen, and never held in her arms. The thought prompted a twisting pang of guilt, Carol and Mark, her thirteen-year-old twins were in the care of Diana Neave in her, and Frank's, prolonged overseas absence.

How much better would it have been to have brought them with her this time...

That said, Frank had felt that it would be good for the twins to be around other 'young people'; the Neave's youngest son, William was the same age as Mark and Carol, and Diana tended to run an 'open house' for all the other youngsters cooped up in the 'Government enclaves' of Oxford.

Her husband was probably right, she was too over-protective and it really was not good for the twins...

There had been no news from Washington since leaving Honolulu and this played on the Prime Minister's mind as the aircraft roared into the air and turned southward, to begin the nine-hundred-mile final 'hop' to its destination.

Once the aircraft reached its cruising altitude, Ian Gow, today attired in his Hussars uniform on account of the full ceremonial welcome awaiting Commonwealth One at Canberra, settled in the seat opposite his principal.

He began his customary briefing.

"Order of events, Prime Minister," he prefaced dutifully. "The

Governor-General and his wife will be at the head of the reception line at the foot of the steps. Sir Peter will escort you and Prime Minister Holyoake down that line, Lady Marija will hang back and attend Sir Robert and Mister Calwell. Our High Commissioner, General Leese, will attach himself to Lord and Lady Harding-Grayson. There will be a guard of honour to inspect. Now then...speeches."

Margaret Thatcher took the two sheets of paper.

She scanned them in a moment.

"Yes, that's fine," she confirmed.

Honestly, she had no idea what she would do without Pat Harding-Grayson, her friend seemed to have an effortlessly light drafting touch. She could always tell when Ian had suggested – he never insisted – on this, of that minor change. If Margaret Thatcher did not know how she would cope without Pat, she would be equally bereft without Ian Gow.

Officially, depending on whether the setting was parliamentary or strictly governmental, Ian Gow was respectively her Parliamentary Private Secretary, or her Appointments Secretary but everybody recognised that he was her de facto Chief of Staff, doorkeeper and ear to the ground within her sporadically fractious National Conservative clan.

'If you didn't have Ian minding the shop,' her husband had once remarked, only half in jest, 'you'd never have a moment to yourself, my dear!'

There were times when the Prime Minister strongly suspected that Ian Gow and Sir Henry Tomlinson, the greying eminence grise of the Home Civil Service, were the ones actually running the country!

"Sir Robert will talk for a little longer," Ian Gow continued, very much in the manner of a reassuring family solicitor, by coincidence the profession the politician-soldier-lawyer had planned to pursue had the October War not intervened. "But he plans to stick to key points only. Likewise, Mister Holyoake. Mister Caldwell will stand beside Sir Robert but he will not speak at the airport. I believe there was some kind of trade-off between the parties and it was agreed that he would have a prime slot at the official homecoming gala. Sir Peter Christopher will do the usual welcoming spiel, I should imagine we can rely upon him to keep things short and sweet. Thereafter, Mister Holyoake and his party will accompany you, the Governor-General and Lady Marija back to Government House at Yarralumla, the Foreign Secretary and others will return to the High Commission with Sir Oliver, et al. I know that you will wish to have a little personal time with Sir Peter and Lady Marija, so I have cleared your diary for the two hours or so between the arrival at Government House and the time scheduled for getting ready for the evening's 'banquet'."

Ian Gow waited a moment.

"Is that satisfactory, Prime Minister?"

"Yes, thank you, Ian."

Blissfully, right then she could think of nothing so guaranteed to if not obviate, then at least, to thoroughly distract her from her worries than the prospect of bouncing her goddaughter, Elisabetta, now over two years old, on her knee and cradling six-month-old godson, Miles Julian in her arms.

While she waited to hear the latest bad news...

Chapter 70

Thursday 16th February 1967
Philip Burton Federal Building, San Francisco

"What are you saying, Lady?" Dwight Christie demanded, careful not to raise his voice because he knew, he just knew, that was not going to cut it with the slim, grey-haired woman whose blue-grey eyes threatened to see straight through him to the wall five feet behind his head.

Professor Caroline Constantis sipped her coffee. Remarkably, it was nowhere near as bad as she had imagined it would be. In her experience FBI coffee was always over-stewed, brutally bitter but this was actually...pleasant.

The deal she had agreed with Special Agent James B. Adams, was that she would present the man who claimed to be Dwight David Christie her 'take' of what she had learned, deduced, intuited from the files she had been allowed to study, and the insights Adams had shared with her. She would confront the man with her version of reality and they would all see how he reacted.

It was hardly a standard diagnostic protocol but then, today, her subject was just about the most atypical 'case' she was ever going to encounter. Caro was about to move on when there was a rap at the door and Adams entered the room.

"A word please, Professor," he apologised, beckoning her to follow him out of the interview room.

Leaving Erin Lambert to keep Dwight Christie company she stepped out into the corridor.

James Adams leaned close, speaking lowly as they wandered a few steps away from the door to the interview suite.

"It has been confirmed that the man shot at the Lincoln Memorial was the Associate Deputy Director of Operations for Counter Intelligence, James Jesus Angleton. He was with Lady Rachel French at the time of the shooting."

Caro was, understandably, nonplussed for several seconds.

"Is she?" She asked, not yet forming coherent thoughts.

"She was uninjured. However, there is speculation that she was part of the assassination plot. Specifically, that she lured Angleton to his death..."

Caro shook her head, emphatically.

"No. The only man she was interested in was Billy the Kid."

"And you know this, how?" The man demanded urgently, his voice a hoarse whisper.

"Because she told me so!"

"And you believed her?"

"Yes, I did!"

"Okay, okay. I had to ask you."

"Rachel French is not the problem," Caro retorted, getting angry. "Hans Mikkelsen and his son are the problems. Whoever thought it was a good idea bringing that poor woman back into this thing – after what she's been through – ought to be ashamed of themselves!"

James Adams backed away, held up his hands.

"Not guilty, Ma'am. All that's way above my pay grade."

"Sorry. I don't usually shoot the messenger," Caro apologised, forcing a tight-lipped smile. "I keep hoping that somebody is going to tell me what's going on, that's all."

The FBI man grinned.

"That's the story of my life, too."

Caro took a few moments to compose herself before she went back into the interview room, settled, took another sip of her coffee and fixed the man on the other side of the table with a quizzical gaze.

"Everybody tells lies," Caro offered gently, "little white lies mostly, we all do it all the time, to avoid embarrassment, often to avoid offending, or injuring the feelings of somebody we care about. Sometimes, the lies are big lies; but not always badly intentioned. The problem comes when those lies, big or small, become incorporated into our pasts as if they were true, real parts of our histories, our lived experiences and personalities. There is nothing worse than not knowing what is true and what is not, of losing a sense of who one was, and is."

"What's your point?" The man calling himself Dwight Christie put to her, irritated.

"Would you agree with the proposition that the FBI is an inherently secretive organisation? That it operates on a need to know basis, especially the closer one moves to day to day operational activities?"

The man nodded.

"Yet the first thing Agent Adams found odd – I won't put it stronger than that – when he got hold of your personnel jacket and began to read the transcripts of your interrogations at Quantico, was that you claimed to know an awful lot about areas of the Bureau's work that you had never had any direct contact with?"

"I keep my ear to the ground and my eyes open."

"Very commendable," Caro breathed. "I was fascinated to digest your own account of how you fell into the 'Red camp'; not to mention your moral justification for betraying your country and, presumably, although you are more reticent about it, or should I say, evasive, in the way you justified your involvement with the so-called 'American Resistance'."

This drew no reply.

"Before the war," Caro went on, "I was developing a diagnostic tool for clinicians to assist in the categorisation of persons with psychopathic personality disorders. Psychopaths were very much 'my thing'; that was how I got to work with Edwin Mertz. There were fifty points on the scale I developed; one day I'll publish my paper on the subject, always assuming the Bureau de-classifies my research." She grimaced. "But I'm not holding my breath on that one. Somewhere along the line I must have upset the Director because most of my work is still embargoed. Anyway, enough of my troubles. We're here to talk about you, *Dwight.*"

The man was giving her the silent routine.

That was okay, he was a fascinating subject; she would love to know, to be able to establish it, on the record, if his psychosis had morphed from relatively benign narcissistic delusions to full blown psychopathy – from a harmless Walter Mitty type character to a sociopathic killer – before or since, or perhaps, as a consequence of the October War.

Caro did not go along with James Adam's idea that the man across the table from her was not the real Dwight Christie.

That was too much of a stretch.

Entia non sunt multiplicanda praeter necessitatem.

More things should not be used than are necessary; or more prosaically, given two or more explanations for a given circumstance or event, the simpler is more likely to be true.

For the man sitting in front of her to be somebody other than Dwight David Christie, a lot of complicated, unlikely things would have needed to have happened and this thing was already, far too messed up...

"The way this works," she explained, "is that I'm going to tell you a story. Your story. If you want, you can put me right as we go along. Trust me, that will be less painful for you. Or, I can tell you," she hesitated, "well, take intelligent guesses, as to which parts of the history are pure baloney. Then you'll feel really dumb and hate me for it. Whatever, the reason Captain Lambert is sitting next to me is that Edwin Mertz's ghost put a curse on me. It's not true that psychopaths don't have a sense of humour. It's just not funny, that's all. That's how I already know, that unlike Mertz, you are way down on the psychopathy scale."

"I'm not a..."

"I didn't say you were a psychopath, Dwight. The problem with you is that one minute I'm talking to a former patriotic FBI agent and the next I'm looking into the eyes of a narcissistic traitor with delusions of grandeur, who is displaying unmistakable, identifiable signatures of sociopathic-psychopathic behaviour. One day you demonstrate empathy, selfless comradeship; the next, I concede, not routinely, you cold-bloodedly murder men you've worked with for years."

Dwight Christie shrugged, feigned indifference, yawned.

"Do what you've got to do, lady."

Caro turned to Erin. "More coffee would be good. Where on earth did you find this stuff?"

"One of the secretaries was feeling sisterly. She put fresh grounds into her boss's machine. I'll go see her again."

Caro drained her cup.

She waited until she was alone again with Dwight Christie.

"Okay, we shall begin at the beginning. Once upon a time there was an idealistic kid called Dwight," she commenced, wryly. "He was bright, too. In fact, *he's* always reckoned he was the sharpest knife in the drawer, isn't that right, Dwight?"

The man shrugged with carefully understated contempt.

"Life was good and then one day the Japanese bombed Pearl Harbour. His folks wanted him to go to Law School; he walked through the Army's officer candidate selection board. He figured he'd be a hero; but the Army saw his IQ scores and made damned sure none of those pesky Japs or Nazis got a chance to shoot him; because, like all armies, it needed its best and brightest men fighting the good fight at home because it always knew, that its biggest problem was not the 'official' enemy abroad but those grasping, amoral profiteering bastards at home in corporate America."

Dwight Christie had been an acting Captain, attached to the Department of Defense Procurement Office by the end of the war. All his commanding officers spoke highly of him but he had never uncovered any huge scam, or managed to highlight a particularly grotesque example of industrial-scale profiteering. No, he had kept his nose clean and lived the good life in the American North West and DC while tens of thousands of other young Americans had fought and died on foreign beaches, islands, lands, or in the air or on the seas of the world. There had clearly been times when he thought his superiors were giving certain contractors an 'easy ride' but he had never been prepared to go to the wall over it. Perhaps, that was when the well of guilt began to overflow?

"I guess," Caro continued, "you'd been having the time of your life, working in Seattle, at Hanford, spending one week in every four or five back in DC reporting to the Pentagon. That must have been a real buzz for a young guy? You were having a great time right up until you got the news your kid brother, Vernon, had died in Normandy. You still hadn't got over that when your big brother, the guy who'd always protected you – the clever, sensitive kid all the bullies picked on – was killed on Iwo Jima. Your parents never got over that, and neither did you. They died young, you didn't know how to cope, or to go on living with the reality of your life, so," Caro quirked a sympathetic smile, "over the years, you invented a new world. Bit by bit your damaged psyche constructed an altered, safer, better reality in which you lived, quite harmlessly, I imagine, until the Cuban Missiles War."

"I'm not crazy," Dwight Christie muttered.

"I agree, and I disagree. I'm describing a psychosis arising out of your mind attempting to heal itself, in which you began to live in your own, increasingly separate world. Once you do that it is relatively easy to lose empathy, connection with the people around you. It becomes easy to think of them as 'things', pieces on a chess board which exist only for your convenience."

"Psycho-babble," the man grunted derisively as Erin Lambert returned with three cups on a metal tray.

"Have I missed anything?" She inquired, picking up her cup and stepping away from the table to stand next to the mirror on the wall.

"The professor has me down for a psycho," Dwight Christie

complained.

"On a bad day," Caro agreed, with an apologetic grimace. "You see, I don't think you recognised what was happening to you. Not for a while, and by the time you did, well, by that time not knowing what was real and what was fantasy didn't seem to matter anymore. Tell me I'm wrong?"

"You're wrong!"

"Okay, that makes you a run of the mill psychopath," Caro retorted matter of factly. "If there is such a thing, which strictly speaking, there probably isn't. Be that as it may, contrary to your carefully constructed back story I don't believe that you were ever that comic-book all-American kid traduced by some kind of 'Communistic dream'. That stuffs purely for the movies. You didn't grow up a closet Red or any other kind of rebel. During the Second War I don't even think you were very shocked to discover that American industry routinely – gratuitously, in fact – systematically fleeces and gouges the American taxpayer. Like most Americans you accept the venality of the system because, in the scale of things, it benefits the greatest number of people. All that polemic you gave those dopes at Quantico about obscene fortunes being shamelessly built upon the bodies of dead GIs; that's just crap, Dwight!"

Caro recognised what had shouted so loudly at James Adams as he forensically deconstructed Dwight Christie's personal history and career in the FBI.

It was far too pat. Too clean, too...organised.

Dwight Christie's whole thesis was flawed.

And besides, while his association with criminal figures on the West Coast and his loose affiliation with several outlandish characters who together, had come to form, in the FBI's files and the wider public imagination, 'the resistance' were demonstrable, documented post-October 1962, there was no evidence other than his own highly suspect testimony, linking him to Soviet Intelligence, Red Dawn or to any other leftist subversive group.

Problematically, J. Edgar Hoover's FBI expected to, badly wanted to and therefore, often assumed that what it was looking for, and now and then seeing, was evidence of 'reds under the bed'. Dwight Christie wholly understood that mentality; and he had played to his audience with marvelous adroitness and adaptability.

But now the game was over.

James Adams had briefed Caro that Christie had been a 'star member' of a special FBI team digging up and feeding, sometimes legally, other times not, 'evidence' to the House Un-American Activities Committee in the 1950s. His work in the American North West, and spells on detachment investigating the Hollywood milieu of Los Angeles, had identified him as a future high-flyer to the 'big chiefs' in DC, and earned him a series of promotions which had eventually put him in line to take over as Head of the San Francisco Field Office in 1963.

Dwight Christie had been living a dual life for a long time: that of the proto-typical FBI man parallel to that of a facilitator and sometime co-conspirator with a gang of 'crazies' ultimately led by Galen Cheney, the evangelical berserker who had terrorised parts of West Texas in the chaos after the October War, and died having led the mob that seized the Wister Park Embassy compound in July 1964.

He had never been a 'deep sleeper' Red spy, that was simply a constructed rationalisation which had come to underpin his alternative reality.

Dwight Christie said he had tried to stop that atrocity at the Wister Park compound; and even when he failed, had attempted – in the event, ineffectually - to stop the rape, torture and murder of the surviving female staff held as hostages. Some of that might even be true. He might, as he claimed, have tried to kill Cheney down in Texas the year before, or not, after he had spirited away several members of the madman's 'family' around the time Cheney and his son had attempted to assassinate the Reverend King at Bedford Pines Park in Atlanta.

Caro sighed, and pushed back her chair.

"I think we're done here," she declared, rising to her feet. "Looking down at Christie she hesitated: "We probably won't meet again. I honestly don't know if you are a bad man, Mister Christie. I suspect you are sick, but honestly and truly, I don't think anybody cares about that anymore."

James Adams had a theory that Hans Mikkelsen was the man with whom Christie and another one of Galen Cheney's disciples, or perhaps one of the maniac's sons, had lured a joint FBI-US Army team into a trap which had claimed the lives of seven federal agents and eleven soldiers, and wounded another dozen, in Texas prior to the Wister Park atrocity.

It was the one thing Dwight Christie refused to talk about.

When shown a mug shot of Hans Mikkelsen he had simply shrugged and looked away.

Caro had no intention, or inclination to go there.

Anybody seriously trying to get to the root of Dwight Christie's psychosis would need to study him for weeks, months perhaps, and having royally screwed up at Quantico, the FBI was never going to allow that to happen.

James Adams had needed an expert second opinion.

She would give him exactly that.

And wash her hands of the whole thing.

Right now, a few months locked up in officers' married quarters at Offutt Air Force Base catching up on her reading, and writing up the papers she had put on the backburner before the war in the Midwest, pretending to be just another ordinary Project Looking Glass widow, would suit her just fine!

Chapter 71

Friday 17th February 1967
United Kingdom Embassy, Washington DC

Air Marshal Sir Daniel French was ushered straight into the Ambassador's rooms on his arrival from Andrews Air Force Base. It was customary for senior British officers in the United States to travel in mufti; however, for this trip he had made an exception, donning his day uniform, for his first appearance before the cameras of the American TV broadcasters and press photographers on the tarmac at Andrews Field.

Nicko Henderson guessed that his guest's expression had scarcely been less black on the tarmac of Andrews Field as it was when he had swept into the Embassy.

"What the Devil is going on, Henderson?" Dan French demanded angrily. "Nobody will tell me a bloody thing!"

The Ambassador was about to reach for a bottle of Brandy, deeming that the other man could, like him, do with a stiff drink right now. He was about to suggest as much when his wife swept into the room.

"Rachel is sleeping at present, Sir Daniel," she said confidentially, softly as if she was afraid the slumbering wife would overhear, and awake.

Although she hid it well, inwardly, Mary Henderson was still a little shaken up after yesterday.

They all were still suffering the after effects, it was just that Nicko was incredibly good at concealing that sort of thing from casual observers. It was something probably best explained by his public school-upbringing – he had gone to Stowe before going up to Hertford College, Oxford - rather than anything the Diplomatic Service had taught him.

Mary had almost fainted the first time she had seen Rachel at Cleveland Park.

The hospital or the police had taken away Rachel's ruined dress and coat, both of which were covered with unspeakable gore; but there had still been what was probably congealed brain matter in her hair, and when she had changed into the winter frock and coat Mary had brought from the Embassy, she had seen that her under things were stained, soaked with dried blood. Apparently, the Angleton man had collapsed across her and pretty much bled out into her lap.

Back at the Embassy Mary had guided Rachel into a bath, where she had sat, shivering, uncommunicative for over an hour until the water was freezing cold. Mary had washed the offal out of her hair and a doctor had been called, who given Rachel an injection of something to help her sleep. Then, Mary, and a female secretary whom Rachel knew from her time at the Embassy in 1964 and 1965, had sat up with her all night.

In addition, at Nicko's request, two armed Marines had stood sentry outside the bedroom door in case she awakened and ran amok in the night.

God, men were so bloody melodramatic!

Mary Henderson took Dan French's arm.

"Look, sit down and have a drink, Dan. I know Nicko's dying to have one. You both need it."

Regardless of how angry or distraught Dan French was he was far too much of a gentleman to gainsay the mistress of the house. It was a matter of moments before the Ambassador pressed a crystal tumbler into his hands.

"The Queen," Nicko Henderson suggested, pouring himself clumsily into a nearby armchair, to be joined in the blink of an eye by his wife, perching on one arm, anxiously scrutinising Dan French.

"Rachel is physically unhurt, Dan," she said, knowing that was the most important message to communicate and that once that had sunk in, the poor man would feel an awful lot better.

"Airey should never have asked her to come back to America!" Dan French fulminated, pausing only to take a gulp of the Embassy's first-class Brandy. "I knew..."

Nicko Henderson raised a hand.

"It was a mistake," he agreed, "but I'm sure Airey had his reasons."

Airey Neave had, presumably motivated by the natural escaper's sixth sense honed and perfected in extricating himself from Colditz Castle in the Second War, made tracks for the White House shortly before Dan French's plane was due to land.

There was an inordinate amount of smoothing over of wounded sensibilities to be done, and had Dan French's arrival not been imminent, Nicko himself would at this moment, be well and truly 'on the carpet' at the State Department; as, indeed, he would be shortly when he attended Foggy Bottom at the Secretary of State's pleasure.

Or in this case...extreme *displeasure*.

"Reasons?" Dan French grunted, teetering on the edge of being unspeakably rude to his hosts.

No, no, that would never do...

Unconsciously, powered by raw angst he had risen to his feet, clunking his glass down on a table which fortunately, happened to be where his hand released it.

Why are the Ambassador and his charming wife looking towards the door I came in through?

The red mist did not want to clear.

However, he turned.

"Rachel..."

His wife was standing in the open doorway.

Dressed in a white shift-gown that covered her shoulders and fell to her knees, her feet bare she seemed so helplessly pale, and weary. Her hair was tangled, half over her face.

She tried to meet her husband's gaze.

Failed, stared at her feet like a little girl lost.

"I'm, I'm sorry... I..."

Dan French, in no mood to stand on ceremony reached his wife in two, three strides and wrapped her in his arms with such urgent intensity that briefly, he inadvertently crushed the air out of her lungs.

Rachel coughed.

"I can't breathe..."

"Sorry, I..."

She was crying and the man was terrified he was about to break down too.

He buried his face in her hair, clung to her as if he was afraid that if he let go, she would evaporate into thin air.

They swayed, embraced.

Then: "I think I'm going to be sick!"

Dan scrabbled desperately for the Ambassador's wastepaper basket and almost, but not quite placed it in the right place at the right time. In the process the couple ended up on their knees in front of Nicko Henderson's marvellously cluttered desk.

"Oh, God... They gave me an injection of some kind yesterday," Rachel gasped. "And now I've been sick on Nicko's favourite rug..."

The Ambassador and his wife had, meanwhile, absented themselves, thus deferring this new embarrassment a while longer.

Rachel fingered her hair.

And I have been sick in my hair...

"Oh God, I must look as dreadful as I feel."

"You look," Dan French began, contemplating a white lie. "Not so good," he confessed.

She rested her brow on his shoulder, too weak to hold up her head.

"Dan..." She slurred, feeling nauseas again.

"I'm here. I'm here, my love."

Chapter 72

The once scenic village at the foot of the Chaine de Puys lay on the gently rising ground west of Clermont-Ferrand, little more than five kilometres distant from the boundaries of the neighbouring city fought over, looted and now left to dereliction since the October War. Before the war the road from Clermont-Ferrand to Limoges would have been busy, particularly in the summer; now, it was pot-holed, cracked and at the margins, overgrown by weeds and when the trees started coming into leaf in the spring, branches would overhang its nature-narrowed course as it headed up into the mountain passes to the west.

Comrade Agnès thought she had dreamed being picked up, and jolted and bounced on the back of some kind of litter or trailer. She had been cold, wet, slowly succumbing to exposure, hypothermia. Beyond help, beyond caring.

Now, her thin, famished frame ached as she lay, barely sensible on the lumpy straw palliasse on the floor of what, as her eyes blinked in and out of focus, she guessed must have been a stable of some kind in happier times.

No, not a stable.

More a pigsty accommodated in a thatched, smelly hovel!

She thought about it, would have brooded had not somebody put a hand under her head, and held a metal bowl to her lips. She slurped brackish, cold water.

Presently, she sat up, her knees drawn close to her chest with her back to the uneven, unyielding wall.

The company of at least one member of the Suinae subfamily of Artiodactyl Mammalia, Suidae – the domesticated pig – would, she decided, have been infinitely preferable to the two filthy, black-uniformed, stinking Revolutionary Guards with whom she shared her new cell. A few days ago, she would have done anything to hide the way she felt, the bile that rose in her throat every time she saw that evil, neo-Nazi uniform. That's what these people were, Nazis by any other name and she hated all the things she had done to help them stay in power.

One of the pigs was looking at her oddly.

"What the fuck are you looking at, shithead!" She snarled.

Now they'll beat me insensible, kick me on the ground until I'm a bloody, broken mess, probably piss on me for good measure. She shut her eyes waiting for the first blow.

What was that to a woman who had slept with a man who kept a knife *and* a gun under his pillow?

One of the men stuttered: "Sorry, Comrade. I didn't mean anything by it..."

No, now I know I am still dreaming.

She squinted at the man.

He was...terrified.

Literally, scared witless, he was clearly about to wet himself with fright.

She thought about asking what was going on: no, that was a bad idea, and anyway, I know I am going mad already. What is the point of getting her self-diagnosis doubly confirmed?

Neither of the Revolutionary Guards were carrying firearms.

"Where are you rifles?" She demanded.

"Left them behind, Comrade. The Chairman said for us to do it. So, well, we could carry you up that hill out of the city..."

"You don't have guns?"

"No..."

"I want a knife. A sharp one."

It would have been easier, probably a lot less painful to kill herself with a gun. Never mind, one good stroke with a sharp knife ought to slash or at least seriously damage both carotid and jugular, she would pass out within seconds, bleed to death in less than half-a-minute.

Back there in the woods she had been reconciled to death.

Now these bastards had 'saved' her.

What right did they have to do that?

Maxim...

They had said 'the Chairman'.

Machenaud was alive...

"Where is the First Secretary?"

"Resting, Comrade."

In that moment her brain tingled as it had as a child the first time that she began solving complex mathematical puzzles, finding proofs for all those theorems her teachers struggled to grasp. It had been as if for a few seconds she glimpsed the infinite majesty of all the possibilities in the physical world.

The 'memory' did not last long.

Ignited into life, it guttered in a nanosecond.

What rational sentient being existing in a Universe with an average temperature of just two degrees above absolute zero would reasonably expect her dreams to come true?

Her head was clear now.

He was still alive.

She was still alive because *he* willed it.

She was tired of living by *his* will.

"Take me to Comrade Maxim!" She commanded, staggering to her feet.

Chapter 73

Friday 17th February 1967
The White House, Washington DC

There were flakes of snow in the air as Alexander Shelepin stepped out of the second, of the three bullet-proof Lincoln's the Secret Service had provided to convey the Soviet delegation wherever they went in Washington.

The mood of the city had been febrile since the President's return from California, and since Wednesday's shooting, reinforced rings of steel had surrounded the White House, Capitol Hill, the Pentagon, and many foreign embassies. There were soldiers on the streets, everywhere, patrolling with Washington PD officers, and tanks, armoured personnel carriers and a host of other military vehicles were parked up at strategic locations across the city. Overhead, the roar of high-flying jet interceptors circling the capital was ever-present.

The great city might have been under siege...

The Soviet leader had mixed feelings about what he was seeing and hearing about the Americans' response to the assassination of a single CIA officer, granted a senior and in some quarters, one known to be an unprincipled, notorious, formidable operator. The response seemed disproportionate, verging on the paranoid even if one accepted the premise that there was a mad dog killer at loose in the District of Columbia; an inherently improbable scenario.

Nevertheless, no man in Alexander Shelepin's position could fail to be impressed by the quantity, and the potency of the military forces the US Administration had been able to magic out of seemingly thin air, and the speed with which the city had been locked down.

If the KGB thought it had a firm grasp on Sverdlovsk and the Chelyabinsk military district to its south, he was going to have to put his subordinates right about that upon his return! Moreover, there was a lesson to be learned in the way his hosts had flooded the metropolis with military firepower and yet not, as would have happened in the Motherland, brought it to a virtual halt. The busses still ran, the traffic was as previously, very heavy, the sidewalks were jammed with pedestrians and nothing, not even being pushed back several tens of metres behind cordons manned by machine gun-toting grim-faced troopers, diminished the enthusiasm or the persistence of the US media.

Flanked by Sergey Gorshkov and Ambassador Anatoly Dobrynin, Shelepin met Richard Nixon, stepping forward beneath the portals of the neoclassical portico of the North Wing of the Executive Residence.

Dobrynin had insisted on explaining the layout of the White House 'complex' to the First Secretary. Although Shelepin could have told him to desist at any time, he had let the man talk.

'The middle, Executive Residence is the shell of the original White House built between 1792 and 1800 to a design by an Irish architect who drew his inspiration from Leinster House in Dublin, presently the home of the Parliament of the Republic of Ireland. The building you will be entering by its northern entrance, the one visible from Pennsylvania Avenue is simply the facade of the original nineteenth century one burnt down in around 1812 by the British. Strictly speaking, it is the third White House. The first one was rebuilt in the early nineteenth century, and then gutted and reconstructed by President Truman between 1949 and 1952. The Americans were afraid all it would take was one medium-sized bomb and the whole place would collapse, so, apart from the exterior fascia, they built a new, massively steel-reinforced version of what had been there in Roosevelt's day.'

Dobrynin had moved on to talk about the rest of the 'complex'.

'Thomas Jefferson, the first President to occupy the original completed building, added eastern and western colonnades to the first White House. In that period the building stood in relatively open, somewhat swampy countryside. Apparently, George Washington – who was sensitive about such things - had not wanted to 'waste' good agricultural land so he had mandated that 'his' house should be built on land nobody wanted to farm!'

Even Alexander Shelepin had quirked a grimace of amusement at this below the belt jibe.

"The North Portico, where President Nixon will greet you, Comrade First Secretary, was built in 1829 during the term of the 6th President, John Quincy Adams. The East Wing of the White House – built in 1846 - is where ordinary and customary business visitors arrive and enter the complex. This wing also accommodates the First Lady's staff and other minor functionaries of the Administration. The modern West Wing, where you will be escorted, was constructed as recently as 1909, with the Oval Office at its south eastern corner overlooking the South Lawn. Although there was an oval room in the original White House, called the *Yellow Oval Room*, inspired by a room used by the first President, Washington in Philadelphia; in modern times the Oval Office became the workplace of American Presidents only in the early years of this century when Theodore Roosevelt built a one-storey temporary one on the site of the present West Wing in around 1902.'

By then the convoy of loaned-Lincolns and its Marine Corps escort was turning into the grounds of the White House.

'Today, after the greeting ceremony on the steps of the White House, the President will guide you into the building for the short walk along the western colonnade to the West Wing for your meeting in the Oval Office, Comrade Chairman.'

'You are very well-informed, Comrade Anatoly Fyodorovich,' Admiral of the Fleet and Minister of Defence of the USSR Sergey Gorshkov growled sarcastically, as the car cruised into the show of the White House.

'Thank you, Comrade Deputy First Secretary,' Dobrynin retorted with exemplary politeness. 'My wife, a very wise woman, purchased a copy of a guide book when we first arrived in Washington, it has been invaluable!'

Despite himself, Gorshkov relented, chuckled and shook his head.

On the steps the President was flanked by the First Lady, Patricia, and the Nixon's daughters, twenty-year-old Tricia and eighteen-year-old Julie.

Richard Nixon proudly introduced his family to Alexander Shelepin, who was impressed by the way Anatoly Dobrynin seemed to get on well with the President and his wife. Dobrynin was clearly regarded as a gentle giant, entertaining uncle figure by both of the daughters.

Anecdotally, the Dobrynin's and their daughter had lunched more than once at the White House, and 'got on well' with the Nixons. A month ago, that had been a possible black mark on the Ambassador's file; a thing which in the new circumstances needed to be urgently revisited.

Shelepin paused for the obligatory pictures taken by a couple of official White House photographers. There would be a small group of reporters, and a TV crew from the US network ABC, inside in the reception hall; more shaking of hands, and posing for the cameras. Such was unavoidable, this was, after all...America.

It had been agreed that only Shelepin, Gorshkov and Dobrynin, the latter acting as an interpreter, would follow the President and his family into the Oval Office where Vice President Nelson Rockefeller, his wife, Secretary of State Cabot Lodge and the newly appointed US National Security Advisor, Gordon Bell, would form a second welcoming committee.

"Often, we welcome visitors to the White House on the South Lawn," Pat Nixon was explaining to Shelepin as the group began to amble, unhurriedly, deeper into the building. 'But the weather at this time of year has turned the lawn back into the swamp it used to be in George Washington's day!'

Alexander Shelepin was struck by the fundamental unreality of the situation. Here he was, supposedly the ringmaster of the Evil Empire, being greeted like a prodigal returning by the First Family while Richard Nixon's closest military and economic ally, the United Kingdom was in the proverbial doghouse over the fallout from the United Nations farrago in San Francisco, and now the extraordinary incident at the Lincoln Memorial, and positively drowning in a storm of excoriating, jingoistic condemnation in the American media.

A visitor from another planet, stepping foot in Washington DC, could easily get the impression that the Soviet Union was the United States' best global friend. After all, the British leader and her Commonwealth allies had been sent packing from California with their tails between their legs.

However, there was going to be a lot to digest on the way home to Sverdlovsk. One view might be that it had been American intransigence which had stopped the United Nation's re-dedication becoming a farce, and that Richard Nixon had emerged anew in the eyes of his own people – and of so-called Middle America - as the reliable strong man who had won the Civil War only last year.

Already, the firestorm over the Operation Maelstrom revelations was partially extinguished, relegated to the inside pages of the newspapers, and unmentioned until after the first, or second commercial breaks on most TV and radio news broadcasts. As Dobrynin had commented, possibly presciently on the day the delegation left San Francisco: 'Last week's news is old news, the attention span of the people on Main Street is short and already, the agenda has moved on. Yes, the scandals of before still rumble on; just not with anywhere near the intensity of only a few days ago.'

Shelepin characterised it as a form of national schizophrenia!

Anatoly Dobrynin had correctly predicted what would happen next: the Nixon Administration had gone through hours, days of panic, recrimination, of desperately attempting to blame the messenger, gone into denial, then a phase of stubborn, short-lived non-engagement with the media. Subsequently, it had lashed out at its enemies, castigated its allies and basically, weathered the initial storm. It had lived to fight another day. The President's approval ratings were on the slide but not anywhere as catastrophically as the 'liberal intelligentsia' imagined, and events like today's in the Oval Office, although meaningless in terms of actual diplomatic substance, could not help to further enhance Richard Nixon's status as an international statesman.

Alexander Shelepin and Richard Nixon were not here today to heal the world's many, incurable problems; they were here to do each other a huge public relations favour. The mere fact that they were meeting publicly, and with all due fanfare shouted that they were big men on the global stage; and that they were men who could 'do business' together.

As a result of this meeting, in Middle America and back in the Motherland both men would in different ways, be more secure in their positions than they had been yesterday. Both men understood that if they were ever to seriously sit down and talk about peace, or any kind of post Cuban Missiles War settlement, there would first need to be months of bitter, intractable debate between their officials; and that would just be to agree an outline agenda!

However, for today, the pictures beamed around the planet would suffice because neither party was yet ready to contemplate 'talking turkey' with the other.

And in the meantime, global realpolitik would continue to play out. Better by far to engage in a propaganda war than the real thing. The Cold War could thaw a while because in their hearts both men knew that sooner or later, winter was coming again.

Bizarrely, Warsaw Concerto had achieved more than anybody in Sverdlovsk imagined possible!

Chapter 74

Friday 17th February 1967
Orcines, Puy-de-Dôme, the Auvergne

Comrade Agnès was unsurprised to discover that Maxim Machenaud had taken pains to ensure that even here, out in the countryside little more than hours after he had abandoned *his* people to their fate, that he had taken steps to ensure his own physical comfort without a concern for that of his followers.

A straw mattress on the cobbled floor of a pigsty had been good enough for *her*, whereas, *he* had laid his palliasse on the floor of the old cottage, close to where a low fire burned and crackled in an ancient hearth.

The wintery trees and a few firs, evergreens, wrapped the cottage the First Secretary and Chairman of the Front Internationale had requisitioned. From the state of the place, its good repair, its cleanliness and the fact there was still glass in the windows, it must have been occupied until recently.

Agnès did not think to ask what had happened to whoever had been living in it when the great leader and his dwindling retinue had turned up last night. She took it for granted either they had fled for their lives, or their bodies were presently mouldering, unburied in the woods nearby

Agnès shut the rickety oaken door at her back.

"You had them put me in a pigsty?"

"I had them wrap you up warmly, and watch over you in the night," the man said coldly. He had been sitting on a hard, wooden stool, reading from a note book. One of *her* note books. "They found this in the ruins. They brought it to me. They said you had probably been killed in the bombing."

The woman shrugged, raised a hand to her head.

"I think I got concussed, I woke up wandering around in the Place de Jaude," she frowned. "The old Opera House took a direct hit from a big bomb. It was chaos... When I came around the fucking Russians grabbed me and ordered me to lead them out of the city!"

Maxim Machenaud was viewing her with none of the reptilian mistrust he reserved for the majority of his other underlings. As time went by, he had been as mystified as she was by his *consideration* for her. The way he had come to need her near him; calming, chaining the worst of his demons. For a while she had managed to talk down his rage, take the edge off the terror. But ever since the latest Soviet mission had arrived in Clermont-Ferrand he had reverted to type, become again a wild animal. Although, hardly ever with her. It was not as if she was any kind of Greek goddess; she was plain, had few wiles, little or no charm, she was just reliable, loyal, and most of the time, unafraid of him and that had somehow, made an indelible mark on him. He had even fucked her a few times; vaguely affirmatory angry couplings. He had ached for her to be more, alive, not lie there like a lifeless doll but then for all he knew, that was how all copulation was conducted. It was, after all, an animal function; purely satisfying a physiological need...

"Did you?" The man asked.

"Help the bastards? Of course not!" She retorted angrily. "I led them into a cul-de-sac with the mob blocking all the exits and slipped into a doorway before they knew what was happening. I knew those streets as a kid, they never had a clue where I'd gone!"

Maxim Machenaud smiled.

"But you kept on running?"

"People were fucking shooting at me!"

"I needed you," he complained with a hint of petulance.

"Where were you when I needed you?" She snarled back at him, stepping closer.

He was little more than her height.

They stood, eye to eye.

"You know what they'll do to us if they catch us?" She asked, a little breathless. She doubted he would misinterpret her rising excitement for what it really was; she did not care.

"I said I'd cut your throat to save you that," the man shrugged.

"I swore I'd never let them take you alive."

"That was our...tryst," Maxim Machenaud agreed, matter of factly. He put his hands on her breasts, groped for them.

"Not like before," she hissed, slapping his hands away. "And if you've got a knife under your mattress, put it somewhere I'm not going to impale myself the moment we start fucking!"

She had no idea why the man she hated and despised with every fibre of her being, had not had her butchered the first time she had rejected his advances. She had recoiled in revulsion and in the next moment, pity, for a man whom she had realised needed something from her that he simply could not get by force. The chemistry of it defeated her; there had actually been brief interludes when *he* had not disgusted her. In any event, while he needed her, she had continued to survive, life had gone on. So, she had become the maniac's lover, occasional mistress although to this day she had no idea what he saw in her. She was ordinary, always a mess, androgynous with no figure to speak of, and most of the time she was dirty, hungry, as romantic as dead meat. And yet, *he* saw something in her she did not see in herself, and he obviously needed something from her that he could not get from anybody else.

Perhaps, it was just a classic example of chemistry gone wrong. One of those implausible ghosts in the machine that every mathematician or physicist glimpsed, like a spectre now and then. Every time a scientist thought they understood everything; nature proved them wrong. That, after all, was the ultimate challenge which defined the human condition...

"Lie down," she said, hoarsely.

As the man obediently lowered himself to the mattress, he reached under it, retrieved the one-hundred-and-eighty-millimetre hunting knife he always carried close to his skin when he was among *his* people.

She had seen him skewer men, and women with that wicked blade: curved and razor-sharp on one side, serrated from its tip half-way to the haft on the reverse.

Mostly, he just liked slicing off pieces of people who had upset him...

He turned, stabbed the knife into the floor board next to the pillow. She glanced around, saw the blade's sheath resting in his left boot.

He watched her wriggle out of her damp, filthy fatigues.

She enjoyed for a second the radiant heat of the fire in the hearth on her bare skin. Naked from the belly down she knelt down beside Maxim Machenaud, and tugged at his belt.

He pushed down his trousers.

Such a monster; such a small cock.

In a moment she had straddled him.

He stank of sweat and mud, stale cigarette smoke, and piss but then she probably did not smell much better. They had been living like animals back in the city, out here they were like two kinds of beasts of the forest, feral, unwashed inside and out.

She sank onto him, rubbed her groin against his.

There was life between her thighs, modest at first.

She went on grinding against him.

Maxim Machenaud closed his eyes, reached to press her hips down onto his small but rising tumescence.

"Wait... There's something I want to tell you," the woman said quietly.

The man's eye's blinked open. "We can talk later..."

"What makes you think there will be a later?" She asked, ignoring his pathetic attempts to penetrate her.

His fingers were pressing into her flesh and he was becoming urgent, breathless.

"There's always later," he grunted irritably.

"No, that's where you're wrong."

That was when she lurched forward onto her elbows with such force her deadweight expelled the air from Maxim Machenaud's lungs.

Suddenly he was staring, transfixed at the polished blade of the knife.

She jerked upright, clasping the haft in both hands.

Maxim Machenaud opened his mouth to speak as the blade descended in a short, savage, unstoppable arc.

"My name is *not* Comrade Agnès," his executioner said, spitting contempt.

In her head the knife stabbed down in slow motion, and each exquisite millimetre of its inexorable fall, and jerking penetration, juddering briefly as it encountered bone on its unstoppable downward path was beatifically elongated.

Actually, the moment of stabbing happened so fast her conscious mind registered nothing other than the motor command to bring the blade, its haft gripped in two hands, straight down to earth, and the aftermath.

The blade was buried in Maxim Machenaud's chest, all the way to the hilt. She had stabbed him in the right torso, level with his heart, or rather, what passed for a heart in the sad, sick, demented little shit's chest cavity.

She twisted the blade, wanted to gut the beast but the blade grated on bone and briefly, it was stuck.

The man attempted to cry out.

There was an obscene, sucking sound as air and blood bubbled around the half to the wicked hunting knife.

More blood filled the dying man's mouth; he began to choke, drown in his own blood. She watched, knowing that if she pulled out the knife that death would come faster and that was not at all what she planned.

She looked down at her groin.

"What's the problem, little man? Can't you get it up today?"

She had seen a lot of people die very, very bad deaths and had learned to tell from their eyes when they were starting to slip away.

His journey was close to its end but that end was not quite yet.

She gathered her wits.

"My name is *Jacqueline Faure* and I am nobody's fucking *comrade.*"

It ought to have been a revelatory moment. It was not. She would have been sick if there had been anything in her painfully cramping stomach.

She dry-retched painfully.

Maxim Machenaud was trying to say something.

She clamped her left hand over his mouth, the blood instantly foaming between her fingers.

"Enough," she muttered.

The knife would not come out.

She pulled once, there was a sick sucking, squelching noise and the man's body twitched in a spasm of agony. She tried again, now there was blood everywhere.

Jacqueline Faure had no idea if the man who had tormented and butchered tens of thousands of his fellow French men and women, whose wanton cruelty and neglect had depopulated whole tracts of the South of France, wasted and ruined a once beautiful, fertile land beyond measure, was already dead when she finally got the blade out of his chest.

She shrieked and plunged the knife into his Godforsaken heart.

Once, twice, three times...

On and on.

Until with one last final insane cry of existential angst she buried it in him and collapsed, exhausted on top of the wrecked torso of the dead man.

Epilogue

Chapter 75

Saturday 18th February 1967
Toulon, France

Captain Dermot O'Reilly, RN, did not care to be the Military Governor of Toulon. He simply was not the stuff of which dictators or imperial pro-consuls were made, and frankly, he was far too busy to worry about little things like how he fed the starving people of the city and the surrounding countryside.

He had actually been a little irritated when a delegation from Marseilles had come into his makeshift headquarters in the old Dockyard Superintendent's Office, to formally surrender that city.

Mercifully, the assault ship HMS Fearless had docked an hour after daybreak that morning and would soon start landing three hundred Royal Marines, their vehicles, and having flooded down her stern dock launched her four twenty-five-ton LCVP – Landing Craft Vehicle Personnel – to be employed for general harbour duties. Fearless's arrival could not have been better timed, overnight, his people had finally locked down most of the port area, secured weapons and munitions stores and set up safe landing and assembly areas. Presently, every available man, over three-quarters of the crews of the Campbeltown, Stirling and the Galatea – leaving only skeleton complements aboard - were ashore in policing, administrative or humanitarian roles, and an emergency field hospital and a communal soup kitchen had been set up inside the dockyard perimeter.

If nothing else, his people had begun to address the city's most pressing ills. The problem was that there was so much still to be done and only so much a few hundred Royal Naval personnel could, even with the best will in the world, achieve.

People were starving to death in the war plague-wracked streets of parts of the city, too weak to call out for help; and because there were still Red Dawn, or Front Internationale diehards, or just plain maniac enclaves holding out all along the coast, preventing Task Force V1 switching its main effort from war-fighting to civil-assistance, Dermot O'Reilly was being forced to operate with one hand tied behind his back.

Once ashore, the manpower on board either the Kent or the Belfast would make a huge local difference, there was enough oil on the RFA Orangeleaf and a second tanker shortly scheduled to join Rear Admiral Henry Leach's fleet in the Bay of Lions, to fuel the generators needed to restore the electricity supply to parts of Toulon, Marseilles, Nice and a dozen other towns and cities.

Yet, while the diehards fought on, people would go on dying...

The two middle-ranking French naval officers standing in front of O'Reilly's desk wanted to know what had happened to the 'Villefranche

Squadron'.

The embattled Captain (D) of the 21st Destroyer Squadron was tempted to have his visitors summarily ejected from the building.

Instead, he sighed, and looked up from his cluttered desk.

"Jean Bart, Clemenceau and several other vessels," he explained in terse, impatient Quebecois French, "including the cruiser De Grasse were safely escorted to Malta where Contra Amiral Leguay formally surrendered the fleet..."

Suddenly, there was something half-way between horror and shame on both the other men's faces. Neither man bore rank insignia but they were of O'Reilly's generation.

He quickly shook his head.

"No, no, it was nothing like that. The surrender business was just a formality. The C-in-C Mediterranean immediately handed the ships back to Rene Leguay. He now commands the French Mediterranean Fleet at Malta. Naval surveyors and engineers are currently inspecting the ships and all personnel are being cared for, and by order of the British Government, being treated like honoured allies by the people on the Archipelago."

"We heard that the Russians sank the fleet?"

"No, that's a lie."

Dermot O'Reilly decided that he needed to rediscover his sense of humour and stop acting like a grumpy old man. He waved the other men to pull up chairs. Around them the whole building was a constant hive of activity.

"Rene Leguay and his people successfully fought off a Front Internationale attempt to seize the fleet, and together, my ships and his, fought off a Russian bombing raid. After that, we patched up the surviving ships and escorted them to Malta. I say again, until somebody tells me differently, Amiral Leguay is C-in-C all French Naval Forces in the Mediterranean. Once we've got things ship shape here, the plan is to fly him up from Malta to take control. We," he shrugged, spreading his hands, "are here as liberators. We, the British, have no desire whatsoever to be running things a minute longer than absolutely necessary. Obviously, the majority of the task force out at sea must remain focused on subduing the remaining 'hostile' pockets of resistance along the coast before we bring all the available resources ashore to help your people." He thought about it. "Our people, now. As in the north, Frenchman in the south will soon be governed by the Provisional Administration of the Free French under the leadership of General Alain de Boissieu. Hopefully, he will nominate a Governor of this city, district, whatever, in the next few days, so that I can get back to being a destroyer captain again!"

The two French officers stared at him, speechless.

"If that was all, I must get on, gentlemen," O'Reilly said. As an afterthought he added: "On your way out please identify yourselves to my officers. If you inform them of your service specialisations and general technical backgrounds, they will assign you both to appropriate roles within the temporary administration."

Wintery sunshine was filtering into the room.

The windows, cracked and dirty rattled gently as the boom of distant guns fell across the city like the threat of an approaching spring storm.

That would probably be the Kent hurling eight-inch two-hundred-and-sixty pound high-explosive rounds fifteen miles inshore with one of the Victorious's Fairy Gannets doing the artillery spotting.

The people of Toulon had turned on the few remaining FI fanatics around the port area in the hours before Campbeltown nosed into the great, mostly derelict port. That had not been pretty. Bodies still hung from lamp posts, other unfortunates had been beaten to death in the streets, or agonisingly, slowly incinerated with a burning tyre around their necks or torso.

It was gruesome, inevitable and in those now lost, halcyon days before the cataclysm it would have shocked and scarred the liberators. But actually, these days such atrocities were water off a duck's back to most of O'Reilly's men. They had survived the war to end all wars, lived in its aftermath, only to fight more battles, each one not for any great cause, rather, simply to go on living and to ensure that the curse of war was held back from wherever they called home.

O'Reilly had sent patrols into the streets to try to stop the ongoing blood-letting, to little avail. Thankfully, this morning the shore patrols were reporting an exhausted calm and a communal sigh of relief that at last, the darkness might be lifting.

Of more concern were the booby traps, usually grenades triggered by tripwires which the departing Revolutionary Guards had hurriedly planted.

The bastards had attempted to sabotage the dockyards fuel pumps, and in one, intact shell store containing several hundred rounds, including to everybody's astonishment, nearly a hundred 380-millimetre reloads for the Jean Bart's main battery, they had laid demolition charges which thankfully, had failed to explode.

Periodically, there was a faraway detonation as O'Reilly's people, hopefully, disarmed or remotely, safely triggered the booby traps in the streets around the port.

Commander Brynmawr Williams knocked at the open door as the two French officers departed and walked in.

"All the former Navy-types are coming out of the woodwork, now, sir," he reported wryly. "Not all of them are very popular with the locals, I'm afraid."

O'Reilly got to his feet, stretched his stiff limbs.

"I don't care, that's not our problem. If they can help us get this city back on its feet and set up a working food distribution system, they get a free pass. It can't have been much fun for anybody trying to get by with those Krasnaya Zarya zealots."

"That's true," Campbeltown's Executive Officer agreed. He looked meaningfully at his wristwatch. "Fearless will be expecting us aboard for the mid-day sitrep," he reminded his Captain.

The assault ship's commanding officer had volunteered to come ashore; Dermot O'Reilly had told him that he would come to him. Fearless had the most modern C-I-C and communications rig in the Task Force, and he badly needed to know what else was going on around the Toulon-Marseilles 'liberated' zone.

Besides, he needed to get out and about.

His people needed to see him.

And so, probably, did the survivors of the city.

"It's a funny old world," Brynmawr Williams chortled as the two men walked down the quayside towards the towering bulk of the Fearless as a Westland Whirlwind helicopter lifted noisily off her flight deck, a cargo of stores boxes slung beneath her belly in a big net at the end of a three fathom line.

Several Land Rovers had been driven down a broad ramp onto the dock, and men were dragging fuel lines from the assault ship to fill the tanks of a motley collection of rusty cars and lorries pushed and wheeled into a long line.

Getting the city moving again was the number one priority; anything with wheels and an engine that might be pressed into service was being brought down to the harbour, hurriedly resuscitated even if it was only for a few precious hours. There had been no petrol, hardly any diesel in Toulon for months. On the nearby berths both of Dermot O'Reilly's Fletchers had pumped hundreds of tons of bunker oil into the two undamaged tanks of the old Naval Base's oiling 'tanker farm'.

Frustratingly, there were no road tankers to carry the priceless black gold deep into the city, and no way to pipe it to the nearest power station. Worse, all – well, most – of the people who knew how to work and maintain the city's essential services, were gone so with every passing minute the Royal Navy men ashore became ever more dispersed, pulled this way and that.

It was ever thus...

"Funny?" Dermot O'Reilly objected. "I don't know about that, Bryn!"

"In a hundred years all that the history books will remember was that Napoleon stopped the British capturing Toulon in 1793, and another damned Frenchie captured it for the Brits in 1967!"

Dermot O'Reilly gave his Executive Officer a hard look.

Then, unable to contain himself, he laughed.

Loudly.

Chapter 76

Aurélie Faure had followed the Governor's wife, a charming, cultured elderly lady out onto the veranda into the late afternoon sunshine - while Rene Leguay, looking splendid in his newly tailored whites, had gone into conclave with Field Marshal Lord Hull, the Governor of the Maltese Archipelago - where the women were partaking of tea and biscuits in the privacy of the residence's walled garden.

Lady Antoinette had suggested that they converse in French, once her own native language, for she too was a daughter of La belle France, borne Antoinette Labouchére de Rougement, into a banking family. Her husband, then only Sir Richard Amyatt Hull, had been Chief of the Imperial General Staff, a post now re-classified as Chief of the Defence Staff in this decidedly post-imperial era, at the time of the Cuban Missiles War, a disaster the Hulls had only escaped by dint of 'being in the country' at the time.

Aurélie still felt a little over-awed by all the attention she had attracted in the short time since the Villefranche Squadron had arrived in Malta. Oddly, now that she had obtained a couple of new frocks that actually fitted her, and she had been blissfully bathed, clean for several days, she was starting to believe again that the world was her oyster. She had almost forgotten how good it was to be able to wash one's hair – properly – every day, or to find a stylist, a delightful woman from somewhere in the English 'Black Country', who had emigrated to the Mediterranean eighteen months ago with her husband and two young children when he was recruited to work in the Admiralty Dockyards of Malta, to magically 'tidy up' her hopelessly unruly auburn-blond 'mop'.

Rene had just stared at her – open-mouthed, basically – the first time she had presented herself in the modest, grey-green dress with a hem dancing around her calves, and with her hair 'under control again' two days ago.

He said she looked like Audrey Hepburn's sister!

Men were so ridiculous!

The two women sipped their teas, nibbled biscuits, and chatted about Maltese fashions. Soon the conversation moved on. Lady Antoinette was quietly, nevertheless immensely, curious about Aurélie's story.

"My husband had travelled to Paris to stay with some friends," she recollected, knowing that she had put a dishonest gloss on those days just before the cataclysm. "We were living in Lyon. I was teaching, I loved it. And I loved our little cottage just outside the city; we had such nice neighbours. Pierre wanted to go back to Paris; to return to the Sorbonne or if he couldn't get an assistant professor's post, any job would do, just so that we could move back to the north."

"How did you feel about that, my dear?"

Aurélie shrugged, abandoning all the little white lies she had told herself in the last four years.

"I wanted children; Pierre always said 'wait until we are in Paris'. It was different for him, he had family in the north. Me, after the Second War there was only me and my sister, Jacqueline, and we were never that close. She was eight years older; you see. Her father was killed in a flying accident before the Second War. My mother re-married, a sweet man, she said, I never knew him because he was killed in May 1940. A few months after I was born..."

Aurélie explained that her brother, Edward, 'Eddy' had been killed in Algeria soon after their mother's death. He had had been her hero...

"I was miserable for a long time; I think that drove Pierre away in the end..."

"What happened to your mother?"

"She passed away in 1960, before Eddy was killed, thank God. She was not always unhappy; she did not brood about things until near the end. At least, not in front of Jacqueline or I. Jacqueline thinks she had many lovers; that may have started when she was in the Resistance. She never talked about it very much but I think she was in a group which helped British flyers who had been shot down to escape over the border to Switzerland or Spain. She died of a cancer, like we all will, I suppose..."

The Governor's wife was not having any of that kind of talk!

"We don't know that yet," she countered gently.

"I'm sorry," Aurélie apologised instantly. "I picked up a book visiting the hospital at Bighi, where a Russian friend is recovering from his wounds," her thoughts became momentarily distracted, "yes, a book..."

Lady Antoinette waited patiently, intrigued.

"It was a *Times of Malta* book containing all the letters and articles that Lady Marija Calleja-Christopher has submitted to the paper since just after the October War." Aurélie blushed guiltily. "I feel terrible, because I didn't give it back. I will donate another book to the library at the hospital to replace it..."

"Lady Marija has a very particular, refreshingly sanguine view of things," the older woman smiled.

"You must have met her, of course."

"Many times." Lady Antoinette shook her head. "I swear that woman will be this island's patron saint before she's done!" Presently, she picked up the threads of their previous conversation. "What became of your sister, my dear?"

"I don't know." Aurélie hesitated. "Jacqueline was on government work. She was in Algeria when the putsch happened. After that, I think she was at the Academy of Sciences in Paris. Her hero was always Marie Curie. It all went over my head but I remember Mama saying one day, just before she passed away, that Jacqueline was working on *our* bomb."

"Oh, so she was a physicist?"

"I think so. I never saw her after our mother's funeral. I think she thought I was a flighty young thing and she didn't have any time to be 'mothering' me. Things turned out okay. I qualified, I got my teaching certificate, I met Pierre." She shrugged. "We were both very young; we might have worked things out eventually..."

"How is your friend at Bighi?"

"Dmitry? The doctors say he won't be back on his feet for a little while," Aurélie smiled, glad her host had diplomatically changed the subject. "It is awkward. He was a Russian officer. He was a Red Navy KGB man."

The older woman struck a reassuring note.

"I think my husband's predecessor, Sir Daniel French, very wisely took the view and established the, er, very sensible precedent, that former Soviet personnel not known to have been involved in committing war crimes against Allied combatants or civilians, should be," Lady Antoinette smiled, "given the benefit of the doubt, and treated accordingly."

"I worry because Dmitry was a..."

"KGB officer?" The Governor's wife shrugged sympathetically. "I'm sure the people at MI6 will want to interview your friend. I should imagine that so long as he is frank with them that he will be treated fairly."

Aurélie tried and failed to hide her anxiety.

Lady Antoinette touched her hand.

"I am sure that your future husband," she decided, "will have been at pains to clarify Captain Kolokoltsev's *situation* with my husband."

Aurélie blushed.

Since the Jean Bart had anchored in the Grand Harbour, she had punctiliously ceased to be Rene's 'secretary', and as deliberately, ceased to be a crew member. Aboard the battleship she had been 'the Admiral's woman' and neither she, nor her beau, wanted her to be that any more.

Rene had been allocated married quarters at Fort Pembroke, a few miles up the coast and in the last couple of days she had been doing what she could to turn the small apartment – a bedroom, a kitchen, a claustrophobic parlour and a small, marvellously clean and sweet-smelling bathroom – into a home, for as long as they were going to be on the island. Rene, foolish man, insisted on staying on board the Jean Bart, now moored alongside Parlatorio Wharf undergoing emergency repairs, until their wedding night, scheduled for a week hence.

She just wanted to be his wife; not a member of his crew. That life had ended. Now she ached to look forward to being, if such a thing was possible, *just* Rene's wife, and if it happened, the mother of his children.

"Ah, there you are, ladies!" Lord Hull chortled happily as he led the tall, hook-nosed man who had, against the odds, saved the last ships of the French Mediterranean Fleet and their rag-tag crews, and now found himself – much to his surprise – the Commander-in-Chief of all Free French Naval Forces in the Mediterranean, out onto the veranda.

Lady Antoinette rose to her feet, as did Aurélie.

"Dinner will be served in a few minutes, Richard," she reminded her husband.

Aurélie reached out and Rene Leguay took her hand as the couples went back inside.

"British forces have taken Toulon and Marseilles," he said, holding his fiancée's chair for her as she settled at the big, lavishly set table in the relatively small day room she assumed their hosts reserved for private, small-scale functions like tonight's dinner. "Everywhere the Front Internationale is in retreat, routed. The Free French in the north are sweeping all before them and the people of the Auvergne had risen up against their gaolers!"

Aurélie turned her face and looked to the man she loved.

"Can it be true?"

"In the streets of Toulon, the people are acclaiming Captain O'Reilly as 'the Liberator of the South', my love." He bent his head and kissed her forehead, oblivious of the presence of the Governor and his wife.

Lord Hull watched the couple for a moment.

"There are still pockets of resistance," he cautioned solemnly, 'but it may well be that the worst is over and that soon, all of France will be free. My best guess is that President de Boissieu will proclaim the 6th Republic sometime in the next few days."

Stewards hovered in the doorway bearing a soup tureen.

It was all Aurélie could do not to burst into excited, distraught, confused joy and laugh like an idiot as she grinned and smiled, half-guiltily at Rene as he, similarly emotional, met her almond-eyed gaze.

It was like a dream, a fairy tale.

The war was almost over...

Chapter 77

Sunday 18th February 1967
Manassas, Virginia

The Virginia State trooper who had slowly driven up to the lodge in the woods had not been some green behind the ears, rookie. The guy had been paunchy, past middle age, balding beneath his cap and suspicious; because suspicion was just a bad habit with some cops and this guy, Kurt Mikkelsen guessed resignedly, was the kind of man who always told his buddies where to find him if he missed his regular call-in.

That was bad news.

If *this* cop failed to come back to wherever he was based with the state's car, people were going to come looking for him. Worse, they might even know where to start searching.

Kurt had killed him anyway.

He figured the guy probably knew the owners of the cabin; that it was never rented it out to strangers and if he got back to town, he was going to start making calls. Kurt could have brazened it out, high-tailed it the moment the trooper's car turned the bend but he had had enough of being on the run, always looking over his shoulder.

Nothing was for sure; nothing was simple.

He would have liked to have known, for certain, for a fact, if Rachel had been coming after him; just like he would have liked to have understood why he had not ended her when he had her in his sights.

Now he would never know.

He had pulled out the forty-five in his back waistband and plugged the cop twice in the face; eventually – he was a big man, two hundred pounds at least – he had wrestled the body into the trunk of his car, parked up in some woods outside Bull Run, hitched and walked back to the cabin, and waited.

He had a lot of stuff to get straight in his head.

His Pa had been right; it was all over.

The Company ought to have known it was playing with fire bringing him back that way; especially, after it tried to cut him loose after he sliced up that redneck bitch in San Antonio.

Why would they send him to San Antonio to kill old man de Witt?

The man was dying already and the way he had been briefed, *she*, the daughter was the one actually spending her daddy's greenbacks rebuilding the 'West Texas' militia. That was the ''militia' which was supposed to 'step into the shoes' of all those crazies who had died at Wister Park. He had expected her to like it rough; she was supposed to have been one of that maniac preacher Galen Cheney's disciples, the hottest bitch in his god-dammed harem for fuck's sake!

Or, maybe that was just another one of the Company's lies?

At the time it had made a kind of sense.

Jeez, that woman had said a lot of crazy things to him when he started on her...

Like he was going to believe she'd been working for the Company all along?

He had not listened at the time; he had been having too much fun.

It was only later he could not quite, ever get some of the things she said out of his head. She had said she worked for *the Scarecrow*...

How the heck had she even known about Angleton?

Or the Office of Security?

Or Operation Maelstrom...

He had talked to his Pa about it.

He had just told him to 'man up'.

And for a day or two, he had moved on.

But Rachel ought not to have just sat there, not like that, like she was waiting for him to end her. That was just...not her. It was like all the things he had taken for granted were somehow, changed. Suddenly, the world around him was scary.

Hunter turned prey...

Like Marilyn de Witt...

Nothing she had said made sense; it was as if she was talking to him from the other side of a mirror. Everything was the wrong way around, upside down.

It had been easier to go on cutting than listen.

Everybody knew that really rich people – like the de Witts – honestly believed that only poor people should pay taxes. What was so weird about the idea they would try to overthrow the government if they reckoned DC was full of liberal, pinko pricks who ignored what good old boys like old man de Witt had to say?

Only...nothing felt right anymore.

Perhaps, it was seeing Pa again after all these years.

He had had that 'death look' about him, had not wanted him, or anybody to see him that way. He had not expected Kurt to come looking for him.

Thinking about it; nothing had messed with his head as badly as what Pa had had to say to him.

'Dwight Christie screwed the Bureau's West Coast files on you and me in the old days backwards, forwards, every which way but sooner or later, somebody will get his thumb out of his arse and put stuff back together the way it used to be. Then they'll come for me and if you're still around, you too, son.'

That was it; there was no way out this time.

Sitting on that pier watching the USS United States glide between the city and Alcatraz on the way to its anchorage off Alameda already seemed like a memory from a past life, surreal.

'I heard you had plenty of chances to plug that SOB back in sixty-three, Pa?' He had checked, more from idle curiosity than angst.

'Yeah, that was after Cheney and his boy went up to Atlanta to shoot that bastard King. I should have done that job myself, not left it to a couple of crazies,' he had smiled sardonically, for a moment his ashen face that of the iron-hard Marine Corps Gunnery Sergeant. He had coughed a rueful laugh. 'Maybe, I would have taken the contract if the money had been better!'

Kurt had worked it all out by then.

'Christie screwed us all, Pa. That's what guys like him do. His people, their people, people like you and me. I reckon Galen Cheney would have cut him up real slow if he hadn't had other things on his mind at Wister Park.'

If the Company, or Hoover's G-men had pieced it all together, Langley would never have sanctioned bringing him out of retirement. They could have left him hanging, sold him out one day like they really meant it. There had been a price on his head in Brazil, head-hunters on his case. The Company had seen to that; assumed it had him on a nice, short string and that he was going to jump at a chance of rehabilitation.

That was the trouble with people like James Jesus Angleton.

Sooner or later they started to believe the shit they told their clients in the White House; and dangerously, the Ivy League and know nothing West Coast frat buddies around the President. They got so arrogant that they convinced themselves operators like the former Associate Deputy Director of Operations for Counter Intelligence, were the real thing, that they really had magic 'intelligence dust' in their coat pockets capable of, hey presto, making all their problems vanish in a puff of smoke.

Well, around about now all the President's men would be discovering that what they had thought was 'magic dust' was actually, poison and without ever knowing it they had been breathing it in for years!

Kurt knew he could have run.

And gone on running for a long time.

But he was tired and as the pre-dawn twilight began to brighten into full day, throwing a tangle of deep shadows through the still wintery woods around the cabin, he had been listening to the cops, state troopers, likely Army, or National Guard flatfoots too, and their dogs cautiously closing the ring around the log cabin.

He had meant to torment James Jesus Angleton longer, make him live with the fear, the mind-rending terror he had inflicted on so many others.

Rachel had made that impossible.

Maybe, she had returned to DC to hunt him but on balance, he doubted that; more likely, she was like him, to old, too damaged to go on playing the game.   There must have been a moment last Wednesday when she longed for the next bullet, the one that meant the nightmares would finally end.

But he had failed her.

And now it was too late to do anything about it.

For her, or for himself.

The Remington lay in pieces on the neatly made up bed; Kurt sat cross-legged on the hard board floor, mindful that the men outside would shoot him dead the instant his head rose above either of the dusty sills of the cabin's two windows.

His forty-five was in his hand, resting in his lap.

If they got their hooks into him. they would drug him, keep him alive until he had blabbed everything, every dirty little secret just to make absolutely sure they had everything they needed to incriminate the innocent and to protect the guilty. That, as Rachel used to say, was the way things had always, and would always, be for the CIA, the KGB, the FBI or MI5 or Mi6, or any other 'serious' intelligence agency there had ever been in the whole history of the world.

Rachel had always had better 'letters' than him.

He reckoned that was because she had needed to find out why she went through what she had when she was a kid in Poland in the Second War...

The hunters were outside the door now...

He bit down hard on the muzzle of the forty-five.

And as the first smoke grenade smashed, with a shower of glass, through the nearest window, without a moment's hesitation, he squeezed the trigger.

Chapter 78

Tuesday 21st February 1967
Pasadena, California

Alan and Rosa Hannay met their visitors on the path in front of their new, as yet not very homely, bungalow situated within a brisk, twenty-minute walk of the campus of the California Institute of Technology.

Air Marshal Sir Daniel French stepped from behind the wheel of the US Air Force Chrysler and strolled around to the passenger side door to hold it open for his wife to emerge, somewhat diffidently into the bright coolness of the day. A second Chrysler, grey like the French's car, had drawn up behind it. Its occupants, both garbed in USAF day uniforms with subtle, blue tabs on their left lapels, had jackets tailored to conceal the bulge of shoulder-holstered pistols.

Alan and Rosa, accustomed to co-existing with their bodyguards, paused to acknowledge the two Military Policemen with friendly nods and smiles.

Rosa went up to Rachel and embraced her like a long-lost, much loved sister. Momentarily, the older woman was wooden, unsure of herself: she relented, she hugged her Maltese friend, albeit with a little more self-awareness.

Alan, meanwhile, had shaken her husband's hand.

Sir Daniel looked even more 'corporate' in his 'civvy threads' than he did in uniform. The former Lancaster and V-Bomber pilot had, during his time in the Governor's Palace at Malta, morphed into a very modern, business-like administrator and fixer and inevitably, sometime politician. A trim, dapper man he seemed tired, yet somehow, 'on leave', as if a burden had lifted off his shoulders which was odd, given that he and his wife were at the epicentre of the biggest US-UK diplomatic row since the two countries had very nearly, started lobbing thermonuclear bombs at each other's cities in July 1964.

Alan retrieved his hand.

Waiting for his wife to disentangle herself from Rachel, he gallantly stepped forward and planted a peck on her pale cheek before, cautiously, as if she was bruised all over, gently embracing her. To his surprise, she hugged him back.

The two couples stood looking at each other for a few seconds.

"It is damned good to see you both," Alan declared.

"Come inside," Rosa commanded. "You must be desperate for a nice cup of tea, or coffee, after your drive down from Palmdale. They say the mountains are beautiful? Alan and I plan to explore a little when we are more settled."

The Hannays had discovered that the Air Force house came with a young Hispanic part-time maid and nanny, who was employed to be at their disposal from eight in the morning to four in the afternoon weekdays, and for two hours each side of noon at the weekends.

The woman, whose name was Ramona, was about Rosa's age, and at first, shy and nervous, a thing Rosa was working on.

"This is Ramona," she said, introducing the other woman to her guests. "This is Sir Daniel French and his wife, Lady Rachel."

Ramona was astonished, paralysed with indecision as the great man held out his hand and a moment later, his lady, did likewise. The brief handshaking completed, she fled into the back of the bungalow to the security of the kitchen.

The Hannay's son, twenty-month-old Julian, was crawling around the living room floor, gurgling cheerfully as he haltingly explored the family's new home. His sister, Sophia Elisabetta, barely thirteen weeks old, was fast asleep in a nest of blankets in a big, wicker basket on the parlour table.

Rosa was fascinated, and a little taken aback when Rachel leaned over her baby daughter and gazed, lost in her thoughts at the sleeping baby's cherubic face.

"I don't know how you manage all this travelling around, all the new places with two such small children," Rachel sighed.

"Neither do we, to be honest," Alan grinned, looking fondly to his wife.

"I hope we're not putting you out, turning up like this?" Dan French inquired, his concern anything but feigned.

"No, it is lovely to see friends from home," Rosa assured him. "Although, sometimes it is hard to know where home is, don't you think?"

"Yes, indeed."

Rachel had drifted over to the window, eying the Air Force bodyguards, both smoking cigarettes by their car.

Rosa invited everybody to sit down while she went to help Ramona with the 'tea things.'

The furniture was comfortably basic, unfussy by American standards – plush and a little too showy in comparison to what the Hannays had been accustomed to before the war – and still had that leathery, just unpacked feel and smell.

It was Rachel who decided to address the metaphorical eight-hundred-pound brooding silverback gorilla in the room.

"There has been nothing official from Oxford yet," she said with rueful self-deprecation, glancing down at the polished boards at her feet, "but I think I have successfully ruined Dan's career. We will probably be recalled to England." She shrugged. "Always assuming the Americans don't arrest me first. As you know, I have no diplomatic immunity and the people who run the big aircraft companies Dan has been working with, well, they spend a lot of money lobbying on Capitol Hill, many of them would probably prefer a more compliant man at the, er..."

"Control column," her husband offered cheerfully.

"At the control column at Boscombe Down," Rachel went on. "They were already pressing for that as a condition of Lockheed and Grumman prioritising the production of the Kestrel."

Rosa, standing in the kitchen door, was a little baffled by all this.

"The Kestrel is the jet fighter that can take off and land vertically, my love," Alan reminded his wife, whose expression suddenly shouted: "Am I supposed to be hearing this!"

Ramona, who had walked in with a second tray, one bearing small tea plates, homemade cookies and slices of a lemony sponge cake, hesitated.

"None of this is really secret," Dan French laughed, surreally relaxed.

"Dan doesn't care," Rachel explained in a small voice. She seemed smaller, diminished to her friends. "For what it is worth, I have promised him that I am...*retired.*"

Alan Hannay was, meanwhile, swiftly parsing and re-parsing the politics of Dan French's situation. Ultimately, irrespective of what the Americans thought about it, the Prime Minister would be the one who decided his fate.

As he understood it, the US Air Force was still fully invested in the transatlantic aerospace partnership, in exactly the same way parts of the US Navy, notwithstanding its reservations, was committed to patching over its scars, embracing the military-industrial, not to mention the strategic advantages inherent in the creation of the Joint Nuclear Strike Force and enjoying its renewed free access to all British home and Commonwealth overseas bases. Moreover, despite what the McDonnell Douglas, Grumman, Northrup and other US aviation industry moguls thought about Dan French, the people at the Pentagon, including US Air Force Chief of Staff John Anderson had always liked Dan French, precisely because he could be relied upon to stand up to the Boeings, Lockheeds and all the other big aerospace players! Besides, Alan had it on good authority that the people at NASA were also big fans of the beleaguered Air Marshal, whose good offices offered the National Aerospace and Space Agency, potential access to launch and test sites, not to mention technical resources and expertise which otherwise, would be closely scrutinised and their costings inflated by pork barrel politics in Congress, throughout the New Commonwealth.

"I'm not convinced about that, Rachel," Alan remarked, thoughtfully, as Ramona helped Rosa pour the drinks. "The Russian thing is playing well for the Administration right now. Your, er, mishap the other day came at just the right time for the White House. To put it crudely, the fact of the matter is that last week the story was Operation Maelstrom; and this week it...isn't."

Rachel French viewed the absurdly youthful-looking, handsome man sitting beside his wife on the sofa the other side of the low glass coffee table at the centre of the room, with thoughtfully limpid eyes. It was a stretch to remember that only three years ago, Alan Hannay had been just Julian Christopher's trusted flag lieutenant, and later one of the heroes of the Battle of Malta, since then he had been a senior British diplomat and a fast-promoted naval representative operating in the hotbed of US politicking, never once putting a foot wrong.

Belatedly, the Navy was rewarding him by sending him here, to Caltech, Pasadena, to start preparing him for what was likely to be a meteoric career in the service. Peter Christopher might have been the United Kingdom's man in America; but Alan Hannay had been his friend's eyes and ears, his go-between and never-say-die gentlemanly fixer, the man who really had his pulse on the mood of Philadelphia, Washington DC and now...America itself.

"You don't think the Prime Minister will throw my dear, faithful husband to the wolves?" She asked, not worried about how brutally the question was phrased.

Alan smiled.

"No. For what it is worth, I don't. People in the Navy have been trying to torpedo Sir Simon Collingwood from the day he got home from the Dreadnought's second war patrol. I know he's only just been promoted Vice Admiral but the First Sea Lord apart, *he* is the Royal Navy to the Prime Minister, quite apart from being," he grimaced apologetically to his wife, "if you'll forgive my turn of phrase, my love, God in the Nuclear Undersea Fleet Project up in Rosyth. Granted, I don't know it for a fact, but I wouldn't be surprised if Sir Daniel's position in the RAF is somewhat analogous to Admiral Collingwood's in the Navy."

Dan French was laughing.

"See," he turned to his wife, "didn't I say that Alan and Rosa would cheer us up?"

"You did," Rachel confessed, leaning gently against her husband.

Sofia Elisabetta began to gribble, a prelude to a bawling demand for attention. Rosa stood up and swept her daughter up into her arms, soothing her instantly.

She sighed.

"My first husband was a Krasnaya Zarya traitor," she reminded her friends, managing to coo at her daughter at the same time. "You never know what is going to happen. Things haven't turned out so badly for Alan and I," she beamed, "and our beautiful bambinos."

Chapter 79

Tuesday 21st February 1967
Government House, Yarralumla, Australian Capital Territories

Lady Marija Christopher entered her husband's big, airy office without knocking, squeezing the door shut at her back. Instantly, she knew that something was terribly wrong.

Fifty-three-year-old Sir Murray Tyrell, Secretary to the Governor-General of Australia, and her husband rose to their feet from their chairs in front of the great gleaming table beneath the windows overlooking the lush grounds beyond.

The last few days had been a whirl of engagements, luncheons, dinners, galas, visits to the theatre and the opera, state functions hosted by Government House, and exhausting. Of course, the Prime Minister had taken it all, effortlessly, in her stride and found time to spend many blissful hours with Marija and her godchildren, far away from the trials and strife of the outside world.

Marija had decided that she was never going to get used to the seasons being the wrong way around in the Southern Hemisphere; it felt like it ought to be spring but it was still summer 'down under'. The other thing she was reconciled to was that even though they had been in Australia over eight months – eight months in which, mercifully, nobody had tried to kill them – she was never going to be as settled here, as she had been back in the United States. Which was a little bizarre really, thinking of everything they had been through...

"What has happened?" She asked, despite her spiking anxiety remembering to walk carefully, placing one foot in front of the other, knowing that if she attempted to rush, she was just going to fall flat on her face – like she always did - and that was not going to help anybody. Suddenly, the look on her husband's face froze her soul.

"Sit down, my love," Sir Peter Christopher suggested.

Since returning from the Australian Parliament, accompanying the Prime Minister that afternoon, he had discarded his stiflingly hot ceremonial garb, showered and donned slacks, a cotton shirt, a Royal Australian Navy Association tie, and a lightweight pale sports jacket. Marija meanwhile, was still wearing the long, off-white calf-length dress she had worn for the afternoon's engagement, and her hair was still unnaturally, albeit marvellously coiffured, rather than falling in its customary nutmeg-dark tangle about her shoulders. Normally, within a few minutes of getting back to Government House one of the bambinos could normally be relied upon to finger, pull or variously destroy the best her 'hair do'.

Although, not yet today.

"We received an urgent communication from Lord Carington a few minutes ago, Lady Marija," Murray Tyrell reported, troubled and uncharacteristically downcast.

The latest occupants of Government House had unashamedly relied on, and pretty much put themselves in the hands of, truth be known, the Victorian-born Secretary to every Governor-General of Australia from 1947 onwards in their time in Canberra.

"We have just consulted with Sir Oliver..."

Sir Oliver Lease was the United Kingdom's High Commissioner – Ambassador by any other name – to Australia, a wise and greatly respected former general officer who had played a distinguished part in the Second War, to whom, like Murray Tyrell, the couple had had no qualms looking to for advice.

In fact, had it not been for the advice, counsel and moral support of Murray Tyrell, Sir Oliver Leese and Admiral John McCain – a man Marija's husband regarded as one of his personal heroes – the United States Ambassador, they would have been in quite a pickle tiptoeing through the sensibilities of the Australasian social and political minefield.

Marija tried not to jump to conclusions.

If her husband had not spoken to John McCain then whatever had gone wrong did not involve a new crisis with Washington. That had to be good news...

Didn't it?

Marija rested on the arm of the chair her husband had risen from. He handed her a single sheet of paper.

"We chopped off most of the header, coding instructions, all that guff," he explained, distractedly.

FROM: FIRST SECRETARY OF STATE/CARINGTON.

PERSONAL AND MOST SECRET/GOVERNOR GENERAL AND HIGH COMMISSIONER'S EYES ONLY

CONTENTS TO BE NOTIFIED TO THE PRIME MINISTER SOONEST.

DEAR MARGARET, I AM SO SORRY TO BE THE BRINGER OF SUCH SAD NEWS. I REGRET TO REPORT THAT THE CHIEF OF THE DEFENCE STAFF HAS REPORTED TO ME THAT AT ABOUT TWENTY-ONE FORTY-FIVE HOURS LOCAL TIME, MAJOR GENERAL FRANCIS ST JOHN WATERS, VC, WAS A PASSENGER IN A VEHICLE WHICH WAS TARGETTED BY A LARGE ROADSIDE BOMB ON THE ROAD BETWEEN THE VILLAGES OF GUDMONT-VILLIERS AND DOULAINCOURT-SAUCOURT IN THE HAUTE-MARNE DEPARTMENT OF FRANCE. IT IS MY SAD DUTY TO REPORT TO YOU THAT ALL THREE OCCUPANTS OF THE VEHICLE, A LAND ROVER, WERE KILLED INSTANTLY. ALL OUR SYMPATHIES AT HOME AND IN DUE COURSE, I AM SURE, THROUGHOUT THE COMMONWEALTH, ARE WITH YOU AT THIS TERRIBLE TIME. I AM GIVEN TO BELIEVE THAT HER MAJESTY IS SENDING A SEPARATE MESSAGE COMMUNICATING HER DEEPEST SENSE OF LOSS AND SYMPATHY TO YOU AT THIS TIME. SIGNED: CARINGTON.

Marija's vision was a blur and as her husband wrapped her in his arms she realised, as if looking down upon herself from above, that she was sobbing uncontrollably, her chest heaving with agonising despair.

Presently, the worst of it passed.

Marija sniffed, tried to wipe her eyes, knowing her face would be red and blotchy, and her hair, was now almost certainly, a mess.

And that there was now a fourth person in the room.

"What's wrong?" Mary Griffin, Marija's constant companion, intimate and Appointments Secretary asked anxiously, obviously sensing that whatever was going on that this was a situation where they would, in the past, have summoned her husband – if only for moral support - whom, problematically, was presently at sea on board HMS Anzac as the brand-new frigate ran acceptance trials off the coast north of Sydney.

"The Prime Minister's husband has been killed in a bombing in France," Peter told her, very quietly.

"Oh, God..." Mary gasped, shocked as if she had been physically struck.

Marija pulled herself together, and staggered to her feet.

Her husband steadied her.

They looked one to the other.

"Tom and Pat are probably travelling, and out of contact," Marija sniffed, her thoughts turning to practicalities.

The Foreign Secretary and his wife, Pat, the Prime Minister's closest friend and confidante, were visiting old friends in Melbourne.

The news was bound to leak out, sooner rather than later.

They could not wait for Lord Harding Grayson and his wife to return to Canberra.

This had to be done now.

Sir Peter Christopher nodded unspoken agreement to his wife.

He turned to his Secretary, Sir Murray Tyrell.

"Murray," he said sombrely, taking charge. He swallowed hard. "We'll collect Ian Gow on the way. Marija and I will speak to the Prime Minister without delay."

[The End]

Author's End Note

'Eight Miles High' is Book 14 of the alternative history series **Timeline 10/27/62**. I hope you enjoyed it - or if you did not, sorry - but either way, thank you for reading and helping to keep the printed word alive. Remember, civilization depends on people like you.

Coming next: **Book 15: Won't Get Fooled Again** which picks up the story one year hence.

NEXT YEAR I plan to go back to April and October releases for Timeline Main Series offerings.

Book 15: Won't Get Fooled Again is pretty much a standalone piece, will come out in April 2020 (all being well) and **Book 16: Armadas**, the first book of another two-parter in October 2020.

Thereafter: the plan is to write the series at least up to Book 20, set around the tenth anniversary of the October War in 1972; publishing at the rate of at least 2 books per year as below.

Book 17: Smoke on the Water (2021)
Book 18: Cassandra's Song (2021)
Book 19: The Changing of the Guard (2022)
Book 20: Independence Day (2022)

Other Books by James Philip

Other Series and Novels

New England Series

Book 1: Empire Day
Book 2: Two Hundred Lost Years
Book 3: Travels Through the Wind
Book 4: Remember Brave Achilles

Coming in 2020

Book 5: George Washington's Ghost
Book 6: The Imperial Crisis

The River Hall Chronicles

Book 1: Things Can Only Get Better
Book 2: Consenting Adults
Book 3: All Swing Together

Coming in 2020

Book 4: The Honourable Member

The Guy Winter Mysteries

Prologue: Winter's Pearl
Book 1: Winter's War
Book 2: Winter's Revenge
Book 3: Winter's Exile
Book 4: Winter's Return
Book 5: Winter's Spy
Book 6: Winter's Nemesis

The Bomber War Series

Book 1: Until the Night
Book 2: The Painter
Book 3: The Cloud Walkers

Until the Night Series

Part 1: Main Force Country – September 1943
Part 2: The Road to Berlin – October 1943
Part 3: The Big City – November 1943
Part 4: When Winter Comes – December 1943
Part 5: After Midnight – January 1944

The Harry Waters Series

Book 1: Islands of No Return
Book 2: Heroes
Book 3: Brothers in Arms

The Frankie Ransom Series

Book 1: A Ransom for Two Roses
Book 2: The Plains of Waterloo
Book 3: The Nantucket Sleighride

The Strangers Bureau Series

Book 1: Interlopers
Book 2: Pictures of Lily

James Philip's Cricket Books

F.S. Jackson
Lord Hawke

**Audio Books of the following Titles
are available (or are in production) now**

Aftermath
After Midnight
A Ransom for Two Roses
Brothers in Arms
California Dreaming
Empire Day
Heroes
Islands of No Return
Love is Strange
Main Force Country
Operation Anadyr
Red Dawn
The Big City
The Cloud Walkers
The Nantucket Sleighride
The Painter
The Pillars of Hercules
The Plains of Waterloo
The Road to Berlin
Travels Through the Wind
Two Hundred Lost Years
Until the Night
When Winter Comes
Winter's Exile
Winter's Pearl
Winter's Return
Winter's Revenge
Winter's Spy
Winter's War

Cricket Books edited by James Philip

The James D. Coldham Series
[Edited by James Philip]

Books

Northamptonshire Cricket: A History [1741-1958]
Lord Harris

Anthologies

Volume 1: Notes & Articles
Volume 2: Monographs No. 1 to 8

Monographs

No. 1 - William Brockwell
No. 2 - German Cricket
No. 3 - Devon Cricket
No. 4 - R.S. Holmes
No. 5 - Collectors & Collecting
No. 6 - Early Cricket Reporters
No. 7 – Northamptonshire
No. 8 - Cricket & Authors

———

Details of all James Philip's published books and
forthcoming publications can be found on his website
www.jamesphilip.co.uk

———

Cover artwork concepts by James Philip
Graphic Design by
Beastleigh Web Design